'Follett's storytelling skills make their adventures riveting'
The Times

'Follett excels in telling a yarn. Intrigue, double twists,
exciting, satisfying . . . you won't be able to put it down'
Independent

'Enormous and brilliant . . . this mammoth tale seems to touch
all human emotion – love and hate, loyalty and treachery,
hope and despair. This is truly a novel to get lost in'
Cosmopolitan

'A historical saga of such breadth and density . . . Follett
succeeds brilliantly in combining hugeness and detail to create
a novel imbued with the rawness, violence and blind faith
of the era'
Sunday Express

'A tale of human courage and perseverance'
Evening Times

'A highly enjoyable tale . . . this book evokes its period brilliantly'
Sunday Times

'A huge read, perfect for long winter nights'
Choice

'The characters, both fictional and real, are fascinating,
and the Tudor-period setting holds its own special allure.
This is a novel that fans of historical fiction will
savour and cherish'
The National

A COLUMN OF FIRE

KEN FOLLETT was twenty-seven when he wrote *Eye of the Needle*, an award-winning thriller that became an international bestseller. He then surprised everyone with *The Pillars of the Earth*, about the building of a cathedral in the Middle Ages, which continues to captivate millions of readers all over the world, and its long-awaited sequel, *World Without End*, was a number one bestseller in the US, UK and Europe. Recently, he has written the bestselling Century trilogy, which comprises *Fall of Giants*, *Winter of the World* and *Edge of Eternity*. *A Column of Fire* is the third novel in the Kingsbridge series.

KEN FOLLETT

A COLUMN of FIRE

PAN BOOKS

First published 2017 by Macmillan

This paperback edition first published 2018 by Pan Books
an imprint of Pan Macmillan
20 New Wharf Road, London N1 9RR
Associated companies throughout the world
www.panmacmillan.com

ISBN 978-1-4472-7875-7

1 3 5 7 9 8 6 4 2

A CIP catalogue record for this book is available from the British Library.

Map artwork by Stephen Raw
Typeset by Palimpsest Book Production Ltd, Falkirk, Stirlingshire
Printed and bound by CPI Group (UK) Ltd, Croydon, CR0 4YY

Visit **www.panmacmillan.com** to read more about all our books
and to buy them. You will also find features, author interviews and
news of any author events, and you can sign up for e-newsletters
so that you're always first to hear about our new releases.

To Emanuele:
49 years of sunshine

By day the LORD went ahead of them in a column of smoke to lead them on their way. By night he went ahead of them in a column of fire to give them light so that they could travel by day or by night.

Exodus 13:21, God's Word Translation

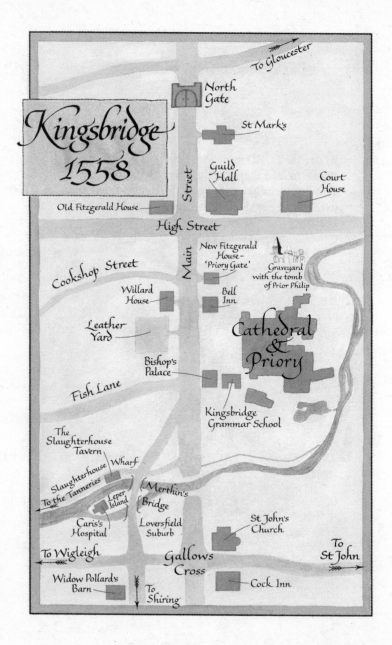

Kingsbridge 1558

To Gloucester

North Gate

St Mark's

Guild Hall

Court House

Old Fitzgerald House

High Street

Street

New Fitzgerald House – 'Priory Gate'

Graveyard with the tomb of Prior Philip

Cookshop Street

Willard House

Bell Inn

Main

Leather Yard

Cathedral & Priory

Bishop's Palace

Fish Lane

Kingsbridge Grammar School

The Slaughterhouse Tavern

Wharf

Slaughterhouse Tanneries

To the Tanneries

Leper Island

Merthin's Bridge

St John's Church

Caris's Hospital

Loversfield Suburb

To Wigleigh

Gallows Cross

To St John

Widow Pollard's Barn

To Shiring

Cock Inn

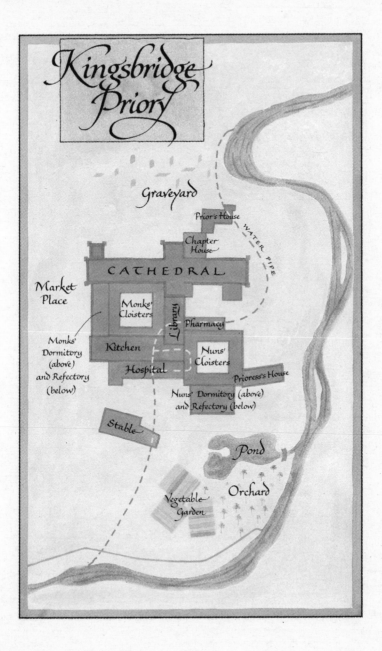

Cast of Characters

I hope you won't need this. Any time I think you might have forgotten a character, I've put in a gentle reminder. But I know that sometimes readers put a book down and don't get another moment to read for a week or more — it happens to me — and then sometimes you forget. So here's a list of the people who pop up more than once, just in case . . .

ENGLAND

Willard household

Ned Willard
Barney, his brother
Alice, their mother
Malcolm Fife, groom
Janet Fife, housekeeper
Eileen Fife, daughter of Malcolm and Janet

Fitzgerald household

Margery Fitzgerald
Rollo, her brother
Sir Reginald, their father
Lady Jane, their mother
Naomi, maid
Sister Joan, Margery's great-aunt

Shiring household

Bart, Viscount Shiring
Swithin, his father, earl of Shiring
Sal Brendon, housekeeper

Cast of Characters

The Puritans

Philbert Cobley, ship owner
Dan Cobley, his son
Ruth Cobley, Philbert's daughter
Donal Gloster, clerk
Father Jeremiah, parson of St John's in Loversfield
Widow Pollard

Others

Friar Murdo, an itinerant preacher
Susannah, Countess of Brecknock, friend of Margery & Ned
Jonas Bacon, captain of the Hawk
Jonathan Greenland, first mate aboard the Hawk
Stephen Lincoln, a priest
Rodney Tilbury, justice

Real historical people

Mary Tudor, queen of England
Elizabeth Tudor, her half-sister, later queen
Sir William Cecil, advisor to Elizabeth
Robert Cecil, William's son
William Allen, leader of the exiled English Catholics
Sir Francis Walsingham, spymaster

FRANCE

Palot family

Sylvie Palot
Isabelle Palot, her mother
Giles Palot, her father

Others

Pierre Aumande
Viscount Villeneuve, fellow student of Pierre's
Father Moineau, Pierre's tutor
Nath, Pierre's maid
Guillaume of Geneva, itinerant pastor

Cast of Characters

Louise, marchioness de Nîmes
Luc Mauriac, cargo broker
Aphrodite Beaulieu, daughter of the count of Beaulieu
René Duboeuf, tailor
Françoise Duboeuf, his young wife
Marquis de Lagny, a Protestant aristocrat
Bernard Housse, a young courtier
Alison McKay, lady-in-waiting to Mary Queen of Scots

Fictional members of the Guise household

Gaston Le Pin, head of the household guard of the Guise family
Brocard and Rasteau, two of Gaston's thugs
Véronique
Odette, maid to Véronique
Georges Biron, a spy

Real historical people: the Guise household

François, duke of Guise
Henri, son of François
Charles, cardinal Lorraine, brother of François

Real historical people: the Bourbons & their allies

Antoine, king of Navarre
Henri, son of Antoine
Louis, prince of Condé
Gaspard de Coligny, admiral of France

Real historical people: others

Henri II, king of France
Caterina de' Medici, queen of France
Children of Henri and Caterina:
Francis II, king of France
Charles IX, king of France
Henri III, king of France
Margot, queen of Navarre
Mary Stuart, queen of Scots
Charles de Louviers, assassin

Prologue

We hanged him in front of Kingsbridge Cathedral. It is the usual place for executions. After all, if you can't kill a man in front of God's face you probably shouldn't kill him at all.

The sheriff brought him up from the dungeon below the Guild Hall, hands tied behind his back. He walked upright, his pale face defiant, fearless.

The crowd jeered at him and cursed him. He seemed not to see them. But he saw me. Our eyes met, and in that momentary exchange of looks there was a lifetime.

I was responsible for his death, and he knew it.

I had been hunting him for decades. He was a bomber who would have killed half the rulers of our country, including most of the royal family, all in one act of bloodthirsty savagery – if I had not stopped him.

I have spent my life tracking such would-be murderers, and a lot of them have been executed – not just hanged but drawn and quartered, the more terrible death reserved for the worst offenders.

Yes, I have done this many times: watched a man die knowing that I, more than anyone else, had brought him to his just but dreadful punishment. I did it for my country, which is dear to me; for my sovereign, whom I serve; and for something else, a principle, the belief that a person has the right to make up his own mind about God.

He was the last of many men I sent to hell, but he made me think of the first . . .

Part One

1558

I

NED WILLARD CAME HOME to Kingsbridge in a snowstorm.

He sailed upstream from Combe Harbour in the cabin of a slow barge loaded with cloth from Antwerp and wine from Bordeaux. When he reckoned the boat was at last nearing Kingsbridge, he wrapped his French cloak more tightly around his shoulders, pulled the hood over his ears, stepped out onto the open deck, and looked ahead.

At first he was disappointed: all he could see was falling snow. But his longing for a sight of the city was like an ache, and he stared into the flurries, hoping. After a while his wish was granted, and the storm began to lift. A surprise patch of blue sky appeared. Gazing over the tops of the surrounding trees, he saw the tower of the cathedral – four hundred and five feet high, as every Kingsbridge Grammar School pupil knew. The stone angel that watched over the city from the top of the spire had snow edging her wings today, turning the tips of her feathers from dove-grey to bright white. As he looked, a momentary sunbeam struck the statue and gleamed off the snow, like a benison; then the storm closed in again and she was lost from view.

He saw nothing except trees for a while, but his imagination was full. He was about to be reunited with his mother after an absence of a year. He would not tell her how much he had missed her, for a man should be independent and self-sufficient at the age of eighteen.

But most of all he had missed Margery. He had fallen for her, with catastrophic timing, a few weeks before leaving Kingsbridge to spend a year in Calais, the English-ruled port on the north coast of France. Since childhood he had known and liked the mischievous, intelligent daughter of Sir

Reginald Fitzgerald. When she grew up, her impishness had taken on a new allure, so that he found himself staring at her in church, his mouth dry and his breath shallow. He had hesitated to do more than stare, for she was three years younger than he, but she knew no such inhibitions. They had kissed in the Kingsbridge graveyard, behind the concealing bulk of the tomb of Prior Philip, the monk who had commissioned the cathedral four centuries ago. There had been nothing childish about their long, passionate kiss: then she had laughed and run away.

But she kissed him again the next day. And on the evening before he left for France they admitted that they loved one another.

For the first few weeks they exchanged love letters. They had not told their parents of their feelings – it seemed too soon – so they could not write openly, but Ned confided in his older brother, Barney, who became their intermediary. Then Barney left Kingsbridge and went to Seville. Margery, too, had an older brother, Rollo; but she did not trust him the way Ned trusted Barney. And so the correspondence ended.

The lack of communication made little difference to Ned's feelings. He knew what people said about young love, and he examined himself constantly, waiting for his emotions to change; but they did not. After a few weeks in Calais, his cousin Thérèse made it clear that she adored him and was willing to do pretty much anything he liked to prove it, but Ned was hardly tempted. He reflected on this with some surprise, for he had never before passed up the chance of kissing a pretty girl with nice breasts.

However, something else was bothering him now. After rejecting Thérèse, he had felt confident that his feelings for Margery would not alter while he was away; but now he asked himself what would happen when he saw her. Would Margery in the flesh be as enchanting as she seemed in his memory? Would his love survive the reunion?

And what about her? A year was a long time for a girl of fourteen – fifteen now, of course, but still. Perhaps her feelings had faded after the letters stopped. She might have kissed someone else behind the tomb of Prior Philip. Ned would be horribly disappointed if she had become indifferent to him. And even if she still loved him, would the real Ned live up to her golden remembrance?

The storm eased again, and he saw that the barge was passing through the western suburbs of Kingsbridge. On both banks were the workshops of industries that used a lot of water: dyeing, fulling of cloth, papermaking and meat slaughtering. Because these processes could be smelly, the west was the low-rent neighbourhood.

Ahead, Leper Island came into view. The name was old: there had been no lepers here for centuries. At the near end of the island was Caris's Hospital, founded by the nun who had saved the city during the Black Death. As the barge drew closer Ned was able to see, beyond the hospital, the graceful twin curves of Merthin's Bridge, connecting the island to the mainland north and south. The love story of Caris and Merthin was part of local legend, passed from one generation to the next around winter fireplaces.

The barge eased into a berth on the crowded waterfront. The city seemed not to have altered much in a year. Places such as Kingsbridge changed only slowly, Ned supposed: cathedrals and bridges and hospitals were built to last.

He had a satchel slung over his shoulder, and now the captain of the barge handed him his only other luggage: a small wooden trunk containing a few clothes, a pair of pistols and some books. He hefted the box, took his leave, and stepped onto the dock.

He turned towards the large stone-built waterside warehouse that was his family's business headquarters, but when he had gone only a few steps, he heard a familiar Scots voice say: 'Well, if it isn't our Ned. Welcome home!'

The speaker was Janet Fife, his mother's housekeeper. Ned smiled broadly, glad to see her.

'I was just buying a fish for your mother's dinner,' she said. Janet was so thin she might have been made of sticks, but she loved to feed people. 'You shall have some, too.' She ran a fond eye over him. 'You've changed,' she said. 'Your face seems thinner, but your shoulders are broader. Did your Aunt Blanche feed you properly?'

'She did, but Uncle Dick set me to shovelling rocks.'

'That's no work for a scholar.'

'I didn't mind.'

Janet raised her voice. 'Malcolm, Malcolm, look who's here!'

Malcolm was Janet's husband and the Willard family's groom. He came limping across the dockside: he had been kicked by a horse years ago when he was young and inexperienced. He shook Ned's hand warmly and said: 'Old Acorn died.'

'He was my brother's favourite horse.' Ned hid a smile: it was just like Malcolm to give news of the animals before the humans. 'Is my mother well?'

'The mistress is in fine fettle, thanks be to God,' Malcolm said. 'And so was your brother, last we heard – he's not a great writer, and it takes a month or two for letters to get here from Spain. Let me help with your luggage, young Ned.'

Ned did not want to go home immediately. He had another plan. 'Would you carry my box to the house?' he said to Malcolm. On the spur of the moment he invented a cover story. 'Tell them I'm going into the cathedral to give thanks for a safe journey, and I'll come home right afterwards.'

'Very good.'

Malcolm limped off and Ned followed more slowly, enjoying the familiar sight of buildings he had grown up with. The snow was still falling lightly. The roofs were all white, but the streets were busy with people and carts, and underfoot there was only slush. Ned passed the notorious White Horse tavern, scene of regular Saturday-night fights, and walked uphill on the main street to the cathedral square. He passed the bishop's palace and paused for a nostalgic moment outside the Grammar School. Through its narrow, pointed windows he could see lamplit bookshelves. There he had learned to read and count, to know when to fight and when to run away, and to be flogged with a bundle of birch twigs without crying.

On the south side of the cathedral was the priory. Since King Henry VIII had dissolved the monasteries, Kingsbridge

Priory had fallen into sad disrepair, with holed roofs, teetering walls and vegetation growing through windows. The buildings were now owned by the current mayor, Margery's father, Sir Reginald Fitzgerald, but he had done nothing with them.

Happily the cathedral was well maintained, and stood as tall and strong as ever, the stone symbol of the living city. Ned stepped through the great west door into the nave. He would thank God for a safe journey and thereby turn the lie he had told Malcolm into a truth.

As always, the church was a place of business as well as worship: Friar Murdo had a tray of vials of earth from Palestine, guaranteed to be genuine; a man Ned did not recognize offered hot stones to warm your hands for a penny; and Puss Lovejoy, shivering in a red dress, was selling what she always sold.

Ned looked at the ribs of the vaulting, like the arms of a crowd of people all reaching up to heaven. Whenever he came into this place he thought of the men and women who had built it. Many of them were commemorated in *Timothy's Book*, a history of the priory that was studied in the school: the masons Tom Builder and his stepson, Jack; Prior Philip; Merthin Fitzgerald, who, as well as the bridge, had put up the central tower; and all the quarrymen, mortar women, carpenters and glaziers, ordinary people who had done an extraordinary thing, risen above their humble circumstances and created something eternally beautiful.

Ned knelt before the altar for a minute. A safe journey was something to be thankful for. Even on the short crossing from France to England, ships could get into trouble and people could die.

But he did not linger. His next stop was Margery's house.

On the north side of the cathedral square, opposite the bishop's palace, was the Bell Inn, and, next to that, a new house was going up. It was on land that had belonged to the priory, so Ned guessed Margery's father was building. It was going to be impressive, Ned saw, with bay windows and many chimneys: it would be the grandest house in Kingsbridge.

He continued up the main street to the crossroads. Margery's current home stood on one corner, across the road from the Guild Hall. Although not as imposing as the new place promised to be, it was a big timber-framed building occupying an acre of the priciest land in town.

Ned paused on the doorstep. He had been looking forward to this moment for a year but, now that it had come, he found his heart full of apprehension.

He knocked.

The door was opened by an elderly maid, Naomi, who invited him into the great hall. Naomi had known Ned all his life, but she looked troubled, as if he were a dubious stranger; and, when he asked for Margery, Naomi said she would go and see.

Ned looked at the painting of Christ on the cross that hung over the fireplace. In Kingsbridge there were two kinds of picture: Bible scenes and formal portraits of noblemen. In wealthy French homes Ned had been surprised to see paintings of pagan gods such as Venus and Bacchus, shown in fantastic forests, wearing robes that always seemed to be falling off.

But here there was something unusual. On the wall opposite the crucifixion was a map of Kingsbridge. Ned had never seen such a thing, and he studied it with interest. It clearly showed the town divided into four by the main street, running north–south, and the high street running east–west. The cathedral and the former priory occupied the south-east quarter; the malodorous industrial neighbourhood the south-west. All the churches were marked and some of the houses too, including the Fitzgeralds' and the Willards'. The river formed the eastern border of the town, then turned like a dog's leg. It had once formed the southern border too, but the town had extended over the water, thanks to Merthin's bridge, and there was now a big suburb on the far bank.

The two pictures represented Margery's parents, Ned noted: her father, the politician, would have hung the map; and her mother, the devout Catholic, the crucifixion.

It was not Margery who came into the great hall but her brother, Rollo. He was taller than Ned, and good-looking, with black hair. Ned and Rollo had been at school together, but they had never been friends: Rollo was four years older. Rollo had been the cleverest boy in the school, and had been put in charge of the younger pupils; but Ned had refused to regard him as a master and had never accepted his authority. To make matters worse, it had soon become clear that Ned was going to be at least as clever as Rollo. There had been quarrels and fights until Rollo went away to study at Kingsbridge College, Oxford.

Ned tried to hide his dislike and suppress his irritation. He said politely: 'I see there's a building site next to the Bell. Is your father putting up a new house?'

'Yes. This place is rather old-fashioned.'

'Business must be good at Combe.' Sir Reginald was Receiver of Customs at Combe Harbour. It was a lucrative post, granted to him by Mary Tudor when she became queen, as a reward for his support.

Rollo said: 'So, you're back from Calais. How was it?'

'I learned a lot. My father built a pier and warehouse there, managed by my Uncle Dick.' Edmund, Ned's father, had died ten years ago, and his mother had run the business ever since. 'We ship English iron ore, tin and lead from Combe Harbour to Calais, and from there it's sold all over Europe.' The Calais operation was the foundation of the Willard family business.

'How has the war affected it?' England was at war with France, but Rollo's concern was transparently fake. In truth he relished the danger to the Willard fortune.

Ned downplayed it. 'Calais is well defended,' he said, sounding more confident than he felt. 'It's surrounded by forts that have protected it ever since it became part of England two hundred years ago.' He ran out of patience. 'Is Margery at home?'

'Do you have a reason to see her?'

It was a rude question, but Ned pretended not to notice. He opened his satchel. 'I brought her a present from France,' he said. He took out a length of shimmering lavender silk, carefully folded. 'I think the colour will suit her.'

'She won't want to see you.'

Ned frowned. What was this? 'I'm quite sure she will.'

'I can't imagine why.'

Ned chose his words carefully. 'I admire your sister, Rollo, and I believe she is fond of me.'

'You're going to find that things have changed while you've been away, young Ned,' said Rollo condescendingly.

Ned did not take this seriously. He thought Rollo was just being slyly malicious. 'All the same, please ask her.'

Rollo smiled, and that worried Ned, for it was the smile he had worn when he had permission to flog one of the younger pupils at the school.

Rollo said: 'Margery is engaged to be married.'

'What?' Ned stared at him, feeling shocked and hurt, as if he had been clubbed from behind. He had not been sure what to expect, but he had not dreamed of this.

Rollo just looked back, smiling.

Ned said the first thing that came into his head. 'Who to?'

'She is going to marry Viscount Shiring.'

Ned said: 'Bart?' That was incredible. Of all the young men in the county, the slow-witted, humourless Bart Shiring was the least likely to capture Margery's heart. The prospect that he would one day be the earl of Shiring might have been enough for many girls – but not for Margery, Ned was sure.

Or, at least, he would have been sure a year ago.

He said: 'Are you making this up?'

It was a foolish question, he realized immediately. Rollo could be crafty and spiteful, but not stupid: he would not invent such a story, for fear of looking foolish when the truth came out.

Rollo shrugged. 'The engagement will be announced tomorrow at the earl's banquet.'

Tomorrow was the twelfth day of Christmas. If the earl of Shiring was having a celebration, it was certain that Ned's family had been invited. So Ned would be there to hear the announcement, if Rollo was telling the truth.

'Does she love him?' Ned blurted out.

Rollo was not expecting that question, and it was his turn to be startled. 'I don't see why I should discuss that with you.'

His equivocation made Ned suspect that the answer was No. 'Why do you look so shifty?'

Rollo bridled. 'You'd better go, before I feel obliged to thrash you the way I used to.'

'We're not in school any longer,' Ned said. 'You might be surprised by which of us gets thrashed.' He wanted to fight Rollo, and he was angry enough not to care whether he would win.

But Rollo was more circumspect. He walked to the door and held it open. 'Goodbye,' he said.

Ned hesitated. He did not want to go without seeing Margery. If he had known where her room was he might have run up the stairs. But he would look stupid opening bedroom doors at random in someone else's house.

He picked up the silk and put it back in his satchel. 'This isn't the last word,' he said. 'You can't keep her locked away for long. I will speak to her.'

Rollo ignored that, and stood patiently at the door.

Ned itched to punch Rollo, but suppressed the urge with an effort: they were men now, and he could not start a fight with so little provocation. He felt outmanoeuvred. He hesitated for a long moment. He could not think what to do.

So he went out.

Rollo said: 'Don't hurry back.'

Ned walked the short distance down the main street to the house where he had been born.

The Willard place was opposite the west front of the cathedral. It had been enlarged, over the years, with haphazard extensions, and now it sprawled untidily over several thousand square feet. But it was comfortable, with massive fireplaces, a large dining room for convivial meals, and good feather beds. The place was home to Alice Willard and her two sons plus Grandma, the mother of Ned's late father.

Ned went in and found his mother in the front parlour, which she used as an office when not at the waterfront warehouse. She leaped up from her chair at the writing table and hugged and kissed him. She was heavier than she had been a year ago, he saw right away; but he decided not to say so.

He looked around. The room had not changed. Her favourite painting was there, a picture of Christ and the

13

adulteress surrounded by a crowd of hypocritical Pharisees who wanted to stone her to death. Alice liked to quote Jesus: 'He that is without sin among you, let him first cast a stone at her.' It was also an erotic picture, for the woman's breasts were exposed, a sight that had at one time given young Ned vivid dreams.

He looked out of the parlour window across the market square to the elegant façade of the great church, with its long lines of lancet windows and pointed arches. It had been there every day of his life: only the sky above it changed with the seasons. It gave him a vague but powerful sense of reassurance. People were born and died, cities could rise and fall, wars began and ended, but Kingsbridge Cathedral would last until the Day of Judgement.

'So you went into the cathedral to give thanks,' she said. 'You're a good boy.'

He could not deceive her. 'I went to the Fitzgerald house as well,' he said. He saw a brief look of disappointment flash across her face, and he said: 'I hope you don't mind that I went there first.'

'A little,' she admitted. 'But I should remember what it's like to be young and in love.'

She was forty-eight. After Edmund died, everyone had said she should marry again, and little Ned, eight years old, had been terrified that he would get a cruel stepfather. But she had been a widow for ten years now, and he guessed she would stay single.

Ned said: 'Rollo told me that Margery is going to marry Bart Shiring.'

'Oh, dear. I was afraid of that. Poor Ned. I'm so sorry.'

'Why does her father have the right to tell her who to marry?'

'Fathers expect some degree of control. Your father and I didn't have to worry about that. I never had a daughter . . . who lived.'

Ned knew that. His mother had given birth to two girls before Barney. Ned was familiar with the two little tombstones in the graveyard on the north side of Kingsbridge Cathedral.

He said: 'A woman has to love her husband. You wouldn't have forced a daughter to marry a brute like Bart.'

'No, I suppose I wouldn't.'

'What is wrong with those people?'

'Sir Reginald believes in hierarchies and authority. As mayor, he thinks an alderman's job is to make decisions and then enforce them. When your father was mayor he said that aldermen should rule the town by serving it.'

Ned said impatiently: 'That sounds like two ways of looking at the same thing.'

'It's not, though,' said his mother. 'It's two different worlds.'

*

'I WILL NOT marry Bart Shiring!' said Margery Fitzgerald to her mother.

Margery was upset and angry. For twelve months she had been waiting for Ned to return, thinking about him every day, longing to see his wry smile and golden-brown eyes; and now she had learned, from the servants, that he was back in Kingsbridge, and he had come to the house, but they had not told her, and he had gone away! She was furious at her family for deceiving her, and she wept with frustration.

'I'm not asking you to marry Viscount Shiring today,' said Lady Jane. 'Just go and talk to him.'

They were in Margery's bedroom. In one corner was a prie-dieu, a prayer desk, where she knelt twice a day, facing the crucifix on the wall, and counted her prayers with the help of a string of carved ivory beads. The rest of the room was all luxury: a four-poster bed with a feather mattress and richly coloured hangings; a big carved-oak chest for her many dresses; a tapestry of a forest scene.

This room had seen many arguments with her mother over the years. But Margery was a woman now. She was petite, but a little taller and heavier than her tiny, fierce mother; and she felt it was no longer a foregone conclusion that the fight would end in victory for Lady Jane and humiliation for Margery.

Margery said: 'What's the point? He's come here to court

me. If I talk to him, he'll feel encouraged. And then he'll be even angrier when he realizes the truth.'

'You can be polite.'

Margery did not want to talk about Bart. 'How could you not tell me that Ned was here?' she said. 'That was dishonest.'

'I didn't know until he'd gone! Only Rollo saw him.'

'Rollo was doing your will.'

'Children should do their parents' will,' her mother said. 'You know the commandment: "Honour thy father and mother". It's your duty to God.'

All her short life Margery had struggled with this. She knew that God wished her to be obedient, but she had a wilful and rebellious nature – as she had so often been told – and she found it extraordinarily difficult to be good. However, when this was pointed out to her, she always suppressed her nature and became compliant. God's will was more important than anything else, she knew that. 'I'm sorry, Mother,' she said.

'Go and talk to Bart,' said Lady Jane.

'Very well.'

'Just comb your hair, dear.'

Margery had a last flash of defiance. 'My hair's fine,' she said, and before her mother could argue she left the room.

Bart was in the hall, wearing new yellow hose. He was teasing one of the dogs, offering a piece of ham then snatching it away at the last moment.

Lady Jane followed Margery down the stairs and said: 'Take Lord Shiring into the library and show him the books.'

'He's not interested in books,' Margery snapped.

'Margery!'

Bart said: 'I'd like to see the books.'

Margery shrugged. 'Follow me, please,' she said, and led the way into the next room. She left the door open, but her mother did not join them.

Her father's books were arranged on three shelves. 'By God, what a lot of them you have!' Bart exclaimed. 'A man would waste his life away reading them all.'

There were fifty or so, more than would normally be seen

outside a university or cathedral library, and a sign of wealth. Some were in Latin or French.

Margery made an effort to play host. She took down a book in English. 'This is *The Pastime of Pleasure*,' she said. 'That might interest you.'

He gave a leer and moved closer. 'Pleasure is a great pastime.' He seemed pleased with the witticism.

She stepped back. 'It's a long poem about the education of a knight.'

'Ah.' Bart lost interest in the book. Looking along the shelf, he picked out *The Book of Cookery*. 'This is important,' he said. 'A wife should make sure her husband has good food, don't you think?'

'Of course.' Margery was trying hard to think of something to talk about. What was Bart interested in? War, perhaps. 'People are blaming the queen for the war with France.'

'Why is it her fault?'

'They say that Spain and France are fighting over possessions in Italy, a conflict that has nothing to do with England, and we're involved only because our Queen Mary is married to King Felipe of Spain and has to back him.'

Bart nodded. 'A wife must be led by her husband.'

'That's why a girl must choose very carefully.' This pointed remark went over Bart's head. Margery went on: 'Some say our queen should not be married to a foreign monarch.'

Bart tired of the subject. 'We shouldn't be talking of politics. Women ought to leave such matters to their husbands.'

'Women have so many duties to their husbands,' Margery said, knowing that her ironic tone would be lost on Bart. 'We have to cook for them, and be led by them, and leave politics to them . . . I'm glad I haven't got a husband, life is simpler this way.'

'But every woman needs a man.'

'Let's talk about something else.'

'I mean it.' He closed his eyes, concentrating, then came out with a short rehearsed speech. 'You are the most beautiful woman in the world, and I love you. Please be my wife.'

Her reaction was visceral. 'No!'

Bart looked baffled. He did not know how to respond. Clearly he had been led to expect the opposite answer. After a pause he said: 'But my wife will become a countess one day!'

'And you must marry a girl who longs for that with all her heart.'

'Don't you?'

'No.' She tried not to be harsh. It was difficult: understatement was lost on him. 'Bart, you're strong and handsome, and I'm sure brave too, but I could never love you.' Ned came into her mind: with him she never found herself trying to think of something to talk about. 'I will marry a man who is clever and thoughtful and who wants his wife to be more than just the most senior of his servants.' There, she thought; even Bart can't fail to understand that.

He moved with surprising speed and grabbed her upper arms. His grip was strong. 'Women like to be mastered,' he said.

'Who told you that? Believe me, I don't!' She tried to pull away from him but could not.

He drew her to him and kissed her.

On another day she might just have turned her face away. Lips did not hurt. But she was still sad and bitter about having missed Ned. Her mind was full of thoughts of what might have happened: how she might have kissed him and touched his hair and pulled his body to hers. His imaginary presence was so strong that Bart's embrace repelled her to the point of panic. Without thinking, she kneed him in the balls as hard as she could.

He roared with pain and shock, released her from his grasp, and bent over, groaning in agony, eyes squeezed shut, both hands between his thighs.

Margery ran to the door, but before she got there her mother stepped into the library, obviously having been listening outside.

Lady Jane looked at Bart and understood immediately what had happened. She turned to Margery and said: 'You foolish child.'

'I won't marry this brute!' Margery cried.

Her father came in. He was tall with black hair, like Rollo, but unlike Rollo he was heavily freckled. He said coldly: 'You will marry whomever your father chooses.'

That ominous statement scared Margery. She began to suspect that she had underestimated her parents' determination. It was a mistake to let her indignation take over. She tried to calm herself and think logically.

Still passionate, but more measured, she said: 'I'm not a princess! We're gentry, not aristocracy. My marriage isn't a political alliance. I'm the daughter of a merchant. People like us don't have arranged marriages.'

That angered Sir Reginald, and he flushed under his freckles. 'I am a knight!'

'Not an earl!'

'I am descended from the Ralph Fitzgerald who became earl of Shiring two centuries ago – as is Bart. Ralph Fitzgerald was the son of Sir Gerald and the brother of Merthin the bridge-builder. The blood of the English nobility runs in my veins.'

Margery saw with dismay that she was up against not just her father's inflexible will but his family pride as well. She did not know how she could overcome that combination. The only thing she was sure of was that she must not show weakness.

She turned to Bart. Surely he would not want to marry an unwilling bride? She said: 'I'm sorry, Lord Shiring, but I'm going to marry Ned Willard.'

Sir Reginald was startled. 'No, you're not, by the cross.'

'I'm in love with Ned Willard.'

'You're too young to be in love with anyone. And the Willards are practically Protestants!'

'They go to Mass just like everyone else.'

'All the same, you're going to marry Viscount Shiring.'

'I will not,' she said with quiet firmness.

Bart was recovering. He muttered: 'I knew she'd be trouble.'

Sir Reginald said: 'She just needs a firm hand.'

'She needs a whip.'

Lady Jane intervened. 'Think of it, Margery,' she said. 'You will be the countess one day, and your son will be the earl!'

'That's all you care about, isn't it?' Margery said. She heard her own voice rising to a defiant yell, but she could not stop.

'You just want your grandchildren to be aristocrats!' She could see from their faces that her surmise had touched the truth. With contempt she said: 'Well, I will not be a broodmare just because you have delusions of nobility.'

As soon as she had said it she knew she had gone too far. Her insult had touched her father where he was most sensitive.

Sir Reginald took off his belt.

Margery backed away fearfully, and found herself up against the writing table. Sir Reginald grabbed her by the back of her neck, using his left hand. She saw that the tongue end of the belt had a brass sleeve, and she was so scared that she screamed.

Sir Reginald bent her over the table. She wriggled desperately, but he was too strong for her, and he held her easily.

She heard her mother say: 'Leave the room, please, Lord Shiring.' That scared her even more.

The door slammed, then she heard the belt whistle through the air. It landed on the backs of her thighs. Her dress was too thin to give her any protection, and she screamed again, in pain this time. She was lashed again, and a third time.

Then her mother spoke. 'I think that's enough, Reginald,' she said.

'Spare the rod and spoil the child,' said Sir Reginald. It was a grimly familiar proverb: everyone believed that flogging was good for children, except the children.

Lady Jane said: 'The Bible verse actually says something different. "He that spareth his rod hateth his son: but he that loveth him chasteneth him betimes." It refers to boys, not girls.'

Sir Reginald countered with a different verse. 'Another biblical proverb says: "Withhold not correction from the child", doesn't it?'

'She's not really a child any more. Besides, we both know this approach doesn't work on Margery. Punishment only makes her more stubborn.'

'Then what do you propose?'

'Leave her to me. I'll talk to her when she's calmed down.'

'Very well,' Sir Reginald said, and Margery thought it was

over; then the belt whistled again, stinging her already painful legs, and she screamed once more. Immediately afterwards she heard his boots stamp across the floor and out of the room, and it really was over.

*

NED WAS SURE he would see Margery at Earl Swithin's feast. Her parents could hardly keep her away. It would be like an announcement that something was wrong. Everyone would be talking about why Margery was not there.

The cartwheel ruts in the mud road were frozen hard, and Ned's pony picked her way daintily along the treacherous surface. The heat of the horse warmed his body, but his hands and feet were numb with cold. Beside him his mother, Alice, rode a broad-backed mare.

The earl of Shiring's home, New Castle, was twelve miles from Kingsbridge. The journey took almost half a short winter day, and made Ned mad with impatience. He had to see Margery, not just because he longed for a sight of her, but also so that he could find out what the devil was going on.

Ahead, New Castle appeared in the distance. It had been new a hundred and fifty years ago. Recently the earl had built a house in the ruins of the medieval fortress. The remaining battlements, made of the same grey stone as Kingsbridge Cathedral, were adorned today with ribbons and swags of freezing fog. As he drew near, Ned heard sounds of festivity: shouted greetings, laughter, and a country band – a deep drum, a lively fiddle, and the reedy whine of pipes drifting through the cold air. The noise bore with it a promise of blazing fires, hot food, and something cheering to drink.

Ned kicked his horse into a trot, impatient to arrive and put an end to his uncertainty. Did Margery love Bart Shiring, and was she going to marry him?

The road led straight to the entrance. Rooks strutting on the castle walls cawed spitefully at the visitors. The drawbridge had gone long ago, and the moat had been filled in, but there were still arrow-slit windows in the gatehouse. Ned rode through to the noisy courtyard, bustling with brightly dressed guests, horses and carts, and the earl's busy servants. Ned entrusted his pony to a groom and joined the throng moving towards the house.

He did not see Margery.

On the far side of the courtyard stood a modern brick mansion, attached to the old castle buildings, the chapel on one side and the brewery on the other. Ned had been here only once in the four years since it had been built, and he marvelled again at the rows of big windows and the ranks of multiple chimneys. Grander than the wealthiest Kingsbridge merchants' homes, it was the largest house in the county, although perhaps there were even bigger places in London, which he had never visited.

Earl Swithin had lost status during the reign of Henry VIII, because he had opposed the king's breach with the Pope; but the earl's fortunes had revived five years ago with the accession of the ultra-Catholic Mary Tudor as queen, and Swithin was once again favoured, rich and powerful. This promised to be a lavish banquet.

Ned entered the house and passed into a great hall two storeys high. The tall windows made the room light even on a winter day. The walls were panelled in varnished oak and hung with tapestries of hunting scenes. Logs burned in two huge fireplaces at opposite ends of the long room. In the gallery that ran around three of the four walls, the band he had heard from the road was playing energetically. High on the fourth wall was a portrait of Earl Swithin's father, holding a staff to symbolize power.

Some guests were performing a vigorous country dance in groups of eight, holding hands to form rotating circles then stopping to skip in and out. Others conversed in clusters, raising their voices over the music and the stomping of the dancers. Ned took a wooden cup of hot cider and looked around the room.

One group stood aloof from the dancing: the ship owner Philbert Cobley and his family, all dressed in grey and black. The Kingsbridge Protestants were a semi-secret group: everyone knew they were there, and could guess who they were, but their existence was not openly acknowledged – a bit like the half-hidden community of men who loved men, Ned thought. The Protestants did not admit to their beliefs, for then they would be tortured until they recanted, and burned to death if they refused. Asked what they believed, they would prevaricate. They went to Catholic services, as they were obliged to by law. But they took every opportunity to object to bawdy songs, bosom-revealing gowns, and drunk priests. And there was no law against dull clothes.

Ned knew just about everyone in the room. The younger guests were the boys with whom he had attended Kingsbridge Grammar School and the girls whose hair he had pulled on Sunday after church. The older generation of local notables were equally familiar; they were in and out of his mother's house all the time.

In the search for Margery his eye lit on a stranger: a long-nosed man in his late thirties, his mid-brown hair already receding, his beard neatly trimmed in the pointed shape that was fashionable. Short and wiry, he wore a dark red coat that was unostentatiously expensive. He was speaking to Earl Swithin and Sir Reginald Fitzgerald, and Ned was struck by the attitudes of the two local magnates. They clearly did not like this distinguished visitor – Reginald leaned back with folded arms, and Swithin stood with legs apart and hands on hips – yet they were listening to him intently.

The musicians ended a number with a flourish, and in the relative quiet Ned spoke to Philbert Cobley's son, Daniel, a couple of years older than himself, a fat boy with a pale round face. 'Who's that?' Ned asked him, pointing at the stranger in the red coat.

'Sir William Cecil. He is estate manager for Princess Elizabeth.'

Elizabeth Tudor was the younger half-sister of Queen Mary. 'I've heard of Cecil,' Ned said. 'Wasn't he secretary of state for a while?'

'That's right.'

At the time Ned had been too young to follow politics closely, but he remembered the name of Cecil being mentioned with admiration by his mother. Cecil had not been sufficiently Catholic for Mary Tudor's taste, and as soon as she became queen she had fired him, which was why he now had the less grand job of looking after Elizabeth's finances.

So what was he doing here?

Ned's mother would want to know about Cecil. A visitor brought news, and Alice was obsessed with news. She had always taught her sons that information could make a man's fortune – or save him from ruin. But as Ned looked around for Alice he spotted Margery, and immediately forgot about William Cecil.

He was startled by Margery's appearance. She looked older by five years, not one. Her curly dark hair was pinned up in an elaborate coiffure and topped by a man's cap with a jaunty plume. A small white ruff around her neck seemed to light up her face. She was small, but not thin, and the fashionably stiff bodice of her blue velvet gown did not quite conceal her delightfully rounded figure. As always, her face was expressive. She smiled, raised her eyebrows, tilted her head, and mimed surprise, puzzlement, scorn and delight, one after another. He found himself staring, just as he had in the past. For a few moments it seemed as if there was no one else in the room.

Waking from his trance, he pushed through the crowd towards her.

She saw him coming. Her face lit up with pleasure, delighting him; then it changed, faster than the weather on a spring day, and her expression became clouded with worry. As he approached, her eyes widened fearfully and she seemed to be telling him to go away, but he ignored that. He had to speak to her.

He opened his mouth, but she spoke first. 'Follow me when they play Hunt the Hart,' she said in a low voice. 'Don't say anything now.'

Hunt the Hart was a hide-and-seek game played by young people at feasts. Ned was bucked by her invitation. But he was not willing to walk away from her without at least some answers. 'Are you in love with Bart Shiring?' he asked.

'No! Now go away – we can talk later.'

Ned was thrilled, but he had not finished. 'Are you going to marry him?'

'Not while I have enough breath to say go to the devil.'

Ned smiled. 'All right, now I can be patient.' He walked away, happy.

*

ROLLO OBSERVED WITH alarm the interaction between his sister and Ned Willard. It did not last long but it was obviously intense. Rollo was concerned. He had been listening outside the library door yesterday, when Margery was beaten by their father, and he agreed with his mother that punishment just made Margery more obstinate.

He did not want his sister to marry Ned. Rollo had always disliked Ned, but that was the least of it. More importantly, the Willards were soft on Protestantism. Edmund Willard had been quite content when King Henry turned against the Catholic Church. Admittedly, he had not seemed very troubled when Queen Mary reversed the process – but that, too, offended Rollo. He could not bear people who took religion lightly. The authority of the Church should be everything to them.

Almost as importantly, marriage with Ned Willard would do nothing for the prestige of the Fitzgeralds: it would merely be an alliance between two prosperous commercial families. However, Bart Shiring would take them into the ranks of the nobility. To Rollo, the prestige of the Fitzgerald family mattered more than anything except the will of God.

The dancing finished, and the earl's staff brought in boards and trestles to make a T-shaped table, the crosspiece at one end and the tail stretching the full length of the room; then they began to lay the table. They went about their work in a somewhat careless spirit, Rollo thought, tossing pottery cups and loaves of bread onto the white tablecloth haphazardly. That would be because there was no woman in charge of the household: the countess had died two years ago, and Swithin had not yet remarried.

A servant spoke to Rollo. 'Your father summons you, Master Fitzgerald. He's in the earl's parlour.'

The man led Rollo into a side room with a writing table and a shelf of ledgers, evidently the place where Earl Swithin conducted business.

Swithin sat on a huge chair that was almost a throne. He was tall and handsome, like Bart, though many years of eating well and drinking plenty had thickened his waist and reddened his nose. Four years ago he had lost most of the fingers of his left hand in the battle of Hartley Wood. He made no attempt to conceal the deficiency – in fact, he seemed proud of his wound.

Rollo's father, Sir Reginald, sat next to Swithin, lean and freckled, a leopard beside a bear.

Bart Shiring was there, too, and to Rollo's consternation so were Alice and Ned Willard.

William Cecil was on a low stool in front of the six local people but, despite the symbolism of the seating, it looked to Rollo as if Cecil was in charge of the meeting.

Reginald said to Cecil: 'You won't mind my son joining us? He has been to Oxford University, and studied law at the Inns of Court in London.'

'I'm glad to have the younger generation here,' Cecil said amiably. 'I include my own son in meetings, even though he's only sixteen – the earlier they begin, the faster they learn.'

Studying Cecil, Rollo noticed that there were three warts on his right cheek, and his brown beard was beginning to turn grey. He had been a powerful courtier during the reign of Edward VI, while still in his twenties, and although he was not yet forty years old he had an air of confident wisdom that might have belonged to a much older man.

Earl Swithin shifted impatiently. 'I have a hundred guests in the hall, Sir William. You'd better tell me what you have to say that is important enough to take me away from my own party.'

'At once, my lord,' Cecil said. 'The queen is not pregnant.'

Rollo let out a grunt of surprise and dismay.

Queen Mary and King Felipe were desperate for heirs to their two crowns, England and Spain. But they spent hardly any time together, being so busy ruling their widely separated kingdoms. So there had been rejoicing in both countries when Mary had announced that she was expecting a baby next March. Obviously something had gone wrong.

Rollo's father, Sir Reginald, said grimly: 'This has happened before.'

Cecil nodded. 'It is her second false pregnancy.'

Swithin looked bewildered. 'False?' he said. 'What do you mean?'

'There has been no miscarriage,' Cecil said solemnly.

Reginald explained: 'She wants a baby so badly, she convinces herself that she's expecting when she's not.'

'I see,' said Swithin. 'Female stupidity.'

Alice Willard gave a contemptuous snort at this remark, but Swithin was oblivious.

Cecil said: 'We must now face the likelihood that our queen will never give birth to a child.'

Rollo's mind was awhirl with the consequences. The longed-for child of the ultra-Catholic Queen Mary and the equally devout King of Spain would have been raised strictly Catholic, and could have been relied upon to favour families such as the Fitzgeralds. But if Mary should die without an heir, all bets were off.

Cecil had figured this out long ago, Rollo assumed. Cecil said: 'The transition to a new monarch is a time of danger for any country.'

Rollo had to suppress a feeling of panic. England could return to Protestantism – and everything the Fitzgerald family had achieved in the last five years could be wiped out.

'I want to plan for a smooth succession, with no bloodshed,' Cecil said in a tone of reasonableness. 'I'm here to speak to you three powerful provincial leaders – the earl of the county, the mayor of Kingsbridge, and the town's leading merchant – and to ask you to help me.'

He sounded deceptively like a diligent servant making careful plans, but Rollo could already see that he was, in fact, a dangerous revolutionary.

Swithin said: 'And how would we help you?'

'By pledging support for my mistress, Elizabeth.'

Swithin said challengingly: 'You assume that Elizabeth is heir to the throne?'

'Henry the Eighth left three children,' Cecil said pedantically, stating the obvious. 'His son, Edward the Sixth, the boy king, died before he could produce an heir, so Henry's elder daughter, Mary Tudor, became queen. The logic is inescapable. If Queen Mary dies childless, as King Edward did, the next in line to the throne is clearly Henry's other daughter, Elizabeth Tudor.'

Rollo decided it was time to speak. This dangerous nonsense could not be allowed to pass unchallenged, and he was the only lawyer in the room. He tried to speak as quietly and as rationally as Cecil but, despite the effort, he could hear the note of alarm in his own voice. 'Elizabeth is illegitimate!' he said. 'Henry was never truly married to her mother. His divorce from his previous wife was disallowed by the Pope.'

Swithin added: 'Bastards cannot inherit property or titles – everyone knows that.'

Rollo winced. Calling Elizabeth a bastard was unnecessary rudeness to her counsellor. Coarse manners were typical of Swithin, unfortunately. But it was rash, Rollo felt, to antagonize the self-possessed Cecil. The man might be out of favour, but still he had an air of quiet potency.

Cecil overlooked the incivility. 'The divorce was ratified by the English parliament,' he said with polite insistence.

Swithin said: 'I hear she has Protestant leanings.'

That was the heart of it, Rollo thought.

Cecil smiled. 'She has told me, many times, that if she should become queen, it is her dearest wish that no Englishman should lose his life for the sake of his beliefs.'

Ned Willard spoke up. 'That's a good sign,' he said. 'No one wants to see more people burned at the stake.'

That was typical of the Willards, Rollo thought: anything for a quiet life.

Earl Swithin was equally irritated by the equivocation. 'Catholic or Protestant?' he said. 'She must be one or the other.'

'On the contrary,' Cecil said, 'her creed is tolerance.'

Swithin was indignant. 'Tolerance?' he said scornfully. 'Of heresy? Blasphemy? Godlessness?'

Swithin's outrage was justified, in Rollo's opinion, but it was no substitute for legal argument. The Catholic Church had its own view on who should be the next ruler of England. 'In the eyes of the world, the true heir to the throne is the other Mary, the queen of the Scots.'

'Surely not,' Cecil argued, clearly having expected this. 'Mary Stuart is no more than the grand-niece of King Henry VIII, whereas Elizabeth Tudor is his daughter.'

'His illegitimate daughter.'

Ned Willard spoke again. 'I saw Mary Stuart when I went to Paris,' he said. 'I didn't talk to her, but I was in one of the outer rooms of the Louvre Palace when she passed through. She is tall and beautiful.'

Rollo said impatiently: 'What's that got to do with anything?'

Ned persisted. 'She's fifteen years old.' He looked hard at Rollo. 'The same age as your sister, Margery.'

'That's not the point—'

Ned raised his voice to override the interruption. 'Some people think a girl of fifteen is too young to choose a husband, let alone rule a country.'

Rollo drew in his breath sharply, and his father gave a grunt of indignation. Cecil frowned, no doubt realizing that Ned's statement had a special meaning hidden from an outsider.

Ned added: 'I was told that Mary speaks French and Scotch, but she has hardly any English.'

Rollo said: 'Such considerations have no weight in law.'

Ned persisted. 'But there's worse. Mary is engaged to marry Prince Francis, the heir to the French throne. The English people dislike our present queen's marriage to the King of Spain, and they will be even more hostile to a queen who marries the King of France.'

Rollo said: 'Such decisions are not made by the English people.'

'All the same, where there is doubt there may be fighting, and then the people may pick up their scythes and their axes and make their opinions known.'

Cecil put in: 'And that's exactly what I'm trying to prevent.'

That was actually a threat, Rollo noted angrily; but before he could say so, Swithin spoke again. 'What is this girl Elizabeth like, personally? I've never met her.'

Rollo frowned in irritation at this diversion from the question of legitimacy, but Cecil answered willingly. 'She is the best-educated woman I have ever met,' he said. 'She can converse in Latin as easily as in English, and she also speaks French, Spanish and Italian, and writes Greek. She is not thought to be a great beauty, but she has a way of enchanting a man so that he thinks her lovely. She has inherited the strength of will of her father, King Henry. She will make a decisive sovereign.'

Cecil was obviously in love with her, Rollo thought; but that was not the worst of it. Elizabeth's opponents had to rely on legalistic arguments because there was little else for them to take hold of. It seemed that Elizabeth was old enough, wise enough, and strong-minded enough to rule England. She might be a Protestant, but she was too clever to flaunt it, and they had no proof.

The prospect of a Protestant queen horrified Rollo. She would surely disfavour Catholic families. The Fitzgeralds might never recover their fortunes.

Swithin said: 'Now, if she were to marry a strong Catholic husband who could keep her under control, she might be more acceptable.' He chuckled lasciviously, making Rollo suppress a shudder. Clearly Swithin was aroused by the thought of keeping a princess under control.

'I'll bear that in mind,' said Cecil drily. A bell rang to tell the guests to take their places at table, and he stood up. 'All I ask is that you don't rush to judgement. Give Princess Elizabeth a chance.'

Reginald and Rollo hung back when the others left the room. Reginald said: 'I think we set him straight.'

Rollo shook his head. There were times when he wished his father's mind were more devious. 'Cecil knew, before he came here, that loyal Catholics such as you and Swithin would never pledge support for Elizabeth.'

'I suppose he did,' said Reginald. 'He's nothing if not well informed.'

'And he's evidently a clever man.'

'Then why is he here?'

'I've been wondering about that,' said Rollo. 'I think he came to assess the strength of his enemies.'

'Oh,' said his father. 'I never thought of that.'

'Let's go in to dinner,' said Rollo.

＊

NED WAS RESTLESS all through the banquet. He could hardly wait for the eating and drinking to end so that the game of Hunt the Hart could begin. But just as the sweets were being cleared away, his mother caught his eye and beckoned him.

He had noticed that she was deep in conversation with Sir William Cecil. Alice Willard was a vigorous, tubby woman, wearing a costly dress of Kingsbridge Scarlet embroidered with gold thread, and a medallion of the Virgin Mary around her neck to ward off accusations of Protestantism. Ned was tempted to pretend that he had not seen her summons. The game would take place while the tables were being cleared and the actors were getting ready to perform the play. Ned was not sure what Margery had in mind but, whatever it was, he was not going to miss it. However, his mother was strict as well as loving, and she would not tolerate disobedience, so he went to her side.

'Sir William wants to ask you a few questions,' Alice said.

'I'm honoured,' Ned said politely.

'I want to know about Calais,' Cecil began. 'I gather you've just returned from there.'

'I left a week before Christmas, and got here yesterday.'

'I need hardly tell you and your mother how vital the city is to English commerce. It's also a matter of national pride that we still rule a small part of France.'

Ned nodded. 'And deeply annoying to the French, of course.'

'How is the morale of the English community there?'

'Fine,' said Ned, but he began to worry. Cecil was not

interrogating him out of idle curiosity: there was a reason. And, now that he thought about it, his mother's face looked grim. But he carried on. 'When I left, they were still rejoicing over the defeat of the French at St Quentin back in August. That made them feel that the war between England and France was not going to affect them.'

'Over-confident, perhaps,' Cecil muttered.

Ned frowned. 'Calais is surrounded by forts: Sangatte, Fréthun, Nielles—'

Cecil interrupted him. 'And if the fortresses should fall?'

'The city has three hundred and seven cannons.'

'You have a good mind for details. But can the people withstand a siege?'

'They have food for three months.' Ned had made sure of his facts before leaving, for he had known that his mother would expect a detailed report. He turned to Alice now. 'What's happened, Mother?'

Alice said: 'The French took Sangatte on the first day of January.'

Ned was shocked. 'How could that happen?'

Cecil answered that question. 'The French army was assembled in great secrecy in nearby towns. The attack took the Calais garrison by surprise.'

'Who leads the French forces?'

'François, duke of Guise.'

'Scarface!' said Ned. 'He's a legend.' The duke was France's greatest general.

'By now the city must be under siege.'

'But it has not fallen.'

'So far as we know, but my latest news is five days old.'

Ned turned to Alice again. 'No word from Uncle Dick?'

Alice shook her head. 'He cannot get a message out of a besieged city.'

Ned thought of his relations there: Aunt Blanche, a much better cook than Janet Fife, though Ned would never tell Janet that; cousin Albin, who was his age and had taught him the French words for intimate parts of the body and other unmentionable things; and amorous Thérèse. Would they survive?

Alice said quietly: 'Almost everything we have is tied up in Calais.'

Ned frowned. Was that possible? He said: 'Don't we have any cargoes going to Seville?'

The Spanish port of Seville was the armoury of King Felipe, with an insatiable appetite for metal. A cousin of Ned's father, Carlos Cruz, bought as much as Alice could send, turning it all into cannons and cannonballs for Spain's interminable wars. Ned's brother, Barney, who was in Seville, was living and working with Carlos, learning another side of the family business, as Ned had done in Calais. But the sea journey was long and hazardous, and ships were sent there only when the much nearer warehouse at Calais was full.

Alice replied to Ned's question: 'No. At the moment we have no ships going to or from Seville.'

'So if we lose Calais . . .'

'We lose almost everything.'

Ned had thought he understood the business, but he had not realized that it could be ruined so quickly. He felt as he did when a trustworthy horse stumbled and shifted under him, making him lose his balance in the saddle. It was a sudden reminder that life was unpredictable.

A bell was rung for the start of the game. Cecil smiled and said: 'Thank you for your information, Ned. It's unusual for young men to be so precise.'

Ned was flattered. 'I'm glad to have been of help.'

Dan Cobley's pretty, golden-haired sister, Ruth, passed by saying: 'Come on, Ned, it's time for Hunt the Hart.'

'Coming,' he said, but he did not move. He felt torn. He was desperate to talk to Margery, but after news like this he was in no mood for a game. 'I suppose there's nothing we can do,' he said to his mother.

'Just wait for more information – which may be a long time coming.'

There was a gloomy pause. Cecil said: 'By the way, I'm looking for an assistant to help me in my work for the lady

Elizabeth; a young man to live at Hatfield Palace as part of her staff, and to act on my behalf when I have to be in London, or elsewhere. I know your destiny is to work with your mother in the family business, Ned, but if you should happen to know a young man a bit like yourself, intelligent and trustworthy, with a sharp eye for detail . . . let me know.'

Ned nodded. 'Of course.' He suspected that Cecil was really offering the job to him.

Cecil went on: 'He would have to share Elizabeth's tolerant attitude to religion.' Queen Mary Tudor had burned hundreds of Protestants at the stake.

Ned certainly felt that way, as Cecil must have realized during the argument in the earl's library about the succession to the throne. Millions of English people agreed: whether Catholic or Protestant, they were sickened by the slaughter.

'As I said earlier, Elizabeth has told me many times that if she should become queen, it is her dearest wish that no Englishman should lose his life for the sake of his beliefs,' Cecil repeated. 'I think that's an ideal worthy of a man's faith.'

Alice looked mildly resentful. 'As you say, Sir William, my sons are destined to work in the family business. Off you go, Ned.'

Ned turned around and looked for Margery.

*

EARL SWITHIN HAD hired a travelling company of actors, and now they were building a raised platform up against one long wall of the great hall. While Margery was watching them, Lady Brecknock stood beside her and did the same. An attractive woman in her late thirties with a warm smile, Susannah Brecknock was a cousin of Earl Swithin's, and was a frequent visitor to Kingsbridge, where she had a house. Margery had met her before and found her amiable and not too grand.

The stage was made of planks on barrels. Margery said: 'It looks a bit shaky.'

'That's what I thought!' said Susannah.

'Do you know what they're going to perform?'

'The life of Mary Magdalene.'

'Oh!' Mary Magdalene was the patron saint of prostitutes. Priests always corrected this by saying: 'Reformed prostitutes,' but that did not make the saint any less intriguing. 'But how can they? All the actors are men.'

'You haven't seen a play before?'

'Not this kind, with a stage and professional players. I've just seen processions and pageants.'

'The female characters are always played by men. They don't allow women to act.'

'Why not?'

'Oh, I expect it's because we're inferior beings, physically weak and intellectually feeble.'

She was being sarcastic. Margery liked Susannah for the candid way she talked. Most adults responded to embarrassing questions with empty platitudes, but Susannah could be relied upon to tell the plain truth. Emboldened, Margery blurted out what was on her mind: 'Did they force you to marry the Lord Brecknock?'

Susannah raised her eyebrows.

Margery realized immediately that she had gone too far. Quickly she said: 'I'm so sorry, I have no right to ask you that, please forgive me.' Tears came to her eyes.

Susannah shrugged. 'You certainly do not have the right to ask me such a question, but I haven't forgotten what it was like to be fifteen.' She lowered her voice. 'Who do they want you to marry?'

'Bart Shiring.'

'Oh, God, poor you,' she said, even though Bart was her second cousin. Her sympathy made Margery feel even more sorry for herself. Susannah thought for a minute. 'It's no secret that my marriage was arranged, but no one forced me,' she said. 'I met him and liked him.'

'Do you love him?'

She hesitated again, and Margery could see that she was torn between discretion and compassion. 'I shouldn't answer that.'

'No, of course not, I apologize – again.'

'But I can see that you're in distress, so I'll confide in you, provided you promise never to repeat what I say.'

'I promise.'

'Brecknock and I are friends,' she said. 'He's kind to me and I do everything I can to please him. And we have four wonderful children. I am happy.' She paused, and Margery waited for the answer to her question. At last Susannah said: 'But I know there is another kind of happiness, the mad ecstasy of adoring someone and being adored in return.'

'Yes!' Margery was so glad that Susannah understood.

'That particular joy is not given to all of us,' she said solemnly.

'But it should be!' Margery could not bear the thought that a person might be denied love.

For a moment, Susannah looked bereft. 'Perhaps,' she said quietly. 'Perhaps.'

Looking over Susannah's shoulder, Margery saw Ned approaching in his green French doublet. Susannah followed her look. Perceptively she said: 'Ned Willard is the one you want?'

'Yes.'

'Good choice. He's nice.'

'He's wonderful.'

Susannah smiled with a touch of sadness. 'I hope it works out for you.'

Ned bowed to her, and she acknowledged him with a nod but moved away.

The actors were hanging a curtain across one corner of the room. Margery said to Ned: 'What do you think that's for?'

'They will put on their costumes behind the curtain, I think.' He lowered his voice. 'When can we talk? I can't wait much longer.'

'The game is about to begin. Just follow me.'

Philbert Cobley's good-looking clerk, Donal Gloster, was chosen to be hunter. He had wavy dark hair and a sensual face. He did not appeal to Margery – too weak – but several of the girls would be hoping to be found by him, she felt sure.

New Castle was the perfect location for the game. It had

more secret places than a rabbit warren. The parts where the new mansion was joined to the old castle were especially rich in odd cupboards, unexpected staircases, niches and irregular-shaped rooms. It was a children's game and Margery, when young, had wondered why nineteen-year-olds were so keen to join in. Now she understood that the game was an opportunity for adolescents to kiss and cuddle.

Donal closed his eyes and began to say the paternoster in Latin, and all the young people scattered to hide.

Margery already knew where she was going, for she had scouted hidey-holes earlier, to be sure of a private place in which to talk to Ned. She left the hall and raced along a corridor towards the rooms of the old castle, trusting to Ned to follow her. She went through a door at the end of the corridor.

Glancing back, she saw Ned – and, unfortunately, several others. That was a nuisance: she wanted him to herself.

She passed through a small storeroom and ran up a twisting staircase with stone steps, then down a short flight. She could hear the others behind her, but she was now out of their sight. She turned into a passageway she knew to be a dead end. It was lit by a single candle in a wall bracket. Halfway along was a huge fireplace: the medieval bakery, long disused, its chimney demolished in the building of the modern house. Beside it, concealed by a stone buttress, was the door to the enormous oven, virtually invisible in the dimness. Margery slipped into the oven, pulling her skirts behind her. It was surprisingly clean, she had noted when scouting. She pulled the door almost shut and peeped through a crack.

Ned came charging along the passageway, closely followed by Bart, then pretty Ruth Cobley, who probably had her eye on Bart. Margery groaned in frustration. How could she separate Ned from the others?

They dashed past the oven without seeing the door. A moment later, having run into the dead end, they returned in reverse order: Ruth, then Bart, then Ned.

Margery saw her chance.

Bart and Ruth disappeared from view, and Margery said: 'Ned!'

He stopped and looked around, puzzled.

She pushed open the oven door. 'In here!'

He did not need to be asked twice. He scrambled in with her and she shut the door.

It was pitch-dark, but they were lying knee to knee and chin to chin, and she could feel the length of his body. He kissed her.

She kissed him back hungrily. Whatever else happened, he still loved her, and for the moment that was all she cared about. She had been afraid that he would forget her in Calais. She thought he would meet French girls who were more sophisticated and exciting than little Marge Fitzgerald from Kingsbridge. But he had not, she could tell, from the way he hugged and kissed and caressed her. Overjoyed, she put her hands on his head and opened her mouth to his tongue and arched her body against his.

He rolled on top of her. At that moment, she would have opened her body to him gladly and let him take her virginity, but something happened. There was a thump, as if his foot had struck something, then a noise that might have been a panel of wood falling to the ground and suddenly she could see the walls of the oven around her.

She and Ned were both sufficiently startled to stop what they were doing and look up. They saw that the back of the oven had fallen away. Clearly it connected with another place that was dimly lit and Margery realized with trepidation that there might be people there who could see what she and Ned were doing. She sat upright and looked through the hole.

There was no one in sight. She saw a wall with an arrow-slit window that was admitting the last of the afternoon light. A small space behind the old oven had simply been closed off by the building of the new house. It led nowhere: the only access was through the oven. On the floor was a panel of wood that must have closed up the hole until Ned kicked it in his excitement. Margery could hear voices, but they came from the courtyard outside. She breathed more easily: they had not been seen.

She crawled through the hole and stood upright in the little space. Ned followed her. They both looked around wonderingly, and Ned said: 'We could stay here for ever.'

That brought Margery back to reality, and she realized how close she had come to committing a mortal sin. Desire had almost overwhelmed her knowledge of right and wrong. She had had a lucky escape.

Her intention in bringing Ned here had been to speak to him, not kiss him. She said: 'Ned, they want to make me marry Bart. What are we going to do?'

'I don't know,' said Ned.

*

SWITHIN WAS quite drunk, Rollo saw. The earl was slumped on a big chair opposite the stage, a goblet in his right hand. A young serving girl refilled his glass, and as she did so he grasped her breast with his maimed left hand. She squealed with horror and pulled away, spilling the wine, and Swithin laughed.

An actor came on stage and began a prologue, explaining that in order to tell a story of repentance it was necessary first to show the sin, and apologizing in advance if this should give offence.

Rollo saw his sister Margery come slinking into the room with Ned Willard, and he frowned in disapproval. They had taken advantage of the game of Hunt the Hart to go off together, Rollo realized, and no doubt they had got up to all kinds of mischief.

Rollo did not understand his sister. She took religion very seriously, but she had always been disobedient. How could that be? For Rollo, the essence of religion was submission to authority. That was the trouble with Protestants: they thought they had the right to make up their own minds. But Margery was a devout Catholic.

On stage a character called Infidelity appeared, identifiable by his oversized codpiece. He winked and spoke behind his hand and looked from left to right as if making sure he was not overheard by any other characters. The audience laughed as they recognized an exaggerated version of a type they all knew.

Rollo had been unnerved by the conversation with Sir William Cecil, but now he thought he might have overreacted. Princess Elizabeth probably was a Protestant, but it was too soon to worry about her: after all, Queen Mary Tudor was only forty-one and in good health, apart from the phantom pregnancies – she could reign for decades more.

Mary Magdalene appeared on stage. Clearly this was the saint before her repentance. She sashayed on in a red dress, fussing with her necklace, batting her eyes at Infidelity. Her lips were reddened with some kind of dye.

Rollo was surprised because he had not seen a woman among the actors. Furthermore, although he had not seen a play before, he was pretty sure women were not allowed to act. The company had appeared to consist of four men and a boy of about thirteen. Rollo frowned at Mary Magdalene, puzzled; then it occurred to him that she was the same size and build as the boy.

The truth began to dawn on the audience, and there were murmurs of admiration and surprise. But Rollo also heard low but clear noises of protest and, looking around, he saw that they came from the corner where Philbert Cobley stood with his family. Catholics were relaxed about plays, provided there was a religious message, but some of the ultra-Protestants disapproved. A boy dressed as a woman was just the kind of thing to make them righteously indignant, especially when the female character was acting sexy. They were all stony-faced – with one exception, Rollo noticed: Philbert's bright young clerk, Donal Gloster, who was laughing as heartily as anyone. Rollo and all the young people in town knew that Donal was in love with Philbert's fair daughter, Ruth. Rollo guessed that Donal was Protestant only to win Ruth.

On stage, Infidelity took Mary in his arms and gave her a long, lascivious kiss. This caused uproarious laughter, hoots and catcalls, especially from the young men, who had by now figured out that Mary was a boy.

But Philbert Cobley did not see the joke. He was a beefy man, short but wide, with thinning hair and a straggly beard. Now he was red in the face, waving his fist and shouting something that could not be heard. At first no one paid him any attention, but when at last the actors broke the kiss and the laughter died down, people turned to look at the source of the shouting.

Rollo saw Earl Swithin suddenly notice the kerfuffle and look angry. Here comes trouble, Rollo thought.

Philbert stopped shouting, said something to the people around him, and moved towards the door. His family fell in behind him. Donal went along too, but Rollo saw that he looked distinctly disappointed.

Swithin got up from his chair and walked towards them. 'You stay where you are!' he roared. 'I gave no one permission to leave.'

The actors paused and turned to watch what was going on in the audience, a reversal of roles that Rollo found ironic.

Philbert stopped, turned, and shouted back at Swithin: 'We will not stay in this palace of Sodom!' Then he continued marching towards the door.

'You preening Protestant!' Swithin yelled, and he ran at Philbert.

Swithin's son, Bart, stepped into his father's way, holding up a placatory hand, and yelled: 'Let them go, Father, they're not worth it.'

Swithin swept him aside with a powerful shove and fell on Philbert. 'I'll kill you, by the cross!' He grabbed him by the throat and began to strangle him. Philbert dropped to his knees and Swithin bent over him, tightening his grip despite his maimed left hand.

Everybody began to shout at once. Several men and women pulled at Swithin's sleeves, trying to get him away from Philbert, but they were constrained by fear of hurting an earl, even one bent on murder. Rollo stayed back, not caring whether Philbert lived or died.

Ned Willard was the first to act decisively. He hooked his right arm around Swithin's neck, getting the crook of his elbow under the earl's chin, and heaved up and back. Swithin could not help but step away and release his hold on Philbert's neck.

Ned had always been like this, Rollo recalled. Even when he

was a cheeky little boy at school he had been a fierce fighter, ready to defy older boys, and Rollo had been obliged to teach him a lesson or two with a bundle of birch twigs. Then Ned had matured and grown those big hands and feet; and, even though he was still shorter than average, bigger boys had learned to respect his fists.

Now Ned released Swithin and smartly stepped away, becoming one of the crowd again. Roaring with fury, Swithin spun around, looking for his assailant, but could not tell who it had been. He might find out, eventually, Rollo guessed, but by then he would be sober.

Philbert got to his feet, rubbing his neck, and staggered to the door unobserved by Swithin.

Bart grabbed his father's arm. 'Let's have another cup of wine and watch the play,' he said. 'In a minute Carnal Concupiscence comes on.'

Philbert and his entourage reached the door.

Swithin stared angrily at Bart for a long moment. He seemed to have forgotten whom he was supposed to be mad at.

The Cobleys left the room and the big oak door slammed shut behind them.

Swithin shouted: 'On with the play!'

The actors resumed.

2

PIERRE AUMANDE made his living by relieving Parisians of their excess cash, a task that became easier on days like today, when they were celebrating.

All Paris was rejoicing. A French army had conquered Calais, taking the city back from the English barbarians who had somehow stolen it two hundred years ago. In every taproom in the capital men were drinking the health of Scarface, the duke of Guise, the great general who had erased the ancient stain on the nation's pride.

The tavern of St Étienne, in the neighbourhood called Les Halles, was no exception. At one end of the room a small crowd of young men played dice, toasting Scarface every time someone won. By the door was a table of men-at-arms celebrating as if they had taken Calais themselves. In a corner a prostitute had passed out at a table, hair soaking in a puddle of wine.

Such festivities presented golden opportunities to a man such as Pierre.

He was a student at the Sorbonne university. He told his fellows that he got a generous allowance from his parents back home in the Champagne region. In fact, his father gave him nothing. His mother had spent her life-savings on a new outfit of clothes for him to wear to Paris, and now she was penniless. It was assumed that he would support himself by clerical work such as copying legal documents, as many students did. But Pierre's open-handed spending on the pleasures of the city was paid for by other means. Today he was wearing a fashionable doublet in blue cloth slashed to show the white silk lining beneath: such clothes could not be paid for even by a year of copying documents.

He was watching the game of dice. The gamblers were the sons of prosperous citizens, he guessed; jewellers and lawyers and builders. One of them, Bertrand, was cleaning up. At first Pierre suspected that Bertrand was a trickster just like himself, and observed carefully, trying to figure out how the dodge was done. But eventually he decided there was no scam. Bertrand was simply enjoying a run of luck.

And that gave Pierre his chance.

When Bertrand had won a little more than fifty livres his friends left the tavern with empty pockets. Bertrand called for a bottle of wine and a round of cheese, and at that point Pierre moved in.

'My grandfather's cousin was lucky, like you,' he said in the tone of relaxed amiability that had served him well in the past. 'When he gambled, he won. He fought at Marignano and survived.' Pierre was making this up as he went along. 'He married a poor girl, because she was beautiful and he loved her, then she inherited a mill from an uncle. His son became a bishop.'

'I'm not always lucky.'

Bertrand was not completely stupid, Pierre thought, but he was probably dumb enough. 'I bet there was a girl who seemed not to like you until one day she kissed you.' Most men had this experience during their adolescence, he had found.

But Bertrand thought Pierre's insight was amazing. 'Yes!' he said. 'Clothilde – how did you know?'

'I told you, you're lucky.' He leaned closer and spoke in a lower voice, as if confiding a secret. 'One day, when my grandfather's cousin was old, a beggar told him the secret of his good fortune.'

Bertrand could not resist. 'What was it?'

'The beggar said to him: "When your mother was expecting you, she gave a penny to me – and that's why you've been lucky all your life." It's the truth.'

Bertrand looked disappointed.

Pierre raised a finger in the air, like a conjurer about to

perform a magic trick. 'Then the beggar threw off his filthy robes and revealed himself to be – an angel!'

Bertrand was half sceptical, half awestruck.

'The angel blessed my grandfather's cousin, then flew up to heaven.' Pierre lowered his voice to a whisper. 'I think *your* mother gave alms to an angel.'

Bertrand, who was not completely drunk, said: 'Maybe.'

'Is your mother kind?' Pierre asked, knowing that few men would answer 'No'.

'She is like a saint.'

'There you are.' Pierre thought for a moment of his own mother, and how disappointed she would be if she knew that he was living by cheating people out of their money. Bertrand is asking for it, he told her in his imagination; he's a gambler and a drunk. But the excuse did not satisfy her, even in his fantasy.

He pushed the thought from his mind. This was not the time for self-doubt: Bertrand was beginning to take the bait.

Pierre went on: 'There was an older man – not your father – who gave you important advice at least once.'

Bertrand's eyes widened in surprise. 'I never knew why Monsieur Larivière was so helpful.'

'He was sent by your angel. Have you ever had a narrow escape from injury or death?'

'I got lost when I was five years old. I decided that my way home was across the river. I almost drowned, but a passing friar saved me.'

'That was no friar, that was your angel.'

'It's amazing – you're right!'

'Your mother did something for an angel in disguise, and that angel has watched over you ever since. I know it.'

Pierre accepted a cup of wine and a wedge of cheese. Free food was always welcome.

He was studying for the priesthood because it was a way up the social ladder. But he had been at the university only a few days when he realized that the students were already dividing into two groups with radically different destinies. The young sons of noblemen and rich merchants were going to be abbots and bishops – indeed, some of them already knew which well-endowed abbey or diocese they would rule, for often such posts were effectively the private property of a particular family. By contrast, the clever sons of provincial doctors and wine merchants would become country priests.

Pierre belonged to the second group, but was determined to join the first.

Initially, the division was only dimly perceptible, and during those early days Pierre had attached himself firmly to the elite. He quickly lost his regional accent and learned to speak with an aristocratic drawl. He had enjoyed a piece of luck when the wealthy Viscount Villeneuve, having carelessly left home without cash, had asked to borrow twenty livres until tomorrow. It was all the money Pierre had in the world, but he saw a unique opportunity.

He handed the money to Villeneuve as if it were a trifle.

Villeneuve forgot to pay him back the next day.

Pierre was desperate, but he said nothing. He ate gruel that evening, because he could not afford bread. But Villeneuve forgot the following day, too.

Still Pierre said nothing. He knew that if he asked for his money back, Villeneuve and his friends would understand immediately that he really was not one of them; and he craved their acceptance more than food.

It was a month later that the young nobleman said to him languidly: 'I say, Aumande, I don't think I ever repaid you those twenty livres, did I?'

With a massive effort of will, Pierre replied: 'My dear fellow, I have absolutely no idea. Forget it, please.' Then he was inspired to add: 'You obviously need the money.'

The other students had laughed, knowing how rich Villeneuve was, and Pierre's witticism had sealed his position as a member of the group.

And when Villeneuve gave him a handful of gold coins, he dropped the money into his pocket without counting it.

He was accepted, but that meant he had to dress like them,

hire carriages for trips, gamble carelessly, and call for food and wine in taverns as if the cost meant nothing.

Pierre borrowed all the time, paid back only when forced, and imitated Villeneuve's financial absent-mindedness. But sometimes he had to get cash.

He thanked heaven for fools such as Bertrand.

Slowly but surely, as Bertrand worked his way down the bottle of wine, Pierre introduced into their chat the unique buying opportunity.

It was different every time. Today he invented a stupid German – the fool in the story was always a foreigner – who had inherited some jewels from an aunt and wanted to sell them to Pierre for fifty livres, not realizing that they were worth hundreds. Pierre did not have fifty livres, he told Bertrand, but anyone who did could multiply his money by ten. The story did not have to be very plausible, but the telling of it was crucial. Pierre had to appear reluctant to let Bertrand get involved, nervous of the idea of Bertrand buying the jewels, perturbed by Bertrand's suggestion that Pierre should take fifty livres of Bertrand's winnings and go away and make the purchase on Bertrand's behalf.

Bertrand was begging Pierre to take his money, and Pierre was getting ready to pocket the cash and disappear from Bertrand's life for ever, when the Widow Bauchene walked in.

Pierre tried to stay calm.

Paris was a city of three hundred thousand people, and he had thought there was no great danger of running into any of his past victims by accident, especially as he was careful to stay away from their usual haunts. This was very bad luck.

He turned his face away, but he was not quick enough, and she spotted him. 'You!' she screeched, pointing.

Pierre could have killed her.

She was an attractive woman of forty with a broad smile and a generous body. Pierre was half her age, but he had seduced her willingly. In return, she had enthusiastically taught him ways of making love that were new to him, and – more importantly – loaned him money whenever he asked.

When the thrill of the affair had begun to wear off, she had got fed up with giving him money. At that point a married woman would have cut her losses, said goodbye, and told herself she had learned a costly lesson. A wife could not expose Pierre's dishonesty, because that would involve confessing her adultery. But a widow was different, Pierre had realized when Madame Bauchene turned against him. She had complained loud and long to anyone who would listen.

Could he prevent her from arousing suspicion in Bertrand? It would be difficult, but he had done more unlikely things.

He had to get her out of the tavern as fast as possible.

In a low tone he said to Bertrand: 'This poor woman is completely mad.' Then he stood up, bowed, and said in a tone of icy politeness: 'Madame Bauchene, I am at your service, as always.'

'In that case, give me the hundred and twelve livres you owe me.'

That was bad. Pierre wanted desperately to glance at Bertrand and measure his reaction, but that would betray his own anxiety, and he forced himself not to look. 'I will bring the money to you tomorrow morning, if you care to name the place.'

Bertrand said drunkenly: 'You told me you didn't have even fifty livres!'

This was getting worse.

Madame Bauchene said: 'Why tomorrow? What's wrong with now?'

Pierre strove to maintain an air of unconcern. 'Who carries that much gold in his purse?'

'You're a good liar,' said the widow, 'but you can't fool me any longer.'

Pierre heard Bertrand give a grunt of surprise. He was beginning to understand.

Pierre kept trying all the same. He stood very upright and looked offended. 'Madame, I am Pierre Aumande de Guise. You may perhaps recognize the name of my family. Kindly be assured that our honour does not permit deception.'

At the table by the door, one of the men-at-arms drinking toasts to 'Calais française' raised his head and looked hard at

Pierre. The man had lost most of his right ear in some fight, Pierre saw. Pierre suffered a moment of unease, but had to concentrate on the widow.

She said: 'I don't know about your name, but I know you have no honour, you young rogue. I want my money.'

'You shall have it, I assure you.'

'Take me to your home now, then.'

'I cannot oblige you, I fear. My mother, Madame de Châteauneuf, would not consider you a suitable guest.'

'Your mother isn't Madame de anything,' said the widow scornfully.

Bertrand said: 'I thought you were a student living in college.' He was sounding less drunk by the minute.

It was over, Pierre realized. He had lost his chance with Bertrand. He rounded on the young man. 'Oh, go to hell,' he said furiously. He turned back to Madame Bauchene. He felt a pang of regret for her warm, heavy body and her cheerful lasciviousness; then he hardened his heart. 'You, too,' he said to her.

He threw on his cloak. What a waste of time this had been. He would have to start all over again tomorrow. But what if he met another of his past victims? He felt sour. It had been a rotten evening. Another shout of 'Calais française' went up. To the devil with Calais, Pierre thought. He stepped towards the door.

To his surprise, the man-at-arms with the mutilated ear now got up and blocked the doorway.

Pierre thought *For God's sake, what now?*

'Stand aside,' Pierre said haughtily. 'This has nothing to do with you.'

The man stayed where he was. 'I heard you say your name was Pierre Aumande de Guise.'

'Yes, so you'd better get out of my way, if you don't want trouble from my family.'

'The Guise family won't cause me any trouble,' the man said, with a quiet confidence that unnerved Pierre. 'My name is Gaston Le Pin.'

Pierre considered shoving the man aside and making a run

for it. He looked Le Pin up and down. The man was about thirty, shorter than Pierre, but broad-shouldered. He had hard blue eyes. The damaged ear suggested he was no stranger to violent action. He would not be shoved aside easily.

Pierre struggled to maintain his tone of superiority. 'What of it, Le Pin?'

'I work for the Guise family. I'm head of their household guard.' Pierre's heart sank. 'And I'm arresting you, on behalf of the duke of Guise, for falsely using an aristocratic name.'

Widow Bauchene said: 'I knew it.'

Pierre said: 'My good man, I'll have you know—'

'Save it for the judge,' said Le Pin contemptuously. 'Rasteau, Brocard, hold him.'

Without Pierre's remarking it, two of the men-at-arms had got up from the table and were standing quietly either side of him, and now they grabbed his arms. Their hands felt like iron bands: Pierre did not bother to struggle. Le Pin nodded to them and they marched Pierre out of the tavern.

Behind him, he heard the widow yell: 'I hope they hang you!'

It was dark, but the narrow, winding medieval streets were busy with revellers and noisy with patriotic songs and shouts of 'Long live Scarface'. Rasteau and Brocard walked fast, and Pierre had to hurry to keep up with them and avoid being dragged along the road.

He was terrified to think what punishment might be imposed on him: pretending to be a nobleman was a serious crime. And even if he got off lightly, what was his future? He could find other fools like Bertrand, and married women to seduce, but the more people he cheated, the more likely he was to be called to account. For how much longer could he maintain this way of life?

He looked at his escorts. Rasteau, the older by four or five years, had no nose, just two holes surrounded by scar tissue, no doubt the result of a knife fight. Pierre waited for them to get bored, relax their vigilance and loosen their grip, so that he might break away, dash off, and lose himself in the crowd; but they remained alert, their grip firm.

'Where are you taking me?' he asked, but they did not trouble to reply.

Instead, they talked about sword fighting, apparently continuing a conversation they had begun in the tavern. 'Forget about the heart,' said Rasteau. 'Your point can slip over the ribs and give the man nothing worse than a scratch.'

'What do you aim for? The throat?'

'Too small a target. I go for the belly. A blade in the guts doesn't kill a man straight away, but it paralyses him. It hurts so much that he can't think of anything else.' He gave a high-pitched giggle, an unexpected sound from such a rough-looking man.

Pierre soon found out where they were going. They turned into the Vieille rue du Temple. Pierre knew that this was where the Guise family had built their new palace, occupying an entire block. He had often dreamed of climbing those polished steps and entering the grand hall. But he was taken to the garden gate and through the kitchen entrance. They went down a staircase into a cheese-smelling basement crowded with barrels and boxes. He was thrust rudely into a room and the door was slammed behind him. He heard a bar drop into a bracket. When he tried the door it would not open.

The cell was cold, and stank like an alehouse privy. A candle in the corridor outside shed a faint light through a barred window in the door. He made out an earth floor and a vaulted ceiling of brick. The only furniture was a chamber pot that had been used but not emptied – hence the smell.

It was amazing how fast his life had turned to shit.

He was here for the night, he assumed. He sat down with his back to the wall. In the morning he would be taken before a judge. He had to think about what he would say. He needed a story to spin to the court. He might still escape serious punishment if he performed well.

But somehow he was too dispirited to dream up a tale. He kept wondering what he would do when this was over. He had enjoyed life as a member of the wealthy set. Losing money betting on dog fights, giving outsize tips to barmaids, buying gloves made from the skins of baby goats – it had all given him a thrill he would never forget. Must he give that up?

The most pleasing thing to him had been the way the others had accepted him. They had no idea that he was a bastard and the son of a bastard. There was no hint of condescension. Indeed, they often called for him on their way to some pleasure outing. If he fell behind the others for some reason, as they walked from one tavern to another in the university quarter, one of them would say: 'Where's Aumande?' and they would stop and wait for him to catch up. Remembering that now, he almost wept.

He pulled his cloak more closely around him. Would he be able to sleep on the cold floor? When he appeared in court he wanted to look as if he might be a *bona fide* member of the Guise family.

The light in his cell brightened. There was a noise in the corridor. The door was unbarred and flung open. 'On your feet,' said a coarse voice.

Pierre scrambled up.

Once again his arm was held in a grip hard enough to discourage fantasies of escape.

Gaston Le Pin was outside the door. Pierre summoned up the shreds of his old arrogance. 'I assume you are releasing me,' he said. 'I demand an apology.'

'Shut your mouth,' said Le Pin.

He led the way along the corridor to the back stairs, then across the ground floor and up a grand staircase. Pierre was now completely bewildered. He was being treated as a criminal, but taken to the *piano nobile* of the palace like a guest.

Le Pin led the way into a room furnished with a patterned rug, heavy brocade curtains that glowed with colour, and a large painting of a voluptuous naked woman over the fireplace. Two well-dressed men sat on upholstered armchairs, arguing quietly. Between them was a small table with a jug of wine, two goblets, and a dish piled with nuts, dried fruits and small cakes. The men ignored the new arrivals and carried on talking, careless of whether anyone heard.

They were obviously brothers, both well built with fair hair and blond beards. Pierre recognized them. They were the most famous men in France after the king.

One had terrible scars on both cheeks, the marks of a lance that had pierced right through his mouth. The legend said that the spearhead had lodged there, and he had ridden back to his tent and had not even screamed when the surgeon pulled out the blade. This was François, duke of Guise, known as Scarface. He was a few days short of his thirty-ninth birthday.

The younger brother, born on the same day five years later, was Charles, cardinal of Lorraine. He wore the bright red robes of his priestly office. He had been made archbishop of Reims at the age of fourteen, and he now had so many lucrative Church positions that he was one of the richest men in France, with an amazing annual income of three hundred thousand livres.

For years Pierre had daydreamed of meeting these two. They were the most powerful men in the country outside the royal family. In his fantasy they valued him as a counsellor, talked to him almost as an equal, and sought his advice on political, financial and even military decisions.

But now he stood before them as a criminal.

He listened to their conversation. Cardinal Charles said quietly: 'The king's prestige has not really recovered from the defeat at St Quentin.'

'But surely my victory at Calais has helped!' said Duke François.

Charles shook his head. 'We won that battle, but we're losing the war.'

Pierre was fascinated, despite his fear. France had been fighting Spain over who was to rule the kingdom of Naples and other states in the Italian peninsula. England had sided with Spain. France had got Calais back but not the Italian states. It was a poor bargain, but few people would dare to say so openly. The two brothers were supremely confident of their power.

Le Pin took advantage of a pause to say: 'This is the imposter, my lords,' and the brothers looked up.

Pierre pulled himself together. He had escaped from awkward situations before, using fast talk and plausible lies. He told himself to regard this problem as an opportunity. If he remained alert and quick-witted he might even gain by the encounter. 'Good evening, my lords,' he said in a dignified tone. 'This is an unexpected honour.'

Le Pin said: 'Speak when you're spoken to, shithole.'

Pierre turned to him. 'Refrain from coarse language in the presence of the cardinal,' he said. 'Otherwise I shall see that you're taught a lesson.'

Le Pin bristled, but hesitated to strike Pierre in front of his masters.

The two brothers exchanged a glance, and Charles raised an amused eyebrow. Pierre had surprised them. Good.

It was the duke who spoke. 'You pretend to be a member of our family. This is a serious offence.'

'I humbly beg your forgiveness.' Before either brother could reply, he went on: 'My father is the illegitimate son of a dairymaid in Thonnance-lès-Joinville.' He hated having to tell this story, because it was true, and it shamed him. However, he was desperate. He went on: 'The family legend is that her lover was a dashing young man from Joinville, a cousin of the Guise family.'

Duke François gave a sceptical grunt. The Guise family seat was at Joinville, in the Champagne region, and Thonnance-lès-Joinville was nearby, as its name implied. But many unmarried mothers put the blame on an aristocratic lover. On the other hand, it was often true.

Pierre went on: 'My father was educated at the Grammar School and became a local priest, thanks to a recommendation from your lordships' father, now in heaven, rest his soul.'

This was perfectly believable, Pierre knew. Noble families did not openly acknowledge their bastards, but they often gave them a helping hand, in the casual way that a man might stoop to draw a thorn from the paw of a limping dog.

Duke François said: 'How can you be the son of a celibate priest?'

'My mother is his housekeeper.' Priests were not allowed to

marry, but they often took mistresses, and 'housekeeper' was the accepted euphemism.

'So you're doubly illegitimate!'

Pierre flushed, and his emotion was genuine. He had no need to pretend to be ashamed of his birth. But the duke's comment also encouraged him. It suggested that his story was being taken seriously.

The duke said: 'Even if your family myth were true, you would not be entitled to use our name – as you must realize.'

'I know I did wrong,' Pierre said. 'But all my life I have looked up to the Guises. I would give my soul to serve you. I know that your duty is to punish me, but please – use me instead. Give me a task, and I will perform it meticulously, I swear. I will do anything you ask – anything.'

The duke shook his head scornfully. 'I cannot imagine there is any service you could do for us.'

Pierre despaired. He had put his heart and soul into his speech – and it had failed.

Then Cardinal Charles intervened. 'As a matter of fact, there might be something.'

Pierre's heart leaped with hope.

Duke François looked mildly irritated. 'Really?'

'Yes.'

The duke made a 'help yourself' gesture with his hand.

Cardinal Charles said: 'There are Protestants in Paris.'

Charles was an ultra-Catholic – which was no surprise, given how much money he made from the Church. And he was right about the Protestants. Even though Paris was a strongly Catholic city, where popular hellfire preachers raged against heresy from the pulpits every Sunday, there existed a minority eager to listen to denunciations of priests who took their Church income and did nothing for their congregations. Some felt strongly enough about Church corruption to take the risk of attending clandestine Protestant services, even though it was a crime.

Pierre pretended to be outraged. 'Such people should be put to death!'

'And they will be,' said Charles. 'But first we have to find them.'

'I can do that!' Pierre said quickly.

'Also the names of their wives and children, friends and relations.'

'Several of my fellow students at the Sorbonne have heretical leanings.'

'Ask where one can buy books and pamphlets dealing with criticism of the Church.'

Selling Protestant literature was a crime punishable by death. 'I'll drop hints,' Pierre said. 'I'll pretend to have sincere doubts.'

'Most of all, I want to know the places where Protestants gather to perform their blasphemous services.'

Pierre frowned, struck by a thought. Presumably the need for such information had not occurred to Charles in the last few minutes. 'Your Eminence must already have people making such inquiries.'

'You need not know about them, nor they about you.'

So Pierre would be joining an unknown number of spies. 'I will be the best of them!'

'You will be well rewarded if you are.'

Pierre could hardly believe his luck. He was so relieved that he wanted to leave now, before Charles could change his mind; but he had to give an impression of calm confidence. 'Thank you for placing your trust in me, Cardinal.'

'Oh, please don't imagine that I trust you,' said Charles with careless contempt. 'But in the task of exterminating heretics, one is obliged to use the tools that come to hand.'

Pierre did not want to leave on that note. He needed to impress the brothers somehow. He recalled the conversation they had been having when he was brought in. Throwing caution to the wind, he said: 'I agree with what you were saying, Cardinal, about the need to boost the popular reputation of his majesty the king.'

Charles looked as if he did not know whether to be offended or merely amused by Pierre's effrontery. 'Do you, indeed?' he said.

Pierre plunged on. 'What we need now is a big, lavish, colourful celebration, to make them forget the shame of St Quentin.'

The cardinal gave a slight nod.

Encouraged, Pierre said: 'Something like a royal wedding.'

The two brothers looked at one another. Duke François said: 'Do you know, I think the rogue might be right.'

Charles nodded. 'I've known better men who have understood politics less well.'

Pierre was thrilled. 'Thank you, my lord.'

Then Charles lost interest in him, picked up his wine, and said: 'You're dismissed.'

Pierre stepped to the door, then his eye fell on Le Pin. Struck by a thought, he turned back. 'Your Eminence,' he said to Charles. 'When I have the addresses where the Protestants hold their services, should I bring them to you, or hand them to one of your servants?'

The cardinal paused with his goblet at his lips. 'Strictly to me in person,' he said. 'No exceptions. Off you go.' He drank.

Pierre caught the eye of Le Pin and grinned triumphantly. 'Thank you, my lord,' he said, and he went out.

*

SYLVIE PALOT had noticed the attractive young man at the fish market the day before. He was not selling fish: he was too well dressed, in a blue doublet slashed to show the white silk lining. Yesterday she had seen him buy some salmon, but he had done so carelessly, without the keen interest of one who was going to eat what he bought. He had smiled at her several times.

She found it difficult not to be pleased.

He was a good-looking man with fair hair and the beginnings of a blond beard. She put his age at twenty, three years older than herself. He had a beguiling air of self-confidence.

She already had one admirer. Among her parents' acquaintances were the Mauriac family. Father and son were both short, and played up to it by being cheery wisecracking chaps: the father, Luc, was a charmer, and everyone liked him, which might have been why he was so successful as a cargo broker; but the son, Georges, who was Sylvie's admirer, was a pale imitation, all poor jokes and clumsy sallies. She really needed him to go away for a couple of years and grow up.

Her new admirer at the fish market spoke to her for the first time on a cold morning in January. There was snow on the foreshore of the River Seine, and thin layers of ice formed on the water in the fishmongers' barrels. Winter-hungry gulls circled overhead, crying in frustration at the sight of so much food. The young man said: 'How can you tell whether a fish is fresh?'

'By the eyes,' she said. 'If they're cloudy, the fish is old. The eyes should be clear.'

'Like yours,' he said.

She laughed. At least he was witty. Georges Mauriac just said stupid things like *Have you ever been kissed?*

'And pull open the gills,' she added. 'They should be pink inside, and wet. Oh, dear.' Her hand went to her mouth. She had given him the cue for a smutty remark about something else that might be pink inside and wet, and she felt herself blush.

He looked mildly amused, but said only: 'I'll bear that in mind.' She appreciated his tact. He was not like Georges Mauriac, evidently.

He stood beside her while she bought three small trout, her father's favourite, and paid one sou and six pennies. He stayed with her as she walked away with the fish in her basket.

'What's your name?' she asked.

'Pierre Aumande. I know you're Sylvie Palot.'

She liked straightforward talk, so she said to him: 'Have you been watching me?'

He hesitated, looked embarrassed, and said: 'Yes, I suppose I have.'

'Why?'

'Because you're so beautiful.'

Sylvie knew she had a pleasant, open face with clear skin and blue eyes, but she was not sure she was beautiful, so she said: 'Is that all?'

'You're very perceptive.'

So there was something else. She could not help feeling disappointed. It was vain of her to have believed, even for a moment, that he had been bewitched by her beauty. Perhaps she would end up with Georges Mauriac after all. 'You'd better tell me,' she said, trying not to reveal her disillusionment.

'Have you ever heard of Erasmus of Rotterdam?'

Of course she had. Sylvie felt the hairs on her forearms rise. For a few minutes she had forgotten that she and her family were criminals, liable to be executed if caught; but now the familiar fear came back.

She was not stupid enough to answer the question, even when it came from such a dreamboat. After a moment she thought of an evasive answer. 'Why do you ask?'

'I'm a student at the university. We're taught that Erasmus was a wicked man, the progenitor of Protestantism, but I'd like to read his work for myself. They don't have his books in the library.'

'How should I know about such things?'

Pierre shrugged. 'Your father's a printer, isn't he?'

He *had* been watching her. But he could not possibly know the truth.

Sylvie and her family had been given a mission by God. It was their holy duty to help their countrymen learn about true religion. They did this by selling books: mainly the Bible, of course, in French so that everyone could easily understand it and see for themselves how wrong the Catholic Church was; but also commentaries by scholars such as Erasmus that explained things clearly, for readers who might be slow to reach the right conclusions unaided.

Every time they sold such a book, they took a terrible risk: the punishment was death.

Sylvie said: 'What on earth makes you think we sell such literature? It's against the law!'

'One of the students thought you might, that's all.'

So it was only rumour – but that was worrying enough. 'Well, please tell him that we don't.'

'All right.' He looked disappointed.

'Don't you know that printers' premises are liable to be searched at any time for illegal books? Our place has been inspected several times. There is no stain on our reputation.'

'Congratulations.'

He walked a few more paces beside her, then stopped. 'It was a pleasure meeting you, anyway.'

Sylvie said: 'Wait.'

Most of the customers for prohibited publications were people they knew, men and women who worshipped side by side with them at illicit services in discreet locations. A few others came with the recommendation of a known co-religionist. Even they were dangerous: if arrested and tortured they would probably tell all.

But Protestants had to take the even greater risk of talking to strangers about their faith: it was the only way to spread the gospel. Sylvie's life's work was to convert Catholics, and she had been presented with an opportunity to do just that. And if she let him walk away she might never see him again.

Pierre seemed sincere. And he had approached her cautiously, as if he was genuinely afraid. He did not seem to be a blabbermouth, a japester, a fool or a drunk: she could think of no excuse for refusing him.

Was she, perhaps, a little more willing than usual to take the risk because this prospective convert was an alluring young man who seemed attracted to her? She told herself that this question was beside the point.

She had to put her life on the line, and pray for God's protection.

'Come to the shop this afternoon,' she said. 'Bring four livres. Buy a copy of *The Grammar of Latin*. Whatever you do, don't mention Erasmus.'

He seemed startled by her sudden decisiveness, but he said: 'All right.'

'Then meet me back in the fish market at nightfall.' The waterfront would be deserted at that hour. 'Bring the *Grammar*.'

'And then what?'

'And then trust in God.' She turned and walked away without waiting for a reply.

As she headed for home, she prayed that she had done the right thing.

Paris was divided into three parts. The largest section, called the Town, was on the north side of the River Seine, known as the right bank. The smaller settlement south of the river, on the left bank, was called the University, or sometimes the Latin Quarter because of all the students speaking Latin. The island in the middle was called the City, and that was where Sylvie lived.

Her home stood in the shadow of the great cathedral of Notre Dame. The ground floor of the house was the shop, the books in mesh-fronted cupboards with locked doors. Sylvie and her parents lived upstairs. At the back was the print works. Sylvie and her mother, Isabelle, took turns minding the store while her father, Giles, who was not a good salesman, toiled in the workshop.

Sylvie fried the trout with onions and garlic in the kitchen upstairs and put bread and wine on the table. Her cat, Fifi, appeared from nowhere: Sylvie gave her the head of a trout, and the cat began to eat it delicately, starting with the eyes. Sylvie worried about what she had done this morning. Would the student show up? Or would a magistrate's officer come instead, with a party of men-at-arms, to arrest the whole family on charges of heresy?

Giles ate first, and Sylvie served him. He was a big man, his arms and shoulders strong from lifting the heavy oak formes full of lead-alloy type. In a bad mood he could knock Sylvie across the room with his left arm, but the trout was flaky and tender, and he was in a cheerful frame of mind.

When he had finished, Sylvie sat in the shop while Isabelle ate, then they changed places; but Sylvie had no appetite.

After the meal was over, Sylvie returned to the shop. There happened to be no customers, and Isabelle said immediately: 'What are you so worried about?'

Sylvie told her about Pierre Aumande.

Isabelle looked anxious. 'You should have arranged to meet him again, and learned more about him, before telling him to come to the shop.'

'I know, but what reason would I have to meet him?' Isabelle gave her an arch look, and Sylvie said: 'I'm no good at flirting, you know that, I'm sorry.'

'I'm glad of it,' Isabelle said. 'It's because you're too honest. Anyway, we must take risks, it's the cross we have to bear.'

Sylvie said: 'I just hope he's not the type to have an attack of guilty conscience and blurt out everything to his confessor.'

'He's more likely to get scared and back out. You'll probably never see him again.'

That was not what Sylvie was hoping for, but she did not say so.

Their conversation was interrupted by a customer. Sylvie looked at him curiously. Most of the people who came into the shop were well dressed, for poor men could not afford books. This young man's clothes were serviceable but plain and well-worn. His heavy coat was travel-stained, and his stout boots were dusty. He must be on a journey. He looked both weary and anxious. Sylvie felt a pang of compassion.

'I would like to speak to Giles Palot,' he said in an out-of-town accent.

'I'll fetch him,' said Isabelle, and she passed from the shop into the factory behind.

Sylvie was curious. What did this traveller want with her father, if not to buy a book? Probing, she said: 'Have you come a long way?'

Before the man could answer, another customer entered. Sylvie recognized him as a clergyman from the cathedral. Sylvie and her mother were careful to bow and scrape to priests. Giles did not, but he was grumpy with everyone. Sylvie said: 'Good afternoon, Archdeacon Raphael, we're very glad to see you, as always.'

The young man in the dirty cloak suddenly looked annoyed. Sylvie wondered if he had a reason to dislike archdeacons.

Raphael said: 'Do you have an edition of the Psalms?'

'Of course.' Sylvie unlocked a cabinet and took out a Latin version, assuming that Raphael would not want a French translation, even one approved by the Faculty of Theology at the Sorbonne. She guessed that the archdeacon was buying a gift, for he must already have the entire Bible. 'This would make a beautiful present,' she said. 'The tooling on the binding is gold leaf, and the printing is in two colours.'

Raphael turned the pages. 'It is very pleasing.'

'Five livres,' said Sylvie. 'A most reasonable price.' It was a small fortune for ordinary people, but archdeacons were not ordinary.

At that moment a third customer entered, and Sylvie recognized Pierre Aumande. She felt a little glow of pleasure at the sight of his smiling face, but she hoped she had been right in thinking him discreet: it would be a catastrophe if he started talking about Erasmus in front of an archdeacon and a mysterious stranger.

Her mother emerged from the back of the premises. She spoke to the traveller. 'My husband will be with you in a moment.' Seeing that Sylvie was serving the archdeacon, she turned to the other customer. 'May I show you something, Monsieur?'

Sylvie caught her mother's attention and slightly widened her eyes in a warning expression, to indicate that the latest arrival was the student they had been talking about. Isabelle responded with an almost imperceptible nod, showing that she understood. Mother and daughter had become skilled in silent communication, living as they did with Giles.

Pierre said: 'I need a copy of *The Grammar of Latin*.'

'At once.' Isabelle went to the appropriate cabinet, found the book, and brought it to the counter.

Giles appeared from the back. There were now three customers, two of whom were being served, so he assumed the third was the one who had asked for him. 'Yes?' he said. His manner was usually gruff: that was why Isabelle tried to keep him out of the shop.

The traveller hesitated, seeming ill at ease.

Giles said impatiently: 'You asked for me?'

'Um . . . do you have a book of Bible stories in French, with pictures?'

'Of course I do,' said Giles. 'It's my best seller. But you could have asked my wife for that, instead of dragging me here from the print works.'

Sylvie wished, not for the first time, that her father could be more charming to customers. However, it was odd that the traveller had asked for him by name before coming up with such a mundane request. She glanced at her mother and saw a slight frown that indicated that Isabelle, too, had heard a wrong note.

She noticed that Pierre was listening to the conversation, apparently as intrigued as she was.

The archdeacon said grumpily: 'People should hear Bible stories from their parish priest. If they start reading for themselves, they're sure to get the wrong idea.' He put gold coins on the counter to pay for the Psalms.

Or they might get the right idea, Sylvie said to herself. In the days when ordinary people had been unable to read the Bible, the priests could say anything – and that was how they liked it. They were terrified of the light of the word of God being shone on their teaching and practices.

Pierre said sycophantically: 'Quite right, your reverence – if a humble student may be permitted to express an opinion. We must stand firm, or we'll end up with a separate sect for every cobbler and weaver.'

Independent craftsmen such as cobblers and weavers seemed especially liable to become Protestants. Their work gave them time alone to think, Sylvie supposed, and they were not as scared as peasants were of priests and noblemen.

But Sylvie was surprised at this smarmy interjection from Pierre after he had shown interest in subversive literature. She looked curiously at him, and he gave her a broad wink.

He did have a very engaging manner.

Sylvie looked away and wrapped the archdeacon's Psalms in a square of coarse linen, tying the parcel with string.

The traveller bridled at the archdeacon's criticism. 'Half the people in France never see their priest,' he said defiantly. It was an exaggeration, Sylvie thought, but the truth was that far too many priests took the income from their post and never even visited their parish.

The archdeacon knew this, and had no answer. He picked up his Psalms and left in a huff.

Isabelle said to the student: 'May I wrap this *Grammar* for you?'

'Yes, please.' He produced four livres.

Giles said to the traveller: 'Do you want this story book, or what?'

The traveller bent over the book Giles showed him, examining the illustrations. 'Don't rush me,' he said firmly. He had not been afraid to argue with the archdeacon, and he seemed unaffected by Giles's bullying manner. There was more to this man than was apparent from his grubby appearance.

Pierre took his parcel and left. Now the shop contained only one customer. Sylvie felt as if the tide had gone out.

The traveller closed the book with a snap, straightened up, and said: 'I am Guillaume of Geneva.'

Sylvie heard Isabelle give a small gasp of surprise.

Giles's attitude changed. He shook Guillaume's hand and said: 'You're very welcome. Come inside.' He led the way upstairs to the private quarters.

Sylvie half understood. She knew that Geneva was an independent Protestant city, dominated by the great John Calvin. But it was two hundred and fifty miles away, a journey of a couple of weeks or more. 'What is that man doing here?' she asked.

'The College of Pastors in Geneva trains missionaries and sends them all over Europe to preach the new gospel,' Isabelle explained. 'The last one was called Alphonse. You were thirteen.'

'Alphonse!' said Sylvie, remembering a zealous young man who had ignored her. 'I never understood why he was living here.'

'They bring us Calvin's writings, and other works, for your father to copy and print.'

Sylvie felt stupid. She had never even wondered where the Protestant books originated.

'It's getting dark outside,' Isabelle said. 'You'd better fetch a copy of Erasmus for your student.'

'What did you think of him?' said Sylvie as she put on her coat.

Isabelle gave a knowing smile. 'He's a handsome devil, isn't he?'

Sylvie's question had been about Pierre's trustworthiness, not his looks; but on reflection she was not keen to get into that conversation, in case it scared her too much. She mumbled a noncommittal reply and went out.

She headed north and crossed the river. The jewellers and milliners on the Notre Dame bridge were getting ready to close their shops. On the Town side she walked along the rue St Martin, the main north–south artery. A few minutes later she reached the rue du Mur. It was a back lane rather than a street. On one side was the city wall; on the other, the rear entrances of a few houses and the high fence of an unkempt garden. She stopped by a stable at the back of a dwelling lived in by an old woman who did not have a horse. The stable was windowless and unpainted, and had a patched and half-derelict look, but it was solidly built, with a strong door and a discreetly heavy lock. Giles had bought it years ago.

Beside the doorpost at waist level was a loose half-brick. After making sure she was not observed, Sylvie pulled it out, reached into the hole, picked up a key, and replaced the brick. She turned the key in the door, entered, then closed and barred the door behind her.

There was a candle lamp in a holder on the wall. Sylvie had brought with her a tinderbox containing a flint, a steel in the shape of a capital letter D that fitted neatly around her slender fingers, some fragments of dry wood, and a twist of linen. When she struck the flint against the steel D, sparks flew into the box and ignited the wood fragments, which flamed rapidly.

She then lit the end of the linen rag and used that to light the lamp.

The flickering light showed a wall of old barrels stacked floor to ceiling. Most were full of sand, and too heavy for one person to lift, but a few were empty. They all looked the same, but Sylvie knew the difference. She quickly moved one stack aside and stepped through the gap. Behind the barrels were wooden boxes of books.

The moment of greatest danger for the Palot family was when contraband books were being printed and bound in Giles's workshop. If the place was raided at just the wrong time, they would all die. But as soon as the books were finished, they were stashed in boxes – always with a layer of innocent Catholic-approved literature on top for camouflage – and trundled in a cart to this warehouse, whereupon the print works reverted to producing legitimate books. Most of the time the premises by the cathedral contained nothing remotely illegal.

And only three people knew about this store: Giles, Isabelle and Sylvie. Sylvie had not been told until she was sixteen. Even the workers in the print factory did not know about it, although they were all Protestants: they were told that the finished books were delivered to a secret wholesaler.

Now Sylvie located a box marked 'SA' for *Sileni Alcibiadis*, probably the most important work of Erasmus. She took out a copy and wrapped it in a square of linen from a stack nearby, then tied up the bundle with string. She replaced the barrels so that the boxes of books were once again out of sight, and all that could be seen was a room apparently half full of barrels.

As she retraced her steps along the rue St Martin, she wondered whether her student would show up. He had come to the shop, as arranged, but he might yet get scared. Worse, he might arrive with some kind of official ready to arrest her. She was not afraid of death, of course, no true Christian was, but she was terrified of being tortured. She had visions of red-hot pincers entering her flesh, and had to thrust the images out of her mind by silent prayer.

The waterfront was quiet at night. The fishmongers' stalls were shuttered and the gulls had gone to scavenge elsewhere. The river lapped softly on the foreshore.

Pierre was waiting for her, holding a lantern. His face lit from below looked sinisterly handsome.

He was alone.

She held up the book, but did not give it to him. 'You must never tell anyone you have this,' she said. 'I could be executed for selling it to you.'

'I understand,' he said.

'You, too, will be risking your life if you accept it from me.'

'I know.'

'If you're sure, take it and give me back the *Grammar*.'

They swapped packages.

'Goodbye,' said Sylvie. 'Remember what I said.'

'I will,' he promised.

Then he kissed her.

*

ALISON MCKAY hurried through the draughty corridors of the palace of Tournelles with startling news for her best friend.

Her friend had to fulfil a promise she had never made. This had been expected for years, but, all the same, it was a shock. It was good news, and it was bad.

The medieval building on the eastern side of Paris was large and decrepit. Despite rich furnishings it was cold and uncomfortable. Prestigious but neglected, it was like its current occupier, Caterina de' Medici, queen of France, the wife of a king who preferred his mistress.

Alison stepped into a side room and found who she was looking for.

Two adolescents sat on the floor by the window, playing cards, by the light of the fitful winter sunshine. Their clothes and jewellery showed them to be among the richest people in the world, but they were excitedly gambling for pennies and having a wonderful time.

The boy was fourteen but looked younger. He was stunted in growth and seemed frail. He was on the verge of puberty, and when he spoke in his cracked voice he stammered. This was Francis, the eldest son of King Henri II and Queen Caterina. He was the heir to the throne of France.

The girl was a beautiful redhead, extraordinarily tall at the age of fifteen, towering over most men. Her name was Mary Stuart, and she was the queen of the Scots.

When Mary was five and Alison eight they had moved from Scotland to France, two terrified little girls in a strange country where they could not understand a word anyone said. The sickly Francis had become their playmate, and the three children had formed the strong mutual attachment of those who live through adversity together.

Alison felt affectionately protective of Mary, who sometimes needed looking after on account of her tendency to be impulsive and foolhardy. Both girls were fond of Francis as of a helpless puppy or kitten. Francis worshipped Mary as a goddess.

Now the triangle of friendship was about to be rocked and perhaps destroyed.

Mary looked up and smiled, then saw Alison's expression and became alarmed. 'What is it?' she said, speaking French with no remaining trace of a Scots accent. 'What's happened?'

Alison blurted it out. 'You two have to get married on the Sunday after Easter!'

'So soon!' said Mary, then they both looked at Francis.

Mary had become engaged to Francis when she was five, just before she moved to France to live. The engagement was political, like all royal betrothals. Its purpose was to cement the alliance of France and Scotland against England.

But as the girls grew older they had come to doubt that the marriage would ever happen. Relations among the three kingdoms shifted constantly. Power brokers in London, Edinburgh and Paris talked frequently about alternative husbands for Mary Stuart. Nothing had seemed certain, until now.

Francis looked anguished. 'I love you,' he said to Mary. 'I want to marry you – when I'm a man.'

Mary reached out to take his hand sympathetically, but he was overcome. He burst into tears and scrambled to his feet.

Alison said: 'Francis—'

He shook his head helplessly, then ran from the room.

'Oh, dear,' said Mary. 'Poor Francis.'

Alison closed the door. Now the two girls were alone and in private. Alison gave Mary her hand and pulled her up from the floor. Still holding hands, they sat together on a sofa covered in rich chestnut-brown velvet. They were quiet for a minute, then Alison said: 'How do you feel?'

'All my life they've been telling me I'm a queen,' Mary said. 'I never was, really. I became queen of the Scots when I was six days old, and people have never stopped treating me like a baby. But if I marry Francis, and he becomes king, then I will be queen of France – the real thing.' Her eyes glittered with desire. 'That's what I want.'

'But Francis . . .'

'I know. He's sweet, and I love him, but to lie down in a bed with him, and, you know . . .'

Alison nodded vigorously. 'It hardly bears thinking about.'

'Perhaps Francis and I could get married and just pretend.'

Alison shook her head. 'Then the marriage might be annulled.'

'And I would no longer be queen.'

'Exactly.'

Mary said: 'Why now? What brought this on?'

Alison had been told by Queen Caterina, the most well-informed person in France. 'Scarface suggested it to the king.' The duke of Guise was Mary's uncle, her mother's brother. The family was riding high after his victory at Calais.

'Why does Uncle Scarface care?'

'Think how the prestige of the Guise family would be boosted if one of them became queen of France.'

'Scarface is a soldier.'

'Yes. This was surely someone else's idea.'

'But Francis . . .'

'It all comes back to little Francis, doesn't it?'

'He's *so* little,' Mary said. 'And so ill. Is he even capable of doing what a man is supposed to do with his wife?'

'I don't know,' said Alison. 'But you're going to find out on the Sunday after Easter.'

3

MARGERY AND HER PARENTS were still deadlocked when January turned into February. Sir Reginald and Lady Jane were determined that Margery should marry Bart, and she had declared that she would never utter the vows.

Rollo was angry with her. She had a chance to take the family into the Catholic nobility, and instead she wanted to ally with the Protestant-leaning Willards. How could she contemplate such a betrayal – especially under a queen who favoured Catholics in every way?

The Fitzgeralds were the leading family in town – and they looked the part, Rollo thought proudly as they stood in the hall putting on their warmest clothes, while the great bell in the cathedral tower boomed its summons to Mass. Sir Reginald was tall and lean, and the freckles that marred his face also gave him a kind of distinction. He put on a heavy cloak of chestnut-brown cloth. Lady Jane, small and thin, had a sharp nose and darting eyes that did not miss much. She wore a coat lined with fur.

Margery, also short, was more rounded. She was in a furious sulk, and had not been allowed out of the house since the earl's party; but she could not be held incommunicado for ever, and this morning the bishop of Kingsbridge would be at Mass, a powerful ally whom the family could not risk offending.

Margery had clearly decided not to look as miserable as she felt. She had put on a coat of Kingsbridge Scarlet and a matching hat. In the past year or so she had grown up to be the prettiest girl in town – even her brother could see that.

The fifth member of the family was Rollo's great-aunt. She had been a nun at Kingsbridge Priory, and had come to live with the Fitzgeralds when the priory was shut down by King

Henry VIII. She had turned her two rooms on the top floor of the house into a little nunnery, the bedroom a bare cell and the parlour a chapel; Rollo was awed by her devotion. Everyone still called her Sister Joan. She was now old and frail, and walked with two sticks, but she insisted on going to church when Bishop Julius was there. The maid Naomi would carry a chair to the cathedral for Sister Joan, for she could not remain standing a whole hour.

They stepped outside together. They lived at the crossroads at the top of the main street, opposite the Guild Hall, a commanding position, and for a moment Sir Reginald paused and looked down over the close-packed streets descending like stairs to the river. A light snow was falling on the thatched roofs and smoking chimneys. My town, his expression said.

As the mayor and his family made their stately procession down the slope of the main street their neighbours greeted them respectfully, the more prosperous ones wishing them good morning, the lower classes silently touching their hats.

In the daylight Rollo noticed that his mother's coat was slightly moth-eaten, and he hoped no one would notice. Unfortunately, his father had no money for new clothes. Business was bad in Combe Harbour, where Sir Reginald was Receiver of Customs. The French had captured the port of Calais, the war dragged on, and Channel shipping was minimal.

As they approached the cathedral, they passed the other cause of the family's financial crisis: the new house, to be called Priory Gate. It stood on the north side of the market square, on land that had been attached to the prior's house in the days when there had been a priory. Construction had slowed almost to a stop. Most of the builders had gone elsewhere, to work for people who could pay them. A crude wooden fence had been erected to discourage curious people from entering the unfinished building.

Sir Reginald also owned the complex of priory buildings on the south side of the cathedral: the cloisters, the monks' kitchen and dormitory, the nunnery and the stables. When Henry VIII had dissolved the monasteries, their property had been given or sold to local magnates, and Sir Reginald had got the priory. These mostly old buildings had been neglected for decades and were now falling down, with birds' nests in the rafters and brambles growing in the cloisters. Reginald would probably sell them back to the chapter.

Between the two shabby lots the cathedral stood proud, unchanged for hundreds of years, just like the Catholic faith it represented. In the last forty years Protestants had tried to alter the Christian doctrines that had been taught here for so long: Rollo wondered how they had the arrogance. It was like trying to put modern windows in the church walls. The truth was for eternity, like the cathedral.

They went in through the great arches of the west front. It seemed even colder inside than out. As always, the sight of the long nave with its ordered lines of precisely repeated columns and arches filled Rollo with a reassuring sense of a systematic universe regulated by a rational deity. At the far end, winter daylight faintly lit the great rose window, its coloured glass showing how all things would end: God sitting in judgement on the last day, evildoers being tortured in Hell, the good entering Heaven, balance restored.

The Fitzgeralds moved down the aisle to the crossing as the prayers began. From a distance they watched the priests perform the service at the high altar. Around them were the other leading families of the town, including the Willards and the Cobleys, and of the county, notably the earl of Shiring and his son Bart, and Lord and Lady Brecknock.

The singing was mediocre. Hundreds of years of thrilling choral music at Kingsbridge Cathedral had come to an end when the priory closed and the choir was disbanded. Some of the former monks had started a new choir, but the spirit had gone. They were not able to recreate the fanatical discipline of a group whose entire lives were dedicated to praising God with beautiful music.

The congregation was still for the dramatic moments, such as the elevation of the Host, and they listened politely to Bishop Julius's sermon – on obedience – but for much of the time they talked among themselves.

Rollo was annoyed to see that Margery had slyly slipped away from the family and was talking animatedly to Ned Willard, the plume on her cap bobbing vigorously with emphasis. Ned, too, was dressed up, in his blue French coat, and he was clearly thrilled to be with her. Rollo wanted to kick him for insolence.

To compensate, Rollo went and spoke to Bart Shiring, and told him it would come right in the end. They spoke about the war. The loss of Calais had damaged more than just trade. Queen Mary and her foreign husband were increasingly unpopular. Rollo still did not think England would ever have another Protestant monarch, but Mary Tudor was doing no good to the Catholic cause.

As the service came to an end, Rollo was approached by Philbert Cobley's plump son, Dan. The puritanical Cobleys were here unwillingly, Rollo felt sure; he guessed they hated the statues and the paintings, and would have liked to hold their noses against the whiff of incense. Rollo was driven mad by the idea that people – ignorant, uneducated, stupid ordinary people – had the right to make up their own minds about religion. If such a naive idea ever gained currency, civilization would collapse. People had to be told what to do.

With Dan was a wiry, weather-beaten man called Jonas Bacon, one of the many sea captains employed by Kingsbridge merchants.

Dan said to Rollo: 'We have a cargo that we want to sell. Might you be interested?'

Ship owners such as the Cobleys often sold their cargoes in advance, sometimes offering quarters or eighths to multiple investors. It was a way of raising the money to finance the voyage and, at the same time, spreading the risk. Stakeholders could sometimes get back ten times the cost of their share – or they could lose it all. In more prosperous days Sir Reginald had made huge profits this way.

'We might be interested,' Rollo said. He was being insincere. His father had no cash to invest in a cargo, but Rollo wanted to know about it anyway.

'The *St Margaret* is on her way back from the Baltic Sea, her hold crammed with furs worth more than five hundred pounds landed,' Dan said. 'I can show you the manifest.'

Rollo frowned. 'How can you know this if she's still at sea?'

Captain Bacon answered the question in a voice hoarse from years of shouting into the wind. 'I overtook her off the Netherlands coast. My ship, the *Hawk*, is faster. I hove to and took the details. The *St Margaret* was about to go into harbour for minor repairs. But she will be in Combe in two weeks.'

Captain Bacon had a bad reputation. Many captains did. There was no one to witness what sailors did at sea, and people said they were thieves and murderers. But his story was credible. Rollo nodded and turned back to Dan. 'So why would you sell the cargo now?'

A sly look appeared on Dan's round white face. 'We need the money for another investment.'

He was not going to say what. That was natural: if he had come across a good business opportunity he would not give others the chance to get in first. All the same, Rollo was suspicious. 'Is there something wrong with your cargo?'

'No. And to prove it we're prepared to guarantee the value of the furs at five hundred pounds. But we'll sell the cargo to you for four hundred.'

It was a large sum. A prosperous farmer owning his land might make fifty pounds a year; a successful Kingsbridge merchant would be proud of an annual income of two hundred. Four hundred was a huge investment – but a guaranteed profit of a hundred pounds in only two weeks was a rare opportunity.

And it would pay off all the Fitzgerald family's debts.

Unfortunately, they did not have four hundred pounds. They did not have four pounds.

Nevertheless, Rollo said: 'I'll put it to my father.' He was sure they could not make this deal, but Sir Reginald might be offended if the son claimed to speak authoritatively for the family.

'Don't delay,' Dan said. 'I came to you first out of respect, because Sir Reginald is the mayor, but there are other people we can go to. And we need the money tomorrow.' He and the captain moved away.

Rollo looked around the nave, spotted his father leaning against a fluted column, and went over. 'I've been talking to Dan Cobley.'

'Oh, yes?' Sir Reginald did not like the Cobleys. Few people did. They seemed to think they were holier than ordinary people, and their walkout at the play had annoyed everybody. 'What did he want?'

'To sell a cargo.' Rollo gave his father the details.

When he had done, Reginald said: 'And they're prepared to guarantee the value of the furs?'

'Five hundred pounds – for an investment of four hundred. I know we don't have the money, but I thought you'd like to know about it.'

'You're right, we don't have the money.' Reginald looked thoughtful. 'But I might be able to get it.'

Rollo wondered how. But his father could be resourceful. He was not the kind of merchant to build up a business gradually, but he was an alert opportunist, keen to grab an unforeseen bargain.

Was it possible he could solve all the family's worries at a stroke? Rollo hardly dared to hope.

To Rollo's surprise Reginald went to speak to the Willards. Alice was a leading merchant, so the mayor often had matters to discuss with her; but the two did not like one another, and relations had not been improved by the Fitzgeralds' rejection of young Ned as a potential son-in-law. Rollo followed his father, intrigued.

Reginald spoke quietly. 'A word with you, Mrs Willard, if I may.'

Alice was a short, stout woman with impeccable good manners. 'Of course,' she said politely.

'I need to borrow four hundred pounds for a short period.'

Alice looked startled. 'You may need to go to London,' she said after a pause. 'Or Antwerp.' The Netherlands city of Antwerp was the financial capital of Europe. 'We have a cousin in Antwerp,' she added. 'But I don't know that even he would want to lend such a large sum.'

'I need it today,' Sir Reginald said.

Alice raised her eyebrows.

Rollo felt a pang of shame. It was humiliating to beg a loan from the family they had scorned so recently.

But Reginald ploughed on regardless. 'You're the only merchant in Kingsbridge who has that kind of money instantly available, Alice.'

Alice said: 'May I ask what you want the money for?'

'I have the chance to buy a rich cargo.'

Reginald would not say from whom, Rollo guessed, for fear that Alice might try to buy the cargo herself.

Reginald added: 'The ship will be in Combe Harbour in two weeks.'

At this point Ned Willard butted into the conversation. Naturally, Rollo thought bitterly, he would enjoy the sight of the Fitzgeralds asking for help from the Willards. But Ned's contribution was businesslike. 'So why would the owner sell it at this point?' he said sceptically. 'He only has to wait two weeks to get the full value of the landed cargo.'

Reginald looked irritated at being questioned by a mere boy, but curbed his displeasure and replied: 'The vendor needs cash immediately for another investment.'

Alice said: 'I can't take the risk of losing such a large amount – you'll understand that.'

'There's no risk,' said Reginald. 'You'll be repaid in little more than two weeks.'

That was absurd, Rollo knew. There was always risk.

Reginald lowered his voice. 'We're neighbours, Alice. We help each other. I ease the way for your cargoes at Combe Harbour, you know that. And you help me. It's how Kingsbridge works.'

Alice looked taken aback, and after a moment Rollo realized why. His father's emollient words about helping neighbours actually constituted a backhand threat. If Alice did not cooperate, it was implied, then Reginald might make trouble for her in the harbour.

There was an extended silence while Alice considered this. Rollo could guess what she was thinking. She did not want to make the loan, but she could not afford to antagonize someone as powerful as Reginald.

At last Alice said: 'I would require security.'

Rollo's hopes sank. A man who has nothing cannot offer security. This was just another way of saying 'No'.

Reginald said: 'I'll pledge my post as Receiver of Customs.'

Alice shook her head. 'You can't dispose of it without royal permission – and you don't have time for that.'

Rollo knew that Alice was right. Reginald was in danger of revealing his desperation.

Reginald said: 'Then how about the priory?'

Alice shook her head. 'I don't want your half-built house.'

'Then the southern part, the cloisters and the monks' quarters and the nunnery.'

Rollo was sure Alice would not accept that as security. The buildings of the old priory had been disused for more than twenty years, and were now beyond repair.

Yet, to his surprise, Alice suddenly looked interested. She said: 'Perhaps . . .'

Rollo spoke up. 'But, Father, you know that Bishop Julius wants the chapter to buy back the priory – and you've more or less agreed to sell it.'

The pious Queen Mary had tried to return all the property seized from the Church by her rapacious father, Henry VIII, but Members of Parliament would not pass the legislation – too many of them had benefited – so the Church was trying to buy it back cheaply; and Rollo thought it was the duty of good Catholics to help that process.

'That's all right,' said Reginald. 'I'm not going to default on the loan, so the security will not be seized. The bishop will have what he wants.'

'Good,' said Alice.

Then there was a pause. Alice was clearly waiting for something, but would not say what. At last Reginald guessed, and said: 'I would pay you a good rate of interest.'

'I would want a high rate,' said Alice. 'Except that to charge interest on loans is usury, which is a crime as well as a sin.'

She was right, but this was a quibble. Laws against usury were circumvented daily in every commercial town in Europe. Alice's prissy objection was only for the sake of appearances.

'Well, now, I'm sure we can find a way around that,' said Reginald in the jocular tone of one who proposes an innocent deception.

Alice said warily: 'What did you have in mind?'

'Suppose I give you use of the priory during the term of the loan, then rent it back from you?'

'I'd want eight pounds a month.'

Ned looked anxious. Evidently he wanted his mother to walk away from this deal. And Rollo could see why: Alice was going to risk four hundred pounds to earn just eight pounds.

Reginald pretended to be outraged. 'Why, that's twenty-four per cent a year – more, compounded!'

'Then let's drop the whole idea.'

Rollo began to feel hopeful. Why was Alice arguing about the rate of interest? It must mean she was going to make the loan. Rollo saw that Ned was looking mildly panicked, and guessed he was thinking the same, but regarding the prospect with dismay.

Reginald thought for a long moment. At last he said: 'Very well. So be it.' He held out his hand, and Alice shook it.

Rollo was awestruck by his father's cleverness. For a man who was virtually penniless to make an investment of four hundred pounds was a triumph of audacity. And the cargo of the *St Margaret* would revive the family finances. Thank heaven for Philbert Cobley's sudden urgent need for money.

'I'll draw up the papers this afternoon,' said Alice Willard, and she turned away.

At the same moment, Lady Jane came up. 'It's time to go home,' she said. 'Dinner will be ready.'

Rollo looked around for his sister.

Margery was nowhere to be seen.

*

As SOON AS the Fitzgeralds were out of earshot, Ned said to his mother: 'Why did you agree to lend so much money to Sir Reginald?'

'Because he would have made trouble for us if I'd refused.'

'But he may default! We could lose everything.'

'No, we'd have the priory.'

'A collection of tumbledown buildings.'

'I don't want the buildings.'

'Then . . .' Ned frowned.

'Think,' said his mother.

If not the buildings, what did Alice want? 'The land?'

'Keep thinking.'

'It's in the heart of the city.'

'Exactly. It's the most valuable site in Kingsbridge, and worth a lot more than four hundred pounds to someone who knows how to make the most of it.'

'I see,' said Ned. 'But what would you do with it – build a house, like Reginald?'

Alice looked scornful. 'I don't need a palace. I would build an indoor market that would be open every day of the week, regardless of the weather. I'd rent space to stallholders – pastry cooks, cheesewrights, glovers, shoemakers. There, right next to the cathedral, it would make money for a thousand years.'

The project was an idea of genius, Ned judged. That was why his mother had thought of it, and he had not.

All the same, a trace of his worry remained. He did not trust the Fitzgeralds.

Another thought occurred to him. 'Is this a contingency plan in case we've lost everything in Calais?'

Alice had made strenuous efforts to get news from Calais, but had learned no more since the French had taken the city. Perhaps they had simply confiscated all English property, including the richly stocked Willard warehouse; perhaps Uncle Dick and his family were on their way to Kingsbridge empty-handed. But the city had prospered mainly because English merchants brought trade, and it was just possible that the French king realized it was smarter to let the foreigners keep what was theirs and stay in business.

Unfortunately, no news was bad news: the fact that no Englishmen had yet escaped from Calais and come home with information, despite the passage of a month, suggested that few were left alive.

'The indoor market is worth doing in any circumstances,' Alice answered. 'But yes, I'm thinking we may well need a whole new business if the news from Calais is as bad as we fear.'

Ned nodded. His mother was always thinking ahead.

'However, it probably won't happen,' Alice finished. 'Reginald would not have lowered himself to beg a loan from me unless he had a really attractive deal lined up.'

Ned was already thinking about something else. The negotiation with Reginald had temporarily driven from his mind the only member of the Fitzgerald family in whom he was really interested.

He looked around the congregation but he could no longer see Margery. She had already left, and he knew where she had gone. He walked down the nave, trying not to appear hurried.

Preoccupied as he was, he marvelled as always at the music of the arches, the lower ones like bass notes repeated in a steady rhythm, the smaller ones in the gallery and the clerestory like higher harmonies in the same chord.

He pulled his cloak closer around him as he stepped outside and turned north, as if heading for the graveyard. The snow was falling more heavily now, settling on the roof of the monumental tomb of Prior Philip. It was so big that Ned and Margery had been able to stand on the far side of it and canoodle without fear of being observed. According to legend, Prior Philip had been forgiving towards those who gave in to sexual temptation, so Ned imagined the soul of the long-dead monk might not have been much troubled by two young people kissing over his grave.

But Margery had thought of a better meeting place than the tomb, and had told Ned her idea in a brief conversation during the service. Following her instructions, Ned now walked around the site of her father's new palace. On the far side he checked that he was unobserved. There was a breach in the fence here, and he stepped through.

Sir Reginald's new house had floors, walls, staircases and a roof, but no doors or windows. Ned stepped inside and ran up the grand stairs of Italian marble to a broad landing. Margery was waiting there. Her body was swathed in a big red coat, but her face was eager. He threw his arms around her and they kissed passionately. He closed his eyes and inhaled the scent of her, a warm fragrance that arose from the skin of her neck.

When they paused for breath, he said: 'I'm worried. My mother has just loaned your father four hundred pounds.'

Margery shrugged. 'They do that sort of thing all the time.'

'Loans lead to quarrels. This could make things worse for us.'

'How could things be worse? Kiss me again.'

Ned had kissed several girls, but none like this. Margery was the only one who came right out and said what she wanted. Women were supposed to be led by men, especially in physical relations, but Margery seemed not to know that.

'I love the way you kiss,' Ned said after a while. 'Who taught you?'

'No one taught me! What do you think I am? Anyway, it's not as if there's one right way. This isn't bookkeeping.'

'I suppose that's true. Every girl is different. Ruth Cobley likes her breasts squeezed really hard, so she can still feel it later. Whereas Susan White—'

'Stop it! I don't want to know about your other girls.'

'I'm teasing. There has never been one like you. That's why I love you.'

'I love you, too,' she said, and they started kissing again. Ned opened his cloak and unbuttoned her coat so that they could press their bodies together. They hardly felt the cold.

Then Ned heard a familiar voice say: 'Stop this right now!'

It was Rollo.

Ned reacted with a guilty start, then suppressed it: there was no reason he should not kiss a girl who loved him. He released Margery from his embrace and turned around with deliberate slowness. He was not afraid of Rollo. 'Don't try to give me orders, Rollo. We're not at school now.'

Rollo ignored him and spoke to Margery, full of righteous indignation. 'You're coming home with me right now.'

Margery had lived a long time with her bullying older brother, and she was practised at resisting his will. 'You go ahead,' she said in a casual tone that sounded only a little forced. 'I'll be there in a minute.'

Rollo reddened. 'I said now.' He grabbed Margery's arm.

Ned said: 'Take your hands off her, Rollo – there's no call for physical force.'

'You shut your mouth. I'll do as I please with my younger sister.'

Margery tried to pull her arm away, but Rollo tightened his grip. She said: 'Stop it, that hurts!'

Ned said: 'I've warned you, Rollo.' He did not want violence, but he would not give in to bullying.

Rollo jerked Margery's arm.

Ned grabbed Rollo by the coat, pulled him away from Margery, and gave him a shove, so that he staggered across the landing.

Then Ned saw Bart coming up the marble staircase.

Rollo recovered his balance. He raised a warning finger, stepped towards Ned, said: 'Now you listen to me!' and then kicked Ned.

The kick was aimed at the groin but Ned moved an inch and took the blow on his thigh. It hurt but he hardly noticed it, he was so angry. He went at Rollo with both fists, hitting Rollo's head and chest three times, four, five. Rollo retreated then tried to hit back. He was taller and had longer arms, but Ned was angrier.

Ned vaguely heard Margery scream: 'Stop it, stop it!'

Ned drove Rollo across the landing then, suddenly, he felt himself seized from behind. It was Bart, he realized. Ned's arms were pressed to his sides as if by a rope: Bart was much bigger and stronger than either Ned or Rollo. Ned struggled furiously but could not break free, and suddenly he realized he was in for a hell of a beating.

As Bart held Ned, Rollo started to hit him. Ned tried to duck and dodge but he was pinned, and Rollo was able to punch his face and belly and kick him in the balls, painfully, again and again. Bart laughed with delight. Margery screamed and tried to restrain her brother, but without much effect: she was fierce enough, but too small to stop him.

After a minute Bart tired of the game and stopped laughing. He shoved Ned aside, and Ned fell on the floor. He tried to get up, but for a moment he could not. One eye was closed, but through the other he saw Rollo and Bart take Margery by either arm and march her away down the stairs.

Ned coughed and spat blood. A tooth came out with the blood and landed on the floor, he saw with his one good eye. Then he vomited.

He hurt all over. He tried again to get up, but it was too agonizing. He lay on his back on the cold marble, waiting for the pain to go away. 'Shit,' he said. 'Shit.'

*

'Where have you been?' Lady Jane asked Margery as soon as Rollo brought her into the house.

Margery yelled: 'Rollo punched Ned while Bart held him still – what kind of animal does that?'

'Calm down,' said her mother.

'Look at Rollo, rubbing his knuckles – he's proud of himself!'

Rollo said: 'I'm proud of doing the right thing.'

'You couldn't fight Ned on your own, though, could you?' She pointed at Bart, who followed Rollo in. 'You had to have his help.'

'Never mind that,' said Lady Jane. 'There's someone to see you.'

'I can't speak to anyone now,' Margery said. She wanted nothing more than to be alone in her room.

'Don't be disobedient,' said her mother. 'Come with me.'

Margery's power of resistance melted away. She had watched the man she loved being beaten up, and it was her fault for loving him. She felt she had lost the ability to do the right thing. She shrugged listlessly and followed her mother.

They went to Lady Jane's parlour, from which she managed

the house and directed the domestic servants. It was an austere room, with hard chairs and a writing table and a prie-dieu. On the table stood Jane's collection of ivory carvings of saints.

The bishop of Kingsbridge was waiting there.

Bishop Julius was a thin old man, perhaps as much as sixty-five, but quick in his movements. His head was bald and Margery always thought his face looked like a skull. His pale blue eyes flashed with intelligence.

Margery was startled to see him. What could he possibly want with her?

Lady Jane said: 'The bishop has something to say to you.'

'Sit down, Margery,' said Julius.

She did as she was told.

'I've known you since you were born,' he said. 'You've been brought up a Christian and a good Catholic. Your parents can be proud of you.'

Margery said nothing. She hardly saw the bishop. In her mind she watched again while Rollo viciously punched Ned's dear face.

'You say your prayers, you go to Mass, you confess your sins once a year. God is pleased with you.'

It was true. Everything else in Margery's life seemed wrong – her brother was hateful, her parents were cruel, and she was supposed to marry a beast – but at least she felt she was right with God. That was some consolation.

'And yet,' said the bishop, 'suddenly you seem to have forgotten everything you were taught.'

Now he had her attention. 'No, I haven't,' she said indignantly.

Her mother said: 'Speak when the bishop asks you to, not otherwise, you impudent child.'

Julius smiled indulgently. 'It's all right, Lady Jane. I understand that Margery is upset.'

Margery stared at him. He was a living icon of Christ and the earthly shepherd of the Christian flock. His words came from God. What was he accusing her of?

He said: 'You seem to have forgotten the fourth commandment.'

Suddenly Margery felt ashamed. She knew what he meant. She looked down at the floor.

'Say the fourth commandment, Margery.'

She mumbled: 'Honour thy father and mother.'

'Say it louder and more clearly, please.'

She lifted her head but could not meet his eye. 'Honour thy father and mother,' she said.

Julius nodded. 'In the last month you have dishonoured your father and mother, haven't you?'

Margery nodded. It was true.

'It's your sacred duty to do as you're told.'

'I'm sorry,' she whispered miserably.

'It's not enough to repent, though, is it, Margery? You know that.'

'What must I do?'

'You must cease to sin. You must obey.'

She looked up and met his eye at last. 'Obey?'

'This is what God wants.'

'Is it, really?'

'It is.'

He was the bishop. He knew what God wanted. And he had told her. She looked down again.

'I want you to speak to your father, now,' said Julius.

'Must I?'

'You know you must. And I think you know what you have to say. Do you?'

Margery was too choked up to speak, but she nodded.

The bishop made a sign to Lady Jane, who went to the door and opened it. Sir Reginald was waiting there, and he stepped in. He looked at Margery and said: 'Well?'

'I'm sorry, Father,' she said.

He said: 'So you should be.'

There was a pause. They were waiting for her.

At last she said: 'I will marry Bart Shiring.'

'Good girl,' he said.

Margery stood up. 'May I go?'

Lady Jane said: 'Perhaps you should thank the bishop for steering you back into the path of God's grace.'

Margery turned to Julius. 'Thank you, bishop.'

'Very well,' said Lady Jane. 'Now you may go.'

Margery left the room.

*

ON MONDAY MORNING Ned looked out of the window and saw Margery, and his heart quickened.

He was standing in the parlour, and his tortoiseshell cat, Maddy, was rubbing her head against his ankle. He had named her Madcap when she was a kitten, but now she was an old lady who was pleased, in a restrained, dignified way, to see him home.

He watched Margery cross the square to the Grammar School. Three mornings a week she held an infants' class, teaching them numbers and letters and the miracles of Jesus, getting them ready for real school. She had been absent from her duties for the whole of January, but now she was returning, Ned assumed. Rollo was with her, apparently as an escort.

Ned had been waiting for this.

He had had romances before. He had never committed the sin of fornication, although he had got close once or twice; he had certainly felt himself very fond of Susan White and Ruth Cobley at different times. However, as soon as he had fallen for Margery he had known this was different. He did not want merely to get Margery behind the tomb of Prior Philip and kiss and caress her. He wanted that, yes, but he also wanted to spend long leisurely hours with her, to talk to her about plays and paintings, Kingsbridge gossip and English politics; or just to lie next to her on a grassy bank by a stream in the sunshine.

He restrained the impulse to rush out of the house now and accost her in the marketplace. He would speak to her when the class ended at noon.

He spent the morning at the warehouse, making entries in ledgers. His older brother, Barney, hated this part of the work – Barney had always struggled with letters and had not learned to read until he was twelve – but Ned liked it: the bills and receipts, the quantities of tin and lead and iron ore, the voyages to Seville and Calais and Antwerp, the prices, and the profits.

Sitting at a table with a quill pen and a bottle of ink and a fat book of lists, he could see an entire international business empire.

However, it was now an empire on the edge of collapse. Most of what the Willard family owned was in Calais, and had probably been confiscated by the king of France. The stocks of materials here in Kingsbridge were valuable, but difficult to sell while cross-Channel shipping was restricted by war. Several employees had been dismissed because there was nothing for them to do. Ned's ledger work consisted of trying to add up what was left and see whether it was enough to pay outstanding debts.

His work was constantly interrupted by people asking him why he had a black eye. He told them the plain truth, just as he had told his mother: Bart and Rollo had beaten him up for kissing Margery. No one was shocked or even surprised: fist fights were not unusual among young men, especially at the end of the week, and it was commonplace to see bruises on Monday morning.

Grandma had been indignant. 'That Rollo is a sly fox,' she had said. 'He was a spiteful little boy and now he's a vindictive big man. You be careful of him.' Alice had cried over Ned's lost tooth.

When the daylight brightened towards midday, Ned left the warehouse and walked up the slushy main street. Instead of going into his home, he went to the entrance of the Grammar School. The cathedral bell struck noon just as he arrived. He felt decades older than the boy who had left that school three years ago. The dramas that had engaged him so powerfully then – tests, sports, rivalries – now seemed ridiculously trivial.

Rollo came across the marketplace to the school. He was here to escort Margery home, Ned guessed. When Rollo saw Ned he looked startled and a bit scared. Then he blustered: 'You stay away from my sister.'

Ned was ready for him. 'You make me stay away, you feeble-minded peasant.'

'Do you want me to black your other eye?'

'I want you to try.'

Rollo backed down. 'I'm not going to brawl in a public place.'

'Of course not,' Ned said contemptuously. 'Especially now that you haven't got your big friend Bart to help you.'

Margery came out of the school. 'Rollo!' she said. 'For heaven's sake, are you trying to start another fight?'

Ned stared at her, his heart in his mouth. She was tiny but magnificent, her chin tilted up, her green eyes radiating defiance, her young voice commanding.

'You are not to speak to the Willard boy,' Rollo said to her. 'Come home with me now.'

'But I want to speak to him,' she said.

'I absolutely forbid you.'

'Don't grab my arm, Rollo,' she said, reading his mind. 'Instead, be reasonable. Stand by the door of the bishop's palace. From there you can see us but not hear us.'

'You have nothing to say to Willard.'

'Don't be stupid. I have to tell him what happened yesterday. You can't deny that, can you?'

'Is that all?' Rollo said sceptically.

'I promise you. I simply have to tell Ned.'

'Don't let him touch you.'

'Go and stand by the bishop's door.'

Ned and Margery watched while Rollo walked twenty paces then turned round and stood glowering.

Ned said: 'What happened yesterday, after the fight?'

'I realized something,' Margery said, and tears came to her eyes.

Ned had a doomed feeling. 'What did you realize?'

'That it is my holy duty to obey my parents.'

She was crying. Ned reached into his pocket and took out a linen handkerchief his mother had made, hemmed and embroidered with acorns. He touched her cheeks gently with it, drying her tears; but she snatched it from him and wiped her eyes roughly, saying: 'There's nothing more to be said, is there?'

'Oh, but there is.' Ned gathered his wits. He knew that

Margery was deeply pious at heart, despite also being passionate and strong-willed. 'Isn't it a sin to lie with a man you hate?'

'No, that's not part of the Church's teaching.'

'Well, it should be.'

'You Protestants always want to revise God's laws.'

'I'm not a Protestant! Is that what this is about?'

'No.'

'What have they done? How did they get to you? Were you threatened?'

'I was reminded of my duty.'

Ned felt she was hiding something. 'Who by? Who reminded you?'

She hesitated, as if she did not want to answer the question; then she gave a little shrug, as if it did not make any real difference, and said: 'Bishop Julius.'

Ned was outraged. 'Well, he was just doing your parents a favour! He's an old crony of your father's.'

'He is a living icon of Christ.'

'Jesus doesn't tell us who we should marry!'

'I believe Jesus wants me to be obedient.'

'This is nothing to do with God's will. Your parents are using your piety to manipulate you into doing what they want.'

'I'm sorry you think that.'

'You're really going to marry Bart Shiring because the bishop told you to?'

'Because God wishes it. I'm leaving now, Ned. In the future it will be best if you and I speak to one another as little as possible.'

'Why? We live in the same town, we go to the same church – why shouldn't we speak?'

'Because my heart is breaking,' said Margery, and then she walked away.

4

Barney Willard walked along the busy Seville waterfront, looking to see whether any English ships had come up the Guadalquivir river on the early tide. He was desperate to learn if his Uncle Dick was still alive, and whether his family had lost everything.

A cold wind blew down the river, but the sky was clear and deep blue, and the morning sun was hot on his tanned face. After this he felt he would never again grow accustomed to the damp cold and cloudy gloom of English weather.

Seville was built astride a bend in the river. On the inside of the curve, a broad beach of mud and sand sloped up from the water's edge to firmer ground where thousands of houses, palaces and churches were packed close together in the largest city in Spain.

The beach was crowded with men, horses and oxen as cargoes were discharged from ships to carts and vice versa, and buyers and sellers haggled at the tops of their voices. Barney surveyed the moored vessels, listening for the broad vowels and soft consonants of English speech.

There was something about ships that made his soul sing. He had never been happier than on the voyage here. Despite the rotten food, the foul drinking water, the stinking bilges, and the frightening storms, he loved the sea. The sensation of speeding across the waves with the wind swelling the sails was a thrill as intense as lying with a woman. Well, almost.

The ships at the water's edge were packed side by side as close as the houses in the town. All were moored prow in, stern out. Barney was used to the docks at Combe Harbour, which would have five or ten ships at anchor on a busy day, but Seville regularly had fifty.

Barney had a practical reason for visiting the waterfront early. He was living with Carlos Cruz, his second cousin, a metal worker. Seville manufactured weapons for the endless wars of King Felipe II, and there was never enough metal. Carlos bought everything exported by Barney's mother: lead from the Mendip Hills for shot, tin from the mines of Cornwall for shipboard food containers and utensils, and – most important – iron ore. But ores and metals came into Seville by ship from other exporters, some in southern England, some in northern Spain, and Carlos needed to buy from them, too.

Barney stopped to watch a new arrival being delicately nosed into a mooring. It looked familiar, and his heart lifted in hope. The ship was about a hundred feet long and twenty feet wide, the narrow shape popular with captains who liked to move fast. Barney guessed it displaced about a hundred tons. There were three masts, with a total of five square sails, for power, plus a triangular lateen on the middle mast for manoeuvrability. It would be an agile vessel.

He thought it might be the *Hawk*, owned by Philbert Cobley of Kingsbridge, and when he heard the sailors calling to one another in English, he felt sure. Then a small man of about forty with a bronzed bald head and a fair beard waded through the shallows to the beach, and Barney recognized Jonathan Greenland, who frequently sailed as first mate with Captain Bacon.

He waited while Jonathan tied a rope to a stake driven deep into the beach. Back at home, men such as Jonathan could always get a glass or two of wine at the Willard house opposite Kingsbridge Cathedral, for Alice Willard had an insatiable appetite for news from anywhere. As a boy, Barney had loved to listen to Jonathan, for he spoke of Africa and Russia and the New World, places where the sun always shone or the snow never melted, and his reports of prices and politics were mixed with tales of treachery and piracy, riots and hijacking.

Barney's favourite story had told how Jonathan had become a seaman. At the age of fifteen he had got drunk in the Jolly Sailor at Combe Harbour on a Saturday night and had woken up the next morning two miles off shore and heading for

Lisbon. He had not seen England again for four years, but when at last he got back he had enough money to buy a house. He recounted this as a cautionary tale, but the boy Barney had thought it a wonderful adventure and had wished it would happen to him. Now a man of twenty, Barney still found the sea exciting.

When the Hawk was securely tied up, the two men shook hands. 'You're wearing an earring,' Jonathan said with a surprised smile. 'You've become exotic. Is that a Spanish fashion?'

'Not really,' said Barney. 'It's more of a Turkish thing. Call it my whim.' He wore it because it made him feel romantic, and because girls found it intriguing.

Jonathan shrugged. 'I haven't been to Seville before,' he said. 'What's it like?'

'I love it – the wine is strong and the girls are pretty,' Barney answered. 'But what's the news of my family? What happened in Calais?'

'Captain Bacon has a letter for you from your mother. But there's not much to tell. We're still waiting for reliable information.'

Barney was downcast. 'If the English in Calais were being treated mercifully, and allowed to continue living and working there, they would have sent messages by now. The longer we wait, the more likely it is that they've been imprisoned, or worse.'

'That's what people are saying.' From the deck of the Hawk someone shouted Jonathan's name. 'I have to get back on board,' he said.

'Do you have any iron ore for my cousin Carlos?'

Jonathan shook his head. 'This cargo is all wool.' His name was called again, impatiently. 'I'll bring you your letter later.'

'Come and dine with us. We're in the nearest quarter of the city, where you can see all the smoke. It's called El Arenal, The Sandpit, and it's where the king's guns are made. Ask for Carlos Cruz.'

Jonathan swarmed up a rope and Barney turned away.

He was not surprised by the news, or lack of it, from Calais, but he was dejected. His mother had spent the best years of her life building up the family business, and it made Barney angry and sad to think everything could just be stolen.

He finished his waterfront patrol without finding any iron ore to buy. At the Triana Bridge he turned back and walked through the narrow zigzag streets of the town, hectic now as people left their homes to begin the day's business. Seville was much wealthier than Kingsbridge, but the people looked sombre by comparison. Spain was the richest country in the world but also the most conservative: there were laws against gaudy clothing. The rich dressed in black while the poor wore washed-out browns. It was ironic, Barney thought, how similar extreme Catholics were to extreme Protestants.

This was the least dangerous time of day to walk through the town: thieves and pickpockets generally slept in the morning, and did their best work in the afternoon and evening when men became careless from wine.

He slowed his pace as he approached the home of the Ruiz family. It was an impressive new brick house with four large windows in a row on the main, upstairs floor. Later in the day those windows would be covered by a grille, and the overweight, breathless Señor Pedro Ruiz would sit behind one like a toad in the reeds, watching the passers-by through the screen; but this early he was still in bed, and all windows and grilles had been thrown open to let in the cool morning air.

Looking up, Barney got what he hoped for: a glimpse of Señor Ruiz's seventeen-year-old daughter, Jerónima. He walked even more slowly and stared at her, drinking in the pale skin, the lush waves of dark hair, and most of all the large, luminous brown eyes accentuated by black eyebrows. She smiled at him and gave a discreet wave.

Well-bred girls were not supposed to stand at windows, let alone wave at passing boys, and she would get into trouble if she were found out. But she took the risk, every morning at this time; and Barney knew, with a thrill, that it was the closest she could get to flirting.

Passing the house he turned and began to walk backwards,

still smiling. He stumbled, almost fell, and made a wry face. She giggled, putting her hand to her red lips.

Barney was not planning to marry Jerónima. At twenty he was not ready for marriage, and if he had been he would not have been sure Jerónima was the one. But he did want to get to know her, and discreetly caress her when no one was looking, and steal kisses. However, girls were supervised more strictly here in Spain than at home and, as he blew her a kiss, he was not sure he would ever get a real one.

Then her head turned, as if she had heard her name called, and a moment later she was gone. Reluctantly, Barney walked away.

Carlos's place was not far, and Barney's thoughts moved from love to breakfast with a readiness that made him feel slightly ashamed.

The Cruz house was pierced by a broad arch leading through to a courtyard where the work was done. Piles of iron ore, coal and lime were stacked against the courtyard walls, separated by rough wooden dividers. In one corner an ox was tethered. In the middle stood the furnace.

Carlos's African slave, Ebrima Dabo, was stoking the fire ready for the first batch of the day, his high dark forehead beaded with perspiration. Barney had come across Africans in England, especially in port cities such as Combe Harbour, but they were free: slavery was not enforceable under English law. Spain was different. There were thousands of slaves in Seville: Barney guessed they were about one in ten of the population. They were Arabs, North Africans, a few Native Americans, and some like Ebrima from the Mandinka region of West Africa. Barney was quick with languages, and had even picked up a few words of Manding. He had heard Ebrima greet people with 'I *be nyaadi?*' which meant 'How are you?'

Carlos was standing with his back to the entrance of the house, studying a newly built structure of bricks. He had heard of a different type of furnace, one that permitted a blast of air to be blown in at the bottom while iron ore and lime were fed into the top. None of the three men had ever seen such a thing, but they were building an experimental prototype, working on it when they had time.

Barney spoke to Carlos in Spanish. 'There's no iron ore to be had at the waterfront today.'

Carlos's mind was on the new furnace. He scratched his curly black beard. 'We have to find a way to harness the ox so that it works the bellows.'

Barney frowned. 'I don't quite see it, but you can get a beast to work any mechanism, if you have enough wheels.'

Ebrima heard them. 'Two sets of bellows,' he said. 'One blowing out while the other breathes in.'

'Good idea,' Carlos said.

The cooking range stood in the courtyard a little nearer the house. Carlos's grandmother stirred a pot and said: 'Wash your hands, you boys. It's ready.' She was Barney's great-aunt, and he called her Aunt Betsy, though in Seville she was known as Elisa. She was a warm-hearted woman, but not beautiful. Her face was dominated by a big, twisted nose. Her back was broad and she had large hands and feet. She was sixty-five, a considerable age, but still full-figured and active. Barney recalled his grandma in Kingsbridge saying: 'My sister Betsy was a handful of trouble when she was a girl – that's why she had to be sent to Spain.'

It was hard to imagine. Aunt Betsy now was cautious and wise. She had quietly warned Barney that Jerónima Ruiz had her eye firmly on her own selfish interests, and would surely marry someone a lot richer than Barney.

Betsy had raised Carlos after his mother died giving birth to him. His father had died a year ago, a few days before Barney's arrival. The men lived on one side of the arch and Betsy, who owned the place, occupied the other half of the house.

The table was in the courtyard. They usually ate out of doors in daylight, unless the weather was exceptionally cold. They sat down to eggs cooked with onions, wheat bread, and a jug of weak wine. They were strong men who did heavy work all day, and they ate a lot.

Ebrima ate with them. A slave would never eat with his owners in the large household of a wealthy family, but Carlos was an artisan who worked with his hands, and Ebrima toiled side by side with him. Ebrima remained deferential, however: there was no pretence that they were equals.

Barney had been struck by Ebrima's clever contribution to the exchange about the new furnace. 'You know a lot about metal working,' Barney said to him as they ate. 'Did you learn from Carlos's father?'

'My own father was an iron maker,' Ebrima said.

'Oh!' Carlos was surprised. 'Somehow I never imagined Africans making iron.'

'How did you think we got swords to fight wars?'

'Of course. Then . . . how did you become a slave?'

'In a war with a neighbouring kingdom. I was captured. Where I come from, prisoners-of-war normally become slaves, working in the fields of the winning side. But my master died, and his widow sold me to an Arab slave trader . . . and, after a long journey, I ended up in Seville.'

Barney had not previously asked Ebrima about his past, and he was curious. Did Ebrima long for home, or prefer Seville? He looked about forty: at what age had he been enslaved? Did he miss his family? But now Ebrima said: 'May I ask you a question, Mr Willard?'

'Of course.'

'Do they have slaves in England?'

'Not really.'

Ebrima hesitated. 'What does that mean, *not really*?'

Barney thought for a moment. 'In my home town, Kingsbridge, there is a Portuguese jeweller called Rodrigo. He buys fine fabrics, lace and silk, then sews pearls into them and makes headdresses, scarves, veils and other such frippery. Women go mad for his things. Rich men's wives come from all over the west of England to buy them.'

'And he has a slave?'

'When he arrived, five years ago, he had a groom from Morocco called Achmed who was clever with animals. Word of this got around, and Kingsbridge people would pay Achmed to doctor their horses. After a while, Rodrigo found out and demanded the money, but Achmed would not hand it over.

Rodrigo went to the court of quarter sessions, and said the money was his because Achmed was his slave; but Justice Tilbury said: "Achmed has broken no English law." So Rodrigo lost and Achmed kept his money. Now he has his own house and a thriving business as an animal doctor.'

'So English people can have slaves, but if the slave walks away, the owner can't force him back?'

'Exactly.'

Barney could see that Ebrima was intrigued by this notion. Perhaps he dreamed of going to England and becoming a free man.

Then the conversation was interrupted. Both Carlos and Ebrima suddenly tensed and looked towards the entrance arch.

Barney followed their gaze and saw three people approaching. In the lead was a short, broad-shouldered man with costly clothes and a greasy moustache. Walking on either side of him and a pace or two behind were two taller men who appeared, from their inexpensive clothing, to be servants, perhaps bodyguards. Barney had never seen any of the three before but he recognized the type. They looked like thugs.

Carlos spoke in a carefully neutral tone. 'Sancho Sanchez, good morning.'

'Carlos, my friend,' said Sancho.

To Barney they did not seem to be friends.

Aunt Betsy stood up. 'Please, sit down, Señor Sanchez,' she said. Her words were hospitable but her tone was not warm. 'Let me get you some breakfast.'

'No, thank you, Señora Cruz,' Sancho said. 'But I'll have a glass of wine.' He took Aunt Betsy's seat.

His companions remained standing.

Sancho began a conversation about the prices of lead and tin, and Barney gathered that he, too, was a metal worker. Sancho went on to discuss the war with France, and then an epidemic of shivering fever that was sweeping the town, taking the lives of rich and poor alike. Carlos responded stiffly. No one ate anything.

At last Sancho got down to business. 'You've done well, Carlos,' he said patronizingly. 'When your father died, rest his soul, I didn't think you would be able to continue to run the enterprise alone. You were twenty-one, and you had finished your apprenticeship, so you were entitled to try; but I thought you would fail. You surprised us all.'

Carlos looked wary. 'Thank you,' he said neutrally.

'A year ago, I offered to buy your business for one hundred escudos.'

Carlos straightened his back, squared his shoulders and raised his chin.

Sancho held up a hand defensively. 'A low price, I know, but that was what I thought it was worth without your father to run it.'

Carlos said coldly: 'The offer was an insult.'

The two bodyguards stiffened. Talk of insults could lead quickly to violence.

Sancho was still being emollient, or as near to it as he could get, Barney thought. He did not apologize for offending Carlos, but rather spoke forgivingly, as if Carlos had slighted him. 'I understand that you should feel that way,' he said. 'But I have two sons, and I want to give them a business each. Now I'm prepared to pay you one thousand escudos.' As if Carlos might not be able to count, Sancho added: 'That's ten times my original offer.'

Carlos said: 'The price is still too low.'

Barney spoke to Sancho for the first time. 'Why don't you just build another furnace for your second son?'

Sancho stared haughtily, as if he had not previously noticed Barney's presence. He seemed to think Barney should not speak until he was spoken to. It was Carlos who answered the question. 'Like most industries in Spain, metal working is controlled by a "corporation", somewhat like an English guild only more conservative. The corporation limits the number of furnaces.'

Sancho said: 'The regulations maintain high standards and keep crooked operators out of the industry.'

Barney said: 'And they ensure that prices are not undermined by cheap alternatives, I suppose.'

Carlos added: 'Sancho is on the council of the Seville metal guild, Barney.'

Sancho was not interested in Barney. 'Carlos, my friend and neighbour, just answer a simple question: what price would you accept for your business?'

Carlos shook his head. 'It's not for sale.'

Sancho visibly suppressed an angry retort and forced a smile. 'I might go to fifteen hundred.'

'I would not sell for fifteen thousand.'

Barney saw that Aunt Betsy was looking alarmed. Clearly she was scared of Sancho and worried that Carlos was antagonizing him.

Carlos saw her look and forced a more amiable tone of voice. 'But I thank you for the courtesy of your proposal, neighbour Sancho.' It was a good try but it did not sound sincere.

Sancho dropped the façade. 'You may regret this, Carlos.'

Carlos's voice became disdainful. 'Why would you say a thing like that, Sancho? It almost sounds like a threat.'

Sancho did not confirm or deny that. 'If business turns bad, you will end up wishing you had taken my money.'

'I will run that risk. And now I have work to do. The king's armourer needs iron.'

Sancho looked furious at being dismissed. He got to his feet.

Aunt Betsy said: 'I hope you enjoyed the wine, Señor – it's our best.'

Sancho did not trouble to reply to such a routine remark from a mere woman. He said to Carlos: 'We'll talk again soon.'

Barney could see Carlos suppressing a sarcastic retort as he responded with a silent nod.

Sancho was turning to leave when he caught sight of the new furnace. 'What's this?' he said. 'Another furnace?'

'My old furnace is due for replacement.' Carlos stood up. 'Thank you for calling on me, Sancho.'

Sancho did not move. 'Your old furnace looks perfectly all right to me.'

'When the new one is ready, the old one will be demolished. I know the rules as well as you do. Goodbye.'

'The new one looks peculiar,' Sancho persisted.

Carlos allowed his irritation to show. 'I'm making some improvements on the traditional design. There's no corporation rule against that.'

'Keep your temper, son, I'm simply asking you questions.'

'And I'm simply saying goodbye.'

Sancho did not even bristle at Carlos's rudeness. He continued to stare at the new furnace for a full minute. Then he turned and left. His two bodyguards followed him. Neither had spoken a word the whole time.

When Sancho was out of earshot, Aunt Betsy said: 'He's a bad man to have as an enemy.'

'I know,' said Carlos.

*

THAT NIGHT Ebrima slept with Carlos's grandmother.

On the men's side of the house, Carlos and Barney had beds on the upstairs floor, while Ebrima slept on a mattress on the ground floor. Tonight Ebrima lay awake for half an hour, until he was quite sure the house was silent; then he got up and padded across the courtyard to Elisa's side. He slid into bed beside her and they made love.

She was an ugly old white woman, but it was dark, and her body was soft and warm. More importantly, she had always been kind to Ebrima. He did not love her, and never would, but it was no hardship to give her what she wanted.

Afterwards, as Elisa dozed off, Ebrima lay awake and remembered the first time.

He had been brought to Seville on a slave ship and sold to Carlos's father ten years ago. He was solitary and homesick and in despair. One Sunday, when everyone else was at church, Carlos's grandmother, whom Barney called Aunt Betsy and Ebrima called Elisa, had come upon him weeping in desolation. To his astonishment she had kissed his tears and pressed his face to her soft breasts, and in his yearning for human affection he had made love to her hungrily.

He realized that Elisa was using him. She could end the relationship any time she pleased, but he could not. However, she was the only human being he could hold in his arms. For a decade of lonely exile she had given him solace.

When she began to snore he returned to his own bed.

Each night, before going to sleep, Ebrima thought about freedom. He imagined himself in a house he owned, with a woman who was his wife, and perhaps some children too. In the vision he had money in his pocket that he had earned by his work, and he wore clothes he had chosen himself and paid for, not hand-me-downs. He left the house when he wanted to, and came back when he pleased, and no one could flog him for it. He always hoped he would go to sleep and dream this vision, and sometimes he did.

He slept for a few hours and woke at first light. It was Sunday. Later he would go to church with Carlos, and in the evening he would go to a tavern owned by a freed African slave and gamble with the little money he made from tips, but now he had a private duty to perform. He put on his clothes and left the house.

He passed through the north gate of the city and followed the river upstream as the daylight grew stronger. After an hour he came to an isolated spot he had visited before, where the river was bordered by a grove of trees. There he performed the water rite.

He had never been observed here, but it would not matter anyway, for he looked as if he was merely bathing.

Ebrima did not believe in the crucified God. He pretended to, because it made life easier, and he had been baptized a Christian here in Spain, but he knew better. The Europeans did not realize that there were spirits everywhere, in the seagulls and the west wind and the orange trees. The most powerful of them all was the river god: Ebrima knew this because he had been raised in a village that stood on the edge of a river. This was a different river, and he did not know how many thousands of miles he was from his birthplace, but the god was the same.

As he entered the water, murmuring the sacred words, tranquillity seeped into his soul, and he allowed his memories to rise from the depths of his mind. He remembered his father, a strong man with black burn scars on his brown skin from accidents with molten metal; his mother, bare-breasted as she weeded her vegetable patch; his sister holding a baby, Ebrima's nephew, whom he would never see grow into a man. None of them even knew the name of the city where Ebrima now made his life, but they all worshipped the same spirit.

In his sadness, the river god comforted him. As the rite came to an end, the god granted his final gift: strength. Ebrima came out of the river, water dripping down his skin, and saw that the sun was up, and he knew that, for a little while longer, he would be able to endure.

*

ON SUNDAY BARNEY went to church with Carlos, Aunt Betsy and Ebrima. They made an unusual group, Barney thought. Carlos looked young to be head of a family, despite his bushy beard and broad shoulders. Aunt Betsy looked neither old nor young: she had grey hair, but she had kept her womanly figure. Ebrima wore Carlos's cast-off clothes, but he walked upright and somehow managed to look neatly dressed for church. Barney himself had a red beard and the golden-brown eyes of the Willards, and his earring was unusual enough to draw glances of surprise, especially from young women; which was why he wore it.

The cathedral of Seville was bigger than that of Kingsbridge, reflecting the fabulous wealth of the Spanish clergy. The extraordinarily high central nave was flanked by two pairs of side aisles plus two rows of side chapels, making the building seem almost as wide as it was long. Any other church in the city would fit inside it, easily. A thousand people looked like a small group, clustered in front of the high altar, their responses to the liturgy lost in the emptiness of the vaults above. There was an immense altarpiece, a riot of gilded carving that was still unfinished after seventy-five years of work.

Mass was a useful social event, as well as an opportunity to cleanse the soul. Everyone had to go, especially the leading citizens. It was a chance to speak to people one would not otherwise meet. A respectable girl might even talk to a single man without compromising her reputation, although her parents would watch closely.

Carlos was wearing a new coat with a fur collar. He had told Barney that today he planned to speak to the father of Valentina Villaverde, the girl he adored. He had hesitated for a year, knowing that the business community were waiting to see whether he could make a success of his father's enterprise; but now he felt he had waited long enough. The visit from Sancho indicated that people recognized the success he had achieved – and that at least one man wanted to take it from him. It was a good moment to propose to Valentina. If she accepted him, not only would he win the bride he loved, but he would also be marrying into the Seville elite, which would protect him from predators such as Sancho.

They met the Villaverde family as soon as they entered the great west doors of the cathedral. Carlos bowed deeply to Francisco Villaverde, then smiled eagerly at Valentina. Barney observed that she was pink-skinned and fair-haired, more like an English girl than a Spaniard. When they were married, Carlos had confided to Barney, he was going to build her a tall, cool house with fountains, and a garden thick with shade trees, so that the sun would never scorch the petals of her cheeks.

She smiled back happily. She was fiercely protected by her father and an older brother, as well as her mother, but they could not stop her showing her pleasure at seeing Carlos.

Barney had courting of his own to do. He scanned the crowd and located Pedro Ruiz and his daughter, Jerónima – the mother was dead. Pushing through the congregation to where they stood, he bowed to Pedro, who was panting after the short walk from his home to the cathedral. Pedro was an intellectual who talked to Barney about whether it was possible that the earth moved around the sun, rather than vice versa.

Barney was more interested in his daughter than his views. He turned his hundred-candle smile on Jerónima. She smiled back.

'I see the service is being conducted by your father's friend Archdeacon Romero,' he said. Romero was a fast-rising churchman said to be close to King Felipe. Barney knew that Romero was a frequent visitor to the Ruiz house.

'Father likes to argue with him about theology,' said Jerónima. She made a disgusted face and lowered her voice. 'He pesters me.'

'Romero?' Barney looked warily at Pedro, but he was bowing to a neighbour and had taken his eyes off his daughter for the moment. 'What do you mean, he pesters you?'

'He says he hopes to be my friend after I'm married. And he touches my neck. It makes my skin crawl.'

Clearly, Barney thought, the archdeacon had developed a sinful passion for Jerónima. Barney sympathized: he had the same feeling. But he knew better than to say so. 'How disgusting,' he said. 'A lascivious priest.'

His attention was caught by a figure ascending the pulpitum in the white robe and black cloak of a Dominican monk. There was going to be a sermon. Barney did not recognize the speaker. He was tall and thin, with pale cheeks and a shock of thick straight hair. He seemed about thirty, young to be preaching in the cathedral. Barney had noticed him during the prayers, for he had seemed possessed of holy ecstasy, saying the Latin words with passion, his eyes closed and his white face lifted to heaven, by contrast with most of the other priests who acted as if they were doing a tedious chore. 'Who's that?' Barney asked.

Pedro answered, having returned his attention to his daughter's suitor. 'Father Alonso,' he said. 'He's the new inquisitor.'

Carlos, Ebrima and Betsy appeared alongside Barney, moving forward to get a closer look at the preacher.

Alonso began by speaking of the shivering fever that had killed hundreds of citizens during the winter. It was a punishment from God, he said. The people of Seville had to learn a lesson from it, and examine their consciences. What terrible sins had they committed, to make God so angry?

The answer was that they had tolerated heathens among them. The young priest became heated as he enumerated the blasphemies of heretics. He spat out Jew, *Muslim* and *Protestant* as if the very words tasted foul in his mouth.

But who was he talking about? Barney knew the history of Spain. In 1492, Ferdinand and Isabella – 'the Catholic monarchs' – had given the Jews of Spain an ultimatum: convert to Christianity or leave the country. Later the Muslims had been offered the same brutal choice. All synagogues and mosques had since been turned into churches. And Barney had never met a Spanish Protestant, to his knowledge.

He thought the sermon was hot air, but Aunt Betsy was troubled. 'This is bad,' she said in a low voice.

Carlos answered her. 'Why? There are no heretics in Seville.'

'If you start a witch hunt, you have to find some witches.'

'How can he find heretics if there are none?'

'Look around you. He'll say that Ebrima is a Muslim.'

'Ebrima is a Christian!' Carlos protested.

'They will say he has gone back to his original religion, which is the sin of apostasy, much worse than never having been a Christian in the first place.'

Barney thought Betsy was probably right: the dark colour of Ebrima's skin would throw suspicion on him regardless of the facts.

Betsy nodded towards Jerónima and her father. 'Pedro Ruiz reads the books of Erasmus and disputes with Archdeacon Romero about the teachings of the Church.'

Carlos said: 'But Pedro and Ebrima are here, attending Mass!'

'Alonso will say they practise their heathen rites at home after dark, with the shutters closed tightly and the doors locked.'

'Surely Alonso would need evidence?'

'They will confess.'

Carlos was bewildered. 'Why would they do that?'

'You would confess to heresy if you were stripped naked and bound with cords that were slowly tightened until they burst through your skin and began to strip the flesh from your body—'

'Stop it, I get it.' Carlos shuddered.

Barney wondered how Betsy knew about the tortures of the inquisition.

Alonso reached his climax, calling for every citizen to join in a new crusade against the infidels right here in their midst. When he had finished, communion began. Looking at the faces of the congregation, Barney thought they seemed uneasy about the sermon. They were good Catholics but they wanted a quiet life, not a crusade. Like Aunt Betsy, they foresaw trouble.

When the service ended and the clergy left the nave in procession, Carlos said to Barney: 'Come with me while I speak to Villaverde. I feel the need of friendly support.'

Barney willingly followed him as he approached Francisco and bowed. 'May I beg a moment of your time, Señor, to discuss a matter of great importance?'

Francisco Villaverde was the same age as Betsy: Valentina was the daughter of his second wife. He was sleek and self-satisfied, but not unfriendly. He smiled amiably. 'Of course.'

Barney saw that Valentina looked bashful. She could guess what was about to happen, even if her father could not.

Carlos said: 'A year has passed since my father died.'

Barney expected the murmured prayer that his soul would rest in peace that was a conventional courtesy whenever a dead relative was mentioned, but to his surprise Francisco remained silent.

Carlos went on: 'Everyone can see that my workshop is well run and the enterprise is prospering.'

'You are to be congratulated,' said Francisco.

'Thank you.'

'What's your point, young Carlos?'

'I'm twenty-two, healthy and financially secure. I'm ready to marry. My wife will be loved and cared for.'

'I'm sure she will. And . . . ?'

'I humbly ask your permission to call at your house, in the hope that your wonderful daughter, Valentina, might consider me as a suitor.'

Valentina flushed crimson. Her brother gave a grunt that might have been indignation.

Francisco Villaverde's attitude changed instantly. 'Absolutely not,' he said with surprising force.

Carlos was astonished. For a moment he could not speak.

'How dare you?' Francisco went on. 'My daughter!'

Carlos found his voice. 'But . . . may I ask why?'

Barney was asking himself the same question. Francisco had no reason to feel superior. He was a perfume maker, a trade that was perhaps a little more refined than that of metal worker; but still, like Carlos, he manufactured his wares and sold them. He was not nobility.

Francisco hesitated, then said: 'You are not of pure blood.'

Carlos looked baffled. 'Because my grandmother is English? That's ridiculous.'

The brother bristled. 'Have a care what you say.'

Francisco said: 'I will not stand here to be called ridiculous.'

Barney could see that Valentina was distraught. Clearly she, too, had been astonished by this angry refusal.

Carlos said desperately: 'Wait a minute.'

Francisco was adamant. 'This conversation is over.' He turned away. Taking Valentina's arm, he moved towards the west door. The mother and brother followed. There was no point in going after them, Barney knew: it would only make Carlos look foolish.

Carlos was hurt and angry, Barney could see. The accusation of impure blood was silly, but probably no less wounding for that. In this country, 'impure' usually meant Jewish or Muslim, and Barney had not heard it used of someone with English forebears; but people could be snobbish about anything.

Ebrima and Betsy joined them. Betsy noticed Carlos's mood immediately, and looked enquiringly at Barney. He murmured: 'Valentina's father rejected him.'

'Hell,' said Betsy.

She was angered but did not seem surprised, and the thought crossed Barney's mind that somehow she had expected this.

*

EBRIMA FELT SORRY for Carlos, and wanted to do something to cheer him up. When they got home, he suggested trying out the new furnace. This was as good a time as any, he thought, and it might take Carlos's mind off his humiliation. It was forbidden for Christians to work or do business on a Sunday, of course, but this was not really work: it was an experiment.

Carlos liked the idea. He fired up the furnace while Ebrima put the ox into the harness they had devised and Barney mixed crushed iron ore with lime.

There was a snag with the bellows, and they had to redesign the mechanism driven by the ox. Betsy abandoned her plans for an elegant Sunday dinner, and brought out bread and salt pork, which the three men ate standing up. The afternoon light was fading by the time they had everything working again. When the fire was burning hot, fanned by the twin bellows, Ebrima started shovelling in the iron ore and lime.

For a while nothing seemed to be happening. The ox walked in a patient circle, the bellows puffed and panted, the chimney radiated heat, and the men waited.

Carlos had heard about this way of making iron from two people, a Frenchman from Normandy and a Walloon from the Netherlands; and Barney had heard something similar talked of by an Englishman from Sussex. They all claimed the method produced iron twice as fast. That might be an exaggeration, but even so it was an exciting idea. They said that molten iron would emerge from the bottom of the furnace, and Carlos had duly built a stone chute to carry the flow to ingot-shaped depressions in the earth of the courtyard. But no one had been able to draw a plan of the furnace, so the design was guesswork.

Still no iron emerged. Ebrima began to wonder what might have gone wrong. Maybe the chimney should be taller. Heat was the key, he thought. Perhaps they should have used wood charcoal, which burned hotter than coal, though it was expensive in a country where all the trees were needed to build the king's ships.

Then it began to work. A half-moon of molten iron appeared at the outlet of the furnace and inched into the stone chute. A hesitant protuberance became a slow wave, then a gush. The men cheered. Elisa came to look.

The liquid metal was red at first, but quickly turned grey. Looking hard at it, Ebrima thought it was more like pig iron, and would need to be smelted again to refine it, but that was not a major problem. On top of the iron was a layer like molten glass which was undoubtedly slag, and they would have to find a way to skim that off the top.

But the process was fast. Once it got started, the iron came out as if a tap had been turned. All they had to do was keep putting coal, iron ore and lime into the top of the furnace, and liquid wealth would pour out the other end.

The three men congratulated one another. Elisa brought them a bottle of wine. They stood with cups in their hands, drinking and staring in delight at the iron as it hardened. Carlos looked more cheerful: he was recovering from the shock of his rejection. Perhaps Carlos would choose this celebratory moment to tell Ebrima that he was a free man.

After a few minutes Carlos said: 'Stoke the furnace, Ebrima.'

Ebrima put down his cup. 'Right away,' he said.

*

THE NEW FURNACE was a triumph for Carlos, but not everyone was happy about it.

The furnace worked from sunrise to sunset, six days a week. Carlos sold the pig iron to a finery forge, so that he did not have to refine it himself, and could concentrate on production, while Barney secured the increased supplies of iron ore they needed.

The king's armourer was pleased. He struggled constantly to buy enough weapons for warfare in France and Italy, for sea battles with the Sultan's fleet, and for protection against pirates for galleons from America. The forges and workshops of Seville could not produce enough, and the corporations opposed any expansion of capacity, so the armourer had to buy much of what he needed from foreign countries – which was why the American silver that came into Spain went out again so quickly. He was thrilled to see iron being produced so fast.

But other iron makers in Seville were not so glad. They could see that Carlos was making twice as much money as they were. Surely there was a rule against this? Sancho Sanchez lodged an official complaint with the corporation. The council would have to make a decision.

Barney was worried, but Carlos said the corporation could not possibly go against the king's armourer.

Then they were visited by Father Alonso.

They were working in the courtyard when Alonso marched in, followed by a small entourage of younger priests. Carlos leaned on his shovel and stared at the inquisitor, trying to look unworried, but failing, Barney thought. Aunt Betsy came out of the house and stood with her big hands on her broad hips, ready to take Alonso on.

Barney could not imagine how Carlos could be accused of being a heretic. On the other hand, why else would Alonso be here?

Before saying anything, Alonso looked slowly around the courtyard with his narrow, beaked nose in the air, like a bird of prey. His gaze rested on Ebrima, and at last he spoke. 'Is that black man a Muslim?'

Ebrima answered for himself. 'In the village where I was born, Father, the gospel of Jesus Christ had never been heard, nor had the name of the Muslim prophet ever been spoken. I was raised in heathen ignorance, like my forefathers. But throughout a long journey God's hand guided me, and when I was taught the sacred truth here in Seville I became a Christian, baptized in the cathedral, for which I thank my heavenly father every day in my prayers.'

It was such a good speech that Barney guessed Ebrima must have made it before.

But it was not enough for Alonso. He said: 'Then why do you work on Sundays? Is it not because your Muslim holy day is Friday?'

Carlos said: 'No one here works on Sundays, and we all work all day every Friday.'

'Your furnace was seen to be lit on the Sunday I preached my first sermon in the cathedral.'

Barney cursed under his breath. They had been caught out. He surveyed the surrounding buildings: the courtyard was overlooked by numerous windows. One of the neighbours had made the accusation – probably a jealous metal worker, perhaps even Sancho.

'But we weren't working,' said Carlos. 'We were conducting an experiment.'

It sounded thin, even to Barney.

Carlos went on, with a note of desperation: 'You see, Father, this type of furnace has air blown in at the bottom of the chimney—'

'I know all about your furnace,' Alonso interrupted.

Aunt Betsy spoke up. 'I wonder how a priest would know all about a furnace? Perhaps you've been talking to my grandson's rivals. Who denounced him to you, Father?'

Barney could see from Alonso's face that Aunt Betsy was right, but the priest did not answer the question. Instead he went on the offensive. 'Old woman, you were born in Protestant England.'

'I most certainly was not,' Betsy said with spirit. 'The good Catholic King Henry the Seventh was on the throne of England when I was born. His Protestant son, Henry the Eighth, was still pissing in his bed when my family left England and brought me here to Seville. I've never been back.'

Alonso turned on Barney, and Barney felt the deep chill of fear. This man had the power to torture and kill people. 'That's certainly not true of you,' Alonso said. 'You must have been born and raised Protestant.'

Barney's Spanish was not good enough for a theological argument, so he kept his response simple. 'England is no longer Protestant, nor am I. Father, if you search this house, you will see that there are no banned books here, no heretical texts, no Muslim prayer mats. Over my bed is a crucifix, and on my wall a picture of St Hubert of Liège, patron saint of metal workers. It was St Hubert who—'

'I know about St Hubert.' Clearly Alonso was offended by any suggestion that someone else might have something to teach him. However, Barney thought he might have run out of steam. Each of his accusations had been parried. All he had was men doing something that might or might not count as working on a Sunday, and Carlos and his family were surely not the only people in Seville who bent that rule. 'I hope everything you have said to me today is the pure truth,' Alonso said. 'Otherwise you will suffer the fate of Pedro Ruiz.'

He turned to go, but Barney stopped him, concerned for Jerónima and her father. 'What happened to Pedro Ruiz?'

Alonso looked pleased to have shocked him. 'He was arrested,' he said. 'In his house I found a translation of the Old Testament into Spanish, which is illegal, and a copy of the heretical *Institutes of the Christian Religion* by John Calvin, the Protestant leader of the abominable city of Geneva. As is normal, all the possessions of Pedro Ruiz have been sequestrated by the Inquisition.'

Carlos did not seem surprised by this, so Alonso must be telling the truth when he said it was normal, but Barney was shocked. 'All his possessions?' he said. 'How will his daughter live?'

'By God's grace, as we all do,' said Alonso, and then he walked out, followed by his entourage.

Carlos looked relieved. 'I'm sorry about Jerónima's father,' he said. 'But I think we got the better of Alonso.'

Betsy said: 'Don't be so sure.'

'Why do you say that?' Carlos asked.

'You don't remember your grandfather, my husband.'

'He died when I was a baby.'

'Rest his soul. He was raised Muslim.'

All three men stared at her in astonishment. Carlos said incredulously: 'Your husband was a Muslim?'

'At first, yes.'

'My grandfather, José Alano Cruz?'

'His original name was Youssef al-Khalil.'

'How could you marry a Muslim?'

'When they were expelled from Spain he decided to convert to Christianity rather than leave. He took instruction in the religion and was baptized as an adult, just like Ebrima. José was his new name. To seal his conversion, he decided to marry a Christian girl. That was me. I was thirteen.'

Barney said: 'Did many Muslims marry Christians?'

'No. They married within their community, even after converting. My José was unusual.'

Carlos was more interested in the personal side. 'Did you know he had been raised Muslim?'

'Not at first, no. He had moved here from Madrid and told no one. But people come here from Madrid all the time, and eventually there was someone who had known him as a Muslim. After that it was never quite secret, though we tried to keep it quiet.'

Barney could not restrain his curiosity. 'You were thirteen? Did you love him?'

'I adored him. I was never a pretty girl, and he was handsome and charming. He was also affectionate and kind and caring. I was in heaven.' Aunt Betsy was in a confiding mood.

Carlos said: 'And then my grandfather died . . .'

'I was inconsolable,' said Betsy. 'He was the love of my life. I never wanted another husband.' She shrugged. 'But I had my children to take care of, so I was too busy to die of grief. And then there was you, Carlos, motherless before you were a day old.'

Barney had an instinctive feeling that, although Betsy was speaking candidly, there was something she was holding back. She had not wanted another husband, but was that the whole story?

Carlos made a connection. 'Is this why Francisco Villaverde won't let me marry his daughter?'

'It is. He doesn't care about your English grandmother. It's your Muslim grandfather he considers impure.'

'Hell.'

'That's not the worst of your problems. Obviously Alonso, too, knows about Youssef al-Khalil. Today's visit was just the beginning. Believe me, he will be back.'

*

AFTER ALONSO'S VISIT Barney went to the home of the Ruiz family to see what had happened to Jerónima.

The door was opened by a young woman who looked North African and was evidently a slave. She was probably beautiful, he thought, but now her face was swollen and her eyes were red with grief. 'I must see Jerónima,' he said in a loud voice. The woman put her finger to her lips in a shushing gesture, then beckoned him to follow her and led him into the back of the house.

He expected to see a cook and a couple of maids preparing dinner, but the kitchen was cold and silent. He recalled Alonso saying that the inquisition routinely confiscated a suspect's goods, but Barney had not realized how fast it would happen. Now he saw that Pedro's employees had already been dismissed. Presumably his slave was going to be sold, which would be why she was crying.

She said: 'I am Farah.'

Barney said impatiently: 'Why have you brought me here? Where is Jerónima?'

'Speak quietly,' she said. 'Jerónima is upstairs, with Archdeacon Romero.'

'I don't care, I want to speak to her,' said Barney, and he stepped to the door.

'Please don't,' said Farah. 'It will cause trouble if Romero sees you.'

'I'm ready for trouble.'

'I'll bring Jerónima here. I'll say a neighbour woman has called and insists on seeing her.'

Barney hesitated, then nodded assent, and Farah went out.

He looked around. There were no knives, pots, jugs or plates. The place had been cleared out. Did the inquisition even sell people's kitchenware?

Jerónima appeared a couple of minutes later. She was different: she looked a lot older than seventeen suddenly. Her beautiful face was an impassive mask, and her eyes were dry, but her olive skin seemed to have turned grey, and her slim body trembled all over as if shivering. He could see the enormous effort it took to bottle up her grief and rage.

Barney moved towards her, intending to embrace her, but she stepped back and held up her hands as if to push him away.

He looked at her helplessly and said: 'What's going on?'

'I am destitute,' she said. 'My father is in prison, and I have no other family.'

'How is he?'

'I don't know. Prisoners of the inquisition are not allowed to communicate with their families, or with anyone else. But his health is poor – you've heard him panting after even a short walk – and they will probably—' She became unable to speak, but it lasted only a moment. She looked down, breathed in, and regained control. 'They will probably put him to the water torture.'

Barney had heard of this. The victim's nostrils were closed to prevent him breathing through his nose, and his mouth was forced open, then jar after jar of water was poured down his throat. What he swallowed distended his stomach agonizingly, and the water that got into his windpipe choked him.

'It will kill him,' Barney said in horror.

'They have already taken all his money and possessions.'

'What are you going to do?'

'Archdeacon Romero has offered to take me into his household.'

Barney felt bewildered. Things were moving too fast. Several questions occurred to him at the same time. He said: 'In what role?'

'We are discussing that right now. He wants me to take charge of his wardrobe, ordering and caring for his vestments, supervising his laundress.' Speaking of such practical matters clearly helped her control her feelings.

'Don't go,' Barney said. 'Come away with me.'

It was a reckless offer, and she knew it. 'Where? I can't live with three men. It's all right for your grandmother.'

'I have a home in England.'

She shook her head. 'I know nothing about your family. I hardly know anything about you. I don't speak English.' Her face softened briefly. 'Perhaps, if this had not happened, you might have courted me, and made a formal offer to my father, and perhaps I would have married you, and learned to speak English . . . who knows? I admit I have thought about it. But to run away with you to a strange country? No.'

Barney could see that she was being much more sensible than he. But all the same he blurted: 'Romero wants to make you his secret mistress.'

Jerónima looked at Barney, and he saw in her big eyes a hardness he had never noticed before. He was reminded of Aunt Betsy's words: 'Jerónima Ruiz has her eye firmly on her own selfish interests.' But surely there were limits? Jerónima now said: 'And if he does?'

Barney was dumbfounded. 'How can you even say it?'

'I've been thinking about this for forty-eight sleepless hours. I have no alternative. You know what happens to homeless women.'

'They become prostitutes.'

This seemed not to shake her. 'So my choice is flight with you into the unknown, prostitution on the streets, or a dubious position in the affluent household of a corrupt priest.'

'Has it occurred to you', Barney said tentatively, 'that Romero might even have denounced your father himself, with the intention of forcing you into this position?'

'I'm sure he did.'

Barney was astonished again. She was always ahead of him.

She said: 'I've known for months that Romero wanted to make me his mistress. It was the worst life I could imagine for myself. Now it's the best life I can hope for.'

'And he has done that to you!'

'I know.'

'And you're going to accept it, and go to his bed, and forgive him?'

'Forgive him?' she said, and a new light came into her brown eyes, a look of hatred like boiling acid. 'No,' she said. 'I might pretend. But one day I will have power over him. And when that day comes, I will take revenge.'

*

EBRIMA HAD DONE as much as anyone to make the new furnace work, and he harboured a secret hope that Carlos would reward him by giving him his freedom. But as the furnace burned for days and weeks his hopes faded, and he realized that the thought had not even crossed Carlos's mind. Loading cold ingots of iron onto a flatbed cart, stacking them in an interlocking web so that they would not shift in transit, Ebrima considered what to do next.

He had hoped Carlos would make the offer spontaneously, but as that had not happened he would have to ask outright. He did not like to beg: the very act of pleading would suggest that he was not entitled to what he wanted – but he *was* entitled, he felt that strongly.

He might try to recruit Elisa to support him. She was fond of him, and wanted the best for him, he felt sure; but did her affection extend so far as to free him, in which case he would no longer be there when she needed love at night?

On balance, it would probably be best to take her into his confidence before he spoke to Carlos. At least then he would know which way she was going to jump when the decision was made.

When should he tell her? After making love one night? It might be smarter to raise the subject *before* lovemaking, when her heart was full of desire. He nodded to himself, and at that moment the attack began.

There were six men, and they all carried clubs and hammers. They did not speak, but immediately began to beat Ebrima and Carlos with clubs. 'What's happening?' Ebrima yelled. 'Why are you doing this?' They did not speak. Ebrima put up an arm to protect himself and suffered an agonizing blow to his hand, then another to his head, and he fell down.

His assailant then went after Carlos, who was retreating across the yard. Ebrima watched, trying to recover from the daze induced by the blow to his head. Carlos seized a shovel, dipped it in the molten metal coming out of the furnace, and threw a shower of droplets at the attackers. Two of them screamed in pain.

For a moment Ebrima thought perhaps he and Carlos might

prevail, despite the odds; but, before Carlos could scoop up more metal, two others got to him and knocked him down.

They then attacked the new furnace, smashing its brickwork with iron-headed sledgehammers. Ebrima saw his creation being destroyed, and found the strength to get to his feet. He rushed at the attackers, screaming: 'No – you can't do this!' He shoved one so that he fell to the ground, and pulled the other away from the precious furnace. He used only his right hand, because he could no longer grip with the left, but he was strong. Then he was forced to scurry backwards out of the way of a lethally swinging sledgehammer.

Desperate to save the furnace, he picked up a wooden shovel and went at them again. He hit one over the head, then he was hit from behind, a blow that landed on his right shoulder and caused him to drop the shovel. He turned to face his assailant and dodged the next blow.

As he backed away, desperately leaping out of the way of a down-swinging club, he could see from the corner of his eye that the furnace was being demolished. The contents poured out, burning coal and red-hot minerals spilling over the ground. The ox began to grunt raucously in panic, a pitiful noise.

Elisa came running out of the house, screaming at the men: 'Leave them alone! Get out of here!' The attackers laughed at the old woman, and one of the men Ebrima had knocked down got up, seized her from behind, and lifted her off her feet. He was big – they all were – and he easily restrained her writhing struggles.

Two men were sitting on Carlos, one was holding Elisa, and one was keeping Ebrima cornered. The remaining two went to work with their sledgehammers. They smashed the bellows mechanism that Ebrima and Carlos and Barney had puzzled over for so long. Ebrima could have wept.

When the furnace and the bellows mechanism were flattened, one of them pulled a long dagger and tried to cut the throat of the ox. It was not easy: the beast's neck was thickly muscled, and he had to saw through the flesh with his knife, while the ox tried to kick free of the wreckage. At last he severed the jugular. The bellowing stopped abruptly. Blood came like a fountain from the wound. The ox sank to the ground.

And then, as quickly as they had come, the six men left.

*

JERÓNIMA HAD BECOME a calculating shrew, Barney thought as he left the Ruiz house in a daze. Perhaps she had always had a hard streak, and he had never noticed it; or perhaps people could be transformed by a terrible ordeal – he did not know. He felt he knew nothing. Anything could happen: the river might rise up and drown the city.

His feet took him automatically to Carlos's house, and there he suffered another shock: Carlos and Ebrima had been beaten up.

Carlos was sitting on a chair in the courtyard while Aunt Betsy tended to his wounds. One eye was closed, his lips were swollen and bloody, and he sat half bent over as if his belly hurt. Ebrima lay on the ground, clutching one hand under the opposite armpit, a bloodstained bandage around his head.

Behind them was the wreckage of the new furnace. It had been ruined, and was now a pile of bricks. The bellows mechanism was a tangle of ropes and firewood. The ox lay dead in a pool of blood. There was a lot of blood in an ox, Barney thought disjointedly.

Betsy had been bathing Carlos's face with a scrap of linen soaked in wine. Now she stood upright and tossed the rag on the ground in a gesture of disgust. 'Listen to me,' she said, and Barney realized she had been waiting only for his return before making a speech.

All the same he forestalled her. 'What happened here?'

'Don't ask stupid questions,' she said impatiently. 'You can see what happened here.'

'I mean, who did this?'

'They were men we've never seen before, and almost certainly they're not from Seville. The real question is who hired them, and the answer is Sancho Sanchez. He's the one who's been whipping up resentment of Carlos's success, and he's the one who wants to buy the business. I've no doubt it was he who told Alonso that Ebrima is a Muslim and works on Sundays.'

'What are we going to do?'

Carlos answered Barney's question. Standing up, he said: 'We're going to give in.'

'What do you mean?'

'We could fight Sancho, or we could fight Alonso, but we can't fight both.' He went over to where Ebrima lay, grasped his right hand – the left was evidently injured – and pulled him to his feet. 'I'm going to sell the business.'

Betsy said: 'That may not be enough, now.'

Carlos was startled. 'Why?'

'Sancho will be satisfied with the business, but Alonso will not. He needs a human sacrifice. He can't admit to having made a mistake. Now that he's accused you, he has to punish you.'

Barney said: 'I've just seen Jerónima. She thinks they will put her father to the water torture. We'll all confess to heresy if that happens to us.'

Betsy said: 'Barney is right.'

Carlos said: 'What can we do?'

Betsy sighed. 'Leave Seville. Leave Spain. Today.'

Barney was shocked, but he knew she was right. Alonso's men might come for them any time, and when that happened, it would be too late to flee. He looked apprehensively at the archway entrance to the courtyard, fearing that they might already be there; but there was no one, not yet.

Was it even possible to go today? Perhaps – if there was a ship leaving on the afternoon tide, and if that ship needed crew. They would probably have no choice about where they went. Barney glanced up at the sun. It was after midday. 'If we're really going to do this, we need to hurry,' he said.

Despite the danger he was in, his spirits lifted at the prospect of going to sea.

Ebrima spoke for the first time. 'If we don't go, we're dead men,' he said. 'And I'll be the first.'

Barney said: 'What about you, Aunt Betsy?'

'I'm too old to go far. Besides, they don't really care about me – I'm a woman.'

'What will you do?'

'I have a sister-in-law in Carmona.' Barney recalled Betsy going there for a few weeks in the summer. 'I can walk to Carmona in a morning. Even if Alonso finds out where I am, I doubt that he'll bother with me.'

Carlos made up his mind. 'Barney, Ebrima, get whatever you want from the house and be back by a count of a hundred.'

None of them had many possessions. Barney tucked a small purse of money into his waist under his shirt. He put on his best boots and his heavy cloak. He did not own a sword: the heavy longsword was made for the battlefield, designed to be thrust into the vulnerable spots in the enemy's suit of armour, but unwieldy at close quarters. Barney sheathed a two-foot-long Spanish dagger with a disc-shaped hilt and a double-edged steel blade. In a street brawl, a big knife such as this was more lethal than a sword.

Back in the courtyard, Carlos was wearing a sword under his new coat with the fur collar. He hugged his grandmother, who was weeping. Barney kissed her on the cheek.

Then Aunt Betsy said to Ebrima: 'Kiss me one more time, my love.'

Ebrima took her in his arms.

Barney frowned, and Carlos said: 'Hey—'

Aunt Betsy kissed Ebrima passionately, her hand buried in his dark hair, while Carlos and Barney stared in astonishment. When they broke the kiss, she said: 'I love you, Ebrima. I don't want you to go. But I can't let you stay here to die in the torture chamber of the inquisition.'

'Thank you, Elisa, for being kind to me,' said Ebrima.

They kissed again, then Betsy turned away and ran into the house.

Barney thought: *What the hell . . . ?*

Carlos looked amazed, but there was no time for questions. 'Let's go,' he said.

'One second,' said Barney. He showed them his dagger. 'If we meet Alonso's men on the way, I won't be taken alive.'

'Nor will I,' said Carlos, touching the hilt of his sword.

Ebrima pulled aside his cloak to reveal an iron-headed hammer thrust into his belt.

The three men left, heading for the waterfront.

They were alert for Alonso's men, but as they moved farther from the house the danger receded. All the same, people stared at them, and Barney realized that they looked scary, with both Carlos and Ebrima bruised and still bleeding from the fight.

After a few minutes, Carlos said to Ebrima: 'Grandma?'

Ebrima spoke calmly. 'Slaves are always used for sex. You must know that.'

Barney said: 'I didn't know it.'

'We talk to one another in the marketplace. Just about every one of us is somebody's whore. Not the old ones, but slaves don't often live to be old.' He looked at Barney. 'Pedro Ruiz, your girlfriend's father, fucks Farah, though she has to get on top.'

'Is that why she was crying? Because she's lost him?'

'She was crying because now she will be sold, and a stranger will fuck her.' Ebrima turned to Carlos. 'Francisco Villaverde, who is too proud to be your father-in-law, always buys slaves as small boys, and buggers them until they grow up. Then he sells them to a farmer.'

Carlos was still incredulous. 'So every night, when I'm asleep, you've been going to Grandma's bedroom?'

'Not every night. Just when she asked me.'

Barney said: 'Did you mind?'

'Elisa is an old woman, but she's warm and loving. And I was glad it wasn't a man.'

Barney felt as if he had been a child until today. He had known that priests could put a man in prison and torture him to death, but not that they could also take all his possessions and make his family destitute. He had not imagined that an archdeacon would take a girl into his house and make her his mistress. And he had had no idea what men and women did with their slaves. It was as if he had been living in a house with rooms he had never entered, sharing it with strange people he had never previously set eyes on. He was disoriented by the discovery of his own ignorance. It threw him off balance. And now his life was in danger and he was trying to leave Seville, leave Spain, all in a headlong rush.

They arrived at the waterfront. The beach was busy, as always, with stevedores and carts. At first glance, Barney reckoned there were about forty ships moored. The morning tide was preferred for departure, for then the ship had a whole day of sailing ahead; but usually one or two would leave in the afternoon. However, the tide was already on the turn: they would soon be away.

The three men hurried to the water's edge and scanned the vessels, looking for signs of imminent departure: hatches closed, captain on deck, crew in the rigging. A ship called *Ciervo* was already moving out of its berth, the crew using long poles to keep it away from the barks on either side. There was still time to get aboard, just. Carlos cupped his hands around his mouth and shouted: 'Skipper! Do you want three strong deck hands?'

'No!' came the answer. 'I've got a complete crew.'

'How about three passengers? We can pay.'

'No room!'

He was probably planning something illegal, Barney speculated, and did not want it to be witnessed by people he did not know or trust. The commonest crime, in these waters, was offshore dealing in American silver, to evade the king's taxes in Seville. But straightforward piracy was not unusual.

They hurried along the river bank, but their luck was out. No one else seemed to be leaving. Barney felt desperate. Now what would they do?

They reached the downstream limit of the harbour. It was marked by a fortress called the Golden Tower. At this point an iron chain could be stretched from one bank to the other, so that raiders coming upstream from the sea could not attack the ships at anchor.

Outside the fortress, a recruiter was at work, standing on a barrel, calling on young men to join the army. 'There's a hot meal and a bottle of wine for every man who enlists now,' he shouted to a crowd of onlookers. 'Over there is a ship called *José y María*, and the two blessed saints watch over her and guard all who sail in her.' He pointed, and Barney saw that he had an iron hand, presumably the artificial replacement for a real one lost in battle.

Barney looked in the direction indicated and saw a big three-masted galleon bristling with cannons, its deck already crowded with young men.

The recruiter went on: 'We're sailing this afternoon to a place where there are wicked heathens to be killed, and where the girls are as willing as they are pretty, as I can tell you, my lads, from personal experience, if you know what I mean.'

There was a knowing laugh from the crowd.

'I don't want you if you're weak,' he said scornfully. 'I don't want you if you're timid. I don't want you if you're a girlie-boy, and you know what I mean by that. This is only for the strong, the brave and the tough. This is for real men.'

On the deck of the *José y María* someone shouted: 'All aboard!'

'Last chance, lads,' the recruiter called. 'What is it to be? Stay at home with your Mama, eating bread-and-milk and doing as you're told? Or come with me, Captain Ironhand Gómez, for a man's life, travel and adventure, fame and fortune. All you have to do is walk up that gangway, and the world is yours.'

Barney, Carlos and Ebrima looked at one another. Carlos said: 'Yes or no?'

Barney said: 'Yes.'

Ebrima said: 'Yes.'

The three men walked to the ship, climbed the gangway, and went on board.

*

TWO DAYS LATER they were on the open sea.

Ebrima had sailed many miles, but always as a captive, chained in the hold. Seeing the sea from the deck was a new and exhilarating experience.

The recruits had nothing to do but speculate on their destination, which still had not been revealed: it was a military secret.

Ebrima had an additional unanswered question: his future.

When they had boarded the *José y María* they had been met by an officer seated at a table with a ledger. 'Name?' he had said.

'Barney Willard.'

The officer wrote in the book then looked at Carlos. 'Name?'

'Carlos Cruz.'

He wrote down the name, glanced at Ebrima, then put down his pen. Looking from Carlos to Barney and back, he had said: 'You can't have a slave in the army. An officer can, though he has to feed and clothe the man out of his own money. But an enlisted soldier obviously can't do that.'

Ebrima had studied Carlos's face closely. A look of desperation had come into Carlos's eyes: he saw his escape route closing. After only a moment's hesitation he said the only thing he could say: 'He's not a slave, he's a free man.'

Ebrima's heart had stopped.

The officer had nodded. Freed slaves were rare, but by no means unknown. 'Fine,' he had said. He had looked at Ebrima and said: 'Name?'

It had all been very quick, and when it was over, Ebrima still was not sure where he stood. Barney had not congratulated him on being freed, and Carlos had not acted like a man who has given a great gift. Clearly Ebrima was to be *treated* as a free man in the army, but how real was it?

Was he free or not?

He did not know.

5

MARGERY'S WEDDING WAS POSTPONED.

After the fall of Calais, England expected to be invaded, and Bart Shiring was deputed to raise a hundred men-at-arms and garrison Combe Harbour. The wedding would have to wait.

For Ned Willard, postponement was hope.

Towns such as Kingsbridge were hastily repairing their walls, and earls reinforcing their castles. Ports scraped the rust off the ancient cannons on their sea fronts, and demanded that the local nobility do their duty and defend the population against the dreaded French.

People blamed Queen Mary Tudor. It was all her fault, for marrying the king of Spain. Were it not for him Calais would still be English, England would not be at war with France, and there would be no need for city walls and waterfront cannons.

Ned was glad. While Margery and Bart remained unmarried, anything could happen: Bart could change his mind, or be killed in battle, or die of the shivering fever that was sweeping the country.

Margery was the woman Ned wanted, and that was that. The world was full of attractive girls, but none of them counted: she was the one. He did not really understand why he was so sure. He just knew that Margery would always be there, like the cathedral.

He regarded her engagement as a setback, not a defeat.

Bart and his squadron mustered in Kingsbridge to travel by barge to Combe Harbour on the Saturday before Holy Week. That morning, a crowd gathered at the river to cheer the men off. Ned joined them. He wanted to be sure that Bart really went.

It was cold but sunny, and the waterfront looked festive.

Downstream of Merthin's Bridge, boats and barges were moored on both banks and all around Leper Island. On the far side, in the suburb of Loversfield, warehouses and workshops jostled for space. From Kingsbridge the river was navigable, by shallow-draught vessels, all the way to the coast. Kingsbridge had long been one of the biggest market towns in England; now it did business with Europe, too.

A big barge was docking on the near bank when Ned arrived at Slaughterhouse Wharf. This had to be the vessel that would take Bart and his company to Combe Harbour. Twenty men had rowed upriver, assisted by a single sail. Now they rested on their oars while the barge was poled into a berth. The downriver voyage would be easier, even with a hundred passengers.

The Fitzgeralds came down the main street to give an enthusiastic send-off to the man who was set to become their son-in-law. Sir Reginald and Rollo walked side by side, old and new editions of the same tall, thin, self-righteous book; Ned stared at them with hatred and contempt. Margery and Lady Jane were behind them, one small and sexy, one small and mean.

Ned believed that Rollo saw Margery as nothing more than a means to power and prestige. Many men had this attitude to the girls in their family, but in Ned's eyes it was the opposite of love. If Rollo was fond of his sister, it was no more than the emotion he might have felt towards a horse: he might like it, but he would sell or trade it if necessary.

Sir Reginald was no better. Ned suspected that Lady Jane was not quite so ruthless, but she would always put the interests of the family before the happiness of any individual member, and in the end that led her to the same cruelty.

Ned watched Margery go up to Bart. He was preening, proud to have the prettiest girl in Kingsbridge as his fiancée.

Ned studied her. It almost seemed as if there was a different person wearing the bright coat of Kingsbridge Scarlet and the little hat with the feather. She stood straight and still, and although she was talking to Bart, her face was like that of a statue. Everything about her expressed resolution, not animation. The imp of mischief had vanished.

But no one could change so quickly. That imp must still be inside her somewhere.

He knew she was miserable, and that made him angry as well as sad. He wanted to pick her up and run away with her. At night he elaborated fantasies in which the two of them slipped out of Kingsbridge at dawn and disappeared into the forest. Sometimes they walked to Winchester and got married under false names; or they made their way to London and set up in some business; they even went to Combe Harbour and took ship to Seville. But he could not save her unless she wanted to be saved.

The oarsmen disembarked and went into the nearest tavern, the Slaughterhouse, to quench their thirsts. A passenger got off the barge, and Ned stared at him in surprise. Wrapped in a grubby cloak and carrying a battered leather satchel, the man had the wearily dogged look of the long-distance traveller. It was Ned's cousin Albin from Calais.

They were the same age, and had become close while Ned was living with Uncle Dick.

Ned hurried to the quay. 'Albin?' he said. 'Is it you?'

Albin replied in French. 'Ned, at last,' he said. 'What a relief.'

'What happened in Calais? We still haven't had definite information, even after all this time.'

'It's all bad news,' Albin said. 'My parents and my sister are dead, and we've lost everything. The French crown seized the warehouse and handed over everything to French merchants.'

'We were afraid of that.' It was the news the Willards had been dreading for so long, and Ned felt deeply dispirited. He was particularly sad for his mother, who had lost her life's work. She would be devastated. But Albin had suffered a much greater loss. 'I'm so sorry about your parents and Thérèse.'

'Thank you.'

'Come to the house. You have to tell my mother everything.' Ned dreaded the moment, but it had to be done.

They walked up the main street. 'I managed to escape from the town,' Albin said. 'But I had no money, and, anyway, it's impossible to get passage from France to England now because of the war. That's why you've had no news.'

'So how did you get here?'

'First I had to leave France, so I crossed the border into the Netherlands. But I still didn't have the fare to England. So I had to get to our uncle in Antwerp.'

Ned nodded. 'Jan Wolman, our fathers' cousin.' Jan had visited Calais while Ned was there, so both he and Albin had met him.

'So I walked to Antwerp.'

'That's more than a hundred miles.'

'And my feet felt every yard. I took a lot of wrong turnings, and I nearly starved to death, but I got there.'

'Well done. Uncle Jan took you in, no doubt.'

'He was wonderful. He fed me beef and wine, and Aunt Hennie bandaged my feet. Then Jan bought me passage from Antwerp to Combe Harbour, and a new pair of shoes, and gave me money for the journey.'

'And here you are.' They arrived at the door of the Willard house. Ned escorted Albin into the parlour. Alice was sitting at a table placed near the window for light, writing in a ledger. There was a big fire in the grate, and she was wrapped in a fur-lined cloak. No one ever got warm keeping books, she sometimes said. 'Mother, here's Albin, arrived from Calais.'

Alice put down her pen. 'Welcome, Albin.' She turned back to Ned. 'Fetch your cousin something to eat and drink.'

Ned went to the kitchen and asked the housekeeper, Janet Fife, to serve wine and cake.

Back in the parlour, Albin told his story. He spoke French, with Ned translating the parts his mother did not understand.

It brought tears to Ned's eyes. The portly figure of his mother seemed to shrink in the chair as the grim details came out: her brother-in-law dead, with wife and daughter; the warehouse given to a French merchant, with all its contents; strangers living in Dick's house. 'Poor Dick,' Alice said quietly. 'Poor Dick.'

Ned said: 'I'm so sorry, Mother.'

Alice made an effort to sit upright and be positive. 'We're

not ruined, not quite. I still have this house and four hundred pounds. And I own six houses by St Mark's church.' The St Mark's cottages were her inheritance from her father, and brought a small income in rents. 'That's more wealth than most people see in a lifetime.' Then she was struck by a worrying thought. 'Though now I wish my four hundred pounds were not on loan to Sir Reginald Fitzgerald.'

'All the better,' said Ned. 'If he doesn't pay it back, we get the priory.'

'Speaking of that,' said his mother, 'Albin, do you know anything of an English ship called the *St Margaret*?'

'Why, yes,' said Albin. 'It came into Calais for repairs the day before the French attack.'

'What happened to the ship?'

'It was seized by the French crown, like all the other English property in Calais – spoils of war. The hold was full of furs. They were auctioned on the quayside; they sold for more than five hundred pounds.'

Ned and Alice looked at each other. This was a bombshell. Alice said: 'So Reginald has lost his investment. My goodness, I'm not sure he can survive this.'

Ned said: 'And he'll forfeit the priory.'

Alice said grimly: 'There will be trouble.'

'I know,' said Ned. 'He'll squeal. But we will have a new business.' He began to brighten. 'We can make a fresh start.'

Alice, always courteous, said: 'Albin, you may like a wash and a clean shirt. Janet Fife will give you everything you need. And then we'll have dinner.'

'Thank you, Aunt Alice.'

'It is I who thank you for making this long journey and bringing me the facts at last, terrible though they are.'

Ned studied his mother's face. She had been rocked by the news, even though it was not unexpected. He felt desperate to do something to renew her spirits. 'We could go and look at the priory now,' he said. 'We can begin to figure out how we'll parcel out space, and whatnot.'

She looked apathetic, then she made an effort. 'Why not?' she said. 'It's ours now.' She got to her feet.

They left the house and crossed the market square to the south side of the cathedral.

Ned's father, Edmund, had been mayor of Kingsbridge when King Henry VIII began to abolish the monasteries. Alice had told Ned that Edmund and Prior Paul – the last prior of Kingsbridge, as things turned out – had seen what was coming, and conspired together to save the school. They had separated the school from the priory and given it self-government and an endowment. Two hundred years earlier, something similar had been done with Caris's Hospital, and Edmund had taken that as a model. So the town still had a great school and a famous hospital. The rest of the priory was a ruin.

The main door was locked, but the walls were falling down, and they found a place at the back of the old kitchen where they could clamber over rubble into the premises.

Other people had had the same idea. Ned saw the ashes of a recent fire, a few scattered meat bones, and a rotted-out wineskin: someone had spent a night here, probably with an illicit lover. There was a smell of decay inside the buildings, and the droppings of birds and rodents were everywhere. 'And the monks were always so clean,' Alice said dismally, looking around. 'Nothing is permanent, except change.'

Despite the dilapidation, Ned felt a keen sense of anticipation. All this now belonged to his family. Something wonderful could be made of it. How clever his mother was, to think of it – and just when the family needed a rescue plan.

They made their way to the cloisters and stood in the middle of the overgrown herb garden, by the ruined fountain where the monks used to wash their hands. Looking all around the arcade, Ned saw that many of the columns and vaults, parapets and arches were still sound, despite decades of neglect. The Kingsbridge masons had built well.

'We should start here,' said Alice. 'We'll knock an archway through the west wall, so that people can see in from the market square. We can divide the cloisters up into small shops, one to each bay.'

'That would give us twenty-four,' Ned said, counting. 'Twenty-three, if we use one for the entrance.'

'The public can come into the quadrangle and look around.'

Ned could picture it, just as his mother obviously could: the stalls with bright textiles, fresh fruits and vegetables, boots and belts, cheese and wine; the stallholders calling their wares, charming their customers, taking money and making change; and the shoppers in their best clothes, clutching their purses, looking and touching and sniffing while they gossiped with their neighbours. Ned liked markets: they were where prosperity came from.

'We don't need to do a lot of work, initially,' Alice went on. 'We'll have to clean the place up, but the stallholders can bring their own tables, and anything else they need. Once the market is up and running, and making money, we can think about repairing the stonework, renewing the roof, and paving the quadrangle.'

Suddenly Ned felt they were being watched. He turned around. The south door of the cathedral was open, and Bishop Julius stood in the cloister, hands like claws on his bony hips, blue eyes glaring at them balefully. Ned felt guilty, though he had no reason to: priests had that effect, he had noticed.

Alice saw the bishop a moment later. She grunted with surprise. Then she muttered: 'I suppose we might as well get this over with.'

Julius shouted indignantly: 'What do you two think you're doing here?'

'Good day, my lord bishop.' Alice walked towards him, and Ned followed. 'I'm examining my property.'

'What on earth do you mean?'

'I own the priory now.'

'No, you don't. Sir Reginald does.' The bishop's cadaverous face registered scorn, but Ned could see that beneath the bluster he was worried.

'Reginald pledged the priory to me as security for a loan he can't repay. He bought the cargo of a ship called the *St Margaret* that has been confiscated by the French king, and he'll never get his money back. So now the property becomes mine. Naturally, I want us to be good neighbours, bishop, and I look forward to discussing my plans—'

'Wait a minute. You can't enforce that pledge.'

'On the contrary. Kingsbridge is a trading city with a reputation for respecting contracts. Our prosperity depends on that. So does yours.'

'Reginald promised to sell the priory back to the Church – to which it rightfully belongs.'

'Then Sir Reginald broke his promise to you when he pledged it as security for his loan. All the same, I'd be happy to sell the property to you, if that's what you would like.'

Ned held his breath. He knew his mother did not really want to do this.

Alice went on: 'Pay me the amount Reginald owes me, and the place is yours. Four hundred and twenty-four pounds.'

'Four hundred and twenty-four?' Bishop Julius repeated, as if there was something odd about the number.

'Yes.'

The priory was worth more than that, Ned thought. If Julius had any sense he would snap up this offer. But perhaps he did not have the money.

The bishop said indignantly: 'Reginald offered it to me at the price he paid for it – eighty pounds!'

'That would have been a pious gift, not a business transaction.'

'You should do the same.'

'Reginald's habit of selling things for less than they're worth may be the reason he's now penniless.'

The bishop shifted his ground. 'What would you propose to do with these ruins?'

'I'm not sure,' Alice lied. 'Let me develop some ideas, then come and talk to you.' Ned guessed she did not want to give Julius the chance to start a campaign against the market even before the plans were finished.

'Whatever you try to do, I'll stop you.'

That was not going to happen, Ned thought. Every alderman on the council knew how badly the town needed more space for citizens to sell their goods. Several of them were desperate for premises themselves, and would be the first to rent space in the new market.

'I hope we can work together,' Alice said pacifically.

Julius said intemperately: 'You could be excommunicated for this.'

Alice remained calm. 'The Church has tried everything to get the monastic properties back, but Parliament won't permit it.'

'Sacrilege!'

'The monks became rich, lazy and corrupt, and the people lost respect for them. That's why King Henry was able to get away with dissolving the monasteries.'

'Henry the Eighth was a wicked man.'

'I want to be your friend and ally, my lord bishop, but not at the price of impoverishing myself and my family. The priory is mine.'

'No, it's not,' said Julius. 'It belongs to God.'

*

ROLLO BOUGHT DRINKS for all Bart Shiring's men-at-arms before they embarked for Combe Harbour. He could not afford it, but he was keen to stay on good terms with his sister's fiancé. He did not want the engagement to be broken off. The marriage was going to transform the fortunes of the Fitzgerald family. Margery would be a countess, and if she gave birth to a son he would grow up to become an earl. The Fitzgeralds would almost be aristocracy.

However, they had not yet made that coveted leap: an engagement was not a marriage. The wilful Margery could renew her mutiny, encouraged by the detestable Ned Willard. Or her ill-concealed reluctance could offend Bart and cause him to break it off in a fit of wounded pride. So Rollo spent money he could not spare to foster his friendship with Bart.

It was not easy. The camaraderie of brothers-in-law had to be mixed with deference and laced with flattery. But Rollo could do that. Raising his tankard, he said: 'My noble brother! May God's grace protect your strong right arm and help you repel the stinking French!'

That went down well. The men-at-arms cheered and drank. A handbell was rung, and they emptied their cups and went on board the barge. The Fitzgeralds waved from the quayside. When the barge was out of sight, Margery and the parents went home, but Rollo went back into the Slaughterhouse.

In the tavern he had noticed one man who was not celebrating, but sitting in a corner on his own looking depressed. He recognized the dark lustrous hair and full lips of Donal Gloster. He was interested: Donal was weak, and weak men could be useful.

He bought two fresh tankards and went to sit with Donal. They were too far apart socially to be close friends, but they were the same age and had attended Kingsbridge Grammar School together. Rollo lifted his beer and said: 'Death to the French.'

'They won't invade us,' said Donal, but he drank anyway.

'What makes you so sure?'

'The King of France can't afford it. They might talk about an invasion, and they could do hit-and-run raids, but a real cross-Channel armada would cost more than they have to spend.'

Rollo thought Donal might know what he was talking about. His employer, Philbert Cobley, was more familiar with the costs of ships than anyone else in Kingsbridge, and as an international trader he probably also understood the finances of the French crown. 'So we should celebrate!' he said.

Donal grunted.

Rollo said: 'You look like a man who has had bad news, old schoolmate.'

'Do I?'

'None of my business, of course . . .'

'You might as well know. Everyone will, soon. I proposed to Ruth Cobley, and she turned me down.'

Rollo was surprised. Everyone expected Donal to marry Ruth. It was the commonest thing in the world for an employee to marry the boss's daughter. 'Doesn't her father like you?'

'I'd make a good son-in-law for him, because I know the business so well. But I'm not religious enough for Philbert.'

'Ah.' Rollo recalled the play at New Castle. Donal had clearly been enjoying it, and had seemed reluctant to join the Cobleys in their outraged walk-out. 'But you said Ruth turned you down.' Rollo would have thought Donal was attractive to girls, with his dark, romantic good looks.

'She says I'm like a brother to her.'

Rollo shrugged. There was no logic to love.

Donal looked at him shrewdly. 'You're not very interested in girls.'

'Nor boys either, if that's what you were thinking.'

'It crossed my mind.'

'No.' The truth was that Rollo did not know what all the fuss was about. Masturbation for him was a mild pleasure, like eating honey, but the idea of sex with a woman, or another man, just seemed slightly distasteful. His preference was for celibacy. If the monasteries still existed he might have been a monk.

'Lucky you,' Donal said bitterly. 'When I think of all the time I've spent trying to be the right husband for her – pretending not to like drinking and dancing and seeing plays, going to their boring services, talking to her mother . . .'

Rollo felt goosebumps at the back of his neck. Donal had said *going to their boring services*. Rollo had long known that the Cobleys belonged to that dangerous class of people who thought they had the right to their own opinions about religion, but he had not previously come across evidence that they actually practised their profanation here in Kingsbridge. He tried not to show his sudden excitement. 'I suppose those services were pretty dull,' he said, endeavouring to sound casual.

Donal immediately backtracked. 'I should have said meetings,' he said. 'Of course they don't hold services – that would be heresy.'

'I know what you mean,' Rollo said. 'But there's no law against people praying together, or reading from the Bible, or singing hymns.'

Donal raised his tankard to his mouth, then put it down again. 'I'm talking nonsense,' he said. His eyes showed the shadow of fear. 'I must have had too much to drink.' He got to his feet with an effort. 'I'm going home.'

'Don't go,' said Rollo, eager to know more about Philbert Cobley's meetings. 'Finish your tankard.'

But Donal was scared. 'Need to take a nap,' he mumbled. 'Thanks for the beer.' He staggered away.

Rollo sipped meditatively. The Cobleys and their friends were widely suspected of secretly having Protestant beliefs, but they were careful, and there was never the least evidence of illicit behaviour. As long as they kept their thoughts to themselves they committed no offence. However, holding Protestant services was another matter. It was a sin and a crime, and the punishment was to be burned alive.

And Donal, drunk and embittered, had momentarily lifted the veil.

There was nothing much Rollo could do about it, for tomorrow Donal would surely deny everything and plead intoxication. But this information would prove useful one day.

He decided to tell his father about it. He finished his drink and left.

He arrived at the family home on the high street at the same time as Bishop Julius. 'We gave our soldiers a jolly good send-off,' he said cheerfully to the bishop.

'Never mind about that,' said Julius irascibly. 'I've got something to tell Sir Reginald.' Clearly he was angry, though fortunately his ire did not seem to be directed at the Fitzgeralds.

Rollo led him into the great hall. 'I'll fetch my father at once,' Rollo said. 'Please sit here in front of the fire.'

Julius gave a dismissive wave and began to pace up and down impatiently.

Sir Reginald was taking a nap. Rollo woke him and told him the bishop was downstairs. Reginald groaned and got out of bed. 'Give him a cup of wine while I dress,' he said.

A few minutes later the three men were seated in the hall. Julius began immediately. 'Alice Willard has heard from Calais. The *St Margaret* has been confiscated by the French and her cargo sold.'

Despair seized Rollo. 'I knew it,' he said. It had been his father's last throw of the dice, and he had lost. What would they do now?

Sir Reginald flushed with anger. 'What the devil was the ship doing in Calais?'

Rollo answered him. 'Jonas Bacon told us that when he met the ship, its captain was intending to go into port for minor repairs. Hence the delay.'

'But Bacon didn't say the port was Calais.'

'No.'

Reginald's freckled face twisted with hatred. 'He knew, though,' he said. 'And I'll bet Philbert did, too, when he sold us the cargo.'

'Of course Philbert knew, the lying hypocritical Protestant swindler.' Rollo was boiling with rage. 'We've been robbed.'

The bishop said: 'If that's so, can you get your money back from Philbert?'

'Never,' said Reginald. 'A town like this can't let people renege on contracts, even when there has been sharp practice. The contract is sacred.'

Rollo, who had studied law, knew he was right. 'The court of quarter sessions will uphold the validity of the transaction,' he said.

Bishop Julius said: 'If you've lost that money, will you be able to repay Alice Willard?'

'No.'

'And you pledged the priory as security for the loan.'

'Yes.'

'Alice Willard told me this morning that the priory is hers, now.'

'Damn her eyes,' said Reginald.

'So she's right.'

'Yes.'

'You were going to let the Church have the priory back, Reginald.'

'Don't ask for sympathy from me, Julius. I've just lost four hundred pounds.'

'Four hundred and twenty-four, Willard told me.'

'Correct.'

Julius seemed to think the exact figure was significant, and Rollo wondered why, but he did not get a chance to ask. His father stood up restlessly and walked across the room and back again. 'I'll get Philbert for this, I swear it. He'll find out that no one swindles Reginald Fitzgerald and gets away with it. I'll see him suffer. I don't know how . . .'

Rollo experienced a flash of inspiration, and he said: 'I do.'

'What?'

'I know how to get revenge on Philbert.'

Reginald stopped pacing and stared at Rollo with narrowed eyes. 'What have you got in mind?'

'Philbert's clerk, Donal Gloster, was drunk in the Slaughterhouse this afternoon. He's been rejected by Philbert's daughter. Drink loosened his tongue and resentment made him malicious. He told me that the Cobleys and their friends hold services.'

Bishop Julius was outraged. 'Services? With no priest? That's heresy!'

'As soon as I took him up on it, Donal changed his story, and said they were only meetings; then he looked guilty and clammed up.'

The bishop said: 'I've long suspected that the rats perform Protestant rites in secret. But where? And when? And who attends?'

'I don't know,' said Rollo. 'But Donal does.'

'Will he tell?'

'Perhaps. Now that Ruth has rejected him, he no longer has any loyalty to the Cobley family.'

'Let's find out.'

'Let me go and see him. I'll take Osmund.' Osmund Carter was the head of the watch. He was a big man with a brutal streak.

'What will you say to Donal?'

'I'll explain that he is suspected of heresy, and he's going to be put on trial unless he tells all.'

'Will that scare him?'

'He'll shit.'

Bishop Julius said thoughtfully: 'This could be a good moment to strike against the Protestants. The Catholic Church is sadly on the defensive. Queen Mary Tudor is unpopular because of the loss of Calais. Her rightful heir, Mary Stuart, the queen of the Scots, is about to get married in Paris, and a French husband will turn the English against her. Sir William Cecil and his pals are going around the country trying to drum up support for the illegitimate Elizabeth Tudor as heir to the throne. So a clampdown on Kingsbridge heretics now would be a useful boost to Catholic morale.'

So, Rollo thought, we will be doing God's will as well as getting our revenge. He felt ferocity boil up in his heart.

His father clearly felt the same. 'Do it, Rollo,' Reginald said. 'Do it now.'

Rollo put on his coat and left the house.

The Guild Hall was right across the street. Sheriff Matthewson had a room on the ground floor, with a clerk, Paul Pettit, who wrote letters and kept documents in careful order in a chest. Matthewson could not always be relied upon to do the bidding of the Fitzgerald family: he would occasionally defy Sir Reginald, saying that he served the queen, not the mayor. Happily, the sheriff happened to be away from his room today, and Rollo had no intention of sending for him.

Instead he went down to the basement, where Osmund and the rest of the watchmen were preparing for their Saturday night duties. Osmund wore a close-fitting leather helmet that made him look even more pugnacious. He was lacing up knee boots.

'I need you to come with me to question someone,' Rollo said to Osmund. 'You won't need to say anything.' He was going to add *Just look menacing*, but that would have been superfluous.

They walked down the main street together in late-afternoon light. Rollo wondered whether he had been right to assure his father and the bishop that Donal would crack. If Donal had sobered up by now he might be tougher. He could apologize for talking trash while drunk and deny point-blank that he had ever been to any kind of Protestant service. Then it would be hard to prove anything.

Passing the wharves, Rollo was greeted by Susan White, a baker's daughter of his own age. She had a heart-shaped face and a sweet nature. When they were both younger they had kissed, and tried other mild experiments. That was when Rollo had realized that sex did not have the power over him that it had over boys such as Donal Gloster and Ned Willard, and his dalliance with Susan had come to nothing. He might marry anyway, one day, in order to have someone to manage his household, but in that event he would hope for someone of higher rank than a baker's daughter.

Susan bore him no resentment: she had had plenty of boyfriends. Now she looked sympathetic. 'I'm sorry you lost your cargo,' she said. 'It seems unfair.'

'It is unfair.' Rollo was not surprised that the story was getting around. Half of Kingsbridge was involved, one way or another, in trading by sea, and everyone was interested in good or bad shipping news.

'You're due for some good luck next,' Susan said. 'That's what people say, anyway.'

'I hope it's true.'

Susan looked with curiosity at Osmund, evidently wondering what he and Rollo were up to.

Rollo did not want to have to explain, so he brought the conversation to an end. 'Forgive me, I'm in a hurry.'

'Goodbye!'

Rollo and Osmund walked on. Donal lived in the south-west of the city, the industrial quarter known as the Tanneries. The north and east had long been the desirable neighbourhoods. The priory had always owned the land upstream of Merthin's Bridge, and there the water was clean. The borough council directed industry downstream, and all of Kingsbridge's dirty enterprises – leather tanning, textile dyeing, coal washing, paper making – sluiced their filth into the river here, as they had done for centuries.

Tomorrow was Sunday, and people would be exchanging news at church, Rollo reflected. By the evening everyone in Kingsbridge would know what had happened to the St Margaret. They might sympathize, like Susan, or they might think Sir Reginald was a fool to let himself be cheated, but either way they would regard the Fitzgeralds with a mixture of pity and scorn. Rollo could hear them being wise after the event, saying: 'That Philbert's a sly one. He never sold anyone a bargain. Sir Reginald should have known that.' The thought made Rollo cringe. He hated the idea of people looking down on his family.

But they would change their tune when Philbert was arrested for heresy. It would be seen as Philbert's punishment. People would say: 'It doesn't pay to swindle Sir Reginald – Philbert should have known that.' The honour of the family would be restored, and once again Rollo's chest would swell with pride when he told people his name.

If he could get Donal to talk.

Rollo led the way to a small house beyond the docks. The woman who opened the door had Donal's sensual good looks. She recognized Osmund and said: 'Mercy! What's my boy done?'

Rollo pushed past her into the house, and Osmund followed.

'I'm sorry he got drunk,' she said. 'He suffered a terrible disappointment.'

Rollo said: 'Is your husband at home?'

'He's dead.'

Rollo had forgotten that. It made things easier. 'Where's Donal?'

'I'll fetch him.' She turned away.

Rollo caught her arm. 'When I speak to you, you must listen to what I say. I didn't tell you to get him. I asked you where he is.'

Her brown eyes flashed anger, and for a moment Rollo thought she was going to tell him she would do as she pleased in her own house; then she got herself under control, no doubt fearing that defiance would make things worse for her son. Eyes downcast, she said: 'In bed. First door at the top of the stairs.'

'You wait here. Osmund, come with me.'

Donal was prone on the bed, fully dressed except for his boots. There was a smell of puke, though it seemed his mother might have cleaned up the worst of it. Rollo shook him awake.

He came round blearily. When he saw Osmund he sat bolt upright and said: 'Jesus Christ save me!'

Rollo sat on the edge of the bed and said: 'Christ will save you, if you tell the truth. You're in trouble, Donal.'

Donal was bewildered. 'What kind of trouble?'

'Don't you recall our talk in the Slaughterhouse?'

Donal looked panicky as he tried to remember. 'Um . . . vaguely . . .'

'You told me you attended Protestant services with the Cobley family.'

'I never said anything of the kind!'

'I've already spoken to Bishop Julius. You're going to stand trial for heresy.'

'No!' Trials rarely found men not guilty. The general view was that if a man were innocent he would not have got into trouble in the first place.

'You'll be better off if you tell the truth.'

'I am telling the truth!'

Osmund said: 'Shall I beat it out of him?'

Donal looked terrified.

Then his mother's voice was heard from the doorway. 'You're not going to beat anyone, Osmund. My son is a law-abiding citizen and a good Catholic boy, and if you touch him you're the one who'll be in trouble.'

It was a bluff – Osmund never got into trouble for beating people – but it gave heart to Donal. Looking braver, he said: 'I have never attended a Protestant service, with Philbert Cobley or anyone else.'

Mrs Gloster said: 'You can't hold a man to account for what he says when drunk, and if you try to, you'll make a fool of yourself, young Rollo.'

Rollo cursed inwardly. Mrs Gloster was getting the better of him. He saw that he had made a mistake in questioning Donal here at home, with his mother to stiffen his nerve. But he could soon put that right. He was not going to let a woman stand in the way of the Fitzgerald family revenge. He stood up. 'Get your boots on, Donal. You'll have to come with us to the Guild Hall.'

Mrs Gloster said: 'I'll come, too.'

'No, you won't,' said Rollo.

Mrs Gloster's eyes flashed mutiny.

Rollo added: 'And if I see you there, you will be arrested too. You must have known Donal was going to blasphemous services – so you're guilty of concealing his crime.'

Mrs Gloster lowered her eyes again.

Donal put his boots on.

Rollo and Osmund escorted him up the main street to the crossroads and took him into the Guild Hall through the basement entrance. Rollo sent one of the watchmen to fetch Sir Reginald, who arrived a few minutes later accompanied by Bishop Julius. 'Well, young Donal,' said Reginald with a pretence of affability. 'I hope you've seen the sense of making a clean breast of things.'

Donal's voice was shaky, but his words were brave enough. 'I don't know what I said when drunk, but I know the truth. I've never been to a Protestant service.'

Rollo began to worry that he might not crack after all.

'Let me show you something,' said Reginald. He went to a massive door, lifted the heavy bar, and opened it. 'Come here and look.'

Donal obeyed reluctantly. Rollo followed. They looked into a windowless room with a high ceiling and an earth floor. It smelled of old blood and shit, like an abattoir.

Reginald said: 'You see that hook in the ceiling?'

They all looked up.

Reginald said: 'Your hands will be tied behind your back. Then the rope from your wrists will be looped around that hook, and you will be hoisted up.'

Donal groaned.

'The pain is unbearable, of course, but at first your shoulders will not dislocate – it doesn't happen that quickly. Heavy stones will be attached to your feet, increasing the agony in your joints. When you pass out, cold water will be thrown in your face to bring you round – there's no relief. As the weights get heavier, so the pain gets worse. Eventually your arms spring from their sockets. Apparently that is the most dreadful part.'

Donal was white, but he did not give in. 'I'm a citizen of Kingsbridge. You can't torture me without a royal command.'

That was true. The Privy Council had to give permission for torture. The rule was often broken, but Kingsbridge people knew their rights. There would be an outcry if Donal was tortured illegally.

'I can get permission, you young fool.'

'Then do,' Donal said in a voice shrill with fear but still determined.

Rollo was downcast to think that they might have to give up. They had done everything possible to scare Donal into a confession, but it had not quite worked. Perhaps Philbert would not be punished after all.

Then Bishop Julius spoke. 'I think you and I had better have a quiet talk, young Donal,' he said. 'But not here. Come with me.'

'All right,' said Donal nervously. He was apprehensive, but Rollo guessed he would agree to anything that would get him out of that basement.

Julius escorted Donal out of the Guild Hall. Rollo and Reginald followed a few yards behind. Rollo wondered what the bishop had in mind. Could he save the dignity of the Fitzgerald family after all?

They went down the main street to the cathedral. Julius led them through a small door in the north side of the nave. The choir was singing evensong. The interior of the church was dimly lit by candles that sent dancing shadows across the arches.

Julius picked up a candle, then took Donal into a side chapel with a small altar and a large painting of Christ crucified. He put the candle on the altar so that it lit up the picture. He stood with his back to the altar, and made Donal face him, so that Donal could see Jesus on the cross.

Julius motioned Rollo and Reginald to keep their distance. They remained outside, but they could see into the chapel and hear what was said.

'I want you to forget about earthly punishments,' Julius said to Donal. 'Perhaps you will be tortured, and burned at the stake as a heretic, but that is not what you should be in fear of this evening.'

'Isn't it?' Donal was mystified as well as scared.

'My son, your soul is in mortal danger. Whatever you said earlier today in the Slaughterhouse doesn't matter – because God knows the truth. He knows what you have done. The pain you would suffer in hell would be so much worse than anything that could happen to you here on earth.'

'I know.'

'But God gives us hope of forgiveness, you know. Always.'

Donal said nothing. Rollo stared at his face in the unsteady candlelight, but could not read his expression.

Julius said: 'You must tell me three things, Donal. If you do, I will forgive your sins, and so will God. If you lie to me, you will go to hell. That's the decision you must make, here and now.'

Rollo saw Donal's head tilt back slightly as he looked at the picture of Jesus.

Julius said: 'Where do they hold their services? When? And who goes? You must tell me, right now.'

Donal gave a sob. Rollo held his breath.

'Let's start with where,' Julius said.

Donal said nothing.

'Last chance of forgiveness,' Julius said. 'I won't ask you again. Where?'

Donal said: 'In Widow Pollard's cowshed.'

Rollo expelled his breath silently. The secret was out.

Mrs Pollard had a smallholding at the southern edge of the city, on the Shiring road. There were no other houses close by, which would be why the Protestants had not been overheard.

Julius said: 'And when?'

'Tonight,' said Donal. 'Always on Saturday evening, at twilight.'

'They creep through the streets in the dusk so that they won't be noticed,' Julius said. 'Men love the darkness rather than the light, because their deeds are evil. But God sees them.' He glanced up at the pointed arch of the window. 'It's almost nightfall. Will they be there now?'

'Yes.'

'Who?'

'Philbert, and Mrs Cobley, and Dan and Ruth. Philbert's sister and Mrs Cobley's brother, and their families. Mrs Pollard. Ellis the brewer. The Mason brothers. Elijah Cordwainer. That's all I know. There might be others.'

'Good lad,' Julius said. 'Now, in a few minutes I'm going to give you my blessing and you can go home.' He raised a warning finger. 'Don't tell anyone we've had this conversation – I don't want people to know where my information comes from. Just go back to your normal life. Do you understand?'

'Yes, lord bishop.'

Julius looked towards where Rollo and Reginald stood, just outside the chapel. His voice changed from low and friendly to brisk and commanding. 'Get down to that cowshed now,' he said. 'Arrest the heretics – every one of them. Go!'

As Rollo turned to leave, he heard Donal say in a low voice: 'Oh, God, I've betrayed them all, haven't I?'

Bishop Julius said smoothly: 'You have saved their souls – and your own.'

Rollo and Reginald left the cathedral at a run. They went up the main street to the Guild Hall and summoned the men of the watch from the basement. They crossed the street to their house and buckled on their swords.

The watchmen all carried home-made clubs of different shapes and sizes. Osmund had a roll of stout cord for tying people's wrists. Two of the men brought lanterns on poles.

Widow Pollard's place was a mile away. 'It would be quicker to ride,' Rollo said.

'Not much quicker, in the dark,' his father replied. 'And the sound of the horses would forewarn the Protestants. I don't want any of those devils to slip through our fingers.'

They all marched down the main street, past the cathedral. People looked apprehensively at them. Clearly someone was in big trouble.

Rollo worried that someone friendly to the Protestants might guess what was happening. A fast runner could warn them. He quickened his pace.

They crossed Merthin's double bridge to the suburb of Loversfield, then followed the Shiring road south. The outskirts of the city were quieter and darker. Fortunately, the road was straight.

Widow Pollard's house gave on to the street, but her cowshed was set well back in an acre or so of land. The late Walter Pollard had kept a small dairy herd. After he died, his widow had sold the cattle. That was why she had a fine brick cowshed standing empty.

Osmund opened a wide gate, and they all followed the track the cows had used to take to milking. No light showed from the building: a cowshed had no need of windows. Osmund whispered to one of the lantern bearers: 'Walk around quickly and see if there's another way out.'

The rest went up to the wide double door. Sir Reginald put his finger to his lips, miming silence, and they all listened. From inside they could hear a murmur of several voices chanting something. After a minute Rollo recognized the Lord's Prayer.

In English.

That was heresy. No more proof was needed.

The lantern bearer returned and whispered: 'No other way in or out.'

Reginald tried the door. It seemed to be barred from the inside.

The sound alerted the people in the cowshed, and they fell silent.

Four of the watchmen charged the door, and it flew open. Reginald and Rollo stepped inside.

Twenty people sat on four benches. In front of them was a plain square table, covered with a white cloth, bearing a loaf of bread and a jug that presumably contained wine. Rollo was horrified: they were celebrating their own version of the Mass! He had heard that this went on but never thought he would see it with his own eyes.

Philbert stood behind the table, wearing a white smock over his doublet and hose. He was playing the part of a priest, even though he had never been ordained.

The intruders stared at the blasphemy going on in front of them. The congregation stared back, both sides equally stunned.

Then Reginald found his voice. 'This is heresy, plain to see. You're under arrest, every last one of you.' He paused. 'Especially you, Philbert Cobley.'

6

On the day before the wedding, Alison McKay was called to see the queen of France.

When the summons arrived Alison was with the bride, Mary Stuart, the queen of the Scots. Alison had been painstakingly shaving Mary's underarms, and she had managed to remove the hair without drawing blood. She was putting on oil to soothe the skin when there was a tap at the door and one of Mary's ladies-in-waiting came in. It was Véronique de Guise: sixteen years old, she was a distant cousin, and therefore not very important, but she made up for that by being beautiful, poised and alluring. 'A page came from Queen Caterina,' she said to Alison. 'Her majesty would like to see you right away.'

Véronique tagged on as Alison left Mary's quarters and hurried through the gloomy rooms of the old palace of Tournelles towards Caterina's apartment. 'What do you think her majesty wants?' Véronique asked.

'I have no idea,' Alison said. Véronique might be merely curious – or something more sinister, a spy reporting back to Mary's powerful uncles.

'Queen Caterina likes you,' Véronique said.

'She likes anyone who is kind to poor Francis.' All the same, Alison felt apprehensive. Royal people were not obliged to be consistent, and a summons meant bad news as often as good.

They were stopped on their way by a young man Alison did not recognize. He made a deep bow and said to Véronique: 'What a pleasure to see you, Mademoiselle de Guise. You are a ray of sunshine in this dismal castle.'

Alison had not met him before. She would have remembered him, for he was attractive-looking with waves of fair hair, and well dressed in a green-and-gold doublet. He was charming, too, though he was clearly more interested in Véronique than in Alison. He said: 'Is there any way I can be of use to you, Mademoiselle Véronique?'

'No, thank you,' Véronique said with a touch of impatience.

He turned to Alison and bowed again, saying: 'And I'm honoured to meet you, Miss McKay. I am Pierre Aumande. I have the honour to serve Mademoiselle de Guise's Uncle Charles, the cardinal of Lorraine.'

'Indeed?' said Alison. 'In what capacity?'

'I help with his very extensive correspondence.'

It sounded as if Pierre was a mere clerk, in which case it was ambitious of him to set his cap at Véronique de Guise. However, sometimes fortune favoured the bold, and Monsieur Aumande certainly was bold.

Alison took the opportunity to shake off her shadow. 'I mustn't keep her majesty waiting,' she said. 'Goodbye, Véronique.' She slipped away before Véronique could reply.

She found the queen reclining on a divan. Beside her were half a dozen kittens, rolling and tumbling and chasing the end of a pink ribbon that Caterina dangled in front of them. She looked up and gave Alison a friendly smile, and Alison breathed a silent sigh of relief: she was not in trouble, it seemed.

Queen Caterina had been plain when young and now, in her fortieth year, she was also fat. But she loved dressing up, and today she wore a black dress covered with enormous pearls, unflattering but extravagant. She patted the divan and Alison sat down, with the kittens between them. Alison was pleased by this sign of intimacy. She picked up a tiny black-and-white kitten. It licked the jewel on her ring finger, then bit her in an exploratory way. Its little teeth were sharp, but its jaw was too weak for the bite to hurt.

'How is the bride-to-be?' Caterina asked.

'Surprisingly calm,' Alison answered, stroking the kitten. 'A little nervous, but looking forward to tomorrow.'

'Does she know that she will have to lose her virginity in front of witnesses?'

'She does. She's embarrassed, but she will bear it.'

Immediately the thought came into Alison's head: If *Francis is capable*. She suppressed it for fear of offending Caterina.

But Caterina voiced the concern herself. 'We don't know whether poor Francis can do it.'

Alison said nothing: this was dangerous territory.

Caterina leaned forward and spoke in a low, intense voice. 'Listen to me. Whatever happens, Mary must pretend that the marriage has been consummated.'

Alison was deeply gratified to be having this intimate, confidential conversation with the queen of France; but she foresaw problems. 'That may be difficult.'

'The witnesses will not be able to see everything.'

'Still . . .' Alison saw that the kitten had fallen asleep in her lap.

'Francis must get on top of Mary, and either fuck her or pretend to fuck her.'

Alison was startled by Caterina's blunt words, but she realized that this subject was too important for inexact euphemisms. 'Who will tell Francis what to do?' she said in the same practical vein.

'I will. But you must talk to Mary. She trusts you.'

It was true, and Alison was pleased that the queen had noticed it. She felt proud. 'What am I to say to Mary?'

'She must announce, loudly, that she has lost her virginity.'

'What if they decide to have the doctors examine her?'

'We're going to take precautions. That's why I've summoned you.' Caterina took something small from her pocket. 'Look at this.' She handed it to Alison.

It was a tiny bag, no bigger than the ball of her thumb, made of some kind of soft leather, with a narrow neck folded over and tied with a little silk thread. 'What is it?'

'The bladder of a swan.'

Alison was mystified.

Caterina said: 'It's empty now. Tomorrow evening I will give it to you filled with blood. The thread will be tied tightly to prevent a leak. Mary must conceal the bladder under her nightdress. After the act – real or pretended – she must pull the thread and spill the blood on the sheets, then make sure everyone sees it.'

Alison nodded. This was good. Blood on the sheets was the traditional proof of consummation. Everyone would know what it meant, and no further doubts need be entertained.

This was how women such as Caterina exercised power, she realized with admiration. They moved cleverly but invisibly, working behind the scenes, managing events while the men imagined they had total control.

Caterina said: 'Will Mary do it?'

'Yes,' Alison said confidently. Mary did not lack courage. 'But . . . the witnesses may see the bladder.'

'When it has been emptied, Mary must push it up her cunt as far as it will go, and leave it there until she gets a private moment to throw it away.'

'I hope it doesn't fall out.'

'It won't – I know.' Caterina gave a humourless smile. 'Mary will not be the first girl to use this trick.'

'All right.'

Caterina took the kitten from Alison's lap, and it opened its eyes. 'Have you got everything clear?'

Alison stood up. 'Oh, yes. It's quite straightforward. It will take nerve, but Mary has plenty of that. She won't let you down.'

Caterina smiled. 'Good. Thank you.'

Alison thought of something, and frowned. 'The blood will need to be fresh. Where will you get it?'

'Oh, I don't know.' Caterina tied the pink ribbon in a bow around the neck of the black-and-white kitten. 'I'll think of something,' she said.

*

PIERRE CHOSE the day of the royal wedding to speak to Sylvie Palot's formidable father about marrying his beloved daughter.

Everyone in Paris dressed up that morning, Sunday 24 April 1558. Pierre put on the blue doublet slashed to show the white silk lining. He knew that Sylvie liked that outfit. It was a lot more dashing than anything worn in her parents' circle of sobersided friends. He suspected that his clothes were part of his appeal for her.

He left his college in the University district, on the left bank of the river, and walked north towards the Île de la Cité. Anticipation seemed to saturate the air of the narrow, crowded streets. Vendors of gingerbread, oysters, oranges and wine were setting up temporary stalls to take advantage of the crowds. A hawker offered him an eight-page printed pamphlet about the wedding, with a woodcut on the front purporting to show the happy couple, though the likenesses were approximate. Beggars, prostitutes and street musicians were heading the same way as Pierre. Paris loved a pageant.

Pierre was pleased about the royal wedding. It was a coup for the Guise family. Mary's uncles, Duke Scarface and Cardinal Charles, were already powerful, but they had rivals: the linked families of Montmorency and Bourbon were their enemies. However, the marriage would boost the Guises above the others. In the natural course of events, their niece Mary would become the queen of France, and then the Guises would be part of the royal family.

Pierre yearned to share in their power. For that, he needed to do a great job for Cardinal Charles. He had already collected the names of many Paris Protestants, some of them friends of Sylvie's family. He listed them all in a notebook with a leather cover – black, appropriately, since everyone in it was liable to be burned at the stake. But what Charles wanted to know most of all was where the Protestants held their services, and Pierre had not yet discovered the address of a single clandestine church.

He was getting desperate. The cardinal had paid him for the names he had handed over, but had promised a bonus for a location. And it was not just the money, though Pierre was always in dire need of that. Charles had other spies: Pierre did not know how many, but he knew he did not want to be just one of the team – he had to stand out as incomparably the best. He must become not just useful but essential to the cardinal.

Sylvie and her family disappeared every Sunday afternoon,

undoubtedly to attend a Protestant service somewhere; but, frustratingly, Giles Palot had not yet invited Pierre to go along, despite increasingly broad hints. So today Pierre planned a drastic step. He was going to propose to Sylvie. He reckoned that if the family accepted him as Sylvie's fiancé they would have to take him to services.

He had already asked Sylvie: she was ready to marry him tomorrow. But her father was not so easily fooled. Pierre would speak to Giles today, Sylvie had agreed. It was a good day for a proposal. The royal wedding would put everyone in a romantic mood – perhaps even Giles.

Pierre had no intention of marrying Sylvie, of course. A Protestant wife would end his nascent career with the Guise family. Besides, he did not even like her: she was too earnest. No, he needed a wife who would lift him up the social ladder. He had his eye on Véronique de Guise, a member of an obscure branch of the family and, he guessed, a girl who understood aspiration. If he became engaged to Sylvie today, he would have to rack his brains for reasons to postpone the marriage. But he would think of something.

In the back of his mind a quiet but irritating voice pointed out that he was going to break the heart of a perfectly nice young woman, which was wicked and cruel. His previous victims, such as the Widow Bauchene, had been more or less asking to be cheated, but Sylvie had done nothing to deserve what was happening to her. She had just fallen in love with the man Pierre was skilfully pretending to be.

The voice would not change his plans. He was on the high road to fortune and power, and such quibbles could not be allowed to get in his way. The voice remarked how much he had changed since he had left Thonnance-lès-Joinville and gone to Paris; it almost seemed as if he was becoming a different person. I hope so, he thought; I used to be nothing but the bastard son of a poor country priest, but I'm going to be a man of consequence.

He crossed the Petit Pont to the City, the island in the Seine river where the cathedral of Notre Dame de Paris stood. Francis and Mary would be married in the square before the west front of the great church. An enormous scaffold stage had been built for the ceremony, twelve feet high and running from the archbishop's palace across the square to the cathedral door, so that the people of Paris could watch the ceremony but would be unable to touch the royal family and their guests. Spectators were already gathering around the stage, making sure of positions with clear views. At the cathedral end was a billowing canopy made of countless yards of blue silk embroidered with fleurs-de-lys to keep the sun off the bridal couple. Pierre shuddered to think of the cost.

Pierre saw Scarface, the duke of Guise, on the stage: he was master of ceremonies today. He appeared to be arguing with some minor gentlemen who had come early to secure good places, ordering them to move. Pierre went close to the stage and bowed deeply to Duke François, but the duke did not see him.

Pierre made his way to the row of houses north of the cathedral. Giles Palot's bookshop was closed for the Sabbath, and the street door was locked, but Pierre knew his way to the factory entrance at the back.

Sylvie came running down the stairs to greet him. That gave them a few seconds unobserved in the silent print shop. She threw her arms around his neck and kissed him with her mouth open.

He found it surprisingly difficult to fake reciprocal passion. He tongued her energetically, and squeezed her breasts through the bodice of her dress, but he felt no arousal.

She broke the kiss to say excitedly: 'He's in a good mood! Come on up.'

Pierre followed her to the living quarters on the upstairs floor. Giles and his wife, Isabelle, were seated at the table with Guillaume.

Giles was an ox, all neck and shoulders. He looked as if he could lift a house. Pierre knew, from hints dropped by Sylvie, that Giles could be violent with his family and with his apprentices. What would happen if Giles ever found out that Pierre was a Catholic spy? He tried not to think about it.

Pierre bowed to Giles first, acknowledging his position as

head of the family, and said: 'Good morning, Monsieur Palot. I hope I find you well.' Giles replied with a grunt, which was not particularly offensive as it was how he greeted everyone.

Isabelle was more responsive to Pierre's charm. She smiled when he kissed her hand, and invited him to sit down. Like her daughter, Isabelle had a straight nose and a strong chin, features that suggested strength of character. People probably called her handsome, but not pretty, and Pierre could imagine her being seductive, in the right mood. Mother and daughter were alike in personality, determined and bold.

Guillaume was a mystery. A pale man of twenty-five, he had an aura of intensity. He had come to the bookshop on the same day as Pierre, and had immediately moved into the family quarters upstairs. His fingers were inky, and Isabelle said vaguely that he was a student, though he was not attached to any of the colleges in the Sorbonne, and Pierre had never seen him in a class. Whether he was a paying lodger or an invited guest was not clear. In conversation with Pierre he gave nothing away. Pierre would have liked to press his questions, but he was afraid of seeming to pry and thereby arousing suspicion.

As Pierre walked into the room he had noticed Guillaume closing a book, with a casual air that was not quite convincing; and it now lay on the table with Guillaume's hand resting on top, as if to prevent anyone opening it. Perhaps he had been reading aloud to the rest of the family. Pierre's intuition told him the book was an illicit Protestant volume. He pretended not to notice.

When the greetings were over, Sylvie said: 'Pierre has something to say to you, Papa.' She was unfailingly direct.

Giles said: 'Well, go ahead, lad.'

Pierre hated to be condescended to with words such as 'lad', but this was not the moment to show it.

Sylvie said: 'Perhaps you'd rather talk in private.'

'I don't see why,' said Giles.

Pierre would have preferred privacy, but he put on a show of insouciance. 'I'd be happy to be heard by everyone.'

'All right, then,' said Giles, and Guillaume, who had half stood up, sat down again.

Pierre said: 'Monsieur Palot, I humbly ask permission to marry Sylvie.'

Isabelle gave a little cry – not of surprise, presumably, since she must have seen this coming; perhaps of pleasure. Pierre caught a shocked look from Guillaume and wondered whether he harboured secret romantic thoughts of Sylvie. Giles just looked annoyed that his peaceful Sunday had been disturbed.

With a barely suppressed sigh, Giles turned his mind to the task now before him: the interrogation of Pierre. 'You're a student,' he said derisively. 'How can you propose marriage?'

'I understand your concern,' Pierre said amiably. He was not going to be blown off course by mere rudeness. He began to tell lies, which was what he was good at. 'My mother owns a little land in Champagne – just a few vineyards, but the rents are good, so we have an income.' His mother was the penniless housekeeper of a country priest, and Pierre lived on his wits. 'When my studies are over, I hope to follow the profession of lawyer, and my wife will be well looked after.' That part was closer to the truth.

Giles did not comment on that response, but asked another question. 'What is your religion?'

'I'm a Christian seeking enlightenment.' Pierre had anticipated Giles's questions and rehearsed the deceitful answers. He hoped they did not come out too pat.

'Tell me about the enlightenment you seek.'

It was a shrewd question. Pierre could not simply claim to be a Protestant, for he had never been part of a congregation. But he needed to make it clear that he was ready to convert. 'I'm concerned by two things,' he said, trying to sound thoughtfully troubled. 'First, the Mass. We're taught that the bread and wine are transformed into the body and blood of Jesus. But they do not look like flesh and blood, nor smell or taste like it, so in what sense are they transformed? It seems like pseudo-philosophy to me.' Pierre had heard these arguments put by fellow-students who leaned towards Protestantism. Personally, he found it barely comprehensible that men should quarrel over such abstractions.

Giles surely agreed wholeheartedly with the argument, but he did not say so. 'What's the second thing?'

'The way that priests so often take the income paid to them in tithes by poor peasants and use the money to live a life of luxury, not troubling to perform any of their holy duties.' This was something even the most devout Catholics complained about.

'You can be thrown in jail for saying these things. How dare you utter heresy in my house?' Giles's indignation was poorly acted, but somehow no less threatening for that.

Sylvie said bravely: 'Don't pretend, Papa, he knows what we are.'

Giles looked angry. 'Did you tell him?' He clenched a meaty fist.

Pierre said hastily: 'She didn't tell me. It's obvious.'

Giles reddened. 'Obvious?'

'To anyone who looks around – at all the things missing from your home. There is no crucifix over your bed, no statue of the Virgin in a niche by the door, no painting of the Holy Family above the mantelpiece. Your wife has no pearls sewn into the fabric of her best dress, although you could afford a few. Your daughter wears a brown coat.' He reached across the table with a swift movement and snatched the book from under Guillaume's hand. Opening it, he said: 'And you read the Gospel of St Matthew in French on a Sunday morning.'

Guillaume spoke for the first time. 'Are you going to denounce us?' He looked scared.

'No, Guillaume. If that was my intention, I would have come here with officers of the city guard.' Pierre returned his gaze to Giles. 'I want to join you. I want to become a Protestant. And I want to marry Sylvie.'

Sylvie said: 'Please say yes, Papa.' She knelt in front of her father. 'Pierre loves me and I love him. We're going to be so happy together. And Pierre will join us in our work of spreading the true gospel.'

Giles's fist unclenched and his colour returned to normal. He said to Pierre: 'Will you?'

'Yes,' said Pierre. 'If you'll have me.'

Giles looked at his wife. Isabelle gave an almost imperceptible nod. Pierre suspected that she was the real power in this family, despite appearances. Giles smiled – a rare thing – and spoke to Sylvie. 'Very well, then. Marry Pierre, and may God bless your union.'

Sylvie jumped up, hugged her father, then exuberantly kissed Pierre. By coincidence there was a cheer from the crowd in front of the cathedral. 'They approve of our engagement,' Pierre said, and everyone laughed.

They all went to the windows, which overlooked the square. The wedding procession was moving along the scaffolded stage. It was led by a company of soldiers known as the Hundred Swiss, identifiable by their striped sleeves and the feathers in their helmets. As Pierre watched, a large group of musicians came into view, playing flutes and drums, then the gentlemen of the court, every one of them in new clothes, a riot of red, gold, bright blue, yellow and lavender. Sylvie said excitedly: 'It's as if they're doing it for you and me, Pierre!'

The crowd fell silent and bowed their heads as the bishops appeared carrying jewelled crucifixes and holy relics housed in gorgeous gold reliquaries. Pierre spotted Cardinal Charles in his red robes bearing a gold chalice decorated with precious stones.

At last the bridegroom appeared. The fourteen-year-old Francis looked terrified. He was thin and frail, and all the jewels in his hat and coat could not make him into a kingly figure. Beside him was King Antoine of Navarre, head of the Bourbon family, the enemies of the Guises. Pierre guessed that someone – perhaps the ever-careful Queen Caterina – had given Antoine this privileged placement as a counterweight to the Guise family, who threatened to dominate the ceremony.

Then the spectators went wild to see the king himself, Henri II, and their war hero, Duke Scarface, walking on either side of the bride.

She wore a dress of pure white.

'White?' said Isabelle, standing behind Pierre and looking over his shoulder. White was the colour of mourning. 'She's wearing white?'

*

ALISON MCKAY had been against the white wedding dress. White was the colour of mourning in France. She feared it would shock people. And it made Mary Stuart look even paler than usual. But Mary could be stubborn, and was as opinionated as any fifteen-year-old, especially about clothing. She had wanted white, and would not even discuss alternatives.

And it had worked. The silk seemed to glow with the purity of Mary's virginity. Over it she wore a mantle of pale blue-grey velvet that shimmered in the April sunlight like the surface of the river that ran alongside the cathedral. The train, of the same material, was heavy, as Alison knew well, for she was one of the two girls carrying it.

Mary wore a golden coronet studded with diamonds, pearls, rubies and sapphires: Alison guessed she must be desperate to take the weight off her head. Around her neck Mary had an enormous jewelled pendant that she had named 'Great Harry' because it was a gift from King Henri.

With her red hair and white skin Mary looked like an angel, and the people loved her. As she advanced on the raised platform, holding the king's arm, the roar of approval moved like a slow wave along the massed ranks of spectators, keeping pace with the progress of the bride.

Alison was a minor figure in this galaxy of royal and noble people, but she basked in the reflected glory of her best friend. Mary and Alison had talked and dreamed of their weddings for as long as she could remember, but this outshone anything they had imagined. It was the justification of Mary's existence. Alison rejoiced for her friend and for herself.

They reached the canopied dais where the groom was waiting.

When the bride and groom stood side by side it was comically obvious that she was a foot taller than he, and there was laughter and some jeering from unruly elements in the crowd. Then the couple knelt down in front of the archbishop of Rouen, and the tableau became less risible.

The king took a ring from his own finger and handed it to the archbishop, and the ceremony began.

Mary made her responses loudly and clearly, while Francis spoke in a low voice so that the crowd would not laugh at his stammer.

Alison recalled, in a flash of memory, that Mary had been wearing white the first time they met. Both Alison's parents had just died of the plague, and she was living in the cold house of her widowed Aunt Janice, a friend of Mary's mother, Marie de Guise. As a kindness, the new orphan was taken to play with the four-year-old queen of Scotland. Mary's nursery was a place of blazing fires and soft cushions and beautiful toys, and while there Alison could forget that she had no mother.

Her visits became frequent. Little Mary looked up to her six-year-old friend. Alison felt rescued from the solemn atmosphere of Aunt Janice's house. After a happy year, they were told that Mary was going away, to live in France. Alison was heartbroken. But Mary, showing early signs of the imperious adult she would become, threw a tantrum and insisted that Alison had to go to France with her; and in the end she got her way.

They had shared a bunk on the rough sea voyage, clinging together for comfort at night, something they still did when they were troubled or scared. They had held hands as they met dozens of colourfully dressed French people who laughed at them for speaking the guttural Scots dialect. Everything was frighteningly strange, and it was the older Alison's turn to be Mary's rescuer, helping her learn unfamiliar French words and refined court manners, comforting her when she cried at night. Alison knew that neither of them would ever forget their childhood devotion to one another.

The ceremony came to an end. At last the gold ring was placed on Mary's finger and they were declared man and wife, and a cheer went up.

At that point two royal heralds carrying leather bags began to toss handfuls of money into the crowd. The people roared their approval. Men leaped into the air to catch the coins, then fell to the ground, scrabbling for those that had escaped their grasp. People in other parts of the square clamoured for their share. Fights broke out. The fallen were trampled while those who remained standing were crushed. Injured ones screamed in pain. Alison found it distasteful, but many of the noble wedding guests laughed uproariously as the commoners fought viciously for loose change: they thought it was better than a bullfight. The heralds threw money until their bags were empty.

The archbishop led the way into the cathedral for the wedding Mass, followed by the newlyweds, two people hardly more than children who were now trapped in a marriage that was hopelessly wrong for both of them. Alison walked behind them, carrying Mary's train. As they all passed out of the sunshine into the cold gloom of the enormous church, she reflected that royal children enjoyed every good thing in life, except freedom.

*

Sylvie held Pierre's arm possessively as they walked south across the Petit Pont bridge. He belonged to her now. She would hold his arm for ever. He was clever, as clever as her father and so much more charming. And wonderfully handsome, with his thick hair and hazel eyes and winning smile. She even liked his clothes, though she felt guilty about being attracted by the flamboyant kind of garments that Protestants disdained.

Most of all, she loved him because he was as serious as she was about the true gospel. All on his own he had come to question the treacherous teachings of Catholic priests. With only a little encouragement from her he had seen his way to the truth. And he was willing to risk his life by coming with her to a secret Protestant church.

The wedding was over, the crowds had dispersed, and the Palot family, now including Pierre Aumande, were heading for their own, Protestant, church.

Now that Sylvie was engaged, she found that she had new

worries. What would it be like to lie with Pierre? Her mother had told her, years ago when her monthly cycles began, what men and women did in bed together, but Isabelle had been uncharacteristically coy about how it made her feel. Sylvie was eager to find out, to have Pierre's hands all over her naked body, to feel his weight on top of her, to see what his private parts looked like.

She had won him, but could she hold his love for a lifetime? Isabelle said that Giles had never even flirted with anyone else, but some men did lose interest in their wives after a time, and Pierre was always going to be attractive to other women. Sylvie might have to work hard to keep him as enchanted as he was now. Their faith would help, especially as they would be working together to spread the gospel.

When would they wed? She wanted to do it as soon as possible. Pierre had mentioned that he would like to bring his mother here from Champagne for the ceremony, if she was well enough to travel. He had been a bit vague, and Sylvie hesitated to press him, feeling bashful about being so impatient.

Isabelle was delighted about the engagement. Sylvie had a feeling that Mama would quite like to marry Pierre herself. Not really, of course, but still . . .

Papa was more pleased than he wanted to reveal, Sylvie guessed. He seemed relaxed and good-tempered, which was the nearest he ever got to happy.

Guillaume was in a sour frame of mind, and Sylvie realized he must be attracted to her himself. Perhaps he had nurtured secret plans to propose. Well, he was too late. If she had never met Pierre she might, perhaps, have liked Guillaume, who was clever and serious. But he would never have looked at her in a way that made her feel that her head was spinning and her legs were weak and she needed to sit down.

What pleased her most was how happy Pierre was this morning. He walked with an eager step, he smiled constantly, and he made her laugh with wry observations about the people and buildings they passed as they walked along the rue

St Jacques through the University district. He was visibly delighted to be engaged to her.

She also knew that he was glad to be invited to a Protestant service at last. More than once he had asked her where her church was, and he had looked hurt when she said she was not allowed to tell him. Now the secrecy could be dropped.

She was impatient to show him off. She felt proud of him and looked forward to introducing him to everyone. They were sure to like him. She hoped he would like them.

They walked out through the St Jacques gate and into the suburbs, where they turned off the road onto a barely perceptible track into a wood. A hundred yards along, out of sight of the road, stood two burly men who had the air of guards even though they did not carry weapons. Giles nodded to them, then jerked a thumb at Pierre and said: 'He's with us.' The group walked past the guards without pausing.

Pierre said to Sylvie: 'Who are those men?'

'They stop anyone they don't know,' she explained. 'If casual strollers wander randomly in this direction, they're told the wood is private.'

'And whose wood is it?'

'It belongs to the marquess of Nîmes.'

'Is he one of the congregation?'

She hesitated. But she could tell him now. No more secrets. 'Yes.'

There were many aristocratic Protestants, Sylvie knew. They could be burned at the stake just like anyone else; although, for heresy as for any crime, noblemen had more chance of escaping punishment through the intervention of powerful friends.

The little group came to what looked like a disused hunting lodge. The lower windows were shuttered, and the weeds flourishing around the main door showed that it had not been opened for years.

Sylvie knew that in a few French towns, where Protestants formed a majority, they had taken over real churches and held services openly, albeit protected by armed guards. But that was not the case in Paris. The capital city was a Catholic stronghold, full of people who made their living serving the Church and the monarchy. Protestants were hated here.

They went around the building to a small side door and entered a great hall where, Sylvie guessed, lavish picnics had once been spread for hunting parties. Now it was silent and dim. Chairs and benches were set out in rows facing a table with a white cloth. About a hundred people were present. As always, there was bread on a plain crockery plate and wine in a jug.

Giles and Isabelle took their seats, and Sylvie and Pierre followed. Guillaume took a single chair facing the congregation.

Pierre whispered: 'So Guillaume is a priest?'

'Pastor,' Sylvie corrected him. 'But he's a visitor. Bernard is the regular pastor.' She pointed to a tall, solemn-looking man in his fifties with thinning grey hair.

'Is the marquess here?'

Sylvie looked around and spotted the portly figure of the marquess of Nîmes. 'Front row,' she murmured. 'Big white collar.'

'Is that his daughter, in the dark green cloak and hat?'

'No, that's the marchioness, Louise.'

'She's young.'

'Twenty. She's his second wife.'

The Mauriac family were there, Luc and Jeanne and their son, Georges, Sylvie's admirer. Sylvie noticed Georges staring at Pierre with surprise and envy. She saw by his face that he knew he could not compete with Pierre. She permitted herself a sinful moment of pride. Pierre was so much more desirable than Georges.

They began by singing a psalm. Pierre whispered: 'No choir?'

'We are the choir.' Sylvie loved being able to sing hymns in French at the top of her voice. It was one of the joys of being a follower of the true gospel. In normal churches she felt like a spectator at a performance, but here she was a participant.

Pierre said: 'You have a beautiful voice.'

It was true, she knew; in fact, it was so good that she was frequently in danger of the sin of pride on that account.

Prayers and Bible readings followed, all in French; then communion. Here the bread and wine were not actually flesh and blood, just symbols, which seemed so much more sensible. Finally, Guillaume preached a fiery sermon about the wickedness of Pope Paul IV. Eighty-one years old, Paul was an intolerant conservative who had beefed up the Inquisition and forced Jews in Rome to wear yellow hats. He was hated by Catholics as well as Protestants.

When the service was over, the chairs were moved into a rough circle, and a different kind of meeting began. 'This part is called fellowship,' Sylvie explained to Pierre. 'We exchange news and discuss all sorts of things. Women are allowed to speak.'

It began with Guillaume making an announcement that surprised Sylvie and everyone else: he was leaving Paris.

He was pleased, he said, that he had been able to help Pastor Bernard and the elders to restructure the congregation along the lines laid down by John Calvin in Geneva. The remarkable spread of Protestantism in France in the last few years was in part due to tight organization and discipline in Calvinist communities such as this one in the Paris suburb of St Jacques. Guillaume was especially thrilled that they had had the confidence to discuss holding the first national Protestant synod the following year.

But he had an itinerant mission, and other congregations needed him. He would be gone by next Sunday.

They had not expected him to stay for ever, but this was abrupt. He had not talked about his departure at all until now. Sylvie could not help thinking that the reason for his sudden decision might be her engagement. She told herself she was veering dangerously close to vanity, and she said a quick prayer for more humility.

Luc Mauriac introduced a note of conflict. 'I'm sorry you're leaving us so soon, Guillaume, because there is an important matter that we haven't yet discussed: the question of heresy within our movement.' Luc had the chin-up pugnaciousness of many small men, but in fact he was an advocate of tolerance. He went on: 'Many of us in this congregation were shocked when Calvin ordered that Michel Servet should be burned at the stake.'

Sylvie knew what he was talking about, as did everyone else in the room. Servet was a Protestant intellectual who had clashed with Calvin over the doctrine of the Trinity. He had been executed in Geneva, to the dismay of Protestants such as Luc Mauriac, who had believed it was only Catholics who would kill those who disagreed with them.

Guillaume said impatiently: 'That happened five years ago.'

'But the question remains unresolved.'

Sylvie nodded vigorously. She felt passionately about this. Protestants demanded tolerance from kings and bishops who disagreed with them: how could they then persecute others? Yet there were many who wanted to be as harsh as the Catholics, or worse.

Guillaume waved a dismissive hand. 'There must be discipline within our movement.' He clearly did not want to have this argument.

His glib tone infuriated Sylvie, and she said loudly: 'But we should not kill one another.' She did not normally say anything during fellowship. Although women could speak, youngsters were not encouraged to voice their opinions. But Sylvie was almost a married woman now and, anyway, she could not remain silent while this issue was the topic. She went on: 'When Servet fought with reason and writing, he should have been repulsed by reason and writing – not violence!'

Luc Mauriac nodded enthusiastic agreement, pleased to be supported so energetically; though some of the older women looked disapproving.

Guillaume said disdainfully: 'Those words are not yours: you're quoting Castellio – another heretic.'

He was right: Sylvie was repeating a sentence from Sebastian Castellio's pamphlet *Should Heretics be Persecuted?*, but she had other resources. She read the books her father printed, and she knew as much as Guillaume about the works of Protestant theologians. 'I'll quote Calvin, if you like,' she said.

'Calvin wrote: "It is unchristian to use arms against those who have been expelled from the Church." Of course, that was when he himself was being persecuted as a heretic.'

She saw several people frown censoriously, and she realized she had gone a little too far, in implying hypocrisy on the part of the great John Calvin.

Guillaume said: 'You're too young to understand.'

'Too young?' Sylvie was outraged. 'You never said I was too young to risk my life selling copies of the books you bring from Geneva!'

Several people began speaking at once, and Pastor Bernard stood up to appeal for calm. 'We're not going to resolve this issue in one afternoon,' he said. 'Let us ask Guillaume to communicate our concerns to John Calvin when he returns to Geneva.'

Luc Mauriac was dissatisfied with that, and said: 'But will Calvin answer us?'

'Of course he will,' Bernard said, without giving any reason why he felt so confident. 'And now let us close our fellowship with a final prayer.' He shut his eyes, tilted his face up to heaven, and began to pray extempore.

In the quietness, Sylvie calmed down. She remembered how much she had looked forward to introducing Pierre to everyone, and hearing herself say the words: *my fiancé*.

After the final amen, the congregation began to talk among themselves. Sylvie led Pierre around the room. She was bursting with pride to have such an attractive man, and she tried hard not to look overly pleased with herself, but it was difficult: she was too happy.

Pierre was as engaging as ever. He spoke respectfully to the men, flirted harmlessly with the older women, and charmed the girls. He paid close attention to Sylvie's introductions, concentrating on remembering all the names, and taking a polite interest in the details of where they lived and what work they did. The Protestants were always pleased by a new convert, and they made him feel welcome.

Things went wrong only when Sylvie introduced Pierre to Louise, the marchioness of Nîmes. She was the daughter of a prosperous wine merchant in Champagne. She was attractive, with a big bust, which was probably what had caught the attention of the middle-aged marquess. She was a tense girl, and had a haughty manner that she had adopted, Sylvie guessed, because she was not an aristocrat by birth, and felt unsure in her role as marchioness. But she could be witheringly sarcastic if crossed.

Pierre made the mistake of amiably treating her as a compatriot. 'I'm from Champagne too,' he said; then, with a smile, he added: 'We're country bumpkins in the city, you and I.'

He did not mean it, of course. There was nothing unsophisticated about him or Louise. His remark was a facetious pleasantry. But he had chosen the wrong subject for a joke. He could hardly have known it, but Sylvie understood that Louise's greatest fear was that she would strike people as a country bumpkin.

Her reaction was instant. She paled, and her face froze into an expression of disdain. She tilted her head back as if there was a bad smell. Raising her voice so that people nearby could hear, she said frostily: 'Even in Champagne, they should teach young men to be respectful to their superiors.'

Pierre went red.

Louise turned away and spoke quietly to someone else, leaving Pierre and Sylvie staring at her back.

Sylvie was mortified. The marchioness had taken against her fiancé, and Sylvie felt sure she would never change her mind. Worse, many in the congregation had heard, and everyone would know about it before the hall was empty. Sylvie feared that now they might never accept Pierre as one of them. She was crestfallen.

Then she looked at Pierre, and saw on his face an expression he had never previously worn. His mouth was twisted into a line of resentment, and hatred blazed from his eyes. He looked as if he could have killed Louise.

My goodness, Sylvie thought, I hope he never looks at me like that.

*

By BEDTIME ALISON was exhausted, and she felt sure Mary must feel the same, but the greatest trial was yet to come.

The celebrations were lavish, even by the standards of royal Paris. After the wedding there was a banquet at the archbishop's palace, followed by a ball. Then the entire wedding party moved to the Palais de la Cité – a short journey that took hours because of the crowds – for a masked ball, with special entertainments including twelve mechanical horses on which the royal children could ride. Finally, there was a buffet supper featuring more pastries than Alison had ever seen in one room. But now, at last, all was quiet, and there was only one ceremony left to perform.

Alison pitied Mary this last duty. The idea of lying with Francis as a woman lies with a man was unpleasant, like doing it with a brother. And if anything went wrong it would be a public catastrophe, talked about in every city in Europe. Mary would want to die. Alison dreaded the thought of her friend suffering such humiliation.

Royal people had to bear this kind of burden, she knew; that was part of the price they paid for their privileged lives. And Mary had to go through it all without her mother. Marie de Guise ruled Scotland, standing in for Mary, and could not risk leaving that country even for her daughter's wedding, so tenuous was the hold of the Catholic monarchy on the quarrelsome, rebellious Scots. Sometimes Alison wondered if it would not be better to be the carefree daughter of a baker, petting in a doorway with a randy apprentice.

Alison was only one of the ladies of the court assembled to wash and dress the bride for her deflowering. But she needed just a minute alone with Mary before the big moment.

They undressed her. Mary was nervous and shivering, but she looked beautiful: tall, pale and slim, with perfect shallow breasts and long legs. The women washed her with warm water, trimmed her fair pubic hair, and doused her with perfume. Finally they helped her dress in a nightgown embroidered with gold thread. She put on satin slippers, a lace nightcap, and a light cloak of fine wool to keep her warm between the dressing room and the bedchamber.

She was ready, but none of the women showed any inclination to withdraw. Alison was forced to speak to her in a whisper. 'Tell them all to wait outside – I *must* speak to you alone!'

'Why?'

'Trust me – please!'

Mary rose to the occasion. 'Thank you, ladies, all,' she said. 'Now please give me a few moments alone with Alison while I prepare my mind.'

The women looked resentful – most of them were superior in rank to Alison – but no one could refuse such a request from the bride, and reluctantly they trooped out.

At last Alison and Mary were alone.

Alison spoke in the same plain language Queen Caterina had used. 'If Francis doesn't fuck you, the marriage will be unconsummated, and that would mean it could be annulled.'

Mary understood. 'And if that happens, I will never be queen of France.'

'Exactly.'

'But I don't know if Francis can manage it!' Mary looked distraught.

'Nobody knows,' Alison said. 'So, whatever happens tonight, you're going to *pretend* he's done it.'

Mary nodded, and her face took on the determined expression that was one of the reasons Alison loved her. She said: 'All right, but will people believe me?'

'Yes, if you follow the advice of Queen Caterina.'

'Is this why she summoned you yesterday?'

'Yes. She says you must make sure Francis lies on top of you and at least pretends to fuck you.'

'I can do that, but it may not be enough to convince the witnesses.'

Alison put a hand into her gown and withdrew what she had been carrying there. 'The queen gave me this for you,' she said. 'There's a pocket for it in your nightdress.'

'What's in it?'

'Blood.'

'Whose?'

'I don't know,' Alison said, although she could guess. 'Never mind where it comes from, the important thing is where it goes – onto the sheets of the bridal bed.' She showed Mary the end of the thread that sealed the neck. 'One pull on this will untie the knot.'

'So they will all think I've lost my maidenhead.'

'But no one must see the bag – so stuff it up inside yourself immediately, and leave it there until later.'

Mary looked horrified and disgusted, but only for a moment; and her brave spirit took over. 'All right,' she said, and Alison wanted to cry.

There was a knock at the door, and a woman's voice called: 'Prince Francis is ready for you, Queen Mary.'

'One more thing,' said Alison in a low voice. 'If Francis fails, you must never tell anyone the truth – not your mother, not your confessor, not even me. You will always smile shyly and say that Francis did what a bridegroom should do, and he did it perfectly.'

Mary nodded slowly. 'Yes,' she said thoughtfully. 'You're right. The only sure way to keep a secret is eternal silence.'

Alison hugged Mary, then said: 'Don't worry. Francis will do anything you say. He adores you.'

Mary composed herself. 'Let us go.'

Surrounded by ladies-in-waiting, Mary walked slowly down the staircase to the principal floor. She had to pass through the large guardroom of the Swiss mercenaries, then the king's antechamber, stared at by everyone she passed, until she came to the royal bedchamber.

In the middle of the room was a four-poster bed covered only with fine white sheets. At each corner were heavy brocade and lace curtains, tied back to the posts. Francis stood waiting, dressed in a gorgeous gown over a cambric nightshirt, looking boyish in a nightcap too big for his head.

Standing and sitting around the bed were fifteen or so men and a handful of women. Mary's uncles, Duke François and

Cardinal Charles, were there, with the king and queen and a selection of important courtiers and senior priests.

Alison had not realized there would be so many.

They were talking in low voices, but fell silent when they saw Mary.

She stopped and said: 'Are they going to draw the drapes?'

Alison shook her head. 'Just the lace curtains,' she said. 'The act must be witnessed.'

Mary swallowed, then bravely moved forward. She took Francis's hand and smiled encouragingly. He looked scared.

She stepped out of her slippers and let her cloak fall to the floor. Standing in front of all these fully dressed people, wearing only a white nightdress of fine fabric, she looked to Alison like a sacrifice.

Francis seemed paralysed. Mary helped him out of his gown, then led him to the bed. The two young people climbed onto the high mattress and pulled the single sheet over themselves.

Alison drew the lace curtains around them. It gave them only token privacy. Their heads were visible and the shapes of their bodies showed clearly under the sheet.

Alison could hardly breathe as she watched Mary snuggle up to Francis, murmuring in his ear, words that no one else could hear, probably telling him what he had to do or pretend to do. They kissed. The sheet moved, but it was not possible to see exactly what was going on. Alison felt painfully sorry for Mary. She imagined herself making love for the first time in front of twenty witnesses. It seemed impossible. But Mary was bravely going ahead. Alison could not read the expressions on the faces of the bridal couple, but she guessed Mary was trying to reassure Francis and get him to relax.

Then Mary rolled on her back and Francis clambered on top of her.

Alison found the tension almost unbearable. Would it happen? And, if not, would Mary succeed in pretending it had? Could all these older people be fooled?

The room was dead silent except for Mary's words to Francis, murmured so low that the sense could not be made out. They could have been loving endearments or, equally, detailed instructions.

The two bodies manoeuvred awkwardly. From the position of Mary's arms, it looked as if she was guiding Francis inside her – or pretending to.

Mary gave a short, sharp cry of pain. Alison could not tell whether it was genuine, but the audience muttered approval. Francis looked shocked and stopped moving, but Mary embraced him comfortingly under the sheets, pulling his body to her own.

Then the couple began to move together. Alison had never watched people doing this, so she had no idea whether it looked real. She glanced at the faces of the men and women around her. They were tense, fascinated and embarrassed, but not, she felt, sceptical. They seemed to believe they were watching actual intercourse, not a pantomime.

She did not know how long it was supposed to last. She had not thought to ask that question. Nor had Mary. Instinct told Alison that the first time might be quick.

After a minute or two there was a sudden movement, as if Francis's body was convulsing – or Mary was jerking her own body to make it look that way. Then the two of them relaxed and the movement stopped.

The audience looked on in silence.

Alison stopped breathing. Had they done it? If not, would Mary remember the little bag?

After a pause, Mary pushed Francis off her and sat upright. She wriggled under the sheet, apparently pulling her nightgown down around her legs, and Francis did something similar.

Mary spoke in a commanding tone. 'Draw back the lace curtains!'

Several ladies hurried to do her bidding.

When the lace was tied back, Mary dramatically threw off the top sheet.

There was a small red bloodstain on the bottom sheet.

The courtiers burst into applause. The deed was done. The marriage had been consummated, and all was well.

Alison felt helpless with relief. She clapped and cheered along with the others, while wondering what had really happened.

She would never know.

7

NED WAS FURIOUS WHEN Sir Reginald Fitzgerald refused
to sign the papers transferring ownership of the old priory to
Alice Willard.

Reginald was the mayor of a trading city: it was shockingly
bad for the town's reputation. Most citizens were on Alice's
side. They, too, had contracts which they could not afford to see
broken.

Alice had to go to court to force Sir Reginald to fulfil his
promise.

Ned had no doubt that the court would uphold the contract,
but the delay was maddening. He and his mother were keen to
inaugurate their indoor market. While they waited for the
hearing, days and weeks went by when the Willard family
was not making money. It was fortunate that Alice had a
modest income from the row of cottages in the parish of St
Mark's.

'What's the point?' Ned asked in frustration. 'Reginald can't
win.'

'Self-deception,' said Alice. 'He made a bad investment, and
he wants to blame everyone but himself.'

Four times a year, important cases were heard at the Quarter
Sessions by two Justices of the Peace assisted by a Clerk of the
Peace. Alice's lawsuit was put down for the June Quarter
Sessions, and was the first case of the day.

The Kingsbridge courthouse was a former dwelling house
on the high street, next to the Guild Hall. The court sat in what
had been the dining hall of the house. Other rooms were
offices for the justices and clerks. The basement served as a jail.

Ned arrived at the court with his mother. A crowd of
townspeople stood around the room, talking. Sir Reginald was

already there, with Rollo. Ned was glad Margery was not present: he did not want her to see her father's humiliation.

Ned nodded stiffly to Rollo. He could no longer act friendly with the Fitzgerald family: the lawsuit had put an end to that pretence. He still greeted Margery when he saw her in the street. She reacted with embarrassment. But Ned loved her, and he believed she felt the same, despite everything.

Dan Cobley and Donal Gloster were also in court. The ill-fated ship the *St Margaret* might be mentioned, and the Cobleys would want to hear anything that was said about them.

Dan and the other Protestants arrested in Widow Pollard's barn had been released on bail, all but Philbert, who was undoubtedly the leader. Philbert was in the basement jail, having been interrogated by Bishop Julius. They would all be tried tomorrow, not at the Quarter Sessions but at the independent church court.

Donal Gloster had escaped arrest. He had not been with his employer at Widow Pollard's barn: the story going around town was that he had been at home drunk, luckily for him. Ned might have suspected that Donal was the one who had betrayed the location of the Protestant service, except that his story had been confirmed by several people who had seen him staggering out of the Slaughterhouse that afternoon.

The clerk, Paul Pettit, called for silence, and the two justices came in and took their seats at one end of the room. The senior justice was Rodney Tilbury, a retired cloth merchant. He wore a rich blue doublet and several large rings. He had been appointed by Queen Mary Tudor, being a staunch Catholic, but Ned did not think that would make any difference today, for the case had nothing to do with religion. The second justice, Seb Chandler, was friendly with Sir Reginald, but again Ned did not see how he could go against the plain facts of the case.

The jury were sworn in: twelve men, all Kingsbridge citizens.

Rollo stepped forward immediately and said: 'I will speak for my father this morning, with your worships' permission.'

Ned was not surprised. Sir Reginald was irascible, and quite likely to spoil his own case by bad temper. Rollo was just as clever as Reginald, but better controlled.

Justice Tilbury nodded. 'As I recall, you studied law at Gray's Inn in London, Mr Fitzgerald.'

'Yes, your worship.'

'Very well.'

As the proceedings were beginning, in walked Bishop Julius, dressed in his priestly robes. His presence was no mystery. He wanted the priory buildings for himself, and Reginald had promised to sell them to him cheaply. He must be hoping that Reginald would find a way to wriggle out of his contract.

Alice stepped forward. She presented the case herself, and handed the signed and sealed contract to the clerk. 'Sir Reginald cannot deny the three key facts,' Alice said. She spoke in the mild, reasonable tone of one who merely wishes to point out the truth. 'One, that he signed the contract; two, that he took the money; and three, that he has not paid it back within the promised time. I ask the court to rule that he has quite clearly forfeited the security. That, after all, is what a security is for.'

Alice was confident of victory, and Ned did not see how any court could possibly rule for Reginald, unless the judges were bribed – and where would Reginald get the money for a bribe?

Tilbury thanked Alice politely and turned to Rollo. 'What have you got to say to that, Mr Fitzgerald? It seems pretty clear-cut.'

But Reginald did not give his son time to reply. 'I was cheated!' he burst out, his freckled face turning pink. 'Philbert Cobley knew perfectly well that the St Margaret had gone into Calais and was likely to be lost.'

Ned thought that was probably true. Philbert was as slippery as a live fish. All the same, Reginald's demand was outrageous. Why should the Willard family pay for Philbert's dishonesty?

Philbert's son, Dan Cobley, shouted out: 'That's a lie! How could we possibly have known what the French king would do?'

'You must have known something!' Reginald shot back.

Dan replied with a quotation from the Bible. 'The book of Proverbs tells us: "A prudent man concealeth knowledge".'

Bishop Julius pointed a bony finger at Dan and said furiously: 'This is what happens when ignorant fools are allowed to read the Bible in English – they cite God's word to justify their crimes!'

The clerk stood up and shouted for quiet, and they all calmed down.

Tilbury said: 'Thank you, Sir Reginald. Even if it were true that Philbert Cobley, or any other third party, cheated you out of money, that would not release you from your contract with Alice Willard. If that is the basis of your argument, you are clearly in the wrong, and the court will rule against you.'

Exactly, Ned thought with satisfaction.

Rollo spoke immediately. 'No, your worships, that is not our argument, and I beg your pardon for my father's intervention, but you will understand that he feels very angry.'

'So what *is* your argument? I'm eager to hear, and I'm sure the jury are too.'

So was Ned. Did Rollo have something up his sleeve? He was a nasty bully, but he was no fool.

'Simply that Alice Willard is guilty of usury,' said Rollo. 'She loaned Sir Reginald four hundred pounds, but she demanded to be repaid four hundred and twenty-four pounds. She is charging interest, which is a crime.'

Suddenly Ned recalled his mother's conversation with Bishop Julius in the cloisters of the ruined priory. Alice had told Julius the exact amount of the debt, and Julius had seemed momentarily struck by the figure, though in the end he had not commented. And here Julius was in court for the hearing. Ned frowned anxiously. The contract between Alice and Sir Reginald had been drawn carefully, so that there was no reference to interest; but the definition of usury was notoriously a grey area of law.

Alice said firmly: 'No interest was payable. The contract states that Sir Reginald will pay rent of eight pounds a month for the continued use of the priory until the loan is repaid or the property is forfeited.'

Reginald protested: 'Why would I pay rent? I never use the place! This was nothing less than concealed usury.'

Alice said: 'But you proposed it!'

'I was misled.'

The clerk interrupted: 'Please! Address the court, not each other.'

Justice Tilbury said: 'Thank you, Mr Pettit. Quite right.'

Rollo said: 'The court cannot enforce a contract that requires a party to commit a crime.'

Tilbury said: 'Yes, I have grasped that point. So you're asking the court to decide whether the extra money payable under the contract is genuinely rent or a concealed form of usury.'

'No, your worship, I am not asking you to decide. With your permission, I will bring an authoritative witness who will testify that this is usury.'

Ned was bewildered. What was he talking about?

The two justices seemed equally puzzled. Tilbury said: 'An authoritative witness? Who do you have in mind?'

'The bishop of Kingsbridge.'

A murmur of surprise went up from the watching crowd. No one had anticipated this. Justice Tilbury looked as startled as anyone. However, after a few moments he said: 'Very well. What have you got to say, my lord bishop?'

Ned was dismayed: everyone knew whose side Julius was on.

Julius walked slowly to the front, his bald head high, making the most of the dignity of his office. As expected, he said: 'The so-called rent is clearly disguised interest. Sir Reginald did not use the land and buildings during the period in question, and had never intended so to do. This was nothing but a flimsy cover for the sin and crime of usury.'

Alice said: 'I protest. The bishop is not an unbiased witness. Sir Reginald has promised the priory to him.'

Rollo said: 'Surely you do not accuse the bishop of dishonesty?'

Alice replied: 'I accuse you of asking the cat whether the mouse should be allowed to go free.'

The crowd laughed: they appreciated wit in argument. But Justice Tilbury did not. 'This court can hardly contradict the bishop on a question of sin,' he said severely. 'It seems the jury will have to rule that the contract is invalid.' He looked unhappy about it, for he knew as well as anyone that many contracts made by Kingsbridge traders might be undermined by such a ruling; but Rollo had backed him into a corner.

Now Rollo said: 'It is no longer a matter merely of invalidating the contract, your worships.' The look of malicious satisfaction on his face worried Ned. Rollo went on: 'Alice Willard has been proved guilty of a crime. I submit that it is the duty of the court to impose the punishment laid down in the Act of 1552.'

Ned did not know what punishment was specified by the law.

Alice said: 'I will plead guilty to usury – on one condition.'

Tilbury said: 'All right, what?'

'There is another person in this court who is as guilty as I am, and he must be punished too.'

'If you're referring to Sir Reginald, the crime attaches to the lender, not the borrower—'

'Not Sir Reginald.'

'Who, then?'

'The bishop of Kingsbridge.'

Julius looked angry. 'Take care what you say, Alice Willard.'

Alice said: 'Last October you pre-sold the fleeces of a thousand sheep to Widow Mercer for ten pence each.' Widow Mercer was the biggest wool dealer in town. 'The sheep were sheared this April, and Mrs Mercer sold the fleeces to Philbert Cobley for twelve pence each, two pence more than she paid you. You forfeited two pence per fleece in order to have your money six months earlier. You paid forty per cent annual interest.'

There was a mutter of approval. Most of the leading citizens were traders, and they understood percentages.

Julius said: 'I am not on trial here, you are.'

Alice ignored that. 'In February you bought stone from the earl's quarry for the extension to your palace. The price was three pounds, but the earl's quarrymaster offered you a reduction of a shilling in the pound for advance payment, which you accepted. The stone was delivered by barge a month later. In effect, you charged the earl sixty per cent interest on the money you paid early.'

The crowd were beginning to enjoy this, and Ned heard laughter and a ripple of applause. Pettit shouted: 'Silence!'

Alice said: 'In April you sold a flour mill in Wigleigh—'

'This is irrelevant,' Julius said. 'You cannot excuse yourself by claiming, plausibly or otherwise, that other people have committed similar crimes.'

Tilbury said: 'The bishop is right about that. I direct the jury to declare Alice Willard guilty of usury.'

Ned harboured a faint hope that the businessmen in the jury might protest, but they did not have the nerve to challenge such a clear direction from the justices, and after a moment they all nodded agreement.

Tilbury said: 'We will now consider the question of punishment.'

Rollo spoke again. 'The Act of 1552 is very clear, your worships. The culprit must lose both interest and principal of the loan and, in addition, "fines and ransom at the king's will or pleasure", to quote the exact words of the law.'

Ned shouted: 'No!' Surely his mother could not forfeit the four hundred pounds as well as the interest?

The Kingsbridge folk felt the same, and there was a mutinous hubbub. Paul Pettit had to call for silence again.

The crowd eventually went quiet, but Tilbury did not immediately speak. He turned to his fellow justice, Seb Chandler, and they held a murmured conversation. Then Tilbury summoned Pettit to join them. The silence grew tense. The justices talked to Pettit, who was a qualified lawyer, as were all Clerks of the Peace. They appeared to be arguing, with Pettit shaking his head in negation. Finally, Tilbury shrugged and turned away, Seb Chandler nodded agreement, and Pettit returned to his seat.

At last Tilbury spoke. 'The law is the law,' he said, and Ned knew at once that his mother was ruined. 'Alice Willard must forfeit both the amount of the loan and the additional rent or interest demanded.' He had to raise his voice over the noise of protest. 'No further punishment will be necessary.'

Ned stared at his mother. Alice was stricken. Until now she had been defiant. But she had been up against the full power of the Church, and her resistance had been hopeless. Now she was suddenly diminished: dazed, pale, bewildered. She looked like one who has been knocked off her feet by a charging horse.

The clerk said: 'Next case.'

Ned and his mother left the court and walked down the main street to their house without speaking. Ned's life had been turned upside down and he could hardly digest the implications. Six months ago he had been sure of spending his life as a merchant, and almost sure of marrying Margery. Now he had no employment and Margery was engaged to Bart.

They went into the parlour. 'At least we won't starve,' Alice said. 'We've still got the houses in St Mark's.'

Ned had not expected his mother to be so pessimistic. 'Won't you find a way to start again?'

Alice shook her head wearily. 'I'll be fifty soon – I haven't got the energy. Besides, when I look back over the past year, I seem to have lost my judgement. I should have moved some of the traffic away from Calais when the war broke out last June. I should have developed the Seville connection more. And I should never have lent money to Reginald Fitzgerald, no matter how much pressure he put on me. Now there's no business left for you and your brother to inherit.'

'Barney won't mind,' Ned said. 'He'd rather be at sea anyway.'

'I wonder where he is now. We must tell him, if we can locate him.'

'He's probably in the Spanish army.' They had received a letter from Aunt Betsy. Barney and Carlos had got into trouble with the Inquisition and had been forced to leave Seville in a hurry. Betsy was not sure where they had gone, but a neighbour thought he had seen them listening to a recruiting captain down at the dockside.

Alice said glumly: 'But I don't know what you'll do, Ned. I've brought you up to be a merchant.'

'Sir William Cecil said he needed a young man like me to work for him.'

She brightened. 'So he did. I had forgotten.'

'He may have forgotten, too.'

Alice shook her head. 'I doubt he ever forgets anything.'

Ned wondered what it might be like, working for Cecil, being part of Elizabeth Tudor's household. 'I wonder if Elizabeth will be queen one day?'

His mother spoke with sudden bitterness. 'If she is, perhaps she'll get rid of some of these arrogant bishops.'

Ned began to see a glimmer of hope.

Alice said: 'I'll write to Cecil for you, if you like.'

'I don't know,' Ned said. 'I might simply show up on his doorstep.'

'He might simply send you home again.'

'Yes,' said Ned. 'He might.'

*

THE REVENGE OF the Fitzgeralds continued the next day.

The weather was hot, but the south transept of Kingsbridge Cathedral was cool in the afternoon. All the leading citizens were there for the Church court. The Protestants arrested in Widow Pollard's barn were on trial for heresy. Few people were ever found not guilty, everyone knew that. The main question was how harsh the punishments would be.

Philbert Cobley faced the most serious charges. He was not in the cathedral when Ned arrived, but Mrs Cobley stood there weeping helplessly. Pretty Ruth Cobley was red-eyed, and Dan's round face looked uncharacteristically grim. Philbert's sister and Mrs Cobley's brother were trying to give comfort.

Bishop Julius was in charge. This was his court. He was prosecutor as well as judge – and there was no jury. Beside him sat Canon Stephen Lincoln, a young sidekick, handing him documents and making notes. Next to Stephen was the dean of

Kingsbridge, Luke Richards. Deans were independent of bishops and did not always follow their orders: Luke was the only hope for mercy today.

One by one the Protestants confessed their sins and recanted their beliefs. By doing so they escaped physical punishment. They were given fines, which most of them paid to the bishop immediately.

Dan Cobley was their deputy leader, according to Julius, and he was given an additional, humiliating sentence: he had to parade through the streets of Kingsbridge wearing only a nightshirt, carrying a crucifix, and chanting the paternoster in Latin.

But Philbert was the leader, and everyone was waiting to see what his sentence would be.

Suddenly the crowd's attention turned to the nave of the church.

Following the direction in which they were looking, Ned saw Osmund Carter approaching, in his leather helmet and laced knee boots. He was with another member of the watch, and they were carrying between them a wooden chair that had on it some kind of bundle. Looking more closely, Ned saw that the bundle was Philbert Cobley.

Philbert was stocky, an imposing figure in spite of being short. Or he had been. Now his legs hung loose over the edge of the chair and his arms dangled limply at his sides. He groaned in pain constantly, his eyes closed. Ned heard Mrs Cobley scream at the sight.

The watchmen put the chair down in front of Bishop Julius and stood back.

The chair had arms that prevented Philbert from falling sideways, but he could not hold himself upright, and he began to slip down in the chair.

His family rushed to him. Dan took him under the arms and lifted him back: Philbert screamed in agony. Ruth pushed at Philbert's hips to keep him in a sitting position. Mrs Cobley moaned: 'Oh, Phil, my Phil, what have they done to you?'

Ned realized what had happened: Philbert had been tortured on the rack. His wrists had been attached to two posts, then his ankles had been tied with ropes that were wrapped around a geared wheel. As the gears were turned, the wheel tightened the rope and the victim's body was stretched agonizingly. This form of torment had been devised because priests were forbidden to shed blood.

Philbert had obviously resisted, and refused to recant his beliefs, despite the pain, so the torture had continued until the shoulder and hip joints had been completely dislocated. He was now a helpless cripple.

Bishop Julius said: 'Philbert Cobley has admitted to leading gullible fools into heresy.'

Canon Lincoln brandished a document. 'Here is his signed confession.'

Dan Cobley approached the judges' table. 'Show me,' he said.

Lincoln hesitated and looked at Julius. The court was under no obligation to the son of the accused man. But Julius probably did not want to provoke further protests from the crowd. He shrugged, and Lincoln gave the papers to Dan.

Dan looked at the last page and said: 'This is not my father's signature.' He showed it to the men nearest him. 'Any one of you knows my father's hand. This is not it.'

Several of them nodded agreement.

Julius said irritably: 'He was not able to sign unassisted, obviously.'

Dan said: 'So you stretched him until—' He choked, tears rolling down his face, but he forced himself to go on. 'You stretched him until he was unable to write – and yet you pretend that he signed this.'

'Pretend? Are you accusing a bishop of lying?'

'I'm saying my father never admitted to heresy.'

'How could you possibly know—'

'He did not believe himself to be a heretic, and the only reason he would have said the opposite was torture.'

'He was prayerfully persuaded of the error of his ways.'

Dan pointed dramatically to his father's hideous form. 'Is this what happens to a man when the bishop of Kingsbridge prays for him?'

'The court will not hear any more of this insolence!'

Ned Willard spoke up. 'Where is the rack?'

The three priests looked at him in silence.

'Philbert has been racked, that's obvious – but where?' Ned said. 'Here in the cathedral? In the bishop's palace? Underneath the courthouse? Where is the rack kept? I think the citizens of Kingsbridge are entitled to know. Torture is a crime in England, except when licensed by the Privy Council. Who has been given permission to carry out torture in Kingsbridge?'

After a long pause, Stephen Lincoln said: 'There is no rack in Kingsbridge.'

Ned digested this fact. 'So Philbert was tortured elsewhere. Do you imagine that makes it all right?' He pointed a finger at Bishop Julius. 'It doesn't matter if he was tortured in Egypt – if you sent him there, you are the torturer.'

'Be silent!'

Ned decided he had made his point. He turned his back and stepped away.

At that point Dean Luke stood up. He was a tall, stooped man of forty with a mild manner and thinnish greying hair. 'My lord bishop, I urge you to be merciful,' he said. 'Philbert is undoubtedly a heretic and a fool, but he is also a Christian, and in his misguided way he seeks to worship God. No man should be executed for that.' He sat down.

There was a collective sound of agreement from the watching citizens. They were mostly Catholics, but they had been Protestants under the two previous monarchs, and none of them felt entirely safe.

Bishop Julius gave the dean a look of withering contempt, but did not reply to his plea. He said: 'Philbert Cobley is guilty, not just of heresy but of spreading heresy. As is usual in such cases, he is sentenced to be excommunicated and then burned to death. The execution will be carried out by the secular authorities tomorrow at dawn.'

There were several different methods of execution. Noblemen normally benefited from the quickest, having their heads chopped off, which was instant if the executioner was skilled, and took only a minute if he was clumsy and needed several blows with the axe before the neck was fully severed. Traitors were hung, disembowelled while still living, then hacked into pieces. Anyone who robbed the Church was flayed, his skin cut off him with a very sharp knife while he was still alive: an expert could take off the skin in one piece. Heretics were burned alive.

The townspeople were not completely taken by surprise, but all the same they greeted the sentence with a horrified silence. No one had yet been burned in Kingsbridge. Ned thought that a ghastly line was being crossed, and he sensed that his neighbours felt the same.

Suddenly Philbert's voice was heard, loud and surprisingly strong: he must have been saving his remaining energy for this. 'I thank God that my agony has almost ended, Julius – but yours has yet to begin, you blaspheming devil.' There was a gasp of shock at this insult, and Julius leaped to his feet, outraged; but a condemned man was traditionally allowed his say. 'Soon you will go to hell, where you belong, Julius, and your torment will *never* end. And may God damn your eternal soul.'

The curse of a dying man was especially potent, and though Julius would have scorned such superstition, nevertheless he was trembling with rage and fear. 'Take him away!' he shouted. 'And clear the church – this court is closed!' He turned and stormed out through the south door.

Ned and his mother went home in a grim silence. The Fitzgeralds had won. They had killed the man who cheated them; they had stolen the Willards' fortune; and they had kept their daughter from marrying Ned. It was total defeat.

Janet Fife served them a desultory supper of cold ham. Alice drank several glasses of sherry wine. 'Will you go to Hatfield?' she asked him as Janet cleared away.

'I still haven't decided. Margery isn't married yet.'

'But even if Bart were to drop dead tomorrow, they still wouldn't let her marry you.'

'She turned sixteen last week. In five years' time, she'll be able to marry whoever she likes.'

'But you can't stand still, like a ship becalmed, for so long. Don't let this blight your life.'

She was right, he knew.

He went to bed early and lay awake. Today's dreadful proceedings made him more inclined to go to Hatfield, but still he could not make up his mind. It would be giving up hope.

He drifted off to sleep in the small hours, and was awakened by sounds outside. Looking out of his bedroom window he saw men in the market square, their movements illuminated by half a dozen flaming torches. They were bringing dry sticks for the execution. Sheriff Matthewson was there, a big man wearing a sword, supervising the preparations: a priest could condemn a man to death, but could not carry out the sentence himself.

Ned put on a coat over his nightshirt and went outside. The morning air smelled of wood smoke.

The Cobley family were there, and most of the other Protestants arrived shortly afterwards. The crowd swelled within minutes. By first light, as the torch flames seemed to fade, there were at least a thousand people in the square in front of the cathedral. The men of the watch forced the spectators to keep their distance.

The crowd was noisy, but they fell silent when Osmund Carter appeared from the direction of the Guild Hall, with another watchman, the two men again carrying Philbert between them on a wooden chair. They had to force their way through the crowd, who made way reluctantly, as if they would have liked to obstruct the progress of the chair but did not quite have the courage.

The women of the Cobley family wailed piteously as the helpless man was tied upright to a wooden stake in the ground. He kept slipping down on his useless legs, and Osmund had to bind him tightly to keep him in place.

The watchmen piled firewood around him while Bishop Julius intoned a prayer in Latin.

Osmund picked up one of the torches that had lit their night-time labours. He stood in front of Philbert and looked at Sheriff Matthewson, who held up a hand indicating that Osmund should wait. Matthewson then looked at Julius.

In the pause, Mrs Cobley started screaming, and her family had to hold her.

Julius nodded, Matthewson dropped his arm, and Osmund put the torch to the firewood around Philbert's legs.

The dry wood caught quickly and the flames crackled with hellish merriment. Philbert cried out feebly at the heat. Wood smoke choked the nearest watchers, who backed away.

Soon there was another smell, one that was at once familiar and sickening, the smell of roasting meat. Philbert began to scream in pain. In between screams he yelled: 'Take me, Jesus! Take me, Lord! Now, please, now!' But Jesus did not take him yet.

Ned had heard that merciful judges sometimes allowed the family to hang a bag of gunpowder around the neck of the condemned man so that his end would be quick. But Julius evidently had not permitted that kindness. The lower half of Philbert's body burned while he remained alive. The noise he made in his agony was unbearable to hear, more like the squealing of a terrified animal than the sound of a man.

At last Philbert fell silent. Perhaps his heart gave out; perhaps the smoke suffocated him; perhaps the heat boiled his brain. The fire continued to burn, and the dead body of Philbert turned into a blackened ruin. The smell was disgusting, but at least the noise had stopped. Ned thanked God it was over at last.

*

In my short life I had never seen anything so dreadful. I did not know how men could do such things, and I did not understand why God would let them.

My mother said something that I have remembered all the subsequent years: 'When a man is certain that he knows God's will, and is resolved to do it regardless of the cost, he is the most dangerous person in the world.'

When the spectators began to drift away from the marketplace I remained. The sun rose, though it did not shine on the smouldering remains, which were in the cold shadow of the cathedral. I was thinking about Sir William Cecil, and our conversation about Elizabeth on the Twelfth Day of Christmas. He had said, 'She has told me many times that if she should become queen, it is her dearest wish that no Englishman should lose his life for the sake of his beliefs. I think that's an ideal worthy of a man's faith.'

At the time it had struck me as a pious hope. But after what I had just seen, I thought again. Was it even possible that Elizabeth would get rid of dogmatic bishops such as Julius and end scenes such as the one I had just witnessed? Might there come a time when people of different faiths did not kill one another?

But would Elizabeth become queen when Mary Tudor died? That would depend, I supposed, on what kind of help she got. She had the formidable William Cecil, but one man was not enough. She needed an army of supporters.

And I could be one.

The prospect lifted my heart. I stared at the ashes of Philbert Cobley. I felt sure it did not have to be like this. There were people in England who wanted to stop this happening.

And I wanted to be with them. I wanted to fight for Elizabeth's tolerant ideals.

No more burnings.

I decided to go to Hatfield.

8

NED WALKED FROM Kingsbridge to Hatfield, a journey of a hundred miles, not knowing whether he would be welcomed and given employment, or sent ignominiously home.

For the first two days he was with a group of students going to Oxford. Everyone travelled in groups: a man on his own was in danger of being robbed; a woman on her own was more vulnerable to worse dangers.

As he had been taught by his mother, Ned talked to everyone he met, acquiring information that might or might not be useful: prices of wool, leather, iron ore, and gunpowder; news of plagues and storms and floods; bankruptcies and riots; aristocratic weddings and funerals.

Each night he stayed in taverns, often sharing beds, an unpleasant experience for a boy from the merchant class used to his own room. However, the students were lively companions on the road, switching from coarse jokes to theological arguments and back again effortlessly. The July weather was warm, but at least it did not rain.

During pauses in the conversation, Ned worried about what awaited him at Hatfield Palace. He hoped to be greeted as just the young assistant they were looking for. But Cecil might say: 'Ned who?' If he was rejected, he did not know quite what he would do next. It would be humiliating to return to Kingsbridge with his tail between his legs. Perhaps he would go to London, and try his luck in the big city.

In Oxford he stayed at Kingsbridge College. Established by the great Prior Philip as an outpost of Kingsbridge Priory, it had become independent of the monastery, but it still provided accommodation for students from Kingsbridge, and hospitality to Kingsbridge citizens.

It was more difficult to find travelling companions for the journey from Oxford to Hatfield. Most people were going to London, which was out of Ned's way. While waiting he fell under the spell of the university. He liked the lively discussions about all kinds of topics, from where the Garden of Eden was to how the Earth could be round without people falling off it. Most students would become priests, a few lawyers or doctors; Ned's mother had told him he would learn nothing at a university that could be of use to a merchant. Now he wondered if she had been right. She was wise, but not omniscient.

After four days he joined a group of pilgrims going to St Albans Cathedral. That took another three days. Then he took a chance and walked alone the last seven miles from St Albans to his destination.

King Henry VIII had confiscated Hatfield Palace from the bishop of Ely, and had used it as an occasional nursery for his children. Elizabeth had spent much of her childhood there, Ned knew. Now Queen Mary Tudor, Elizabeth's older half-sister, liked to keep her there. Hatfield was twenty miles north of London, a day's walk or half a day's fast ride: Elizabeth was out of London, where she might have been a nuisance, but close enough to be watched. Elizabeth was not exactly a prisoner, but she was not free to come and go as she pleased.

The palace was visible from a distance, atop a rise. It looked like an enormous barn built of red brick with leaded windows. As he climbed the slope to the entrance arch, Ned saw that in fact it was four linked buildings in a square, enclosing a courtyard big enough to hold several tennis courts.

His apprehension grew as he saw the busy crowd in the yard, grooms and laundresses and delivery boys. He realized that even though Elizabeth was out of favour she was still royal, and she maintained a large household. Probably lots of people would like to work for her. Perhaps the servants turned applicants away every day.

He walked into the courtyard and looked around. Everyone was busy, no one noticed him. Cecil might be away, he realized:

one reason the man needed an assistant was that he could not be at Hatfield all the time.

Ned went up to an older woman placidly shelling peas. 'Good day, mistress,' he said politely. 'Where might I find Sir William Cecil?'

'Ask the fat man,' she said, jerking a thumb at a well-dressed heavy-set figure Ned had not previously noticed. 'Tom Parry.'

Ned approached the man. 'Good day, Master Parry,' he said. 'I'm here to see Sir William Cecil.'

'A lot of people would like to see Sir William,' said Parry.

'If you tell him Ned Willard from Kingsbridge is here, he will be glad of the information.'

'Will he, now?' Parry was sceptical. 'From Kingsbridge?'

'Yes. I walked here.'

Parry was unimpressed. 'I didn't think you'd flown.'

'Will you be so kind as to give him my name?'

'And if he asks me what business Ned Willard has with him, what shall I say?'

'The confidential matter he and I discussed with the earl of Shiring on the Twelfth Day of Christmas.'

'Sir William, and the earl, and you?' said Parry. 'What were you doing – serving the wine?'

Ned smiled thinly. 'No. But the topic was, as I mentioned, confidential.' He decided that if he submitted himself to any further rude interrogation he would begin to seem desperate, so he ended the conversation. 'Thank you for your courtesy,' he said, and turned his back.

'All right, no need to take umbrage. Come with me.'

Ned followed Parry into the house. The place was gloomy and somewhat decrepit: Elizabeth might have a royal income, but clearly it did not stretch to refurbishing a palace.

Parry opened a door, looked in, and said: 'Do you want to receive a Ned Willard from Kingsbridge, Sir William?'

A voice inside answered: 'Very well.'

Parry turned to Ned. 'Go in.'

The room was large, but not richly decorated; a working office, with ledgers on shelves, rather than a reception room. Cecil sat at a writing table, with pens and ink, paper and sealing-wax. He wore a black velvet doublet that looked too warm for summer weather – but he was sedentary, and Ned had been walking in the sun.

'Ah, yes, I remember,' Cecil said when he saw Ned. 'Alice Willard's boy.' His tone was neither friendly nor unfriendly, just a little wary. 'Is your mother well?'

'She's lost all her money, Sir William,' Ned replied. 'Most of our fortune was in Calais.'

'Several good men have suffered a similar fate. We were foolish to declare war on France. But why have you come to me? I can't get Calais back.'

'When we met, at the earl of Shiring's banquet, you said you were looking for a young man a bit like myself, to help you in your work for the lady Elizabeth. My mother told you I was destined to work in the family business, and therefore unavailable – but now there is no business. I don't know whether you found someone . . .'

'I did,' said Cecil, and Ned was crestfallen. Then Cecil added: 'But he turned out to be a bad choice.'

Ned brightened again. 'I would be honoured and grateful if you would consider me for the position,' he said eagerly.

'I don't know,' Cecil said. 'This is not one of those posts that exists to provide an income for a courtier. It requires real work.'

'I'm prepared to work.'

'Perhaps, but to be frank, a boy from a rich background whose family have fallen on bad times does not usually make a good assistant: he's liable to be too accustomed to giving the orders himself, and he may find it strange that anyone should expect him to do what he's told promptly and conscientiously. He just wants the money.'

'I want more than the money.'

'You do?'

'Sir William, two weeks ago we burned a Protestant in Kingsbridge – our first.' Ned knew he should not get emotional, but he could hardly help it. 'As I watched him die screaming, I remembered what you said to me about Elizabeth's wish that no one should be killed for his faith.'

Cecil nodded.

'I want her to be queen one day,' Ned said passionately. 'I want our country to be a place where Catholics and Protestants don't kill one another. When the moment comes, I want to be with you as you help Elizabeth to win the throne. That's the real reason I'm here.'

Cecil stared hard at Ned, as if trying to look into his heart and determine whether he was sincere. After a long pause he said: 'All right. I'll give you a trial.'

'Thank you,' Ned said fervently. 'I promise you won't regret it.'

*

NED WAS STILL in love with Margery Fitzgerald, but he would have gone to bed with Elizabeth in a heartbeat.

And yet she was not beautiful. She had a big nose and a small chin, and her eyes were too close together. But, paradoxically, she was irresistibly alluring: astonishingly clever, as charming as a kitten, and shamelessly flirtatious. The effect was hardly reduced by her imperiousness and her occasional bad temper. Men and women adored her even after she had scolded them cruelly. Ned had never met anyone remotely like her. She was overpowering.

She spoke French to him, mocked his hesitant Latin, and was disappointed that he could not help her practise her Spanish. She let him read any of her books that he fancied, on condition that he discussed them with her. She asked him questions about her finances that made it clear she understood accounts as well as he did.

Within a few days he learned the answers to two key questions.

First, Elizabeth was not plotting against Queen Mary Tudor. In fact, she expressed a horror of treason that seemed genuine to Ned. However, she was preparing, quite methodically, to make a bid for the throne after Mary's death, whenever that might be. Cecil's Christmas trip to Kingsbridge had been part of a programme in which he, and other allies of Elizabeth, visited the most important cities in England to assess her support – and opposition. Ned's admiration for Cecil grew fast:

the man thought strategically, judging every issue by its long-term effect on the destiny of the princess he served.

Second, Elizabeth was a Protestant, despite Cecil's pretence that she had no strong religious convictions. She went to Mass and performed every Catholic ritual that was expected of her, but that was for show. Her favourite book was *Paraphrases of the New Testament* by Erasmus. Most telling was her bad language. She used swear words that Catholics considered offensive. In polite company she chose phrases that were not quite blasphemous: 'blood' instead of 'God's blood'; 'zounds' for 'God's wounds'; and 'marry' for 'Mary'. But in private she was more profane, saying: 'by the Mass' and – her favourite – 'God's body!'

In the mornings she studied with her tutor, and Ned sat in Cecil's office with the ledgers. Elizabeth had a lot of property, and a major part of Ned's job was making sure that she was paid the rents due to her in full and on time. After the midday meal Elizabeth relaxed, and sometimes she liked her favourite servants to chat with her. They would sit in a room known as the bishop's parlour, which had the most comfortable chairs, a chess board, and a virginal on which Elizabeth would sometimes pick out tunes. Her governess, Nell Baynsford, was always there, and sometimes Tom Parry, who was her treasurer.

Ned was not a member of this exclusive inner circle, but one day, when Cecil was absent, he was called in to talk about plans for Elizabeth's twenty-fifth birthday on 7 September, a couple of weeks away. Should they try to arrange a big celebration in London, which would require the permission of the queen, or something more modest here at Hatfield, where they could do what they liked?

They were deep in discussion when a surprise visitor arrived.

They heard the clatter of hooves as several horses came through the arched gateway into the central courtyard. Ned went to the leaded window and peered out through the smoky glass. There were six riders, and their mounts were powerful, costly beasts. Elizabeth's grooms came out of the stables to deal with the horses. Ned looked harder at the leader of the group and was astonished to recognize him. 'It's Earl Swithin!' he said. 'What does he want here?'

Ned's first thought was that the visit must have something to do with the coming marriage of the earl's son, Bart, to the girl Ned loved, Margery. But this was a fantasy. Even if the engagement had been broken off, the earl would not trouble to tell Ned.

What, then?

The visitors were ushered into the house, taking off their dusty cloaks. A few minutes later a servant came into the parlour to say that the earl of Shiring would like to speak to the lady Elizabeth, and Elizabeth ordered that he should be shown in.

Earl Swithin was a big man with a loud voice, and when he entered, he filled the room with his presence. Ned, Nell and Tom stood up, but Elizabeth remained sitting, perhaps to emphasize that her royal blood counted for more than Swithin's greater age. He made a deep bow, but spoke in familiar tones, like an uncle to a niece. 'I'm pleased to see you looking so well, and so beautiful,' he said.

'This is an unexpected delight,' Elizabeth said. The compliment was fulsome but her tone was wary. Clearly she mistrusted Swithin – and so she should, Ned thought. Loyal Catholics such as Swithin had prospered under Queen Mary Tudor, and they feared a return to Protestantism, so they did not want Elizabeth to become queen.

'So beautiful, and almost twenty-five years old!' Swithin went on. 'A red-blooded man such as myself cannot help thinking that such beauty should not be wasted – you will forgive me for saying so.'

'Will I?' Elizabeth replied frostily. She never was amused by vague sexual innuendo uttered in tones of jollity.

Swithin sensed Elizabeth's coolness and looked at the servants standing in the background. Clearly he was wondering if he might get on better without them listening. He was mildly startled when his eye fell on Ned, but he said nothing to him. Turning back to Elizabeth he said: 'May I speak privately to you, my dear?'

Assuming unwarranted familiarity was not the way to charm Elizabeth. She was a younger daughter, some said illegitimate, and that made her ultra-sensitive to any sign of disrespect. But Swithin was too stupid to grasp that.

Tom Parry said: 'The lady Elizabeth must never be alone with a man – on the instructions of the queen.'

'Nonsense!' said Swithin.

Ned wished that Cecil had been here for this visit. It was risky for servants to stand up to an earl. The thought crossed his mind that Swithin might deliberately have arranged to come on a day when none of Elizabeth's senior staff were at the house.

What was he up to?

Swithin said: 'Elizabeth has nothing to fear from me,' and he chortled heartily. It made Ned's skin crawl.

But Elizabeth took offence. 'Fear?' she said, raising her voice. She resented any suggestion that she was a fragile woman in need of protection. 'Why should I be afraid? Of course I will speak to you privately.'

Reluctantly, her servants left the room.

When the door was closed, Tom said to Ned: 'You know him – what is he like?'

'Swithin is a violent man,' Ned said. 'We must stay close.' He realized that Tom and Nell were looking to him for guidance. He thought fast. 'Nell, will you tell the kitchen to send wine for the guest?' If it became necessary to enter the room, the wine would provide a pretext.

Tom said: 'What will he do if we go back in?'

Ned thought of Swithin's reaction to the Puritan walk-out at the play. 'I've seen him try to kill a man who offended him.'

'God save us.'

Ned touched his head to the door. He could hear the two voices: Swithin's was loud and Elizabeth's was penetrating. He could not make out the words, but the tones were calm, if not very amiable, and he felt that for the moment Elizabeth was in no danger.

Ned tried to figure out what was going on. Swithin's surprise visit must have something to do with the succession to the throne. It was the only reason a powerful courtier would be interested in Elizabeth.

Ned recalled that a much-discussed solution to the problem of the succession was to marry Elizabeth to a strong Catholic. It was assumed that she would be led by her husband in religious matters. Ned now knew Elizabeth well enough to realize that such a plan would not work, but others thought it would. King Felipe had proposed his cousin, the duke of Savoy, but Elizabeth had refused.

Did Swithin want to marry Elizabeth himself? It was possible. He might hope to seduce her on this visit. More likely, he might think that if he spent enough time alone with her the suspicion of fornication would make a marriage the only way to rescue her reputation.

He would not be the first to try. When Elizabeth had been only fourteen Thomas Seymour – a man of forty – had indulged in sexual petting with her and schemed to marry her. Seymour had ended up executed for treason, though his designs on Elizabeth had not been his only offence. Ned thought it was quite possible that the foolhardy Earl Swithin might be prepared to risk the same fate.

The tones of voice within the room changed. Elizabeth began to sound commanding. Swithin went the other way, countering her coldness with a voice so amiable it was almost lecherous.

If something unpleasant should happen, Elizabeth could shout for help. Except that she never admitted needing help. And Swithin might be able to silence her anyway.

Nell reappeared carrying a tray with a jug of wine, two goblets, and a plate of cakes. Ned held up a hand to stop her entering the room. 'Not yet,' he murmured.

A minute later Elizabeth made a noise that was almost a scream. It was followed by a crash and a tinkling sound that Ned guessed was a bowl of apples being knocked to the floor. He hesitated, waiting for Elizabeth to shout. But there followed a silence. Ned did not know what to do. He found the silence more sinister than anything.

Unable to bear the suspense, he threw open the door, seized the tray from Nell, and stepped inside.

On the far side of the room, Earl Swithin held Elizabeth in a bear hug, kissing her. Ned's worst fears had been justified.

Elizabeth turned her head from side to side, trying to escape his mouth, and Ned saw her small fists beating ineffectually on Swithin's broad back. Clearly she was unwilling. But this would be Swithin's idea of courtship, Ned thought. He would imagine that a woman might be overcome by the strength of his passion, yield to his embraces, and fall in love with him for his forceful masculinity.

Elizabeth would not be won that way if Swithin were the last man on earth.

In a loud voice Ned said: 'Some refreshments for you, Earl.' He was shaking with fear but he managed to make his voice jovial. 'A glass of sherry wine, perhaps?' He put the tray down on a table beside the window.

Swithin turned to Ned but kept tight hold of Elizabeth's slim wrist in his deformed left hand. 'Get out of here, you little turd,' he said.

His persistence shocked Ned. How could Swithin continue now that he had been seen? Even an earl could be executed for rape, especially if there were three independent witnesses – and both Tom and Nell were in the doorway, watching, though too terrified to enter.

But Swithin was nothing if not headstrong.

Ned realized he could not leave now, no matter what.

With an effort he controlled the shaking of his hands enough to pour wine into a goblet. 'And the kitchen has kindly sent some cakes. You must be hungry after your journey.'

Elizabeth said: 'Let go of my arm, Swithin.' She tugged, but even though he was holding her with his mutilated hand, the one that had lost two and a half fingers, she could not free herself.

Swithin put his hand on the dagger at his belt. 'Leave the room instantly, young Willard, or by God I'll slit your throat.'

Ned knew he was capable of it. At New Castle, in his rages, he had injured servants in several incidents that had been smoothed over, later, with a combination of threats and compensation. And if Ned defended himself, he could be hanged for wounding an earl.

But he could not leave Elizabeth now.

The mention of a knife inspired him. 'There's been a fight in the stables,' he said, extemporizing. 'Two of your companions got into an argument. The grooms managed to pull them apart, but one seems badly injured – a knife wound.'

'Bloody liar,' said Swithin, but clearly he was not sure, and the indecision cooled his ardour.

Behind Ned, Nell and Tom at last came hesitantly into the room. Nell knelt down and started to pick up pieces of the broken fruit bowl. Tom cottoned on to Ned's story and said: 'Your man is bleeding quite badly, Earl Swithin.'

Common sense began to prevail. Swithin seemed to realize that he could not stab three of Elizabeth's servants without getting into trouble. And his plan of seduction had collapsed. He looked furious, but let go of Elizabeth. She immediately moved away from him, rubbing her wrist.

With a grunt of frustration, Swithin strode from the room.

Ned almost collapsed with relief. Nell began to cry. Tom Parry took a gulp of sherry directly from the jug.

Ned said: 'My lady, you should go to your private chamber with Nell and bar the door. Tom, you and I should vanish too.'

'I agree,' said Elizabeth, but she did not leave immediately. She moved closer to Ned and said quietly: 'There was no fight in the stables, was there?'

'No. It was the only thing I could think of on the spur of the moment.'

She smiled. 'How old are you, Ned?'

'Nineteen.'

'You risked your life for me.' She stood on tiptoe and kissed him on the lips briefly but tenderly. 'Thank you,' she said.

Then she left the room.

*

MOST PEOPLE bathed twice a year, in spring and autumn, but princesses were fastidious, and Elizabeth bathed more often. It was a major operation, with maidservants carrying big two-handled laundry tubs of hot water from the kitchen fire to her bedchamber, hurrying up the stairs before the water cooled.

She took a bath the day after Swithin's visit, as if to wash away her disgust. She had said no more about Swithin, after kissing Ned, but Ned thought he had won her trust.

Ned knew he had made an enemy of a powerful earl, but he hoped it would not last: Swithin was quick-tempered and vengeful but, Ned thought, he had a short attention span. With luck he would nurse his grudge against Ned only until a better one came along.

Sir William Cecil had arrived shortly after Swithin left, and next morning he got down to work with Ned. Cecil's office was in the same wing as Elizabeth's private suite. He sent Ned to Tom Parry's office to fetch a ledger of expenditure for another house Elizabeth owned. Coming back with the heavy book in his hand, Ned walked along Elizabeth's corridor, where the floorboards were puddled with water spilled by the maids. As he passed her suite, he saw that the door was open, and – stupidly – he glanced in.

Elizabeth had just got out of her bath. The tub itself was screened off, but she had stepped across the room to pick up a large white linen sheet with which to dry herself. There should have been a maid waiting beside the tub holding the towel, and of course the door should have been shut; but someone had been dilatory, and Elizabeth was impatient with dozy servants.

Ned had never seen a woman naked. He had no sisters, he had never gone that far with a girlfriend, and he had not visited a brothel.

He froze, staring. The hot bathwater, steaming faintly, ran from her dainty shoulders down her small breasts to her rounded hips and her strong thighs, muscular from riding. Her skin was creamy white and her pubic hair was a wonderful red-gold. Ned knew he should look away instantly, but he was enchanted, and could not move.

She caught his eye and was startled, but only for a moment. She reached out and grabbed the edge of the door.

Then she smiled.

A moment later she slammed the door.

Ned hurried along the corridor, his heart beating like a big drum. For what he had just done he could be sacked from his job, put in the stocks, or flogged – or all three.

But she had smiled.

The smile had been warm, friendly, and a little coquettish. Ned could imagine a naked woman smiling like that at her husband or lover. The smile seemed to say that this glimpse of forbidden loveliness was a boon she was happy to grant him.

He told nobody what had happened.

That evening he waited for an explosion of anger, but none came. Elizabeth did not mention the incident, to him or anyone else. Slowly Ned became sure he was not going to be punished. Then he began to doubt whether it had really happened. It was more like something he might have dreamed.

But he would remember that vision for the rest of his life.

*

MARGERY WAS KISSED by Bart for the first time in the new house, Priory Gate.

Sir Reginald Fitzgerald, Lady Jane and Rollo were proudly showing Earl Swithin around. Margery followed with Bart, who was back from his posting to Combe Harbour now that the threat of a French invasion seemed to have faded. Margery knew that Reginald had sold the rest of the priory back to the cathedral chapter, as promised. The price had been low, but enough to pay for the building work on the new house to be completed.

It was a grand, impressive modern structure on the market square, made of the same pale limestone as the cathedral. It had rows of large windows and tall clustered chimneys. Inside there seemed to be staircases everywhere and dozens of fireplaces. It smelled of new paint, some of the chimneys smoked, and several of the doors would not close properly, but it was habitable, and servants were already moving furniture here from the old house on the high street.

Margery did not want to live here. For her, Priory Gate

would always smell of bloodshed and fraud. Philbert Cobley
had been burned to death and Alice Willard had been ruined
so that this house could be finished. Philbert and Alice had
committed sins, of course, and so had to be punished, but
Margery's sharp moral discrimination would not permit her to
content herself with such blurring of distinctions: the severe
sentences had been prompted by impure motives. Bishop
Julius had got the priory back for the cathedral and Margery's
father had gained a lot of money that was not really his.

A mere girl had no business thinking such thoughts, but
she could not help it, and it made her angry. Bad behaviour
by bishops and leading Catholics was part of what drove
Protestantism – could they not see that? However, there was
nothing she could do but seethe.

As the party entered the Long Gallery, Bart lagged behind,
grabbed Margery's elbow, and pulled her back; then, when the
others were out of sight, he kissed her.

Bart was tall and handsome and well dressed, and Margery
knew that she must love him, for he had been chosen as her
husband by her parents, who had been set in authority over
her by God. So she kissed him back, opening her mouth, and
let him explore her body, feel her breasts and even press his
hand between her legs. It was difficult, especially as she kept
remembering that Ned had kissed her in this house when it
was half built. She tried to summon the feelings that used to
come over her with Ned. It did not really work, but it made the
ordeal a little easier to bear.

She broke the embrace and saw Swithin watching them.

'We were wondering where you two had got to,' he said,
then he gave a conspiratorial grin and a lascivious wink.
Margery found it creepy that he had stood there, watching,
until she had noticed him.

The party sat down in the room designated as Sir Reginald's
parlour to talk about the wedding. It was just a month away.
Margery and Bart would be married in Kingsbridge Cathedral,
and there would be a banquet here in the new house. Margery
had ordered a dress in pale blue silk and an elaborate headdress
in the jaunty style she loved. Earl Swithin wanted to know all

the details of her outfit, almost as if he would be marrying her himself. Her parents had to have new clothes, too, and there were a hundred other decisions to be made. There would be entertainment as well as food and drink for the guests, and Sir Reginald would have to provide free beer for all comers at the gate.

They were discussing what play would be appropriate to finish the festivities when the head groom, Percy, came in followed by a young man with the dust of the road on his clothes. 'A courier from London, Sir Reginald,' said Percy. 'He assures me you would not want to delay hearing his news.'

Sir Reginald looked at the courier. 'What is it?'

'I bring a letter from Davy Miller, sir.' Miller was Reginald's business representative in London. The courier held out a slim leather wallet.

'Tell me what it says, man,' said Sir Reginald impatiently.

'The queen is ill.'

'What's wrong with her?'

'The doctors say there is a malignant growth in her female parts that is causing her belly to swell.'

Rollo said: 'Ah. Those false pregnancies . . .'

'It is so bad that she sometimes falls unconscious.'

'The poor queen,' said Margery. She had mixed feelings about Mary Tudor. The queen was an admirably strong-willed and devout woman, but the burnings of Protestants were wrong. Why could people not be devout and merciful at the same time, like Jesus?

Rollo said worriedly: 'What's the prognosis?'

'We understand that she may take some months to die, but she will not recover.'

Margery saw Rollo turn a little pale, and a moment later she understood why. 'This is the worst possible news,' he said. 'Mary Tudor has no child, and young Mary Stuart has made herself a less attractive successor by marrying the wretched French boy. That makes Elizabeth Tudor the leading candidate – and all our efforts to bring her under control have failed.'

Rollo was right. Margery had not seen it as quickly as he had, but as soon as he said it she understood, and so did her father and the earl. England was in danger of falling back into the swamp of heresy. She shivered.

Swithin said: 'Elizabeth must not become queen! That would be a catastrophe.'

Margery looked at Bart, but he seemed bored. Her husband-to-be was impatient with politics. He preferred to talk about horses and dogs. She felt annoyed with him: the topic was their future!

Reginald said: 'Mary Stuart is married to a French prince, and the English people don't want another foreign king.'

'The English people will have no say in the matter,' Swithin grunted. 'Tell them now that their next monarch will be Mary Stuart. By the time it happens they will have got used to the idea.'

Margery thought that was wishful thinking, and her father showed, by his next remark, that he agreed. 'We can tell them anything,' said Reginald. 'But will they believe us?'

Rollo answered the question. 'They might,' he said with a speculative air. He was thinking on his feet, Margery could tell, but what he was saying made sense. 'Especially if the announcement was endorsed by King Felipe.'

'Perhaps,' said Sir Reginald. 'First we would have to get King Felipe to agree.'

Margery began to see a glimmer of hope.

Rollo said: 'Then we will go and see King Felipe.'

'Where is he now?'

'In Brussels, leading his army against the French. But that war is almost over.'

'We may have to be quick, if the queen is as ill as she seems.'

'Indeed. We can get passage from Combe Harbour to Antwerp – Dan Cobley has ships going every week. From Antwerp to Brussels is a day's ride. We'll be back for the wedding.'

It was ironic, Margery thought, that they would have to rely on the ultra-Protestant Dan Cobley to transport them on this mission.

Rollo said: 'Would King Felipe receive us?'

Swithin answered the question. 'He would receive me.

England is one of his kingdoms, and I'm one of its greatest noblemen. And he stayed at New Castle once, after the marriage, on his way from Winchester to London.'

The three men looked at one another: Reginald, Rollo and Swithin. 'Very well,' said Reginald. 'We'll go to Brussels.'

Margery felt better. At least they were doing something.

Rollo stood up. 'I'll go and see Dan about a ship,' he said. 'We can't afford to lose any time.'

*

NED WILLARD DID NOT want to go to Kingsbridge for Margery's wedding, but he had to. The ceremony provided too good a pretext for his undercover mission.

In October he retraced the steps of his July journey, but this time on horseback. His mission was urgent. The queen was dying, and everything was urgent.

His mother seemed shrunken. It was not so much physical – she was still quite heavy – but the spirit had gone out of her. Ned had not really believed her, back in June, when she had said: 'I'll be fifty soon – I haven't got the energy.' But three months later she was still despondent and lethargic. Ned felt sure now that Alice would never revive the family enterprise. It made him grind his teeth with rage.

But things were going to change. Ned was part of the force that would break the power of men such as Bishop Julius and Sir Reginald. Ned was thrilled to be part of Elizabeth's household. Both Cecil and Elizabeth liked him, especially since he had defied Swithin. He felt a surge of eager anticipation every time he thought about how they would change the world together. But first they had to put Elizabeth on the throne of England.

He stood with his mother in the market square, waiting for the bride. A brisk north wind blew across the open space. As always, the couple would exchange vows in the porch of the church, then go inside for the wedding Mass. Kingsbridge people greeted Ned warmly. Most of them felt that his family had been severely mistreated.

Swithin and Bart stood at the front of the crowd, Bart

wearing a new yellow doublet. There was no sign of the bride yet. Would she look happy or sad? Was she heartbroken, her life ruined because she was not marrying Ned? Or was she by now getting over her love for him and beginning to enjoy her new role with Viscount Bart? Ned was not sure which he would find harder to bear.

But he was not really here for Margery. He raked the crowd, looking for the Protestants. He spotted Dan Cobley and began his mission.

Faking a casual air, he strolled across the square to speak to Dan, who was standing outside the north-west corner of the cathedral. Dan seemed changed, although it had been only three months: he had lost some weight, and his face looked harder as well as leaner. Ned was pleased by the change, for his mission was to turn Dan into a military leader.

It would not be easy.

Exchanging pleasantries, he drew Dan behind a mighty buttress, then spoke in a low voice. 'The queen is fighting for her life.'

'So I hear,' said Dan warily.

Ned was disheartened to see that Dan did not trust him, but he understood why. The Willards had switched from Catholicism to Protestantism and back again too easily for Dan's liking. Now Dan was not sure where they really stood.

Ned said: 'The succession is a contest between Elizabeth Tudor and Mary Stuart. Now, Mary is fifteen years old and married to a sickly husband who is even younger: she would be a weak queen, dominated by her French uncles, the Guises – who are ultra-Catholic. You need to fear her.'

'But Elizabeth goes to Mass.'

'And she may continue to do so after she becomes queen – no one really knows.' This was not true. Ned and everyone close to Elizabeth knew she would become openly Protestant as soon as she could, for that was the only way to break the stranglehold of the Church. But they were pretending otherwise to disarm the opposition. In the world of kings and courtiers, Ned had learned, no one told all of the truth all of the time.

Dan said: 'In that case, why should I care whether our next monarch is Elizabeth Tudor or Mary Stuart?'

'If Elizabeth becomes queen, she will not burn Protestants for their beliefs.' That part *was* true.

Fury blazed in Dan's eyes at this reminder of his father's dreadful death; but he controlled his emotions. 'That's easy to say.'

'Be realistic. You want the slaughter of Protestants to stop. Elizabeth is not just your best hope, she's your only hope.' Dan did not want to believe this, Ned guessed, but he saw in Dan's eyes an acknowledgement of the truth, and had the satisfaction of feeling one step closer to his goal.

Reluctantly, Dan said: 'Why are you telling me this?'

Ned answered Dan's question with a question. 'How many Protestants are there in Kingsbridge now?'

Dan looked stubborn and said nothing.

'You have to trust me,' Ned said urgently. 'Come on!'

'At least two thousand,' Dan said at last.

'What?' Ned was pleasantly surprised. 'I imagined a few hundred at most.'

'There's more than one group. And the numbers have increased since June.'

'Because of what happened to your father?'

Dan looked bitter. 'More because of what happened to your mother. They're scared to do business. No deal is safe now. Most of these people don't care about a Protestant martyr, but they can't live with a Church that steals their money.'

Ned nodded. He suspected Dan was right. Few people became passionate about doctrinal disputes, but everyone had to make a living, and a Church that stopped them doing that was bound to run into trouble.

Ned said: 'I've come here from Hatfield with one question for you, Dan, and I could be in danger just for asking it, so please think before you answer.'

Dan looked scared. 'Don't involve me in anything treasonable!'

That was exactly what Ned was about to do. He said: 'Out of those two thousand Protestants, how many able-bodied men could you muster, when the queen dies, to fight for Elizabeth against the supporters of Mary Stuart?'

Dan looked away. 'I have no idea.'

He was prevaricating, Ned knew. He moved closer to Dan, pressing the point. 'What if a group of Catholic noblemen, led perhaps by Earl Swithin, were to muster an army to march on Hatfield, intending to take Elizabeth prisoner while they wait for Mary Stuart and her hard-line uncles to arrive from France? Would you stand by and let that happen?'

'Four hundred Kingsbridge men won't make any difference.'

So it was four hundred, Ned thought. That was the information he needed. He was pleased: it was more than he had expected. He said: 'Do you imagine you're the only brave Protestants in England?' He lowered his voice more. 'Every city in the land has a group like yours, ready to march to Hatfield and defend Elizabeth, waiting only for the word from her.'

For the first time, Dan's face was lit by hope – albeit hope of revenge. 'Is that true?' he said.

It was something of an exaggeration, but not entirely untrue. Ned said: 'If you want the freedom to worship in the way you so passionately believe is right – and to do so without the fear, every minute, that you might be burned alive for it – then you must be ready to fight, and I mean fight with swords.'

Dan nodded thoughtfully.

'And there's one other thing you have to do,' Ned went on. 'Watch what Earl Swithin and Sir Reginald are up to. Send a fast messenger to me at Hatfield as soon as they do anything unusual, such as stockpiling weapons. Early information is the key.'

Dan said nothing. Ned stared at him, waiting for a reply, hoping for assent. At last Dan said: 'I'll think about what you've said.' Then he walked away.

Ned was frustrated. He had felt confident that Dan would be eager to revenge the killing of his father by leading a Kingsbridge militia to fight for Elizabeth, and he had assured Sir William Cecil of it. Perhaps he had been overconfident.

Discouraged, Ned made his way back across the square, heading for where his mother stood. Halfway there he found himself facing Rollo Fitzgerald, who said: 'What news of the queen?'

It was on everyone's minds, of course.

Ned said: 'She is gravely ill.'

'There are rumours that Elizabeth intends to permit Protestantism if she becomes queen.' Rollo made it sound like an accusation.

'Rumours, indeed?' Ned had no intention of getting into that kind of discussion. He moved to step around Rollo.

But Rollo blocked his way. 'Or even that she wants to turn England to heresy, as her father did.' Rollo lifted his chin aggressively. 'Is it true?'

'Who told you that?'

'Consider this,' said Rollo, who could ignore a question as effortlessly as Ned. 'If she tries it, who will oppose her? Rome, of course.'

'Indeed,' said Ned. 'The Pope's policy on Protestants is extermination.'

Rollo put his hands on his hips and leaned forward belligerently. The stance was familiar to Ned from their schooldays: this was Rollo playing the bully. 'She will also be opposed by the king of Spain, who is the richest and most powerful man in the world.'

'Perhaps.' The position of Spain was not that simple, but there was certainly some danger that King Felipe would try to undermine Elizabeth.

'And the king of France, probably the second most powerful.'

'Hmm.' That, too, was a real danger.

'Not to mention the king of Portugal and the queen of Scots.'

Ned was pretending to be indifferent to this argument, but Rollo was dismayingly right. Almost all Europe was going to turn on Elizabeth if she did what Ned knew perfectly well she intended to do. He had known all this, but Rollo's summation was hammering the points home with chilling effect.

Rollo went on: 'And who would support her? The king of

Sweden and the queen of Navarre.' Navarre was a small kingdom between Spain and France.

'You paint a dramatic picture.'

Rollo came uncomfortably close. He was tall, and loomed threateningly over Ned. 'She would be very foolish indeed to quarrel with so many powerful men.'

Ned said: 'Take a step back, Rollo. If you don't, I promise you, I will pick you up with both hands and throw you.'

Rollo looked uncertain.

Ned put a hand on Rollo's shoulder, in a gesture that might have been friendly, and said: 'I won't tell you twice.'

Rollo pushed Ned's hand off his shoulder, but then he turned away.

'That's how Elizabeth and I deal with bullies,' said Ned.

There was a fanfare of trumpets, and the bride appeared.

Ned caught his breath. She looked wonderful. Her dress was a pale sky-blue with a dark blue underskirt. It had a high collar that stood up dramatically behind like a fan, framing her curly hair. Her jewelled headdress had a plume at an angle.

Ned heard a group of girls nearby murmur approval. Glancing at their faces, he saw mainly envy. It occurred to him that Margery had hooked the man they all wanted. Bart must be the most eligible bachelor in the county. They thought she had won first prize. How wrong they were.

Sir Reginald walked beside her, looking proud in a doublet of gorgeous red silk embroidered with gold thread, and Ned thought angrily: *He paid for all this with my mother's money.*

Ned studied Margery's expression as she came across the square, looking tiny and helpless as she approached the massive stones of the west front. What was she thinking? Her lips were set in a half-smile, and she looked from side to side, nodding at friends. She seemed confident and proud. But Ned knew her better. Serenity was not her mode. The natural Margery was playful, mischievous, amused and amusing. There was no laughter in her today. She was putting on an act, like the boy impersonating Mary Magdalene in the play.

As she passed where he stood, she caught his eye.

She had not known he would be here, and she was shocked.

Her eyes widened in dismay. She looked away from him immediately, but she had lost her self-possession. Her fixed smile faltered, and a moment later she stumbled.

Ned stepped forward automatically to help her, but he was five yards away. Sir Reginald, next to her, caught her arm. But his reaction was late and his arm was not strong enough to save her. She lost her balance and went down on her knees.

The crowd gasped. It was bad luck. A fall on the way to your wedding was the worst possible omen for your married life.

Margery remained on her knees for a few seconds, catching her breath and trying to regain her composure, while her family clustered around her. Ned was one of many people trying to look over their shoulders to see if she was all right. Those farther away in the crowd were asking each other what had happened.

Then Margery stood upright again, and seemed steady enough on her feet. Her face assumed the same controlled expression. She looked around, smiling ruefully as if at her own clumsiness.

At last she stepped forward, and continued towards the cathedral porch.

Ned stayed where he was. He did not need to see the ceremony close up. The woman he loved was committing her life to another man. Margery was serious about promises: for her, a vow was sacred. When she said: 'I do,' she meant it. Ned knew he was losing her permanently.

After the exchange of vows, everyone proceeded into the cathedral for the wedding Mass.

Ned intoned the responses and looked at the sculpted pilasters and soaring arches, but today the timeless rhythm of the repeated columns and curves failed to soothe his wounded soul. Bart was going to make Margery miserable, Ned knew that. The thought that kept recurring, and that Ned could not completely suppress no matter how hard he tried, was that tonight Bart, that wooden-headed fool in a yellow doublet, would lie in bed with Margery and do with her all the things Ned himself longed for.

Then it was over, and they were husband and wife.

Ned left the cathedral. Now there was no uncertainty and no hope. Ned was going to spend his life without her.

He felt sure he would never love anyone else. He would be a lifelong bachelor. He was glad that at least he had a new career that engaged him so powerfully. His work for Elizabeth quite possessed him. If he could not spend his life with Margery, he would dedicate himself to Elizabeth. Her ideal of religious tolerance was outrageously radical, of course. Almost the whole world thought that the notion of letting everyone worship as they wished was disgustingly permissive and completely mad. But Ned thought the majority were mad, and people who believed as Elizabeth did were the only sane ones.

Life without Margery would be sad, but not pointless.

He had impressed Elizabeth once, by the way he had dealt with Earl Swithin, and now he needed to do it again, by recruiting Dan Cobley and the Kingsbridge Protestants as soldiers in her army.

He stopped in the windy square and looked around for Dan, who had not come into the cathedral for the wedding Mass. Presumably Dan had spent the hour thinking about Ned's proposition. How long did he need? Ned spotted him in the graveyard, and went to join him.

Philbert Cobley had no grave, of course: heretics did not benefit from Christian burial. Dan was standing at the tomb of his grandparents, Adam and Deborah Cobley. 'We gathered some ashes, furtively, after the burning,' Dan said. His face was wet with tears. 'We brought them here that evening and dug them into the soil at dusk. We'll see him again, on the Last Day.'

Ned did not like Dan, but could not help feeling sad for him. 'Amen,' he said. 'But it's a long time until Judgement Day, and in the meantime we have to do God's work here on earth.'

'I'll help you,' Dan said.

'Good man!' Ned was happy. His mission had been accomplished. Elizabeth would be pleased.

'I should have said yes right away, but I've become cautious.'

Understandably, Ned thought. But he did not want to dwell on the past, now that Dan had committed himself. He adopted a briskly practical tone. 'You'll need to appoint ten captains, each in charge of forty men. They won't all have swords, but tell them to find good daggers or hammers. An iron chain can make a useful weapon.'

'Is this the advice you're giving to all the Protestant militias?'

'Exactly. We need disciplined men. You need to take them to a field somewhere and march them up and down. It sounds stupid, but anything that gets them used to moving in unison is good.' Ned was not speaking from his own knowledge or experience: he was repeating what Cecil had told him.

'We might be seen, marching,' Dan said dubiously.

'Not if you're discreet.'

Dan nodded. 'There's something else,' he said. 'You want to know what Swithin and the Fitzgeralds do.'

'Very much.'

'They went to Brussels.'

Ned was rocked. 'What? When?'

'Four weeks ago. I know because they travelled on a ship of mine. We took them to Antwerp, and heard them hiring a guide to take them on to Brussels. They came back on one of my ships, too. They were afraid they might have to postpone the wedding, but they got here three days ago.'

'King Felipe is in Brussels.'

'So I gather.'

Ned tried to analyse this as William Cecil would, and in his mind the dominoes fell one by one. Why did Swithin and the Fitzgeralds want to see King Felipe? To talk about who would rule England when Mary Tudor died. What had they said to Felipe? That Mary Stuart should be queen, not Elizabeth Tudor.

They must have asked Felipe to support Mary.

And if Felipe had said yes, Elizabeth was in trouble.

*

NED BECAME EVEN more worried when he saw Cecil's reaction.

'I didn't expect King Felipe to support Elizabeth, but I did hope he might stay out of it,' Cecil said anxiously.

'Why wouldn't he support Mary Stuart?'

'He's worried about England coming under the control of

her French uncles. He doesn't want France to become too powerful. So, much as he wants us to be Catholic again, he's in two minds. I don't want him to be talked into making a decision for Mary Stuart.'

Ned had not thought of that. It was remarkable how often Cecil pointed out things he had not thought of. He was learning fast, but he felt he would never master the intricacies of international diplomacy.

Cecil was moody for an entire day, trying to think of something he could do or say to discourage the Spanish king from interfering. Then he and Ned went to see the count of Feria.

Ned had met Feria once before, back in the summer, when the Spanish courtier had come to Hatfield. Elizabeth had been pleased to see him, taking his visit as a sign that his master, King Felipe, might not be implacably opposed to her. She had turned the full force of her charm on Feria, and he had gone away half in love with her. However, nothing was quite what it seemed in the world of international relations. Ned was not sure how much it meant that Feria was smitten with Elizabeth. He was a smooth diplomat, courteous to all, ruthless beneath the surface.

Cecil and Ned found Feria in London.

The city of London was small by comparison with Antwerp, Paris or Seville, but it was the beating heart of England's growing commercial life. From London a road ran west, along the river, through palaces and mansions with gardens running down to the beach. Two miles from London was the separate city of Westminster, which was the centre of government. White Hall, Westminster Yard and St James's Palace were where noblemen, councillors and courtiers gathered to thrash out the laws that made it possible for the merchants to do business.

Feria had an apartment in the sprawl of assorted buildings known as White Hall Palace. Cecil and Ned were lucky: they caught him as he was about to return to his master in Brussels.

Cecil was not fluent in Spanish, but happily Feria spoke good English. Cecil pretended he had been passing Feria's door and had merely dropped in to pay his respects. Feria politely pretended to believe him. They danced around each other for a few minutes, speaking platitudes.

A lot was at stake underneath the courtesies. King Felipe believed it was his holy duty to support the Catholic Church: it was perfectly possible for Swithin and Sir Reginald to talk the Spanish king into opposing Elizabeth.

Once the formalities were done, Cecil said: 'Between us, England and Spain have very nearly defeated France and Scotland.'

Ned noted the odd emphasis. England had had little to do with the war: it was Spain that was winning. And Scotland was almost irrelevant. But Cecil was reminding Feria who his friends were.

Feria said: 'The war is almost won.'

'King Felipe must be pleased.'

'And most grateful for the assistance of his English subjects.'

Cecil nodded acknowledgement and got down to business. 'By the way, count, have you been in touch recently with Mary Stuart, the queen of the Scots?'

Ned was surprised by the question. Cecil had not told him in advance what he planned to say.

Feria was surprised, too. 'Good lord, no,' he said. 'Why on earth do you want me to communicate with her?'

'Oh, I'm not saying you should – although I would, if I were you.'

'Why?'

'Well, she may be the next queen of England, even though she's a mere girl.'

'One could say the same of Princess Elizabeth.'

Ned frowned. Feria had misjudged Elizabeth if he thought she was a mere girl. Perhaps he was not as sharp as people said.

Cecil ignored the remark. 'In fact, I understand that King Felipe has been asked to support Scottish Mary's claim to the throne.'

Cecil paused, giving Feria the chance to deny this. Feria said nothing. Ned concluded that his guesswork had been accurate: Swithin and Reginald had asked Felipe to support Mary Stuart.

Cecil went on: 'In your place, I would ask Mary Stuart for a very specific commitment. I would want her to guarantee that under her rule England will not change sides, to join forces with France and Scotland against Spain. After all, at this stage that's just about the only development that could prevent Spain winning this war.'

Ned marvelled. Cecil's imagination had come up with just the right fantasy to scare Feria – and his master, the king of Spain.

Feria said: 'Surely you don't think that's likely?'

'I think it's inevitable,' Cecil said, though Ned felt sure he thought no such thing. 'Mary Stuart is technically ruler of Scotland, though her mother acts as regent on her behalf. And Mary's husband is heir to the throne of France. How could she be disloyal to both her countries? She is sure to turn England against Spain – unless you do something now to prevent it.'

Feria nodded thoughtfully. 'And I'm guessing you have a suggestion,' he said.

Cecil shrugged. 'I hardly dare offer advice to the most distinguished diplomat in Europe.' Cecil, too, could be smooth when necessary. 'But, if King Felipe really is considering a request from English Catholics to support Mary Stuart as heir to the throne of England, I do think his majesty might first ask her for a guarantee that, as queen of England, she will not declare war on Spain. He could make that a condition of his support.'

'He could,' Feria said neutrally.

Ned was confused. Cecil was supposed to be talking Feria out of supporting Mary Stuart. Instead he seemed to be suggesting how King Felipe might overcome the main problem. Was there yet again something here Ned was not seeing?

Cecil stood up. 'I'm glad we had the chance to chat,' he said. 'I only looked in to say bon voyage.'

'It's always a pleasure to see you. Please give my respects to the lovely Elizabeth.'

'I'll tell her. She'll be glad.'

As soon as they were outside, Ned said: 'I don't understand!

Why did you make that helpful suggestion about asking Mary Stuart for a guarantee?'

Cecil smiled. 'First of all, King Henri of France will never allow his daughter-in-law to make such a promise.'

Ned had not thought of that. She was still only fifteen: she could not do anything without approval.

Cecil went on: 'Second, her guarantee would be worthless. She would just break it after she took the throne. And there would be nothing anyone could do to hold her to it.'

'And King Felipe will see both of those snags.'

'Or, if he doesn't, Count Feria will point them out to him.'

'So why did you suggest it?'

'As the fastest way to alert Feria and Felipe to the hazards of supporting Mary Stuart. Feria won't take up my suggestion, but he's now thinking hard about what else he could do to protect Spain. And soon Felipe will be thinking about it, too.'

'And what will they do?'

'I don't know – but I know what they *won't* do. They won't help Earl Swithin and Sir Reginald. They won't throw their weight behind the campaign for Mary Stuart. And that makes things a lot more hopeful for us.'

*

QUEEN MARY TUDOR departed her earthly life gradually and majestically, like a mighty galleon inching out of its berth.

As she got weaker, lying in bed in her private apartment in St James's Palace, London, Elizabeth at Hatfield received more and more visitors. Representatives of noble families and rich businesses came to tell her how unhappy they were about religious persecution. Others sent messages offering to do anything they could for her. Elizabeth spent half the day dictating to secretaries, sending a blizzard of short notes thanking people for their loyalty, firming up friendships. The implied message in every letter was I *will be an energetic monarch, and I will remember who helped me at the start.*

Ned and Tom Parry were in charge of military preparations. They commandeered a nearby house, Brocket Hall, and made it their headquarters. From there, they liaised with Elizabeth's backers in the provincial towns, preparing to deal with a Catholic uprising. Ned added up the number of soldiers they could muster, calculated how long it would take each group to get to Hatfield, and wrestled with the problem of finding weapons for them all.

Cecil's sly intervention with Count Feria had been effective. Feria was back in England in the second week of November. He met with the Privy Council – the monarch's most powerful group of advisors – and told them that King Felipe supported Elizabeth as heir to the throne. Queen Mary, in so far as she was able to do anything at all, seemed to have accepted her husband's decision.

Then Feria came to Hatfield.

He walked in all smiles, a man with good news for a captivating woman. The Spanish were the richest people in the world, and Feria wore a red doublet delicately pinked to show the gold lining. His black cloak had a red lining and gold embroidery. Ned had never seen anyone looking quite so pleased with himself.

'Madam, I bring you a gift,' he said.

In the room with Elizabeth and Feria were Cecil, Tom Parry and Ned.

Elizabeth liked presents but hated surprises, and she said guardedly: 'How kind.'

'A gift from my master and yours, King Felipe,' Feria went on.

Felipe was still Elizabeth's master, technically, for Mary Tudor was still alive, still queen of England, and therefore her husband was king of England. But Elizabeth was not pleased to be reminded of this. Ned saw the signs – her chin raised a fraction, the ghost of a frown on her pale brow, a barely perceptible stiffening of her body in the carved-oak chair – but Feria missed them.

He went on: 'King Felipe gives you the throne of England.' He took a step back and bowed, as if expecting a round of applause, or a kiss.

Elizabeth looked calm, but Ned could tell she was thinking

hard. Feria brought good news, but delivered it with magnificent condescension. What would Elizabeth say?

After a moment Feria added: 'May I be the first to congratulate you – your majesty.'

Elizabeth nodded regally, but still said nothing. Ned knew such a silence to be ominous.

'I have informed the Privy Council of King Felipe's decision,' Feria added.

'My sister is dying, and I am to be queen,' Elizabeth said. 'I feel a kind of defeated joy, gladness and sorrow equal in the balance.'

Ned thought she had probably prepared those words.

Feria said: 'Queen Mary, despite her illness, was able to ratify her husband's choice.'

Something had changed subtly in his manner, and Ned instinctively suspected that Feria was now lying.

Feria went on: 'She designates you her heir, on condition that you promise to keep England Catholic.'

Ned's spirits fell again. Elizabeth's hands would be tied from the start of her reign if she agreed to this. Bishop Julius and Sir Reginald would continue to do anything they pleased in Kingsbridge.

Ned glanced at Cecil. He did not seem dismayed. Perhaps he, too, thought Feria was lying. Cecil's expression showed faint amusement, and he was looking expectantly at Elizabeth.

There was a long silence. Feria broke it by saying: 'May I tell the king and queen that you consent to their decision?'

When Elizabeth spoke at last, her voice was like the crack of a whip. 'No, sir, you may not.'

Feria looked as if he had been slapped. 'But . . .'

Elizabeth did not give him the chance to protest. 'If I become queen, it will be because I have been chosen by God, not King Felipe,' she said.

Ned wanted to cheer.

She went on: 'If I rule, it will be by the consent of the English people, not of my dying sister.'

Feria was thunderstruck.

Elizabeth's scorn became vitriolic. 'And when I am crowned

I will take the oath customary to an English sovereign – and will not add extra promises proposed to me by the count of Feria.'

For once Feria did not know what to say.

He had played his cards in the wrong order, Ned realized. Feria should have demanded a promise of Catholicism from Elizabeth *before* endorsing her to the Privy Council. Now it was too late. Ned guessed that at their first meeting Feria had been misled by Elizabeth's alluring manner into thinking she was a weak female who could be manipulated by a strong-minded man. But she had played him, instead of the other way around.

Feria was not a fool, and he saw all this in a flash, Ned could tell. Suddenly Feria looked deflated, an empty wineskin. He made as if to speak then changed his mind, several times: Ned guessed he could think of nothing to say that would make any difference.

Elizabeth put him out of his misery. 'Thank you for coming to visit us, Count,' she said. 'Please give our best greetings to King Felipe. And though hope is slender, we will pray for Queen Mary.'

Ned wondered whether she meant to include her staff in the good wishes, or was already using the royal 'we'. Knowing her, he decided the ambiguity was probably intentional.

Feria took his dismissal as graciously as he could and backed out of the room.

Ned grinned happily. He thought of Earl Swithin and said quietly to Cecil: 'Well, Count Feria isn't the first man to suffer for underestimating Elizabeth.'

'No,' said Cecil, 'and I don't suppose he'll be the last.'

*

WHEN MARGERY WAS nine years old, she had announced that she was going to be a nun.

She was awestruck by the devout life led by her great-aunt, Sister Joan, living on the top floor of the house with her altar and her prayer beads. Joan had dignity and independence and a purpose in life.

All the nunneries had been abolished, along with the

monasteries, by Henry VIII, and Queen Mary Tudor had failed to restore them; but that was not the reason Margery abandoned her ambition. The truth was that as soon as she reached puberty she knew that she could never live a life of celibacy. She loved boys, even when they acted stupid. She liked their boldness and their strength and their humour, and she was excited by the yearning stares they directed at her body. She even liked how blind they were to subtleties and hidden meanings: there was something attractive about their straightforwardness, and sometimes girls were so sly.

So she had given up on the plan of becoming a nun, but she was still drawn to the idea of a life devoted to a mission. She confessed this to Sister Joan, on the day she was to move to New Castle, while her clothes, books and jewellery were being loaded onto a four-wheeled cart for the journey. 'Don't worry about it,' Sister Joan said, sitting on a wooden stool, straight-backed and alert despite her age. 'God has a purpose for you. He has a purpose for all of us.'

'But how can I find out what his purpose is for me?'

'Why, you can't find out!' said Sister Joan. 'You must just wait for him to reveal it. God won't be hurried.'

Margery vowed to use self-control, although she was beginning to feel that her life was an exercise in self-control. She had submitted to her parents in marrying Bart. With her new husband she had spent the last two weeks at a house on Leper Island owned by the earl, and during that time Bart had made it clear that he expected Margery to submit to him in the same way she had submitted to her parents. He decided on his own where they would go and what they would do and then simply issued instructions to her as he might have done to a steward. She had expected their marriage to be more of a partnership, but that thought seemed never to have crossed Bart's mind. She hoped she might change him, gradually and subtly, but he was awfully like his father.

Her proud family came with her on the journey to New Castle: Sir Reginald, Lady Jane and Rollo. They were related to the earl, now, and revelling in their connection with the aristocracy.

Also, the men were eager to confer with Earl Swithin. Their trip to Brussels had failed. King Felipe had seemed to listen to them and agree with their point of view, but someone else must have got to him, for in the end he had thrown the weight of his support behind Elizabeth. Rollo was bitterly disappointed, Margery could see.

On the journey Reginald and Rollo discussed what to do next. The only recourse left to them was an armed uprising against Elizabeth immediately after the death of Mary Tudor. They needed to know how many men-at-arms Earl Swithin could muster, and who among the Catholic nobility could be relied upon to support Swithin.

Margery was troubled. She saw Protestantism as an arrogant heresy favoured by men who imagined they were clever enough to find fault with hundreds of years of Church teaching, but she also believed that Christians should not kill one another. However, as New Castle loomed up ahead, her mind was on more mundane worries. Earl Swithin was a widower, so Margery – now titled Viscountess Shiring – was going to be the lady of the house. She was only sixteen, and hardly knew what it took to manage a castle. She had talked it over at length with Lady Jane, and made some plans, but she was anxious about facing the reality.

Bart had gone ahead, and when the Fitzgerald party arrived, about twenty servants were waiting for them in the courtyard. They clapped and cheered when Margery rode in, and she felt welcomed. Perhaps they disliked working for an all-male family, and looked forward to a woman's touch. She hoped so.

Swithin and Bart came out to greet them. Bart kissed her, then Swithin did the same, letting his lips linger on her cheek and pressing her body to his. Then Swithin introduced a voluptuous woman of about thirty. 'Sal Brendon is my housekeeper, and she will help you with everything,' he said. 'Show the viscountess around, Sal. We men have a lot to talk about.'

As he turned away to usher Reginald and Rollo into the house, he gave Sal a pat on her ample bottom. Sal did not seem surprised or displeased. Both Margery and Lady Jane noticed this and looked at one another. Sal was obviously more than a housekeeper.

'I'll take you to your quarters,' Sal said. 'This way.'

Margery wanted more of a tour. She had been here before, most recently on the Twelfth Day of Christmas, but it was a big place and she needed to refamiliarize herself with the layout. She said: 'We'll look at the kitchen first.'

Sal hesitated, looking annoyed, then said: 'As you wish.'

They entered the house and went to the kitchen. It was hot and steamy and not too clean. An older servant was sitting on a stool, watching the cook work and drinking from a tankard. When Margery entered, he got to his feet rather slowly.

Sal said: 'This is the cook, Mave Brown.'

There was a cat sitting on the table picking delicately at the remains of a knuckle of ham. Margery lifted the cat up with a swift movement and dropped it on the floor.

Mave Brown said resentfully: 'She's a good mouser, that cat.'

Margery said: 'She'll be a better mouser if you don't let her eat ham.'

The older manservant began to prepare a tray with a plate of cold beef, a jug of wine and some bread. Margery took a slice of the beef and ate it.

The man said: 'That's for the earl.'

'And very good it is, too,' Margery said. 'What's your name?'

'Colly Knight,' he said. 'Worked for Earl Swithin forty years, man and boy.' He said it with an air of superiority, as if to let Margery know that she was a mere latecomer.

'I am the viscountess,' Margery said. 'You should say "my lady" when you speak to me.'

There was a long pause, then at last Colly said: 'Yes, my lady.'

'Now we will go to the viscount's quarters,' Margery said.

Sal Brendon led the way. They passed through the great hall, where a girl of ten or eleven was sweeping the floor in a desultory way, holding the brush with one hand. 'Get both your hands on that broom handle,' Margery snapped at her as they passed. The girl looked startled but did as she was told.

They went up the stairs and along the corridor to the end. The bedchamber was a corner room with communicating doors to two side rooms. Margery immediately liked that arrangement: it meant that Bart could have a dressing room for his muddy boots, and Margery could have a boudoir where maids could help with her clothes and hair.

But all the rooms were filthy. The windows seemed not to have been washed for a year. There were two big dogs lying on a blanket, an old one and a young one. Margery saw dog shit on the floor – Bart obviously let his pets do as they pleased in his rooms. On the wall was a painting of a naked woman, but the room contained no flowers or greenery, no plates of fruit or raisins, no fragrant bowls of dried herbs and petals to scent the air. On a chair was a tangle of laundry, including a bloodstained shirt, that seemed to have been there a long time.

'This is disgusting,' Margery said to Sal Brendon. 'We're going to clean the place up before I open my trunks. Go and fetch brooms and a shovel. The first thing you'll do is clean up the dog shit.'

Sal put her hand on her hip and looked mutinous. 'Earl Swithin is my master,' she said. 'You'd better speak to him.'

Something in Margery snapped. She had been deferring to people too long: her parents, Bishop Julius, Bart. She was not going to defer to Sal Brendon. All the bottled fury of the past year boiled over inside her. She drew back her arm and gave Sal a terrific slap across the face. The crack of palm on cheek was so loud that one of the dogs jumped. Sal fell back with a cry of shock.

'Don't ever speak to me like that again,' Margery said. 'I know your type. Just because the earl gives you a fuck when he's drunk you think you're the countess.' Margery saw a flare of recognition in Sal's eyes that confirmed the truth of the accusation. 'I am mistress of this house now, and you'll obey me. And if you give trouble, you'll be out of here so fast your feet won't touch the ground until you land in the Kingsbridge whorehouse, which is probably where you belong.'

Sal was visibly tempted to defy her. Her face was suffused with rage and she might even have hit back. But she hesitated. She had to realize that if the earl's new daughter-in-law were to ask him to get rid of an insolent servant, today of all days, he could not possibly refuse. Sal saw sense and her face changed. 'I . . . I ask your pardon, my lady,' she said humbly. 'I'll fetch the brooms right away.'

She left the room. Lady Jane said quietly to Margery: 'Well done.'

Margery spotted a riding whip on a stool beside a pair of spurs, and picked it up. She crossed the room to where the dogs lay. 'Get out, you filthy beasts,' she said, and gave each of them a smart smack. More shocked than hurt, both dogs jumped up and scampered from the room, looking indignant.

'And stay out,' said Margery.

*

ROLLO REFUSED TO believe that the tide was turning against Mary Stuart. How could it, he asked himself indignantly, when England was a Catholic country and Mary had the support of the Pope? So that afternoon he wrote a letter for Earl Swithin to send to the archbishop of Canterbury, Cardinal Pole.

The letter asked for the archbishop's blessing on an armed insurrection against Elizabeth Tudor.

Violence was now the only hope. King Felipe had turned against Mary Stuart and backed Elizabeth. That meant disaster for Rollo, the Fitzgerald family and the true Catholic Christian faith in England.

'Is this treason?' Swithin asked as he picked up the pen.

'No,' said Rollo. 'Elizabeth is not queen yet, so no one is conspiring to rebel against the sovereign.' Rollo knew that if they lost and Elizabeth won the crown, she would consider that a distinction without a difference. So they were all risking execution. But at moments such as this men had to take sides.

Swithin signed it – not without difficulty, for he found it easier to break in a wild horse than to write his name.

Pole was ill, but he could surely dictate a letter, Rollo thought. What would he say in reply to Swithin? Pole was the most hard-line Catholic of all the English bishops, and Rollo felt almost certain that he would support a revolt. Then the actions of Swithin and his supporters would be legitimized by the Church.

Two of Swithin's trusted men were given the letter to carry to Lambeth Palace, the archbishop's residence near London.

Meanwhile, Sir Reginald and Lady Jane returned to Kingsbridge. Rollo stayed with the earl. He wanted to make sure there was no backsliding.

While waiting for the archbishop's reply, Swithin and Bart set about mustering a force of armed men. Other Catholic earls must be doing the same thing all over England, Rollo reckoned, and their combined forces would be irresistible.

In a hundred villages in the county of Shiring, Earl Swithin was lord and master with much of the same absolute authority that his ancestors had wielded in the Middle Ages. Swithin and Bart visited some of these places personally. The earl's servants read a proclamation in others, and parish priests gave the same message in their sermons. Single men between eighteen and thirty were summoned to New Castle, and ordered to bring with them axes, scythes and iron chains.

Rollo had no experience of anything like this, and could not guess what would happen.

The response thrilled him. Every village sent half a dozen lads. They were keen to go. The makeshift weapons, and the young men carrying them, were not much needed in the fields in November. And Protestantism was an urban movement: it had never taken hold in the conservative countryside. Besides, this was the most exciting thing that had happened in living memory. Everyone was talking about it. Beardless boys and old men wept that they were not wanted.

The army could not remain many days at New Castle, and anyway it was a long march to Hatfield, so they set off, even though they had not heard back from Cardinal Pole. Their route would take them through Kingsbridge, where they would receive the blessing of Bishop Julius.

Swithin rode at the head of the column, with Bart at his side and Rollo behind. They reached Kingsbridge on the third day. Entering the city, they were stopped at Merthin's Bridge by Rollo's father, Sir Reginald, who was the mayor. He was accompanied by the aldermen of the borough.

'I'm sorry,' Reginald said to Swithin. 'There's a difficulty.'

Rollo eased his horse forward so that he was at the front with Swithin and Bart. 'What on earth is the matter?' he said.

His father seemed in despair. 'If you will dismount and come with me, I'll show you,' he said.

Swithin said irascibly: 'This is a poor way to welcome a holy crusade!'

'I know,' said Reginald. 'Believe me, I am mortified. But come and look.'

The three leaders got off their horses. Swithin summoned the captains, gave them money, and told them to get barrels of beer sent over from the Slaughterhouse tavern to keep the men happy.

Reginald led them across the double bridge into the city, and up the main street to the market square.

There they saw an astonishing sight.

The market stalls were closed, the temporary structures having been removed, and the square had been cleared. Forty or fifty stout tree trunks, all six or eight inches in diameter, had been firmly planted in the hard winter earth. Several hundred young men stood around the stakes, and Rollo saw, with increasing astonishment, that all of them had wooden swords and shields.

It was an army in training.

As they watched, a leader performed a demonstration on a raised stage, attacking the stake with wooden sword and shield, using right and left arms alternately in a rhythm that – Rollo could imagine – would have been effective on the battlefield. When the demonstration was over, all the others tried to imitate his actions, taking it in turns.

Rollo recalled seeing similar exercises in Oxford, when Queen Mary Tudor had been preparing to send an English army to France to support the Spanish war. The stakes were called pells. They were firmly seated and difficult to knock over. At first, he remembered, untrained men's swings were so wild that they sometimes missed the pell entirely. They quickly learned to aim carefully and hit harder. He had heard military men say that a few afternoons of pell practice could turn a hopeless yokel into a halfway dangerous soldier.

Rollo saw Dan Cobley among the trainees, and the last piece of the puzzle fell into place.

This was a Protestant army.

They would not call themselves that, of course. They would claim to be preparing to resist a Spanish invasion, perhaps. Sir Reginald and Bishop Julius would not have believed them, but what could they do? The dozen or so men of the city watch could not arrest and jail several hundred, even if the trainees had been breaking the law, which they probably were not.

Rollo watched in despair as the young men attacked the pells, rapidly becoming more focussed and effective. 'This is not a coincidence,' he said. 'They heard of the approach of our army, and mustered their own to obstruct us.'

Reginald said: 'Earl Swithin, if your army enters the town, there will be a pitched battle in the streets.'

'My strong-armed village lads will smash these puny city Protestants.'

'The aldermen will not admit your men.'

'Overrule the cowards,' Swithin said.

'I don't have the right. And they have said they will arrest me if I try.'

'Let them. We'll get you out of jail.'

Bart said: 'We'll have to fight our way across that damn bridge.'

'We can do that,' Swithin blustered.

'We'd lose a lot of men.'

'That's what they're for.'

'But then who would we take to Hatfield?'

Rollo watched Swithin's face. It was not in his character to yield, even when the odds were against him. His expression showed furious indecision.

Bart said: 'I wonder if the same thing is happening elsewhere – Protestants getting ready to fight, I mean.'

This had not occurred to Rollo. When he had proposed that Swithin raise a small army, he should have guessed that the Protestants would be thinking the same way. He had foreseen a neat coup d'état, but instead he was facing a bloody civil war. And instinct told him that the English people did not want a civil war – and might well turn on men who started one.

It was beginning to look as if the peasant lads would have to be sent home.

Two men emerged from the nearby Bell Inn and came hurrying over. Seeing them, Reginald remembered something. 'There's a message for you, earl,' he said. 'These two men got here an hour ago. I told them to wait rather than risk missing you on the road.'

Rollo recognized the men Swithin had sent to Lambeth Palace. What had Archbishop Pole said? That could prove crucial. With his encouragement, perhaps Swithin's army could continue to Hatfield. Without it, they might be wiser to disband.

The older of the two couriers spoke. 'There's no reply from the cardinal,' he said.

Rollo's heart sank.

'What do you mean, no reply?' Swithin said angrily. 'He must have said something.'

'We spoke to his clerk, Canon Robinson. He told us the cardinal was too ill to read your letter, let alone reply to it.'

'Why, he must be at death's door!' said Swithin.

'Yes, my lord.'

This was catastrophic, Rollo thought. England's leading ultra-Catholic was dying at this turning point in the country's history. The fact changed everything. The idea of kidnapping Elizabeth and sending for Mary Stuart had seemed, until now, like a hopeful enterprise with a great chance of success. Now it looked suicidal.

Sometimes, Rollo reflected, fate seemed to be on the side of the devil.

*

NED MOVED TO London and haunted St James's Palace, waiting for news of Queen Mary Tudor.

She weakened dramatically on 16 November, a day that Protestants began to call Hope Wednesday even before the sun went down. Ned was in the shivering crowd outside the tall red-brick gatehouse the following morning, just before dawn, when a servant, hurrying out with a message, whispered: 'She's gone.'

Ned ran across the road to the Coach and Horses tavern. He ordered a horse to be saddled, then woke his messenger, Peter Hopkins. While Hopkins was getting dressed and drinking a flagon of ale for breakfast, Ned wrote a note telling Elizabeth that Mary Tudor was dead. Then he saw the man off to Hatfield.

He returned to the gatehouse and found the crowd grown larger.

For the next two hours he watched important courtiers and less important messengers hurry in and out. But when he saw Nicholas Heath emerge, he followed him.

Heath was probably the most powerful man in England. He was archbishop of York, Queen Mary's Chancellor, and the holder of the Great Seal. Cecil had tried to win him to the cause of Elizabeth, but Heath had remained uncommitted. Now he would have to jump – one way or the other.

Heath and his entourage rode the short distance to Westminster, where members of Parliament would be gathering for the morning session. Ned and others ran behind them. Another crowd was already forming at Westminster. Heath announced that he would address the lords and commons together, and they assembled in the House of Lords.

Ned tried to slip in with Heath's entourage, but a guard stopped him. Ned pretended to be surprised, and said: 'I represent the princess Elizabeth. She has ordered me to attend and report to her.'

The guard was disposed to make trouble, but Heath heard the altercation and intervened. 'I've met you, young man,' he said to Ned. 'With Sir William Cecil, I think.'

'Yes, my lord archbishop.' It was true, though Ned was surprised that Heath remembered.

'Let him in,' Heath said to the guard.

The fact that Parliament was sitting meant that the succession could happen quickly, especially if Heath backed

Elizabeth. She was popular, she was the sister of Queen Mary Tudor, and she was only twenty miles away. Mary Stuart, by contrast, was unknown to the English, she had a French husband, and she was in Paris. Expediency favoured Elizabeth.

But the Church favoured Mary Stuart.

The debating chamber resounded with animated conversation as everyone in the room discussed the same question. Then they fell silent when Heath stood up.

'God this present morning called to his mercy our late sovereign lady, Queen Mary,' he said.

The assembly gave a collective sigh. All of them either knew this or had heard rumours, but the confirmation was heavy.

'But we have cause to rejoice with praise to Almighty God for that he left us a true, lawful and right inheritress to the crown.'

The chamber went dead silent. Heath was about to name the next queen. But which one would it be?

'Lady Elizabeth,' he said, '*whose most lawful right and title we need not doubt!*'

The room exploded in uproar. Heath carried on speaking, but no one heard. The archbishop had endorsed Elizabeth, calling her title 'lawful' – in direct contradiction of the Pope's ruling. It was all over.

A few of the members of Parliament were shouting in protest, but Ned could see that most of them were cheering. Elizabeth was Parliament's choice. Perhaps they had been afraid to reveal their feelings while the issue was in doubt, but now their inhibitions fell away. Cecil might even have underestimated Elizabeth's popularity, Ned saw. Although there were some long faces in the chamber, men neither applauding nor cheering but sitting silent with folded arms, they were a minority. The rest were delighted. Civil war had been avoided, there would be no foreign king, the burnings would end. Ned realized that he was cheering, too.

Heath left the chamber, followed by most of the Privy Council, and stood on the steps outside to repeat his proclamation to the waiting crowd.

He then announced that he would read it again in the city of London. But before he left he beckoned to Ned. 'I expect you'll ride to Hatfield now with the news,' he said.

'Yes, my lord archbishop.'

'You may tell Queen Elizabeth that I will be with her before nightfall.'

'Thank you.'

'Don't stop to celebrate until after you have delivered the message.'

'Certainly not, sir.'

Heath left.

Ned ran back to the Coach and Horses. A few minutes later he was on the road to Hatfield.

He had a good, steady mare which he trotted and walked alternately. He was afraid to push her too hard for fear she would break down. Speed was not crucial, as long as he got there before Heath.

He had set off at mid-morning, and it was mid-afternoon when he saw the red-brick gables of Hatfield Palace ahead.

Hopkins was there already, presumably, so everyone already knew that Queen Mary Tudor was dead. But no one knew who was the new monarch.

As he rode into the courtyard, several grooms shouted at once: 'What's the news?'

Ned decided that Elizabeth herself must be the first to know. He said nothing to the grooms and kept his face expressionless.

Elizabeth was in her parlour with Cecil, Tom Parry and Nell Baynsford. They all stared at him in tense silence as he walked in, still wearing his heavy riding cloak.

He walked up to Elizabeth. He tried to remain solemn, but he could not help smiling. She read his expression and he saw her lips move slightly in a responding smile.

'You are the queen of England,' he said. He took off his hat, bent his knee and made a deep, sweeping bow. 'Your Majesty,' he said.

*

We were happy, because we had no idea how much trouble we were causing. It was not just me, of course: I was the junior partner with others who were older and a good deal wiser. But none of us saw the future.

We had been warned. Rollo Fitzgerald had lectured me on how much opposition Queen Elizabeth would face, and what a pitiful few European leaders would support her. I paid him no heed, but he was right, the sanctimonious bastard.

What we did in that momentous year of 1558 caused political strife, revolt, civil war and invasion. There were times, in later years, when in the depths of despair I would wonder whether it had been worth it. The simple idea that people should be allowed to worship as they wished caused more suffering than the ten plagues of Egypt.

So, if I had known then what I know now, would I have done the same?

Hell, yes.

Part Two

1559 to 1563

9

STROLLING ALONG THE SOUTHERN side of the Île de la
Cité on a sunny Friday in June, with the winged cathedral on
one side and the sparkling river on the other, Sylvie Palot said
to Pierre Aumande: 'Do you want to marry me, or not?'

She had the satisfaction of seeing a flash of panic in his eyes.
This was unusual. His equanimity was not easily disturbed: he
was always controlled.

He regained his composure so quickly that she might
almost have imagined the lapse. 'Of course I want to marry
you, my darling,' he said, and he looked hurt. 'How could you
ask such a question?'

She regretted it instantly. She adored him, and hated to see
him upset in any way. He looked especially lovable now, with
the breeze off the river ruffling his blond mane. But she
hardened her heart and persisted with her question. 'We've
been betrothed for more than a year. It's too long.'

Everything else in Sylvie's life was good. Her father's
bookshop was booming, and he was planning to open a second
store on the other side of the river, in the university quarter.
His illegal trade in French-language Bibles and other banned
books was going even better. Hardly a day went by when Sylvie
did not go to the secret warehouse in the rue du Mur for a
book or two to sell to a Protestant family. New Protestant
congregations were coming up like bluebells in spring, in Paris
and elsewhere. As well as spreading the true gospel, the Palots
were making healthy profits.

But Pierre's behaviour puzzled and troubled her.

'I need to finish my studies, and Father Moineau refused to
allow me to continue as a married student,' he said now. 'I
explained that to you, and you agreed to wait.'

'For a year. And in a few days' time lectures will be over for the summer. We have my parents' consent. We have enough money. We can live over the shop, at least until we have children. But you haven't said anything.'

'I've written to my mother.'

'You didn't tell me.'

'I'm waiting for her answer.'

'What was the question?'

'Whether she's well enough to travel to Paris for the wedding.'

'And if she's not?'

'Let's not worry about that unless it happens.'

Sylvie was not happy with this response, but she let it drop for the moment, and said: 'Where shall we have the official ceremony?' Pierre glanced up at the towers of Notre Dame, and she laughed and said: 'Not there. That's for the nobility.'

'At the parish church, I assume.'

'And then we'll have our real wedding at our own church.' She meant the old hunting lodge in the forest. Protestants still could not worship openly in Paris, though they did in some French cities.

'I suppose we'll have to invite the marchioness,' Pierre said with a grimace of dislike.

'As the building belongs to her husband ...' It was unfortunate that Pierre had got off on the wrong foot with Marchioness Louise, and afterwards had not been able to win her round. In fact, the more he tried to charm her, the frostier she became. Sylvie had expected him to brush this aside with a laugh, but it seemed he could not. It made him furious, and Sylvie realized that her outwardly self-assured fiancé was, in fact, deeply sensitive to any kind of social slight.

His vulnerability made her love him more, but it also troubled her, though she was not sure why.

'I suppose it can't be helped,' Pierre said, his tone light but his look dark.

'Will you have new clothes?' She knew how much he liked buying clothes.

He smiled. 'I should have a sombre coat of Protestant grey, shouldn't I?'

'Yes.' He was a faithful worshipper, attending every week. He had quickly got to know everyone in the congregation, and had been keen to meet people from other groups in Paris. He had even attended services with other congregations. He had badly wanted to go to the national synod in Paris in May – the first time French Protestants had dared to hold such a conference – but the arrangements were highly secret and only longstanding Protestants were invited. Despite this rebuff, he was a thoroughly accepted member of the community, which delighted Sylvie.

'There's probably a tailor specializing in dark clothing for Protestants,' he said.

'There is: Duboeuf in the rue St Martin. My father goes there, though only when Mother forces him. He could afford a new coat every year, but he won't spend money on what he calls frippery. I expect he'll buy me a wedding dress, but he won't be happy about it.'

'If he won't, I will.'

She grabbed his arm, stopped him walking, and kissed him. 'You're wonderful,' she said.

'And you're the most beautiful girl in Paris. In France.'

She laughed. It wasn't true, although she did look fetching in the black dress with a white collar: Protestant colours happened to suit her dark hair and fresh complexion. Then she recalled her purpose, and became solemn again. 'When you hear back from your mother . . .'

'Yes?'

'We must set a date. Whatever she says, I don't want to wait any longer.'

'All right.'

For a moment she was not sure whether to believe he had assented, and she hesitated to rejoice. 'Do you mean it?'

'Of course. We'll set a date. I promise!'

She laughed with delight. 'I love you,' she said, and she kissed him again.

*

I DON'T KNOW how much longer I can keep this up, Pierre fretted as he left Sylvie at the door to her father's shop and walked north across the Notre Dame bridge to the right bank. Away from the river there was no breeze, and soon he was perspiring.

He had already made her wait longer than was reasonable. Her father was even more grumpy than usual and her mother, who had always favoured Pierre, was inclined to speak curtly to him. Sylvie herself was besotted with him, but even she was discontented. They suspected he was dallying with her – and, of course, they were right.

But she was bringing him such a rich harvest. His black leather-bound notebook now contained hundreds of names of Paris Protestants and the addresses where they held their heretical services.

Even today she had given him a bonus: a Protestant tailor! He had made the suggestion half in jest, but his speculation had been right, and foolish Sylvie had confirmed it. This could be a priceless lead.

The files of Cardinal Charles were already bulging. Surprisingly, Charles had not yet arrested any of the Protestants. Pierre planned to ask him, before long, when he intended to pounce.

He was on his way to meet Cardinal Charles now, but he had time to spare. He went along the rue St Martin until he found the establishment of René Duboeuf. From outside it looked much like a regular Paris house, though the windows were larger than usual and there was a sign over the door. He went in.

He was struck by the air of neatness and order. The room was crammed, but everything was tidy: rolls of silk and woollen cloth on shelves, precisely aligned; bowls of buttons arranged by colour; drawer stacks all with little signs indicating their contents.

A bald man was stooping over a table, carefully cutting a length of cloth with a huge pair of spring scissors that looked very sharp. At the back a pretty woman sat under an iron chandelier, sewing in the light of a dozen candles: Pierre wondered if she bore a label that read 'Wife'.

One more Protestant couple did not amount to much, but Pierre hoped to meet some of the customers.

The man put down his scissors and came forward to greet Pierre, introducing himself as Duboeuf. He looked hard at Pierre's slashed doublet, apparently appraising it with an expert eye, and Pierre wondered if he thought it too ostentatious for a Protestant.

Pierre gave his name. 'I need a new coat,' he said. 'Not too gaudy. Dark grey, perhaps.'

'Very good, sir,' said the tailor warily. 'Did someone recommend me to you, perhaps?'

'Giles Palot, the printer.'

Duboeuf relaxed. 'I know him well.'

'He is to be my father-in-law.'

'Congratulations.'

Pierre was accepted. That was the first step.

Duboeuf was a small man, but he lifted the heavy rolls of cloth down from the shelves with practised ease. Pierre picked out a grey that was almost black.

No other customers came in, disappointingly. Pierre wondered just how he could make use of this Protestant tailor. He could not stay in the shop all day waiting to meet clients. He could set a watch on the place – Gaston Le Pin, the captain of the Guise household guard, could find a discreet man – but the watcher would not know the names of the men who came and went, so the exercise would be pointless. Pierre racked his brains: there had to be a way of exploiting this discovery.

The tailor picked up a long strip of fine leather and began to measure Pierre's body, sticking coloured pins into the strip to record the width of his shoulders, the length of his arms, and the circumference of his chest and waist. 'You have a fine physique, Monsieur Aumande,' he said. 'The coat will look very distinguished on you.' Pierre ignored this piece of shopkeeper's flattery. How was he going to get the names of Duboeuf's customers?

When all the measurements had been made, Duboeuf took a notebook from a drawer. 'If I might take down your address, Monsieur Aumande?'

Pierre stared at the book. Of course, Duboeuf had to know where his customers lived, otherwise it would be too easy for someone to order a coat then change his mind and simply not return. And even if Duboeuf had a phenomenal memory, and could remember every customer and every order, the lack of a written record would surely lead to disputes about bills. No, the obsessively neat Duboeuf would have to keep notes.

Pierre had to get a look inside that book. Those names and addresses belonged in his own ledger, the one with the black leather cover, that listed all the Protestants he had discovered.

'The address, Monsieur?' Duboeuf repeated.

'I'm at the College des Ames.'

Duboeuf found his inkwell dry. With a faintly embarrassed laugh, he said: 'Excuse me one moment while I get a bottle of ink.' He disappeared through a doorway.

Pierre saw his chance to look inside the book. But it would be better to get rid of the wife. He went to the back of the room and spoke to her. She was about eighteen, he guessed, younger than her husband, who was in his thirties. 'I wonder – might I ask you for a small cup of wine? It's a dusty day.'

'Of course, Monsieur.' She put down her sewing and went out.

Pierre opened the tailor's notebook. As he had hoped, it listed the names and addresses of customers, together with details of garments ordered and fabric specified, and sums of money owed and paid. He recognized some of the names as those of Protestants he had already identified. He began to feel excited. This book probably listed half the heretics in Paris. It would be a priceless asset to Cardinal Charles. He wished he could slip it inside his doublet, but that would be rash. Instead, he began to memorize as many names as he could.

He was still doing so when he heard the voice of Duboeuf behind him. 'What are you doing?'

The tailor looked pale and scared. So he should, Pierre thought: he had made a dangerous error in leaving the book on the table. Pierre closed the book and smiled. 'Idle curiosity. Forgive me.'

Duboeuf said severely: 'The notebook is private!' He was unnerved, Pierre saw.

Pierre said lightly: 'It turns out that I know most of your customers. I'm glad to see that my friends pay their bills!' Duboeuf did not laugh. But what could he do?

After a moment, Duboeuf opened the new ink bottle, dipped his pen, and wrote down Pierre's name and address.

The wife came in. 'Your wine, sir,' she said, handing Pierre a cup.

Duboeuf said: 'Thank you, Françoise.'

She had a nice figure, Pierre noted. He wondered what had attracted her to the older Duboeuf. The prospect of a comfortable life with a prosperous husband, perhaps. Or it might even have been love.

Duboeuf said: 'If you would be so kind as to come back a week from today, your new coat will be ready for you to try on. It will be twenty-five livres.'

'Splendid.' Pierre did not think he would learn much more from Duboeuf today. He drank the wine and took his leave.

The wine had not quenched his thirst, so he went into the nearest tavern and got a tankard of beer. He also bought a sheet of paper and borrowed a quill and ink. While drinking the beer he wrote neatly: 'René Duboeuf, tailor, rue St Martin. Françoise Duboeuf, wife.' Then he added all the names and addresses he could remember from the notebook. He dried the ink and put the sheet inside his doublet. He would transfer the information to his black book later.

Sipping his beer, he wondered impatiently when Cardinal Charles was going to make use of all this information. For the present, the cardinal seemed content to accumulate names and addresses, but the time would come when he would swoop. That would be a day of carnage. Pierre would share in Charles's triumph. However, he shifted uneasily on his tavern stool as he thought of the hundreds of men and women who would be imprisoned, tortured and perhaps even burned alive. Many of the Protestants were self-righteous prigs, and he would be glad to see them suffer – especially Marchioness Louise – but others had been kind to him, made him welcome at the hunting-lodge church, invited him into their homes, and answered his sly questions with a frank honesty that made him wince when he thought how he was deceiving them. Only eighteen months ago, the worst thing he had ever done was sponge off a randy widow. It seemed longer.

He emptied his tankard and left. It was a short distance to the rue Saint-Antoine, where a tournament was being held. Paris was partying, again. The treaty with Spain had been signed, and King Henri II was celebrating the peace, and pretending he had not lost the war.

The rue Saint-Antoine was the widest street in Paris, which was why it was used for tournaments. Along one side was the massive, ramshackle Palace of Tournelles, its windows crowded with royal and aristocratic spectators, the colours of their costly clothes making a row of bright pictures. On the opposite side of the road the common people jostled for space, their cheap garments all in shades of faded brown, like a ploughed field in winter. They stood or sat on stools they had brought with them, or perched precariously on window ledges and rooftops. A tournament was a grand spectacle, with the added attraction of possible injury or even death to the high-born competitors.

As Pierre entered the palace he was offered a tray of cakes by Odette, a maid of about twenty, voluptuous but plain. She smiled flirtatiously at him, showing crooked teeth. She had a reputation for being easy, but Pierre was not interested in girls of the servant class – he could have got one of those back in Thonnance-lès-Joinville. All the same he was pleased to see her, for it meant that the adorable Véronique was nearby. 'Where is your mistress?' he said.

Odette pouted and said: 'Mademoiselle is upstairs.'

Most of the courtiers were on the upper floor, which had windows overlooking the jousting ground. Véronique was sitting at a table with a gaggle of aristocratic girls, drinking fruit cordial. A distant cousin of the Guise brothers, she was among the least important family members, but nevertheless noble. She wore a pale green dress made of some mixture of silk and linen, so light it seemed to float around her perfect figure. The thought of having such a high-born woman naked in his arms made Pierre feel faint. This was who he wanted to marry – not the bourgeoise daughter of a Protestant printer.

Véronique had treated him with mild disdain when he had first met her, but she had gradually warmed to him. Everyone knew he was only the son of a country priest, but they also knew he was close to the powerful Cardinal Charles, and that gave him a special status.

He bowed to her and asked if she was enjoying the tournament.

'Not much,' she said.

He gave her his most charming smile. 'You don't like watching men ride too fast and knock each other off their horses? How strange.'

She laughed. 'I prefer dancing.'

'So do I. Happily there's a ball tonight.'

'I can hardly wait.'

'I look forward to seeing you there. I must speak with your Uncle Charles. Excuse me.'

Walking away, he felt good about that brief encounter. He had made her laugh, and she had treated him almost as an equal.

Charles was in a side room with a small boy who had the blond hair of the Guises. This was his nephew Henri, aged eight, eldest son of Scarface. Knowing that the boy might one day be the duke of Guise, Pierre bowed to him and asked if he was having a good time. 'They won't let me joust,' Henri said. 'But I bet I could. I'm a good rider.'

Charles said: 'Run along, now, Henri – there'll be another bout in a minute and you don't want to miss it.'

Henri left and Charles waved Pierre to a chair.

In the year and a half that Pierre had been spying for Charles, their relationship had altered. Charles was grateful for the names and addresses Pierre had brought him. The cardinal's file on clandestine Paris Protestants was far better than it had been before Pierre had come along. Charles could still be scornful and patronizing, but he was like that with everyone, and he seemed to respect Pierre's judgement. They sometimes talked about general political issues and Charles even listened to Pierre's opinion.

'I made a discovery,' Pierre said. 'Many of the Protestants use a tailor in the rue St Martin who keeps a little book with all their names and addresses.'

'A gold mine!' said Charles. 'Dear God, these people are getting brazen.'

'I was tempted to pick it up and run off down the street with it.'

'I don't want you to reveal yourself yet.'

'No. But one day I'll get hold of that book.' Pierre reached inside his doublet. 'Meanwhile, I wrote down as many of the names and addresses as I could memorize.' He handed the sheet to Charles.

Charles read the list. 'Very useful.'

'I had to order a coat from the tailor.' Pierre raised the price. 'Forty-five livres.'

Charles took coins from a purse. He gave Pierre twenty gold ecus, each worth two and a half livres. 'Should be a nice coat,' he said.

Pierre said: 'When will we pounce on these deviants? We have hundreds of Paris Protestants in our records.'

'Be patient.'

'But every heretic is one less enemy. Why not get rid of them?'

'When we crack down, we want everyone to know it's the Guises who are doing it.'

That made sense to Pierre. 'So that the family wins the loyalty of the ultra-Catholics, I suppose.'

'And people who advocate tolerance – the middle-of-the-roaders, the *moyenneurs* – will be labelled Protestant.'

That was subtle, Pierre thought. The Guise family's worst enemies were people who advocated tolerance. They would undermine the entire basis of the family's strength. Such people had to be pushed to one extreme or the other. Charles's political shrewdness impressed him repeatedly. 'But how will we come to be in charge of stamping out heresy?'

'One day young Francis will be king. Not yet, we hope – we need him first to establish his independence from Queen Caterina, and come completely under the influence of his wife, our niece, Mary Stuart. But when it happens . . .' Charles waved Pierre's sheet of paper. 'That's when we use this.'

Pierre was downcast. 'I hadn't realized your thinking was so long-term. That gives me a problem.'

'Why?'

'I've been engaged to Sylvie Palot for more than a year, and I'm running out of excuses.'

'Marry the bitch,' said Charles.

Pierre was horrified. 'I don't want to get stuck with a Protestant wife.'

Charles shrugged. 'Why not?'

'There's someone I *would* like to marry.'

'Oh? Who?'

It was time to tell Charles what reward he wanted for his work. 'Véronique de Guise.'

Charles laughed loudly. 'You cocky little upstart! You, marry my relation? It's the arrogance of the devil! Don't be absurd.'

Pierre felt himself flush from forehead to throat. He had made an error of timing, and in consequence he was humiliated. 'I didn't think it too ambitious,' he protested. 'She's only a distant relative.'

'She's a second cousin of Mary Stuart, who will probably be queen of France one day! Who do you think you are?' Charles waved a hand in dismissal. 'Go on, get out of here.'

Pierre got up and left.

*

ALISON McKAY WAS enjoying life. Since Mary Stuart had become Francis's wife, rather than merely his fiancée, her status had risen, and consequently so had Alison's. They had more servants, more dresses, more money. People bowed and curtseyed to Mary deeper and longer. She was now incontestably French royalty. Mary loved it, and so did Alison.

And the future held more of the same, for one day Mary would be the queen of France.

Today they were in the grandest room of the Tournelles Palace, in front of the largest window, where Mary's mother-in-law, Queen Caterina, was holding court. Caterina wore a voluminous confection of gold and silver cloth that must have cost a fortune. It was late afternoon, but the weather was hot, and the window was open to welcome a light breeze.

The king came in, bringing with him a strong odour of warm sweat. Everyone except Caterina stood up. Henri looked happy. He was the same age as his wife, forty, and in his prime: handsome, strong, and full of energy. He loved jousting, and he was winning today. He had even unseated Scarface, the duke of Guise, his great general. 'Just one more,' he said to Caterina.

'It's getting late,' she protested, speaking French with the strong Italian accent she had never lost. 'And you're tired. Why don't you rest now?'

'But it's for you that I fight!' he said.

This piece of gallantry did not go down well. Caterina looked away, and Mary frowned. Everyone had already seen that Henri was wearing on his lance ribbons of black and white, the colours of Diane of Poitiers. She had seduced Henri within a year of his marriage, and Caterina had spent the last twenty-five years pretending not to know. Diane was much older – she would be sixty in a few weeks' time – and Henri had other mistresses now, but Diane was the love of his life. Caterina was used to it, but he could still wound her carelessly.

Henri left to put his armour back on, and a buzz of conversation arose from the ladies. Caterina beckoned to Alison. The queen was always warm to Alison because she had been a good friend to the sickly Francis. Now Caterina half turned her back on the rest of the group, indicating that their conversation was private, and said in a low voice: 'It's been fourteen months.'

Alison knew what she was talking about. That was how long Francis and Mary had been married. 'And she's not pregnant,' Alison said.

'Is something wrong? You would know.'

'She says not.'

'But you don't believe her.'

'I don't know what to believe.'

'I had trouble getting pregnant when I was first married,' Caterina said.

'Really?' Alison was astonished. Caterina had borne ten children for Henri.

The queen nodded. 'I was distraught – especially after my husband was seduced by Madame.' This was what everyone called Diane. 'I adored him – I still do. But she won his heart away. I believed I might win him back with a baby. He still came to my bed – she ordered him to, I found out later.' Alison winced: this was painful to hear. 'But I did not conceive.'

'What did you do?'

'I was fifteen years old, and my family were hundreds of miles away. I felt desperate.' She lowered her voice. 'I spied on them.'

Alison was shocked and embarrassed by this intimate revelation, but Caterina was in the mood to tell the story. Henri's thoughtless *It's for you that I fight* had put the queen in an odd frame of mind.

'I thought perhaps I was doing something wrong with Henri, and I wanted to see whether Madame had some different method,' Caterina went on. 'They used to go to bed in the afternoon. My maids found a place from which I could watch them.'

What an astonishing picture, Alison thought: the queen gazing through some kind of peephole at her husband in bed with his mistress.

'It was very hard for me to look, because he obviously adored her. And I didn't learn anything. They played some games I didn't know about, but in the end he fucked her the same way he fucked me. The only difference was how much more he enjoyed it with her.'

Caterina spoke in a dry, bitter voice. She was not emotional, but Alison was close to tears. It must have broken Caterina's heart, she thought. She wanted to ask questions, but she was afraid of disturbing this confiding mood.

'I tried all kinds of remedies, some of them utterly disgusting – poultices of dung on my vagina, that kind of thing. Nothing worked. Then I met Dr Fernel, and I found out what was stopping me getting pregnant.'

Alison was fascinated. 'What was it?'

'The king's cock is short and fat – adorable, but not long. He wasn't putting it in far enough, and my maidenhead had never been broken, so the spunk didn't go all the way up. The doctor broke the membrane with a special implement, and a month later I was pregnant with Francis. *Pronto*.'

There was a huge cheer from the crowd outside, as if they had been listening to the story and heard its happy ending. Alison guessed that the king must have mounted his horse for the next bout. Caterina put a hand on Alison's knee, as if to detain her a moment longer. 'Dr Fernel is dead, but his son is just as good,' she said. 'Tell Mary to see him.'

Alison wondered why the queen did not give this message to Mary herself.

As if reading her mind, Caterina said: 'Mary is proud. If I give her the impression that I think she might be barren, she could take offence. Advice such as this comes better from a friend than from a mother-in-law.'

'I understand.'

'Do this as a kindness to me.'

It was courteous of the queen to request what she might command. 'Of course,' Alison said.

Caterina stood up and went to the window. The others in the room crowded around her, Alison included, and looked out.

Along the middle of the road, two fences enclosed a long, narrow track. At one end was the king's horse, called Malheureux; at the other, the mount of Gabriel, count of Montgomery. Down the middle of the track ran a barrier to keep the two horses from colliding.

The king was talking to Montgomery in the middle of the field. Their words could not be heard from the palace window, but they seemed to be arguing. The tournament was almost over, and some spectators were already leaving, but Alison guessed the combative king wanted to play a final bout. Then the king raised his voice, and everyone heard him say: 'That's an order!'

Montgomery gave a bow of obedience and put his helmet on. The king did the same, and both men returned to the ends of the track. Henri lowered his visor. Alison heard Caterina murmur: 'Fasten it shut, *chérie*,' and the king turned the catch that prevented the eyepiece flying up.

Henri was impatient, and did not wait for the trumpet, but kicked his horse and charged. Montgomery did the same.

The horses were destriers, bred for war, big and tremendously strong, and their hooves made a noise like a titan beating the earth with giant drumsticks. Alison felt her pulse quicken with exhilaration and fear. The two riders picked up speed. The crowd cheered wildly as the warhorses pounded towards one another, ribbons flying. The two men angled their wooden lances across the central barrier. The weapons had blunted tips: the object was not to injure the opponent but simply to knock him from his saddle. All the same Alison was glad that only men played this sport. She would have been terrified.

At the last moment both men clamped their legs tightly into their horses and leaned forward. They met with a terrific crash. Montgomery's lance struck the king's head. The lance damaged the helmet. The king's visor flew up, and Alison understood in a flash that the impact had snapped the visor catch. The lance broke in two.

The tremendous momentum of the horses continued to carry both men forwards, and a fraction of a second later the broken end of Montgomery's lance struck the king's face again. He reeled in the saddle, looking as if he might be losing consciousness. Caterina screamed in fear.

Alison saw Duke Scarface leap the fence and run to the king. Several more noblemen did the same. They steadied the horse, then lifted the king from the saddle, with great effort because of his heavy armour, and lowered him to the ground.

*

CARDINAL CHARLES ran after his brother Scarface, and
Pierre followed close on his heels. When the king's helmet was
gingerly removed they saw immediately that he had suffered a
serious wound. His face was covered in blood. A long, thick
splinter of wood was sticking out of his eye. Other splinters
were lodged in his face and head. He lay still, apparently numb
to pain and barely conscious. His doctor was in attendance in
case of just such an incident as this, and he now knelt beside
the patient.

Charles looked hard at the king for a long moment then
backed away. 'He will die,' he murmured to Pierre.

Pierre was thrown. What did this mean for the Guise family,
whose future was Pierre's future? The long-term plan that
Charles had only just outlined to him was now in ruins. Pierre
felt a degree of anxiety close to panic. 'It's too soon!' he said. He
realized that his voice was oddly high-pitched. Making an
effort to speak more calmly, he said: 'Francis cannot rule this
country.'

Charles moved farther away from the crowd, to make sure
they could not be overheard, though no one was paying
attention to anyone but the king now. 'According to French
law, a king can rule at fourteen. Francis is fifteen.'

'True.' Pierre began to think hard. His panic evaporated and
logic took over his brain. 'But Francis will have help,' he said.
'And whoever becomes his closest advisor will be the true king
of France.' Throwing caution to the winds, he moved closer to
Charles and spoke in a low, urgent voice. 'Cardinal, *you must be
that man.*'

Charles gave him a sharp look of a kind that Pierre
recognized. It indicated that he had surprised Charles by
saying something Charles had not thought of. 'You're right,'
Charles said slowly. 'But the natural choice would be Antoine
of Bourbon. He is the first prince of the blood.' A prince of the
blood was a direct male descendant of a French king. Such
men were the highest aristocracy outside the royal family
itself. They took precedence over all other noblemen. And
Antoine was the most senior among them.

'God forbid,' said Pierre. 'If Antoine becomes the principal advisor to King Francis II, the power of the Guise family will be at an end.' And so will my career, he added silently.

Antoine was king of Navarre, a small country between France and Spain. More importantly, he was head of the Bourbon family who, together with the Montmorency clan, were the great rivals of the Guises. Their religious policies were fluid, but the Bourbon–Montmorency alliance tended to be less hard-line on heresy than the Guises, and were therefore favoured by the Protestants – a type of support that was not always welcome. If Antoine controlled the boy king, the Guises would become impotent. It did not bear thinking about.

Charles said: 'Antoine is stupid. And a suspected Protestant.'

'And, most importantly, he's out of town.'

'Yes. He's at Pau.' The residence of the kings of Navarre was in the foothills of the Pyrenees Mountains, five hundred miles from Paris.

'But messengers will be on their way to him before nightfall,' Pierre said insistently. 'You can neutralize Antoine, but only if you act fast.'

'I must speak to my niece, Mary Stuart. She will be queen of France. She must persuade the new king to reject Antoine as advisor.'

Pierre shook his head. Charles was thinking, but Pierre was ahead of him. 'Mary is a beautiful child. She cannot be relied upon in something as important as this.'

'Caterina, then.'

'She is soft on Protestants and might have no objection to Antoine. I have a better idea.'

'Go on.'

Charles was listening to Pierre as he might to an equal. Pierre felt a glow of pleasure. His political acumen had won the respect of the most able politician in France. 'Tell Caterina that if she will accept you and your brother as the king's leading counsellors, you will banish Diane of Poitiers from the court for the rest of her life.'

Charles thought for a long moment then he nodded, very slowly, once.

*

Alison was secretly thrilled by the injury to King Henri. She put on plain white mourning clothes and even managed to force tears occasionally, but that was for show. In her heart she rejoiced. Mary Stuart was about to be queen of France, and Alison was her best friend!

The king had been carried into the Palace of Tournelles, and the court gathered around his sick room. He took a long time dying, but there was little doubt about the eventual outcome. Among his doctors was Ambroise Paré, the surgeon who had removed the spearhead from the cheeks of Duke François of Guise, leaving the scars that had given the duke his nickname. Paré said that if the splinter had penetrated only the king's eye he might have survived, provided the wound did not become fatally infected; but in fact the point had gone farther and entered the brain. Paré conducted experiments on four condemned criminals, sticking splinters into their eyes to replicate the wound, but all of them died, and there was no hope for the king.

Mary Stuart's fifteen-year-old husband, soon to be King Francis II, became infantile. He lay in bed, moaning incomprehensibly, rocking in a lunatic rhythm, and had to be restrained from banging his head against the wall. Even Mary and Alison, who had been his friends since childhood, resented that he was so useless.

Queen Caterina, who had never really possessed her husband, was nevertheless distraught at the prospect of losing him. However, she showed her ruthless side by banning her rival, Diane of Poitiers, from the king's presence. Twice Alison saw Caterina deep in conversation with Cardinal Charles, who might have been giving her spiritual consolation but more probably was helping her plan a smooth succession. Both times they were attended by Pierre Aumande, the handsome, mysterious young man who had appeared from nowhere a year or so ago and was at Charles's side more and more often.

King Henri was given extreme unction on the morning of 9 July.

Shortly after one o'clock that day, Mary and Alison were at lunch in their rooms at the château when Pierre Aumande came in. He bowed deeply and said to Mary: 'The king is sinking fast. We must act now.'

This was the moment they had all been waiting for.

Mary did not pretend to be distraught or to have hysterics. She swallowed, put down her knife and spoon, patted her lips with a napkin, and said: 'What must I do?' Alison felt proud of her mistress's composure.

Pierre said: 'You must help your husband. The duke of Guise is with him now. We are all going immediately to the Louvre with Queen Caterina.'

Alison said: 'You're taking possession of the person of the new king.'

Pierre looked sharply at her. He was the kind of man, she realized, who saw only important people: the rest were invisible. Now he gave her an appraising look. 'That's exactly right,' he said. 'The queen mother is in agreement with your mistress's Uncle François and Uncle Charles. At this moment of danger, Francis must turn for help to his wife, Queen Mary – and no one else.'

Alison knew that was rubbish. François and Charles wanted the new king to turn to François and Charles. Mary was merely their cover. In the moment of uncertainty that always followed the death of a king, the man with the power was not the new king himself but whoever had him in his hands. That was why Alison had said *possession of the person* – the phrase that had alerted Pierre to the fact that she knew what was going on.

Mary would not have figured this out, Alison guessed; but that did not matter. Pierre's plan was good for Mary. She would be all the more powerful in alliance with her uncles. By contrast, Antoine of Bourbon would surely try to sideline Mary if he gained control of Francis. So, when Mary looked at Alison enquiringly, Alison gave a slight nod.

Mary said: 'Very well,' and stood up.

Watching Pierre's face, Alison saw that he had not missed that little interaction.

Alison went with Mary to Francis's room, and Pierre followed. The door was guarded by men-at-arms. Alison recognized their leader, Gaston Le Pin, a tough-looking character who was chief of the Guise family's paid roughnecks. They were willing to hold Francis by force if necessary, Alison deduced.

Francis was weeping, but getting dressed, helped by his servants. Both Duke Scarface and Cardinal Charles were there, watching impatiently, and a moment later Queen Caterina came in. This was the group taking power, Alison realized. Francis's mother had made a deal with Mary's uncles.

Alison considered who might try to stop them. The leading candidate would be the duke of Montmorency, who held the title of Constable of France. But Montmorency's royal ally, Antoine of Bourbon, never quick off the mark, had not yet arrived in Paris.

The Guises were in a strong position, Alison saw. All the same, they were right to act now. Things could change quickly. An advantage was no use unless it was seized.

Pierre said to Alison: 'The new king and queen will occupy the royal apartments at the Louvre palace immediately. The duke of Guise will move into the suite of Diane of Poitiers, and Cardinal Charles will occupy the rooms of the duke of Montmorency.'

Clever, Alison thought. 'So the Guise family will have the king *and* the palace.'

Pierre looked pleased with himself, and Alison guessed that might have been his idea.

She added: 'So you have effectively neutralized the rival faction.'

Pierre said: 'There is no rival faction.'

'Of course not,' she said. 'Silly me.'

He looked at her with something like respect. That pleased her, and she realized that she was drawn to this clever, confident young man. You and I could be allies, she thought; and perhaps something more. Living most of her life at the French court, she had come to regard marriage the way noblemen did, as a strategic alliance rather than a bond of love. She and Pierre Aumande might be a formidable couple. And, after all, it would be no hardship to wake up in the morning next to a man who looked like that.

The party went down the grand staircase, crossed the hall, and walked out onto the steps.

Outside the gate, a crowd of Parisians waited to see what was going to happen. They cheered when they saw Francis. They, too, knew he would soon be their king.

Carriages stood in the forecourt, guarded by more of the Guises' bully boys. Alison noticed that the vehicles were placed so that everyone in the crowd would see who got in.

Gaston Le Pin opened the door of the first carriage. The duke of Guise walked slowly forward with Francis. The crowd knew Scarface and they could all see that he had the king in his charge. This had been carefully choreographed, Alison realized.

Francis walked to the carriage, went up the single step, and got inside without making a fool of himself, to Alison's great relief.

Caterina and Mary went next. At the step, Mary held back to let Caterina go first. But Caterina shook her head and waited.

Holding her head high, Mary got into the carriage.

*

PIERRE ASKED HIS confessor: 'Is it a sin to marry someone you don't love?'

Father Moineau was a square-faced, heavy-set priest in his fifties. His study in the College des Ames contained more books than Sylvie's father's shop. He was a rather prissy intellectual, but he enjoyed the company of young men, and he was popular with the students. He knew all about the work Pierre was doing for Cardinal Charles.

'Certainly not,' Moineau said. His voice was a rich baritone somewhat roughened by a fondness for strong Canary wine. 'Noblemen are obliged so to do. It might even be a sin for a king to marry someone he *did* love.' He chuckled. He liked paradoxes, as did all the teachers.

But Pierre was in a serious mood. 'I'm going to wreck Sylvie's life.'

Moineau was fond of Pierre, and clearly would have liked

their intimacy to be physical, but he had quickly understood that Pierre was not one of those men who loved men, and had never done anything more than pat him affectionately on the back. Now Moineau caught his tone and became sombre. 'I see that,' he said. 'And you want to know whether you would be doing God's will.'

'Exactly.' Pierre was not often troubled by his conscience, but he had never done anyone as much harm as he was about to do to Sylvie.

'Listen to me,' said Moineau. 'Four years ago a terrible error was committed. It is known as the Pacification of Augsburg, and it is a treaty that allows individual German provinces to choose to follow the heresy of Lutheranism, if their ruler so wishes. For the first time, there are places in the world where it is not a crime to be a Protestant. This is a catastrophe for the Christian faith.'

Pierre said in Latin: 'Cuius regio, eius religio.' This was the slogan of the Augsburg treaty, and it meant: 'Whose realm, his religion.'

Moineau continued: 'In signing the agreement, the emperor Charles V hoped to end religious conflict. But what has happened? Earlier this year the accursed Queen Elizabeth of England imposed Protestantism on her wretched subjects, who are now deprived of the consolation of the sacraments. Tolerance is spreading. This is the horrible truth.'

'And we have to do whatever we can to stop it.'

'Your terminology is precise: Whatever we can. And we now have a young king much under the influence of the Guise family. Heaven has sent us an opportunity to crack down. Look, I know how you feel: no man of sensibility likes to see people burned to death. You've told me about Sylvie, and she seems to be a normal girl. Somewhat too lascivious, perhaps.' He chuckled again, then resumed his grave tone. 'In most respects, poor Sylvie is no more than a victim of her wicked parents, who have brought her up in heresy. But this is what Protestants do. They convert others. And their victims lose their immortal souls.'

'So you're saying I will not be doing anything wrong by marrying Sylvie and then betraying her.'

'On the contrary,' said Moineau, 'you will be doing God's will – and you will be rewarded in heaven, I assure you.'

That was what Pierre had wanted to hear. 'Thank you,' he said.

'God bless you, my son,' said Father Moineau.

*

Sylvie married Pierre on the last Sunday in September.

Their Catholic wedding took place on the Saturday, in the parish church, but Sylvie did not count that: it was a legal requirement, nothing more. They spent Saturday night apart. On Sunday they had their real wedding at the forest hunting lodge that served as a Protestant church.

It was a mild day between summer and autumn, cloudy but dry. Sylvie's dress was a soft dove-grey, and Pierre said the colour made her skin glow and her eyes shine. Pierre himself was devastatingly handsome in his new coat from Duboeuf. Pastor Bernard conducted the service, and the marquess of Nîmes was the witness. When Sylvie made her vows, she was overcome by a feeling of serenity, as if her life had at last begun.

Afterwards the entire congregation was invited back to the bookshop. They filled the shop and the apartment upstairs. Sylvie and her mother had spent all week preparing food: saffron broth, pork pies with ginger, cheese-and-onion tarts, custard pastries, apple fritters, quince cheese. Sylvie's father was uncharacteristically genial, pouring wine into flat-bottomed glasses and offering platters of food. Everyone ate and drank standing up, except for the bridal couple and the marquess and marchioness, who were privileged to sit at the dining table.

Sylvie thought Pierre seemed a little tense, which was unusual for him: in general he was at his relaxed best on big social occasions, listening attentively to the men and charming the women, never failing to say that a new baby was beautiful, no matter what it looked like. But today he was restless. He went to the window twice, and when the cathedral bells struck the hour, he jumped. Sylvie guessed he was worried about being at a Protestant gathering in the heart of the city. 'Relax,' she said to him. 'This is just an ordinary wedding celebration. No one knows we're Protestants.'

'Of course,' he said, and smiled anxiously.

Sylvie was thinking mainly about tonight. She was looking forward to it eagerly, but she was also just a little nervous. 'Losing your virginity doesn't hurt much, and it's only for a second,' her mother had said. 'Some girls hardly feel it. And don't worry if you don't bleed – not everyone does.' Sylvie was not actually worried about that. She was longing for the physical intimacy of lying in bed with Pierre, kissing him and touching him to her heart's content, without having to hold back. Her anxiety was about whether he would love her body. She felt it was not perfect for him. Statues of women always had perfectly matched breasts, whereas hers were not quite the same. And naked women in paintings had almost-invisible private parts, sometimes covered just with a faint down, but hers were plump and hairy. What would he think when he looked for the first time? She was too embarrassed to share these worries with her mother.

It crossed her mind to ask Marchioness Louise, who was only three years older, and had a conspicuously large bust. Then, just as she decided that Louise was not approachable enough, her thoughts were interrupted. She heard raised voices down in the shop, then someone screamed. Strangely, Pierre went to the window again, though the noise undoubtedly came from inside the building. She heard breaking glass. What was going on? It sounded more and more like a fight. Had someone got drunk? How could they spoil her wedding day?

The marquess and marchioness looked fearful. Pierre had turned pale. He stood with his back to the window, looking through the open door to the landing and the staircase. Sylvie ran to the top of the stairs. Through a rear window she saw some of the guests fleeing through the backyard. As she looked down the stairs, a man she did not know started to come up. He wore a leather jerkin and carried a club. She realized with horror that this was worse than a drunken brawl among the wedding guests; it was an official raid. Her anger turned to fear. Scared by the brute coming up the stairs, she ran back into the dining room.

The man followed her. He was short and powerfully built, and he had lost most of one ear: he looked terrifying. All the same, Pastor Bernard, who was a frail fifty-five-year-old, stood in front of him and said bravely: 'Who are you and what do you want?'

'I'm Gaston Le Pin, captain of the Guise family household guard, and you're a blaspheming heretic,' the man said. He raised his club and struck the pastor. Bernard turned away from the blow, but it caught him across the shoulders and he fell to the floor.

Le Pin looked at the other guests, who were trying to press themselves into the walls. 'Anyone else got any questions?' he said. No one spoke.

Two more thugs came into the room and stood behind Le Pin.

Then, incomprehensibly, Le Pin addressed Pierre. 'Which one is the marquess?' he said.

Sylvie was bewildered. What was going on?

Even more bafflingly, Pierre pointed to the marquess of Nîmes.

Le Pin said: 'And I suppose the bitch with the big tits is the marchioness?'

Pierre nodded dumbly.

Sylvie felt as if the world had been turned upside down. Her wedding had become a violent nightmare in which no one was what they seemed.

Marchioness Louise stood up and said indignantly to Le Pin: 'How dare you?'

Le Pin slapped her face hard. She screamed and fell back. Her cheek reddened instantly, and she began to cry.

The portly old marquess half rose from his chair, realized it was pointless, and sat back down again.

Le Pin spoke to the men who had followed him in. 'Take those two and make sure they don't get away.'

The marquess and marchioness were dragged from the room.

Pastor Bernard, still on the floor, pointed at Pierre and said: 'You devil, you're a spy!'

Everything fell into place in Sylvie's mind. Pierre had organized this raid, she realized with horror. He had infiltrated the congregation in order to betray them. He had pretended to fall in love with her only to win their trust. That was why he had dithered so long about the date of the wedding.

She stared at him aghast, seeing a monster where once there had been the man she loved. It was as if her arm had been chopped off and she was looking at the bleeding stump – except that this hurt more. It was not just her wedding day that was ruined, it was her whole life. She wanted to die.

She moved towards Pierre. 'How could you?' she screamed, advancing on him, not knowing what she intended to do. 'Judas Iscariot, how could you?'

Then something hit her on the back of the head, and the world went black.

*

'ONE THING TROUBLED ME about the coronation,' said Pierre to Cardinal Charles.

They were at the vast Guise family palace in the Vieille rue du Temple, in the opulent small parlour where Pierre had first met Charles and his scarred elder brother, François. Charles had bought more paintings since then, all biblical scenes but highly charged with sexuality: Adam and Eve, Susanna and the elders, Potiphar's wife.

Sometimes Charles was interested in what Pierre had to say; at other times he would shut Pierre up with a casually dismissive flick of his long, elegant fingers. Today he was in a receptive mood. 'Go on.'

Pierre quoted: 'Francis and Mary, by the grace of God king and queen of France, Scotland, England and Ireland.'

'As indeed they are. Francis is king of France. Mary is the queen of Scots. And, by right of inheritance and by the authority of the Pope, Mary is queen of England and Ireland.'

'And they have those words carved on their new furniture and embossed on the queen's new dining plates for all to see – including the English ambassador.'

'Your point is?'

'By encouraging Mary Stuart to tell the world she is the rightful queen of England, we have made an enemy of Queen Elizabeth.'

'So what? Elizabeth is hardly a threat to us.'

'But what have we achieved? When we make an enemy there should be some benefit to us. Otherwise we have harmed only ourselves.'

A look of greed came over Charles's long face. 'We're going to rule over the greatest European empire since Charlemagne,' he said. 'It will be greater than that of Felipe of Spain, because his dominions are scattered and therefore impossible to govern, whereas the new French empire will be compact, its wealth and strength concentrated. We will hold sway from Edinburgh to Marseilles, and control the ocean from the North Sea to the Bay of Biscay.'

Pierre took the risk of arguing. 'If we're serious, we would have done better to conceal our intentions from the English. Now they're forewarned.'

'And what will they do? Elizabeth rules a poor and barbarous country that has no army.'

'It has a navy.'

'Not much of one.'

'But, given the difficulty of attacking an island . . .'

Charles gave the flick of the fingers that indicated he had lost interest. 'On to a more immediate topic,' he said. He handed Pierre a sheet of heavyweight paper with an official seal. 'There it is,' he said. 'The annulment of your marriage.'

Pierre took the paper gratefully. The grounds were clear – the marriage had never been consummated – but even so it could be difficult to get an annulment. He felt relieved. 'That was quick.'

'I'm not a cardinal for nothing. And it was gutsy of you to go through with the ceremony.'

'It was worth it.' Hundreds of Protestants had been arrested all over the city in a co-ordinated series of raids planned by Charles and Pierre. 'Even if most of them have been let off with fines.'

'If they recant their beliefs we can't burn them to death – especially if they're aristocrats, like the marquess of Nîmes and his wife. Pastor Bernard will die – he refused to recant, even under torture. And we found parts of a French Bible in the print shop, so your ex-wife's father can't escape punishment by recanting. Giles Palot will burn.'

'All of which makes the Guise family Catholic heroes.'

'Thanks to you.'

Pierre bowed his head in acknowledgement, glowing with pride. His satisfaction was profound. This was what he had wanted: to be the trusted aide to the most powerful man in the land. It was his moment of triumph. He tried not to show just how exultant he felt.

Charles said: 'But there's another reason why I was in a hurry to get you an annulment.'

Pierre frowned. What now? Charles was the only man in Paris who was as devious as Pierre himself.

Charles went on: 'There's someone else I want you to marry.'

'Good God!' Pierre was rocked. He had not been expecting that. His thoughts immediately flew to Véronique de Guise. Had Charles changed his mind about letting Pierre marry her? His heart filled with hope. Was it possible that two dreams could come true?

Charles said: 'My nephew Alain, who is only fourteen, has seduced a maid and got her pregnant. He can't possibly marry her.'

Pierre's spirits fell with a painful crash. 'A maid?'

'Alain will have an arranged political marriage, like all Guise men except those of us who are called to the priesthood. But I'd like to take care of the maid. I feel sure you'll understand that, having been born in similar circumstances.'

Pierre felt sick. He had thought the triumph he and Charles had enjoyed might elevate his status closer to that of a member of the family. Instead, he was being reminded of how far below them he really was. 'You want me to marry a maid?'

Charles laughed. 'Don't speak as if it's a death sentence!'

'More like life imprisonment.' What was he going to do about this? Charles did not like to be thwarted. If Pierre refused this demand it could blight his flowering career.

'We'll give you a pension,' Charles said. 'Fifty livres a month—'

'I don't care about money.'

Charles raised his eyebrows at the insolence of an interruption. 'Indeed? What do you care about?'

Pierre realized there was one reward that might make the sacrifice worthwhile. 'I want the right to call myself Pierre Aumande de Guise.'

'Marry her, and we'll see.'

'No.' Pierre knew he was risking everything now. 'My name on the marriage certificate must be Pierre Aumande de Guise. Otherwise I will not sign it.' He had never been this audacious with Charles. He held his breath, waiting for the reaction, dreading an explosion.

Charles said: 'You're a determined little bastard, aren't you?'

'I wouldn't be so useful to you otherwise.'

'That's true.' Charles was silent and thoughtful for a minute. Then he said: 'All right, I'll agree.'

Pierre felt weak with relief.

Charles said: 'From now on you are Pierre Aumande de Guise.'

'Thank you.'

'The girl is in the next room along the corridor. Go and see her. Get acquainted.'

Pierre got up and went to the door.

'Be nice to her,' Charles added. 'Give her a kiss.'

Pierre left the room without replying. Outside the door he stood still for a moment, feeling shaky, trying to take it all in. He did not know whether to be elated or dismayed. He had escaped from one unwanted marriage only to fall into another. But he was a Guise!

He pulled himself together. He had better take a look at his wife-to-be. She was low-class, obviously. But she might be pretty, given that she had enticed Alain de Guise. On the other hand, it did not take much to win the sexual interest of a boy of fourteen: willingness was the most important attraction.

He walked along the passage to the next door and went in without knocking.

A girl sat on the sofa with her head in her hands, weeping. She wore the plain dress of a servant. She was quite plump, Pierre saw, perhaps on account of the pregnancy.

When he closed the door behind him she looked up.

He knew her. It was plain Odette, the maid of Véronique. She would forever remind him of the girl he had not been allowed to marry.

Odette recognized him and smiled bravely through her tears, showing her crooked teeth. 'Are you my saviour?' she said.

'God help me,' said Pierre.

*

AFTER GILES PALOT was burned to death, Sylvie's mother went into a depression.

For Sylvie this was the most shocking of the traumas she suffered, more seismic than Pierre's betrayal, even sadder than her father's execution. In Sylvie's mind, her mother was a rock that could never crumble, the foundation of her life. Isabelle had put salve on her childish injuries, fed her when she was hungry, and calmed her father's volcanic temper. But now Isabelle was helpless. She sat in a chair all day. If Sylvie lit a fire, Isabelle would look at it; if Sylvie prepared food, Isabelle would eat it mechanically; if Sylvie did not help her get dressed, Isabelle would spend all day in her underclothes.

Giles's fate had been sealed when a stack of newly printed sheets for Bibles in French had been found in the shop. The sheets were ready to be cut into pages and bound into volumes, after which they would have been taken to the secret warehouse in the rue du Mur. But there had not been time to finish them. So Giles was guilty, not just of heresy but of promoting heresy. There had been no mercy for him.

In the eyes of the Church, the Bible was the most dangerous of all banned books – especially translated into French or

English, with marginal notes explaining how certain passages proved the correctness of Protestant teaching. Priests said that ordinary people were unable to rightly interpret God's word, and needed guidance. Protestants said that the Bible opened men's eyes to the errors of the priesthood. Both sides saw reading the Bible as the central issue of the religious conflict that had swept Europe.

Giles's employees had claimed they knew nothing of these sheets. They had only worked on Latin Bibles and other permitted works, they said; Giles must have printed the others himself, at night, after they had gone home. They had been fined just the same, but had escaped the death penalty.

When a man was executed for heresy, all his goods were confiscated. This law was applied patchily, and interpretation could vary, but Giles lost everything, and his wife and daughter were left destitute. They managed to escape with the cash in the shop before it was taken over by a rival printer. Later they went back to beg for their clothes and learned they had been sold – there was a big market for second-hand garments. They were now living in one room of a tenement.

Sylvie was a poor seamstress – she had been raised to sell books, not to make clothes – so she could not even take in sewing, the traditional last resort of the penniless middle-class woman. The only work she could get was doing laundry for Protestant families. Despite the raids, most of them still adhered to the true religion, and after paying their fines they had swiftly restarted their congregations, finding new places to worship in secret. People who knew Sylvie from the old days often paid her more than the usual price for laundry, but still it was not enough to keep two people in food and fuel, and gradually the money they had brought from the shop was spent. It ran out in a bitterly cold December, with an icy wind knifing through the high, narrow Paris streets.

One day when Sylvie was washing a bedsheet for Jeanne Mauriac in the freezing water of the Seine river, the cold hurting her hands so badly that she could not stop crying, a man passing by offered her five sous to suck his cock.

She shook her head silently and carried on washing the sheet, and he went away.

But she could not stop thinking about it. Five sous, sixty pennies, a quarter of a livre. It would buy a load of firewood, a leg of pork and bread for a week. And all she had to do was put a man's thing in her mouth. How could that be worse than what she was doing now? It would be a sin, of course, but it was hard to care about sin when her hands were in such agony.

She took the sheet home and hung it across the room to dry. The last lot of wood was almost gone: tomorrow she would not be able to dry laundry, and even Protestants would not pay if she delivered their sheets wet.

She did not sleep much that night. She wondered why anyone would desire her. Even Pierre had only been pretending. She had never thought herself beautiful, and now she was thin and unwashed. Yet the man at the waterside had wanted her, so perhaps others would.

In the morning, she bought two eggs with the last of her money. She put the remaining fragments of wood on the fire and cooked the eggs, and she and her mother had one each, with the stale remains of last week's bread. Then they had nothing. They would just starve to death.

God will provide, the Protestants always said. But he had not.

Sylvie combed her hair and washed her face. She had no mirror, so she did not know what she looked like. She turned her stockings inside out to hide the dirt. Then she went out.

She was not sure what to do. She walked along the street, but no one propositioned her. Of course not, why would they? She had to proposition them. She tried smiling at men as they walked by, but none responded. To one she said: 'I'll suck your cock for five sous,' but he just looked embarrassed and hurried on. Perhaps she should show her breasts, but it was cold.

She saw a young woman in an old red coat hurrying along the street with a well-dressed middle-aged man, holding his arm as if afraid he might escape. The woman gave her a hard look that might have signified recognition of a rival. Sylvie would have liked to speak to her, but the woman seemed intent on going somewhere with the man, and Sylvie heard her say to him: 'It's just around the corner, my darling.' Sylvie realized that if she succeeded in getting a customer she would have nowhere to take him.

She found herself in the rue du Mur, across the street from the warehouse where the Palot family had stored illegal literature. It was not a busy thoroughfare, but perhaps men would be more willing to deal with prostitutes in back streets. And, sure enough, a man stopped and spoke to her. 'Nice tits,' he said.

Her heart leaped. She knew what she had to say next: *I'll suck your cock for five sous.* She felt nauseated. Was she really going to do this? But she was hungry and cold.

The man said: 'How much for a fuck?'

She had not thought about that. She did not know what to say.

The man was irritated by her hesitation. 'Where's your room?' he said. 'Nearby?'

Sylvie could not take him back to where her mother was. 'I haven't got a room,' she said.

'Stupid cow,' the man said, and he walked away.

Sylvie could have cried. She was a stupid cow. She had not worked this out.

Then she looked across the road at the warehouse.

The illegal books had presumably been burned. The new printer might be using the warehouse, or he might have leased it to someone else.

But the key might still be behind the loose brick. Perhaps the warehouse could be her 'room'.

She crossed the road.

She pulled out the loose half-brick next to the doorpost and reached inside. The key was there. She took it out and replaced the brick.

She cleared some rubbish from in front of the warehouse door with her foot. She turned the key in the lock, went inside, closed and barred the door behind her, and lit the lamp.

The place looked the same. The floor-to-ceiling barrels were still there. Between them and the wall there was enough space to do what Sylvie planned. There was a rough stone floor. This would be her secret room of shame.

The barrels looked dusty, as if the warehouse was no longer used much. She wondered whether the empty barrels were still in the same place. She tried moving one, and lifted it easily.

She saw that there were still boxes of books behind the barrels. A bizarre possibility occurred to her.

She opened a box. It was full of French Bibles.

How had this happened? She and her mother had assumed the new printer had seized everything. But clearly he had never found out about the warehouse. Sylvie frowned, thinking. Father had always insisted on secrecy. Even the men working for him had not known about the warehouse. And Sylvie had been ordered not to tell Pierre until after they were married.

Nobody knew except Sylvie and her mother.

So all the books must still be here – hundreds of them.

And they were valuable, if she could find people with the courage to buy them.

Sylvie took out a French Bible. It was worth a lot more than the five sous she had hoped to get on the street.

As in the past, she wrapped it in a square of coarse linen and tied it up with string. Then she left the warehouse, carefully locking it behind her and hiding the key.

She walked away full of new hope.

Back at the tenement, Isabelle was staring into a cold fire.

Books were costly, but to whom could Sylvie sell? Only Protestants, of course. Her eye fell on the sheet she had washed yesterday. It belonged to Jeanne Mauriac, a member of the congregation that used to worship at the hunting lodge in the suburb of St Jacques. Her husband, Luc, was a cargo broker, whatever that meant. She had not previously sold him a Bible, she thought, though he could certainly afford one. But would he dare, only six months after Cardinal Charles's raids?

The sheet was dry. She made her mother help her fold it. Then she wrapped it around the book and took the package to the Mauriac house.

She timed her visit so that she would catch the family at

the midday meal. The maid looked at her shabby dress and told her to wait in the kitchen, but Sylvie was too desperate to be thwarted by a maid. She pushed her way into the dining room. The smell of pork cutlets made her stomach hurt.

Luc and Jeanne were at the table with Georges, their son. Luc greeted Sylvie cheerily: he was always lively. Jeanne looked wary. She was the anchor of the family, and often seemed pained by the humorous banter of her husband and son. Young Georges had once been an admirer of Sylvie's, but now he could hardly bring himself to look at her. She was no longer the well-dressed daughter of a prosperous printer: she was a grubby pauper.

Sylvie unwrapped the sheet and showed the book to Luc, who, she reckoned, was most likely to buy. 'As I recall, you don't have a Bible in French yet,' she said. 'This is a particularly beautiful edition. My father was proud of it. Take it, have a look.' She had learned long ago that a customer was more likely to buy once he had held the book in his hands.

Luc leafed through the volume admiringly. 'We should have a French Bible,' he said to his wife.

Sylvie smiled at Jeanne and said: 'It would surely please the Lord.'

Jeanne said: 'It's against the law.'

'It's against the law to be Protestant,' her husband said. 'We can hide the book.' He looked at Sylvie. 'How much is it?'

'My father used to sell this for six livres,' she said.

Jeanne made a sound of disapprobation, as if the price was far too high.

Sylvie said: 'Because of my circumstances, I can let you have it for five.' She held her breath.

Luc looked dubious. 'If you could say four . . .'

'Done,' Sylvie said. 'The book is yours, and may God bless it to your heart.'

Luc took out his purse and counted eight of the silver coins called testons, each worth ten sous, half a livre.

'Thank you,' said Sylvie. 'And ten pennies for the sheet.' She no longer needed the pennies, but she remembered how her hands had hurt washing it, and she felt the money was hers.

Luc smiled and gave her a small coin called a dixain, worth ten pennies.

Luc opened the book again. 'When my partner Radiguet sees this, he'll be envious.'

'I don't have any more,' Sylvie said quickly. The rarity of Protestant books kept the price high, and her father had taught her never to let people know there were plenty. 'If I come across another one, I'll go and see Radiguet.'

'Please do.'

'But don't tell him how cheaply you got it!'

Luc smiled conspiratorially. 'Not until after he's paid you, anyhow.'

Sylvie thanked him and left.

She was so weak with relief that she could not find the energy to feel exultant. She went into the next tavern she saw and ordered a tankard of beer. She drank it quickly. It eased the pain of hunger. She left feeling light-headed.

Closer to home she bought a ham, cheese, butter, bread and apples, and a small jar of wine. She also bought a sack of firewood and paid a boy ten pennies to carry it for her.

When she entered the tenement room, her mother gazed in astonishment at her purchases.

'Hello, Mother,' Sylvie said. 'Our troubles are over.'

*

IN A MONUMENTAL sulk, Pierre got married for the second time three days after Christmas, 1559.

He was determined that the wedding would be a perfunctory affair: he was not going to pretend to celebrate. He invited no guests and planned no wedding breakfast. He did not want to look like a poor man, so he wore his new dark grey coat, which was appropriately sombre, fitting his mood. He arrived at the parish church as the clock was striking the appointed hour.

To his horror, Véronique de Guise was there.

She was sitting at the back of the little church with half a dozen Guise maids, presumably friends of Odette's.

Nothing could be worse, to Pierre, than for Véronique to

witness his humiliation. She was the woman he really wanted to marry. He had talked to her, charmed her, and done his best to give her the impression that they were on the same social level. This had been a fantasy, as Cardinal Charles had made brutally clear. But for Véronique to actually see Pierre marrying her maid was too excruciatingly painful. He wanted to walk out of the church.

Then he thought of his reward. At the end of this ordeal he would sign the register with his new name, Pierre Aumande de Guise. It was his dearest wish. He would be a recognized member of the lofty Guise family, and no one would be able to take that away from him. He would be married to an ugly maid who was pregnant with someone else's child, but he would be a Guise.

He gritted his teeth and vowed to bear the pain.

The ceremony was short, the priest having been paid the minimum fee. Véronique and the other girls giggled during the service. Pierre did not know what was so funny, but he could not help feeling that they were laughing at him. Odette kept looking back over her shoulder at them and grinning, showing her crooked teeth, tombstones in an old graveyard, tightly packed and tilting in all directions.

When it was over, she looked proud to be walking out of the church on the arm of a handsome and ambitious bridegroom. She seemed to have forgotten that she had been foisted on him against his will. Did she pretend to herself that she had somehow won his love and affection?

As if that were possible.

They walked from the church to the modest house Cardinal Charles had provided for them. It was near the tavern of St Étienne in the neighbourhood of Les Halles, where Parisians did their everyday shopping: meat, wine and the second-hand clothes that all but the wealthy wore. Without invitation, Véronique and the maids followed. One of them had a bottle of wine, and they insisted on entering the house and drinking the health of the bride and groom.

At last they left, with many crude jokes about the couple

being in a hurry to do what bridal couples are expected to do on the wedding night.

Pierre and Odette went upstairs. There was one bedroom and one bed. Until this moment, Pierre had not confronted the question of whether he would have normal sexual relations with his wife.

Odette lay down. 'Oh, well, we're married now,' she said. She threw up her dress to reveal her nakedness. 'Come on, let's make the best of it.'

Pierre was utterly revolted. The sheer vulgarity of her pose disgusted him beyond measure. He was appalled.

At that moment he knew he could not have sex with her, today or ever.

10

BARNEY WILLARD HATED being in the army. The food was disgusting, he was cold all the time except when he was too hot, and for long periods the only women he saw were camp-following prostitutes, desperate and sad. The captain in charge of Barney's company, Gómez, was a big, vicious bully who enjoyed using his iron hand to punish breaches of discipline. Worst of all, no one had been paid for months.

Barney could not understand how King Felipe of Spain could have money troubles. He was the richest man in the world, yet he was always broke. Barney had seen the galleons loaded with silver from Peru sail into the harbour at Seville. Where did it all go? Not to the troops.

After leaving Seville, two years earlier, the *José y María* had sailed to a place called the Netherlands, a loose federation of seventeen provinces on the north coast of Europe between France and Germany. For historical reasons that Barney had never quite untangled, the Netherlands was ruled by the Spanish king. Felipe's army stationed here had fought in Spain's war against France.

Barney, Carlos and Ebrima were expert metalworkers, and so they had been made gunners, maintaining and firing the big artillery pieces. Although they had seen some action, gunners did not usually become involved in hand-to-hand fighting, and all three had survived the war without suffering injury.

The peace treaty between Spain and France had been signed in April 1559, almost a year ago, and Felipe had gone home, but he had left his army behind. Barney guessed the king wanted to make sure that the incredibly prosperous Netherlanders paid their taxes. But the troops were bored, resentful and mutinous.

Captain Gómez's company was garrisoned at the town of Kortrijk on the river Leie. The citizens did not like the soldiers. They were foreigners, they carried arms, they got noisily drunk and, because they got no pay, they stole. The Netherlanders had a streak of obstinate insubordination. They wanted the Spanish army gone, and they let the soldiers know it.

The three friends wanted to get out of the army. Barney had a family and a comfortable home in Kingsbridge, and he wanted to see them again. Carlos had invented a new type of furnace that was going to make him a fortune one day, and he needed to get back into the iron-making industry. What Ebrima saw in his future Barney was not sure, but it certainly was not a life of soldiering. However, escape was not easy. Men deserted every day, but, if caught, they could be shot. Barney had been alert for an opportunity for months, but none had offered itself, and he was beginning to wonder whether he was being too cautious.

Meanwhile, they spent too much time in taverns.

Ebrima was a gambler, obsessively risking what little money he had in a dream of getting more. Carlos drank wine whenever he could afford it. Barney's vice was girls. The tavern of St Martin in the Old Market of Kortrijk had something for each of them: a card game, Spanish wine and a pretty barmaid.

Barney was listening to the barmaid, Anouk, complaining in French about her husband while Carlos made a single glass last all afternoon. Ebrima was winning money from Ironhand Gómez and two other Spanish soldiers. The other players were drinking hard, shouting loudly when they won or lost, but Ebrima was quiet. He was a serious gambler, always careful, never betting very high or very low. Sometimes he lost, but often he won just because others took foolish risks. And today luck was with him.

Anouk disappeared into the kitchen, and Carlos said to Barney: 'There should be standard sizes of cannonball throughout the Spanish army and navy. That's what the English do. Making a thousand iron balls the same size is cheaper than making twenty different sizes for twenty different guns.' As usual, they spoke Spanish to one another.

Barney said: 'And then you'd never find yourself trying to use a ball one inch too large for your barrel – as has happened to us more than once.'

'Exactly.'

Ebrima stood up from the table. 'I'm through,' he said to the other players. 'Thank you for the game, gentlemen.'

'Wait a minute,' said Gómez bad-temperedly. 'You have to give us a chance to win our money back.'

The other two players agreed. One shouted: 'Yes!' and the other banged the table with his fist.

'Tomorrow, maybe,' said Ebrima. 'We've been playing all afternoon, and I want a drink, now that I can afford one.'

'Come on, one more hand, double or nothing.'

'You don't have enough money left for that bet.'

'I'll owe you.'

'Debts make enemies.'

'Come on!'

'No, Captain.'

Gómez stood up, knocking the table over. He was six feet tall, and broad in proportion, and he was flushed with sherry wine. He raised his voice. 'I say yes!'

The others in the tavern moved away, seeing what was coming.

Barney stepped towards Gómez and said in a quiet voice: 'Captain, let me buy you another drink, yours has spilled.'

'Go to hell, you English savage,' Gómez roared. Spaniards considered Englishmen to be northern barbarians, just as the English regarded the Scots. 'He has to play on.'

'No, he doesn't.' Barney spread his arms in a let's-be-reasonable gesture. 'The game has to stop some time, doesn't it?'

'I'll say when it stops. I'm the captain.'

Carlos joined in. 'That's not fair,' he said indignantly. He was quick to be angered by injustice, perhaps because he had suffered so much himself. 'We're all equal when the cards are dealt.' He was right – it was the rule when officers gambled with enlisted men. 'You know that, Captain Gómez, and you can't pretend you don't.'

Ebrima said: 'Thank you, Carlos,' and he stepped away from the fallen table.

'Get back here, you black devil,' said Gómez.

On the rare occasions when Ebrima got into an argument, sooner or later his antagonist would use skin colour in an insult. It was tediously predictable. Fortunately, Ebrima's self-control was formidable, and he never took the bait. He did not respond to Gómez's jibe, except to turn his back.

Like all bullies, Gómez hated to be ignored. Furious, he hit Ebrima from behind. It was a wild, drunken punch, and it only clipped Ebrima's head, but the fist at the end of the arm was the iron artificial hand, and Ebrima staggered and fell to his knees.

Gómez came after Ebrima, obviously intending to hit him again. Carlos grabbed the captain from behind, trying to restrain him. Gómez was now enraged and out of control. He struggled. Carlos was strong, but Gómez was stronger, and he fought free of Carlos's grasp.

Then, with his good hand, he drew his dagger.

Barney now joined in. He and Carlos tried desperately to restrain Gómez while Ebrima struggled to his feet, still dazed. Gómez threw off both his assailants and stepped towards Ebrima, raising his knife arm high in the air.

Barney realized fearfully that this was no longer a mere tavern brawl: Gómez was intent on murder.

Carlos made a grab for Gómez's knife arm, but Gómez batted him sideways with a sweeping blow of his iron-handed arm.

But Carlos had delayed Gómez for two seconds, just enough time for Barney to draw his own weapon, the two-foot-long Spanish dagger with the disc-shaped hilt.

Gómez's knife arm was high in the air, his iron hand extended outwards for balance. His front was undefended.

As Gómez brought his knife down, aiming for the exposed neck of the dazed Ebrima, Barney swung his dagger in a wide arc and stabbed Gómez in the left side of his chest.

It was a lucky stroke, or perhaps a very unlucky one. Although Barney had swung wildly, the sharp double-edged steel blade slipped neatly between Gómez's ribs and penetrated deep into his chest. His roar of pain ended abruptly after half a second. Barney jerked out the blade, and a gush of bright red blood came out after it. He realized the blade had reached Gómez's heart. A moment later Gómez collapsed, his knife falling from limp fingers. He hit the floor like a felled tree.

Barney stared in horror. Carlos cursed. Ebrima, coming out of his daze, said: 'What have we done?'

Barney knelt down and felt Gómez's neck for a pulse. There was none. The blood had stopped pumping from the wound. 'Dead,' Barney said.

Carlos said: 'We've killed an officer.'

Barney had stopped Gómez murdering Ebrima, but that would be difficult to prove. He looked around the room and saw that the witnesses were leaving as fast as they could go.

No one would bother to investigate the rights and wrongs of this. It was a tavern brawl and an enlisted man had killed an officer. The army would have no mercy.

Barney noticed the owner of the tavern giving instructions, in the West Flemish dialect, to a teenage boy who hurried away a moment later. 'They'll be sending for the city guard,' Barney said.

Carlos said: 'The men are probably stationed in the city hall. In five minutes we'll be under arrest.'

Barney said: 'And I'll be as good as dead.'

'Me, too,' said Carlos. 'I helped you.'

Ebrima said: 'There'll be scant justice for an African.'

Without further discussion they ran to the door and out into the marketplace. Behind a cloudy sky, the sun was setting, Barney saw. That was good. Twilight was only a minute or two away.

He shouted: 'Head for the waterfront!'

They dashed across the square and turned into Leiestraat, the street that ran down to the river. It was a busy thoroughfare in the heart of a prosperous city, full of people and horses, loaded handcarts, and porters struggling under heavy burdens. 'Slow down,' Barney said. 'We don't want everyone to remember which way we went.'

At a brisk walk they were still somewhat conspicuous.

People would know they were soldiers by their swords. Their clothes were mismatched and unmemorable, but Barney was tall, with a bushy red beard, and Ebrima was African. But it would soon be night.

They reached the river. 'We need a boat,' Barney said. He could handle most types of craft: he had always loved sailing. There were plenty of vessels in sight, tied up at the water's edge or anchored in mid-river. However, few people were foolish enough to leave a boat unprotected, especially in a city full of foreign troops. All the larger craft had watchmen, and even small rowing boats were chained up with their oars removed.

Ebrima said: 'Get down. Whatever happens, we don't want people to see.'

They knelt down in the mud.

Barney looked around desperately. They did not have much time. How long would it be before the city guard began to search the riverside?

They could free a small boat, breaking the attachment of chain to wood, but without oars they would be helpless, drifting downstream, unable to steer, easy to catch. It might be better to swim to a barge, overcome the watchman, and raise the anchor, but did they have time? And the more valuable the craft, the more intense would be the pursuit. He said: 'I don't know, maybe we should cross the bridge and take the first road out of town.'

Then he saw the raft.

It was an almost worthless vessel, just a dozen or so tree trunks roped together, with a low shed in which one man might sleep. Its owner stood on deck, letting the current carry him, using a long pole to steer. Beside him was a pile of gear that looked, in the twilight, like ropes and buckets that might have been used for fishing.

'That's our boat,' said Barney. 'Softly does it.'

Still on his knees, he slipped into the river. The others followed.

The water got deeper quickly, and soon they were up to their necks. Then the raft was almost upon them. All three grabbed its edge and hauled themselves up. They heard the voice of the old man yelling in shock and fear. Then Carlos was on him, wrestling him to the deck, covering his mouth so that he could not call for help. Barney managed to grab the pole he had dropped before it was lost, and he steered the boat into midstream. He saw Ebrima rip off the man's shirt and stuff it in his mouth to silence him, then pick a length of rope from the tangle and bind the man's wrists and ankles. The three friends worked well as a team, Barney reflected, no doubt because of the time they had spent jointly managing and firing a heavy cannon.

Barney looked around. As far as he could see, no one had witnessed their hijack of the raft. What now?

Barney said: 'We're going to have—'

'Shut up,' said Ebrima.

'What?'

'Be careful what you say. Give nothing away. He may understand Spanish.'

Barney saw what he meant. Sooner or later the old man was going to tell someone what had happened to him – unless they killed him, which none of them would want to do. He would be questioned about his captors. The less he knew, the better. Ebrima was twenty years older than the other two, and this was not the first time his wisdom had restrained their impulses.

Barney said: 'But what will we do with him?'

'Keep him with us until we're out in the fields. Then dump him on the river bank, bound and gagged. He'll be all right, but he won't be found until morning. By then we'll be well away.'

Ebrima's plan made sense, Barney thought.

Then what would they do? Travel by night and hide in the daytime, he thought. Every mile farther away from Kortrijk made it more difficult for the authorities to find them. And then what? If he remembered aright, this river flowed into the Scheldt, which went to Antwerp.

Barney had a relative in Antwerp: Jan Wolman, his late father's cousin. Come to think of it, Carlos, too, was related to Jan Wolman. The trading nexus Melcombe–Antwerp–Calais–Seville had been set up by four cousins: Barney's father,

Edmund Willard; Edmund's brother, Uncle Dick; Carlos's father; and Jan.

If the three fugitives could reach Antwerp, they would probably be safe.

Darkness fell. Barney had blithely assumed they would travel by night, but steering the raft was difficult in the dark. The old man had no lantern and, anyway, they would not want to show a flame for fear of being spotted. The faintest imaginable starlight penetrated the clouds. Sometimes Barney was able to see the river ahead, and sometimes he blindly ran the raft into the bank and had to push off again.

Barney felt strange, and wondered why, then remembered that he had killed a man. Odd how such a dreadful thing could fall from his consciousness, only to return as a shock. His mood was as dark as the night and he felt edgy. His mind returned to the way Gómez had fallen, as if life had left him even before he hit the floor.

It was not the first time Barney had killed. He had fired cannonballs from a distance into advancing troops and had seen them fall by the dozen, dead or fatally wounded; but somehow that had not touched his soul, perhaps because he could not see their faces as they died. Killing Gómez, by contrast, had been a horribly intimate act. Barney could still feel the sensation in his wrist as the blade of his dagger first met and then penetrated Gómez's body. He could see the gush of bright blood from a living, beating heart. Gómez had been a hateful man, and his death was a blessing to the human race, but Barney could not feel good about it.

The moon rose, and shone fitfully through gaps in the clouds. During a period of better visibility they dumped the old man at a spot that seemed, as best they could judge, to be far from habitation. Ebrima carried him to a dry place well above the river, and made him comfortable. From the boat, Barney heard Ebrima speak to the man in low tones, perhaps apologizing. That was reasonable: the old fellow had done nothing to deserve this. Barney heard the chink of money.

Ebrima got back on board and Barney poled away.

Carlos said to Ebrima: 'You gave him the money you won from Gómez, didn't you?'

Ebrima shrugged in the moonlight. 'We stole his raft. It was his living.'

'And now we're broke.'

'You were broke already,' Ebrima said sharply. 'Now I'm broke too.'

Barney thought some more about pursuit. He was not sure how energetically they would be chased. The city authorities did not like a murder, but victim and perpetrators were Spanish soldiers, and the Kortrijk town council would not spend much money chasing foreigners who had killed a foreigner. The Spanish army would execute them, given the chance, but once again Barney wondered whether they would care enough to organize a murder hunt. The army might well go through the motions and give up quite soon.

Ebrima was quiet and thoughtful for a while, then he spoke solemnly. 'Carlos, there's something we need to get straight.'

'What?'

'We've left the army now.'

'If they don't catch us, yes.'

'When we boarded the _José y María_, you told the officer I was a free man.'

Carlos said: 'I know.'

Barney sensed the tension. For two years Ebrima had been treated as a regular soldier – an exotic-looking one, but no more a slave than the rest of them. What was his position now?

Ebrima said: 'Am I a free man in your eyes, Carlos?'

Barney noted that phrase _in your eyes_. It meant that Ebrima was a free man in his own eyes.

Barney was not sure how Carlos felt about this. Ebrima's slavery had not been discussed since that moment on the _José y María_.

There was a long pause, then Carlos said: 'You're a free man, Ebrima.'

'Thank you. I'm glad we understand each other.'

Barney wondered what Ebrima would have done if Carlos had said no.

The clouds began to break. In the better light, Barney was able to keep the raft in midstream, and they moved faster.

After a while Carlos said: 'Where does this river lead, anyway?'

'Antwerp,' said Barney. 'We're going to Antwerp.'

*

EBRIMA DID NOT know whether to believe Carlos. It was not wise to put your trust in friendly words from your owner: that was an article of faith among the Seville slaves. A man who was happy to keep you prisoner, force you to work for no pay, flog you for disobedience and rape you any time he felt like it would not hesitate to lie to you. Carlos was different from the norm, but how different? The answer to that question would determine the course of the rest of Ebrima's life.

His head hurt from Gómez's blow. Touching his skull gingerly, he felt a lump where the iron hand had struck him. But he was not confused or dizzy, and he thought he would recover.

When dawn broke they stopped where the river ran through a grove of trees. They pulled the raft out of the water and concealed it with branches. Then they took turns to watch while the other two slept. Ebrima dreamed that he woke up in chains.

On the morning of the third day they saw the tall tower of Antwerp's cathedral in the distance. They abandoned the raft, letting it float free, and walked the last few miles. They were not yet out of trouble, Ebrima reckoned. They might be seized immediately and thrown in jail, then handed over to the Spanish military, to be hastily tried and speedily executed for the murder of Ironhand Gómez. However, on the busy roads leading to the city no one seemed to have heard about three Spanish soldiers – one with a red beard, one African – who had killed a captain in Kortrijk then fled.

News went from city to city mainly in merchants' bulletins, which contained mostly commercial information. Ebrima could not read, but he understood from Carlos that such newsletters included details of crimes only if they were politically significant: assassinations, riots, coups. A tavern brawl in which all involved were foreign soldiers would be of little interest.

Antwerp was surrounded by water, he realized as they explored the outskirts. To the west was the broad sweep of the river Scheldt. On the other three sides, the city was separated from the mainland by a walled channel. The waterway was crossed by bridges, each leading directly to a fortified gate. It was said to be the richest town on earth, so, naturally, it was well defended.

Even if the guards knew nothing of what had happened in Kortrijk, would they admit ragged, starving men with swords? The friends approached with trepidation.

However, the guards gave no sign that they were looking for three fugitives from justice, to Ebrima's relief. They did look askance at the appearance of the three – who were wearing the clothes in which they had boarded the *José y María* two years ago – but then Barney said they were relatives of Jan Wolman, and suspicion melted away. The guards even gave them directions to his address, near the high cathedral they had seen from so far away.

The island was indented with long, narrow docks and latticed with winding canals. Walking through the busy streets, Ebrima wondered how Jan Wolman would receive two penniless second cousins and an African. They might not be the most welcome of surprise visitors.

They found his home, a fine tall house in a row. They knocked at the door with apprehension, and were regarded doubtfully by the servants. But then Jan appeared and welcomed them with open arms. He said to Barney: 'You look exactly like my late father when he was young and I was a boy.' Jan himself had the red hair and golden-brown eyes of the Willards.

They had decided not to burden Jan with the whole truth about their flight from Kortrijk. Instead, they said they had deserted from the Spanish army because they had not been paid. Jan believed them, and even seemed to think that soldiers who had not been paid had a right to desert.

Jan gave them wine, bread and cold beef, for they were starving. Then he made them wash and loaned them clean shirts because, he said with amiable candour, they stank.

Ebrima had never been in a house like Jan's. It was not big enough to be called a palace, though it had plenty of room, especially for a city dwelling. However, it was crammed with costly furniture and objects: large, framed wall mirrors; Turkish rugs; decorated glassware from Venice; musical instruments; and delicate ceramic jugs and bowls that seemed to be for show rather than use. The paintings were also unlike anything Ebrima had seen. Netherlanders seemed to enjoy pictures of people like themselves, relaxing with books and cards and music in comfortable rooms similar to the ones they lived in, as if they found their own lives more interesting than those of the biblical prophets and figures of legend more common in Spanish art.

Ebrima was given a room smaller than those of Barney and Carlos, but he was not asked to sleep with the servants, and he concluded from this that Jan was not certain of his status.

That evening they sat around the table with the family: Jan's wife, Hennie; his daughter, Imke; and three small boys, Frits, Jef and Daan.

They used a mixture of languages. French was the main medium in the south and west of the Netherlands, and various Dutch dialects were spoken elsewhere. Jan, like many merchants, could get by in several languages, including Spanish and English.

Jan's daughter, Imke, was seventeen and attractive, with a wide happy smile and curly fair hair; a junior version of Hennie. She took an immediate shine to Barney, and Ebrima noticed that Carlos competed in vain for her attention. Barney had a roguish grin that girls loved. In Ebrima's opinion steady, reliable Carlos would make the better husband, but few teenage girls would be so wise as to see that. Ebrima himself had no interest in young girls, but he liked Hennie, who seemed intelligent and kind.

Hennie asked how they had come to join the Spanish army, and Ebrima began to tell the story, in mixed Spanish and

French with a few dialect words when he knew them. He made the most of the drama, and soon the whole table was listening to him. He included the details of the new furnace, emphasizing that he had been an equal partner with Carlos in its invention. He explained how the blast of air made the fire burn so hot that the iron was produced in molten form and flowed out continuously, allowing the furnace to produce a ton of metal per day; and as he did so he observed Jan looking at him with new respect.

The Wolmans were Catholics, but they were horrified to learn how the Church in Seville had treated Carlos. Jan said that kind of thing would never happen in Antwerp, but Ebrima wondered if he was right, given that the Church in both countries was ruled by the same Pope.

Jan was excited by the blast furnace, and said that Ebrima and Carlos must meet his main supplier of metals, Albert Willemsen, as soon as possible – in fact, tomorrow.

Next morning, they all walked to a less affluent neighbourhood near the docks. Albert lived in a modest house with his wife, Betje; a solemn little eight-year-old daughter, Drike; his attractive widowed sister, Evi; and Evi's son, Matthus, who was about ten. Albert's premises were strikingly like Carlos's old home in Seville, with a passage leading to a backyard workplace with a furnace and stocks of iron ore, limestone and coal. He readily agreed that Carlos, Ebrima and Barney could build a blast furnace in his yard, and Jan promised to lend them the money needed.

Over the following days and weeks, they got to know the city. Ebrima was struck by how hard the Netherlands people worked – not the poor, who worked hard everywhere, but the rich. Jan was one of the wealthiest men in town, but he worked six days a week. A Spaniard with that much money would have retired to the countryside, bought a hacienda and paid a steward to collect rents from peasants so that his own lily-white fingers did not have to touch grubby money, while seeking an aristocratic match for his daughter in the hope that his grandchildren would have titles. Netherlanders did not seem to care much about titles, and they liked money. Jan bought iron and bronze and manufactured guns and ammunition; he bought fleeces from England and turned them into woollen cloth that he sold back to the English; he bought profitable shares in cargoes, workshops, farms and taverns; and he loaned money to expanding businesses, to bishops who had overspent their incomes, and to princes. He always charged interest, of course. The Church's prohibition against usury was ignored here.

Heresy was another thing that did not trouble the people of Antwerp. The city was thronged with Jews, Muslims and Protestants, all cheerfully identifying themselves by their clothing, all doing business on an equal footing. There were folk of many complexions: redbeards like Barney, Africans like Ebrima, light-brown Turks with wispy moustaches, and beige Chinamen with straight blue-black hair. The Antwerpers hated nobody, except those who did not pay their debts. Ebrima liked the place.

Nothing was said about Ebrima's freedom. Every day he went with Carlos and Barney to Albert's yard, and every evening they all ate at Jan's house. On Sundays Ebrima went to church with the family, then slipped away in the afternoon – when the other men were sleeping off the wine they had drunk with the midday meal – and found a place out in the countryside where he could perform the water rite. No one called Ebrima a slave, but in other respects his life was worryingly similar to how it had been in Seville.

While they were working in the yard Albert's sister Evi often sat with them when they took a break. She was about forty, a little on the heavy side – as were many well-fed Netherlands women in their middle years – with a distinct twinkle in her blue-green eyes. She talked to them all, but especially to Ebrima, who was close to her own age. She had a lively curiosity, and questioned him about life in Africa, pressing him for details, some of which he had to strain to remember. As a widow with a child, she was probably looking for a husband; and since both Carlos and Barney were too young to be interested in her, Ebrima had to wonder whether she had a speculative eye on him. He had not been intimate with a woman since parting with Elisa, but he hoped that was a temporary state: he certainly did not intend to live the life of a monk.

Building the blast furnace took a month. When they were ready to test it, both Jan's family and Albert's came to watch.

Ebrima recollected that they had done this only once before, and so they could not be sure that it would work a second time. The three of them would look stupid if it failed. Worse, a fiasco would blight their future – which made Ebrima realize that he had been half-consciously hoping to stay and make a living here. And he hated the thought of making a fool of himself in front of Evi.

Carlos lit the fire, Ebrima poured in the iron ore and lime, and Barney whipped on the two harnessed horses that drove the bellows mechanism.

As before, there was a long, nail-biting wait.

Barney and Carlos fidgeted nervously. Ebrima struggled to maintain his habitual impassivity. He felt as if he had staked everything on the turn of a single card.

The spectators became a bit bored. Evi started talking to Hennie about the problems of having adolescent children. Jan's three sons chased Albert's daughter around the yard. Albert's wife, Betje, offered oranges on a tray. Ebrima was too tense to eat.

Then the iron began to flow.

The molten metal inched slowly from the base of the furnace into the prepared stone channels. At first, the motion was agonizingly slow, but soon the flow strengthened, and began to fill the ingot-shaped hollows in the ground. Ebrima poured more raw materials into the top of the furnace.

He heard Albert say wonderingly: 'Look at that – it just keeps coming!'

'Exactly,' Ebrima said. 'As long as you keep feeding the furnace, it will keep giving you iron.'

Carlos warned: 'It's pig iron – it has to be purified before it can be used.'

'I can see that,' Albert said. 'But it's still impressive.'

Jan said incredulously: 'Are you telling me that the king of Spain turned up his nose at this invention?'

Carlos replied: 'I don't suppose King Felipe even heard of it. But the other iron makers in Seville felt threatened. Spanish people don't like change. The people who run our industries are very conservative.'

Jan nodded. 'I suppose that's why the king buys so many cannons from foreigners like me – because Spanish industry doesn't produce enough.'

'And then they complain that the silver from America arrives in Spain only to leave again right away.'

Jan smiled. 'Well, as we're Netherlands merchants rather than Spanish grandees, let's go into the house, have a drink, and talk business.'

They went inside and sat around the table. Betje served them beer and cold sausage. Imke gave the children raisins to keep them quiet.

Jan said: 'The profits from this new furnace will be used first to pay off my loan, with interest.'

Carlos said: 'Of course.'

'Afterwards, the money should be shared out between Albert and yourselves. Is that how you see it?'

Ebrima realized that the word 'yourselves' was deliberately vague. Jan did not know whether Ebrima was to be included as an equal partner with Carlos and Barney.

This was no time for humility. Ebrima said: 'The three of us built the furnace together: Carlos, Barney and me.'

Everyone looked at Carlos, and Ebrima held his breath. Carlos hesitated. This was the real test, Ebrima realized. When they had been on the raft, it had cost Carlos nothing to say *You're a free man, Ebrima*, but this was different. If Carlos acknowledged Ebrima as an equal, in front of Jan Wolman and Albert Willemsen, he would be committed.

And Ebrima would be free.

At last Carlos said: 'A four-way split, then. Albert, Barney, Ebrima and me.'

Ebrima's heart bounded, but he kept his face expressionless. He caught Evi's eye, and saw that she was looking pleased.

That was when Barney dropped his bombshell. 'Count me out,' he said.

Carlos said: 'What are you talking about?'

'You and Ebrima invented this furnace,' Barney said. 'I hardly did anything. Anyway, I'm not staying in Antwerp.'

Ebrima heard Imke gasp. She would be disappointed: she had fallen in love with Barney.

Carlos said: 'Where will you go, Barney?'

'Home,' said Barney. 'I've had no contact with my family for more than two years. Since we arrived in Antwerp, Jan has confirmed that my mother lost everything when Calais fell. My brother, Ned, no longer works in the family business – there is no business – and he's some kind of secretary in the court of Queen Elizabeth. I want to see them both. I want to make sure they're all right.'

'How will you get to Kingsbridge?'

'There's a Combe Harbour ship docked here in Antwerp at the moment – the *Hawk*, owned by Dan Cobley, captained by Jonas Bacon.'

'You can't afford passage – you haven't got any money.'

'Yesterday I spoke to the first mate, Jonathan Greenland, who I've known since I was a boy. One of the crew died on the voyage here, the ship's blacksmith and carpenter, and I've taken his job, just for the journey home.'

'But how will you make a living back in England, if your family business is gone?'

Barney gave the devil-may-care grin that broke the hearts of girls like Imke. 'I don't know,' he said. 'I'll think of something.'

＊

BARNEY QUESTIONED Jonathan Greenland as soon as the *Hawk* was out at sea and the crew were able to think about something other than steering the ship.

Jonathan had spent last winter in Kingsbridge, and had left to rejoin the ship only a few weeks ago, so he had all the latest news. He had called on Barney's mother, expecting Alice to be as eager as ever for reports from overseas. He had found her sitting in the front parlour of the big house, looking out at the west front of the cathedral, doing nothing; surrounded by old ledgers but never opening them. Apparently, she attended meetings of the borough council, but did not speak. Barney found it hard to imagine his mother not doing business. For as long as he could remember, Alice had lived for deals, percentages and profits; the challenge of making money by trading absorbed her completely. This transformation was ominous.

Sir Reginald Fitzgerald, who had plotted Alice's ruin, was still mayor of Kingsbridge, and living in Priory Gate, his vast new palace, Jonathan said. However, Bishop Julius had been brought down. Queen Elizabeth had broken all her promises and returned England to Protestantism. She required all priests to take the Oath of Supremacy, swearing allegiance to her as the supreme governor of the Church of England: refusal was treason. Almost all the lower clergy had agreed, but most of the old Catholic bishops had not. They could have been executed, but Elizabeth had vowed not to kill people for their faith, and she was keeping to that – so far. Most of the bishops were merely dismissed from their posts. Julius was living with two or three former monks in a house attached to St Mark's church in northern Kingsbridge. Jonathan had seen him drunk in the Bell Inn on a Saturday night, telling anyone who would listen that the true Catholic faith would return soon. He made a sad figure, Jonathan said, but Barney thought the malevolent old priest deserved a worse fate.

Jonathan also explained to Barney the attractions of life at sea. Jonathan was at home on board ship: he was sunburned and wiry, with hard hands and feet, as nimble as a squirrel in the rigging. Towards the end of the war against France, the *Hawk* had captured a French vessel. The crew had shared the profits with Captain Bacon and Dan Cobley, and Jonathan had got a bonus of sixty pounds on top of his wages. He had bought a house in Kingsbridge for his widowed mother and had rejoined the crew in the hope of more of the same.

'But we're no longer at war,' Barney said. 'If you capture a French ship now, you're guilty of piracy.'

Jonathan shrugged. 'We'll be at war with someone before

too long.' He tugged at a rope, checking the security of a knot that was evidently as tight as it could be, and Barney guessed that he did not want to be questioned too closely about piracy.

Barney changed the subject and asked about his brother.

Ned had come to Kingsbridge for Christmas, wearing an expensive new black coat and looking older than twenty. Jonathan knew that Ned worked with Sir William Cecil, who was Secretary of State, and people in Kingsbridge said Ned was an increasingly powerful figure at court, despite his youth. Jonathan had talked to him in the cathedral on Christmas Day, but had not learned much: Ned had been vague about exactly what he did for the queen, and Jonathan guessed he was involved in the secretive world of international diplomacy.

'I can't wait to see them,' Barney said.

'I can imagine.'

'It should be only a couple of days now.'

Jonathan checked another rope, then looked away.

No one expected to get into a fight on the journey along the Channel from Antwerp to Combe Harbour, but Barney felt he ought to work his passage by making sure the Hawk's armaments were ready for action.

Merchant ships needed guns as much as any other vessel. Seafaring was a dangerous business. In wartime, ships of one combatant nation could legitimately attack ships of the enemy; and all the major countries were at war as often as they were at peace. In peacetime, the same activity was called piracy, but it went on almost as much. Every ship had to be able to defend itself.

The Hawk had twelve guns, all bronze minions, small cannons that fired a four-pound shot. The minions were on the gun deck, immediately below the top deck, six on each side. They fired through square holes in the woodwork. Ship design had changed to accommodate this need. In older ships, such gun ports would have seriously weakened the structure. But the Hawk was carvel-built, an internal skeleton of heavy timbers providing its strength, with the planks of the hull fastened to the skeleton like skin over ribs. This type of structure had the additional advantage that enemy cannonballs could make multiple holes in the hull without necessarily sinking the ship.

Barney cleaned and oiled the guns, making sure they were running freely on their wheels, and made some small repairs, using the tools left behind by the previous smith, who had died. He checked stocks of ammunition: all the guns had the same size barrel and fired interchangeable cast-iron balls.

His most important job was to keep the gunpowder in good condition. It tended to absorb moisture – especially at sea – and Barney made sure that there were string bags of charcoal hanging from the ceiling on the gun deck to dry the air. The other hazard was that the ingredients of gunpowder – saltpetre, charcoal and sulphur – would separate over time, the heavier saltpetre sinking to the bottom, making the mixture harmless. In the army Barney had learned to turn the barrels upside down once a week.

He even ranged the guns. He did not want to waste ammunition, but Captain Bacon let him fire a few balls. All cannon barrels rested on trunnions, like handles sticking out both sides, which fitted into grooved supports in the gun carriage, making it easy to tilt the barrel up and down. With the barrel at an angle of forty-five degrees – the attitude for maximum distance – the minions would fire a four-pound ball almost a mile, about one thousand six hundred yards. The angle was changed by propping up the rear end of the barrel with wedges. With the barrel level, the ball splashed into the water about three hundred yards away. That told Barney that each seven degrees of elevation from the horizontal added just over two hundred yards to the range. He had brought with him from the army an iron protractor with a plumb line and a curved scale for measuring angles. With its long arm thrust into the barrel, he could measure the gun's angle precisely. On land it worked well. At sea, the constant motion of the ship made shooting less accurate.

On the fourth day, Barney had nothing more to do, and he found himself on deck with Jonathan again. They were crossing a bay. The coast was on the port bow, as it had been ever since the Hawk had left the Westerschelde estuary and entered the English Channel. Barney was no expert in navigation, but he thought that by now they should have the English coast on the starboard bow. He frowned. 'How long do you think it will be before we reach Combe Harbour?'

Jonathan shrugged. 'I don't know.'

An unpleasant possibility crossed Barney's mind. 'We are headed for Combe Harbour, aren't we?'

'Eventually, yes.'

Barney's alarm grew. 'Eventually?'

'Captain Bacon doesn't confide his intentions to me. Nor to anyone else, come to that.'

'But you seem to think we might not be going home.'

'I'm looking at the coastline.'

Barney looked harder. Deep in the bay, just off the coast, a small island rose steeply out of the water to a precarious summit where a great church was perched like a giant seagull. It was familiar, and he realized, with dismay, that he had seen it before – twice. It was called Mont St Michel, and he had passed it once on his way to Seville, three years ago, and again on his way back from Spain to the Netherlands two years ago. 'We're going to Spain, aren't we?' he said to Jonathan.

'Looks like it.'

'You didn't tell me.'

'I didn't know. And besides, we need a gunner.'

Barney could guess what they needed a gunner for. And that explained why Bacon had hired him when there was so little work for him to do as ship's blacksmith. 'So Bacon and you have tricked me into becoming a member of the crew.'

Jonathan shrugged again.

Barney looked north. Combe Harbour was sixty miles in that direction. He turned his gaze to the island church. It was a mile or two away, in waves of at least three feet. He could not swim it, he knew. It would be suicide.

After a long moment, he said: 'But we'll come back to Combe Harbour from Seville, won't we?'

'Maybe,' said Jonathan, 'maybe not.'

II

WHILE ODETTE GAVE BIRTH, painfully and loudly, Pierre planned how to get rid of the baby.

Odette was suffering God's punishment for her unchastity. She deserved it. There was some justice on earth, after all, Pierre thought.

And as soon as the baby arrived, she would lose it.

He sat downstairs in the small house, leafing through his black leather-bound notebook, while the midwife attended to Odette in the bedroom. The remains of an interrupted breakfast were on the table in front of him: bread, ham and some early radishes. The room was dismal, with bare walls, a flagstone floor, a cold fireplace and one small window on to a narrow, dark street. Pierre hated it.

Normally he left straight after breakfast. He usually went first to the Guise family palace in the Vieille rue du Temple, a place where the floors were marble and the walls were hung with splendid paintings. Most often he spent the day there or at the Louvre palace, in attendance on Cardinal Charles or Duke François. In the late afternoon he frequently had meetings with members of his rapidly growing network of spies, who added to the list of Protestants in the black leather notebook. He rarely returned to the little house in Les Halles until bedtime. Today, however, he was waiting for the baby to come.

It was May 1560, and they had been married five months.

For the first few weeks Odette had tried to cajole him into a normal sexual relationship. She did her best to be coquettish, but it did not come naturally to her, and when she wiggled her broad behind and smiled at him, showing her crooked teeth, he was repelled. Later she began to taunt him with impotence and, as an alternative jibe, homosexuality. Neither arrow struck home – he thought nostalgically of long afternoons in the widow Bauchene's feather bed – but Odette's insults were nevertheless irritating.

Their mutual resentment hardened into cold loathing as her belly swelled through the end of a harsh winter and the beginning of a rainy spring. Their conversation shrank to terse exchanges about food, laundry, housekeeping money, and the performance of their sulky adolescent maid, Nath. Pierre found himself festering with rage. Thoughts of his hateful wife poisoned everything. The prospect of having to live, not only with Odette but also with her baby, the child of another man, came to be so odious as to seem impossible.

Perhaps the brat would be stillborn. He hoped so. That would make everything easy.

Odette stopped screaming, and a few moments later Pierre heard the squalling of a baby. He sighed: his wish had not been granted. The little bastard sounded repulsively healthy. Wearily, he rubbed his eyes with his hands. Nothing was easy, nothing ever went the way he hoped. There were always disappointments. Sometimes he wondered if his entire philosophy of life might be faulty.

He put the notebook in a document chest, locked the chest, and slipped the key into his pocket. He could not keep the book at the Guise palace, for he did not have a room of his own there.

He stood up. He had planned what to do next.

He climbed the stairs.

Odette lay in the bed with her eyes closed. She was pale, and bathed in perspiration, but breathing normally, either asleep or resting. Nath, the maid, was rolling up a sheet stained with blood and mucus. The midwife was holding the tiny baby in her left arm and, with her right hand, washing its head and face with a cloth that she dipped into a bowl of water.

It was an ugly thing, red and wrinkled with a mat of dark hair, and it made an irritating noise.

As Pierre watched, the midwife wrapped the baby in a little

blue blanket – a gift to Odette, Pierre recalled, from Véronique de Guise.

'It's a boy,' the midwife said.

He had not noticed the baby's gender, even though he had seen it naked.

Without opening her eyes, Odette said: 'His name is Alain.'

Pierre could have killed her. Not only was he expected to raise the child, she wanted him to have a daily reminder of Alain de Guise, the pampered young aristocrat who was the real father of the bastard. Well, she had a surprise coming.

'Here, take him,' said the midwife, and she handed the bundle to Pierre. He noticed that Véronique's blanket was made of costly soft wool.

Odette muttered: 'Don't give the baby to him.'

But she was too late. Pierre was already holding the child. It weighed next to nothing. For a moment he experienced a strange feeling, a sudden urge to protect this helpless little human being from harm; but he quickly suppressed the impulse. I'm not going to let my life be blighted by this worthless scrap, he thought.

Odette sat up in bed and said: 'Give me the baby.'

The midwife reached for the bundle, but Pierre withheld it. 'What did you say its name was, Odette?' he said in a challenging tone.

'Never mind, give him here.' She threw back the covers, evidently intending to get out of bed, but then she cried out, as if at a spasm of pain, and fell back on the pillow.

The midwife looked worried. 'The baby should suckle now,' she said.

Pierre saw that the child's mouth had puckered into a sucking shape, though it was taking in only air. Still he kept it in his arms.

The midwife made a determined attempt to wrest the baby from his grasp. Holding the child in one arm, he slapped the midwife's face hard with the other hand, and she fell back. Nath screamed. Odette sat up again, white with pain. Pierre went to the door, carrying the child.

'Come back!' Odette screamed. 'Pierre, please don't take away my baby!'

He went out and slammed the bedroom door.

He went down the stairs. The baby cried. It was a mild spring evening, but he threw on a cloak so that he could hide the baby underneath it. Then he left the house.

The baby seemed to like motion: when Pierre started walking steadily, it stopped crying. That came as a relief, and Pierre realized the child's noise had been bothering him, as if he was supposed to do something about it.

He headed for the Île de la Cité. Getting rid of the child would be easy. There was a particular place in the cathedral where people left unwanted babies, at the foot of a statue of St Anne, the mother of Mary and the patron saint of mothers. By custom, the priests would put the abandoned baby in a crib for all to see, and sometimes the child would be adopted by a soft-hearted couple as an act of charity. Otherwise it would be raised by nuns.

The baby moved under his arm, and once again he had to suppress an irrational feeling that he ought to love it and take care of it.

More challenging was the problem of explaining the disappearance of a Guise infant, albeit a bastard; but Pierre had his story ready. As soon as he returned he would dismiss the midwife and the maid. Then he would tell Cardinal Charles that the child had been stillborn, but the trauma had driven Odette mad, and she refused to accept that the baby was dead. Walking along, Pierre invented a few details: she had pretended to suckle the corpse, she had dressed it in new clothes, she had put it in a crib and said it was sleeping.

Charles would be suspicious, but the story was plausible, and there would be no proof of anything. Pierre thought he would get away with it. He had realized, at some point in the last two years, that Charles did not like him and never would, but found him too useful to be discarded. Pierre had taken the lesson to heart: as long as he was indispensable, he was safe.

The streets were crowded, as always. He passed a tall pile of refuse: ashes, fish bones, night soil, stable sweepings, worn-out shoes. It occurred to him that he could just leave the baby on such a rubbish tip, though he would have to make sure no one saw him. Then he noticed a rat nibbling the face of a dead cat, and he realized the baby would suffer the same fate, but alive. He did not have the stomach for that. He was not a monster.

He crossed the river by the Notre Dame Bridge and entered the cathedral; but when he reached the nave, he began to have doubts about his plan. As usual, there were people in the great church: priests, worshippers, pilgrims, hucksters and prostitutes. He walked slowly up the nave until he came level with the little side chapel dedicated to St Anne. Could he discreetly put the baby on the floor in front of the statue without being observed? He did not see how. For a destitute woman, perhaps it would hardly matter if she were noticed: no one would know who she was and she might slip away and vanish before anyone had the presence of mind to question her. But it was a different matter for a well-dressed young man. He might get into trouble if the baby so much as cried. Under his cloak, he pressed the warm body closer to him, hoping to muffle any noise as well as keeping it out of sight. He realized he should have come here late at night or very early in the morning – but what would he have done with the child in the meantime?

A thin young woman in a red dress caught his eye, and he was inspired. He would offer one of the prostitutes money to take the baby from him and put it into the chapel. Such a woman would not know him, and the baby would remain unidentified. He was about to approach the one in the red dress when, to his shock, he heard a familiar voice. 'Pierre, my dear chap, how are you?'

It was his old tutor. 'Father Moineau!' he said, horrified. This was calamitous. If the baby cried, how would Pierre explain what he was doing?

The priest's square, reddish face was creased with smiles. 'I'm glad to see you. I hear you're becoming a man of consequence!'

'Something like that,' Pierre said. Desperately he added:

'Which means, unfortunately, that I am pressed for time and must leave you.'

Moineau looked thunderous at this brush-off. 'Please, don't allow me to detain you,' he said curtly.

Pierre longed to confess his troubles, but he felt a more urgent need to get himself and the baby out of the cathedral. 'I do beg your pardon, Father,' he said. 'I will call on you before too long.'

'If you have time,' Moineau said sarcastically.

'I'm sorry. Goodbye!'

Moineau did not say goodbye, but turned away petulantly.

Pierre hurried down the nave and out through the west door. He was dismayed to have offended Moineau, the only person in the world he could tell his troubles to. Pierre had his masters and his servants, but he did not cultivate friends; Moineau was the exception. And now he had offended him.

He put Moineau out of his mind and retraced his steps across the bridge. He wished he could have thrown the baby into the river, but he would have been seen. Anyway, he knew that Father Moineau would not have reassured him that such a murder was God's will. Sins committed in a good cause might be indulged, but there was a limit.

If he could not leave the baby in the cathedral, he would take it directly to the nuns. He knew one of the convents that acted as an orphanage: it was in the affluent east of the city, not far from the Guise family palace. He turned in that direction. He probably should have chosen this plan in the first place: the cathedral had been a mistake.

The place he was thinking of was called the Convent of the Holy Family. As well as an orphanage, the nuns ran a school for girls and small boys. As Pierre approached he heard the unmistakable sound of children at play. He went up the front steps to a tall carved door and stepped into a cool, quiet hall with a stone floor.

He took the baby from under his cloak. Its eyes were closed but it was still breathing. It waved its tiny fists in front of its face as if trying to get its thumb in its mouth.

After a few moments a young nun glided silently into the hall. She stared at the baby.

Pierre used his most authoritative voice. 'I must speak with your Mother Superior immediately.'

'Yes, sir,' said the nun. She was polite but not intimidated: a man with a baby in his arms cannot be fearsome, Pierre realized. The nun said: 'May I ask who wishes to see her?'

Pierre had anticipated this question. 'My name is Doctor Jean de la Rochelle, and I am attached to the College of the Holy Trinity at the university.'

The nun opened a door. 'Please be so kind as to wait in here.'

Pierre went into a pleasant small room with a painted wooden sculpture of Mary, Joseph and the baby Jesus. The only other furniture was a bench, but Pierre did not sit down.

An older nun came in a few minutes later. 'Doctor Roche?' she said.

'De la Rochelle,' Pierre corrected her. It was just possible that her mistake with his name was a deliberate error intended to test him.

'Forgive me. I am Mother Ladoix.'

Pierre said dramatically: 'The mother of this boy child is possessed by the devil.'

Mother Ladoix was as shocked as he intended. She crossed herself and said: 'May God protect us all.'

'The mother cannot possibly raise the baby. It would die.'

'And the family?'

'The child is illegitimate.'

Mother Ladoix began to recover from her shock and looked at Pierre with a touch of scepticism. 'And the father?'

'Not me, I assure you, in case that was what you were thinking,' he said haughtily.

She looked embarrassed. 'Certainly not.'

'However, he is a very young nobleman. I am the family's physician. Naturally, I cannot reveal their name.'

'I understand.'

The baby began to cry. Almost automatically, Mother Ladoix took the bundle from Pierre and rocked the baby. 'He's hungry,' she said.

'No doubt,' said Pierre.

'This blanket is very soft. It must have been costly.'

It was a hint. Pierre took out his purse. He had not prepared for this contingency, but fortunately he had money. He counted out ten gold ecus, worth twenty-five livres, enough to feed a baby for years. 'The family asked me to offer you ten ecus, and to say they would guarantee the same amount every year that the child is here.'

Mother Ladoix hesitated. Pierre guessed that she did not know how much of his story to believe. But caring for unwanted children was her mission in life. And ten ecus was a lot of money. She took the coins. 'Thank you,' she said. 'We will take good care of this little boy.'

'I will pray for him and for you.'

'And I look forward to seeing you one year from today.'

For a moment Pierre was thrown. Then he realized she expected him to return with another ten ecus, as promised. It would never happen. 'I will be here,' he lied. 'One year from today.'

He opened the door and held it for the nun. She left the room and silently disappeared into the nunnery.

Pierre went out with a light heart and walked away rapidly. He was exultant. He had got rid of the bastard. There would be a thunderstorm when he got home, but that was all right. There was no longer anything to tie him to the repellent Odette. Perhaps he could get rid of her, too.

To postpone the confrontation, he went into a tavern and ordered a celebratory cup of sherry. As he sat alone, sipping the strong, tawny wine, he turned his mind to his work.

It was more difficult now than when he had started. King Francis II had stepped up trials of Protestants, perhaps under the guidance of his Scottish wife, Mary Stuart, but more likely influenced by her Guise uncles. The heightened persecution had made the Protestants more cautious.

Several of Pierre's spies were Protestants who had been arrested and threatened with torture unless they turned traitor. But the heretics were getting wise to this, and no longer automatically trusted their co-religionists. Nowadays they often knew each other only by first names, not revealing their surnames or addresses. It was like a game in which the Church's moves were always countered by the heretics. However, Charles was patient, and Pierre was relentless; and it was a game that ended in death.

He finished his wine and walked the rest of the way home.

When he got there, he was shocked to find Cardinal Charles sitting in his living room, in a red silk doublet, waiting for him.

The midwife stood behind the cardinal with her arms folded and her chin raised defiantly.

Without preamble, Charles said: 'What have you done with the baby?'

Pierre got over his shock rapidly and thought hard. Odette had acted faster than he had anticipated. He had underestimated the resourcefulness of a desperate woman. She must have recovered from childbirth sufficiently to send a message to the cardinal, probably by Nath, pleading for help. Nath had been lucky to find Charles at home and willing to come immediately. The upshot was that Pierre was in trouble. 'Somewhere safe,' he said in answer to the cardinal's question.

'If you've killed a Guise child, by God you'll die for it, no matter how good you are at catching blasphemers.'

'The baby is alive and well.'

'Where?'

There was no point in resistance. Pierre gave in. 'At the Convent of the Holy Family.'

The midwife looked triumphant. Pierre felt humiliated. He now regretted that slap in the face.

Charles said: 'Go back and get him.'

Pierre hesitated. He could hardly bring himself to return, but he could not defy the cardinal without ruining everything.

Charles said: 'You'd better bring him here alive.'

Pierre realized that if the baby should die of natural causes now – as they often did in the first few hours – he would be blamed, and probably executed for murder.

He turned and went to the door.

'Wait,' said Charles. 'Listen to me. You are going to live with

Odette, and take care of her and her child for the rest of your life. That is my will.'

Pierre was silent. No one could defy Charles's will, not even the king.

'And the child's name is Alain,' said Charles.

Pierre nodded assent, and left the house.

*

SYLVIE'S LIFE WENT WELL for half a year.

With the proceeds of book sales she and her mother rented a pleasant small house with two bedrooms in the rue de la Serpente, a street in the University district south of the river, and opened a shop in the front parlour. They sold paper, ink and other writing necessities to teachers, students and the literate general public. Sylvie bought the paper in Saint-Marcel, a suburb outside the city wall to the south, where the manufacturers had the unlimited water they needed from the Bièvre river. She made the ink herself using oak galls, the wart-like growths she picked from the bark of trees in the woods. Her father had taught her the recipe. Printing ink was different, made with oil to be more viscous, but she also knew how to prepare a more dilute ink for ordinary writing. The shop did not really make enough money for the two of them to live on, but it served as a plausible cover for their more important business.

Isabelle recovered from her depression, but she had aged. The horror the two women had experienced seemed to have weakened the mother and strengthened the daughter. Sylvie now took the initiative.

Sylvie led a dangerous life as a criminal and a heretic but, paradoxically, she was happy. Reflecting on why this was, she suspected that for the first time in her life she did not have a man telling her what to do. She had decided to open the shop, she had chosen to rejoin the Protestant congregation, she had continued selling banned books. She talked to her mother about everything, but she made the decisions. She was happy because she was free.

She longed for a man to hold at night, but not at the price

of her liberty. Most men treated their wives like children, the only difference being that women could work harder. Perhaps there were men somewhere who did not regard wives as property, but she had never met one.

Sylvie had invented new names for them both, so that the authorities would not connect them with the executed heretic Giles Palot. They now called themselves Thérèse and Jacqueline St Quentin. The Protestants understood why and went along with the pretence. The two women had no friends who were not Protestants.

Their aliases had fooled a man from the city government who had visited the shop soon after it opened. He had looked all over the premises and asked a lot of questions. He might even have been one of Pierre Aumande's informants, Sylvie thought; although any paper shop might have been checked for illegal literature. There were no books in the building, other than notebooks and ledgers, and he had gone away satisfied.

The contraband books were at the warehouse in the rue du Mur, and Sylvie withdrew one only when she had a buyer lined up, so that the incriminating objects were never at the house for more than a few hours. Then, one Sunday morning in the summer of 1560, she went to the warehouse for a French-language Geneva Bible and found that there was only one left in the box.

Checking the other boxes, she discovered that most contained obscure texts, such as the works of Erasmus, which she was able to sell only occasionally, to broad-minded priests or curious university students. She might have guessed: the books were still in the warehouse because they did not sell well. Other than the Bible, the only moderately popular book was John Calvin's manifesto *Institutes of the Christian Religion*. That was why her father had been printing more Bibles last September, when the Guises had pounced. But those Bibles, found in the shop and fatally incriminating for Giles, had been burned.

She realized that she had failed to plan ahead. What was she going to do now? She thought with horror of the profession she had almost taken up back in the winter, when she and her mother had been close to starving. Never again, she vowed.

On her way home she passed through Les Halles, the district where Pierre lived. Despite her loathing of Pierre, she tried to keep an eye on him. His master, Cardinal Charles, was responsible for the royal crackdown on Paris Protestants, and Sylvie felt sure Pierre must still be involved in finding them. He could no longer be a spy himself, because so many people knew who he was, but he was probably a spymaster.

Sylvie had discreetly watched Pierre's house, and talked to people in the nearby tavern of St Étienne. Members of the Guise household guard often drank there, and she sometimes picked up useful chatter about what the family was up to. She had also learned that Pierre had remarried quickly after the annulment. He now had a wife called Odette, a baby boy called Alain, and a maid called Nath: the tavern gossip was that both Odette and Nath hated Pierre. Sylvie had not yet spoken to Odette or Nath, but she was on nodding terms, and she hoped they might one day be persuaded to betray his secrets. Meanwhile, Pierre was watched at court by the young marchioness of Nîmes, who kept a note of the people she saw him talking to. So far her only moderately interesting identification had been Gaston Le Pin, the captain of the Guise family guard, who was too well known to have a clandestine role.

When she got home and told her mother they were out of Bibles, Isabelle said: 'We could forget about the books, and just sell stationery.'

'The stationery doesn't make enough money,' Sylvie said. 'Anyway, I don't want to spend my life selling paper and ink. We have a mission to enable our fellow men and women to read God's word for themselves, and to find their way to the true gospel. I want to go on doing that.'

Her mother smiled. 'Good girl.'

'But how will I get the books? We can't print them. Father's machinery belongs to someone else now.'

'There must be other Protestant printers in Paris.'

'There are – I've seen their books in customers' homes. And

we've got plenty of money from past sales to buy new stock. But I can't find out where the printers are – it's a secret, obviously. Anyway, they can sell the books themselves, so why would they need me?'

'There's only one place where it's possible to buy large quantities of Protestant books, and that's Geneva.' Isabelle said it as if Geneva were as remote as the moon.

But Sylvie was not easily discouraged. 'How far is it?'

'You can't go! It's a long way, and a dangerous journey. And you've never travelled farther than the outskirts of Paris.'

Sylvie pretended to be less daunted than she felt. 'Other people do it. Remember Guillaume?'

'Of course I remember him. You should have married him.'

'I should never have married anyone. How do people get from Paris to Geneva?'

'I have no idea.'

'Maybe Luc Mauriac will know.' Sylvie knew the Mauriac family well.

Isabelle nodded. 'He's a cargo broker.'

'I've never understood exactly what a cargo broker does.'

'Imagine that a captain comes from Bordeaux and up the Seine river to Paris with a cargo of wine. Then he gets a shipment of cloth to take back to Bordeaux, but it fills only half of his hold. He doesn't want to wait around, he needs another half-cargo as soon as possible. So he goes to Luc, who knows every merchant in Paris and every port in Europe. Luc will find the captain a load of coal, or leather, or fashionable hats, that someone in Bordeaux wants.'

'So Luc knows how to go everywhere, including Geneva.'

'He'll tell you that a young woman can't possibly do it.'

'The days of men telling me what I can and can't do are over.'

Isabelle stared at her. To Sylvie's astonishment, tears came to her mother's eyes. 'You're so brave,' Isabelle said. 'I can hardly believe you came from me.'

Sylvie was moved by her mother's emotion. She managed to say: 'But I'm just like you.'

Isabelle shook her head. 'As the cathedral is like the parish church, perhaps.'

Sylvie was not sure how to respond to Isabelle. A parent was not supposed to look up to a child: it should be the other way around. After an awkward moment she said: 'It's time to go to the service.'

The congregation from the hunting lodge had found a new location for what they sometimes called their temple. Sylvie and Isabelle entered a large yard where horses and carriages could be hired. They were wearing drab clothes so that they did not look dressed up for church. The business, owned by a Protestant, was closed today, Sunday, but the doors were not locked. They entered the stable, a big stone building. A burly young groom was combing a horse's mane. He looked hard at them, ready to challenge them, then recognized them and stepped aside to let them pass.

At the back of the stable a door opened on a concealed staircase leading up to a large attic. This was where the group worshipped. As always, the room was bare of pictures or statues and furnished simply with chairs and benches. One great advantage here was that there were no windows, so the room was soundproof. Sylvie had stood outside in the street while the congregation sang at the tops of their voices and had not been able to hear anything more than a distant strain of music that might have come from any one of several nearby religious buildings: the parish church, a monastery, or a college.

Everyone in the room knew Sylvie. She was a pivotal member of the congregation because of her role as the bookseller. In addition, during the discussion sessions that they called fellowship she often expressed trenchant views, especially on the emotive subject of tolerance. Her views, like her singing voice, could not go unnoticed. She would never be an elder, for that role was reserved for men, but, nevertheless, she was treated as one of the leaders.

She and her mother took front-row seats. Sylvie loved Protestant services – although, unlike many of her co-worshippers, she did not despise the Catholic rites: she understood that for many people the whiff of incense, the Latin words and the eerie singing of a choir were part of the spiritual experience. However, she was moved by other things: plain language, logical beliefs and hymns that she could sing herself.

All the same, today she found herself impatient for the service to end. Luc Mauriac was in the congregation with his family and she was eager to question him.

She did not forget business. Immediately after the final Amen, she gave her last French Bible to Françoise Duboeuf, the tailor's young wife, and took five livres in payment.

Then she was approached by Louise, the young marchioness of Nîmes. 'The court is moving to Orléans,' Louise said.

It was normal for the king and his entourage to move around the country from time to time. 'Perhaps there will be a respite for Parisian Protestants,' Sylvie said hopefully. 'What's happening in Orléans?'

'The king has called a meeting of the Estates-General there.' This was a traditional national assembly. 'Cardinal Charles and Pierre Aumande are going with the court.'

Sylvie frowned. 'I wonder what new mischief those two devils are planning.'

'Whatever it is, it won't be good for us.'

'Lord protect us.'

'Amen.'

Sylvie left Louise and sought out Luc. 'I need to go to Geneva,' she said.

Luc was a small man with a jolly manner, but he frowned disapprovingly. 'May I ask why, Sylvie? Or Thérèse, I should say.'

'We've sold all our French Bibles and I have to buy more.'

'God bless you,' he said. 'I do admire your guts.'

For the second time that morning, Sylvie was thrown off balance by unexpected admiration. She was not brave, she was scared. 'I just do what has to be done,' she said.

'But you can't do this,' Luc said. 'There's no safe route, and you're a young woman who can't afford a bodyguard of men-at-arms to protect you from bandits, thieving tavern-keepers and randy peasants armed with wooden shovels.'

Sylvie frowned at the image of randy peasants. Why did men so often speak of rape as if it were a joke? But she refused to be distracted. 'Humour me,' she said. 'How do people get to Geneva?'

'The quickest way is to go up the Seine from here as far as Montereau, which is about sixty miles. The rest of the journey, another two hundred and fifty miles or so, is mostly overland, all right if you have no goods to transport. Two to three weeks, with no serious delays, although there are always delays. Your mother will go with you, of course.'

'No. She needs to stay here and keep the shop open.'

'Seriously, Sylvie, you can't do this alone.'

'I may have to.'

'Then you must attach yourself to a large party at every stage of the journey. Families are safest. Avoid all-male groups, for obvious reasons.'

'Of course.' All this was new to Sylvie. The prospect was terrifying. She felt foolish for having spoken glibly of going to Geneva. 'I still want to do it,' she said, trying to sound more confident than she felt.

'In that case, what's your story?'

'What do you mean?'

'You'll be in company. Travellers have nothing to do but talk. They will ask you questions. You're not going to admit that you're on your way to Geneva to buy illegal books. In fact, you'd better not say you're going to Geneva at all, since everyone knows it's the world capital of heresy. You need a story.'

Sylvie was stumped. 'I'll think of something.'

He looked thoughtful. 'You could say you're on a pilgrimage.'

'To where?'

'Vézelay, which is halfway to Geneva. The abbey has relics of Mary Magdalene. Women often go there.'

'Perfect.'

'When do you want to go?'

'Soon.' She did not want to spend too long worrying about the trip. 'This week.'

'I'll find a trustworthy captain to take you to Montereau. At least you'll get that far safely. Then just keep your wits about you.'

'Thank you.' She hesitated, thinking she should say

something polite after picking his brains. 'How is Georges? I haven't seen him for a while.'

'Fine, thank you, and opening a branch of our business at Rouen now.'

'He was always clever.'

Luc smiled wryly. 'I love my son dearly, but he was never a match for you, Sylvie.'

That was true, but embarrassing, so Sylvie let it pass without comment, and said: 'Thank you for your help. I'll call at your office tomorrow, if I may.'

'Come on Tuesday morning. By then I will have found you a captain.'

Sylvie extracted her mother from a group of women. She was impatient to get home and start making preparations.

On the way back to the rue de la Serpente, she found a cheap draper's store and bought a length of coarse grey cloth, ugly but hard-wearing. 'When we get home, I need you to sew me a nun's costume,' she said to her mother.

'Of course, though I'm almost as bad a seamstress as you.'

'That's fine. The cruder the better, as long as it doesn't fall apart.'

'All right.'

'But first I need you to cut off my hair. All of it. It must be less than an inch long all over.'

'You're going to look hideous.'

'Exactly,' said Sylvie. 'That's what I want.'

*

In Orléans, Pierre was planning a murder.

He would not wield the knife himself, but he would make it happen.

Cardinal Charles had brought him to Orléans for that purpose. Charles was still angry with Pierre over his attempt to get rid of Odette's baby but, as Pierre had calculated, his usefulness saved him.

In other circumstances he would have drawn the line at murder. He had never committed such a terrible sin, though he had come close: he had been sorely tempted to kill baby

Alain, but had not seen how he could get away with it. He had been responsible for many deaths, including that of Giles Palot, but they were all legitimate executions. He knew he was about to cross a dreadful line.

However, he had to win back Charles's confidence, and this was the way to do it. And he hoped that Father Moineau would agree it was the will of God. If not, Pierre was damned.

The intended victim was Antoine de Bourbon, the king of Navarre. And the assassination was the key element in a coup that would at the same time neutralize the two other most important enemies of the Guise family: Antoine's younger brother Louis, the prince of Condé; and the Bourbons' most important ally, Gaspard de Coligny, admiral of France and the most energetic member of the Montmorency family.

These three, who rarely went anywhere together for fear of exactly this kind of plot, had been lured to Orléans by the promise of a debate about freedom of worship at a meeting of the Estates-General. As leaders of the tolerance faction they could not possibly be absent from such an important occasion. They had to take the risk.

Orléans was on the north bank of the Loire. It was two hundred miles from the sea, but the river was busy with traffic, mostly flat-bottomed boats with fold-down masts that could negotiate shallow waters and go under bridges. In the heart of the city, across the street from the cathedral, was a newly built palace called Château Groslot, whose proud owner, Jacques Groslot, had been turfed out of his gorgeous new house to make way for the royal party.

It was a splendid building, Pierre thought, approaching it at daybreak on the morning of the murder. Its red bricks were mixed with black in a lozenge pattern around rows of tall windows. Twin flights of steps swept up in mirror-image curves to the main entrance. It was clever and innovative in a conservative way that Pierre admired.

Pierre was not staying there. As usual he was lodged with the servants, even though his name was now de Guise. But one day he would have a palace like this of his own.

He went in with Charles de Louviers, the assassin.

Pierre felt strange in de Louviers's company. Louviers was well dressed, and his manners were courtly, but, all the same, there was something thuggish about the set of his shoulders and the look in his eye. There were many murderers, of course, and several times Pierre had watched such men hang at the place de Grève in Paris. But Louviers was different. He came from the gentry, hence the 'de' in his full name, and he was willing to kill people of his own social class. It seemed strange, but everyone agreed that a prince of the blood such as Antoine could not be slain by a common criminal.

The interior of the palace gleamed with new wealth. The panelling shone, the rich colours of the tapestries had not had time to fade, and the massive candelabra were untarnished. The elaborate paintwork of the coffered ceilings was vividly fresh. Monsieur Groslot was a local politician and businessman, and he wanted the world to know he had prospered.

Pierre led Louviers to the suite occupied by the queen. Once there, he asked a servant to tell Alison McKay that he had arrived.

Alison was very grand indeed, now that her close companion Mary Stuart had become the queen of France. Pierre had watched the two girls, draped in priceless dresses and glittering with jewellery, acknowledging the deep bows and low curtsies of the nobility with a casual nod or a condescending smile, and he had thought how quickly people could get used to lofty status and universal deference; and how badly he himself longed to be the object of such veneration.

It was impudent of him to ask for Alison so early in the morning. But he had got to know her since the day, more than a year ago, when he had brought Mary the news of the imminent death of King Henri II. Alison's future, like his, was tied to the fate of the Guise family. She knew that he came as an emissary of Cardinal Charles, and she trusted him. She would know he would not waste her time.

A few minutes later, the servant showed them into a small side room. Alison was sitting at a round table. She had obviously dressed hurriedly, putting on a brocade coat over her nightdress. With her dark hair hastily combed and her blue eyes heavy with sleep, she looked charmingly dishevelled.

'How is King Francis?' Pierre asked her.

'Not well,' she said. 'But he's never well. He had smallpox as a child, you know, and that stunted his growth and left him permanently sickly.'

'And Queen Mary? I imagine she's still grieving for her mother.' Mary Stuart's mother, Marie de Guise, had died in Edinburgh in June.

'As much as one can mourn a mother one hardly knew.'

'I trust there is no question of Queen Mary going to Scotland.' This was a niggling worry for Pierre and the Guise brothers. If Mary Stuart should capriciously decide that she wanted to rule Scotland, it might be hard for the Guises to stop her, for she was the Queen of Scots.

Alison did not immediately agree, increasing Pierre's unease. 'The Scots certainly need a firm hand,' she said.

It was not the answer Pierre wanted, but it was true. Their Protestant-dominated Parliament had just passed a bill making it a crime to celebrate Mass. Pierre said: 'But Mary's first duty lies here in France, surely.'

Happily, Alison agreed with that. 'Mary must stay with Francis until she has borne him a son, ideally two. She understands that assuring the succession in France is more important than pacifying the seditious Scots.'

'Besides,' Pierre said with a relieved smile, 'why would someone who is queen of France want to exchange that for being queen of Scotland?'

'Indeed. We both have only the vaguest memories of Scotland: when we left, Mary was five and I was eight. Neither of us can speak the Scots dialect. But you didn't get me out of bed this early to talk about Scotland.'

Pierre realized he had been avoiding the real subject. Don't be afraid, he told himself. You are Pierre Aumande de Guise. 'Everything is ready,' he said to Alison. 'Our three enemies are in town.'

She knew exactly what he meant. 'Do we move immediately?'

'We already have. Louis de Bourbon is in custody, accused

of high treason and facing the death penalty.' He was probably guilty, Pierre thought, not that it mattered. 'Gaspard de Coligny's lodging is surrounded by armed men who follow him everywhere. He is a prisoner in all but name.' Gaston Le Pin had managed this with the Guise family's household guard, a private army several hundred strong. 'Antoine de Bourbon has been summoned to see King Francis this morning.' Pierre indicated Louviers with a gesture. 'And Charles de Louviers is the man who will kill him.'

Alison did not flinch. Pierre was impressed with her coolness. She said: 'What do you need from me?'

Louviers spoke for the first time. His voice was cultivated and precise, his accent that of the gentry. 'The king must give me a signal when he is ready for me to do the deed.'

'Why?' Alison asked.

'Because a prince of the blood cannot be killed except on the authority of the king.'

What Louviers meant was that it had to be clear, to everyone in the room, that King Francis was responsible for the murder. Otherwise it would be too easy for the king to repudiate the assassination afterwards, proclaim his innocence, and execute Louviers, Pierre, Cardinal Charles, and anyone else who could plausibly be linked to the plot.

'Of course,' said Alison, getting the point quickly, as usual.

Pierre said: 'Louviers must have a few quiet moments with his majesty, so that they can agree on a signal. Cardinal Charles has already explained this to the king.'

'Very well.' Alison stood up. 'Come with me, Monsieur de Louviers.'

Louviers followed her to the door. There she turned. 'Do you have your weapon?'

He reached under his coat, revealing a dagger two feet long in a sheath hanging from his belt.

'You'd better leave it with Monsieur Aumande de Guise for now.'

Louviers removed the knife and sheath from his belt, put them on the table, and followed Alison from the room.

Pierre went to the window and looked across the square to

the tall pointed arches of the west front of the cathedral. He was nervous and guilt-stricken. I'm doing this for that church, he told himself, and for the God whose house it is, and for the old, authentic faith.

He was relieved when Alison reappeared. She stood close to him, her shoulder touching his, and looked in the same direction. 'That's where Joan of Arc prayed, during the siege of Orléans,' she said. 'She saved the city from the savagery of the English army.'

'Saved France, some say,' said Pierre. 'As we are trying to save France today.'

'Yes.'

'Is all well between King Francis and Louviers?'

'Yes. They're talking.'

Pierre's spirits lifted. 'We're about to get rid of the Bourbon menace – permanently. I thought I'd never see the day. All our enemies will be gone.' Alison did not reply, but looked uneasy, and Pierre said: 'Don't you agree?'

'Beware of the queen mother,' Alison said.

'What makes you say that?'

'I know her. She likes me. When we were children I used to take care of Francis and Mary – especially him, because he was so feeble. Queen Caterina has always been grateful to me for that.'

'And . . . ?'

'She talks to me. She thinks what we're doing is wrong.' When Alison said 'we' she meant the Guise family, Pierre knew.

'Wrong?' he said. 'How?'

'She believes we will never stamp out Protestantism by burning people to death. It just creates martyrs. Rather, we should remove the impulse that creates Protestants by reforming the Catholic Church.'

She was right about martyrs. No one had even liked the overbearing Giles Palot during his lifetime but now, according to Pierre's spies, he was almost a saint. However, reformation of the Church was a counsel of perfection. 'You're talking about taking away the wealth and privileges of men such as Cardinal Charles. It will never happen, because they are too powerful.'

'Caterina thinks that's the problem.'

'People will always find fault with the Church. The answer is to teach them that they have no right to criticize.'

Alison shrugged. 'I didn't say Queen Caterina was right. I just think we have to be on our guard.'

Pierre made a doubtful face. 'If she had any power, yes. But with the king married to a Guise-family niece, we're in control. I don't think we have anything to fear from the queen mother.'

'Don't underestimate her because she's a woman. Remember Joan of Arc.'

Pierre thought Alison was wrong, but he said: 'I never underestimate a woman,' and gave his most charming smile.

Alison turned a little, so that her breast was pressing against Pierre's chest. Pierre believed firmly that women never did such things by accident. She said: 'We're alike, you and I. We have dedicated ourselves to serving very powerful people. We're counsellors to giants. We should always work together.'

'I'd like that.' She was talking about a political alliance, but under her words was another message. The tone of her voice and the look on her face said she was attracted to him.

He had not thought of romance for a year. His disappointment over Véronique and his revulsion for the ghastly Odette left no room in his heart for feelings about other women.

For a moment he was unable to think how he should respond to Alison. Then he realized that Alison's talk of working together was not merely empty chatter to cover romantic interest. More likely it was the other way around: she was being flirtatious in order to lure him into a working partnership. Normally it was Pierre who pretended to be in love with a woman in order to get something out of her. He smiled at the irony, and she mistook that for encouragement. She tilted her head back a fraction so that her face was slightly turned up to his. The invitation was unmistakable.

Still he hesitated. What was in this for him? The answer came immediately: control of the queen of France. If Mary Stuart's best friend was his paramour, he could become even more powerful than Duke François and Cardinal Charles.

He leaned down and kissed her. Her lips were soft and yielding. She put her hand behind his head, pressing him closer, and opened her mouth to his tongue. Then she pulled away. 'Not now,' she said. 'Not here.'

Pierre tried to figure out what that meant. Did she want to go to bed with him somewhere else, later? A single girl such as Alison could not sacrifice her virginity. If it became known – as such things usually did at court – it would forever ruin her prospects of making a good marriage.

However, an upper-class virgin might well permit liberties with a man she expected to marry.

And then it struck him. 'Oh, no,' he said.

'What?'

'You don't know, do you?'

'What don't I know?'

'That I'm married.'

Her face fell. 'Good God, no.'

'It was arranged by Cardinal Charles. A woman who needed a husband in a hurry, for the usual reason.'

'Who?'

'Alain de Guise impregnated a maid.'

'Yes, I heard about that – oh! You're the one who married Odette?'

Pierre felt foolish and ashamed. 'Yes.'

'But why?'

'My reward was the right to call myself Pierre Aumande de Guise. It's on the marriage certificate.'

'Hell.'

'I'm sorry.'

'I'm sorry, too – though I might have done the same, for the sake of such a name.'

Pierre felt a bit better. He had rapidly gained and lost a remarkable opportunity to get close to the queen, but at least Alison did not despise him for marrying Odette. Her contempt would have been agony.

The door opened, and Pierre and Alison moved apart guiltily. Louviers came in and said: 'All is arranged.' He picked up the knife from the table, reattached the sheath to his belt, and drew his coat about him to cover the weapon.

Alison said: 'I'm going to dress. You two should wait in the reception room.' She left by the inner door.

Pierre and Louviers walked along a corridor and through a lobby to an ornate room with gilded panelling, richly coloured wallpaper and a Turkish carpet. This was only a waiting room. Beyond it was the presence chamber, where the king would actually give audiences, and a guard room occupied by twenty or thirty soldiers, then finally the royal bedchamber.

They were early, but a few courtiers had already gathered. Louviers said: 'He'll be an hour or two – he's not even dressed.'

Pierre settled down to wait, brooding. Reflecting on his conversation with Alison, his stomach burned with the acid thought that the best friend of the queen of France might have married him if he had been single. What a team they would have made: both smart, good-looking, ambitious. He might have ended up a duke. He felt the lost opportunity like a bereavement. And he hated Odette all the more. She was so vulgar and low-class, she took him all the way back down to the social level he had worked so hard to escape from. She defeated his entire life mission.

Gradually the room filled up. Antoine de Bourbon arrived at mid-morning. His face was handsome but weak, with heavy-lidded eyes and a downturned moustache that gave him a look of sulky lethargy. With his brother imprisoned and Coligny effectively under arrest, Antoine had to know there was a serious plot against him. Watching him, Pierre got the feeling he knew he could die today. His manner seemed to say *Do your worst, and see if I care.*

Duke Scarface and Cardinal Charles arrived. Nodding to acquaintances, they passed into the inner rooms without pausing.

A few minutes later, the waiting courtiers were beckoned into the presence chamber.

King Francis sat on an elaborately carved throne. He was leaning sideways, as if needing to support himself on the arm of the chair. His face was pale and moist. 'He's never well,' Alison had said, but this seemed worse than his usual frailty.

Cardinal Charles stood next to the throne.

Pierre and Louviers positioned themselves at the front of the crowd, making sure the king could see them clearly. Antoine de Bourbon was a few steps away.

Now they just needed the king to give the signal.

Instead, Francis beckoned to a courtier, who stepped forward and answered a desultory question. Pierre could not take in the conversation. The king should have ordered the execution immediately. It was bizarre to deal with minor business first, as if the murder were merely one item on a full agenda. But the king went on to ask a second courtier about another equally routine matter.

Cardinal Charles whispered in the king's ear, presumably telling him to get on with it, but Francis made a dismissive gesture with his hand, as if to say, *I'm coming to that.*

The bishop of Orléans began to make a speech. Pierre could have strangled the man. The king leaned back on his throne and closed his eyes. He probably imagined that people thought he must be concentrating hard on what the bishop was saying. It looked more as if he was going to sleep . . . or even fainting.

After a minute he opened his eyes and looked around. His gaze fastened on Louviers, and Pierre felt sure this was the moment; but the king's regard moved on.

Then he started to shiver.

Pierre stared in horror. The shivering fever was a plague that had ravaged France and other European countries for three years. Sometimes it was fatal.

He thought: *Give the signal, for God's sake – then you can collapse!*

Instead the king started to rise. He seemed too weak to get up, and fell back into a sitting position. The bishop droned on, either not noticing or not caring that the king seemed ill; but Cardinal Charles was more quick-witted. He murmured something to Francis, who shook his head feebly in negation. With a helpless expression, Charles assisted him to his feet.

The king moved towards the inner door on the arm of the cardinal.

Pierre looked at Antoine de Bourbon. He seemed as surprised as anyone else. Clearly this was not the result of some elaborate plot of his. He was out of danger, for the moment, but he evidently did not know why.

Charles beckoned to his brother, Duke Scarface; but, to Pierre's astonishment, the duke looked thoroughly disgusted and turned his back on Charles and the king – a discourtesy for which a stronger king would have thrown him in jail.

Leaning heavily on Charles, King Francis left the room.

*

THE WEATHER BECAME colder as Sylvie climbed through the foothills of the Alps towards Geneva. It was winter, and she needed a fur coat. She had not anticipated this.

There were many things she had not anticipated. She had had no idea how fast shoes would wear out when she was walking all day, every day. She was shocked by the rapacity of tavern-keepers, especially in locations where there was only one such establishment: they charged exorbitant rates, even though she was a 'nun'. She expected unwelcome advances from men, and dealt with them briskly, but was surprised one night to be mauled by a woman in the communal bedroom of a hostelry.

She felt profoundly relieved when the spires of Geneva's Protestant churches appeared in the distance. She was also proud of herself. She had been told it could not be done, but she had done it, with God's help.

The city stood at the southern tip of the lake of the same name, at the spot where the Rhône river flowed out of the lake on its way to the distant Mediterranean Sea. As she got closer, she saw that it was a small town in comparison to Paris. But every town she had seen was small in comparison to Paris.

The sight was pretty as well as welcome. The lake was clear, the surrounding mountains were blue-and-white, and the sky was a pearly grey.

Before presenting herself at the city gate, Sylvie took off her nun's cap, hid her pectoral cross under her dress, and wound a yellow scarf around her head and neck, so that she no longer looked like a nun, just a badly dressed laywoman. She was admitted without trouble.

She found lodging at an inn where the landlord was a woman. The next day, she bought a red wool cap. It covered her nun-like cropped hair, and was warmer than the yellow scarf.

A hard, cold wind came from the Rhône valley, lashed the surface of the lake into foaming wavelets, and chilled the city. The people were as cold as the climate, Sylvie found. She wanted to tell them that one did not have to be grumpy to be a Protestant.

The town was full of printers and booksellers. They produced Bibles and other literature in English and German as well as French, and sent their books to be sold all over Europe. She went into a printer's nearest to her lodging and found a man and his apprentice working at a press with books stacked all around them. She asked the price of a Bible in French.

The printer looked at her coarse dress and said: 'Too expensive for you.'

The apprentice sniggered.

'I'm serious,' she said.

'You don't look it,' the man said. 'Two livres.'

'And if I buy a hundred?'

He half turned away to show lack of interest. 'I don't have a hundred.'

'Well, I'm not going to give my business to someone so apathetic,' she said tartly, and she went out.

But the next printer was the same. It was maddening. She could not understand why they did not want to sell their books. She tried telling them she had come all the way from Paris, but they did not believe her. She said she had a holy mission to bring the Bible to misguided French Catholics, and they laughed.

After a fruitless day she went back to the inn, feeling frustrated and helpless. Had she come all this way for nothing? Tired out, she slept heavily, and woke determined to take a different approach.

She found the College of Pastors, figuring that their mission was to spread the true gospel, and they would surely want to help her. There, in the hall of the modest building, she saw someone she knew. It took her a few moments to figure out that it was the young missionary who had come into her father's bookshop almost three years ago and said: 'I am Guillaume of Geneva.' She greeted him with relief.

For his part, he regarded her sudden appearance in Geneva as some kind of godsend. Having done two tours of missionary duty in France, he was now teaching younger men to follow in his footsteps. In this easier way of life he had lost his intensity, and he was no longer as thin as a sapling: in fact, he looked contentedly plump. And Sylvie's arrival completed his happiness.

He was shocked to hear of Pierre's treachery, but he failed to conceal a feeling of satisfaction that his more glamorous rival had turned out to be a fraud. Then tears came to his eyes when she told him of the martyrdom of Giles.

When she related her experiences with Geneva booksellers, he was unsurprised. 'It's because you treat them as equals,' he said.

Sylvie had learned to appear unafraid and in command, as the only way to discourage men from trying to exploit her. 'What's wrong with that?' she said.

'They expect a woman to be humble.'

'They like deferential women in Paris, too, but they don't turn customers away on that account. If a woman has money, and they have goods to sell, they do business.'

'Paris is different.'

Evidently, she thought.

Guillaume eagerly agreed to help her. He cancelled his lectures for the day and took her to a printer he knew. She stood back and let him do the talking.

She wanted two kinds of Bible: one cheap enough for almost anyone to buy, and a luxury edition, expensively printed and bound, for wealthier customers. Following her instructions, Guillaume bargained hard, and she got both at a price she could treble in Paris. She bought a hundred prestige editions and a thousand cheap ones.

She was excited to see, in the same workshop, copies of the

Psalms in the translation by the French poet Clément Marot. This had been a big success for her father and she knew she could sell many more. She bought five hundred.

She felt a thrill as she watched the boxes being brought out from the storeroom at the back of the shop. Her journey was not over yet, but she had succeeded so far. She had refused to abandon her mission, and she had been right. Those books would take the true religion into the hearts of hundreds of people. They would also feed her and her mother for a year or more. It was a triumph.

But first she had to get them to Paris, and that required a degree of deception.

She also bought a hundred reams of paper to sell in the shop on the rue de la Serpente. On her instructions, Guillaume told the printer to cover the books in each box with packages of paper, so that if a box was opened for any reason the contraband books would not be visible immediately. She also had the boxes marked with the Italian words 'Carta di Fabriano'. The town of Fabriano was famous for high-quality paper. Her deception might satisfy a casual inspection. If her boxes were subjected to a more serious search then, of course, she would be finished.

That evening, Guillaume took her to his parents' house for supper.

She could not refuse the invitation, for he had been kind, and without his help she might well have failed in her mission. But she was uncomfortable. She knew he had had romantic feelings for her, and he had left Paris abruptly as soon as she had become engaged to Pierre. Clearly those feelings had now returned – or perhaps they had never left him.

He was an only child, and his parents doted on him. They were warm, kind people, and they obviously knew that their son was smitten. Sylvie had to tell again the story of her father's martyrdom, and how she and her mother had rebuilt their lives. Guillaume's father, a jeweller, was as proud of Sylvie as if she were already his daughter-in-law. His mother admired her courage, but in her eyes was the knowledge, sad but incontestable, that her son had failed to capture Sylvie's heart.

They invited her to lodge with them, but she declined, not wanting to encourage false hopes.

That night she wondered why she did not love Guillaume. They had much in common. They came from prosperous middle-class families. They were both committed to spreading the true gospel. Both had experienced the deprivations and hazards of long-distance travel. Both knew danger and had seen violence. Yet she had rejected this brave, intelligent, decent man for a smooth-talking liar and spy. Was there something wrong with her? Perhaps she was just not destined for love and marriage.

Next day, Guillaume took her to the docks and introduced her to a bargee whom he believed to be trustworthy. The man attended the same church as Guillaume, and so did his wife and children. Sylvie thought he could be trusted as far as any man.

She now had a heavy consignment, very difficult to transport overland by cart on country roads, so she had to return to Paris by ship. The barge would take her downstream to Marseilles, where she would transfer her books to an oceangoing vessel bound for Rouen, on the north French coast. From there she would sail upstream to Paris.

Her boxes were loaded the next day, and on the following morning Guillaume escorted her on board. She felt bad about accepting so much help from him while having no intention of giving him what he really wanted. She told herself that Guillaume had been an eager volunteer, and she had not manipulated him, but all the same she felt guilty.

'Write to me when you've sold all the books,' he said. 'Tell me what you want, and I'll bring the next consignment to Paris myself.'

She did not want Guillaume to come to Paris. He would court her persistently, and she would not be able to quit his company so easily. She saw this embarrassing scenario in a flash, but she could not turn down his offer. She would have a supply of books without making this long and difficult journey.

Would it be disingenuous of her to accept? She knew

perfectly well why he was doing it. But she could not think only of herself. She and Guillaume shared a holy duty. 'That would be wonderful,' she said. 'I will write.'

'I'm going to look forward to that letter,' he said. 'I'll pray for it to come soon.'

'Goodbye, Guillaume,' said Sylvie.

*

ALISON FEARED THAT King Francis would die. Mary would be a widow, an ex-queen, and Alison would be no more than the ex-queen's friend. Surely they deserved longer in the sun?

Everyone was on edge because of Francis's illness. The death of a king was always a moment of terrible uncertainty. Once again the Guise brothers would struggle with the Bourbons and the Montmorencys for dominance; once again the true religion would have to battle with heresy; once again power and wealth would go to those who moved fastest and fought hardest.

As Francis sank lower, Queen Caterina summoned Alison McKay. The queen mother wore an imposing black silk dress with priceless diamond jewellery. 'Take a message to your friend Pierre,' she said.

Caterina had a woman's intuition, and had undoubtedly guessed at Alison's warm feelings for Pierre. The queen mother knew all the gossip, so she probably also understood that Pierre was married and the romance was doomed.

Alison had been upset by Pierre's revelation. She had allowed herself to fall for him. He was clever and charming as well as handsome and well dressed. She had a daydream in which the two of them were the powerful couple behind the throne, devoted to each other and to the king and queen. Now she had to forget that dream.

'Of course, your majesty,' she said to Caterina.

'Tell him I need to see Cardinal Charles and Duke Scarface in the presence room in one hour.'

'What shall I say it's about?'

The queen mother smiled. 'If he asks you,' she said, 'say you don't know.'

Alison left Caterina's suite and walked through the corridors of the Château Groslot. Men bowed and women curtsied as she passed. She could not help enjoying their deference, especially now that she knew it might be so short-lived.

As she walked she wondered what Caterina might be up to. The queen mother was shrewd and tough, she knew. When Henri had died, Caterina had felt weak, and so had allied herself with the Guise brothers; but that now looked like a mistake, for Charles and François had sidelined Caterina and dominated the king through Queen Mary. Alison had a feeling that Caterina would not be so easily fooled a second time.

The Guise brothers had rooms in the palace, along with the royal family. They understood the crucial importance of being physically close to the king. Pierre, in turn, knew he had to stay close to Cardinal Charles. He was lodging at the St Joan Tavern, next to the cathedral, but – Alison knew – every day he arrived here at Groslot before the Guise brothers got up in the morning and stayed until they had gone to bed at night. So he did not miss anything.

She found him in Cardinal Charles's parlour, along with several other aides and servants. Pierre was wearing a blue sleeveless jerkin over a white shirt embroidered in blue with a ruff. He always looked dashing, especially in blue.

The cardinal was still in his bedroom, although he was undoubtedly dressed and seeing people: Charles was anything but lazy. 'I'll interrupt him,' Pierre said to Alison, standing up. 'What does Caterina want?'

'She's being mysterious,' Alison told him. 'Ambroise Paré examined the king this morning.' Paré was the royal surgeon. 'But so far only Caterina knows what he said.'

'Perhaps the king is recovering.'

'And perhaps he's not.' Alison's happiness, and that of Mary Stuart, depended on the uncertain health of Francis. It might have been different if Mary had had a child, but she still had not become pregnant. She had seen the doctor recommended by Caterina, but she would not tell Alison what he had said.

Pierre said thoughtfully: 'If King Francis dies without fathering a child, his brother Charles will become king.'

Alison nodded. 'But Charles is ten years old, so someone else would have to rule as regent on his behalf.'

'And that position goes automatically to the first prince of the blood, who happens to be Antoine of Bourbon.'

'Our great enemy.' Alison foresaw a nightmare in which the Guise family lost all influence, and she and Mary Stuart became nobodies to whom people hardly bothered to bow.

She felt sure that Pierre shared the nightmare, but she saw that he was already thinking about how to deal with it. He never seemed daunted: she liked that. Now he said: 'So the challenge for us, if Francis dies, will be to neutralize Antoine. Do you think that's what Caterina wants to discuss with the Guise brothers?'

Alison smiled. 'If anyone asks you, say you don't know.'

An hour later, Alison and Pierre were standing side by side with Duke Scarface and Cardinal Charles amid the gorgeous décor of the presence room. A fire blazed in a massive fireplace. To Alison's surprise, Antoine of Bourbon was also there. The rivals stared at each other across the room. Scarface was flushed with anger, and Charles was stroking his beard into a point as he did when he was truly furious. Antoine looked frightened.

Why was Caterina bringing these mortal enemies together? Would she instigate a gladiatorial combat to decide which faction would prevail if Francis died?

The others in the room were leading courtiers, most of them members of the king's Privy Council, all of them looking bemused. Nobody seemed to have any idea what was going on. Was Antoine to be murdered in front of all these people? The assassin, Charles de Louviers, was not present.

Clearly something big was going to happen, but Caterina had been at great pains to keep it secret. Even Pierre did not know, and he usually knew everything.

It was unusual, Alison reflected, for Caterina to take the initiative like this. But the queen mother could be crafty. Alison recalled the little vial of fresh blood that Caterina had provided for Mary Stuart's wedding night. She recalled the kittens, too, and realized that Caterina had a tough streak that she habitually concealed.

Caterina came in, and everyone bowed low. Alison had never before seen her look so commanding, and she realized that the black silk and the diamonds had been deliberately chosen to project authority. She was wearing the same outfit now but had added a headdress that looked like a crown. She crossed the room followed by four men-at-arms whom Alison had not seen before. Where had they come from? Also following her were two clerks with a writing desk and stationery.

Caterina sat on the throne normally used by Francis. Someone gasped.

Caterina was carrying two sheets of paper in her left hand.

The clerks set up the writing table and the bodyguards stood behind Caterina.

'My son Francis is very ill,' she said.

Alison and Pierre exchanged a glance. My son? Not his majesty the king?

She went on: 'The surgeons can do nothing for him.' Her voice faltered, in a moment of maternal weakness, and she touched a lace handkerchief to her eyes. 'Dr Paré has told me that Francis is certain to die in the next few days.'

Aha, thought Alison; this is about the succession.

Caterina said: 'I have brought my second son, Charles-Maximilien, from the Château of Saint-Germain-en-Laye, and he is here with me now.'

That was news to Alison. Caterina had moved fast and shrewdly. In the dangerous moment when one king succeeded another, power could lie with whomever had possession of the person of the new monarch. Caterina had stolen a march on everyone.

Alison looked at Pierre again. His mouth was open in surprise.

Next to him, Cardinal Charles whispered angrily: 'None of your spies told us this!'

Pierre said defensively: 'They're paid to spy on Protestants, not the royal family.'

Caterina separated the two papers in her hand and held one up. 'However,' she said, 'King Francis has found sufficient strength to sign the death warrant of Louis of Bourbon, prince of Condé.'

Several courtiers gasped. Louis had been convicted of treason, but until now the king had hesitated to have him executed. To kill a prince of the blood was an extreme measure: all Europe would be horrified. Only the Guise brothers were keen to see Louis dead. But it looked as if they would get their way, as they usually did. It seemed as if Caterina was going to make sure that the dominance of the Guise family would continue.

Caterina waved the paper. Alison wondered whether the king really had signed it. No one could actually see.

Antoine spoke up. 'Your majesty, I beg you,' he said, 'please do not execute my brother. I swear he is innocent.'

'Neither of you is innocent!' Caterina snapped. Alison had never heard her use this tone of voice. 'The main question confronting the king is whether you *both* should die.'

Antoine was bold on the battlefield and timid everywhere else, and now he became cringing. 'I beg you, your majesty, spare our lives. I swear we are loyal to the king.'

Alison glanced at the Guise brothers. They could hardly hide their elation. Their enemies were being roasted – at just the right moment.

Caterina said: 'If King Francis dies, and my ten-year-old second son becomes King Charles IX, how could you, Antoine, possibly act as regent, when you have taken part in a conspiracy against his predecessor?'

There was no proof that either Antoine or Louis had conspired against King Francis, but Antoine took a different line. 'I don't want to be regent,' he said desperately. 'I'll renounce the regency. Just spare my brother's life, and mine.'

'You would give up the regency?'

'Of course, your majesty, whatever is your wish.'

Alison suspected that Caterina's purpose, from the start of

the meeting, had been to get Antoine to say what he had just said. The guess was confirmed by what Caterina did next.

The queen mother brandished the second sheet of paper. 'In that case, I want you to sign this document, in front of the court here today. It states that you relinquish your right of regency to ... another person.' She looked significantly at Duke Scarface, but did not name him.

Antoine said: 'I'll sign anything.'

Alison saw that Cardinal Charles was smiling broadly. This was exactly what the Guise brothers wanted. They would control the new king, and continue to pursue their policy of exterminating Protestants. But Pierre was frowning. 'Why did she do this on her own?' he whispered to Alison. 'Why not bring the Guises in on the plot?'

'Perhaps she's making a point,' Alison said. 'They have rather ignored her since King Henri died.'

Caterina handed the document to the clerk, and Antoine stepped forward.

Antoine read the document, which was short. At one point he seemed surprised, and raised his head to look at Caterina.

In her new, sharp voice she said: 'Just sign!'

A clerk dipped a quill in ink and offered it to Antoine.

Antoine signed.

Caterina got up from the throne with the death warrant in her hand. She walked over to the fireplace and threw the document on the burning coals. It flamed for a second and vanished.

Now, Alison thought, no one will ever know whether King Francis really signed it.

Caterina resumed her place on the throne. Clearly she had not yet finished. She said: 'The accession of King Charles IX will begin a time of reconciliation in France.'

Reconciliation? This did not seem to Alison like any kind of bringing together. It looked more like a resounding victory for the Guise family.

Caterina went on: 'Antoine of Bourbon, you will be appointed Lieutenant of France, in recognition of your willingness to compromise.'

That was his reward, Alison thought; the consolation prize. But it might help keep him from rebellion. She looked at the Guise brothers. They were not pleased by this development, but it was a small thing by comparison with the regency.

Caterina said: 'Antoine, please read out the document you have just signed in front of the court.'

Antoine picked up the sheet of paper and turned to the audience. He looked pleased. Perhaps the post of Lieutenant of France was one he had longed for. He began: 'I, Antoine of Bourbon, King of Navarre—'

Caterina interrupted: 'Skip to the important part.'

'I renounce my claim to the regency, and transfer all my powers in that regard to her royal majesty Queen Caterina, the queen mother.'

Alison gasped.

Duke Scarface leaped to his feet. 'What?' he roared. 'Not me?'

'Not you,' said Antoine quietly.

Scarface stepped towards him. Antoine handed the document to Caterina. Scarface turned towards her. Her bodyguards moved closer, clearly having been forewarned of this possibility. Scarface stood helpless. The scars on his face turned liver-coloured as he flushed with fury. He shouted: 'This is outrageous!'

'Be silent!' Caterina snapped. 'I have not called upon you to speak!'

Alison was flabbergasted. Caterina had fooled everyone and seized control. She had made herself effectively the monarch of France. The new power in France would not be Guise or Bourbon-Montmorency: it would be Caterina herself. She had slipped in between the two giants and disabled them both. How devious! There had been no hint of this plan. With skill and confidence she had carried out a manoeuvre that was nothing less than a coup d'état. Angry and disappointed though Alison was, in a part of her mind she could not help admiring Caterina's strategy.

Still Caterina had not quite done.

'And now,' she said, 'to seal the peace that has been won today, the duke of Guise will embrace the king of Navarre.'

For Scarface, this was the ultimate humiliation.

Scarface and Antoine glared at one another.

'Go ahead, please,' said Caterina. 'It is my command.'

Antoine moved first, stepping across the multicoloured tiled floor towards Scarface. The two men were almost the same age, but the resemblance ended there. Antoine had an apathetic air, and now underneath his moustache he wore what men sometimes called a shit-eating grin; Scarface was tanned, gaunt, disfigured and vicious. Antoine was not stupid, however. He stopped a yard from Scarface, spread his arms wide, and said: 'I obey her majesty the queen mother.'

Scarface could not possibly say I *don't*.

He stepped towards Antoine and the two men exchanged the briefest possible hug, then separated as if they feared catching the plague.

Caterina smiled and clapped, and the rest of the court followed suit.

*

IN THE TEEMING Mediterranean port of Marseilles, Sylvie transferred her cargo from the river barge to an oceangoing merchant ship. It took her through the Strait of Gibraltar, across the Bay of Biscay where she was miserably seasick, along the English Channel and then up the river Seine as far as Rouen, the most important northern port in France.

The city was one-third Protestant, and Sylvie attended a Sunday service that hardly troubled to hide its nature and took place in a real church. She could have sold all her books here. But the need was greater in Catholic Paris. And prices were higher in Paris too.

It was January, 1561, and in France the news was all good. After King Francis II died his mother, Queen Caterina, had taken charge and dismissed the Guise brothers from some of their political offices. She had issued new regulations that made life easier for Protestants, though these were not yet formally laws. All religious prisoners were to be released, heresy trials were suspended, and the death penalty for heresy was abolished. The Protestants, whom Sylvie now heard referred to by their new nickname of Huguenots, were rejoicing.

However, selling banned books was aggravated heresy, and still a crime.

Sailing upstream on a river boat to Paris, with the hold full of her boxes, she felt hope and fear in equal measure. She arrived on a cold February morning at the quai de la Grève, where dozens of ships and boats were moored along the banks or anchored in midstream.

Sylvie sent a message to her mother that she had arrived, and a note to Luc Mauriac saying she hoped to see him soon to thank him personally for helping her plan her successful trip. Then she walked the short distance to the customs house in the place de Grève. If she was going to have trouble, it would begin here.

She brought with her false receipts, carefully forged with Guillaume's help, showing that she had bought one hundred and ten boxes of paper from a fictional manufacturer in Fabriano. She also brought her purse, ready to pay the import tax.

She showed the receipts to a clerk. 'Paper?' he said. 'Plain paper, with nothing written or printed on it?'

'My mother and I sell paper and ink to students,' she explained.

'You've bought a lot.'

She tried a smile. 'There are a lot of students in Paris – luckily for me.'

'And you went a long way to get it. Don't we have our own paper manufacturers, in Saint-Marcel?'

'Italian paper is better – and cheaper.'

'You'll have to talk to the boss.' He gave her back her receipts and pointed to a bench. 'Wait there.'

Sylvie sat down with a sense of inevitable doom. All they had to do was open the boxes and look carefully! She felt as if she had already been found guilty and was awaiting sentence.

The tension was hard to bear. She almost wished they would put her in jail and get it over with.

She tried to distract herself by watching the way business was done here, and realized that most of the men who came through the door were known to the clerks. Their papers were handled with casual efficiency and they paid their dues and left. Lucky them.

An agonizing hour later she was shown upstairs to a larger office occupied by the Deputy Receiver of Customs, Claude Ronsard, a sour-looking individual in a brown doublet and a velvet cap. While he was asking her all the same questions, she wondered uneasily whether she was supposed to bribe any of these people. She had not noticed this happening downstairs but it would not be done openly, she supposed.

Eventually Ronsard said: 'Your cargo must be inspected.'

'Very well,' she said, trying to affect a light tone of voice, as if this were a minor inconvenience; but her heart was pounding. She jingled her purse discreetly, hinting at bribery, but Ronsard seemed not to notice. Perhaps he took bribes only from people he knew well. Now she did not know what she had to do to save her cargo – and perhaps her life.

Ronsard stood up and they left his office. Sylvie felt shaky and walked unsteadily, but Ronsard seemed oblivious to any signs of her distress. He summoned the clerk whom Sylvie had spoken to first, and they walked along the quay to the boat.

To Sylvie's surprise, her mother was there. She had hired a porter with a heavy four-wheeled cart to take the boxes to the warehouse in the rue du Mur. Sylvie explained what was happening, and Isabelle looked frightened.

Ronsard and the clerk went on board and selected a box to be unloaded and inspected. The porter carried it onshore and put it down on the quayside. It was made of light wood, nailed, and on its side were the Italian words: 'Carta di Fabriano.'

Now, Sylvie thought, they were hardly likely to go to all this trouble without emptying the box – and then they would find inside forty Geneva Bibles in French, complete with inflammatory Protestant comments in the margins.

The porter prised open the box with a crowbar. There, on top, were several packages of plain paper.

At that moment, Luc Mauriac arrived.

'Ronsard, my friend, I've been looking for you,' he said breezily. He was carrying a bottle. 'There's a consignment of wine from Jerez, and I thought you ought to try some, just to make sure it's, you know, what it should be.' He winked broadly.

Sylvie could not take her eyes off the box. Just under those reams of paper were the Bibles that would condemn her.

Ronsard shook Luc's hand warmly, took the bottle, and introduced the clerk. 'We're just inspecting the cargo of this person,' he said, indicating Sylvie.

Luc looked at Sylvie and pretended surprise. 'Hello, Mademoiselle, are you back? You don't need to worry about her, Ronsard. I know her well – sells paper and ink to the students on the Left Bank.'

'Really?'

'Oh, yes, I'll vouch for her. Listen, old pal, I've just got a cargo of furs from the Baltic, and there's a blond wolf that would look wonderful on Madame Ronsard. I can just see her hair against that fur collar. If you like it, the captain will give it to you – gesture of goodwill, you know what I mean. Come with me and take a look.'

'By all means,' Ronsard said eagerly. He turned to his clerk. 'Sign her papers.' He and Luc went off arm in arm.

Sylvie almost fainted with relief.

She paid the customs duty to the clerk. He asked for one gold ecu 'for ink', an obvious shakedown, but Sylvie paid without protest, and he went away happy.

Then the porter began to load the boxes onto the cart.

*

EARLY IN 1561, Ned Willard was given his first international mission for Queen Elizabeth. He was daunted by the weight of responsibility, and desperately keen to succeed.

He was briefed by Sir William Cecil at Cecil's fine new house in the Strand, sitting in a bay window at the rear that looked over the fields of Covent Garden. 'We want Mary Stuart to stay in France,' Cecil said. 'If she goes to Scotland as queen, there will be trouble. The religious balance there is delicate, and a strongly Catholic monarch will probably start a civil war. And then, if she should defeat the Protestants and win the civil war, she might turn her attention to England.'

Ned understood. Mary Stuart was the rightful queen of England in the eyes of most European leaders. She would be even more of a threat to Elizabeth if she crossed the Channel. He said: 'And for that same reason, I suppose the Guise family want her in Scotland.'

'Exactly. So your job will be to persuade her that she's better off staying where she is.'

'I'll do my best,' Ned said, though for the moment he could not imagine how he could do it.

'We're sending you with her brother.'

'She doesn't have a brother!' Ned knew that Mary was the only child of King James V of Scotland and his queen, Marie de Guise.

'She has many brothers,' Cecil said with a disapproving sniff. 'Her father was unfaithful to his wife on a scale that was spectacular even by the standards of kings, and he had at least nine bastard sons.' Cecil, the grandson of an innkeeper, had a middle-class disdain for royal shenanigans. 'This one is called James Stuart. Mary Stuart likes him, even though he's a Protestant. He, too, wants her to stay in France, where she can't cause much trouble. You will pose as his secretary: we don't want the French to know that Queen Elizabeth is interfering in this.'

James turned out to be a solemn sandy-haired man of twenty-eight or twenty-nine, wearing a chestnut-brown doublet studded with jewels. All Scottish noblemen spoke French, but some did so better than others: James's French was hesitant and heavily accented, but Ned would be able to help him out.

They went by ship to Paris, a relatively easy journey now that England and France were no longer at war. There Ned was disappointed to learn that Mary Stuart had gone to Reims for Easter. 'The Guise dynasty have retired en masse to Champagne to lick their wounds,' he was told by Sir Nicholas Throckmorton, the English ambassador. Throckmorton was a sharp-eyed man in his forties with a beard that was still a youthful red-brown. He wore a black doublet with small but exquisitely embroidered ruffs at the neck and sleeves. 'Queen Caterina outmanoeuvred them brilliantly in Orléans, and, since then, she has encountered no serious opposition, which has left the Guises frustrated.'

Ned said: 'We hear there were Protestant riots at Easter.'

Throckmorton nodded. 'In Angers, Le Mans, Beauvais and Pontoise.' Ned was impressed by his mastery of detail. 'As you're aware, superstitious Catholics like to hold parades in which sacred objects are carried through the streets. We enlightened Protestants know that to venerate images and relics constitutes the sin of idolatry, and some of our more passionate brethren attacked the processions.'

Violent Protestants angered Ned. 'Why can't they be content merely to do without idols in their own places of worship? They should leave God to judge those who disagree with them.'

'Perhaps,' said Throckmorton. He was a more extreme Protestant than Ned – as were many of Elizabeth's key men, including Cecil, though Elizabeth herself was moderate.

'But Caterina seems to have kept the lid on it,' Ned said.

'Yes. She is reluctant to meet violence with violence. She always tries to avoid escalation. After Easter, people calmed down.'

'Sensible woman.'

'Perhaps,' Throckmorton said again.

As Ned was leaving, Throckmorton said: 'In Reims, watch out for Pierre Aumande de Guise, a chap a couple of years older than you who does the dirty work for the family.'

'Why should I watch out?'

'He's utterly poisonous.'

'Thank you for the warning.'

Ned and James travelled to Reims by a river boat that took them up the Seine and then the Marne: a slow way to travel, but more comfortable than spending three or four days in the saddle. However, another disappointment awaited them in the great Champagne city: Mary Stuart had left, and was on her way to visit her cousin Charles, duke of Lorraine.

Following her trail, on horseback now, Ned talked to everyone he met, as always, gathering news. He was disconcerted to learn that they were not the only people chasing Mary Stuart. Ahead of them by a day or so was John Leslie, a Scottish priest who he guessed must be an envoy from the Scottish Catholics. Presumably his message for Mary would be the contrary of Ned's.

Ned and James finally caught up with Mary at the royal castle of St Dizier, a walled fortress with eight towers. They gave their names and were shown into the great hall. A few minutes later they were confronted by a handsome young man with an arrogant air who seemed displeased to see them. 'I am Pierre Aumande de Guise,' he said.

James and Ned stood up. James answered: 'A relative of my sister, Queen Mary?'

'Of course.' Pierre turned to Ned. 'And you, sir?'

'Ned Willard, secretary to James Stuart.'

'And what are two Scottish Protestants doing here?'

Ned was pleased that Pierre had accepted his cover story. Mary might be easier to persuade if she believed the message came from a Scottish relative rather than an English rival.

James did not react to Pierre's rude manner. 'I've come to talk to my sister,' he said calmly.

'For what purpose?'

James smiled. 'Just tell her James Stuart is here.'

Pierre put his nose in the air. 'I will ask whether Queen Mary is willing to give you audience.' It was clear to Ned that Pierre would do what he could to prevent the meeting.

James sat down and turned away. He had royal blood, after all, and he had already expended more courtesy than was strictly necessary on a young aide.

Pierre looked cross but left without saying more.

Ned settled down to wait. The castle was busy, and servants

fetching and carrying for the royal visitor criss-crossed the hall constantly. An hour went by, then two.

A young woman of about Ned's age came into the hall. It was obvious from her pink silk dress and the pearl headdress that decorated her dark hair that she was no servant. There was a look of shrewd alertness in the blue-eyed gaze she turned on Ned. But when she saw James she smiled. 'What a surprise!' she said. 'Lord James! Do you remember me? Alison McKay – we met at Mary's wedding.'

James stood up and bowed, and Ned did the same. 'Of course I remember you,' James said.

'We didn't know you were here!'

'I gave my name to a man called Pierre something.'

'Oh! He has been sent to keep people like you away from Mary. But she'll see you, of course. Let me tell her you're here, then I'll send someone to fetch you . . . both.' She gave Ned an enquiring look.

James explained: 'My secretary, Ned Willard.'

Ned bowed again. Alison gave him the briefest nod of acknowledgement then left.

James said: 'That Pierre character didn't even tell Mary we had arrived!'

'I was warned about him.'

A few minutes later, a servant led them from the hall to a small, comfortable parlour. Ned felt nervous. This was the meeting for which he had travelled so far. Both his queen, Elizabeth, and his master and mentor, Cecil, had placed their faith in him. He only wished he had as much faith in himself.

Soon afterwards Mary Stuart came in.

Ned had seen her once before, but he was startled all over again by how tall she was, and how strikingly beautiful. She had dramatically pale skin and red hair. She was only eighteen, yet she had tremendous poise, and moved like a ship on a calm sea, her head held high on a long, graceful neck. Her official mourning period was over, but she was still wearing white, the symbol of grief.

Alison McKay and Pierre Aumande de Guise walked in behind her.

James bowed deeply, but Mary immediately went to him and kissed him. 'You are clever, James,' she said. 'How did you know I was at St Dizier?'

'It's taken me a while to catch up with you,' he said with a smile.

Mary took a seat and told them all to sit also. She said: 'I have been told that I should return to Scotland like a newly risen sun, to scatter the clouds of religious tumult from the land.'

James said: 'You've been talking to John Leslie, I suppose.' This was what Ned had feared. Leslie had got to her first, and what he had said had clearly enthralled her.

'You know everything!' Mary said. Evidently, she admired her half-brother. 'He says that if I sail to Aberdeen, he will have an army of twenty thousand men waiting to march with me to Edinburgh and overthrow the Protestant parliament in a blaze of Christian glory.'

James said: 'You don't believe it, do you?'

Ned very much feared that she did believe it. He was rapidly getting the impression that Mary was impressionable. Her physical poise and grace were queenly, but so far there was no sign that she had the sceptical wisdom so essential to much-flattered monarchs.

Mary gaily ignored James's question. 'If I do return to Scotland,' she said, 'I'm going to make you an archbishop.'

Everyone in the room was surprised. As queen of Scotland she would not appoint bishops – unlike the monarch of France, who had that power. But James mentioned a different snag. 'I'm not a Catholic,' he said.

'But you must become one,' Mary said brightly.

James resisted her breezy manner. Sombrely he said: 'I came here to ask you to become a Protestant.'

Ned frowned. This was *not* the mission.

Mary's answer was firm. 'I'm Catholic and my family is Catholic. I cannot change.'

Ned saw Pierre nodding. No doubt the idea of a Guise becoming Protestant would fill him with horror.

James said: 'If you won't become Protestant, will you at least become tolerant? The Protestants would give you their loyalty if you left them alone to worship as they wish.'

Ned did not like this line of argument. Their mission was to persuade Mary to stay in France.

Pierre, too, looked uneasy, but surely for a different reason: the notion of tolerance was abhorrent to ultra-Catholics.

Mary said to James: 'And would the Protestants treat Catholics with the same tolerance?'

Ned spoke for the first time. 'Absolutely not,' he said. 'It is now a crime to celebrate the Mass in Scotland.'

Pierre contradicted him. 'You're wrong, Monsieur Willard,' he said. 'The Mass is not a crime.'

'The Scottish Parliament has passed an act!'

'The self-constituted parliament may have passed a *bill*,' Pierre argued, 'but only the monarch can turn a bill into law, and her majesty Queen Mary has not given her royal assent.'

'Technically, you're right,' Ned conceded. 'I just don't want her majesty to be misled about the extent to which tolerance prevails in Scotland.'

'And for whom do you speak when you say that, Monsieur Willard?'

Pierre seemed to have guessed that Ned was more than a secretary. Ned did not answer his question. He spoke directly to Mary. 'Your majesty, here in France you are a duchess, you have lands, money and the support of wealthy and powerful relatives. In Scotland all that awaits you is conflict.'

Mary said: 'In France I am the widow of the king. In Scotland I am queen.'

Ned saw that he was failing to persuade her.

Pierre said: 'What would Queen Elizabeth think, Monsieur Willard, if her majesty Queen Mary were to return to Scotland?'

It was a trick question. If Ned answered it knowledgeably, he would reveal himself as Elizabeth's envoy. He pretended ignorance. 'We Scots know only what we hear. Bear in mind that in Reims you are nearer to London than we are in Edinburgh.'

Pierre was not to be diverted by mileages. 'So what do you Scots hear?'

Ned replied carefully. 'No monarch likes to be told that someone else claims the throne, and apparently Queen Elizabeth was distressed when King Francis and Queen Mary called themselves the monarchs of England and Ireland as well as France and Scotland. Nevertheless, we understand that Elizabeth believes firmly in Mary's right to rule Scotland, and would not stand in her way.'

That was not really true. Elizabeth was torn. Her ideological belief in the primacy of royal inheritance was in conflict with her fear of Mary as a rival to her own throne. That was why she wanted Mary to remain quietly in France.

Pierre probably knew that, but he pretended to take Ned seriously. 'That's good to know,' he said, 'because the Scots love their queen.' He turned to Mary. 'They will welcome her with cheers and bonfires.'

Mary smiled. 'Yes,' she said. 'I believe they will.'

Ned thought: You poor fool.

James began to speak, no doubt intending to say tactfully what Ned had thought bluntly, but Mary interrupted him. 'It's midday,' she said. 'Let's have dinner. We can continue our discussion.' She stood up, and they all did the same.

Ned knew he had lost, but he made one last try. 'Your majesty,' he said, 'I believe it would be most unwise of you to return to Scotland.'

'Do you?' Mary said regally. 'All the same, I think I shall go.'

*

PIERRE REMAINED in Champagne for most of the following year. He hated it. He was powerless in the countryside. The Guises had lost all influence at court, and Queen Caterina was keeping the peace – just – between Catholics and Protestants; and he could do nothing about that while he was a hundred miles away from Paris. Besides, he did not like being so near the place of his birth, where people knew all about his humble origins.

In late February of 1562, when duke Scarface set off from

his country seat of Joinville and headed for the capital, Pierre eagerly joined him. This was Pierre's chance to get back into the game.

The journey began on narrow dirt roads winding between newly ploughed fields and leafless winter vineyards. It was a cold, sunny day. Scarface was escorted by two hundred armed men led by Gaston Le Pin. Some of the men-at-arms carried the newly fashionable long swords called rapiers. They had no uniform as such, but many wore the duke's bright colours of red and yellow. They looked like the host of an invading army.

Scarface spent the last night of February at the village of Dommartin. He was joined there by a younger brother, Cardinal Louis, nicknamed Cardinal Bottles for his love of wine. The armed force was enlarged by Louis's body of gunmen with arquebuses. These were long-barrelled firearms, sometimes called hook-butts because they were J-shaped. They were light enough to be fired from the shoulder, unlike muskets, which had to be supported by a forked rest stuck in the ground.

The next day, 1 March, was a Sunday, and they started early. They were due to pick up a squadron of heavy cavalry at the town of Wassy. By the time Scarface arrived in Paris, he would have enough soldiers to discourage his enemies from making a move against him.

Wassy was a small town on the Blaise river, with forges in the suburbs and watermills along the river bank. As the Guise army approached the south gate, they heard bells. The sound of church bells rung at the wrong time was often a sign of trouble, and Scarface asked a passer-by what was going on. 'It'll be the Protestants, summoning their folk to the service,' the man said.

The duke flushed with anger, his facial scars darkening. 'Protestant bells?' he said. 'How did they get bells?'

The passer-by looked scared. 'I don't know, lord.'

This was the kind of Protestant provocation that started riots. Pierre began to feel hopeful. It could lead to an inflammatory incident.

Scarface said: 'Even if the edict of tolerance becomes law –

which may never happen – they are supposed to perform their blasphemous rites discreetly! What's discreet about this?'

The man said nothing, but Scarface was no longer addressing him, just expressing outrage. Pierre knew why he was so mad. The town of Wassy was the property of Mary Stuart and, now that she had gone back to Scotland, Scarface, as her senior uncle, was in charge of her estates. This was therefore his territory.

Pierre rubbed it in. 'The Protestants, like everyone in town, must know that your grace is due here this morning,' he said. 'This looks very much like a deliberate personal insult.'

Gaston Le Pin was listening. He was a soldier who believed in avoiding violence if possible – which may have been why he was still alive at thirty-three. Now he said: 'We could bypass the town, duke. We don't want to risk losing men before we even get to Paris. We need a good show of strength there.'

Pierre did not like that line of argument. 'You can't overlook this affront, your grace,' he murmured. 'It would appear weak.'

'I don't intend to appear weak,' Scarface said hotly, and he kicked his horse on.

Le Pin gave Pierre a black look, but his soldiers followed Scarface eagerly, their spirits lifting at the prospect of action. Pierre decided to encourage them tactfully. He dropped back and spoke to a group. 'I smell loot,' he said, and they laughed. He was reminding them that when there was violence, there was usually pillage too.

As they entered the town, the bells stopped. 'Send for the parish priest,' the duke ordered.

The host moved slowly along the street to the town centre. Within a walled precinct stood a royal law court, a castle and a church. In the market square to the west of the church they found, waiting for them, the squadron of heavy cavalry they had come here to pick up: fifty men, each with two warhorses and a pack animal loaded with armour. The big horses whinnied and shifted as they smelled the newcomers.

Gaston Le Pin ordered the duke's men-at-arms to dismount in the partly roofed market, and parked Cardinal Louis's gunmen in the cemetery on the south side of the church.

Some of the men went into the Swan tavern, on the square, to breakfast on ham and beer.

The parish priest came hurrying with crumbs of bread on his surplice. The provost of the castle was close behind him. Scarface said: 'Now, tell me, are Protestants holding a blasphemous service here in Wassy this morning?'

'Yes,' said the priest.

'I can't stop them,' said the provost. 'They won't listen.'

Scarface said: 'The edict of tolerance – which has not been ratified – would permit such services only outside the town.'

The provost said: 'Strictly speaking, they aren't in the town.'

'Where are they, then?'

'Within the precincts of the castle, which is not considered part of the town, legally speaking. At least, that's what they argue.'

Pierre commented: 'A contentious legal quibble.'

Impatiently, Scarface said: 'But where are they, exactly?'

The provost pointed across the graveyard to a large, dilapidated barn with holes in its roof, standing up against the castle wall. 'There. That barn is within the grounds of the castle.'

'Which means it's my barn!' said Scarface angrily. 'This is intolerable.'

Pierre saw a way to escalate the situation. 'The edict of tolerance gives royal officials the right to oversee Protestant assemblies, duke. You would be within your rights to inspect the service going on over there.'

Again Le Pin tried to avoid conflict. 'That would be sure to cause unnecessary trouble.'

But the provost liked the idea. 'If you were to speak to them today, duke, with your men-at-arms behind you, perhaps it would scare them into obeying the law in the future.'

'Yes,' said Pierre. 'You have a duty, duke.'

Le Pin rubbed his mutilated ear as if it itched. 'Better to let sleeping dogs lie,' he said.

Scarface looked thoughtful, weighing up the conflicting advice, and Pierre feared he might be calming down and leaning towards Le Pin's cautious approach; then the Protestants started to sing.

Communal singing was not part of normal Catholic services, but the Protestants loved it, and they sang psalms loudly and enthusiastically – and in French. The sound of hundreds of voices raised in song carried clearly across the cemetery to the market square. Scarface's indignation boiled up. 'They think they're all priests!' he said.

Pierre said: 'Their insolence is insufferable.'

'It certainly is,' said Scarface. 'And I shall tell them so.'

Le Pin said: 'In that case, let me go ahead with just a couple of men to forewarn them of your arrival. If they understand that you have the right to speak to them, and they are prepared to listen to you in peace, perhaps bloodshed can be avoided.'

'Very well,' said Scarface.

Le Pin pointed to two men armed with rapiers. 'Rasteau and Brocard, follow me.'

Pierre recognized them as the pair who had marched him through the streets of Paris from the tavern of St Étienne to the Guise family palace. That had been four years ago, but he would never forget the humiliation. He smiled to think how far above these thugs he stood now. How his life had changed!

They headed across the graveyard, and Pierre went with them.

'I didn't ask you to accompany me,' Le Pin muttered.

'I didn't ask what you wanted,' Pierre replied.

The barn was a ramshackle building. Some of the timbers of the walls were missing, the door hung askew, and there was a large pile of broken masonry outside. As they approached, he was aware that they were being watched intently by the men-at-arms outside the church and the gunmen in the graveyard.

The psalm came to an end, and silence fell as they reached the door of the barn.

Le Pin motioned to the others to stand back, then opened the door.

Inside the barn were about five hundred men, women and children, all standing – there were no pews. It was evident from their clothing that rich and poor were mixed promiscuously, unlike in a Catholic church where the elite had special seats. At one end of the barn Pierre could see a makeshift pulpit and, as he looked, a pastor in a cassock began to preach.

A moment later, several men near the door spotted the newcomers and moved to bar their way.

Le Pin took several paces back, to avoid a nose-to-nose confrontation. Rasteau and Brocard did the same. Then Le Pin announced: 'The duke of Guise is coming to speak to you. Prepare the congregation to receive him.'

'Hush!' said a young man with a black beard. 'Pastor Morel is preaching!'

'Take care,' Le Pin warned. 'The duke is already displeased that you're holding this service illegally in his barn. I advise you not to anger him further.'

'Wait until the pastor has finished.'

Pierre said loudly: 'The duke does not wait for such people as you!'

More of the congregation looked towards the door.

Blackbeard said: 'You can't come in!'

Le Pin stepped forward, slowly and purposefully, heading directly for him. 'I will come in,' he said deliberately.

The young man shoved Le Pin away with surprising force. Le Pin staggered back a pace.

Pierre heard shouts of indignation from the watching men-at-arms in the marketplace. Out of the corner of his eye he saw some of them begin to move into the graveyard.

'You shouldn't have done that,' said Le Pin. With sudden speed he lashed out with his fist, hitting the young man squarely on the jaw. The beard provided negligible protection from such a powerful blow. The man fell down.

'Now,' said Le Pin, 'I'm coming in.'

To Pierre's astonishment and delight the Protestants did not have the sense to let him in. Instead, they all picked up stones, and Pierre realized that he had been wrong to assume that the pile was merely debris from the tumbledown building. He watched in disbelief. Were they really going to start a fight with hundreds of armed men?

'Out of my way,' said Le Pin, and he stepped forward.

The Protestants threw their stones.

Le Pin was hit by several. One struck his head and he fell.

Pierre, who did not carry a sword, stepped back out of the way.

Rasteau and Brocard roared with outrage at the assault on their captain. Both drew their rapiers and dashed forward.

The Protestants threw again. The two men-at-arms were hit by a hail of rocks. One gashed the cheek of Rasteau, the older of the two, the one with no nose. Another hit Brocard's knee, causing him to fall. More men came out of the church and picked up stones.

Rasteau ran forward, bleeding from the wound to his face, rapier held in front of him, and thrust the blade into the belly of the young man with the black beard. The man screamed horribly in pain. The slim blade went through his body and the bloody point came out the other side. In a flash of memory, Pierre recalled hearing Rasteau and Brocard discuss sword fighting, on that fateful day four years ago. *Forget about the heart,* Rasteau had said. *A blade in the guts doesn't kill a man straight away, but it paralyses him. It hurts so much he can't think of anything else.* Then he had giggled.

Rasteau pulled his blade out of the man's intestines with a sucking sound that made Pierre want to vomit. Then the Protestants were on Rasteau, six or seven of them, beating him with stones. Defending himself desperately, Rasteau retreated.

The duke's men-at-arms were now running at top speed across the graveyard, leaping over tombstones, unsheathing their weapons as they came, yelling for revenge on their fallen comrades. Cardinal Louis's gunmen were readying their arquebuses. More men came out of the barn and, suicidally fearless, picked up stones to throw at the advancing soldiers.

Pierre saw that Le Pin had recovered from the blow to his head and was getting to his feet. He dodged two flying stones in a way that told Pierre he was again in full possession of his faculties. Then he drew his rapier.

To Pierre's dismay, Le Pin made another attempt to prevent further bloodshed. Lifting his sword high he yelled: 'Stop! Lay down your arms! Sheath your swords!'

No one took any notice. A huge stone was thrown at Le Pin. He dodged it, then charged.

Pierre was almost horrified by the speed and violence of Le Pin's attack. His blade flashed in the sunlight. He stabbed, sliced and hacked, and with each swing of his arm a man was maimed or killed.

Then the other men-at-arms arrived. Pierre yelled encouragement to the newcomers, shouting: 'Kill the heretics! Kill the blasphemers!'

The slaughter became general. The duke's troops forced their way into the barn and began to butcher men, women and children. Pierre saw Rasteau attack a young woman with ghastly savagery, slashing her face again and again with his dagger.

Pierre followed the press of men-at-arms, always careful to be several steps behind the front line: it was not his role to risk his life in battle. Inside, a few Protestants were fighting back with swords and daggers, but most were unarmed. Hundreds of people were screaming in terror or in agony. Within seconds the barn walls were splashed with blood.

Pierre saw that at the far end of the barn there were wooden steps up to a hayloft. The steps were crammed with people, some carrying babies. From the loft they were escaping through the holes in the roof. Just as he noticed that, he heard a volley of gunfire. Two people fell back through the roof and crashed down to the barn floor. The arquebusiers of Cardinal Bottles had deployed their weapons.

Pierre turned, pushed against the press of soldiers still coming in, and fought his way outside for a better look.

The Protestants were still escaping through the roof, some of them trying to make their way down to the ground and others jumping onto the castle ramparts. The cardinal's gunmen were shooting the escapers. The light guns with their modern firing mechanisms were easy to deploy and quick to reload, and the result was a constant hail of bullets that brought down just about everyone who ventured onto the roof.

Pierre looked across the cemetery to the market square. Townspeople were running into the square, alerted, no doubt, by the sound of gunfire. At the same time, more men-at-arms were coming out of the Swan, some still chewing their breakfasts. Clashes began as soldiers tried to prevent townspeople coming to the rescue of the Protestants. A cavalryman sounded a trumpet to muster his comrades.

Then it ended as fast as it had begun. Gaston Le Pin came out of the barn with the pastor, holding his prisoner's arm in an iron grip. Other men-at-arms followed them out. The flight of people through holes in the roof came to an end, and the arquebusiers stopped shooting. Back in the market square, captains were marshalling their men into squads to keep them under control, and ordering townspeople back to their homes.

Looking into the barn, Pierre saw that the fighting was over. Those Protestants still able to move were bending over those on the ground, trying to help the wounded and weeping over the dead. The floor was puddled with blood. Groans of agony and sobs of grief replaced the screaming.

Pierre could not have hoped for anything better. He reckoned that about fifty Protestants had been killed and more than a hundred wounded. Most had been unarmed, and some had been women and children. The news would be all over France in a few days.

It struck Pierre that four years ago he would have been horrified by the slaughter he had seen, yet today he was pleased. How he had changed! Somehow it was difficult to see how God could approve of this aspect of the new Pierre. A dim and nameless fear trickled into the depths of his mind like the darkening blood on the barn floor. He suppressed the thought. This was God's will; it had to be.

He could envisage the eight-page pamphlets that would soon pour from Protestant printing presses, each with a grisly front-page woodcut illustration of the slaughter in the barn. The obscure town of Wassy would be the subject of a thousand sermons all over Europe. Protestants would form armed militias, saying they could not be safe otherwise. Catholics would muster their forces in response.

There would be civil war.

Just as Pierre wanted.

*

SITTING IN THE tavern of St Étienne, with a plate of smoked fish and a cup of wine in front of her, Sylvie felt hopeless.

Would there ever be an end to the violence? Most French people just wanted to live in peace with their neighbours of both religions, but every effort at reconciliation was sabotaged by men such as the Guise brothers, for whom religion was a means to power and wealth.

What Sylvie and her friends needed most was to find out how much the authorities knew about them. Whenever she could, she came to places like this tavern and talked to people involved in trying to catch heretics: members of the city militia, Guise family hangers-on, and anyone associated with Pierre. She picked up a lot of information from their loose gossip. But what she really needed was a sympathizer on the inside.

She looked up from her lunch and saw Pierre's maid, Nath, walking in with a black eye.

Sylvie had a nodding acquaintance with Nath, but had never said more than hello to her. Now she reacted fast. 'That looks sore,' she said. 'Let me buy you a drink of wine to ease the pain.'

Nath burst into tears.

Sylvie put her arm around the girl. Her sympathy was not pretended: both Sylvie and her mother had suffered violence from the two-fisted Giles Palot. 'There, there,' Sylvie murmured.

The barmaid brought some wine and Nath took a large swallow. 'Thank you,' she said.

'What happened to you?' Sylvie asked.

'Pierre hit me.'

'Does he hit Odette too?'

Nath shook her head. 'He's too scared. She'd hit him back.'

Nath herself was about sixteen, small and thin, probably

incapable of hitting a man – just as Sylvie had been unable to fight back against her father. The memory made Sylvie angry.

'Drink some more wine,' Sylvie said.

Nath took another gulp. 'I hate him,' she said.

Sylvie's pulse raced. For more than a year she had been waiting for a moment such as this. She had known it would come, if she was patient, because everyone hated Pierre, and sooner or later someone was bound to betray him.

Now at last the opportunity had arrived, but she had to handle it right. She could not be too eager or too obvious. All the same, she would have to take risks.

'You're not the only one who hates Pierre,' she said cautiously. 'They say he is the main spy behind the persecution of Protestants.' This was not inside information: half Paris knew it.

'It's true,' Nath said. 'He's got a list.'

Sylvie felt suddenly breathless. Of course he had a list, but what did Nath know about it? 'A list?' Sylvie said in a voice so low it was almost a whisper. 'How do you know?'

'I've seen it. A black notebook, full of names and addresses.'

This was gold dust. It would be risky to try to subvert Nath, but the reward was irresistible. Making an instant decision, Sylvie took the plunge. Pretending to speak light-heartedly, she said: 'If you want revenge, you should give the notebook to the Protestants.'

'I would if I had the courage.'

Sylvie thought: Would you, really? How would you square that with your conscience? She said carefully: 'That would go against the Church, wouldn't it?'

'I believe in God,' Nath said. 'But God isn't in the church.'

Sylvie could hardly breathe. 'How can you say that?'

'I was fucked by the parish priest when I was eleven. I didn't even have any hair between my legs. Was God there? I don't think so.'

Sylvie emptied her cup, put it down, and said: 'I've got a friend who would pay ten gold ecus for a look at that notebook.' Sylvie could find the money: the business made a profit, and her mother would agree that this was a good way to spend it.

Nath's eyes widened. 'Ten gold ecus?' It was more than she earned in a year – much more.

Sylvie nodded. Then she added a moral justification to the monetary incentive. 'I suppose my friend thinks she might save a lot of people from being burned to death.'

Nath was more interested in the money. 'But do you mean it about the ten ecus?'

'Oh, absolutely.' Sylvie pretended to realize suddenly that Nath was speaking seriously. 'But surely ... you couldn't get hold of the notebook ... could you?'

'Yes.'

'Where is it?'

'He keeps it at the house.'

'Where in the house?'

'In a locked document chest.'

'If the chest is locked, how could you get the notebook?'

'I can unlock the chest.'

'How?'

'With a pin,' said Nath.

*

THE CIVIL WAR was everything Pierre had hoped for. A year after the Massacre of Wassy the Catholics, led by Duke Scarface, were on the brink of winning. Early in 1563, Scarface besieged Orléans, the last Protestant stronghold, where Gaspard de Coligny was holed up. On 18 February, a Thursday, Scarface surveyed the defences and announced that the final attack would be launched tomorrow.

Pierre was with him, feeling that total victory was now within their grasp.

As dusk fell they headed back towards their quarters at the Château des Vaslins. Scarface was wearing a buff-coloured doublet and a hat with a tall white feather: too highly visible to be sensible battlefield clothing, but he was expecting to meet his wife, Anna, tonight. Their eldest son, Henri, now twelve years old, would also be at the château. Pierre had been careful to ingratiate himself with the duke's heir ever since they had met, four years ago, at the tournament at which King Henri II had received his fatal eye wound.

They had to cross a small river by a ferry that took only three people. Pierre, Scarface and Gaston Le Pin stayed back while the others in the entourage led the horses across. Scarface said conversationally: 'You've heard that Queen Caterina wants us to make peace.'

Pierre laughed scornfully. 'You make peace when you're losing, not when you're winning.'

Scarface nodded. 'Tomorrow we'll take Orléans and secure the line of the river Loire. From there we will drive north into Normandy and crush the remnants of the Protestant army.'

'And that's what Caterina is afraid of,' Pierre said. 'When we've conquered the country and wiped out the Protestants, you, duke, will be more powerful than the king. You will rule France.'

And I will be one of your inner circle of advisors, he thought.

When all the horses were safe on the far bank, the three men boarded the little ferry. Pierre said: 'I hear nothing from Cardinal Charles.'

Charles was in Italy, at the city of Trento, attending a council convened by Pope Pius IV. Scarface said contemptuously: 'Talk, talk, talk. Meanwhile, we're killing heretics.'

Pierre dared to differ. 'We need to make sure the Church takes a tough line. Otherwise your triumphs could be undermined by weak men with notions of tolerance and compromise.'

The duke looked thoughtful. Both he and his brother listened when Pierre spoke. Pierre had proved the value of his political judgement several times, and he was no longer treated as a cheeky upstart. It gave him profound satisfaction to reflect on that.

Scarface opened his mouth to respond to Pierre's point, then a shot rang out.

The bang seemed to come from the river bank they had just left. Pierre and Le Pin turned together. Although it was evening, Pierre saw the figure at the water's edge quite clearly.

It was that of a small man in his middle twenties with a dark complexion and a tuft of peaked hair in the middle of his forehead. A moment later he ran off, and Pierre saw that he clutched a pistol in his hand.

Duke Scarface collapsed.

Le Pin cursed and bent over him.

Pierre could see that the duke had taken a bullet in the back. It had been an easy shot from a short range, helped by the duke's light-coloured clothing.

'He's alive,' said Le Pin. He looked again at the bank, and Pierre guessed he was calculating whether he could wade or swim the few yards back and catch the shooter before he got away. Then they heard hoof beats, and realized that the man must have tethered a horse not far off. All their mounts were already on the opposite bank. Le Pin could not catch him now. The shooting had been planned well.

Le Pin shouted at the ferryman: 'Forward, go forward!' The man began to pole his raft more energetically, no doubt fearful that he might be accused of being in on the plot.

The wound was just below the duke's right shoulder. The ball had probably missed the heart. Blood was oozing onto the buff-coloured doublet – a good sign, Pierre knew, for dead men did not bleed.

All the same, the duke might not recover. Even superficial wounds could become infected, causing fever and often death. Pierre could have wept. How could they lose their heroic leader when they were on the point of winning the war?

As the ferry approached the far bank, the men waiting there shouted a storm of questions. Pierre ignored them. He had questions of his own. What would happen if Scarface died?

Young Henri would become duke at the age of twelve, the same age as King Charles IX, and too young to take any part in the civil war. Cardinal Charles was too far away; Cardinal Louis was too drunk. The Guise family would lose all their influence in a moment. Power was terrifyingly fragile.

Pierre fought down despair and made himself continue to think ahead logically. With the Guise family helpless, Queen Caterina would make peace with Gaspard de Coligny and revive the edict of toleration, curse her. The Bourbons and the Montmorencys would be back in favour and the Protestants would be allowed to sing their psalms as loudly as they liked. Everything Pierre had striven for over the past five years would be wiped out.

Again he suppressed the feeling of hopeless despair. What could he do?

The first necessity was to preserve his position as key advisor to the family.

As soon as the raft touched the far bank, Pierre started giving orders. In a crisis, frightened people would obey anyone who sounded as if they knew what they were doing. 'The duke must be carried to the château as quickly as possible without jolting him,' he said. 'Any bumping may cause him to bleed to death. We need a flat board.' He looked around. If necessary, they could break up the timbers of the little ferry. Then he spotted a cottage nearby and pointed to its entrance. 'Knock that front door off its hinges and put him on that. Then six men can carry him.'

They hurried to obey, glad to be told what to do.

Gaston Le Pin was not as easily bossed around, so to him Pierre gave suggestions rather than orders. 'I think you should take one or two men and horses, go back across the river, and chase the assassin. Did you get a good look at him?'

'Small, dark, about twenty-five, with a small tuft of hair at the front.'

'That's what I saw, too.'

'I'll get after him.' Le Pin turned to his henchmen. 'Rasteau, Brocard, put three horses back on the ferry.'

Pierre said: 'I need the best horse. Which of these is fastest?'

'The duke's charger, Cannon, but why do you need him? I'm the one who has to chase the shooter.'

'The duke's recovery is our priority. I'm going to ride ahead to the château to send for surgeons.'

Le Pin saw the sense of that. 'Very well.'

Pierre mounted the stallion and urged it on. He was not an expert horseman, and Cannon was high-spirited, but, fortunately, the beast was tired after a long day, and submitted wearily to Pierre's will. It trotted off, and Pierre cautiously urged it into a canter.

He reached the château in a few minutes. He leaped off Cannon and ran into the hall. 'The duke has been wounded!' he shouted. 'He will be here shortly. Send at once for the royal surgeons! Then prepare a bed downstairs for the duke.' He had to repeat the orders several times to the stunned servants.

The duchess, Anna d'Este, came hurrying down the stairs, having heard the commotion. The wife of Scarface was a plain-looking Italian woman of thirty-one. The marriage had been arranged, and the duke was no more faithful than other men of wealth and power; but, all the same, he was fond of Anna and she of him.

Young Henri was right behind her, a handsome boy with fair curly hair.

Duchess Anna had never spoken to Pierre or even acknowledged his existence, so it was important to present himself to her as an authoritative figure who could be relied upon in this crisis. He bowed and said: 'Madame, young Monsieur, I'm sorry to tell you that the duke is hurt.'

Henri looked frightened. Pierre remembered him at the age of eight, complaining that he was considered too young to take part in the jousting. He had spirit, and might become a worthy successor to his warrior father, but that day was far off. Now the boy said in a voice of panic: 'How? Where? Who did it?'

Pierre ignored him and spoke to his mother. 'I have sent for the royal surgeons, and I have ordered your servants to prepare a bed here on the ground floor so that the duke will not have to be carried upstairs.'

She said: 'How bad is the injury?'

'He has been shot in the back, and when I left him he was unconscious.'

The duchess gave a sob, then controlled herself. 'Where is he? I must go to him.'

'He will be here in minutes. I ordered the men to improvise a stretcher. He should not be jolted.'

'How did this happen? Was there a battle?'

Henri said: 'My father would never be shot in the back during a battle!'

'Hush,' said his mother.

Pierre said: 'You are quite right, Prince Henri. Your father never fails to face the enemy in battle. I have to tell you there was treachery.' He recounted how the assassin had hidden himself, then fired as soon as the ferry left the shore. 'I sent a party of men-at-arms to chase after the villain.'

Henri said tearfully: 'When we catch him he must be flayed alive!'

In a flash, Pierre saw that if Scarface died, the catastrophe could yet be turned to advantage. Slyly he said: 'Flayed, yes – but not before he tells us whose orders he is following. I predict that the man who pulled the trigger will turn out to be a nobody. The real criminal is whoever sent him.'

Before he could say whom he had in mind, the duchess said it for him, spitting the name in hatred: 'Gaspard de Coligny.'

Coligny was certainly the prime suspect, with Antoine de Bourbon dead and his brother Louis a captive. But the truth hardly mattered. Coligny would make a useful hate figure for the Guise family – and especially for the impressionable boy whose father had just been shot. Pierre's plan was firming up in his mind when shouts from outside told him the duke had arrived.

Pierre stayed close to the duchess as the duke was brought in and settled in a bed. Every time Anna expressed a wish, Pierre repeated it loudly as an order, giving the impression that he had become her right-hand man. She was too distraught to care what he might be scheming, and in fact appeared glad to have someone beside her who seemed to know what needed to be done.

Scarface had recovered consciousness, and was able to speak to his wife and son. The surgeons arrived. They said that the wound did not appear fatal, but everyone knew how easily such wounds turned lethally putrescent, and no one rejoiced yet.

Gaston Le Pin and his two henchmen returned at midnight empty-handed. Pierre got Le Pin in a corner of the hall and said: 'Resume the search in the morning. There'll be no battle tomorrow: the duke will not recover overnight. That means you'll have plenty of soldiers to help you. Start early and spread your net wide. We must find the little man with the tuft.'

Le Pin nodded agreement.

Pierre stayed at the duke's bedside all night.

When dawn broke, he met Le Pin in the hall again. 'If you catch the villain, I will be in charge of the interrogation,' he said. 'The duchess has decreed it.' This was not true, but Le Pin believed it. 'Lock him up somewhere nearby then come to me.'

'Very well.'

Pierre saw him off with Rasteau and Brocard. They would recruit all the helpers they needed along the way.

Pierre went to bed soon afterwards. He would need to be quick-witted and sure-footed over the next few days.

Le Pin woke him at midday. 'I've got him,' he said with satisfaction.

Pierre got up immediately. 'Who is he?'

'Says his name is Jean de Poltrot, sieur de Méré.'

'I trust you didn't bring him here to the château.'

'No – young Henri might try to kill him. He's in chains at the priest's house.'

Pierre dressed quickly and followed Le Pin to the nearby village. As soon as he was alone with Poltrot, he said: 'It was Gaspard de Coligny, wasn't it, who ordered you to kill Duke Scarface?'

'Yes,' said Poltrot.

It soon became evident that Poltrot would say anything. He was a type Pierre had come across before, a fantasist.

Poltrot probably had worked as some kind of spy for the Protestants, but it was anyone's guess who had told him to kill Scarface. It might have been Coligny, as Poltrot sometimes said; it might have been another Protestant leader; or Poltrot might have had the idea himself.

That afternoon and over the next few days he talked volubly. Most likely half of what he said was invented to please his interrogator, and the other half to make himself look better.

The story he told one day was contradicted by what he said the next. He was completely unreliable.

Which was not a problem.

Pierre wrote out Poltrot's confession, saying that Gaspard de Coligny had paid him to assassinate the duke of Guise, and Poltrot signed it.

The following day, Scarface developed a high fever, and the doctors told him to prepare to meet his maker. His brother, Cardinal Louis, gave him the last rites, then he said goodbye to Anna and young Henri.

When the duchess and the next duke came out of the sick room in tears, Pierre said: 'Coligny killed Duke Scarface,' and he showed them the confession.

The result exceeded his hopes.

The duchess became vituperative, sputtering: 'Coligny must die! He must die!'

Pierre told her that Queen Caterina was already making overtures of peace to the Protestants, and Coligny would probably escape punishment as part of any treaty.

At that Henri became nearly hysterical, crying in his boyish treble: 'I will kill him! I will kill him myself!'

'I believe you will, one day, Prince Henri,' Pierre said to him. 'And when you do, I will be by your side.'

Duke Scarface died the next day.

Cardinal Louis was responsible for the funeral arrangements, but was rarely sober long enough to get much done, and Pierre took charge without difficulty. With Anna's support he devised a magnificent send-off. The duke's body would be conveyed first to Paris, where his heart would be interred in the cathedral of Notre Dame. Then the coffin would travel in state across the country to Champagne, where the body would be buried at Joinville. Such grand obsequies were normally only for kings. No doubt Queen Caterina would have preferred less ostentation, but Pierre did not consult her. For her part, Caterina always avoided a quarrel when she could, and she probably figured that Scarface could do no more harm now, even if he did have a royal funeral.

However, Pierre's scheme to make Coligny a hate figure did

not go so smoothly. Once again Caterina showed that she could be as cunning as Pierre. She sent a copy of Poltrot's confession to Coligny, who had retreated to the Protestant hinterland of Normandy, and asked him to respond to it. She was already planning his rehabilitation.

But the Guises would never forget.

Pierre went to Paris ahead of the duke's body to finalize arrangements. He had already sent Poltrot there, and imprisoned him in the Conciergerie, at the western tip of the Île de la Cité. Pierre insisted on a heavy guard. The ultra-Catholic people of Paris had worshipped Scarface, and if the mob got hold of Poltrot, they would tear him to pieces.

While the duke's corpse was on its way to Paris, Coligny made a deposition denying his involvement in the assassination, and sent copies to Queen Caterina and others. It was a vigorous defence, and Pierre had to admit – only to himself, of course – that it carried conviction. Gaspard was a heretic, not a fool, and if he had planned to assassinate Scarface, he would probably have chosen as killer someone better than the unstable Poltrot.

The last part of Gaspard's deposition was particularly dangerous. He pointed out that in natural justice he had the right to confront his accuser in court, and he begged Queen Caterina to ensure the safety of Poltrot, and make sure he survived to give evidence to a formal investigation.

An unbiased inquiry was the last thing Pierre wanted.

To make matters worse, in the Conciergerie Poltrot retracted his confession.

Pierre had to stop the rot quickly. He went to the supreme court called the Parlement of Paris and proposed that Poltrot should be tried immediately. He pointed out that if the murderer remained unpunished, riots would break out when the hero's body came to Paris. The judges agreed.

In the early hours of 18 March, the duke's coffin arrived in the southern suburbs of Paris and was lodged at a monastery.

Next morning, Poltrot was found guilty and sentenced to be dismembered.

The sentence was carried out in the place de Grève in front

of a wildly cheering mob. Pierre was there to make sure he died. Poltrot's arms and legs were tied to four horses facing the four points of the compass, and the horses were whipped into motion. Theoretically, his limbs should have been torn from his torso, leaving the stump of his body to bleed to death. But the executioner botched the knots, and the ropes slipped. Pierre sent for a sword, and the executioner then began to hack off Poltrot's arms and legs with the blade. The crowd egged him on, but it was an awkward procedure. At some point during the half-hour that it took, Poltrot stopped screaming and lost consciousness. Finally, his head with its distinctive tuft at the front was chopped off and fixed to a post.

Next day the body of Duke Scarface was brought into the city.

*

SYLVIE PALOT WATCHED the procession, feeling optimistic.

It entered Paris from the south, by the St Michel Gate, and passed through the University district, where Sylvie had her shop. The cortege began with twenty-two town criers dressed in mourning white, ringing solemn handbells and calling upon the grieving citizens to pray for the departed soul of their great hero. Then came priests from every parish in the city, all holding crosses. Two hundred elite citizens were next, carrying blazing torches that sent up a black funeral pall of smoke and darkened the sky. The armies that had followed Scarface to so many victories were represented by six thousand soldiers with lowered banners, playing muffled drums that sounded like faraway gunfire. Then came the city militia with a host of black flags fluttering in the March wind that came off the cold river.

The streets were lined with crowds of mourning Parisians, but Sylvie knew that some of them were like her, secretly elated that Scarface was dead. The assassination had brought peace, at least for now. Within days Queen Caterina had met with Gaspard de Coligny to discuss a new edict of tolerance.

Persecution had increased during the civil war, although Protestants in Sylvie's circle now had some protection. Sylvie had sat at Pierre's writing desk one day, when he was away with

Scarface and Odette was dining with her girlfriends, and copied out every word of his little black book while Nath played with two-year-old Alain, who could not yet talk well enough to betray the secret of Sylvie's visit.

Most of the names were not known to her. Many would be false, for the Protestants knew they might be spied upon and often gave made-up names and other misleading information: Sylvie and her mother called themselves Thérèse and Jacqueline, and told no one about their shop. Sylvie had no way of knowing which of the unfamiliar names were real.

However, many in the book were her friends and fellow-worshippers. Those people had been discreetly warned. A few had left the congregation in fear and had become Catholic again; others had moved house and changed their names; several had left Paris and gone to more tolerant cities.

More important in the long term, Nath had become a regular member of the congregation in the attic over the stable, singing the psalms loudly and tunelessly. With her ten gold ecus in her hand she had talked about leaving Pierre's employment, but Sylvie had persuaded her to stay and continue to spy on him for the Protestants.

The safer atmosphere was good for book sales, and Sylvie was glad to have new stock brought from Geneva by Guillaume. Poor boy, he was still in love with Sylvie. She liked him, and was grateful to have him as an ally, but could not find it in her heart to love him back. Her mother was frustrated by her rejection of an apparently ideal match. He was an intelligent, prosperous, handsome young man who shared her religion and her ideals: what more did she want? Sylvie was as mystified as Isabelle by this question.

At last the coffin came by, draped with a banner displaying the heraldic arms of the Guises, resting on a gun-carriage drawn by six white horses. Sylvie did not pray for the soul of Scarface. Instead she thanked God for ending his life. Now she dared to hope that there would be peace and tolerance.

Behind the coffin rode the widow, Anna, all in white, with ladies-in-waiting either side of her. Finally, there was a pretty-faced boy with fair hair who had to be Scarface's heir, Henri.

Beside him, wearing a white doublet with a pale fur collar, was a handsome man of twenty-five with thick blond hair.

Sylvie was overwhelmed by shock, disgust and horror as she recognized the man at the right hand of the new duke of Guise.

It was Pierre.

12

BARNEY THOUGHT THE Caribbean island of Hispaniola must be the hottest place on earth.

In the summer of 1563 he was still master gunner on the *Hawk*, three years after he had boarded the ship in Antwerp wanting to go only as far as Combe Harbour. He longed to go home and see his family but, strangely, he was not very angry about having been tricked into joining the crew. Life at sea was dangerous and often cruel, but there was something about it that suited Barney. He liked waking up in the morning not knowing what the day would bring. More and more, he felt that the sad collapse of his mother's business had been, for him, an escape.

His main complaint was all-male society. He had always loved the company of women, and they, in turn, often found him attractive. Unlike many crew, he did not resort to dockside whores, who often gave men horrible infections. He yearned just to stroll along a street with a girl at his side, flirting and looking for a chance to snatch a kiss.

The *Hawk* had sailed from Antwerp to Seville, then to the Canary Islands. There followed a series of lucrative round trips, taking knives and ceramic tiles and clothing from Seville to the islands and bringing back barrels of strong Canary wine. It was a peaceful trade, so Barney's expertise in gunnery had not been required, although he had kept the armaments in constant readiness. The crew had shrunk from fifty to forty through accidents and disease, the hazards of normal life at sea, but there had been no fighting.

Then Captain Bacon had decided that the big money was in slaves. At Tenerife he had found a Portuguese pilot called Duarte who was familiar with both the African coast and the transatlantic crossing. The crew had become restive at this dangerous prospect, especially after so long at sea; so Bacon had promised that they would return home after one trip, and get a bonus.

Slavery was a major industry in West Africa. Since before anyone could remember, the kings and chieftains of the region had sold their fellow men to Arab buyers who took them to the slave markets of the Middle East. The new European traders horned in on an existing business.

Bacon bought three hundred and twenty men, women and children in Sierra Leone. Then the *Hawk* headed west across the Atlantic Ocean to the vast unmapped territory called New Spain.

The crew did not like the slave business. The wretched victims were crammed together in the hold, chained up in filthy conditions. Everyone could hear the children crying and the women wailing. Sometimes they sang sad songs to keep up their spirits, and that was even worse. Every few days one of them would die, and the body would be thrown overboard with no ceremony. 'They're just cattle,' Bacon said, if anyone complained; but cattle did not sing laments.

The first Europeans to cross the Atlantic had thought, when they made landfall, that they were in India, so they had called these islands the West Indies. They knew better now that Magellan and Elcano had circumnavigated the globe, but the name stuck.

Hispaniola was the most developed of many islands, few of which were even named. Its capital, Santo Domingo, was the first European city in New Spain, and even had a cathedral, but to his disappointment Barney did not get to see it. The pilot Duarte directed the *Hawk* away from the city because what the ship was doing was illegal. Hispaniola was governed by the king of Spain, and English merchants were forbidden to trade there. So Duarte advised Captain Bacon to head for the northern coast, as far away as possible from the forces of law and order.

The sugar planters were desperate for labour. Barney had heard that something like half of all Europeans who migrated to the West Indies died within two years, and the death rate was almost as bad among Africans, who seemed resistant to some but not all the diseases of New Spain. As a result, the planters did not scruple to buy from illicit English traders, and the day after the Hawk docked at a little place with no name, Bacon sold eighty slaves, taking payment in gold, pearls and hides.

Jonathan Greenland, the first mate, bought supplies in the town and the crew enjoyed their first fresh food in two months.

The following morning Barney was standing in the waist, the low, middle part of the deck, talking anxiously to Jonathan. From where they were, they could see most of the small town where they had at last made landfall. A wooden jetty led to a little beach, beyond which was a square. All the buildings were of wood but one, a small palace built of pale-gold coral limestone.

'I don't like the illegality of this,' Barney said quietly to Jonathan. 'We could end up in a Spanish jail, and who knows how long it would take to get out?'

'And all for nothing,' Jonathan said. The crew did not share in the profits of regular trading, just the prize money from captured ships, and he was disappointed that the voyage had been peaceful.

As they talked, a young man in clerical black came out of the main door of the palace and walked, looking important, across the square, down the beach and along the jetty. Coming to the gangplank he hesitated, then stepped onto it and crossed to the deck.

In Spanish he said: 'I must speak to your master.'

Barney replied in the same language. 'Captain Bacon is in his cabin. Who are you?'

The man looked offended to be questioned. 'Father Ignacio, and I bring a message from Don Alfonso.'

Barney guessed that Alfonso was the local representative of authority, and Ignacio was his secretary. 'Give me the message, and I'll make sure the captain gets it.'

'Don Alfonso summons your captain to see him immediately.'

Barney was keen to avoid offending the local authorities, so he pretended not to notice Ignacio's arrogance. Mildly he said: 'Then I'm sure my captain will come. If you'll wait a moment, I'll find him.'

Barney went to Bacon's cabin. The captain was dressed and eating fried plantains with fresh bread. Barney gave him the message. 'You can come with me,' Bacon said. 'Your Spanish is better than mine.'

A few minutes later they stepped off the ship onto the jetty. Barney felt the warmth of the rising sun on his face: today would be very hot again. They followed Ignacio up the beach. A few early-rising townspeople stared at them with lively interest: clearly strangers were rare enough here to be fascinating.

As they crossed the dusty square, Barney's eye was caught by a girl in a yellow gown. She was a golden-skinned African, but too well-dressed to be a slave. She rolled a small barrel from a doorway to a waiting cart, then looked up at the visitors. She met Barney's gaze with a fearless expression, and he was startled to see that she had blue eyes.

With an effort Barney returned his attention to the palace. Two armed guards, their eyes narrowed against the glare, watched silently as he and Bacon followed Ignacio through the gate. Barney felt like a criminal, which he was, and he wondered whether he would get out as easily as he had got in.

The palace was cool inside, with high ceilings and stone floors. The walls were covered with tiles of bright blue and golden yellow that Barney recognized as coming from the potteries of Seville. Ignacio led them up a wide staircase and told them to sit on a wooden bench. Barney figured this was a snub. The mayor of this place did not have a string of people to see every morning. He was making them wait just to show that he could. Barney thought this was a good sign. You do not bother to slight a man if you are about to throw him in jail.

After a quarter of an hour, Ignacio reappeared and said: 'Don Alfonso will see you now.' He showed them into a spacious room with tall shuttered windows.

Alfonso was obese. A man of about fifty, with silver hair and blue eyes, he sat in a chair that appeared to have been made specially to fit his unnatural girth. Two stout walking-sticks on a table beside him suggested that he could not walk around unaided.

He was reading a sheaf of papers, and once again Barney thought this was for show. He and Bacon stood with Ignacio, waiting for Alfonso to speak. Barney sensed Bacon becoming angry. The disdainful treatment was getting to him. Barney willed him to stay calm.

At last Alfonso looked up. 'You're under arrest,' he said. 'You have been trading illegally.'

That was what Barney had been afraid of.

He translated, and Bacon said: 'If he tries to arrest me, the Hawk will flatten his town.'

This was an exaggeration. The Hawk's guns were minions, small cannons that would not destroy any well-built masonry structure. They were too small even to sink a ship, unless by extraordinary luck. The four-pound cannonballs were designed to paralyse an enemy vessel by wrecking its masts and rigging, and killing or demoralizing the crew, thereby depriving the captain of all control. Just the same, the Hawk could inflict a good deal of unpleasant damage on the little town square.

Barney scrambled for a more conciliatory way of phrasing Bacon's rejoinder. After a moment he said to Alfonso in Spanish: 'Captain Bacon suggests that you send a message to his crew, telling them that he has been detained quite lawfully, and that they should not fire the ship's guns at your town, no matter how angry they may feel.'

'That's not what he said.' Clearly Alfonso understood some English.

'It's what he meant.'

Bacon said impatiently: 'Ask him how much he needs to be bribed.'

Again Barney's translation was more tactful. 'Captain Bacon asks what it would cost to purchase a licence to trade here.'

There was a pause. Would Alfonso angrily refuse, and jail them for corruption as well as illegal trading?

The fat man said: 'Five escudos per slave, payable to me.'

Thank heaven, Barney thought.

The price was high, but not unreasonable. A Spanish escudo was a coin containing one-eighth of an ounce of gold.

Bacon's reply was: 'I can't pay more than one escudo.'

'Three.'

'Done.'

'One more thing.'

'Damn,' Bacon muttered. 'I agreed too easily. Now there'll be some supplementary charge.'

Barney said in Spanish: 'Captain Bacon will not pay more.'

Alfonso said: 'You have to threaten to destroy the town.'

Barney had not expected that. 'What?'

'When the authorities in Santo Domingo accuse me of permitting illicit trade, my defence will be that I had to do it to save the town from the wrath of the savage English pirates.'

Barney translated, and Bacon said: 'Fair enough.'

'I'll need it in writing.'

Bacon nodded agreement.

Barney frowned. He did not like the idea of a written confession of crime, even if it was true. However, he saw no way around it.

The door opened and the girl in the yellow dress walked in. Ignacio glanced at her without interest. Alfonso smiled fondly. She crossed the room to his chair as casually as if she were family, and kissed him on the forehead.

Alfonso said: 'My niece, Bella.'

Barney guessed that 'niece' was a euphemism for 'illegitimate daughter'. Alfonso had fathered a child with a beautiful slave, it seemed. Barney recalled the words of Ebrima: *Slaves are always used for sex.*

Bella was carrying a bottle, and now she put it on the table with the walking-sticks. 'I thought you might need some rum,' she said, speaking the Spanish of an educated woman with just the hint of an accent Barney did not recognize. She gave him a direct look, and he realized her eyes were the same bright blue as Alfonso's. 'Enjoy it in good health,' she said, and she went out.

'Her mother was a spitfire, rest her soul,' Alfonso said

nostalgically. For a moment he was silent, remembering. Then he said: 'You should buy Bella's rum. It's the best. Let's have a taste.'

Barney began to relax. The atmosphere had changed completely. They were now collaborators, not adversaries.

The secretary got three glasses from a cupboard, drew the stopper from the bottle, and poured generous measures for the other men. They drank. It was very good rum, spicy but smooth, with a kick in the swallow.

Bacon said: 'A pleasure to do business with you, Don Alfonso.'

Alfonso smiled. 'I believe you have sold eighty slaves.'

Barney began to make an excuse. 'Well, we weren't aware of any prohibition—'

Alfonso ignored him. 'So that means you owe me two hundred and forty escudos already. You can settle the account here and now.'

Bacon frowned. 'It's a bit difficult—'

Alfonso interrupted him before Barney had time to translate. 'You got four thousand escudos for the slaves.'

Barney was surprised: he had not known that Bacon had made so much. The captain was secretive about money.

Alfonso went on: 'You can afford to pay me two hundred and forty right now.'

He was right. Bacon got out a heavy purse and laboriously counted out the money, mostly in the larger coins called doubloons, each containing a quarter of an ounce of gold and therefore worth two escudos. His face was twisted in a grimace of discomfort, as if he had a stomach-ache. It hurt him to pay such a large bribe.

Ignacio checked the amount and nodded to Alfonso.

Bacon stood up to leave.

Alfonso said: 'Let me have your threatening letter before you sell any more slaves.'

Bacon shrugged.

Barney winced. Rough manners irritated the Spanish, who valued formalities. He did not want Bacon to spoil everything by offending Alfonso's sensibilities just before leaving. They were still under Spanish jurisdiction. He said politely: 'Thank you, Don Alfonso, for your kindness in receiving us. We are honoured by your courtesy.'

Alfonso made a grandly dismissive gesture, and Ignacio led them out.

Barney felt better, though he was not sure that they were completely in the clear. However, he wanted to see Bella again. He wondered whether she was married, or courting. He guessed she was about twenty – she might have been less, but dark skin always looked younger. He was eager to know more about her.

Outside in the square, he said to Bacon: 'We need rum on board – we're almost out. Should I buy a barrel from that woman, his niece, Bella?'

The captain was not fooled. 'Go on, then, you randy young bastard.'

Bacon headed back towards the *Hawk*, and Barney went to the doorway from which he had seen Bella emerge earlier. The house was of wood, but otherwise built on the same pattern as Carlos Cruz's home in Seville, with a central arch leading through to a courtyard workshop – a typical craftsman's dwelling.

Barney smelled the earthy odour of molasses, the bitter black treacle that was produced by the second boiling of sugar cane and was mainly used to make rum. He guessed the smell came from the huge barrels lined up along one side of the yard. On the other side were smaller barrels and stacked bottles, presumably for rum. The yard ended in a little orchard of lime trees.

In the middle of the space were two large tanks. One was a waist-high square of caulked planks, full of a sticky mixture that was being stirred by an African with a large wooden paddle. The brew gave off the bready smell of yeast, and Barney assumed this was a fermentation tank. Alongside it was an iron cauldron perched over a fire. The cauldron had a conical lid with a long spout, and a dark liquid dripped from the spout into a bucket. Barney guessed that in this cauldron the fermented mash was distilled to produce the liquor.

Bella stood over the bucket, sniffing. Barney watched her, admiring her concentration. She was slim but sturdy, with strong legs and arms, no doubt from manhandling barrels. Something about her high forehead reminded him of Ebrima, and on impulse he spoke to her in Manding. He said: 'I *be nyaadi?*' which meant *How are you?*

She jumped with shock and turned around. Recovering, she spoke a stream of Manding.

Barney replied in Spanish. 'I don't really speak the language, I'm sorry. I learned a few words from a friend in Seville.'

'My mother spoke Manding,' Bella said in Spanish. 'She's dead. You spooked me.'

'I'm sorry.'

She looked thoughtfully at him. 'Not many Europeans bother to pick up even a few words of any African languages.'

'My father taught us to learn as much as possible of any tongue we came across. He says it's better than money in the bank.'

'Are you Spanish? You don't look it, with that ginger beard.'

'English.'

'I never met an English person before.' She picked up the bucket at her feet, sniffed it, and threw its contents on the ground.

Barney said: 'Something wrong with the rum?'

'You always have to discard the first fractions of the distillate. They're poisonous. You can save the stuff and use it for cleaning boots but, if you do, sooner or later some idiot will try drinking it and kill himself. So I throw it away.' She touched the tip of a slender finger to the spout and sniffed it. 'That's better.' She rolled an empty barrel under the spout, then turned her attention back to Barney. 'Do you want to buy some rum?'

'Yes, please.'

'Come with me. I want to show you the best way to drink it.'

She led him to the far end of the yard. She picked small pale-green limes from the trees and handed them to him. Barney watched her, mesmerized. All her movements were fluid and graceful. She stopped when he was holding a dozen or so of the fruits. 'You have big hands,' she said. Then she looked more closely. 'But damaged. What happened?'

'Scorch marks,' he said. 'I used to be a gunner in the Spanish army. It's like being a cook – you're always getting minor burns.'

'Shame,' she said. 'Makes your hands ugly.'

Barney smiled. She was sassy, but he liked that.

He followed her into the house. Her living room had a floor of beaten earth, and the furniture was evidently home-made, but she had brightened the place with bougainvillea blossom and colourful cushions. There was no sign of a husband: no boots in the corner, no sword hanging from a hook, no tall, feathered hat. She pointed to a crude wooden chair and Barney sat down.

Bella took two tall glasses from a cupboard. Barney was surprised: glass was an expensive luxury. But selling rum was her business, and all drinks tasted better out of glassware.

She took the limes from him and halved them with a knife, then squeezed their juice into a pottery jug. She knew he was staring at her, and did not seem to mind.

She put an inch of rum into each glass, stirred in a spoonful of sugar, then topped up the glasses with lime juice.

Barney took a glass and sipped. It was the most delicious drink he had ever tasted. 'Oh, my soul,' he said. 'That really is the best way to take it.'

'Shall I send some rum to the Hawk this afternoon? My best is half an escudo for a thirty-four gallon barrel.'

That was cheap, Barney thought; about the same price as beer in Kingsbridge. Presumably molasses cost next to nothing on this sugar-growing island. 'Make it two barrels,' he said.

'Done.'

He sipped more of the zesty drink. 'How did you get started in this business?'

'When my mother was dying, Don Alfonso offered her anything she wanted. She asked him to give me my freedom and set me up with some way of making a living.'

'And he came up with this.'

She laughed, opening her mouth wide. 'No, he suggested needlework. The rum was my idea. And you? What brought you to Hispaniola?'

'It was an accident.'

'Really?'

'Well, more a series of accidents.'

'How so?'

Barney thought of Sancho in Seville, the *José y María*, the killing of Ironhand Gómez, the raft down the river Leie, the Wolman family in Antwerp, and Captain Bacon's deceit. 'It's a long story.'

'I'd love to hear it.'

'And I'd love to tell you, but I'm needed on board ship.'

'Does the captain ever give you time off?'

'In the evenings, usually.'

'If I make you supper, will you tell me your story?'

Barney's heart beat faster. 'All right.'

'Tonight?'

'Yes.' He stood up.

To his surprise, she kissed his lips, briefly and softly. 'Come at sundown,' she said.

*

'Do you believe in love at first sight?' Barney said to Bella three weeks later.

'Maybe, I don't know.'

They were in bed at her house, and the sun had just risen. The new day was already warm, so they had thrown off the bedclothes. They slept naked: there was no need for nightwear in this climate.

Barney had never set eyes on anything as lovely as Bella's golden-brown body carelessly splayed across a linen sheet in the morning light. He never tired of gazing at her, and she never minded.

He said: 'The day that I went to speak to Don Alfonso, and I glanced across the square and saw you come out of this house rolling a barrel, and you looked up and met my eye – I fell for you right then, not knowing anything at all about you.'

'I might have turned out to be a witch.'

'What did you think, when you saw me staring at you?'

'Well, now, I can't say too much, in case you get a swollen head.'

'Go on, take the risk.'

'At that moment, I couldn't really think at all. My heart started beating fast and I couldn't seem to catch my breath. I told myself it was just a white man with peculiar-coloured hair and a ring in his ear, nothing to get excited about. Then you just looked away, as if you hadn't really noticed me, and I figured it really was nothing to get excited about.'

Barney was deeply in love with her, and she with him, and they both knew it, but he had no idea what they were going to do about it.

Bacon had sold almost all the slaves, and those that remained were mostly rejects, men who had fallen ill on the voyage, pregnant women, children who had pined away after separation from their parents. The hold of the *Hawk* was bursting with gold, sugar and hides. Soon the ship would sail for Europe, and this time it seemed Bacon really did mean to go to Combe Harbour.

Would Bella go home with Barney? It would mean giving up everything she knew, including a successful business. He was afraid to ask her the question. He did not even know whether Bacon would permit a woman on board for the voyage home.

So should Barney give up his old life and settle here in Hispaniola? What would he do? He could help Bella expand the rum business. He could become a sugar planter, perhaps, though he had no capital to invest. It was a big step to take after less than a month in a place. But he wanted to spend his life with Bella.

He had to talk to her about the future. The unasked question was always in his mind, and perhaps hers too. They had to face it.

He opened his mouth to speak, and Jonathan Greenland walked in.

'Barney!' he said. 'You have to come, now!' Then he saw Bella and said: 'Oh, my good God, she's gorgeous.'

It was a clumsy remark, but Bella's beauty could have a distracting effect on a normally intelligent man even when she was fully clothed. Barney smothered a grin and said: 'Get out of here! This is a lady's bedroom!'

Jonathan turned his back, but did not leave. 'I'm sorry, Señorita, but it's an emergency,' he said.

'It's all right,' Bella said, pulling the sheet over her. 'What's the crisis?'

'A galleon approaching, fast.'

Barney leaped out of bed and pulled on his breeches. 'I'll be back,' he said to Bella as he pushed his feet into his boots.

'Be careful!' she said.

Barney and Jonathan ran out of the house and across the square. The *Hawk* was already lifting its anchor. Most of the crew were on deck and in the rigging, unfurling the sails. The mooring ropes had been untied from the jetty, and the two latecomers had to leap across a gap of a yard onto the deck.

Once safely on board, Barney looked across the water. A mile to the east was a Spanish galleon bristling with guns, coming at them fast with a following wind. For three weeks he had forgotten about the danger he and the rest of the crew were in. But now the forces of law and order had arrived.

The crew used long poles to push the *Hawk* away from the jetty and out towards deeper water. Captain Bacon turned the ship west, and the wind filled the sails.

The galleon was riding high in the water, suggesting it carried little or no cargo. It had four masts, with more sails than Barney could count at a glance, giving it speed. It was broad in the beam, and had a high aft castle, which would make it relatively clumsy to turn; but in a straight race it could not fail to catch the *Hawk*.

Barney heard a distant bang that he immediately recognized as cannon fire. There was a nearby crash, a cacophony of breaking timbers, and a chorus of shocked yells from the crew. A huge cannonball passed a yard from Barney, smashed through the woodwork of the forecastle, and disappeared.

The ball had been much bigger than the four-pounders with which the Hawk was armed, so the galleon must have heavier guns. Even so, Barney thought their gunner must have been lucky to score a hit at the range of a mile.

A moment later the Hawk turned sharply, throwing Barney off balance. He was suddenly afraid that the ship had been badly damaged and was out of control, perhaps sinking. The prospect of dying at sea terrified him – but only for a moment. He saw that Captain Bacon was spinning the wheel, intentionally turning north, broadside to the wind. Fear was replaced by bafflement. Clearly Bacon had realized that he could not outrun the Spaniard – but what was his alternative plan?

'Stop staring, you bloody idiot,' Jonathan roared at Barney. 'Get down on the gun deck where you belong!'

Barney realized he was about to experience his first sea battle. He wondered if it would also be his last. He wished he had been able to go home to Kingsbridge one more time before dying.

He had been under fire before. He was scared, but he knew how to control his fear and do his job.

He went first to the galley, in the forecastle. The cook was bleeding from a flying splinter, but the kitchen had not been wrecked, and Barney was able to light a taper at the fire. He heard a second bang and tensed, waiting for the impact, terrified all over again; but the ball had missed.

Down in the hold, the few remaining slaves figured out what was going on, and they began to scream in terror, no doubt fearing that they were about to die chained to a sinking ship.

There was a third explosion, again without impact, and Barney's guess was confirmed: the first shot had been lucky. The gunner of the galleon must have made the same deduction, and decided to save his ammunition for better opportunities, for there was no fourth explosion.

Barney returned to the waist, shielding his flame with his hand. Most of the crew were on deck or up in the rigging, adjusting the sails in accordance with Captain Bacon's shouted orders. Barney ran across to the companionway, the hooded hatch leading to the lower decks, and scrambled down the ladder, carrying his burning taper.

The crew had already opened the gun ports and untied the ropes that kept the minions in position when not being used. Now the heavy gun carriages could roll back on their wheels under the recoil from the shot. Sensible men took great care walking around the gun deck when the cannons were untied: someone standing behind a gun at the moment of firing could be crippled or killed.

Each gun had beside it a chest containing most of what was needed to fire: a leather gunpowder bucket with a lid; a pile of rags for wadding; a slow-burning match made of three woven strands of cotton rope soaked in saltpetre and lye; tools for loading the gun and cleaning it between shots; and a bucket of water. The ammunition was in a big chest in the middle of the deck next to a barrel of gunpowder.

There were two men to each gun. One used a long-handled ladle to scoop up exactly the right quantity of gunpowder – an amount weighing the same as the ball, although good men made small adjustments when they knew the weapon. Then the other rammed some wadding down the barrel, followed by the ball.

In a few minutes, all the starboard guns were loaded. Barney went around with his taper lighting the slow matches. Most of the men wound a rope match around a forked stick, called a linstock, so that they could stand well clear of the gun when putting the flame to the touchhole.

Barney peered through a gun port. The Hawk was now side-on to the stiff easterly breeze, bowling along at eight or nine knots, with the faster galleon half a mile away and bearing down on its starboard side.

Barney waited. At this range he might hit the galleon, and he might do some minor damage, but it would not be the best use of his armaments.

The attacking ship was approaching nose-on to the Hawk, so could not use its powerful broadside cannons. Two small explosions indicated that the gunner was trying out his foredeck guns, but Barney saw from the splashes that both balls had landed harmlessly in the sea.

However, the fast vessel would soon come close enough to turn at an angle and deploy its broadside guns, and then the Hawk would be in trouble. What the hell was Captain Bacon's plan? Perhaps the old fool had none. Barney fought down panic.

A crewman called Silas said impatiently: 'Shall we fire, sir?'

Barney held his nerve with an effort. 'Not yet,' he said with more assurance than he felt. 'They're too far off.'

Up on deck, Bacon yelled: 'Hold your fire, gunners!' He could not have heard Silas, but his instinct had told him the gun deck would be getting restless.

As the galleon came closer, the angle improved for shooting. At six hundred yards, it fired.

There was a bang and a puff of smoke. The ball moved slowly enough to be visible, and Barney saw it rise on a high trajectory. He resisted the temptation to duck. Before the ball came close he saw that it was going to hit. But the Spanish gunner had aimed a fraction too high, and the ball flew through the rigging. Barney heard canvas and rope rip, but it sounded as if no woodwork was damaged.

Barney was about to fire back, but he hesitated when he heard Bacon yelling a stream of orders. Then the Hawk lurched again and turned to leeward. For a few moments it had the wind behind it, but Bacon continued turning through one hundred and eighty degrees and then headed south, back towards the island.

Without needing to be told, all the gunners switched to the port side of the gun deck and loaded the other six minions.

But what was Bacon up to?

Looking out, Barney saw the galleon change direction, its prow swinging around to intercept the Hawk's new course. And then he understood what Bacon was doing.

He was presenting Barney with the perfect target.

In a minute or two the Hawk would be broadside-on to the nose of the enemy ship, and three hundred yards away. Barney would be able to attack with raking fire, putting one ball after another into the vulnerable bow of the galleon and all along the length of its deck to the stern, causing maximum damage to its rigging and crew.

If he did it right.

The range was so close that he had no need of the wedges that elevated the gun barrels. Firing dead level, their range should be perfect. But the target was narrow.

Silas said: 'Now, sir?'

'No,' Barney replied. 'Stay ready, stay calm.'

He knelt beside the foremost gun and stared out, watching the angle of the galleon, his heart thudding. This was so much easier on land, when gun and target were not rising and falling on waves.

The enemy ship seemed to turn slowly. Barney fought the temptation to start firing too soon. He watched the four masts. He would fire when they were in a straight line so that the first obscured the rest. Or just before, to allow for the time it would take the ball to travel.

Silas said: 'Ready when you are, sir!'

'Get set!' The masts were almost in line. 'Fire one!' He tapped Silas on the shoulder.

Silas put the burning tip of his rope match to the touchhole in the gun barrel.

The explosion was deafening in the confined space of the gun deck.

The cannon sprang backwards with the recoil.

Barney peered out and saw the ball smash into the forecastle of the galleon. A cheer went up from the crew of the *Hawk*.

Barney moved to the next gun and tapped the man's shoulder. 'Fire!'

This ball went higher, and crashed into the galleon's masts.

Barney could hear tremendous cheering from on deck. He moved sternwards down the line, concentrating on trying to time the shots to a fraction of a second, until all six guns had fired.

He returned to the first gun, expecting to find Silas reloading. To his dismay, Silas and his mate were shaking hands, congratulating each other. 'Reload!' Barney screamed. 'The swine aren't dead yet!'

Hastily, Silas picked up a gun-worm, a long-handled tool with a pointed spiral blade. He used it to extract residual wadding from the barrel. The detritus came out smouldering and sparking. Silas trod on the embers with a horny bare foot, apparently feeling no pain. His mate then picked up a long stick thickly wrapped in rags. He dipped it in the water bucket then plunged it down the barrel to extinguish any remaining sparks or burning fragments that might, otherwise, have ignited the next charge of gunpowder prematurely. He withdrew the sponge, and the heat of the barrel quickly evaporated any traces of water. The two men then reloaded the cleaned gun.

Barney looked out. The bow of the galleon was holed in two places and its foremast was leaning sideways. From the deck – now only two hundred yards away – came the screams of the wounded and the panicked cries of the survivors. But the ship had not been crippled, and the captain kept his nerve. The galleon came on at barely reduced speed.

Barney was dismayed by how long his gunners took to reload. He knew, from battlefield experience, that a single volley never won a fight. Armies could recover. But repeated volleys, one after another, decimating their ranks and felling their comrades, destroyed morale and caused men to run away or surrender. Repetition was everything. However, the crew of the Hawk were sailors, not artillerymen, and no one had taught them the importance of rapid, disciplined reloading.

The galleon came straight at the Hawk. Its captain no longer wanted to fire his broadside guns. Of course not, Barney thought: the Spaniards did not want to sink the Hawk. They would prefer to capture the ship and confiscate its illegally acquired treasure. They were firing the small foredeck guns, and some shots were hitting the rigging; but the Hawk was narrow, making it easy to overshoot or undershoot. The galleon's tactic, Barney now saw, would be to ram the Hawk then board.

By the time the Hawk's guns were ready, the galleon would

be less than a hundred yards away. But it was taller than the Hawk, and Barney wanted to hit the deck rather than the hull, so he needed to elevate his guns slightly. He ran along the line adjusting the wedges.

The next few moments felt long. The galleon was moving fast, nine or ten knots, its prow foaming the swell, but it seemed to approach by inches. Its deck was crowded with sailors and soldiers, apparently eager to leap aboard the Hawk and kill everyone. Silas and the gunners kept looking from the galleon to Barney and back: they were itching to put their matches to gunpowder. 'Wait for my word!' he shouted. Slightly premature shooting was the greatest possible gift to the enemy, allowing him to get close in safety while the gunners were reloading.

But then the galleon was a hundred yards away, and Barney fired.

Once again Captain Bacon had presented him with the perfect target. The galleon was heading straight for the guns of the Hawk. At such close range Barney could not miss. He fired all six guns in rapid succession, then yelled: 'Reload! Reload!'

Then he looked out, and saw that his shooting had been even better than he had hoped. One ball must have struck the main mast, for, as he watched, it was falling forward, pushed by the wind. The pace of the galleon slowed as some of its sails collapsed. The main mast fell into the rigging of the damaged foremast and that, too, began to topple. The ship was now only fifty yards away, but still too far for its men to board the Hawk. It was crippled – but, Barney saw, it was nevertheless drifting into collision with the Hawk, which would then be boarded anyway.

But Bacon acted again. He turned the Hawk to leeward. The east wind filled the sails. The ship picked up pace. In moments the Hawk was speeding westward.

The crippled galleon could not catch up.

Could it be over?

Barney went up on deck, and the crew cheered him. They had won. They had beaten off a larger, faster vessel. Barney was their hero, though he knew the battle had really been won by Bacon's skill and his quick, agile ship.

Barney looked back. The galleon was limping towards the harbour. Hispaniola was already receding.

And so was Bella.

Barney went to Bacon at the wheel. 'Where are we heading, Captain?'

'Home,' said Bacon. 'To Combe Harbour.' When Barney said nothing, he added: 'Isn't that what you wanted?'

Barney looked back at Hispaniola, disappearing now into a haze under the Caribbean sun. 'It was,' he said.

13

MARGERY KNEW SHE WAS committing a serious crime when she picked up a broom and began to sweep the floor of the chapel, preparing it for Mass.

The small village of Tench had no church, but this chapel was within the manor house. Earl Swithin rarely went to Tench, and the building was in bad repair, dirty and damp. When Margery had cleaned the floor she opened a window to let in some fresh air, and in the dawn light it began to feel more like a holy place.

Stephen Lincoln put candles on the altar, either side of a small jewelled crucifix he had purloined from Kingsbridge Cathedral, way back in the early days of Elizabeth's reign, before he had officially left the priesthood. Around his shoulders he was wearing a magnificent cope he had rescued from a Protestant bonfire of priestly vestments. It was gorgeously embroidered with gold and silver thread and coloured silk. The embroidery depicted the martyrdom of Thomas Becket. It also showed random foliage and, for some reason, several parrots.

Margery brought a wooden chair from the hall and sat down to prepare herself for Mass.

There were no clocks in Tench but everyone could see sunrise and, as the pale light of a summer morning crept through the east window and turned the grey stone walls to gold, the villagers came into the chapel in their family groups, quietly greeting their neighbours. Stephen stood with his back to the congregation and they stared, mesmerized, at the colourful images on his cope.

Margery knew how many people lived in Tench, for it was part of the Shiring earldom, and she was pleased to see that every inhabitant showed up, including the oldest resident, Granny Harborough, who was carried in, and was the only other member of the congregation who sat down for the service.

Stephen began the prayers. Margery closed her eyes and let the familiar sound of the Latin words penetrate her mind and submerge her soul in the precious tranquillity of feeling right with the world and with God.

Travelling around the county of Shiring, sometimes with her husband Bart and sometimes without him, Margery would talk to people about their religious feelings. Men and women liked her, and were more willing to open up to her because she was an unthreatening young woman. She generally targeted the village steward, a man paid to take care of the earl's interests. He would already know that the earl's family were staunch Catholics and, if handled gently, he would soon tell Margery where the villagers stood. In poor, remote places such as Tench it was not unusual to find that they were all Catholic. And then she would arrange for Stephen to bring them the sacraments.

It was a crime, but Margery was not sure how dangerous this was. In the five years since Elizabeth had come to the throne, no one had been executed for Catholicism. Stephen had the impression, from talking to other ex-priests, that clandestine services such as this one were, in fact, common; but there was no official reaction, no campaign to stamp them out.

It seemed that Queen Elizabeth was willing to tolerate such things. Ned Willard hinted as much. He came home to Kingsbridge once or twice a year, and Margery usually saw him in the cathedral, and spoke to him even though his face and his voice provoked wicked thoughts in her mind. He said that Elizabeth had no interest in punishing Catholics. However, he added, as if warning her personally, anyone who challenged Elizabeth's authority as head of the Church of England – or, even worse, questioned her right to the throne – would be treated harshly.

Margery had no wish to make any kind of political

statement. All the same, she could not feel safe. She thought it would be a mistake to relax vigilance. Monarchs could change their minds.

Fear was always present in her life, like a bell ringing for a distant funeral, but it did not keep her from her duty. She was thrilled that she had been chosen as the agent who would preserve the true religion in the county of Shiring, and she accepted the danger as part of the mission. If one day it got her into serious trouble, she would find the strength to deal with that, she felt sure. Or nearly sure.

The congregation here would protect themselves by walking, later in the morning, to the next village, where a priest would hold a Protestant service using the prayer book authorized by Elizabeth and the English-language Bible introduced by her heretical father, King Henry VIII. They had to go, anyway: the fine for not attending church was a shilling, and no one in Tench could spare a shilling.

Margery was the first to receive Holy Communion, to give courage to the others. Then she stood aside to watch the congregation. Their weathered peasant faces glowed as they received the sacrament that had been denied them for so long. Finally, Granny Harborough was carried to the front. Almost certainly this would be the last time for her here on earth. Her wrinkled visage was suffused with joy. Margery could imagine what she was thinking. Her soul was saved, and she was at peace.

Now she could die happy.

*

ONE MORNING IN BED Susannah, the dowager countess of Brecknock, said: 'I'd marry you, Ned Willard, if I was twenty years younger, I really would.'

She was forty-five years old, a cousin of Earl Swithin. Ned had known her by sight since childhood, and had never dreamed that he might be her lover. She lay beside him with her head on his chest and one plump thigh thrown over his knees. He could easily imagine being married to her. She was clever and funny and as lustful as a tomcat. She had ways in bed that he had never heard of, and she made him play games he had not even imagined. She had a sensual face and warm brown eyes and big soft breasts. Most of all, she helped him to stop thinking about Margery in bed with Bart.

She said: 'But it's a terrible idea, of course. I'm past the age when I could give you children. I could help a young man's career, but with Sir William Cecil as your mentor you don't need any help. And I don't even have a fortune to leave you.'

And we're not in love, Ned thought, though he did not say it. He liked Susannah enormously, and she had given him intense pleasure for a year, but he did not quite love her, and he was pretty sure she did not love him. He had not known that a relationship such as this was even possible. He had learned so much from her.

'Besides,' she said, 'I'm not sure you'll ever get over poor Margery.'

The one drawback of an older lover, Ned had learned, was that nothing could be concealed from her. He was not sure how she did it but she guessed everything, even things he did not want her to know. Especially things he did not want her to know.

'Margery is a lovely girl, and she deserved you,' Susannah went on. 'But her family were desperate to join the nobility, and they just used her.'

'The Fitzgerald men are the scum of the earth,' Ned said with feeling. 'I know them too damn well.'

'Doubtless. Unfortunately, marriage is not just about being in love. For instance, I really need to be married.'

Ned was shocked. 'Why?'

'A widow is a nuisance. I could live with my son, but no boy really wants his mother around all the time. Queen Elizabeth likes me, but a single woman at court is assumed to be a busybody. And if she's attractive, she makes the married women nervous. No, I need a husband, and Robin Twyford will be perfect.'

'You're going to marry Lord Twyford?'

'I think so, yes.'

'Does he know about this?'

She laughed. 'No, but he thinks I'm wonderful.'

'You are, but you might be wasted on Robin Twyford.'

'Don't condescend. He's fifty-five, but he's sprightly and smart and he makes me laugh.'

Ned realized he should be gracious. 'My darling, I hope you'll be very happy.'

'Bless you.'

'Are you going to the play tonight?'

'Yes.' She loved plays, as he did.

'I'll see you then.'

'If Twyford is there, be nice to him. No silly jealousy.'

Ned's jealousy was focussed elsewhere, but he did not say so. 'I promise.'

'Thank you.' She sucked his nipple.

'That feels good.' He heard the bell of St Martin-in-the-Fields. 'But I have to attend upon her majesty.'

'Not yet, you don't.' She sucked the other nipple.

'But soon.'

'Don't worry,' she said, rolling on top of him. 'I'll be quick.'

Half an hour later, Ned was walking briskly along the Strand.

Queen Elizabeth had not yet appointed a new bishop of Kingsbridge to replace Julius, and Ned wanted the dean of Kingsbridge, Luke Richards, to get the job. Dean Luke was the right man – and also a friend of the Willard family.

Everyone at court wanted jobs for their friends, and Ned hesitated to pester the queen with his own personal preferences. He had learned, during five years in Elizabeth's service, how quickly her amity could turn sour if a courtier lost sight of who served whom. So he had bided his time. However, today the queen planned to discuss bishops with her secretary of state, Sir William Cecil, and Cecil had told Ned to be there.

The palace called White Hall was a sprawl of dozens of buildings, courtyards and gardens, including a tennis court. Ned knew his way to the royal apartment and went quickly through the guardroom to a large waiting room. He was relieved to find that Cecil had not yet arrived. Susannah had been quick, as promised, and she had not delayed Ned too much.

Also in the outer chamber was the Spanish ambassador, Álvaro de la Quadra. He was pacing restlessly and looked angry, though Ned suspected the emotion might be at least partly faked. An ambassador's job was difficult, Ned reflected: when his master was impassioned he had to convey that emotion, whether he shared it or not.

It was only a few minutes before the secretary of state came in and swept Ned along with him to the presence chamber.

Queen Elizabeth was now thirty, and she had lost the girlish bloom that had once made her almost beautiful. She was heavier, and her fondness for sugary treats had damaged her teeth. But she was in a good mood today.

'Before we get on to bishops, let's have the Spanish ambassador in,' she said. Ned guessed that she had been waiting for Cecil, not wanting to be alone for a confrontation with Quadra, who represented the most powerful monarch in Europe.

Quadra's greetings to the queen were so brisk as to be almost offensive, then he said: 'A Spanish galleon has been attacked by English pirates.'

'I'm very sorry to hear that,' said the queen.

'Three noblemen were killed! Several sailors also died, and the ship was severely damaged before the pirates fled.'

Reading between the lines, Ned guessed that the galleon had got the worst of the encounter. King Felipe's pride was hurt, hence his ire.

Elizabeth said: 'I'm afraid I can't control what my subjects do when they're at sea and far from home. No monarch can.'

What Elizabeth said was only half the truth. It was difficult to control ships at sea, but the other side of the story was that Elizabeth did not try very hard. Merchant ships could get away with murder, often literally, because of the role they played in the security of her kingdom. In times of war the monarch could order merchant ships to join forces with the royal navy. Together they formed the main defence of an island nation with no standing army. Elizabeth was like the owner of a vicious dog that is useful in scaring off intruders.

Elizabeth went on: 'Anyway, where did this happen?'

'Off the coast of Hispaniola.'

Cecil, who had studied law at Gray's Inn, asked: 'And who fired the first shot?'

That was an astute question. 'I do not have that information,' said Quadra, and Ned took that to mean the Spaniards had fired first. Quadra came close to confirming his suspicion when he blustered: 'However, a ship of his majesty King Felipe would be entirely justified in firing on any vessel involved in criminal activity.'

Cecil said: 'What sort of crime are we talking about?'

'The English ship did not have permission to sail to New Spain. No foreign ships may do so.'

'And do we know what the captain was up to in the New World?'

'Selling slaves!'

Elizabeth said: 'Let me make sure I understand you,' and Ned wondered if Quadra could hear, as clearly as Ned could, the dangerous note in her voice. 'An English vessel, innocently doing business with willing buyers in Hispaniola, is fired upon by a Spanish galleon – and *you* are complaining to *me* because the English fired back?'

'They were committing a crime just by being there! Your majesty is well aware that his holiness the Pope has granted jurisdiction over the entire New World to the kings of Spain and Portugal.'

The queen's voice became icy. 'And his majesty King Felipe is well aware that the Pope does not have the authority to grant this or that part of God's earth to one monarch or another at his pleasure!'

'The holy father in his wisdom—'

'God's body!' Elizabeth exploded, using a curse that deeply offended Catholics such as Quadra. 'If you fire upon Englishmen just for being in the New World, your ships must take their chances! Don't complain to me of the consequences. You are dismissed.'

Quadra bowed, then looked sly. 'Don't you want to know the name of the English ship?'

'Tell me.'

'It was the *Hawk*, based at Combe Harbour, and its captain is Jonas Bacon.' Quadra looked at Ned. 'The master gunner is someone called Barnabas Willard.'

Ned gasped. 'My brother!'

'Your brother,' said Quadra with evident satisfaction, 'and, by generally accepted laws, a pirate.' He bowed again to the queen. 'I humbly bid your majesty good day.'

When he had gone, Elizabeth said to Ned: 'Did you know?'

'Some of it,' said Ned, trying to collect his thoughts. 'Three years ago, my uncle Jan in Antwerp wrote to say that Barney was on his way home aboard the *Hawk*. We guessed that he got diverted. But we had no idea that he might have crossed the Atlantic!'

'I hope he gets home safely,' the queen said. 'Now, speaking of Kingsbridge, who can we have as bishop?'

Ned missed his cue, still being dazed by the news of Barney; but after a pause Cecil prompted him by saying: 'Ned knows of a suitable candidate.'

Ned shook himself. 'Luke Richards. Aged forty-five. He's already the dean.'

'A friend of yours, I suppose,' the queen said sniffily.

'Yes, your majesty.'

'What's he like?'

'A moderate man. He is a good Protestant – although honesty compels me to tell your majesty that five years ago he was a good Catholic.'

Cecil frowned in disapproval, but Queen Elizabeth laughed heartily. 'Excellent,' she said. 'That's just the kind of bishop I like!'

*

MARGERY HAD BEEN married for five years, and every day of those years she had thought about running away.

Bart Shiring was not a bad husband by general standards. He had never beaten her. She had to submit to sex with him now and again, but most of the time he took his pleasure elsewhere, so in that respect he was like most noblemen. He was disappointed that they had no children, and all men believed that such a failure was the woman's fault, but he did not accuse her of witchcraft, as some husbands would have. All the same, she hated him.

Her dream of escape took many forms. She thought about entering a French nunnery, but of course Bart would find her and bring her back. She could cut her hair, dress as a boy, and run away to sea; but there was no privacy on a ship and she would be discovered within a day. She could saddle her favourite horse one morning and just never come back, but where would she go? London appealed, but how would she make a living? She knew a little of how the world worked, and it was common knowledge that girls who fled to the big city usually ended up as prostitutes.

There were times when she was tempted to commit the sin of suicide.

What kept her alive was her clandestine work for England's deprived Catholics. It gave meaning to her existence, and in addition it was exciting, though frightening. Without it she would have been nothing more than a sad victim of circumstance. With it she was an adventurer, an outlaw, a secret agent for God.

When Bart was away from home she was almost happy. She liked having the bed to herself: no one snoring, belching or lurching out of bed in the middle of the night to piss in the pot. She enjoyed being alone in the morning while she washed and dressed. She liked her boudoir, with its little shelf of books and sprays of greenery in jugs. She could come back to her room in the afternoon, to sit alone and read poetry or study her Latin Bible, without being asked scornfully why any normal person would want to do such a thing.

It did not happen often enough. When Bart travelled it was usually to Kingsbridge, and then Margery went with him, taking the opportunity to see friends and connect with the clandestine Catholics there. But this time Bart had gone to Combe Harbour, and Margery was enjoying her own company.

She appeared at supper, of course. Earl Swithin had married a second time, to a girl younger than Margery, but the teenage countess had died giving birth to her first, stillborn child. So Margery was again the lady of the house, and meals were her responsibility. Tonight she had ordered mutton with cinnamon and honey. At table were just Earl Swithin and Stephen Lincoln, who now lived at New Castle: officially he was the secretary, but in fact he was the earl's priest. He said Mass in the chapel for the family and their servants every Sunday, except when he and Margery were away doing the same thing somewhere else.

Although everyone was discreet, such a practice could not remain hidden for ever. By now a lot of people knew or guessed that Catholic services were going on at New Castle and, probably, all over England. The Puritans in Parliament – all men, of course – were infuriated by this. But Queen Elizabeth refused to enforce the laws. It was a compromise that Margery was beginning to recognize as typical of Elizabeth. The queen was a heretic, but she was also a sensible woman, and Margery thanked God for that.

She left the supper table as soon as it was polite to. She had a genuine excuse: her housekeeper was ill, and probably dying, and Margery wanted to make sure the poor woman was as comfortable as possible for the night.

She made her way to the servants' quarters. Sal Brendon was lying in an alcove to one side of the kitchen. She and Margery had got off to a rocky start, five years ago, but Margery had slowly made an ally of her, and eventually they had run the house as a team. Sadly, Sal had developed a lump in one of her ample breasts, and over the past year had been transformed from a fleshy middle-aged sexpot into a skeleton with skin.

Sal's tumour had broken through the skin and spread to her shoulder. It was heavily bandaged in an attempt to suppress the bad smell. Margery encouraged her to drink some sherry wine, and sat talking to her for a while. Sal told her, with bitter resignation, that the earl had not bothered to come to see her for weeks. She felt she had wasted her life trying to make an ungrateful man happy.

Margery retired to her room and cheered herself up with an outrageously funny French book called *Pantagruel*, about a race of giants, some of whom had testicles so large that three would fill a sack. Stephen Lincoln would have disapproved of the book, but there was no real harm in it. She sat by her candle for an hour, chuckling now and again; then she undressed.

She slept in a knee-length linen shift. The bed was a four-poster, but she kept the curtains tied back. The house had tall windows, and there was a half-moon, so the room was not completely dark. She climbed under the bedclothes and closed her eyes.

She would have liked to show *Pantagruel* to Ned Willard. He would delight in the author's fantastic comic inventions the way he had in the Mary Magdalene play here at New Castle. Whenever she came across something interesting or unusual she wondered what Ned would have to say about it.

She often thought of him at night. Foolishly, she felt that her wicked ideas were more secret when she was lying in the dark. Now she remembered the first time Ned and she had kissed and petted, in the disused old oven, and she wished they had gone farther. The memory made her feel warm and cosy inside. She knew it was a sin to touch herself down there, but – as sometimes happened – tonight the feeling came over her without touching, and she could not help pressing her thighs together and riding the waves of pleasure.

Afterwards she felt sad. She thought about Sal Brendon's regrets, and she pictured herself on her own deathbed and wondered if she would feel as bitter as Sal. Tears came to her eyes. She reached out to a small chest beside the bed where she kept her private things and took out a linen handkerchief embroidered with acorns. It was Ned's: she had never given it back. She buried her face in it, imagining that she was with him again, and he was gently touching it to her cheeks, drying her tears.

Then she heard breathing.

There were no locks at New Castle, but she normally shut her door. However, she had not heard it open. Perhaps she had left it ajar. But who would enter silently?

The breathing could come from a dog: the earl's hounds were allowed to roam the corridors at night, and one might have nosed in curiously. She listened: the breathing was restrained, like that of a man trying to be quiet – dogs could not do that.

She opened her eyes and sat upright, her heart beating fast. In the silver moonlight she made out the figure of a man in a nightshirt. 'Get out of my room,' she said firmly, but there was a tremor in her voice.

A moment of silence followed. It was too dark to identify the man. Had Bart come home unexpectedly? No – no one travelled after dark. It could not be a servant: one of them would risk death entering a noblewoman's bedroom at night. It could not be Stephen Lincoln, for she felt sure he was not drawn to women's beds – if he were to sin in that way it would be with a pretty boy.

The man spoke. 'Don't be afraid.'

It was Swithin.

'Go away,' said Margery.

He sat on the edge of her bed. 'We're both lonely,' he said. His speech was a little slurred, as it always was by the end of the evening.

She moved to get up, but he stopped her with a strong arm.

'You know you want it,' he said.

'No, I don't!' She struggled against his grip, but he was big and powerful, and had not drunk enough to weaken him.

'I like a bit of resistance,' he said.

'Let me go!' she cried.

With his free hand he pulled the bedclothes off. Her shift was rucked up around her hips, and he stared hungrily at her thighs. Irrationally, she felt ashamed, and tried to cover her nakedness with her hands. 'Ah,' he said with pleasure. 'Shy.'

She did not know what to do to get rid of him.

With surprising swiftness he grabbed her by both ankles and pulled sharply. She was dragged down the bed and her shoulders fell back onto the mattress. While she was still shocked he jumped onto the bed and lay on her. He was heavy and his breath was foul. He groped her breasts with his mutilated hand.

Her voice came out in a high squeal. 'Go away now or I'll scream and everyone will know.'

'I'll tell them you seduced me,' he said. 'They'll believe me, not you.'

She froze. She knew he was right. People said that women could not control their desires, but men could. Margery thought it was the other way round. But she could imagine the scenes of accusation and counter-accusation, the men all siding with the earl, the women looking at her with suspicion. Bart would be torn, for he knew his father well, yet in the end he might not have the courage to go against the earl.

She felt Swithin fumble to pull up his nightshirt. Perhaps he would be impotent, she thought in desperate hope. It happened sometimes with Bart, usually because he had drunk too much wine, though he always blamed her for putting him off. Swithin had certainly drunk a lot.

But not too much. She felt his penis pushing against her and that hope faded.

She pressed her legs close together. He tried to force them apart. But it was awkward: he had to rest his considerable weight on one elbow while shoving the other hand between her thighs. He grunted in frustration. Perhaps she could make it so difficult that he would lose his erection and give up in disgust.

He hissed: 'Open your legs, bitch.'

She pressed them closer together.

With his free hand, he punched her face.

It was like an explosion. He was powerfully built, with big shoulders and strong arms, and he had done a lot of punching in his lifetime. She had no idea that such a blow could hurt so much. She felt as if her head would come off her neck. Her mouth filled with blood. Momentarily she lost all power of resistance, and in that second he forced her thighs apart and shoved his penis into her.

After that it did not take long. She endured his thrusts in a daze. Her face hurt so much that she could hardly feel the rest of her body. He finished and rolled off her, breathing hard.

She got off the bed, went into the corner of the room, and sat on the floor, holding her aching head. A minute later she heard him pad out of the room, still panting.

She wiped her face with the handkerchief that was, to her surprise, still clutched tightly in her hand. When she was sure he had gone she returned to the bed. She lay there, crying softly, until at last sleep brought blessed unconsciousness.

In the morning she might have thought she had dreamed it, except that one side of her face was agony. She looked in a glass and saw that it was swollen and discoloured. At breakfast she made up a story about having fallen out of bed: she did not care whether anyone believed it, but for her to accuse the earl would get her into even more trouble.

Swithin ate a hearty breakfast and acted as if nothing had happened.

As soon as he left the table, Margery told the servant to leave the room and went to sit next to Stephen. 'Swithin came to my room last night,' she said in a low voice.

'What for?' he said.

She stared at him. He was a priest, but he was twenty-eight years old and had been a student at Oxford, so he could not be completely innocent.

After a moment he said: 'Oh!'

'He forced himself on me.'

'Did you struggle?'

'Of course, but he's stronger than I am.' She touched her swollen face with her fingertips, careful not to press. 'I didn't fall out of bed. His fist did this.'

'Did you scream?'

'I threatened to. He said he would tell everyone that I seduced him. And that they would believe him and not me. He was right about that – as you must know.'

Stephen looked uncomfortable.

There was a silence. At last Margery said: 'What should I do?'

'Pray for forgiveness,' said Stephen.

Margery frowned. 'What on earth do you mean?'

'Ask forgiveness for sin. God will be merciful.'

Margery's voice rose. 'What sin? I haven't committed a sin! I am the victim of a sin – how can you tell me to ask forgiveness?'

'Don't shout! I'm telling you that God will forgive your adultery.'

'What about his sin?'

'The earl's?'

'Yes. He has committed a sin much worse than adultery. What are you going to do about it?'

'I'm a priest, not a sheriff.'

She stared at him in disbelief. 'Is that it? Is that your response to a woman who has been raped by her father-in-law? To say that you're not a sheriff?'

He looked away.

Margery stood up. 'You worm,' she said. 'You utter worm.' She left the room.

She felt like renouncing her religion, but that did not last long. She thought of Job, whose tribulations had been a test of his faith. 'Curse God, and die,' his wife had said, but Job had refused. If everyone who met a pusillanimous priest rejected God, there would not be many Christians. But what was she going to do? Bart was not due back until tomorrow. What if Swithin came again tonight?

She spent the day making her plans. She ordered a young maid, Peggy, to sleep in her room, on a palliasse at the foot of her bed. It was common for single women to have a maidservant with them at night, though Margery herself had never liked the practice. Now she saw the point.

She got a dog. There were always a few puppies around the castle, and she found one young enough to be taught to be loyal to her personally. He had no name, and she dubbed him Mick. He could make a noise now, and in time he might be trained to protect her.

She marvelled over Swithin's behaviour during the day. She saw him again at dinner and supper. He hardly spoke to her, which was normal; and he talked to Stephen Lincoln about current affairs: the New World, the design of ships, and Queen Elizabeth's continuing indecision about whom she should marry. It was as if he had forgotten the wicked crime he had committed during the night.

When she went to bed, she closed her door firmly, then, with the help of Peggy, dragged a chest across the doorway. She wished it was heavier, but then they would not have been able to move it.

Finally, she put a belt on over her nightdress and attached a small knife in a sheath. She resolved to get herself a bigger dagger as soon as she could.

Poor Peggy was terrified, but Margery did not explain her actions, for that would require that she accuse the earl.

She got into bed. Peggy blew out the candles and curled up on her mattress. Mick was evidently puzzled by his new quarters but took the change with canine stoicism, and went to sleep in front of the fireplace.

Margery got into bed. She could not lie on her left side because contact, even with a feather pillow, hurt her bruised face too much. She lay on her back with her eyes wide open. She knew she was not going to sleep, as surely as she knew she was not going to fly out of the window.

If only she could get through tonight, she thought. Tomorrow Bart would be home, and after that she would make sure she was never left alone with Swithin. But even as she said that to herself she realized it was not possible. Bart decided whether or not she would accompany him, and he did not always consult her wishes. Probably, he left her behind when he planned to see one of his mistresses, or to take all his friends to a brothel, or to indulge in some other entertainment at which a wife would be an embarrassment. Margery could not go against his wishes without a reason, and she could not reveal her reason. She was trapped, and Swithin knew it.

The only way out was for her to kill Swithin. But if she did so, she would be hanged. No excuses would help her escape punishment.

Unless she could make it look like an accident . . .

Would God forgive her? Perhaps. Surely he did not intend her to be raped.

As she contemplated the situation, the door handle rattled.

Mick barked nervously.

Someone was trying to get in. In a frightened voice Peggy said: 'Who can it be?'

The handle was turned again, then there was the sound of a bump as the door hit the chest that was an inch away.

Margery said loudly: 'Go away!'

She heard a grunt outside, like that of a man making an effort, and then the chest moved.

Peggy screamed.

Margery leaped off the bed.

The chest scraped across the floor, the door opened wide enough for a man to enter, and Swithin came in in his nightshirt.

Mick barked at him. Swithin kicked out and caught the dog's chest with his foot. Mick gave a terrified whimper and darted out through the gap.

Swithin saw Peggy and said: 'Get out, before I give you a kicking too.'

Peggy fled.

Swithin stepped closer to Margery.

She drew the knife from her belt and said: 'If you don't go away, I'll kill you.'

Swithin lashed out with his left arm, a sweeping motion that struck Margery's right wrist with the force of a hammer. The knife went flying from her grasp. He grabbed her upper arms, lifted her off the floor effortlessly, and threw her back onto the bed. Then he climbed on top of her.

'Open your legs,' he said. 'You know you want to.'

'I hate you,' she said.

He raised his fist. 'Open your legs, or I'll punch you in the same place again.'

She could not bear for her face to be touched, and she felt that if he punched her she would die. She began to weep, helplessly, and parted her thighs.

*

ROLLO FITZGERALD did all he could to keep tabs on the Kingsbridge Puritans. His main source of information was Donal Gloster, Dan Cobley's chief clerk. Donal had a dual motivation: he hated the Cobley family for spurning him as a suitor for their daughter, and he was greedy for Rollo's money because Dan underpaid him.

Rollo met Donal regularly at a tavern called the Cock at Gallows Cross. The place was in fact a brothel, so Rollo was able to rent a private room where they could talk unobserved. If any of the girls gossiped about their meetings, people would assume they were homosexual lovers. That was a sin and a crime, but men who were on gossiping terms with prostitutes were not generally in any position to make accusations.

'Dan is angry about Dean Luke being made bishop,' Donal said one day in the autumn of 1563. 'The Puritans think Luke turns whichever way the wind blows.'

'They're right,' Rollo said contemptuously. Changing your beliefs with every change of monarch was called 'policy', and people who did it were 'politicians'. Rollo hated them. 'I expect the queen chose Luke for his malleability. Who did Dan want for bishop?'

'Father Jeremiah.'

Rollo nodded. Jeremiah was parson of St John's in Loversfield, a southern neighbourhood of Kingsbridge. He had always been a reformer, though he had stayed in the Church. He would have made an extreme Protestant bishop, highly intolerant of people who missed the old ways. 'Thank heaven Dan didn't get his way.'

'He hasn't given up.'

'What do you mean? The decision is made. The queen has announced it. Luke will be consecrated the day after tomorrow.'

'Dan has plans. That's why I asked to see you. You'll be interested.'

'Go on.'

'For the consecration of a new bishop, the clergy always bring out St Adolphus.'

'Ah, yes.' Kingsbridge Cathedral had possessed the bones of St Adolphus for centuries. They were kept in a jewelled reliquary that was on display in the chancel. Pilgrims came from all over Western Europe to pray to the saint for health and good fortune. 'But perhaps Luke will leave the bones where they are this time.'

Donal shook his head. 'Luke is going to bring them out for the procession, because that's what the people of Kingsbridge want. He says no one is worshipping the bones, so it's not idolatry. They are just revering the memory of the holy man.'

'Always a compromiser, that Luke.'

'The Puritans think it's blasphemy.'

'No surprise.'

'On Sunday they will intervene.'

Rollo raised his eyebrows. This was interesting. 'What are they going to do?'

'When the bones are elevated during the ceremony, they will seize the reliquary and desecrate the remains of the saint – all the while calling on God to strike them dead if he disapproves.'

Rollo was shocked. 'They would do that to relics that have been cherished by the priests of Kingsbridge for five hundred years?'

'Yes.'

Even Queen Elizabeth frowned on this kind of thing. A lot of iconoclasm had gone on during the reign of Edward VI, but Elizabeth had passed a law making it a crime to destroy pictures and objects belonging to the Church. However, the ban had been only partially successful: there were a lot of ultra-Protestants. 'I shouldn't be so surprised,' Rollo said.

'I thought you'd like to know.'

He was right about that. A secret was a weapon. But more than that, the possession of knowledge that others did not share always filled Rollo with elation. He could hug it to himself at night and feel powerful.

He reached into his pocket and handed Donal five of the gold coins called angels, each worth ten shillings or half a pound. 'Well done,' he said.

Donal pocketed the money with a satisfied air. 'Thank you.'

Rollo could not help thinking of Judas Iscariot's thirty pieces of silver. 'Stay in touch,' he said, and left.

He crossed Merthin's bridge to the city centre and walked up the main street. There was a cold autumn bite to the air that seemed to intensify his excitement. As he looked up at the ancient holy stones of the cathedral he thrilled with horror to think of the blasphemy that was planned, and he vowed to prevent it.

Then it occurred to him that he might do more than just prevent it. Was there a way he could turn the incident to advantage?

Walking slowly, thinking hard, he went into Priory Gate, his father's palace. Building it had almost broken the Fitzgerald family. But, in the end, it was the Willard family who had been broken. Now five years old, the house had lost its brand-new sheen and had mellowed. The pale grey of the stones, from the same quarry as those of the cathedral, had darkened a little in the English rain and the smoke of two thousand Kingsbridge fireplaces.

Earl Swithin was visiting, with Bart and Margery. They had come for the consecration of the new bishop. They were staying at the earl's house on Leper Island, but spent much of their time at Priory Gate, and Rollo hoped they were here now, for he was bursting to tell Swithin the news he had heard from Donal. The earl would be even more outraged than Rollo himself.

He went up the marble staircase and entered Sir Reginald's parlour. Although there were grander rooms in the house, this was where people gathered to talk business. Sir Reginald, old enough now to be sensitive to cold weather, had a fire blazing. The guests were there, and a jug of wine stood on a side table.

Rollo felt proud to see the earl of the county making himself comfortable in the house. Rollo knew that his father was equally proud, though he never said so – but in Swithin's presence he became more restrained and judicious in his conversation, presenting himself as a wise and experienced counsellor, repressing the impulsive, belligerent side of his character.

Bart was by Swithin's side, physically a younger version of the earl, though not such a strong character. Bart revered his powerful, assertive father, but he might never match him.

The old guard are still here, Rollo thought, despite Elizabeth. They had suffered reverses but they were not beaten.

He sat next to his sister, Margery, and accepted a cup of wine from his mother. He was vaguely worried about Margery. She was only twenty, but looked older. She had lost weight, there was no colour in her cheeks, and she had a bruise on her jaw. She had always been proud of her appearance, to the point of vanity, in his opinion, but today she wore a drab dress and her hair was greasy and unkempt. He had no doubt that she was unhappy, but he was not sure why. He had asked her directly whether Bart was cruel to her, but she had said firmly: 'Bart is a decent husband.' Perhaps she was disappointed that she had not yet conceived a child. Whatever the reason for her unhappiness, he just hoped she was not going to cause trouble.

He took a gulp of wine and said: 'I've got some disturbing news. I've been talking to Donal Gloster.'

'Despicable character,' said Sir Reginald.

'Contemptible, but useful. Without him we would not know that Dan Cobley and the Puritans are planning an outrage on Sunday, at the consecration of Luke Richards, whom they find insufficiently heretical for their taste.'

'An outrage?' said his father. 'What are they going to do?'

Rollo dropped his bombshell. 'Desecrate the bones of the saint.'

There was a moment of stunned silence.

Margery whispered: 'No.'

Earl Swithin said: 'I'll stick my sword in his guts, if he tries it.'

Rollo's eyes widened. The violence might not be one-sided: he had not thought of that.

His mother spoke up feistily. 'If you kill a man in church, Swithin, you'll be executed. Even an earl can't get away with that.' Lady Jane's perky charm allowed her to speak bluntly.

Swithin looked downcast. 'You're right, damn it.'

Rollo said: 'I think she may be wrong, my lord.'

'How?'

'Yes,' said Lady Jane, arching her eyebrows. 'Tell us how I'm wrong, my clever son.'

Rollo concentrated, the plan forming in his mind while he spoke. 'Committing a premeditated murder in a church: yes, even an earl might be executed for that. But think on. The mayor of Kingsbridge could tell a different story.'

Swithin looked baffled, but Reginald said: 'Go on, Rollo – this is interesting.'

'Any event may be good or evil, depending on the point of view. Consider this: a group of armed toughs enter a city, kill the men, rape the women, and make off with all the valuables; they are wicked criminals – unless the city is in Assyria and the victims are Muslims, in which case the armed men are not criminals but Crusaders and heroes.'

Margery said disgustedly: 'And you're not even being satirical.'

Rollo did not understand that.

Sir Reginald said impatiently: 'So what?'

'What will happen on Sunday is that the Puritans will attack the clergy and attempt to steal the relics, contrary to the law passed by Queen Elizabeth. Then faithful Christians in the congregation will leap to the defence of Elizabeth's new bishop and save the bones of the saint. Even better if no swords are used, though, naturally, men will have with them the everyday knives they use to cut their meat at table. Sadly, in the ensuing melee the leader of the Kingsbridge Puritans, Dan Cobley, will be fatally stabbed; but, as he is the main instigator of the riot, it will be felt that this was God's will. Anyway, it will not be possible to determine who struck the fatal blow. And you, Father, as the mayor of Kingsbridge, will write a report to her majesty the queen telling that plain story.'

Sir Reginald said thoughtfully: 'The death of Dan Cobley would be a godsend. He's the leader of the Puritans.'

'And our family's worst enemy,' Rollo added.

Margery said severely: 'A lot of other people could be killed.'

Rollo was not surprised by her disapproval. She was staunch, but she believed that the Catholic faith should be promoted by all means short of violence.

Earl Swithin said: 'She's right, it's hazardous. But we can't let that stand in our way.' He smiled. 'Women worry about such things,' he said. 'That's why God made man the master.'

*

LYING IN BED, thinking over the day's events, Margery despised Dan Cobley and the Puritans for planning such a dreadful desecration, but she felt almost as much contempt for her father and her brother. Their response was to exploit the sacrilege to strike a political blow.

Both Reginald and Rollo might be hurt in the fracas, but she found herself more or less indifferent to this danger. She had lost all feeling for them. They had used her ruthlessly for their own social advancement – just as they were planning to use the sacrilege of the Puritans. The fact that they had ruined her life meant nothing to them. Their care for her when she was a child had been such as they might have shown for a foal that promised to turn into a useful carthorse one day. Tears came to her eyes when she thought nostalgically of the childhood time when she had thought they really loved her.

She was far from indifferent to the possibility that Swithin might be hurt. She longed with all her heart for him to be killed, or at least maimed so badly that he could never again force himself upon her. In her prayers she begged God to take Swithin to hell on Sunday morning. She went to sleep imagining a time when she was free of her tormentor.

She woke up realizing that it was up to her to make her wish come true.

Swithin was putting himself in danger, but there had to be a way for her to make it more certain that he would suffer injury. Because of her clandestine work with Stephen Lincoln, Rollo and Reginald regarded her as a rock-solid ally, and it never occurred to them to keep anything from her. She knew the secret, and she had to use it.

She got up early. Her mother was already in the kitchen,

giving orders to the staff for the day's meals. Lady Jane was perceptive, so she had to know that something was badly wrong in Margery's life, but she said nothing. She would give advice if asked, but she would not probe uninvited. Perhaps there were things in her own marriage that she preferred to keep to herself.

She asked Margery to go to the riverside and see whether there was some good fresh fish for sale. It was a rainy Saturday morning, and Margery put on an old coat. She picked up a basket for the fish then went out. In the square, the market traders were setting up their stalls.

She had to warn the Puritans of the trap that awaited them, so that they would go to the cathedral armed to defend themselves. But she could not knock on Dan Cobley's door and say she had a secret to impart. For one thing, she would be seen by passers-by, and the fact that Margery of Shiring had called on Dan Cobley would be surprising news that went around town in minutes. For another thing, Dan would not believe her, suspecting a trick. She needed some undercover means of warning him.

She could not think of a way out of this dilemma. She was deep in thought as she crossed the square. Her reverie was disturbed by a voice that made her pulse race. 'I'm very glad to see you!'

She looked up, shocked and thrilled. There, in a costly black coat, looking the same as ever, was Ned Willard. He seemed to Margery to be a guardian angel sent by God.

She realized with dismay that she looked slovenly, her coat unflattering and her hair tied up in a rag. Fortunately, Ned did not appear to care. He stood there as if he would be happy to smile at her for ever.

'You have a sword, now,' she said.

Ned shrugged. 'Courtiers wear swords,' he said. 'I've even had fencing lessons, just so that I know what to do with it.'

Getting over her surprise, she began to think logically. Clearly this was a chance to use the secret. If people noticed her talking to Ned, they would nod sagely and tell each other that she had never really got over him; and her family would think the same if they got to hear of it.

She was not sure how much to tell him. 'There's going to be a fight at the consecration,' she began. 'Dan Cobley is going to seize the bones of the saint.'

'How do you know?'

'Donal Gloster told Rollo.'

Ned raised his eyebrows. Of course he had not known that Dan Cobley's right-hand man was a spy for the Catholics. But he made no comment, seeming to tuck the revelation away for future consideration.

Margery went on: 'Rollo told Swithin, and Swithin is going to use it as an excuse to start a fight and kill Dan.'

'In the church?'

'Yes. He thinks he'll get away with it because he will be protecting the clergy and the relics.'

'Swithin's not smart enough to think of that.'

'No, it was Rollo's idea.'

'The devil.'

'I've been trying to figure out how to warn the Puritans so that they can come armed. But now you can do it.'

'Yes,' he said. 'Leave it to me.'

She resisted the temptation to throw her arms around him and kiss him.

*

'WE MUST CALL off the ceremony,' Dean Luke said when Ned told him what was going to happen.

'But when would you reschedule it?'

'I don't know.'

They were in the chancel, standing next to one of the mighty pillars that held up the tower. Looking up, Ned recalled that this was Merthin's tower, rebuilt by him after the old one caused a collapse, according to the history of Kingsbridge known as Timothy's Book. Merthin must have built well, for that had been two hundred years ago.

Ned turned his gaze to Luke's anxious face and mild blue eyes. He was a priest who would avoid conflict at all costs. 'We can't postpone the consecration,' Ned said. 'It would be a political blow to Queen Elizabeth. People would say that the Kingsbridge Puritans had prevented her from appointing the bishop of her choice. Ultra-Protestants in other cities would think they had the right to say who should be their bishop, and they might start copycat riots. The queen would crucify you and me for letting it happen.'

'Oh, dear,' said Luke. 'Then we'll have to leave the saint inside his railings.'

Ned glanced across at the tomb of St Adolphus. The monument was closed off by locked iron railings. A little group of pilgrims were on their knees, staring through the grille at the reliquary. It was a gold casket in the shape of a church, with archways and turrets and a spire. Set into the gold were pearls, rubies and sapphires, glittering in the watery sunlight that came through the great east window.

'I'm not sure that will be enough,' Ned said. 'Now that they've planned this, they may break down the railings.'

Luke looked panicky. 'I can't have a riot during my consecration!'

'No, indeed. That would be almost as bad as cancellation, from the point of view of the queen.'

'What, then?'

Ned knew what he wanted to do, but he hesitated. There was something Margery was not telling him. She had wanted him to arm the Puritans, not avoid the brawl altogether. It was surprising that she had taken that line, for she was strongly against religious violence of any kind. This thought had occurred to him vaguely while talking to her, but he saw it more clearly now in retrospect. Something else was going on, but he did not know what.

However, he could not base his actions on such nebulous notions. He put thoughts of Margery aside. He needed to offer Luke a safe way out. 'We have to take the gunpowder out of the cannon,' he said.

'What do you mean?'

'We have to get rid of the relics.'

Luke was shocked. 'We can't just throw them away!'

'Of course we can't. But we can bury them – with all due ceremony. Hold a funeral service tomorrow at first light – just you and one or two priests. Tonight, have George Cox dig a hole somewhere inside the cathedral – don't tell anyone where.' George Cox was the gravedigger. 'Bury the bones, in the golden casket, and let George replace the stones of the floor so that no one can tell they've been disturbed.'

Luke was thinking this through with a worried frown. 'When people arrive for the consecration it will already be done. But what will they say? They will see that the saint has gone.'

'Put up a notice on the iron railings saying that St Adolphus is buried here in the cathedral. Then explain, in your sermon, that the saint is still here, blessing us with his presence, but he has been buried in a secret grave to protect his remains from people who might wish to violate them.'

'That's clever,' Luke said admiringly. 'The people will be content, but there will be nothing for the Puritans to object to. Their protest will be like gunpowder that has separated.'

'A good image. Use it in your sermon.'

Luke nodded.

Ned said: 'So that's settled.'

'I have to discuss it with the chapter.'

Ned suppressed an impatient retort. 'Not really. You're the bishop-elect.' He smiled. 'You may command.'

Luke looked uncomfortable. 'It's always better to explain to people the reasons for commands.'

Ned decided not to fight a hypothetical battle. 'Do it your way. I'll come here at dawn to witness the burial.'

'Very well.'

Ned was not totally sure that Luke would go through with it. Perhaps a reminder of Luke's debt to him would help. 'I'm glad I was able to persuade the queen that you're the right man to be bishop of Kingsbridge,' he said.

'I'm deeply grateful to you, Ned, for your faith in me.'

'I believe we'll work well together, in years to come, to prevent religious hatred.'

'Amen.'

Luke could yet change his mind about the whole idea, if one of his colleagues objected to burying the relics, but Ned could do no more for now. He resolved to see Luke again before nightfall and make sure of him.

He took his leave and walked down the nave, between the marching pillars, the leaping arches and the glowing windows, thinking how much good and evil this building had seen in the last four hundred years. When he stepped out of the west door, he saw Margery again, returning to her house with her fish basket over her arm. She caught his eye and turned to meet him.

In the cathedral porch she said: 'Did you do it?'

'I think I've avoided violence,' he said. 'I've persuaded Luke to bury the bones clandestinely, tomorrow morning, so that there will be nothing to fight over.'

He expected her to be pleased and grateful, but to his consternation she stared at him in horror for a long moment then said: 'No! That's not it.'

'What on earth are you talking about?'

'There has to be a fight.'

'But you were always so much against violence.'

'Swithin has to die!'

'Hush!' He took her elbow and led her back inside. In the north aisle was a side chapel dedicated to St Dymphna. She was not a popular figure, and the little space was empty. The painting of the saint being beheaded had been taken down to appease the Puritans.

He stood in front of Margery, holding her hands, and said: 'You'd better tell me what's wrong. Why does Swithin have to die?'

She said nothing, but he could see, watching her face, that a struggle was going on inside her, and he waited.

At last she said: 'When Bart is away from home, Swithin comes to my bed at night.'

Ned stared at her, aghast. She was being raped – by her father-in-law. It was obscene – and brutal. Hot rage possessed him, and he had to quell his emotions and think rationally. Questions leaped to his mind, but the answers were obvious.

'You resist him, but he's too strong, and he tells you that if you scream, he will say you seduced him, and everyone will believe him.'

Tears rolled down her cheeks. 'I knew you'd understand.'

'The man is an animal.'

'I shouldn't have told you. But perhaps God will take Swithin's life tomorrow.'

And if God won't, I will, Ned vowed, but he did not say it out loud. Instead he said: 'I'll talk to Luke again. I'll make sure there's a fight.'

'How?'

'I don't know. I have to think.'

'Don't risk your own life. That would be even worse.'

'Take your fish home,' he said.

She hesitated for a long moment. Then she said: 'You're the only person I can trust. The only one.'

He nodded. 'I know,' he said. 'Go home.'

She wiped her eyes on her sleeve and left the cathedral, and he followed her out a minute later.

If he had seen Swithin at that moment, he would have fallen on the earl and got his hands around the man's throat and choked the life out of him – or, perhaps, been run through by Swithin's sword, though he was too angry to fear that or anything else.

He turned and looked back at the mighty west front of the cathedral, wet now with the persistent slow English rain. That was the doorway through which people went to find God: how could Ned think of murder there? But he could hardly think of anything else.

He struggled to be cogent. Face it, he said to himself, in a fight with Swithin you might not win, and if you did, you would be hanged for murdering a nobleman. But you are smart, and Swithin is stupid, so come up with a clever way to put an end to him.

He turned away and crossed the market square. It was busy every Saturday, but today it was teeming with all the visitors who had come for tomorrow's ceremony. Normally, winding his way between the stalls, he would have automatically noted rising and falling prices, shortages and gluts, how much money people had and what they spent it on; but not now. He was aware of acquaintances greeting him, but he was too deep in thought to respond with more than a vague wave or a distracted nod. He reached the front door of the family house and went inside.

His mother had drifted unhappily into old age. Alice seemed to have shrunk inside her skin, and she walked with a stoop. She seemed to have lost interest in the world outside the house: she asked Ned perfunctory questions about his work with the queen and hardly listened to the answers. In the old days she would have been eager to hear about political manoeuvrings, and wanted to know all about how Elizabeth ran her household.

However, since Ned had left the house this morning, something seemed to have changed. His mother was in the main hall with their three servants: Janet Fife, the housekeeper; her husband, lame Malcolm; and their sixteen-year-old daughter, Eileen. They all looked animated. Ned guessed right away that they had good news. As soon as his mother saw him she said: 'Barney's back in England!'

Some things went right, Ned reflected, and he managed a smile. 'Where is he?'

'He landed at Combe Harbour with the Hawk. We got a message: he's only waiting to collect his pay – three years of it! – then he's coming home.'

'And he's safe and well? I told you he'd been to the New World.'

'But he's come home unhurt!'

'Well, we must prepare to celebrate – kill the fatted calf.'

Alice's jubilation was punctured. 'We haven't got a calf, fatted or otherwise.'

Young Eileen, who had once had a childish crush on Barney, said excitedly: 'We've got a six-month-old piglet out the back that my mother was planning to use for winter bacon. We could roast it on a spit.'

Ned was pleased. The whole family would be together again.

But Margery's torment came back to him as he sat down with his mother for the midday meal. She chatted animatedly, speculating about what kind of adventures Barney might have had in Seville, Antwerp and Hispaniola. Ned let her talk flow over him while he brooded.

Margery's idea had been to warn the Puritans so that they would come armed, and to hope that Swithin would die in the resulting brawl. But Ned had not known the full story, and despite the best of intentions he had put paid to her hopes. There would be no brawl, now: the relics would not be seen in the consecration ceremony, the Puritans would therefore not protest, and Swithin would have no pretext for a fight.

Could Ned now undo what he had done? It was next to impossible. Dean Luke would surely refuse to return to the original timetable in order to guarantee a riot.

Ned realized he could recreate the brawl scenario, simply by telling both sides that the relics would now be buried at dawn. But there was another snag. A brawl was unpredictable. Swithin might be hurt, but he might not. Ned needed to be surer than that, for Margery's sake.

Was there a way to turn tomorrow's burial ceremony into a trap for Swithin?

What if Ned could preserve Rollo's violent plan, but remove the justification?

A scheme began to take shape in his mind. Perhaps he could lure Swithin to the cathedral with false information. But of course the Catholics would not trust Ned. Who would they trust?

Then he remembered what Margery had told him about Donal Gloster being a spy. Rollo would trust Donal.

Ned began to feel hopeful again.

He left his family's dinner table as soon as he could. He walked down the main street, turned along Slaughterhouse Wharf, and went past the moorings to the Tanneries, a riverside neighbourhood of smelly industries and small houses. There he knocked on Donal Gloster's front door. It was opened by Donal's mother, a handsome middle-aged woman with Donal's full lips and thick dark hair. She looked wary. 'What brings you here, Mr Willard?'

'Good afternoon, Widow Gloster,' Ned said politely. 'I want to speak to Donal.'

'He's at work. You know where Dan Cobley's place of business is.'

Ned nodded. Dan had a warehouse down by the docks. 'I shan't disturb Donal at work. When do you expect him home?'

'He'll finish at sundown. But he usually goes to the Slaughterhouse tavern before coming home.'

'Thank you.'

'What do you want him for?'

'I don't mean him any harm.'

'Thank you,' she said, but she said it uncertainly, and Ned suspected she did not believe him.

He returned to the waterfront and sat on a coil of rope, gnawing at his plan, which was uncertain and dangerous, while he watched the bustle of commerce, the boats and carts arriving and leaving, loading and unloading grain and coal, stones from the quarry and timber from the forest, bales of cloth and barrels of wine. This was how his family had prospered: by buying in one place and selling in another, and pocketing the difference in the price. It was a simple thing, but it was the way to become rich – the only way, unless you were a nobleman and could force people to pay you rent for the land they farmed.

The afternoon darkened. The hatches were closed and the warehouses locked up, and men began to leave the docks, their faces eager for home and supper, or tavern and song, or dark lane and lover. Ned saw Donal come out of the Cobley building and head for the Slaughterhouse with the air of one who does not have to make a decision because he does the same thing every day.

Ned followed him into the inn. 'A quiet word with you, Donal, if I may.' These days, no one refused Ned a quiet word. He had become a man of power and importance, and everyone in Kingsbridge knew it. Strangely, this gave him no great satisfaction. Some men craved deference; others craved wine, or the bodies of beautiful women, or the monastic life of order and obedience. What did Ned crave? The answer came into his mind with a speed and effortlessness that took him by surprise: justice.

He would have to think about that.

He paid for two tankards of ale and steered Donal to a corner. As soon as they sat down, he said: 'You lead a dangerous life, Donal.'

'Ned Willard, always the cleverest boy in the class,' said Donal with an unpleasant twist of his lips.

'We're not at the Grammar School any longer. There we were only flogged for our mistakes. Now we get killed.'

Donal looked intimidated, but he put on a brave face. 'Then it's a good thing I don't make any.'

'If Dan Cobley and the Puritans find out about you and Rollo, they'll tear you to pieces.'

Donal turned white.

After a long moment he opened his mouth to speak, but Ned forestalled him. 'Don't deny it. That would be a waste of your time and mine. Focus on what you have to do to make sure that I keep your secret.'

Donal swallowed and managed a nod.

'What you told Rollo Fitzgerald yesterday was correct at the time, but it has changed.'

Donal's mouth dropped open. 'How—?'

'Never mind how I know what you told Rollo. All you need to understand is that the relics of the saint will be desecrated in the cathedral tomorrow – but the time has changed. Now it will be done at dawn, with few people present.'

'Why are you telling me?'

'So that you will tell Rollo.'

'You hate the Fitzgeralds – they ruined your family.'

'Don't try to figure this out. Just do what you're told and save your skin.'

'Rollo will ask how I know about the change.'

'Say you overheard Dan Cobley talking about it.'

'All right.'

'Go and see Rollo now. You must have some means of signalling that you need an urgent meeting.'

'I'll just finish my beer.'

'Wouldn't you rather be stone cold sober?'

Donal looked regretfully at his tankard.

Ned said: 'Now, Donal.'

Donal got up and left.

Ned left a few minutes later. He walked back up the main street. He felt uneasy. He had a plan, but it relied on a lot of people doing what he expected: Dean Luke, Donal Gloster, Rollo Fitzgerald and – most important of all, and most wilful – Earl Swithin. If one part of the chain were to break, the scheme would fail.

And now he had to add one more link.

He walked past the cathedral, the Bell Inn, and the new Fitzgerald palace called Priory Gate, and went into the Guild Hall. There he tapped on the door of Sheriff Matthewson's room and went in without waiting for an invitation. The sheriff was eating an early supper of bread and cold meat. He put down his knife and wiped his mouth. 'Good evening, Mr Willard. I hope you're well.'

'Very well, sheriff, I thank you.'

'Can I be of service to you?'

'To the queen, sheriff. Her majesty has a job for you to do – tonight.'

*

ROLLO NERVOUSLY touched the hilt of his sword. He had never been in battle. As a boy he had practised with a wooden weapon, like most sons of prosperous families, but he had no experience of deadly combat.

Sir Reginald's bedroom was full of people, and unlit, but no one was in bed. From the windows there was a spectacular view of the north and west sides of Kingsbridge Cathedral. It was a clear night, and to Rollo's dark-adapted eyes the glimmering starlight revealed the outline of the church, faint but clear. Under its pointed arches, all doorways and windows were deep pools of gloom, like the eye sockets of a man blinded for forging money. Higher up, the turrets with their crockets and finials were blackly silhouetted against the night sky.

With Rollo were his father, Sir Reginald; his brother-in-law, Bart Shiring; Bart's father, Earl Swithin; and two of Swithin's most trusted men-at-arms. All wore swords and daggers.

When the cathedral bell had struck four, Stephen Lincoln had said Mass and then had given all six of them absolution for the sins they were about to commit. They had been watching since then.

The women of the house, Lady Jane and Margery, were in bed, but Rollo doubted that they were asleep.

The market square, so crowded and noisy in the day, was now empty and silent. On the far side were the Grammar School and the bishop's palace, both now dark. Beyond them the city sloped downhill to the river, and the close-packed roofs of the houses looked like the tiled steps of a giant staircase.

Rollo hoped that Swithin and Bart and the men-at-arms, whose profession was violence, would do any fighting necessary.

First light cracked the dome of stars and turned the cathedral from black to grey. Soon afterwards, someone whispered: 'There.' Rollo saw a silent procession emerge from the bishop's palace, six dark figures, each carrying a candle lamp. They crossed the square and entered the church by the west door, their lamps vanishing as if extinguished.

Rollo frowned. Dan Cobley and the other Puritans must already be inside the cathedral, he supposed. Perhaps they had crept through the ruined monastic buildings and entered by one of the doors on the far side, unseen by the group in Priory Gate. He felt uneasy, not knowing for sure; but if he said so, at this late stage, his doubts would be attributed to mere cowardice, so he kept quiet.

Earl Swithin murmured: 'We'll wait a minute more. Give them time to get started on their satanic business.'

He was right. It would be a mistake to jump the gun, and

burst into the church before the relics were brought out and the desecration had begun.

Rollo imagined the priests walking down the aisle to the east end, unlocking the iron railings, and picking up the reliquary. What would they do next? Throw the bones into the river?

'All right, let's go,' said Swithin.

He led the way, and the others followed him down the stairs and through the front door. As soon as they were outside they broke into a run, and their footsteps seemed thunderous in the silence of the night. Rollo wondered if the people inside the cathedral could hear, and whether they would be sufficiently quick-witted to stop what they were doing and flee.

Then Swithin flung open the great door and they drew their swords and rushed in.

They were only just in time. Dean Luke stood in the middle of the nave, in front of the low altar, where a few candles burned. He had the golden reliquary in his hands, and he was holding it aloft, while the others sang something that was no doubt part of their devil-worshipping ritual. In the dim light it was hard to see just how many people stood in the shadows of the vast church. As the intruders ran along the nave towards the startled group at the altar, Rollo noticed that a hole had been dug in the church floor, and a large paving-stone stood to one side, propped against a pillar. Also beside the pillar was George Cox, the gravedigger, leaning on a shovel. This was not quite the scene Rollo had foreseen, but it hardly mattered: Dean Luke's stance clearly revealed his blasphemous purpose.

At the head of the group, Earl Swithin charged Luke with his sword raised. Luke turned around, still holding the reliquary high.

Then George Cox raised his shovel and ran at the earl.

At that moment, Rollo heard a baffling shout: 'Stop, in the name of the queen!' He could not see where the voice came from.

Swithin slashed at Luke. Luke jerked back at the last instant, but the sword struck his left arm, ripping the black of his robe and slicing deep into the flesh of his forearm. He cried out in pain and dropped the reliquary, which hit the floor with a thud and a crash, dislodging precious jewels that rolled across the stone pavement.

Rollo saw, out of the corner of his eye, a dim sign of movement in the south transept. A moment later, a group of ten or twelve men burst into the nave, wielding swords and clubs. They rushed at the intruders. The same voice repeated the order to stop in the name of the queen, and Rollo saw that the man shouting the pointless instruction was Sheriff Matthewson. What was he doing here?

George Cox swung his shovel, aiming at the earl's head, but Swithin moved and the tool struck his left shoulder. Enraged, Swithin stabbed with his sword, and Rollo was horrified to see the blade pierce the gravedigger's belly and come out of his back.

The other priests knelt beside the dropped reliquary as if to protect it.

The sheriff and his men were rushing at the earl and his group, and Rollo saw the leather helmet of Osmund Carter among the dim-lit heads. And was that the red-brown hair of Ned Willard?

The earl's side was outnumbered two to one. I'm going to die, Rollo thought, but God will reward me.

He was about to rush forward into the fray when he was struck by a thought. The surprise presence of Ned Willard made him suspicious. This could not be a trap, could it? Where were the Puritans? If they had been hiding in the shadows, they would by now have charged into the light. But Rollo saw only the earl's men on one side, the sheriff's on the other, and the frightened priests between.

Perhaps Donal Gloster's information had been wrong. But the priests were here at dawn, as Donal had predicted, and they were undoubtedly doing something sinister with the relics. More likely Dan Cobley had changed his mind, and decided that a protest in an empty church was hardly worthwhile. More puzzling, why was the sheriff here? Had he somehow got wind of the earl's intentions? That seemed impossible: the only people informed, outside the family, had been the two men-at-arms and Stephen Lincoln, all of whom were completely trustworthy. Dean Luke must have decided to be ultra-cautious. A guilty conscience was always full of fear.

A trap, or a foolhardy adventure that had turned into a fiasco? It hardly mattered: the fight was on.

The sheriff and the earl were the first to clash. Swithin was tugging at his sword, trying to pull it out of the body of George Cox, when the sheriff's weapon came down on Swithin's right hand. Swithin roared in pain and let go of the hilt of his weapon, and Rollo saw a detached thumb fall to the floor among the scattered jewels.

Ned Willard came out of the crowd of sheriff's men and dashed at Swithin, sword held high; and Rollo stepped quickly forward and stood in Ned's way, protecting the injured earl. Ned stopped short, and the two young men faced one another.

Rollo was taller and heavier. At school he had been able to persecute little Neddy Willard, but only until he grew up. Now there was something in the way Ned stood and looked that undermined Rollo's sense of superiority.

They moved around one another, swords held forward, looking for a chance. Rollo saw something close to loathing on Ned's face. What have I done to make you hate me? he wondered, and the answers came thick and fast: forcing Margery to marry Bart; the charge of usury that had ruined the Willard family; the failed effort to stop Elizabeth becoming queen; all that on top of school bullying.

Rollo heard a roar behind him and looked over his shoulder quickly. He saw that Earl Swithin was still fighting, despite his injury. He held his sword awkwardly in his left hand but had managed to cut the sheriff's forehead. The wound was superficial but bleeding copiously, and the blood was interfering with the sheriff's vision. Both hurt, they were fighting clumsily, like drunk men.

Rollo's glance behind was a mistake. Ned attacked suddenly and furiously. He came at Rollo fast, the heavy sword flashing in the candlelight as it stabbed and sliced and twisted. Rollo defended himself desperately, blocking the blows and backing away; then something moved under the sole of his right boot

– jewels from the reliquary, he realized despite his fear – and his leg slipped from under him. He fell on his back and dropped his sword. Both his arms spread wide, leaving his body undefended; and he foresaw his own death in the next split-second.

To his astonishment Ned stepped over him.

Rollo sprang to his knees and looked behind him. Ned was attacking the earl with even more ferocity, while the sheriff stood aside and tried to dash the blood from his eyes. Swithin backed until a pillar arrested his retreat. A swipe from Ned knocked the weapon from the earl's left hand, and then suddenly Ned had the point of his sword at the earl's throat.

The sheriff yelled: 'Arrest him!'

Ned's point pierced the skin of Swithin's throat, bringing a trickle of blood, but Ned restrained himself. For a long moment Swithin was an inch from death. Then Ned said: 'Tell your men to drop their weapons.'

Swithin shouted: 'Yield! Yield!'

The noise of fighting died rapidly, to be replaced by the sound of iron swords falling to the stone floor. Rollo looked around and saw that his father, Sir Reginald, was kneeling down, holding his head, which was bloody.

Ned did not take his eyes off Swithin, Rollo saw. Ned said: 'I arrest you in the name of the queen for blasphemy, desecration and murder.'

Rollo jumped to his feet. 'We're not the blasphemers!'

'No?' said Ned with surprising composure. 'But here you are in the church, with your swords unsheathed. You have wounded the bishop-elect and murdered the gravedigger, and you've caused the holy relics to be dropped on the floor.'

'What about yourselves?'

'The sheriff and his men came here to protect the clergy and the relics, and a good thing we did.'

Rollo was baffled. How had this gone so wrong?

Ned said: 'Osmund, tie them up, then take them to the Guild Hall and lock them in the jail.'

Osmund promptly produced a roll of stout cord.

Ned went on: 'Then send for the surgeon, and make sure he treats Dean Luke first.'

As Rollo's hands were tied behind his back, he stared at Ned, whose face registered a savage kind of satisfaction. Rollo's mind thrashed about looking for explanations. Had the sheriff been tipped off about Swithin's intentions, or had the timid Dean Luke summoned them merely out of nervousness? Had the Puritans been warned off, or had they simply decided not to come?

Had Ned Willard planned this whole disaster?

Rollo did not know.

*

Earl Swithin was executed, and I was responsible for his death. I had no idea, then, that he was the first of so many.

Rollo and Bart and Sir Reginald were punished with heavy fines, but one of the group had to die, and the earl had actually murdered a man in church. That was the justification; but what really sealed his fate was that he had tried to defy the will of Queen Elizabeth. The queen wanted England to understand very clearly that she, alone, had the right to appoint bishops, and anyone who interfered with her prerogative risked his life. Shocking though it was to kill an earl, she needed Swithin dead.

I made sure the judge understood her wishes.

As the crowd gathered in front of Kingsbridge Cathedral for the execution, Rollo stared hard at me, and I knew he suspected a trap, but I don't think he ever worked it out.

Sir Reginald was there, too, with a long scar across his head where the hair never grew back. The wound damaged his brain as well as his hair, and he never quite regained his wits. I know Rollo always blamed me for that.

Bart and Margery watched, too.

Bart wept. Swithin was a wicked man, but his father.

Margery looked like someone released from a horrible dungeon into the sunlight and fresh air. She had lost that sickly look, and she was dressed with her former panache, albeit in sombre mourning colours: on her, a black hat with a black feather could still look playful.

Her tormentor was on his way to hell, where he belonged, and she was free of him.

Swithin was brought out of the Guild Hall; and I had no doubt that the worst part of his punishment was the humiliating walk down the main street to the square in front of a jeering throng of people he had always despised as his inferiors. His head was chopped off, decapitation being the mercifully quick death reserved for the nobility; and I imagine the end came as a release.

Justice was done. Swithin was a murderer and a rapist who deserved to die. But I found that my conscience was not untroubled. I had lured him into an ambush. In a way the death of poor George Cox was my responsibility. I had meddled in things that should be left to the law or, failing that, to God.

I may yet go through anguish in hell for my sin. But if I had to live that time again I would do the same, to end Margery's ordeal. I preferred to suffer myself than to know that her agony continued. Her wellbeing was more important to me than my own.

I have learned, during the course of a long life, that that is the meaning of love.

Part Three

1566 to 1573

14

EBRIMA DABO WAS living his dream. He was free, rich and happy.

On a Sunday afternoon in the summer of 1566 he and his partner, Carlos Cruz, walked out of the city of Antwerp into the countryside. They were two prosperous, well-dressed inhabitants of one of the richest cities in the world. Together they owned the largest iron-making concern in Antwerp. In brains they were about equal, Ebrima thought: he was older and wiser, but Carlos had the bold imagination of youth. Carlos was married to Imke, the daughter of his distant cousin Jan Wolman, and they had two small children. Ebrima, who would be fifty next year, had married Evi Dirks, a widow his own age, and had a teenage stepson who was employed in the ironworks.

Ebrima often thought nostalgically of the village where he had been born. If he could have turned back the years, and avoided being taken as a prisoner-of-war and sold into slavery, he would have had a long, uneventful and contented life in that village. When he thought this way he felt sad. But he could not go back. For one thing, he had no idea how to get there. But there was something else. He knew too much. He had eaten of the fruit of the tree of knowledge, like Eve in the myth the Christians believed, and he could never return to the garden. He spoke Spanish and French and the local Brabant Dutch dialect, and had not uttered a word of Manding for years. He hung oil paintings in his house, he loved to listen to musical groups playing complex scores, and he was particular about the quality of his wine. He was a different man.

With brains and hard work and luck he had forged a new

life. All he wanted, now, was to keep what he had won. But he feared he would not be able to.

He and Carlos were not the only people leaving the city. Antwerpers often walked into the countryside in good weather, but today's crowds were abnormal. There were hundreds of people on the narrow country road. Ebrima knew many of them: men who supplied him with ore, others who bought his iron, families who lived in his street, keepers of shops where he bought meat and gloves and glassware. All were heading for the same place, a broad meadow known as Lord Hubert's Pasture. It was Carlos's children's favourite place to picnic. But the crowd on the road were not picnickers.

They were Protestants.

Many carried copies of the same small book, the Psalms translated into French by the poet Clément Marot, printed in Antwerp. It was a crime to own the book, and the penalty for selling it was death, but it was easily available and cost a penny.

Most of the younger men also carried weapons.

Ebrima guessed that Lord Hubert's Pasture had been chosen for the meeting because it was outside the jurisdiction of the Antwerp city council, so the city watch had no authority there, and the rural police did not have the manpower to disperse such a crowd. Even so, there was always the danger of violence: everyone had heard of the Massacre of Wassy. And some of the younger men were undoubtedly in an aggressive mood.

Carlos was a Catholic. Ebrima was what the Christians would have called a pagan, if they had known what was in his heart, but of course they did not, for he pretended to be a devout Catholic like Carlos. Even his wife, Evi, did not know, and if she wondered why he liked to go for riverside walks at dawn on Sunday mornings she was tactful enough not to ask. Ebrima and Carlos both went regularly, with their families, to their parish church and, on big occasions, to Antwerp Cathedral. Both feared that religious warfare in the Netherlands could destroy their happiness as it had done for so many people across the border in France.

Carlos was a simple soul, philosophically, and he could not

understand why anyone wanted to take up an alternative religion. But Ebrima saw, with sadness and alarm, what attracted so many Netherlanders to Protestantism. Catholicism was the creed of their Spanish overlords, and many Dutch people resented foreign domination. Also, Netherlanders were innovators, whereas the Catholic Church was conservative about everything, quick to condemn new ideas, slow to change. Worst of all, the clergy were not friendly to the commercial activities that had made so many Netherlanders rich, especially banking, which could not exist unless men committed the sin of usury. By contrast the influential John Calvin, leader of the Geneva Protestants until his death two years ago, had allowed interest to be charged on loans.

This summer, as a fresh wave of itinerant Calvinist pastors from Geneva gave informal sermons in the forests and fields of the Netherlands, the trickling spread of Protestantism had turned into a flood.

Persecution was fierce, but intermittent. The governor of the Netherlands was Margherita, duchess of Parma, the illegitimate half-sister of King Felipe of Spain. She was inclined to go easy on heretics for the sake of a quiet life, but her brother was determined to wipe out heresy in all his domains. When she became too tolerant, the bloodthirsty Chief Inquisitor Pieter Titelmans would crack down: Protestants would be tortured, mutilated and burned to death. But the hard line got little support even from Catholics. Most of the time, the laws were enforced lightly. Men such as Carlos were more interested in making and selling things. The new religion grew.

How big was it now? Ebrima and Carlos were on their way to the open-air meeting to find out. City councillors wanted to know just how popular the alternative religion was. It was difficult to tell, normally, because Protestantism was semi-hidden; today's meeting would be a rare chance to see how many Protestants there really were. So a councillor had unofficially asked Carlos and Ebrima, as solid Catholic citizens without official status, to discreetly count them.

Judging by the numbers on the road, the total was going to be higher than expected.

As they walked, Ebrima asked: 'How is the painting coming along?'

'It's almost finished.' Carlos had commissioned a top Antwerp artist to paint a picture for the cathedral. Ebrima knew that in his prayers Carlos thanked God for his gifts and asked that he would be allowed to keep them. Like Ebrima, he did not take his prosperity for granted. He often mentioned the story of Job, the man who had everything and lost it all, and he would quote: 'The Lord giveth, and the Lord taketh away.'

Ebrima was intrigued that Carlos did not reject the Church after the persecution he had suffered in Seville. Carlos was not very forthcoming about his spiritual life, but over the years Ebrima had gathered, from casual remarks and hints, that Carlos found great consolation in Catholic services, something similar to what Ebrima got from the water rite. Neither of them felt the same at an earnest Protestant service in a whitewashed church.

Now Ebrima said: 'What subject did you decide upon, for the painting, in the end?'

'The miracle at Cana, when Jesus turned the water into wine.'

Ebrima laughed. 'Your favourite Bible story. I wonder why.' Carlos's love of wine was well known.

Carlos smiled. 'It will be unveiled in the cathedral next week.'

The painting would, technically, be a gift from the city's metalworkers, but everyone would know that it had been bought with Carlos's money. This was a measure of how quickly Carlos had become one of Antwerp's leading citizens. He was amiable and gregarious and very smart, and might be a city councillor one day.

Ebrima was a different kind of man, introverted and cautious. He was just as smart as Carlos but he had no political ambitions. Also, he preferred to keep his money for himself.

Carlos added: 'We'll have a big party afterwards. I hope you and Evi will come.'

'Of course.'

They heard the singing before they reached their destination. Ebrima felt the hairs on the back of his neck stand up. The sound was awesome. He was used to chorus singing by choirs in Catholic churches – quite large choirs in cathedrals – but this was different. He had never before heard thousands of voices raised in the same song.

The road passed through a little wood then emerged at the top of a shallow rise from where they could see the whole of the meadow. It sloped down to a shallow stream and up the far side, and the entire space of ten acres or more was covered with men, women and children. On the far side a pastor stood on a makeshift platform, leading the singing.

The hymn was in French:

> Si seurement, que quand au val viendroye
> D'umbre de mort, rien de mal ne craindroye . . .

Ebrima understood the French words and recognized them as a translation from the familiar Latin of the twenty-third psalm, which he had heard in church – but not like this. The sound seemed a mighty phenomenon of nature, making him think of a gale over the ocean. They really believed what they were singing, that as they walked through the valley of the shadow of death they would fear no evil.

Ebrima spotted his stepson, Matthus, not far away. Matthus still worshipped with his mother and stepfather every Sunday but, lately, he had started to criticize the Catholic Church. His mother urged him to keep his doubts to himself, but he could not: he was seventeen, and for him right was right and wrong was wrong. Now Ebrima was troubled to see him with a group of youths, all carrying unpleasant-looking clubs.

Carlos saw him at the same time. 'Those boys seem to be looking for a fight,' he said anxiously.

But the atmosphere in the meadow was peaceful and happy, and Ebrima said hopefully: 'I think they'll be disappointed today.'

'What a lot of people,' Carlos said.

'How many, do you think?'

'Thousands.'

'I don't know how we're going to count.'

Carlos was clever with numbers. 'Let's say there's half this side of the stream and half the other. Now imagine a line from here to the preacher. How many in the near quarter? Divide it into four again.'

Ebrima took a guess. 'Five hundred in each sixteenth?'

Carlos did not respond to that, but said: 'Here comes trouble.'

He was staring over Ebrima's shoulder, and Ebrima turned to look for the cause. He saw at once what had alerted Carlos. Coming along the road through the wood was a small group of clergy and men-at-arms.

If they had come to break up the meeting, they were too few. This armed crowd, full of righteousness, would wipe them out.

In the centre of the group was a priest in his mid-sixties wearing an ostentatious silver cross outside his black robe. As he came closer, Ebrima saw that he had dark, deep-set eyes either side of a high-bridged nose, and a mouth set in a hard, determined line. Ebrima did not recognize the man, but Carlos did. 'That's Pieter Titelmans, dean of Ronse,' he said. 'The Grand Inquisitor.'

Ebrima looked anxiously at Matthus and his friends. They had not yet spotted the newcomer. What would they do when they realized that the Grand Inquisitor had come to spy on their meeting?

As the group approached, Carlos said: 'Let's stay out of his way – he knows me.'

But he was too late. Titelmans met his eye, registered surprise, and said: 'I'm disappointed to see you in this nest of ungodliness.'

'I'm a good Catholic!' Carlos protested.

Titelmans tilted back his head, like a hungry hawk spotting movement in the grass. 'What would a good Catholic be doing at a Protestant psalm-singing orgy?'

Ebrima answered him. 'The city council needs to know how many Protestants there are in Antwerp. We've been sent here to count them.'

Titelmans looked sceptical and spoke to Carlos. 'Why would I take the word of that Ethiopian? He's probably a Muslim.'

If only you knew, thought Ebrima. Then he recognized one of Titelmans's entourage, a middle-aged man with salt-and-pepper hair and the flushed complexion of one who loves wine. 'Father Huus, there, knows me,' he said. Huus was a canon of Antwerp Cathedral.

Huus said quietly: 'Both these men are good Catholics, Dean Pieter. They go to St James's parish church.'

The psalm came to an end and the preacher began to speak. Some people pressed closer to hear his words shouted across the field. Others noticed Titelmans with his big silver cross, and there were angry mutterings.

Huus said nervously: 'Sir, there are more Protestants here than we imagined possible and, if violence were to break out, we have too few men to protect you.'

Titelmans ignored him. Looking sly, he said: 'If you two are what you claim to be, you can tell me the names of some of these wicked men.' He indicated the congregation with a wide sweep of his arm.

Ebrima was not going to betray his neighbours to a torturer, and he knew Carlos would feel the same. He saw that Carlos was about to make an indignant protest, and forestalled him. 'Of course, Dean Pieter,' he said. 'We'll be glad to give you names.' He made a pantomime of looking around, then said: 'At the moment I don't see anyone I know, unfortunately.'

'That's unlikely. There must be seven or eight thousand people here.'

'Antwerp is a city of eighty thousand inhabitants. I don't know them all.'

'Just the same, you must recognize a few.'

'I don't think so. Perhaps it's because all my friends are Catholics.'

Titelmans was stumped, and Ebrima was relieved. He had survived the interrogation.

Then he heard a voice cry out, in the local Brabant Dutch dialect: 'Carlos! Ebrima! Good day!'

Ebrima spun around to see Albert Willemsen, his brother-in-law, the iron maker who had helped them when they first came to Antwerp six years ago. Albert had built a blast furnace just like theirs, and all had done well. With Albert were his wife, Betje, and their daughter, Drike, now fourteen, a slim adolescent with an angelic face. Albert and his family had embraced Protestantism.

'Don't you think this is great?' Albert enthused. 'All these people singing God's word, and no one to tell them to shut up!'

Carlos said quietly: 'Careful what you say.'

But the ebullient Albert had not noticed Titelmans or his cross. 'Oh, come on, now, Carlos, you're a man of tolerance, not one of those hardliners. You can't possibly see anything here that would displease the God of love.'

Ebrima said urgently to Albert: 'Shut up.'

Albert looked hurt and puzzled, then Betje pointed to the Grand Inquisitor, and Albert turned pale.

But others were noticing Titelmans, and most of the nearby Protestants had now turned away from the preacher to stare. Matthus and his friends were approaching, clubs in hands. Ebrima called out: 'Stay back, you boys, I don't want you here.'

Matthus ignored his stepfather and stood close to Drike. He was a big lad who had not yet grown used to his size. His adolescent face wore a look that was part threatening, part fearful. However, his attitude to Drike seemed protective, and Ebrima wondered if the boy might be in love. I must ask Evi, he thought.

Father Huus said: 'We should return to the city now, Dean Pieter.'

Titelmans seemed determined not to go away empty-handed. Pointing to Albert, he said: 'Tell me, Father Huus, what is that man's name?'

Huus said: 'I'm sorry, dean, I don't know the man.'

Ebrima knew that was a brave lie.

Titelmans turned to Carlos. 'Well, *you* obviously know him – he speaks to you like an old friend. Who is he?'

Carlos hesitated.

Titelmans was right, Ebrima thought: Carlos could not pretend not to know Albert, after such an effusive greeting.

Titelmans said: 'Come, come! If you're as good a Catholic as you claim to be, you'll be glad to identify such a heretic. If you don't, you shall be questioned in another place, where we have means of making you honest.'

Carlos shuddered, and Ebrima guessed he was thinking of Pedro Ruiz undergoing the water torture in Seville.

Albert spoke bravely. 'I shan't allow my friends to be tortured on my account,' he said. 'My name is Albert Willemsen.'

'Profession?'

'Iron maker.'

'And the women?'

'Leave them out of this.'

'No one is left out of God's mercy.'

'I don't know who they are,' Albert said desperately. 'They're two prostitutes I met on the road.'

'They don't look like prostitutes. But I shall learn the truth.' Titelmans turned to Huus. 'Make a note of the name: Albert Willemsen, iron maker.' He gathered up the skirts of his robe, turned, and walked back the way he had come, followed by his little entourage.

The others watched him go.

Carlos said: 'Shit.'

*

THE NORTH TOWER of Antwerp Cathedral was more than four hundred feet high. It had been designed as one of a pair, but the south tower had not been built. Ebrima thought it was more impressive on its own, a single finger pointing straight up to heaven.

He could not help feeling awestruck as he entered the nave. The narrow central aisle had a vaulted ceiling that seemed impossibly high. It sometimes made him wonder if the god of the Christians might be real, after all. Then he would remember that nothing they built could compete with the power and majesty of a river.

Above the high altar was the pride of the city, a large carving of Christ crucified between two thieves. Antwerp was wealthy and cultured, and its cathedral was rich in paintings, sculptures, stained glass, and precious objects. And today Ebrima's friend and partner, Carlos, would add to that treasure.

Ebrima hoped that this would make up for their abrasive encounter with the loathsome Pieter Titelmans. It was a bad thing to have the Grand Inquisitor for an enemy.

On the south side was a chapel dedicated to Urban, the patron saint of winemakers. There the new painting hung, covered by a red velvet cloth. Seats in the little chapel had been reserved for Carlos's friends and family and for the officials of the metalworkers' guild. Standing nearby, eager to see the new picture, were a hundred or so neighbours and fellow businessmen, all in their best clothes.

Ebrima saw that Carlos was glowing with happiness. He was seated in a place of honour in the church that was the centre of the great city. This ceremony would confirm that he belonged here. He felt loved and respected and safe.

Father Huus arrived to perform the service of dedication. In his short sermon he said what a good Christian Carlos was, raising his children in piety and spending his money to enrich the cathedral. He even hinted that Carlos was destined to play a part in the city's government one day. Ebrima liked Huus. He often preached against Protestantism, but preaching was as far as he wanted to go. Ebrima felt sure he must be reluctant to help Titelmans, and did so only under pressure.

The children became fidgety during the prayers. It was hard for them to listen for long to someone speaking their own language, let alone Latin. Carlos shushed them, but gently: he was an indulgent father.

As the service came to an end, Huus asked Carlos to step forward and unveil the painting.

Carlos took hold of the red velvet cover, then hesitated.

Ebrima thought he might be about to make a speech, which would be a mistake: ordinary people did not speak out in church, unless they were Protestants. Then Carlos pulled at the velvet, nervously at first, then more vigorously. At last the cover came down like a crimson waterfall, and the picture was revealed.

The wedding was shown taking place in a grand town house that might have been the home of an Antwerp banker. Jesus sat at the head of the table in a blue robe. Next to him, the host of the feast was a broad-shouldered man with a bushy black beard, very like Carlos; and next to Carlos sat a fair smiling woman who might have been Imke. A buzz of comment arose from the group standing in the nave, and there were smiles and laughter as they identified other faces among the guests: there was Ebrima in an Arab-style hat, with Evi next to him in a gown that emphasized her large bust; a richly dressed man next to Imke was clearly her father, Jan Wolman; and the empty wine jars were being examined by a tall, thin, dismayed-looking steward who resembled Adam Smits, Antwerp's best-known wine merchant. There was even a dog that looked just like Carlos's hound, Samson.

The painting looked fine in the chapel, up against the ancient stones of the cathedral, sunnily lit by a south-facing window. The robes of the wealthy guests glowed orange, blue and bright green against the white of the tablecloth and the pale walls of the dining room.

Carlos was visibly thrilled. Father Huus shook his hand then took his leave. Everyone else wanted to congratulate Carlos, and he went around the crowd, smiling and accepting the plaudits of his fellow citizens. Eventually, he clapped his hands and said: 'Everybody! You're invited to my house! And I promise the wine won't run out!'

They walked in procession through the serpentine streets of the town centre to Carlos's house. He led them to the upstairs floor where food and wine stood ready on tables in the grand drawing room. The guests dug in with enthusiasm. They were joined by several Protestants who had not been in the cathedral, including Albert and his family.

Ebrima picked up a goblet and took a long swallow. Carlos's wine was always good. He wiped his mouth with his sleeve. The wine warmed his blood and made him feel mellow. He talked amiably to Jan Wolman about business, to Imke about her children, and to Carlos briefly about a customer who was late paying his bill: the customer was here, enjoying Carlos's hospitality, and Ebrima thought this was the moment to confront him and ask for the money, but Carlos did not want to spoil the mood. The guests became a little raucous. Children squabbled, adolescent boys tried to woo adolescent girls, and married men flirted with their friends' wives. Parties were the same everywhere, Ebrima thought; even Africa.

Then Pieter Titelmans came in.

The first Ebrima knew of it was when a hush fell over the room, starting at the door and spreading to all four corners. He was talking to Albert about the merits of cast-iron cannons as compared with bronze when they both realized something was wrong and looked up. Titelmans stood in the doorway wearing his big silver cross, again accompanied by Father Huus and four men-at-arms.

Ebrima said: 'What does that devil want?'

Albert said with nervous hopefulness: 'Perhaps he's come to congratulate Carlos on the painting.'

Carlos pushed through the quietened crowd and spoke to Titelmans with a show of amity. 'Good day, Dean Pieter,' he said. 'Welcome to my house. Will you take a cup of wine?'

Titelmans ignored the question. 'Are there any Protestants here?' he said.

'I don't think so,' Carlos said. 'We've just come from the cathedral, where we unveiled—'

'I know what you did at the cathedral,' Titelmans interrupted rudely. 'Are there any Protestants here?'

'I can assure you, to the best of my knowledge—'

'You're about to lie to me. I can smell it.'

Carlos's bonhomie began to crack. 'If you don't believe me, why ask the question?'

'To test you. Now shut your mouth.'

Carlos sputtered: 'I'm in my own house!'

Titelmans raised his voice so that everyone could hear. 'I'm here to see Albert Willemsen.'

Titelmans seemed unsure which one was Albert – he had only seen him for a few minutes at Lord Hubert's Pasture – and for a moment Ebrima hoped they might all pretend he was not present. But the crowd was not sufficiently quick-witted, and indeed many of them stupidly turned and looked directly at Albert.

After a moment of fearful hesitation, Albert stepped forward. With a show of bravado he said: 'What do you want with me?'

'And your wife,' said Titelmans, pointing. Unfortunately Betje was standing close to Albert and Titelmans's guess was correct. Looking pale and scared, Betje stepped forward.

'And the daughter.'

Drike was not standing with her parents, and Titelmans surely would not remember a fourteen-year-old girl. 'The child is not here,' Carlos lied bravely. Perhaps she might be saved, Ebrima thought hopefully.

But she did not want to be saved. A girlish voice piped up: 'I am Drike Willemsen.'

Ebrima's heart sank.

He could see her, by the window, in a white dress, talking to his stepson Matthus, with Carlos's pet cat in her arms.

Carlos said: 'She's a mere child, dean. Surely—'

But Drike was not finished. 'And I am a Protestant,' she said defiantly. 'For which I thank the Lord.'

From the guests came a murmur of mixed admiration and dismay.

'Come here,' said Titelmans.

She crossed the room with her head held high, and Ebrima thought: Oh, hell.

'Take the three of them away,' said Titelmans to his entourage.

Someone shouted: 'Why don't you leave us in peace?'

Titelmans looked angrily towards the source of the jeer, but he could not see who had spoken. However, Ebrima knew: he had recognized the voice of young Matthus.

Another man shouted: 'Yeah, go back to Ronse!'

The other guests started to cheer their approval and shout their own catcalls. Titelmans's men-at-arms escorted the Willemsen family out of the room. As Titelmans turned to follow, Matthus threw a bread roll. It hit Titelmans's back. He pretended not to notice. Then a goblet flew through the air and hit the wall close to him, splashing his robe. The booing became louder and cruder. Titelmans barely retained his dignity as he hurried through the door before anything else could threaten him.

The crowd laughed and clapped his exit. But Ebrima knew there was nothing to smile about.

*

THE BURNING OF young Drike was scheduled for two weeks later.

It was announced in the cathedral. Titelmans said that Albert and Betje had recanted their Protestantism, asked God's forgiveness, and begged to be received back into the bosom of the Church. He probably knew their confessions were insincere, but he had to let them off with a fine. However, to everyone's horror, Drike had refused to renounce her religion.

Titelmans would not let anyone visit her in prison, but Albert bribed the guards and got in anyway. However, he was unable to change her mind. With the idealism of the very young, she insisted she was ready to die rather than betray her Lord.

Ebrima and Evi went to see Albert and Betje the day before the burning. They wanted to give support and comfort to their friends, but it was hopeless. Betje wept without stopping, and Albert could barely speak. Drike was their only child.

That day a stake was planted in the pavement in the city centre, overlooked by the cathedral, the elegant Great Market building, and the grand, unfinished city hall. A cartload of dry firewood was dumped next to the stake.

The execution was scheduled for sunrise, and a crowd gathered before dawn. The mood was grim, Ebrima noted. When hated criminals such as thieves and rapists were executed, the spectators mocked them and cheered their death agonies; but that was not going to happen today. Many in the crowd were Protestants, and feared this might one day happen to them. The Catholics, such as Carlos, were angered by the Protestants' troublemaking, and fearful that the French wars of religion would spread to the Netherlands; but few of them believed it was right to burn a girl to death.

Drike was led out of the town hall by Egmont, the executioner, a big man dressed in a leather smock and carrying a blazing torch. She wore the white dress in which she had been arrested. Ebrima saw at once that Titelmans, in his arrogance, had made a mistake. She looked like a virgin, which she undoubtedly was; and she had the pale beauty of paintings of the Virgin Mary. The crowd gave a collective gasp on seeing her. Ebrima said to his wife, Evi: 'This is going to be a martyrdom.' He glanced at Matthus and saw that the boy had tears in his eyes.

One of the two west doors of the cathedral opened, and Titelmans appeared at the head of a little flock of priests like black crows.

Two men-at-arms tied Drike to the stake and piled the firewood around her feet.

Titelmans began to speak to the crowd about truth and heresy. The man had no sense of the effect he had on people, Ebrima realized. Everything about him offended them: his hectoring tone, his haughty look, and the fact that he was not from this city.

Then Drike began to speak. Her treble rose above Titelmans's shout. Her words were in French:

> Mon Dieu me paist soubs sa puissance haute
> C'est mon berger, de rien je n'auray faute . . .

It was the psalm the crowd had sung at Lord Hubert's Pasture, the twenty-third, beginning *The Lord is my shepherd*. Emotion swamped the crowd like a tidal wave. Tears came to Ebrima's eyes. Others in the crowd wept openly. Everyone felt they were present at a sacred tragedy.

Titelmans was furious. He spoke to the executioner, and

Ebrima was close enough to hear his words: 'You were supposed to pull out her tongue!'

There was a special tool, like a claw, for removing tongues. It had been devised as a punishment for liars, but was sometimes used to silence heretics, so that they could not preach to the crowd as they were dying.

Egmont said sullenly: 'Only if specifically instructed.'

Drike said:

> ... En tect bien seur, joignant les beaulx herbages,
> Coucher me faict, me meine aux clairs rivages ...

She was looking up, and Ebrima felt sure she was seeing the green pastures and still waters waiting in the afterlife of all religions.

Titelmans said: 'Dislocate her jaw.'

'Very well,' said Egmont. He was of course a man of blunted sensibility, but this instruction clearly offended even him, and he did not trouble to hide his distaste. Nevertheless, he handed his torch to a man-at-arms.

Next to Ebrima, Matthus turned around and shouted: 'They're going to dislocate her jaw!'

'Be quiet!' said his mother anxiously, but Matthus's big voice had already reached far. There was a collective roar of anger. Matthus's words were repeated throughout the crowd until everyone knew.

Matthus shouted: 'Let her pray!' and the cry was repeated: 'Let her pray! Let her pray!'

Evi said: 'You'll get into trouble!'

Egmont went up to Drike and put his hands to her face. He thrust his thumbs into her mouth and took a firm grip of her jaw, so that he could wrench the bone from its sockets.

Ebrima sensed a sudden violent movement beside him, then Egmont was struck on the back of the head by a stone thrown by Matthus.

It was a big stone, aimed well and hurled hard by a strong seventeen-year-old arm, and Ebrima heard the thud as it hit Egmont's skull. The executioner staggered, as if momentarily losing consciousness, and his hands fell from Drike's face. Everyone cheered.

Titelmans saw the event slipping from his control. 'All right, never mind, light the fire!' he said.

Matthus shouted: 'No!'

More stones were thrown, but they missed.

Egmont took back his torch and put it to the firewood. The dry sticks blazed up quickly.

Matthus pushed past Ebrima and ran out of the crowd towards Drike. Evi shouted: 'Stop!' Her son ignored her.

The men-at-arms drew their swords, but Matthus was too quick for them. He kicked the burning wood away from Drike's feet then ran away, disappearing back into the crowd.

The men-at-arms came after him, swords raised. The crowd scattered before them, terrified. Evi wailed: 'They'll kill him!'

Ebrima saw that there was only one way to save the boy, and that was to start a general riot. It would not be difficult: the crowd was almost there already.

Ebrima pushed forward, and others went with him, surging around the now-undefended stake. Ebrima drew his dagger and cut the ropes that bound Drike. Albert appeared and picked her up – she did not weigh much – and they disappeared into the crowd.

The people turned on the priests, jostling them. The men-at-arms gave up searching for Matthus and returned to defend the clergy.

Titelmans hurried away towards the cathedral, and the priests went after him. Their walk turned into a run. The crowd let them go, jeering, and watched them as they passed through the elaborately carved stone archway, pushed open the great wooden door, and finally vanished into the darkness of the church.

*

ALBERT AND HIS family left Antwerp that night.

Ebrima was one of only a handful of people who knew they were going to Amsterdam. It was a smaller town, but farther to the north-east and therefore more removed from the centre of

Spanish power at Brussels – for which reason it was prospering and growing rapidly.

Ebrima and Carlos bought Albert's ironworks, paying him for it in gold which he took with him in locked saddlebags on a sturdy pony.

The lovelorn Matthus wanted to go with them, and Ebrima – who remembered, albeit dimly, the power of adolescent romance – would have let him; but Albert said that Drike was too young to marry, and they must wait a year. Then Matthus could come to Amsterdam and propose to her, if he still wanted to. Matthus swore that he would, and his mother said: 'We'll see.'

Titelmans went quiet. There were no further confrontations, no more arrests. Perhaps he had realized that Antwerp Catholics disliked his extremism. Or he might just be biding his time.

Ebrima wished the Protestants would quieten down, too, but they seemed to have become more confident, not to say arrogant. They demanded tolerance, and the right to worship as they wished, but they were never satisfied with that, he thought with exasperation. They believed their rivals were not just mistaken but evil. Catholic practices – the ways in which Europeans had worshipped for hundreds of years – were blasphemous, they said, and must be abolished. They did not practise the tolerance they preached.

It worried Ebrima that the Spanish overlords and their allies in the priesthood seemed to be losing their grip on authority. Hatred and violence seethed under the surface of city life. Like all entrepreneurs, he just wanted peace and stability so that he could do business.

He was doing just that, negotiating with a buyer in the ironworks, perspiring a little in the summer heat, on the twentieth day of August, when the trouble boiled over again.

He heard a commotion in the street: running footsteps, breaking glass, and the raucous shouts of over-excited men. He hurried out to see what was going on, and Carlos and Matthus joined him. A couple of hundred youths, including a handful of girls, were hurrying along the street. They carried ladders, pulleys and ropes as well as cruder tools such as wooden staffs, sledgehammers, iron bars and lengths of chain. 'What are you doing?' Ebrima shouted at them, but no one answered his question.

The glass Ebrima had heard breaking was a window in the house of Father Huus, who lived in the same street as the iron-works; but that appeared to have been a passing fancy, and the mob was heading for the city centre in a seemingly purposeful mood.

Carlos said: 'What the hell are they up to?'

Ebrima could guess, and he hoped he was wrong.

The three men followed the crowd to the market square where Drike had been rescued. There the youths gathered in the centre, and one of them asked for God's blessing, speaking Brabant Dutch. Among Protestants, anyone could pray extempore, and they could use their own language, instead of Latin. Ebrima was afraid they had come to the market square because that was where the cathedral stood, and his fear turned out to be right. When the prayer ended they all turned as one, clearly following a prearranged plan, and marched to the cathedral.

The entrance was a pointed gothic arch under an ogee. On the tympanum was carved God in heaven, and the concentric orders of the arch were filled with angels and saints. Next to Ebrima, Carlos gasped with horror as the group began to attack the carvings with their hammers and makeshift weapons. As they smashed the stonework they yelled Bible quotations, making the scriptures sound like curses.

Carlos yelled at them: 'Stop this! There will be retaliation!' No one took any notice.

Ebrima could tell that Matthus was itching to join them. As the boy took a step forward, Ebrima took his arm in a strong iron-maker's grip. 'What would your mother say?' he said. 'She worships here! Stop, and think.'

'They're doing God's work!' Matthus yelled.

The rioters discovered that the big cathedral doors were locked: the priests had seen them coming. Ebrima felt relieved:

at least the damage they could do was limited. Perhaps they would wind down now. He released Matthus's arm.

But the mob ran round to the north of the church, looking for another way in. The onlookers followed. To Ebrima's consternation they found a side door unlocked: the priests in their panic must have overlooked it. The mob pushed through into the church, and Matthus pulled away from Ebrima.

By the time Ebrima got inside, the Protestants were running in all directions, yelling in triumph, lashing out at any carved or painted image. They seemed drunk, though not with wine. They were possessed by a frenzy of destruction. Both Carlos and Ebrima yelled at them to stop, and other older citizens joined in the appeal, but it was useless.

There were a few priests in the chancel, and Ebrima saw some of them fleeing through the south porch. One did the opposite, and came towards the intruders, holding up both hands as if to stop them. Ebrima recognized Father Huus. 'You are God's children,' he kept saying. He walked directly at the charging youths. 'Stop this, and let's talk.' A big lad crashed into him, knocking him to the floor, and the others ran over him.

They pulled down precious hangings and threw them into a pile in the middle of the crossing, where screeching girls set fire to them using lighted candles from an altar. Wooden statues were smashed, ancient books were torn, and costly vestments were ripped up; and the debris was added to the flames.

Ebrima was appalled, not just by the destruction but by its inevitable consequences. This could not be allowed to pass. It was the most outrageous provocation of both King Felipe and Pope Pius, the two most powerful men in Europe. Antwerp would be punished. It might be a long time coming, for the wheels of international politics turned slowly; but when it happened it would be dreadful.

Some of the group were even more serious. They had clearly planned this, and they gathered around the high altar, their target obviously the massive sculpture. They quickly set their ladders and pulleys in positions that they must have prearranged. Carlos was aghast. 'They're going to abuse the crucified Christ!' he said. He stared in horror as they tied ropes around Jesus and hacked at his legs to weaken the structure. They kept shouting about idolatry, but it was clear even to the pagan Ebrima that it was the Protestants who were perpetrating the blasphemy here. They worked the pulleys with determined concentration, tightening the ropes, until at last the dying Jesus tilted forward, cracked at the knees, and was finally torn from his place and thrown to the ground, face down. Not satisfied, the Protestants attacked the fallen monument with hammers, smashing the arms and head with a glee that seemed satanic.

The two carved thieves, crucified either side of where Jesus had been nailed, now seemed to look mournfully down on his shattered body.

Someone brought a flagon of communion wine and a golden chalice, and they all congratulated one another and drank.

A shout from the south side made Ebrima and Carlos turn. With a shock, Ebrima saw that a little group had gathered in the chapel of St Urban, staring up at the painting Carlos had commissioned of the miracle at Cana.

'No!' Carlos roared, but no one heard.

They ran across the church, but before they got there one of the boys had raised a dagger and slashed the canvas from one side to the other. Carlos threw himself at the boy, knocking him to the floor, and the knife went flying; but others grabbed both Carlos and Ebrima and held them fast, struggling but helpless.

The boy Carlos had attacked got up, apparently unhurt. He picked up his knife and slashed the canvas again and again, tearing the images of Jesus and the disciples, and the representations of Carlos and his family and friends among the painted wedding guests.

A girl brought a taper and put it to the shredded canvas. The painted fabric first smouldered and smoked. Then eventually a small flame appeared. It spread rapidly, and soon the entire picture was blazing.

Ebrima ceased to struggle. He looked at Carlos, who had closed his eyes. The young hooligans let them both go and went off to vandalize something else.

Released, Carlos fell to his knees and wept.

15

ALISON MCKAY WAS in prison with Mary Queen of Scots.

They were confined in a castle, on an island, in the middle of a Scottish lake called Loch Leven. They were guarded day and night by fifteen men-at-arms, more than enough to watch over two young women.

And they were going to escape.

Mary was indomitable. She did not have good judgement: Alison admitted to herself, in the darkest hours of the night, that just about every decision the queen had ever taken had turned out badly. But Mary never gave up. Alison loved that about her.

Loch Leven was a grim place. The house was a square tower of grey stone with small, mean windows to keep out the cold wind that blew hard across the water, even in summer. It was set in a compound less than a hundred yards across. Outside was a narrow strip of scrubland, then the lake. When the weather was stormy, the strip was submerged and the waves lashed the stones of the perimeter wall. The lake was broad, and it took half an hour for a strong man to row to the mainland.

This was a hard prison from which to escape, but they had to try. They were miserable. Alison had never imagined, until now, that boredom could drive her to contemplate suicide.

They had been raised in the glittering court of France, surrounded by people in gorgeous clothes and priceless jewels, invited every day to banquets and pageants and plays. Their everyday conversation had been of political plots and social intrigue. The men around them started wars and ended them; the women were queens and the mothers of kings. After that, Loch Leven was purgatory.

It was 1568. Alison was twenty-seven and Mary twenty-five. They had been at Loch Leven almost a year, and Alison had spent much of that time brooding about where they had gone wrong.

Mary's first mistake had been to fall for and then marry Queen Elizabeth's cousin Henry, Lord Darnley, a charming drunk who had syphilis. Alison had felt torn: happy to see Mary in love, but appalled by her choice of man.

Love quickly wore off, and when Mary became pregnant, Darnley murdered her private secretary, whom he suspected of fathering the child.

If there was a nobleman in Scotland even worse than Darnley it was, in Alison's opinion, the quarrelsome and violent Earl of Bothwell, and Mary's second mistake had been to encourage Bothwell to kill Darnley. Bothwell had succeeded, but everyone knew or guessed what had happened.

Neither Mary nor Alison had anticipated the reaction of the Scots. They were an upright nation, and Catholics and Protestants alike disapproved of this royal immorality. Mary's standing with the Scottish people fell off a cliff.

Alison felt that a storm of bad luck was sweeping over them when Bothwell kidnapped them and forced Mary to spend the night with him. In other circumstances the nation would have been outraged by this attack on their queen, and would have rallied to her defence; but by then her reputation was stained, and Mary could not feel sure of popular support. Together they decided the only way to restore Mary's respectability was for her to marry Bothwell, and pretend that he had not really raped her. Bothwell's fed-up wife obtained a quickie divorce that was not recognized by the Catholic Church, and they were married immediately.

That was the third mistake.

Twenty-six outraged Scottish noblemen raised an army and overwhelmed the forces of Bothwell and Mary. They captured her, forced her to abdicate in favour of her one-year-old son, James, and imprisoned her here at Loch Leven – without her baby boy.

All these events were undoubtedly watched avidly by

Queen Elizabeth of England. In principle, Elizabeth supported Mary as the incontestably rightful queen of Scotland; but in practice no rescue party appeared on the horizon. Elizabeth's true attitude was probably that of someone who hears two drunks fighting in the street at night: it did not matter who won so long as neither tried to get into the house.

While Mary was with Darnley, Alison married a good Catholic, a man with hazel eyes and a mane of blond hair who reminded her of Pierre Aumande. He was kind and affectionate, but he expected Alison to serve him, not Mary, which she found difficult, even though she knew she should have anticipated it. She became pregnant but miscarried after four months. Soon afterwards her husband died in a hunting accident, and it was almost a relief to Alison to return to her familiar role as Mary's dedicated right-hand woman.

And now this.

'No one else has loved me the way you love me,' Mary had said during one of the long, dark Scottish evenings at Loch Leven, and Alison had blushed with a vague but strong emotion. 'My father died when I was a baby,' Mary had said. 'My mother mostly lived elsewhere. All three of my husbands have been hopelessly weak in their different ways. You've been mother and father and husband to me. Isn't that strange?' It had made Alison cry.

Their jailer was Sir William Douglas, owner of Loch Leven. Mary had a remarkable power to win affection, and Sir William had fallen for her. He acted like an obliging host entertaining a distinguished house guest. His daughters adored Mary – they found the notion of an imprisoned queen madly romantic – but his wife, Lady Agnes, was not seduced. Agnes had a strong sense of duty, and she remained insistently watchful.

However, Agnes had just given birth to her seventh child and was still confined to her room, which was one reason why this was the moment for an escape bid.

Mary was still being guarded by Captain Drysdale and his men-at-arms. But today was Sunday 2 May, so the soldiers were enjoying the May Day revels – and drinking more than usual.

Alison hoped they would become careless by late afternoon, when she and Mary planned to make their getaway.

It would be difficult, but they had collaborators.

Also resident at Loch Leven were Sir William's handsome half-brother George, nicknamed Pretty Geordie; and Willie Douglas, a tall fifteen-year-old orphan who Alison thought was probably an illegitimate son of Sir William.

Mary had set out to win the heart of Pretty Geordie. She had been allowed to send for her clothes – although not her jewels – and she was able to dress well. In any case, George was no great challenge: Mary had always been alluring, and here on this tiny island she had no rivals. With such a small group of people in a confined space, romantic emotions could heat up fast. Alison guessed it was not difficult for Mary to play the game, for George was charming as well as good-looking. Mary's feelings for him might even have been genuine.

Alison was not sure what favours Mary granted George: more than mere kisses, she assumed, for George was a grown man, but less than sexual intercourse, because Mary, with her besmirched reputation, could not risk the further disgrace of an illegitimate pregnancy. Alison did not ask Mary for the details. It was a long time since the happy days in Paris when they had been adolescent girls who told one another everything. But all that mattered now was that George was so badly smitten that he longed to play the part of the medieval knight and rescue his beloved from the castle of despair.

Alison herself had worked on young Willie. Again it was no great challenge, even though Alison was almost twice his age. Only just out of puberty, Willie would have fallen in love with any attractive woman who paid him attention. Alison needed only to talk to him, and ask him about his life, while standing a little too close to him; and to kiss him in a way that was almost sisterly, though not quite; and to smile when she caught him staring at her breasts; and to make arch remarks about 'you men' to bolster his courage. She had no need to grant sexual favours to this boy who was only just a man. In the deep recesses of her half-conscious mind she felt a tiny regret about this – something she was embarrassed to admit even to herself. But Willie succumbed easily, and was now her slave.

George and Willie had been smuggling Mary's letters in and out of the prison for some months, but with difficulty. Escape would be much harder.

Mary could not cross the little compound without being seen, for it was home to about fifty people: as well as the family and the men-at-arms there were Sir William's secretaries and a large staff of household servants. The gate was kept locked, and anyone who wanted to come and go had to get it unlocked or climb over the wall. Three or four boats were always pulled up on the beach, but Mary would need a strong accomplice to row her, and she could quickly be followed. Then, on the mainland, she would need friends with horses to whisk her away to a hiding place somewhere safe from pursuit.

There was such a lot that could go wrong.

Alison found it hard to sit still during the morning service in the chapel. She was desperate to escape, but she also feared the consequences if they were caught: she and Mary would probably be confined to one room, perhaps even forbidden those walks along the top of the perimeter wall which, though depressing, at least gave them fresh air and a distant sight of the world outside. Worst of all, they might be separated.

Mary was nothing if not bold, and she was ready to take the risk, as Alison was. But the penalty for failure would be dire.

After church there were May Day festivities. Willie excelled himself as Lord of Misrule, doing a hilarious drunk act while shrewdly remaining one of the few people on the island who was completely sober.

Pretty Geordie was on the mainland, and should by now be in the lakeside village of Kinross. It was his job to assemble horses and men to escort Mary and Alison away from there before they could be recaptured. Alison was frantic to know whether he had carried out his part of the plan. She was anxiously awaiting a signal from him.

Mary dined early in the afternoon with Sir William and the family, and Alison and Willie helped to serve. The dining room was on an upper floor of the square tower, with views from the little windows to the mainland; a necessary defensive feature. Alison had to stop herself constantly looking over the water.

At the end of the meal Willie left. The plan was that he would scramble over the wall and wait outside for a boat bringing a message from George saying that all was ready.

During the planning of the escape, young Willie had suggested that Mary should jump off the wall to the ground outside, a drop of seven feet that he did easily. As an experiment Alison had tried it, and had sprained her ankle. They could not risk Mary being slowed by an injury, so Willie's suggestion had been dropped. Instead, they would have to leave by the gate, which meant getting hold of a key.

Alison, as a noblewoman as well as a servant, was permitted to join the others at table as they sat chatting after dinner, eating nuts and fruit, Sir William sipping wine. There was not much to talk about on Loch Leven, but conversation was the main form of entertainment for lack of much else.

It was Sir William's mother, Lady Margaret, who glanced out of the window and noticed something on the far shore. 'Who are those horsemen, I wonder?' she said in a tone of mild curiosity.

Alison froze. How could George be so careless? He was supposed to keep his men out of sight! If Sir William became suspicious, he could easily lock Mary in her room, and then the plan would be wrecked. Surely it could not have failed already?

Sir William looked out and frowned. 'No reason for them that I know of.'

Mary rose to the occasion brilliantly. 'I must speak to you, Lady Margaret, about your son James, my brother,' she said in a challenging voice.

That got everyone's attention. Lady Margaret in her youth had been one of the many mistresses of Mary's father, King James V. She had borne his illegitimate son James Stuart, the half-brother Alison had met at St Dizier with the enigmatic Ned Willard, when the two young men had tried to persuade Mary not to return to Scotland. For Mary to raise this topic was not good manners.

Embarrassed, Lady Margaret said: 'James is in France.'

'Visiting Admiral Coligny – the hero of the Huguenots!'

'Madam, there is nothing I can do about James, as you surely know.'

Mary kept everyone looking at her instead of out of the window. Indignantly she said: 'I have been fond of him. I made him earl of Moray!'

Margaret was intimidated by this suddenly angry young queen. Sounding nervous, she said: 'And I know how grateful he is for your kindness.'

No one was looking out of the window now.

'Then why has James plotted against me?' Mary cried. Alison knew that her anger, though calculated, was genuine. 'Since I was brought here, he has forced me to sign abdication papers, he has crowned my baby son as King James VI, and he has made himself regent. He is now king of Scotland in all but legitimacy!'

The Douglases felt sorry for Mary, but they undoubtedly approved of what James Stuart had done, and they looked awkward – which was fine, Alison thought, for they had forgotten about the horsemen on the shore.

Sir William tried to be pacific. 'Of course this is not how you would wish it, madam,' he said to Mary. 'On the other hand, your child is king and your brother is regent, so the arrangement has a degree of legitimacy that cannot be denied.'

Alison stole a glance out of the window. There was no sign of horsemen now. She imagined that George might have angrily told them to get away from the shore. Perhaps they had been in Kinross for an hour or two and were getting restless, letting discipline slip. But the semblance of normality had been restored.

The crisis was over, but it had underlined how chancy the whole plan was, and it left her feeling even more edgy.

Mary seemed to run out of patience. 'I feel tired, after the May Day festivities,' she said, standing up. 'I'm going to rest.'

Alison went with her. Outside the door, a dark and narrow spiral staircase of stone led up and down to other floors. They climbed to the queen's quarters.

Mary was not in the least tired. She was excited and jittery, constantly getting up from her chair to go to the window, then returning and sitting down again.

Alison checked their disguises, folded in a trunk under Mary's gowns. They had got hold of coarse home-made wool-and-linen kirtles of the kind worn over petticoats by the many serving women at the castle, complete with the type of headdress known as a Flemish hood, which covered the hair and made it difficult for others to see the face except from directly in front. Servants sometimes wore stout leather boots that were so hard Mary and Alison could not even walk in them, but, fortunately, the women also used their mistresses' cast-off silk and satin slippers. For weeks Alison and Mary had been wearing old shoes whenever they were alone, to make them look shabby enough to have been handed down.

Their main problem was Mary's height. That could not be disguised. No other woman on the island was anywhere near so tall. Alison could hardly imagine that they could get away with it.

She put the disguises away again.

They had to be patient for another hour then, at six o'clock, Mary's supper was brought to her room.

As usual, it was served to her by Sir William, a courtesy by a jailer to his royal prisoner. Alison left the room and went looking for Willie to find out what was happening. Outside, a holiday game of handball was in progress, soldiers versus servants, with supporters cheering each side. Alison noticed that Drysdale, who was supposed to keep a close eye on Mary, was captain of the soldiers' team. That was good, she thought; he was distracted.

Willie was coming across the courtyard towards her, looking excited. 'It's come!' he whispered, and showed her a pearl earring.

This was the signal from George on the mainland. The earring meant all was ready for Mary's escape. Alison was thrilled. But Willie had been less than discreet. 'Close your fist!' she hissed at him. 'We don't want anyone asking questions.'

Fortunately, the people in the courtyard were intent on the game.

'Sorry,' said Willie. He closed his fingers around the jewel then passed it to Alison with a display of casualness.

Alison said: 'Now, slip over the wall and sabotage all the boats but one.'

'I'm ready!' he said, pulling aside his coat to reveal a hammer hanging from his belt.

Alison returned to Mary's quarters. Mary had not eaten much. Alison could imagine why. She herself was so tense that she could not have swallowed food. She handed Mary the jewel, saying: 'Here's the earring you lost. One of the boys found it.'

Mary knew what it meant. 'I'm so glad!' she said, beaming.

Sir William looked out of the window and grunted in surprise. 'What is that foolish boy doing with the boats?' he said in a tone that combined fondness with exasperation.

Alison followed his gaze. Willie was on the foreshore, kneeling in one of three boats that were drawn up on the beach. What he was doing was not obvious to a distant observer, but Alison knew he was making a hole in the hull so that the boat could not be used to pursue escapers. Alison suffered a moment of pure panic. She had no idea what to do. She turned to Mary and mouthed: 'Willie!'

Mary knew what Willie was supposed to do to the boats. Once again she showed her ability to think fast in an emergency. 'I feel terribly faint,' she said, and slumped in her chair with her eyes closed.

Alison realized what she was up to and played along. 'Oh, dear God, what's wrong?' she said, putting on a frightened voice.

She knew that Mary was faking, but Sir William did not. Looking fearful, he came at once to Mary's side. If she died in his care he would be in trouble. The regent, James Stuart, would be obliged to deny that he had connived at her murder, and to demonstrate his sincerity he might well have Sir William executed. 'What is it, what has happened?' Sir William said.

Alison said: 'She should have strong wine to revive her. Sir William, do you have some canary?'

'Of course. I'll fetch it at once.' He left the room.

'Well done,' Alison said quietly to Mary.

Mary said: 'Is Willie still at it?'

Alison looked out of the window. Willie was doing the same thing in a different boat. 'Hurry up, Willie!' she murmured. How long did it take to make a hole in a boat?

Sir William returned with a steward carrying a jug of wine and a goblet. Alison said: 'My hands are shaking. Sir William, will you hold the cup to her lips?'

Sir William obliged, taking the opportunity to put a hand tenderly behind Mary's head, and did not think to look out of the window.

Mary took a sip, coughed, and pretended to revive a little.

Alison made a show of touching her forehead and feeling her pulse. 'You'll be all right now, your majesty, but perhaps you should retire for the night.'

'Very well,' said Mary.

Sir William looked relieved. 'Then I'll leave you,' he said. 'Good night, ladies.' He glanced out of the window. Alison looked too. Willie was no longer on the beach. It was not possible to see whether he had succeeded in holing the boats.

Sir William left without making any comment.

The steward cleared the table and went out, then Alison and Mary were alone. Mary said: 'Did we get away with it?'

'I think so. Sir William may forget what he saw from the window: he's been drinking all afternoon, and he must be at least a little fuddled by now.'

'I hope suspicion doesn't make Sir William vigilant. Willie still has to steal the key.'

Sir William kept the gate key close at hand. When someone went to the mainland or came back, he would either open the gate himself or entrust the key to a guard for a few minutes only. Otherwise no one needed to leave the compound: there was nothing outside apart from the boats.

Mary and Alison had to get out of the compound, and Alison's experiment had established that they could not climb over the wall, so they had to unlock the gate. Willie had assured Alison and Mary that he would be able to steal the key without Sir William noticing. They were dependent on him.

'We should be dressed and ready,' said Alison.

They took off their costly gowns and put on the rough kirtles, then changed their shoes for old worn ones. The Flemish hoods covered their heads and usefully concealed Mary's distinctive auburn hair.

Now all they could do was wait.

Sir William liked Willie to serve his supper. His fondness for the orphan boy was what led everyone to speculate that they were father and son. But Willie's loyalty had been undermined by Alison.

She imagined that right now, one floor down, Willie was putting down and picking up plates and napkins and jugs. Perhaps the key lay on the table next to Sir William's wine goblet. She visualized Willie dropping a napkin over the key then picking up both. Would he get away with it? How drunk was Sir William? They could only wait and see.

If the plan worked, Mary's escape would be a political earthquake. She would disavow the abdication papers she had been forced to sign and claim her rightful throne. Her half-brother James would assemble a Protestant army, and Mary's Catholic supporters would rally – those of them who had not lost faith in her. The civil war would be renewed. Mary would be cheered by her brother-in-law the King of France, who was fighting a similar long-running civil war with the Huguenots. The supportive Pope would be glad to annul her marriage with Bothwell. Speculation about possible husbands for her would be renewed in every royal court from Rome to Stockholm. The European balance of power would shift seismically. Queen Elizabeth of England would be furious.

All that depended on Willie Douglas, aged fifteen.

There was a tap at the door, soft but insistent. Alison opened it. Willie stood there, beaming, holding a big iron key.

He stepped inside and Alison closed the door.

Mary stood up. 'Let's go at once,' she said.

Willie said: 'They're still at table. Sir William is asleep over his wine, but Lady Margaret is talking to her granddaughters.

They might see us, through the open door, as we go down.' The spiral staircase went past the doors to each floor of the castle.

Alison said: 'But this is a good time – the soldiers are still playing handball.'

Mary said decisively: 'We have to take chances. We'll go.'

Willie looked woebegone. 'I should have closed the dining-room door. I never thought of it.'

Alison said: 'Never mind, Willie. You're doing wonderfully well.' She gave him a soft kiss on the lips. He looked as if he had gone to heaven.

Alison opened the door, and they went out.

Willie led the way, followed by Mary, with Alison last. They tried to tread softly on the stone of the spiral staircase, hoping not to attract attention. Both women pulled their hoods forward as they approached the open door to the dining room. Light spilled from the doorway, and Alison heard low female voices. Willie went past without looking in. Mary put her hand to her face as the light fell on her. Alison waited to hear a shout of alarm. She walked past the door and went on down the stairs after the others. She heard a peal of laughter, and imagined Lady Margaret chortling scornfully at their pathetic attempt to disguise themselves; but it seemed her amusement had some other cause. They had not been noticed; or, if Lady Margaret had happened to glance up, perhaps she had seen nothing more remarkable than a few servants passing the doorway on some errand.

They went outside.

It was just a few steps from the tower door to the compound gate, but it seemed more. The courtyard was full of people watching the game. Alison spotted Drysdale, hitting the ball with his two hands clamped together, concentrating hard.

Then Willie was at the gate.

He put the iron key into the big lock and turned it. Alison kept her back to the crowd, hiding her face, but that meant she could not tell whether anyone was looking at them. It took an effort of will to resist the temptation to look back over her shoulder. The massive timber gate creaked noisily as Willie pushed it open: did anyone hear that sound over the cheering?

The three fugitives stepped through. No one came after them. Willie closed the gate behind them.

'Lock it,' said Alison. 'It may slow them down.'

Willie locked the gate, then dropped the key into the barrel of the cannon that stood beside the entrance.

No one had seen them.

They ran down to the beach.

Willie took hold of the one undamaged boat and pushed it into the shallows, then held it with its keel just touching the shore. Alison clambered in, then turned to help Mary. The queen stepped into the boat and sat down. Willie pushed it off from the beach, jumped in, and started to row.

Alison looked back. There was no sign that they had been missed: no one on the ramparts, no one leaning out of the castle windows, no one running down to the beach.

Was it possible that they had escaped?

The sun had not yet set, and a long summer evening stretched ahead. The breeze, though stiff, was warm. Willie pulled strongly at the oars. He had long arms and legs, and he was motivated by love. All the same, their progress across the wide lake seemed agonizingly slow. Alison kept looking back, but there was no pursuit yet. Even if they realized the queen had gone, what could they do? They would have to mend one of the remaining boats before they could give chase.

She began to believe they were free.

As they approached the mainland, Alison saw the figure of a man she did not recognize, waiting on the shore. 'Hell,' she said. 'Who's that?' She was possessed by a terrible fear that they had come this far only to be trapped again.

Willie looked over his shoulder. 'That's Alistair Hoey. He's with George.'

Alison's heartbeat slowed again.

They reached the shore and jumped out of the boat. Alistair led them along a path between houses. Alison heard horses stamping and snorting impatiently. The escapers emerged onto the main road through the village – and there was Pretty Geordie, smiling in triumph, surrounded by armed men. Horses were saddled ready for the fugitives. George helped

Mary onto her mount, and Willie had the joy of holding Alison's foot while she swung herself up.

Then they all rode out of the village to freedom.

*

EXACTLY TWO WEEKS later, Alison was convinced that Mary was about to make the greatest mistake of her life.

Mary and Alison were at Dundrennan Abbey, on the south coast of Scotland, across the Solway Firth from England. Dundrennan had been the grandest monastery in Scotland. The monasteries had been secularized, but there was still a magnificent Gothic church and an extensive range of comfortable quarters. Mary and Alison sat alone in what had been the abbot's luxurious suite of rooms, grimly contemplating their future.

Everything had gone wrong for Queen Mary – again.

Mary's army had met the forces of her brother, James Stuart, at a village called Langside, near Glasgow. Mary had ridden with her men, and had been so brave that they had had to restrain her from leading the charge, but she had been defeated, and now she was on the run again. She had ridden south, across bleak windswept moorland, burning bridges behind her to slow pursuit. One miserable evening Alison had cut off all Mary's lovely auburn hair, to make her less easily recognizable, and now she was wearing a dull brown wig. It seemed to complete her wretchedness.

She wanted to go to England, and Alison was trying to talk her out of it.

'You still have thousands of supporters,' Alison said brightly. 'Most Scots people are Catholic. Only upstarts and merchants are Protestant.'

'An exaggeration, but with some truth,' Mary said.

'You can regroup, assemble a bigger army, try again.'

Mary shook her head. 'I had the larger army at Langside. It seems I cannot win the civil war without outside help.'

'Then let us go back to France. You have lands there, and money.'

'In France I am an ex-queen. I feel too young for that role.'

Mary was an ex-queen everywhere, Alison thought, but she did not say it. 'Your French relations are the most powerful family in the country. They might assemble an army to back you, if you ask them personally.'

'If I go to France now, I will never return to Scotland. I know it.'

'So you're determined . . .'

'I will go to England.'

They had had this discussion several times, and each time Mary came to the same conclusion.

She went on: 'Elizabeth may be a Protestant, but she believes that a monarch who has been anointed with holy oils – as I was when I was nine months old – rules by divine right. She cannot validate a usurper such as my brother James – she is in too much danger of being usurped herself.'

Alison was not sure how precarious Elizabeth's position was. She had been queen for ten years without serious opposition. But perhaps all monarchs felt vulnerable.

Mary went on: 'Elizabeth must help me regain my throne.'

'No one else thinks that.'

It was true. All the noblemen who had fought at Langside and had accompanied Mary on her flight south were opposed to her plan.

But she would make up her own mind, as always. 'I'm right,' she said. 'And they're wrong.'

Mary had always been wilful, Alison thought, but this was almost suicidal.

Mary stood up. 'It's time to go.'

They went outside. George and Willie were waiting in front of the church, with a farewell party of noblemen and a small group of servants who would accompany the queen. They mounted horses and followed a grassy track alongside a stream that ran, gurgling and chuckling, through the abbey grounds towards the sea. The path went through spring-green woodland sprinkled with wild flowers, then the vegetation changed to tough gorse bushes splashed with deep-golden-yellow blossoms. Spring blooms signalled hope, but Alison had none.

They reached a wide pebble beach where the stream emptied into the sea.

A fishing boat waited at a crude wooden jetty.

On the jetty, Mary stopped, turned, and spoke directly to Alison in a low voice. 'You don't have to come,' she said.

It was true. Alison could have walked away. Mary's enemies would have left her alone, seeing no danger: they would think a mere lady-in-waiting could not organize a counter-revolution, and they would be right. Alison had an amiable uncle in Stirling who would take her in. She might marry again: she was certainly young enough.

But the prospect of freedom without Mary seemed the most dismal of all possible outcomes. She had spent her life serving Mary. Even during the long empty weeks and months at Loch Leven she had wanted nothing else. She was imprisoned, not by stone walls, but by her love.

'Well?' said Mary. 'Will you come?'

'Of course I will,' Alison said.

They got into the boat.

'We could still go to France,' Alison said desperately.

Mary smiled. 'There is one factor you overlook,' she said. 'The Pope and all the monarchs of Europe believe that Elizabeth is an illegitimate child. Therefore she was never entitled to the throne of England.' She paused, looking across the twenty miles of water to the far side of the estuary. Following her gaze Alison saw, dimmed by haze, the low green hills of England. 'And if Elizabeth is not queen of England,' said Mary, 'then I am.'

*

'SCOTTISH MARY HAS arrived in Carlisle,' said Ned Willard to Queen Elizabeth, in the presence chamber at White Hall palace.

The queen expected Ned to know such things, and he made it his job to have answers ready. That was why she had made him Sir Ned.

'She's moved into the castle there,' Ned went on, 'and the

deputy governor of Carlisle has written to you asking what he should do with her.'

Carlisle was in the far north-west corner of England, and close to the Scottish border, which was why there was a fortress there.

Elizabeth paced the room, her magnificent silk gown rustling with her impatient steps. 'What the devil shall I tell him?'

Elizabeth was thirty-four. For ten years she had ruled England with a firm hand. She had a confident grasp of European politics, navigating those treacherous tides and undercurrents with Sir William Cecil as her pilot. But she did not know what to do about Mary. The queen of the Scots was a problem with no satisfactory solution.

'I can't have Scottish Mary running around England, stirring up discontent among the Catholics,' Elizabeth said with frustration. 'They would start saying she is the rightful queen, and we'd have a rebellion to deal with before you could say transubstantiation.'

Cecil, the lawyer, said: 'You don't have to let her stay. She is a foreign monarch on English soil without your permission, which is at least a discourtesy and could even be interpreted as an invasion.'

'People would call me heartless,' Elizabeth said. 'Throwing her to the Scottish wolves.' Ned knew that Elizabeth could be heartless when it suited her. However, she was always sensitive to what the English people would think of her actions.

Ned said: 'What Mary wants is for you to send an English army to Scotland to help her regain her rightful throne.'

'I haven't got the money,' Elizabeth said quickly. She hated war and she hated spending money. Neither Ned nor Cecil was surprised at her instant rejection of this possibility.

Cecil said: 'Failing your assistance, she may ask her French relatives to help her. And we don't want a French army in Scotland.'

'God forbid.'

'Amen,' said Cecil. 'And let's not forget that when she was married to Francis they called themselves king and queen of

France, Scotland, England and Ireland. She even had it on her tableware. Mary's French family have ambitions without limit, in my opinion.'

'She's a thorn in my foot,' Elizabeth said. 'God's body, what am I to do?'

Ned recalled his encounter with Mary seven years ago at St Dizier. She was striking-looking, taller than Ned and beautiful in an ethereal way. He had thought she was brave but impulsive, and he had imagined she might make decisions that were bold but unwise. Coming to England was almost certainly a wrong move for her. He also remembered her companion, Alison McKay, a woman of about his own age, dark-haired and blue-eyed, not as beautiful as Mary but probably wiser. And there had been an arrogant young courtier with them called Pierre Aumande de Guise: Ned had disliked him instantly.

Cecil and Ned already knew what decision Elizabeth must make. But they knew her too well to try to tell her what to do. So they had taken her through the available choices, letting her rule out the bad ones herself. Now Cecil assumed a casual tone of voice as he put to her the option he wanted her to decide on. 'You could just incarcerate her.'

'Here in England?'

'Yes. Let her stay, but keep her prisoner. It has certain advantages.' Cecil and Ned had made this list together, but Cecil spoke as if the advantages had only just occurred to him. 'You would always know where she is. She would not be free to foment a rebellion. And it would weaken the Scots Catholics if their figurehead were captive in a foreign country.'

'But she would be here, and the English Catholics would know it.'

'That is a drawback,' Cecil said. 'But perhaps we could take steps to prevent her communicating with malcontents. Or with anyone else, come to that.'

In practice, Ned suspected, it might be difficult to keep a prisoner totally incommunicado. But Elizabeth's mind went in a different direction. 'I would be quite justified in locking her up,' she mused. 'She has called herself queen of England. What would Felipe do to a man who said he was the rightful king of Spain?'

'Execute him, of course,' said Cecil promptly.

'In fact,' Elizabeth said, talking herself into doing what she wanted to do, 'it would be merciful of me merely to imprison Mary.'

'I think that's how it would be seen,' Cecil said.

'I think that's the solution,' she said. 'Thank you, Cecil. What would I do without you?'

'Your majesty is kind.'

The queen turned to Ned. 'You'd better go to Carlisle and make sure it's done properly,' she said.

'Very good, your majesty,' said Ned. 'What shall I say is the reason for detaining Mary? We don't want people to say her imprisonment is unlawful.'

'Good point,' said Elizabeth. 'I don't know.'

'As to that,' said Cecil, 'I have a suggestion.'

*

CARLISLE WAS A formidable fortress with a long defensive wall pierced only by a narrow gateway. The castle was made of pinkish-red local sandstone, the same as the cathedral that stood opposite. Within the wall was a square tower with cannons on its roof. The guns were all pointed towards Scotland.

Alison and Mary were housed in a smaller tower in a corner of the compound. It was just as stark as Loch Leven, and cold even in June. Alison wished they had horses, so that they could go for rides, something Mary had always loved and had missed badly at Loch Leven. But they had to content themselves with walking, escorted always by a troop of English soldiers.

Mary decided not to press her complaints to Elizabeth. All that mattered was that the queen of England should help her regain her Scottish throne.

Today they expected the long-awaited emissary from Elizabeth's court. He had arrived late last night and retired immediately.

Alison had managed to get messages to Mary's friends in

Scotland and as a result some clothes and wigs had arrived, though her jewellery – much of it given to her by King Francis II when she was queen of France – was still in the Protestant grasp of her half-brother. However, she had been able to make herself look royal this morning. After breakfast they sat in the mean little room they inhabited at the castle, waiting to hear their fate.

They had discussed Elizabeth night and day for a month, talking over her religious convictions, her beliefs about monarchy, her reputed learning, and her famously imperious personality. They had tried to guess what decision she would make: would she help Mary regain her throne, or not? They had reached no conclusion – or, rather, they had reached a different conclusion every day. But now they would find out.

Elizabeth's messenger was a little older than Alison, almost thirty, she guessed. He was slim, with a pleasant smile and golden-brown eyes. His clothes were good but unostentatious. Looking closely, Alison was surprised to recognize him. She glanced at Mary and saw a slight frown, as if she, too, was trying to place him. As he bowed low to the queen and nodded to Alison she remembered where they had met. 'St Dizier!' she said.

'Seven years ago,' he said. He spoke French: he knew, or had guessed, that Mary was most comfortable in this tongue, Scots being her second language and English a distant third. His manner was polite but relaxed. 'I'm Sir Ned Willard.'

Alison thought his careful good manners cloaked a dangerous toughness, like a velvet scabbard for a sharp-edged sword. She spoke warmly in an attempt to soften him. 'Sir Ned, now!' she said. 'Congratulations.'

'You're very kind.'

Alison remembered that Ned had pretended to be merely a clerk to James Stuart, a pretence that had been revealed when he spoke so challengingly to Pierre Aumande.

Mary said: 'You tried to persuade me not to go to Scotland.'

'You should have taken my advice,' he said unsmilingly.

Mary ignored that and got down to business. 'I am the queen of Scotland,' she said. 'Queen Elizabeth won't deny that.'

'No, indeed,' said Ned.

'I was illegally imprisoned by traitors among my subjects. Again, I feel sure my cousin Elizabeth will agree.'

They were not quite cousins, of course, but more distantly related: Elizabeth's grandfather, King Henry VII of England, was Mary's great-grandfather. But Sir Ned did not quibble.

Mary went on: 'And I came here to England of my own free will. All I ask is the chance to speak to Elizabeth in person, and to beg for her assistance.'

'I will certainly give her that message,' said Ned.

Alison suppressed a groan of disappointment. Ned was prevaricating. That was bad news.

Mary bristled. 'Give her the message?' she said indignantly. 'I expected you to bring me her decision!'

Ned was not flustered. Perhaps it was not the first time he had had to deal with an angry queen. 'Her majesty can't make such a decision immediately,' he said in the calm tones of reason.

'Why not?'

'Other matters must be resolved first.'

Mary was not to be fobbed off that easily. 'What matters?'

Ned said reluctantly: 'The death of your husband, Lord Darnley, the king consort of Scotland and the cousin of Queen Elizabeth, remains . . . unexplained.'

'That is nothing to do with me!'

'I believe you,' said Ned. Alison suspected he did not. 'And her majesty Queen Elizabeth believes you.' That was not true either. 'But we must establish the facts to the satisfaction of the world before you can be received at Elizabeth's court. Her majesty hopes that you, as a queen yourself, will understand that.'

This was rejection, Alison thought, and she wanted to weep. The murder of Darnley was not the real issue; it was a pretext. The plain fact was that Elizabeth did not want to meet Mary.

And that meant she did not want to help Mary.

Mary came to the same conclusion. 'This is cruelly unjust!' she said, standing up. Her face reddened, and tears came to her eyes. 'How can my cousin treat me so coldly?'

'She asks you to be patient. She will provide for all your needs meanwhile.'

'I do not accept this decision. I shall sail to France. My family there will give me the help Elizabeth denies me.'

'Queen Elizabeth would not want you to bring a French army to Scotland.'

'Then I shall simply go back to Edinburgh, and take my chances against my treacherous half-brother, your friend James Stuart.'

Ned hesitated. Alison saw that his face was a little pale, and he clasped his hands behind his back as if to stop himself fidgeting uneasily. The wrath of a queen was a dreadful sight. But Ned held all the cards. His voice, when he spoke, was strong and his words were uncompromising. 'I'm afraid that will not be possible.'

It was Mary's turn to look fearful. 'What on earth can you mean?'

'The queen's orders are that you shall remain here, until the English courts can clear you of complicity in the murder of Lord Darnley.'

Alison felt tears come to her eyes. 'No!' she cried. This was the worst possible outcome.

'I'm sorry to bring you such unwelcome news,' he said, and Alison believed he meant it. He was a kind man with an unkind message.

Mary's voice was shaky. 'So Queen Elizabeth will not receive me at court?'

'No,' said Ned.

'She will not let me go to France?'

'No,' he said again.

'And I may not return home to Scotland?'

'No,' Ned said for the third time.

'So I am a prisoner?'

'Yes,' said Ned.

'Again,' said Mary.

16

WHEN HIS MOTHER DIED, Ned felt sad and bereft and alone but, most of all, he felt angry. Alice Willard's last years should have been luxurious and triumphant. Instead, she had been ruined by a religious quarrel, and had died thinking herself a failure.

It was Easter 1570. By chance Barney was at home, in a short break between sea voyages. On Easter Monday the brothers celebrated the resurrection of the dead in Kingsbridge Cathedral, then the next day they stood side by side in the cemetery as their mother's coffin was lowered into the grave where their father already lay. There was hot resentment in Ned's stomach, bilious and sour, and he vowed again to spend his life making sure that men such as Bishop Julius would not have the power to destroy honest merchants like Alice Willard.

As they walked away from the grave, Ned tried to turn his mind to practical matters, and he said to Barney: 'The house is yours, of course.'

Barney was the elder son. He had shaved off his bushy beard to reveal a face that was prematurely aged, at thirty-two, by cold saltwater winds and the glare of the unshaded sun. He said: 'I know, but I have little use for it. Please live there whenever you're in Kingsbridge.'

'Is seafaring going to be your life, then?'

'Yes.'

Barney had prospered. After leaving the *Hawk*, he had been made captain of another vessel, with a share in the profits, and then he had bought his own ship. He had their mother's knack for making money.

Ned looked across the market square to the house where he had been born. He loved the old place, with its view of the cathedral. 'I'll be glad to take care of it for you. Janet and Malcolm Fife will do the work, but I'll keep an eye on them.'

'They're getting old,' Barney said.

'They're in their fifties. But Eileen is only twenty-two.'

'And perhaps she might marry a man who would like to take over Malcolm's job.'

Ned knew better. 'Eileen will never marry anyone but you, Barney.'

Barney shrugged. Many women had fallen hopelessly in love with him; poor Eileen was just another one.

Ned said: 'Aren't you ever tempted to settle down?'

'There's no point. A sailor hardly ever sees his wife. What about you?'

Ned thought for a minute. The death of his mother had made him aware that his time on earth was limited. Of course he had known that before, but now it was brought home to him; and it made him ask himself if the life he led was the one he really wanted. He surprised himself with his answer to Barney's question. 'I want what they had,' he said, looking back at the grave where both parents lay. 'A lifelong partnership.'

Barney said: 'They started early. They were married at twenty, or thereabouts, weren't they? You're already ten years behind schedule.'

'I don't live the life of a monk . . .'

'I'm glad to hear it.'

'But somehow I never come across a woman I want to spend my life with.'

'With one exception,' said Barney, looking over Ned's shoulder.

Ned turned and saw Margery Fitzgerald. She must have been in church during the service, but he had not seen her in the crowd. Now his heart faltered. She had dressed sombrely for the funeral, but as always she wore a hat, today a purple velvet cap pinned at an angle to her luxuriant curls. She was speaking earnestly to old Father Paul, a former monk at Kingsbridge Priory, now a canon at the cathedral, and probably a secret Catholic. Margery's obstinate Catholicism should have repelled Ned, but on the contrary he admired her idealism. 'I'm afraid there's only one of her, and she married someone else,' he said. This was a fruitless subject of discussion, he thought impatiently. He said: 'Where will your next sea voyage take you?'

'I want to go to the New World again. I don't like the slave trade – the cargo is too liable to die on the voyage – but over there they need just about everything, except sugar.'

Ned smiled. 'And I seem to remember you mentioning a girl . . .'

'Did I? When?'

'That sounds to me like a yes.'

Barney looked bashful, as if he did not want to admit to a deeper feeling. 'Well, it's true that I've never met anyone like Bella.'

'That was seven years ago.'

'I know. She's probably married to a wealthy planter by now, with two or three children.'

'But you want to find out for sure.' Ned was quite surprised. 'You're not very different from me after all.'

They drifted towards the ruined monastery. 'The Church never did anything with these old buildings,' Ned said. 'Mother had a dream of turning them into an indoor market.'

'She was smart. It's a good idea. We should do it one day.'

'I'll never have enough money.'

'I might, though, if the sea is kind to me.'

Margery approached, followed by a lady-in-waiting and a man-at-arms: she rarely went anywhere alone, now that she was the countess of Shiring. Her little retinue stood a few yards off as she shook Barney's hand, then Ned's, and said: 'What a sad day.'

Barney said: 'Thank you, Margery.'

'But a wonderful crowd for the funeral. Your mother was very much loved.'

'Indeed.'

'Bart begs your pardon for not being here – he had to go to Winchester.'

Barney said: 'Will you excuse me? I have to speak to Dan

Cobley. I want him to invest in my next voyage – to spread the risk.' He moved away, leaving Ned alone with Margery.

Margery's voice changed to a low, intimate tone. 'How are you, Ned?'

'My mother was sixty, so it wasn't a shock to me,' Ned said. That was what he told everyone, but it was glib, and he felt an urge to say more to Margery. He added bleakly: 'But you only get one mother.'

'I know. I didn't even like my father, especially after he made me marry Bart, but still I cried when he passed away.'

'That generation has almost gone.' Ned smiled. 'Remember that Twelfth Night party, twelve years ago, when William Cecil came? In those days they seemed to rule the world: your father, my mother and Bart's father.'

Margery's eyes glinted with mischief. 'Of course I remember.'

Ned knew she was thinking of the fevered minutes they had spent kissing in the disused bread oven. He smiled at the memory. On impulse he said: 'Come to the house for a cup of wine. Let's talk about old times. This is a day for remembering.'

They threaded their way slowly through the market. It was crowded: business did not stop for a funeral. They crossed the main street and went into the Willard house. Ned showed Margery into the little front parlour, where his mother had always sat, with the view of the west front of the cathedral.

Margery turned to the two servants who had followed her in. 'You two can go to the kitchen.'

Ned said: 'Janet Fife will give you a mug of ale and something to eat. And please ask her to bring wine for your mistress and me.'

They went away, and Ned closed the door. 'How is your baby?' he said.

'Bartlet isn't a baby any longer,' she said. 'He's six years old, walking and talking like a grown-up, and carrying a wooden sword.'

'And Bart has no idea . . .'

'Don't even say it.' Margery lowered her voice to a whisper.

'Now that Swithin's dead, you and I are the only people who know. We must keep the secret for ever.'

'Of course.'

Margery was quite sure that Bartlet had been fathered by Swithin, not Bart; and Ned thought she was almost certainly right. In twelve years of marriage she had conceived only once, and that was when her father-in-law raped her.

He said: 'Does it change how you feel?'

'About Bartlet? No. I adored him from the moment I saw him.'

'And Bart?'

'Also dotes on him. The fact that Bartlet looks like Swithin seems quite natural, of course. Bart wants to turn the boy into a copy of himself in every way . . .'

'But that's natural, too.'

'Listen, Ned. I know men think that if a woman conceives that means she enjoyed it.'

'I don't believe that.'

'Because it isn't true. Ask any woman.'

Ned saw that she was desperate for reassurance. 'I don't need to ask anyone. Really.'

'You don't think I lured Swithin, do you?'

'Certainly not.'

'I hope you feel sure.'

'I'm more sure of that than of my own name.'

Tears came to her eyes. 'Thank you.'

Ned took her hand.

After a minute she said: 'Can I ask you another question?'

'All right.'

'Has there been anyone else?'

He hesitated.

The pause was enough for her. 'So there has,' she said.

'I'm sorry, but I'm not a monk.'

'More than one, then.'

Ned said nothing.

Margery said: 'Years ago, Susannah Brecknock told me she had a lover half her age. It was you, wasn't it?'

Ned was amazed by the accuracy of her intuition. 'How did you guess?'

'It just seems right. She said he didn't love her, but she didn't care, because he was such fun to lie with.'

Ned was embarrassed that two women had discussed him in this way. 'Are you angry?' he said.

'I have no right to be. I lie with Bart, why should you be celibate?'

'But you were forced to marry.'

'And you were seduced by a woman with a warm heart and a soft body. I'm not angry, I just envy her.'

Ned raised her hand to his lips.

The door opened and Ned hastily pulled his hand away.

The housekeeper came in with a jug of wine and a plate of nuts and dried fruits. Margery said kindly: 'This is a sad day for you, too, Janet.'

Janet burst into tears and left without speaking.

'Poor thing,' said Margery.

'She's worked for my mother since she was a girl.' Ned wanted to hold Margery's hand again, but he restrained himself. Instead, he brought up a new topic. 'I need to talk to Bart about a small problem.'

'Oh? What?'

'The queen has made me lord of Wigleigh.'

'Congratulations! Now you'll be rich.'

'Not rich, but comfortable.' Ned would collect rents from all the farmers in the village. It was how monarchs often paid their advisors – especially penny-pinching rulers such as Elizabeth.

Margery said: 'So now you're Sir Ned Willard of Wigleigh.'

'My father always said Wigleigh traditionally belonged to our family. He thought we were descended from Merthin the bridge-builder. According to Timothy's Book, Merthin's brother, Ralph, was lord of Wigleigh, and Merthin built the watermill that is still there.'

'So you're descended from nobility.'

'Gentry, at least.'

'So what's the problem you need to discuss with Bart?'

'One of my tenants has cleared some of the forest beyond the stream, on land that belongs to you. He had no right, of course.' Tenants were always trying to increase the size of their holdings surreptitiously. 'But I don't like to punish enterprise, so I want to work out some agreement that will compensate Bart for the loss of a couple of acres.'

'Why don't you come to New Castle for dinner one day next week, and talk to him?'

'All right.'

'Friday at noon?'

Suddenly Ned felt happy. 'Yes,' he said. 'Friday is fine.'

*

MARGERY WAS ASHAMED of how excited she felt about Ned's visit.

She believed in fidelity. Even though she had been forced to marry Bart, her duty was to be loyal to him. It made no difference that he was growing more like his late father, oafish and bullying and promiscuous. There were no excuses for Margery: sin was sin.

She was embarrassed by the flush of desire that had overwhelmed her when Ned promised to visit New Castle. She vowed to treat him with careful courtesy, and no more warmth than any polite hostess would show a distinguished guest. She wished he would fall in love and marry someone else, and lose interest in her. Then perhaps they could think of one another calmly, as old flames that had sputtered out long ago.

The day before she had ordered the cook to kill and pluck a pair of fat geese, and in the morning she was heading for the kitchen to give instructions for the cooking when she saw a girl coming out of Bart's room.

It was Nora Josephs, she saw, the youngest of the housemaids at fifteen. Her hair was untidy and she had evidently dressed in haste. She was not pretty, but she had the plump kind of young body that appealed to Bart.

They had had separate bedrooms for about five years now. Margery preferred it this way. Bart still came to her bed now and again, but less and less often. She knew that he had other women but, she told herself, she did not care, because she did not love him. All the same, she wished with all her heart that she could have had a different kind of marriage.

As far as she knew, none of his mistresses had ever become pregnant. However, Bart seemed never to question why. He did not have a very logical mind, and if he thought about it at all he probably told himself it was God's will.

Margery was prepared to pretend she had not noticed, but young Nora gave her a saucy look, and that was a bad sign. Margery was not willing to be humiliated, and she decided she had better deal with Nora immediately. It was not the first time she had found herself in this situation, and she knew what to do. 'Come with me, girl,' she said in her most authoritative voice, and Nora did not dare to disobey. They went into Margery's boudoir.

Margery sat down and left Nora standing. The girl looked scared now, so perhaps there was hope for her. 'Listen to me carefully, because the whole of the rest of your life depends on how you behave now,' Margery said. 'Do you understand me?'

'Yes, madam.'

'If you choose, you may flaunt your relationship with the earl. You can touch him in front of the other servants. You can show off the gifts he gives you. You can even shame me by kissing him in my presence. Everyone in this house and half the people in the county of Shiring will know that you are the earl's mistress. You will feel proud.'

She paused. Nora could not meet her eye.

'But what will happen when he tires of you? I will throw you out, of course, and Bart won't care. You will try to find work as a maid in another house, and then you'll realize that no woman is going to take you on, because they'll all think you're going to seduce their husbands. And do you know where you'll end up?'

She paused, and Nora whispered: 'No, madam.'

'In a waterfront brothel at Combe Harbour, sucking the cocks of ten sailors a night, and you'll die of a horrible disease.'

Margery did not really know what went on in brothels, but

she managed to sound as if she did, and Nora was fighting back tears.

Margery went on: 'Or you can treat me with respect. If the earl takes you to his bed, leave him as soon as he falls asleep, and return to the servants' quarters. Refuse to answer the questions the others ask you. In the daytime, don't look at him or speak to him, and never touch him in front of me or anyone else. Then, when he tires of you, you will still have a place here, and your life will return to normal. Do you understand the choice in front of you?'

'Yes, madam,' Nora whispered.

'Off you go.' As Nora opened the door, Margery added bitterly: 'And when you take a husband for yourself, pick one who is not like mine.'

Nora scurried away, and Margery went to see about the cooking of the geese.

Ned arrived at midday, wearing a costly black coat and a white lace collar – an outfit that was becoming the uniform for affluent Protestants, Margery had noticed. It looked a bit austere on Ned: she liked him in warm colours, green and gold.

Margery's dog, Mick, licked Ned's hand. Bart, too, welcomed Ned in a friendly way, getting out the best wine for the midday dinner. That was a relief. Perhaps Bart had forgotten that Margery had wanted to marry Ned. Or perhaps he did not care, because he had got her anyway. To men such as Bart, winning was all-important.

Bart was not a deep thinker, and he had never suspected Ned of planning the downfall and execution of Swithin. Bart had a different theory. He was convinced that Dan Cobley, the leader of the Puritans, had set the trap, as revenge on Sir Reginald and Rollo for the execution of his own father. And it was true that Dan still bore a poisonous grudge against Rollo.

Margery also felt nervous about Stephen Lincoln, who joined them at table. Ned would guess Stephen's role in the earl's household, but he would not say anything. The presence of priests in the homes of Catholic noblemen was universally known but never acknowledged. Margery usually frowned on hypocrisy: the orphan whose father was known but never named; the nuns who shared a passionate love that everyone pretended not to notice; the unmarried housekeeper who bore a series of children all resembling the priest who employed her. But in this case, the pretence worked in Margery's favour.

However, she was not sure that Stephen would be as tactful as Ned. Stephen hated Queen Elizabeth, to whom Ned owed his entire career. And Ned had reason to hate the Catholic Church, which had punished his mother so cruelly for usury. It might be a tense dinner.

Bart said amiably: 'So, Ned, you're one of the queen's most important advisors now, people tell me.' There was only a touch of resentment in Bart's tone. He thought the queen's counsellors should be earls, not the sons of merchants; but he also knew in his heart that he could never give the queen guidance on the intricacies of European politics.

'I work with Sir William Cecil, and have done for twelve years,' Ned said. 'He is the important one.'

'But she has made you a knight, and now lord of Wigleigh.'

'I'm very grateful to her majesty.'

An unaccustomed feeling crept over Margery, sitting at the table and watching Ned as he talked. He had a quick intelligence, and his eyes crinkled with humour frequently. She sipped wine and wished this dinner could go on forever.

Stephen Lincoln said: 'What, exactly, do you do for Elizabeth, Sir Ned?'

'I try to give her early warning of burgeoning problems.'

Margery thought this sounded pat, as if Ned had been asked the question many times and always trotted out the same answer.

Stephen gave a twisted grin. 'Does that mean you spy on people who disagree with her?'

Margery groaned inwardly. Stephen was going to be combative and spoil the atmosphere.

Ned sat back and squared his shoulders. 'She doesn't care if people disagree with her, as long as they keep their views to themselves. I would have expected you to know that, Stephen, as Earl Bart regularly pays the fine of one shilling a week for not going to church.'

Bart said grumpily: 'I go to the big events at Kingsbridge Cathedral.'

'And very wise you are, if I may say so. But in Elizabeth's England no one is tortured for their religion, and no one has been burned at the stake – a stark contrast with the reign of her predecessor, Queen Mary.'

Bart spoke again. 'What about the Northern Rebellion?'

Margery knew what he was talking about. Just before Christmas a group of Catholic earls had taken up arms against Queen Elizabeth in the only rebellion of her reign so far. They had celebrated a Latin Mass in Durham Cathedral, occupied several other towns in the north, and marched towards Tutworth, where Mary Queen of Scots was imprisoned, with the evident intention of freeing her and proclaiming her queen of England. But the uprising had gained little support, the queen's forces had put it down quickly, and Mary Stuart remained a prisoner.

Ned said: 'It fizzled out.'

'Five hundred men have been hanged!' Bart said indignantly. 'By the queen who complains of Mary Tudor's cruelty!'

Ned said mildly: 'Men who try to overthrow the monarch are generally executed, in every country in the world, I believe.'

Bart was a poor listener, like his father, and he responded as if he had not heard Ned. 'The north is poor enough already, but it has been looted mercilessly, lands confiscated and all the livestock seized and driven south!'

Margery wondered whether this reminded Ned of how his own family had been mercilessly plundered by her father; but if he thought of that he hid his pain. He was not flustered by Bart's tactless tirade, and Margery supposed that, spending his life among the queen's advisors, Ned had learned how to remain calm during angry arguments. 'I can tell you that the queen has not received much booty,' he said in a reasonable tone of voice. 'Certainly nothing approaching the cost to her of putting down the insurrection.'

'The north is part of England – it should not be plundered like a foreign country.'

'Then its people should behave like Englishmen, and obey their queen.'

Margery decided that this was a good moment to change the subject. 'Ned, tell Bart about the problem in Wigleigh.'

'It's quickly stated, Bart. One of my tenant farmers has encroached on your land, and has cleared a couple of acres of forest on your side of the river.'

'Then throw him off it,' Bart said.

'If you wish, I will simply tell him to stop using that land, of course.'

'And if he disobeys?'

'I'll burn his crop.'

Margery knew that Ned was pretending to be harsh in order to reassure Bart.

Bart did not realize he was being manipulated. 'It's what he deserves,' he said in a tone of satisfaction. 'These peasants know the boundaries better than anyone: if he has encroached, he's done so deliberately.'

'I agree, but there might be a better solution,' Ned said as if he hardly cared one way or the other. 'After all, when peasants prosper, their landlords do too. Suppose I give you four acres of woodland somewhere else, in exchange for the two already cleared? That way, we both gain.'

Bart looked reluctant, but clearly could not think of a counterargument. However, he temporized. 'Let's pay a visit to Wigleigh together,' he said. He was not good at abstract thinking, Margery knew: he would much prefer to make a decision while looking at the land in question.

Ned said: 'Of course, I'd be glad to, especially if we can do so soon – I need to get back to London, now that my mother is buried.'

Margery felt a stab of disappointment, and realized she had been hoping that Ned would stay in Kingsbridge longer.

Bart said: 'How about next Friday?'

Ned felt impatient, but suppressed the feeling: Margery could tell by his face, though probably no one else noticed. Clearly he would have preferred to settle this trivial matter right away so that he could get back to great affairs of state. He said: 'Could you make it Monday?'

Bart looked annoyed, and Margery knew he was offended that he, an earl, should be asked to hurry up by a mere knight. 'No, I'm afraid I can't,' he said mulishly.

'Very well,' said Ned. 'Friday it is.'

*

IN THE DAYS following the funeral, Ned thought ahead to the time when he would meet his maker, and asked himself whether he would be proud of the life he had led. He had dedicated himself to a vision – one he shared with Queen Elizabeth – of an England where no one was killed for his religion. Could he say he had done everything possible to defend that ideal?

Perhaps the greatest danger was King Felipe of Spain. Felipe was constantly at war, often over religious differences. He fought the Ottoman Muslims in the Mediterranean Sea and the Dutch Protestants in the Netherlands. Sooner or later, Ned felt sure, he would turn his attention to England and the Anglican Church.

Spain was the richest and most powerful country in the world, and no one knew how to defend England.

Ned shared his worry with his brother. 'The only thing Queen Elizabeth will spend money on willingly is the navy,' he said. 'But we'll never have a fleet to match King Felipe's galleons.'

They were sitting in the dining room, finishing breakfast. Barney was about to leave for Combe Harbour, where his ship was taking on stores for the next voyage. He had renamed the vessel *Alice* after their mother.

'England doesn't need galleons,' said Barney.

Ned was startled by that. He was in the act of giving a sliver of smoked fish to Maddie, the tortoiseshell cat – daughter or perhaps granddaughter of his childhood pet – but he froze, looked up at Barney and said: 'What *do* we need, in your opinion?'

'The Spanish idea is to have big ships to transport hundreds of soldiers. Their tactic is to ram, so that the soldiers can board the enemy ship and overwhelm the crew.'

'That makes sense.'

'And it often works. But galleons have a high after-castle with cabins for all the officers and noblemen on board. That structure acts like a sail that can't be adjusted, and pushes the ship in the direction of the wind, regardless of where the captain wants to go. In other words, it makes the ship harder to steer.'

The waiting cat made a plaintive noise, and Ned gave her the fish, then said: 'If we don't need galleons, what do we need to protect ourselves?'

'The queen should build ships that are narrow and low, and therefore more manoeuvrable. An agile ship can dance around a galleon, firing at it without letting the galleon get close enough for all those soldiers to board.'

'I have to tell her this.'

'The other main factor in sea battles is speed of reloading.'

'Really?'

'It's more important than having heavy guns. My sailors are trained to clean out the barrel and recharge the cannon rapidly and safely. With practice they can do it in under five minutes. Once you're close enough to hit the enemy ship with every shot, it's all about the number of times you can fire. A relentless barrage of cannonballs will demoralize and devastate the enemy very quickly.'

Ned was fascinated. Elizabeth had no standing army, so the navy was England's only permanent military force. The country was not wealthy, by European standards, but such prosperity as it had came from overseas trade. The navy was a formidable presence on the high seas, making others hesitate before attacking English merchant ships. In particular, the navy gave England dominance in the Channel, the waterway that separated the country from Europe. Elizabeth was parsimonious, but she had an eye for what was really important, and she paid careful attention to her ships.

Barney got up. 'I don't know when I'll see you again,' he said.

I don't know if I'll *ever* see you again, Ned thought. He

picked up Barney's heavy travelling coat and helped him on with it. 'Be safe, Barney,' he said.

They parted company with little ceremony, in the manner of brothers.

Ned went into the front parlour and sat at the writing table his mother had used for so many years. While the conversation was fresh in his mind he made a note of everything Barney had said about the design of fighting ships.

When he had finished, he looked out of the window at the west front of the cathedral. I'm thirty years old, he thought. When my father was this age he already had Barney and me. In another thirty years I may be lying in the cemetery next to my parents. But who will stand at my grave?

He saw Dan Cobley approaching the house, and put morbid thoughts out of his mind.

Dan walked in. 'Barney's just left,' Ned said, assuming that Dan was here to talk about his investment in Barney's voyage. 'He's taking the barge to Combe Harbour. But you might catch him at the dock, if you hurry.'

'My business with Barney is settled, to our mutual satisfaction,' Dan said. 'I've come to see you.'

'In that case, please sit down.'

At thirty-two Dan was plumper than ever, and still had a know-all air that struck Ned as adolescent. But Dan was a good businessman, and had expanded the enterprise he had inherited. He was now probably the richest man in Kingsbridge. He was looking for a bigger house, and had offered a good price for Priory Gate, though Rollo did not want to sell. Dan was also the undisputed leader of the town's Puritans, who liked to worship at St John's church in the suburb of Loversfield.

As Ned feared, Dan had come to talk about religion.

Dan leaned forward dramatically. 'There is a Catholic among the clergy at Kingsbridge Cathedral,' he said.

'Is there?' Ned sighed. 'How could you possibly know a thing like that?'

Dan answered a different question. 'His name is Father Paul.'

Paul Watson was a gentle old priest. He had been the last prior of Kingsbridge, and he had probably never accepted the reformed religion. 'And what is Father Paul's crime, exactly?'

Dan said triumphantly: 'He celebrates Mass, secretly, in the crypt, with the doors locked!'

'He's an old man,' Ned said wearily. 'It's hard for such people to keep changing their religious convictions.'

'He's a blasphemer!'

'Yes, he is.' Ned agreed with Dan about theology; he differed only about enforcement. 'You've actually witnessed these illegal rites?'

'I have watched people creeping furtively into the cathedral by a side door at dawn on Sunday – including several I've long suspected of backsliding into idolatry: Rollo Fitzgerald, for one, and his mother, Lady Jane, for another.'

'Have you told Bishop Luke?'

'No! I'm sure he tolerates it.'

'Then what do you propose?'

'Bishop Luke has to go.'

'And I suppose you want Father Jeremiah from St John's to be made bishop.'

Dan hesitated, surprised that Ned had read his intentions so easily. He cleared his throat. 'That is for her majesty to decide,' he said with insincere deference. 'Only the monarch can appoint and dismiss bishops in the Anglican Church, as you know. But I want you to tell the queen what is going on – and if you don't, I will.'

'Let me explain something to you, Dan – though you're not going to like it. Elizabeth may dislike Catholics but she hates Puritans. If I go to her with this story she'll have me thrown out of the presence chamber. All she wants is peace.'

'But the Mass is illegal, as well as heretical!'

'And the law is not strictly enforced. How could you not have noticed?'

'What is the point of a law if it's not enforced?'

'The point is to keep everyone reasonably content. Protestants are happy because the Mass is illegal. Catholics are happy because they can go to Mass anyway. And the queen is happy because people are going about their business and not killing one another over religion. I strongly advise you not to complain to her. She won't do anything about Father Paul, but she might do something about you.'

'This is outrageous,' said Dan, standing up.

Ned did not want to quarrel. 'I'm sorry to send you away with a dusty answer, Dan,' he said. 'But this is the way things are. I'd be misleading you if I said anything else.'

'I appreciate your frankness,' Dan said grudgingly, and they parted with at least the semblance of cordiality.

Five minutes later, Ned left the house. He walked up the main street, past Priory Gate, the house he would always think of as having been built with money stolen from his mother. He saw Rollo Fitzgerald emerge. Rollo was in his middle thirties now, and his black hair was receding, giving him a high forehead. When Sir Reginald died, Rollo had applied to take his place as Receiver of Customs at Combe Harbour, but such plum posts were used by the sovereign to reward loyalty, and it had gone to a staunch Protestant, not surprisingly. However, the Fitzgerald family still had a large business as wool brokers, and Rollo was running that well enough, more competently than his father ever had.

Ned did not speak to Rollo but hurried on across the high street and went to a large old house near St Mark's church. Here lived what remained of the Kingsbridge monks. King Henry VIII had granted a small stipend to some of those he dispossessed, and the few still alive continued to receive their pensions. Father Paul came to the door, a bent figure with a red nose and wispy hair.

He invited Ned into the parlour. 'I'm sorry you've lost your mother,' Paul said simply. 'She was a good woman.'

The former bishop, Julius, also lived here, and he was sitting in a corner, staring at nothing. He was demented, and had lost all speech, but his face wore a furious expression, and he mumbled angry gibberish at the wall.

'It's good of you to take care of Julius,' Ned said to Father Paul.

'It's what monks are supposed to do – look after the sick, and the poor, and the bereaved.'

If more of them had remembered that we might still have a monastery, Ned thought, but he kept it to himself. 'Of course,' he said. 'The legendary Caris, who founded the hospital, was a nun at Kingsbridge.'

'Rest her soul.' Looking hopeful, Paul said: 'A glass of wine, perhaps?'

Ned hated the fuddling effect of wine in the morning. 'No, thank you. I won't stay long. I came to give you a word of warning.'

An anxious frown crossed Paul's lined face. 'Oh, dear, that sounds ominous.'

'It is, a little. I've been told that something is going on in the crypt at dawn on Sundays.'

Paul paled. 'I have no idea—'

Ned held up a hand to stall the interruption. 'I'm not asking you whether it's true, and there's no need for you to say anything at all.'

Paul was agitated, but quieted himself with a visible effort. 'Very well.'

'Whoever is using the crypt at that hour, for whatever purpose, should be warned that the town's Puritans are suspicious. To avoid trouble, perhaps the services – if that is what they are – should be moved to a different venue.'

Paul swallowed. 'I understand.'

'Her majesty the queen believes that religion was given to us for consolation in this life and salvation in the next, and that we may disagree about it, but we should never let it be a cause of violence between one Englishman and another.'

'Yes.'

'Perhaps I don't need to say any more.'

'I think I understand you perfectly.'

'And it might be best if you don't tell anyone that I came to see you.'

'Of course.'

Ned shook Paul's hand. 'I'm glad we had a chance to talk.'

'Me, too.'

'Goodbye, Father Paul.'

'God bless you, Ned,' said Paul.

*

ON FRIDAY MORNING, Margery's husband felt ill. This was not unusual, especially after a good supper with plenty of wine the night before. However, today Earl Bart was supposed to go to Wigleigh and meet Sir Ned Willard.

'You can't let Ned down,' Margery said. 'He'll have ridden there specially.'

'You'll have to go instead of me,' Bart said from his bed. 'You can tell me what it's all about.' Then he put his head under the blanket.

Margery's spirits lifted at the prospect of spending an hour or two with Ned. Her heart seemed to beat faster and her breath came in shallow gasps. She was glad Bart was not looking at her.

But her reaction showed her how unwise it would be to do this. 'I don't want to go,' she lied. 'I've got so much to do here at the castle.'

Bart's voice was muffled by the blanket, but his words were clear enough. 'Don't be stupid,' he said. 'Go.'

Margery had to obey her husband.

She ordered her best horse saddled, a big mare called Russet. She summoned the lady-in-waiting and the man-at-arms who usually accompanied her: they should be enough to keep her out of trouble. She changed into travelling clothes, a long blue coat and a red scarf and hat to keep the dust out of her hair. It was a practical outfit, she told herself, and she could not help it if the colours suited her complexion and the hat made her look cute.

She kissed Bartlet goodbye. She whistled for her dog, Mick, who loved to accompany her on a ride. Then she set off.

It was a fine spring day, and she decided to stop worrying and enjoy the sunshine and fresh air. She was twenty-seven years old and a countess, rich and healthy and attractive: if she could not be happy, who could?

She stopped at an inn on the road for a glass of beer and a

piece of cheese. Mick, who seemed tireless, drank at the pond. The man-at-arms gave each horse a handful of oats.

They reached Wigleigh in the early afternoon. It was a prosperous village, with some fields still cultivated on the old strip system and others belonging to individual farmers. A fast stream drove an old watermill for fulling cloth, called Merthin's Mill. In the centre were a tavern, a church and a small manor house. Ned was waiting in the tavern. 'Where's Bart?' he said.

'He's sick,' Margery replied.

He looked surprised, then pleased, then apprehensive, all in quick succession, as he digested this news. Margery knew why he might be apprehensive: it was the risk of temptation. She felt the same anxiety.

Ned said: 'I hope it's not serious.'

'No. It's the kind of illness a man suffers after drinking too much wine.'

'Ah.'

'You get me instead – a poor substitute,' she said with facetious modesty.

He grinned happily. 'No complaints here.'

'Shall we go to the site?'

'Don't you want something to eat and drink?'

Margery did not want to sit in a stuffy room with half a dozen peasants staring at her. 'No, thank you,' she said.

They rode a path between fields of spring-green wheat and barley. 'Will you live in the manor house?' Margery asked.

'No. I'm too fond of the old house in Kingsbridge. I'll just use this place for a night or two when I need to visit.'

Margery was seized by a vision of herself creeping into Ned's house at night, and she had to put the wicked thought out of her mind.

They came to the wood. The stream that drove the mill also marked part of the boundary of Wigleigh, and the land beyond belonged to the earl. They followed the stream for a mile, then came to the location in question. Margery could see immediately what had happened. A peasant who was more enterprising than most, or greedier, or both, had cleared the forest on the earl's side of the stream and was grazing sheep on the rough grass that had sprung up there.

'Just beyond here is the patch I'm offering Bart in exchange,' Ned said.

Margery saw a place where the ground on the Wigleigh side was forested. They rode across the stream, then dismounted and walked the horses into the wood. Margery noted some mature oaks that would provide valuable timber. They stopped at a pretty clearing with wild flowers and a grassy bank beside the stream. 'I can't see why Bart would object to the exchange,' Margery said. 'In fact, I think we'll be getting a bargain.'

'Good,' said Ned. 'Shall we rest here a while?'

The prospect was delightful. 'Yes, please,' she said.

They tethered the horses where they could crop some grass.

Ned said: 'We could send your people to the tavern for food and drink.'

'Good idea.' Margery turned to the man-at-arms and the lady-in-waiting. 'You two, go back to the village. You can walk – the horses need a rest. Fetch a jug of ale and some cold ham and bread. And enough for yourselves, of course.'

The two servants disappeared into the woods.

Margery sat on the grass by the stream and Ned lay beside her. The wood was quiet: there was just the shush of the stream and the breath of a light breeze in the spring leaves. Mick lay down and closed his eyes, but he would wake and give warning if anyone approached.

Margery said: 'Ned, I know what you did for Father Paul.'

Ned raised his eyebrows. 'News travels fast.'

'I want to thank you.'

'I suppose you supply the sacramental wafers.' She was not sure what to say to that, but Ned quickly added: 'I don't want to know the details, please forget I asked.'

'Just as long as you know that I would never conspire against Queen Elizabeth.' Margery wanted him to understand that. 'She is our anointed ruler. I may wonder why God in his wisdom chose to set a heretic on the throne, but it is not for me to challenge his choice.'

Ned, still lying down, looked up at her and smiled. 'I'm very glad to hear it.' He touched her arm.

She stared at his kind, clever face. What she saw in his eyes was a yearning so strong it might have broken her heart. No one else had ever felt like this about her, she knew. At that moment it seemed that the only possible sin would be to reject his passion. She lowered her head and kissed his lips.

She closed her eyes and gave herself up to the love that possessed her, filling her soul as the blood filled her body. She had thought about this ever since the last time they had kissed, though now, after such a long wait, it was even sweeter. She sucked his lower lip into her mouth, then teased his upper lip with the tip of her tongue, then pushed her tongue into his mouth. She could not get enough of him.

He grasped her shoulders and pulled her down until she was lying on top of him, putting all her weight on him. She could feel his erection through her petticoats. She worried that she might be hurting him, and moved to roll off, but he held her in place. She relaxed into the feeling of being so close that they might melt into one another. There seemed nothing in the world except him and her, nothing outside their two bodies.

Even this did not satisfy her for long: everything they did made her want more. She knelt up, straddling Ned's knees, and opened the front of his breeches to free his penis. She stared at it, stroking it lovingly. It was pale and slightly curved, springing from a tangle of curly auburn hair. She bent over and kissed it, and heard him gasp with pleasure. A tiny drop of fluid appeared at the end. Unable to resist the temptation, she licked it off.

She could wait no longer. She moved to straddle his hips, tenting the skirt of her dress over the middle of his body, then sank down, guiding his penis inside her. She was impossibly wet, and it slipped in effortlessly. She bent forward so that she could kiss him again. They rocked gently for a long time, and she wanted to do it for ever.

Then he was the one who wanted more. He rolled her over, without withdrawing. She spread her legs wide and lifted her knees. She wanted him deeper inside her, filling her up. She felt him losing control. She looked into his eyes and said: 'It's you, Ned, it's you.' She felt the jerking spasm and the rush of fluid, and that drove her over the edge, and she felt happy, truly happy, for the first time in years.

*

ROLLO FITZGERALD would have died rather than change his religion. For him there was no room for compromise. The Catholic Church was right and all rivals were wrong. It was obvious, and God would not forgive men who ignored the obvious. A man held his soul in his hand like a pearl, and if he were to drop that pearl in the ocean he would never get it back.

He could hardly believe that Elizabeth Tudor had lasted twelve years as the illegitimate queen of England. She had given people a measure of religious freedom and, amazingly, her religious settlement had not yet collapsed. The Catholic earls had failed to overthrow her and all the monarchs of Europe had hesitated while she pretended she might marry a good Catholic. It was a terrible disappointment. Rollo would have believed that God was asleep, were it not a blasphemous thing to say.

Then, in May of 1570, everything changed, not just for Rollo but for everyone in England.

Rollo got the news at breakfast in Priory Gate. Margery was at the table. She was paying an extended visit to Kingsbridge to look after their mother, Lady Jane, who had been ill. Mother had recovered somewhat and was now at breakfast with them, but Margery seemed in no hurry to go home. The maid Peggy came in and handed Rollo a letter, saying a courier had brought it from London. It was a large piece of heavy paper, folded corners-to-middle and closed with a blob of red wax impressed with the Fitzgerald seal. The handwriting was that of Davy Miller, the family's man of business in London.

Davy's letters were normally about the price of wool, but this one was different. The Pope had made a formal announcement, called a Papal Bull. Such messages were not circulated in England, of course. Rollo had heard rumours about it, but now, according to Davy, someone had daringly nailed a copy to the gate of the bishop of London's palace, so everyone knew what was in it. Rollo gasped when he read Davy's summary.

Pope Pius V had excommunicated Queen Elizabeth.

'This is good news!' Rollo said. 'The Pope describes Elizabeth as "the pretended queen of England and the servant of crime". At last!'

'Elizabeth must be furious,' Margery said. 'I wonder if Ned Willard knows about this.'

Lady Jane said darkly: 'Ned Willard knows everything.'

'It gets better,' Rollo said jubilantly. 'Englishmen are released from their allegiance to Elizabeth, even if they have sworn oaths.'

Margery frowned. 'I'm not sure you should be so pleased,' she said. 'This means trouble.'

'But it's true! Elizabeth is a heretic and an illegitimate queen. No one should obey her.'

Lady Jane said: 'Your sister's right, Rollo. This may not be good news for us.'

Rollo carried on reading. 'In fact, people are commanded *not* to obey her, and anyone who does obey is included in the sentence of excommunication.'

Margery said: 'This is a catastrophe!'

Rollo did not understand them. 'It needs to be said, and the Pope is saying it at last! How can this be bad news?'

'Don't you see what it means, Rollo?' said Margery. 'The Pope has turned every English Catholic into a traitor!'

'He's only making plain what everyone knows.'

'Sometimes it's better not to say what everyone knows.'

'How is that possible?'

'Everyone knows that Father Paul celebrates Mass for us, and Stephen Lincoln too, and all the other secret priests – but no one says it. That's the only reason we get away with it. Now it's under threat. We're all potential traitors.'

Rollo saw what they meant, but they were wrong. People were stupid and freedom was dizzyingly perilous. Men had to fight against Elizabeth's heresy, even if it made life uncomfortable or even dangerous. 'You women don't understand politics,' he said.

Margery's son, Bartlet, came into the room. Rollo looked at the boy with pride. Bartlet was his nephew, and would one day be the earl of Shiring.

'Can we play with the kittens today?' Bartlet said.

'Of course, my darling,' said Margery. She explained: 'Ned's tortoiseshell cat has had kittens, and Bartlet's fascinated by them.'

Lady Jane said: 'I wouldn't stay too long at the Willard house, if I were you.'

Rollo wondered why his mother's tone was so frosty, then he recalled the struggle to make Margery marry Bart rather than Ned. That was ancient history, but perhaps Lady Jane feared people would think Margery had an ulterior motive in going to Ned's house.

Perhaps she did.

Rollo dismissed the thought: he had more important things on his mind. 'I've got to go to a meeting of the borough council,' he said. 'I'll see you all at dinner.' He kissed his mother and went out.

Kingsbridge was ruled by a council of twelve aldermen, all local merchants, chaired by the Mayor. Rollo had taken his father's place as an alderman when he inherited the family's wool business, but the current mayor was Elijah Cordwainer, a crony of Dan Cobley's. The council met in the Guild Hall, as they had for hundreds of years.

Rollo walked up the main street to the crossroads, went into the Guild Hall, and climbed the stairs to the council chamber, conscious that he was about to take part in a venerable tradition. The room was panelled in smoke-blackened wood. Leather chairs were arranged around a conference table that was scored with ancient graffiti. On a sideboard was a round of beef and a jug of ale, for anyone who had not had time for breakfast.

Rollo took his place. He was the only Catholic in the room: none of the other aldermen had ever appeared at one of Father Paul's clandestine services. Rollo felt vaguely intimidated, as if he was a spy among enemies. He had not felt this way before, and he wondered if that was because of the Papal Bull. Perhaps Margery was right. He hoped not.

The council regulated commerce and industry in the city, and the morning's business was about weights and measures, wages and prices, masters and apprentices. It was reported that some visiting tradesmen at the market were using the banned Tower Pound, which was lighter than the approved Troy Pound. They discussed a rumour that Queen Elizabeth might standardize a mile at 5,280 feet instead of 5,000. They were about to break up for midday dinner when Mayor Cordwainer announced a last-minute addition to the agenda: the Papal Bull.

Rollo was puzzled. The council never discussed religion. What was this about?

Cordwainer said: 'Unfortunately, the Pope in Rome has seen fit to order Englishmen not to obey her majesty Queen Elizabeth.'

Rollo said irritably: 'What has that to do with this council?'

Cordwainer looked uncomfortable and said: 'Well, er, Alderman Cobley feels it may raise questions . . .'

So Dan Cobley was up to something, Rollo thought. That made him anxious. Dan still blamed him for the execution of Philbert, and lusted for vengeance.

Everyone looked at Dan.

'It would be a bad thing if the shadow of treason were to fall on the borough of Kingsbridge,' Dan said, clearly making a rehearsed speech. 'I'm sure you all agree.'

There was a mutter of agreement around the table. Margery had said at breakfast that the Bull made traitors of all Catholics, and Rollo now felt a dark foreboding.

'To avoid all suspicion,' Dan went on, 'I have a simple suggestion: all Kingsbridge merchants should swear to the Thirty-Nine Articles.'

The room fell silent. Everyone knew what this meant. It was a direct attack on Rollo. The Thirty-Nine Articles defined the doctrine of the Anglican Church. Any Catholic who accepted them would be betraying his faith. Rollo would die rather than take such an oath.

And everyone in the room knew that.

Not all Kingsbridge Protestants were as hard-line as Dan. Most of them wanted nothing more than to do business in peace. But Dan could be slyly persuasive.

Paul Tinsley, the lawyer who was clerk of the peace for the town, said: 'There have been several attempts by Parliament to make all public officials take an oath affirming the Articles, but Queen Elizabeth has always refused to ratify any such legislation.'

Dan said: 'She won't refuse next time it comes up – not after this Bull. She's going to have to clamp down.'

'Perhaps,' said Tinsley. 'But we could wait until Parliament makes a decision, rather than take the matter into our own hands.'

'Why wait?' said Dan. 'Surely there is no one in this room who denies the truth of the Articles? And if there is, should he be allowed to trade in Kingsbridge after this Papal Bull?'

Tinsley persisted in his mild tone of voice. 'You may well be right, Alderman Cobley. I'm suggesting merely that we should not act in haste.'

Rollo spoke up. 'Alderman Tinsley is right. I for one will not sign a religious declaration put in front of me by Alderman Cobley.' Untruthfully he added: 'If her majesty the queen should ask for it, that would be a different matter.' It would not, but Rollo was desperate: his livelihood was at stake.

Dan said: 'What if word got around that we have had this discussion and decided not to act? Won't that put *us* under suspicion?'

Around the table there were several reluctant nods, and Rollo began to think Dan would get his way.

Cordwainer said: 'I think we must take a vote. Those in favour of Alderman Cobley's proposal, please raise your hands.'

Ten hands went up. Only Rollo and Tinsley were against.

Cordwainer said: 'The resolution is passed.'

Rollo stood up and left the room.

*

MARGERY LAY in bed at New Castle early on a July morning, listening to the birds. She felt happy, guilty and scared.

She was happy because she loved Ned and he loved her. He had stayed in Kingsbridge all through May, and they had met several times a week. Then he had been ordered to report on south-coast defences. It was Margery's normal practice to go with Stephen Lincoln at least once a week to celebrate Mass clandestinely in remote villages and suburban barns, and she and Ned contrived to make their paths cross. They would manage to spend a night in the same town, or nearby villages. After dark, when most people had gone to bed, they would rendezvous. If she was staying in a tavern, Ned would creep into her room. On warm nights they sometimes met in woods. The secrecy made their meetings almost unbearably thrilling. Right now he was only a few miles from New Castle, and she was hoping to slip away on some pretext and see him today. She lived in a state of continuous excitement that made it almost impossible for her to eat. She lived on wheat bread with butter and watered wine.

Bart seemed oblivious. It would never occur to him that his wife might be unfaithful, any more than he would expect his own dog to bite him. Margery's mother, Lady Jane, probably had her suspicions, but would not say anything for fear of causing trouble. However, Margery knew she and Ned could not get away with this behaviour indefinitely. It might take a week or a year, but sooner or later they would be found out. Nevertheless, she could not stop.

She was happy, but at the same time tortured by guilt. Often she thought back to where she had gone wrong. It had been the moment when she ordered her lady-in-waiting and man-at-arms to walk back to Wigleigh for food. She must have known, in her heart, that she was going to lie with Ned among the wild flowers beside the stream; and the prospect had been too sweet to resist. She had seen the steep and thorny way to heaven, but had chosen the primrose path of dalliance. She was committing a sin, enjoying it, and repeating it. Every day she vowed to end it, and every time she saw Ned her resolution evaporated.

She was afraid of the consequences, both now and in the

afterlife. God would surely punish her. He might afflict her with a terrible disease, or drive her mad, or strike her blind. She sometimes gave herself a headache thinking about it. And she had additional reasons for fear. Her foreboding about the effects of the Papal Bull had turned out to be tragically accurate. Puritans could now gleefully point to Catholics as a danger to national security. Intolerance had gained a pretext.

Bart now had to pay the large sum of a pound a week, instead of a shilling a week, for not going to church. A pound was the price of a musket, a fancy shirt or a small pony. It made a dent in Bart's income from rents, which came to about fifty pounds a week. The parish churchwarden was naturally afraid of the earl, but summoned up the courage once a week to come to the castle and ask for the money, and Bart had to pay.

Much worse was the effect on Rollo. He had lost his business because he would not swear to the Thirty-Nine Articles. He had been forced to sell Priory Gate, and Dan Cobley had exultantly bought it. Lady Jane was now living at New Castle with Margery and Bart. Rollo himself had gone away, and even his mother did not know where.

Ned was incandescent with rage. Queen Elizabeth had risked everything for the ideal of religious freedom, and had maintained it for a decade, proving that it could be done; but now, he fumed, she was being undermined – by the Pope, of all people. Margery did not like to hear him criticizing the Pope, even though she secretly agreed with him, so she just tried to avoid the topic.

In fact, she avoided all serious thoughts as much as she could, and let her mind dwell on love. When she was not with Ned, she daydreamed about the next time they would meet, and what they would do. Now, as her imagination began to depict them together, and she heard, in the ear of fantasy, the intimate words he would murmur to her as he touched her, she felt the familiar sensation in her loins, and her hand drifted to the place between her legs where delight arose. Strangely, her meetings with Ned did not quench this desire: in fact, she did it more now, as if one sin fed the other.

Her dog, Mick, lying beside the bed, woke up and growled.

'Hush,' she murmured, but then he barked. A moment later, there was a hammering at the door of the house.

The sound itself told Margery that trouble had arrived. The knocking was loud, repeated, demanding, authoritative. Few people dared to knock on an earl's door in that aggressive, arrogant manner. She jumped out of bed and ran to the window. Outside she saw Sheriff Matthewson with a group of nine or ten men.

She could not guess exactly what the sheriff wanted, but she had no doubt it had to do with religion.

She ran from the room, pulling a wrapper over her nightdress. Along the corridor, Bart looked out of his room. 'What is it?' he said thickly.

'Don't open the door,' Margery said.

The knocking continued.

Margery hurried across the landing to Stephen Lincoln's room. She burst in: there was no time for niceties. But he was up and dressed and kneeling at his prie-dieu. 'The sheriff is at the door,' she said. 'Come with me. Bring the sacramentals.'

Stephen picked up a box containing all they needed for the Mass and followed Margery out.

She saw Bartlet, in his nightshirt, followed by a sleepy young nurse. 'Go back to your room, Barty,' she said. 'I'll come for you when breakfast is ready.' She ran down the stairs, praying that the servants had not already let Matthewson in. She was almost too late: young Nora Josephs was in the act of unbarring the door, shouting: 'All right! All right! I'm coming!'

'Wait!' Margery hissed.

All the servants were Catholic. They would understand what was happening and keep silent about what they knew.

With Stephen close behind, Margery ran along the corridor and through a storeroom to a spiral staircase. She went up the stairs and then down a shorter flight into a dead-end passageway that was the bakery of the old castle, now disused. She pulled open the iron door to the massive bread oven where she had kissed Ned all those years ago. 'In here!' she said to Stephen. 'Hide!'

'Won't they look here?'

'Go all the way to the back and push against the wall. It leads to a secret room. Quickly!'

Stephen climbed inside with his box, and Margery shut the door.

Breathing hard, she retraced her steps to the front hall. Her mother was there, hair in a nightcap, looking worried. Margery pulled the wrapper more closely around her, then nodded to Nora. 'Now you can open up.'

Nora opened the door.

Margery said brightly: 'Good morning, Sheriff. How hard you knocked! Are you in a hurry?'

Matthewson was a big man who had a brusque way with malefactors, but he was uneasy confronting a countess. He tipped up his chin defiantly and said in a loud voice: 'Her majesty the queen has ordered the arrest of the Catholic priest Stephen Lincoln, suspected of treasonously conspiring with the Queen of the Scots.'

The charge was ridiculous. Stephen had never met Mary Queen of Scots, and anyway he would not have the nerve for a conspiracy. The accusation was malicious, and Margery suspected that Dan Cobley was behind it. But she smiled and said: 'Then you needn't have woken us up so early. Stephen is not a priest, nor is he here.'

'He lives here!'

'He was the earl's clerk, but he has left.' Improvising desperately, she added: 'I think he may have gone to Canterbury.' That was enough detail, she decided. 'Anyway, I'm quite sure he has never had anything to do with the Queen of the Scots. I'm sorry you've had a wasted journey. But now that you're here, would you and your men like some breakfast?'

'No, thank you.' He turned to his men. 'Search the house.'

Margery heard Bart say: 'Oh, no, you don't.' She turned to see him coming down the stairs. He was wearing his sword as well as his breeches and boots. 'What the devil do you think you're up to, Matthewson?'

'Carrying out orders from the queen, my lord, and I hope you won't offend her majesty by obstructing me.'

Margery stood between Bart and the sheriff and spoke in a

low voice. 'Don't fight him. Don't be executed like your father. Let him search the house. He won't find anything.'

'To hell with that.'

The sheriff said: 'You're suspected of harbouring a Catholic priest called Stephen Lincoln who is a traitor. It will be better for you to give him up now.'

In a louder voice, Margery said to Bart: 'I've already explained that Stephen is not a priest and is no longer here.'

Bart looked mystified. He stepped closer to Margery and whispered: 'But what about—'

'Trust me!' she hissed.

Bart shut up.

Margery raised her voice again. 'Perhaps we should allow the sheriff to satisfy himself that we're telling the truth. Then everyone will be content.'

Enlightenment dawned on Bart. He mouthed: 'In the old oven?'

Margery said: 'Yes, that's what I think, let him search.'

Bart looked at Matthewson. 'All right, but I won't forget this – especially your part in it.'

'It's not my decision, my lord, as you know.'

Bart grunted contemptuously.

'Get going, men,' said the sheriff. 'Pay special attention to the remains of the old castle – it's sure to be full of hiding places.' He was no fool.

Margery said to Nora: 'Serve breakfast in the dining room – just for the family, no one else.' There was now no point in pretending to be hospitable.

Bart went with ill temper to the dining room, and Lady Jane followed, but Margery could not summon enough sang-froid to sit and eat while the men looked for Stephen, so she followed the sheriff around the house.

Although his men searched the halls and parlours of the new house, he was more interested in the old castle, and carried a lantern to light dark places. He examined the church first. The tomb of a forgotten ancestor caught his eye, and he grasped the effigy of the knight on top and tried to move it, to test whether it might have been opened. It was firm.

The bakery was almost the last place he tried. He opened the iron door and shone his lamp inside, and Margery held her breath and pretended insouciance. He leaned forward, head and shoulders in the oven, and waved the lamp around. Was the door at the back as invisible as Margery remembered? Matthewson grunted, but she could not interpret the sound.

Then he withdrew and slammed the door.

Margery said gaily: 'Did you think we might keep priests in the oven?' Then she hoped he had not noticed the slight tremor in her voice.

He looked annoyed and did not trouble to answer her facetious question.

They returned to the entrance hall. Matthewson was angry. He suspected he had been hoodwinked but he could not figure out how.

Just as he was about to leave, the front door opened and Sir Ned Willard walked in.

She stared at him in horror. He knew the secret of the old bakery. Why was he here?

There was a light film of perspiration on his forehead, and he was breathing heavily: clearly he had been riding hard. She guessed that somehow he had heard about the sheriff's mission. But what was his purpose? No doubt he was worried about Margery. But he was a Protestant, too: would he be tempted to flush out the fugitive priest? His loyalty to Queen Elizabeth was profound, almost like love: would it be outweighed by his love for Margery?

He gave Matthewson a hostile glare. 'What's going on here?' he said.

The sheriff repeated his explanation. 'Stephen Lincoln is suspected of treason.'

'I haven't heard of any such suspicion,' Ned said.

'As I understand it, Sir Ned, you haven't been in London since before Easter, so perhaps you haven't heard.' The sheriff's words were polite, but he said them with a sneer.

Ned felt foolish, Margery could tell by his face. He prided himself on knowing everything first. He had slipped – and undoubtedly it was because of her.

Margery said: 'Stephen Lincoln is not here. The sheriff has searched my house very thoroughly. If we'd had a Catholic mouse in the pantry I believe he would have found it.'

'I'm glad to hear the queen's orders are being carried out so meticulously,' Ned said, apparently changing sides. 'Well done, sheriff.'

Margery felt so tense she wanted to scream. Was Ned about to say *But did you find the secret room behind the old oven?* Controlling her voice with an effort she said: 'If that's all, sheriff . . .'

Matthewson hesitated, but he had nothing left to do. Looking like thunder, he walked away, rudely without saying farewell.

One by one his men followed him through the door.

Bart came out of the dining room. 'Have they gone?' he said.

Margery could not speak. She burst into tears.

Bart put his arms around her. 'There, there,' he said. 'You were magnificent.'

She looked over his shoulder at Ned, who wore the face of a man in torment.

*

ROLLO WAS GOING to have his revenge.

He was weary, dusty, and seething with hatred and resentment when he arrived at the university town of Douai, in the French-speaking south-west of the Netherlands, in July of 1570. It reminded him of Oxford, where he had studied: there were many churches, gracious college buildings, and gardens and orchards where teachers and students could walk and talk. That had been a golden age, he thought bitterly; his father had been alive and prosperous, a strong Catholic had sat on the throne of England, and Rollo had seemed to have an assured future.

He had walked a long way across the flat landscape of Flanders, but his feet were not as sore as his heart. The Protestants were never satisfied, he thought furiously. England had a Protestant queen, compliant bishops, an English Bible and a reformed prayer book. The paintings had been taken down, the statues beheaded, the golden crucifixes melted down. And still it was not enough. They had to take away Rollo's business and his home, and drive him out of his own country.

One day they would regret it.

Speaking a mixture of French and English, he found his way to a brick town house, large but not beautiful, in a street of shops and tenements. All his hopes were now invested in this disappointingly ordinary building. If England was to return to the true faith, and if Rollo was to be revenged on his enemies, it would all start here.

The door was open.

In the hall he met a lively pink-faced man about ten years his junior – Rollo was thirty-five. 'Bonjour, monsieur,' he said politely.

'You're English, aren't you?' said the other man.

'Is this the English College?'

'It certainly is.'

'Thank God.' Rollo was relieved. It had been a long journey, but he had arrived. Now he had to find out whether it would live up to his hopes.

'I'm Leonard Price. Call me Lenny. What are you doing here?'

'I lost my livelihood in Kingsbridge because I wouldn't sign the Thirty-Nine Articles.'

'Good man!'

'Thank you. I'd like to help restore the true faith in England, and I've been told that's your mission here.'

'Right again. We train priests then send them back home – clandestinely, of course – to bring the sacraments to loyal Catholics there.'

This was the idea that thrilled Rollo. Now that Queen Elizabeth was beginning to reveal her true, tyrannical nature, the Church would fight back. And so would Rollo. His life had been ruined, so he had nothing to lose. He should have been a prosperous Kingsbridge alderman, living in the best house in the city, destined eventually to be mayor like his father; but instead he was an outcast, walking the dusty roads of a foreign land. However, he would turn the tables one day.

Lenny lowered his voice. 'If you ask William Allen – that's our founder – he'll say that training priests is our only mission. But some of us have bigger ideas.'

'What do you mean?'

'Elizabeth must be deposed, and Mary of Scotland must be queen.'

That was what Rollo wanted to hear. 'Are you really planning that?'

Lenny hesitated, probably realizing he had been indiscreet. 'Call it a daydream,' he said. 'But it's one shared by a lot of people.'

That was indisputable. Mary's right to the throne was a constant topic of discussion at Catholic dinner tables. Rollo said eagerly: 'Can I see William Allen?'

'Let's go and ask. He's with a very important visitor, but perhaps they'd both like to talk to a potential new recruit. Come with me.'

Lenny led Rollo up the stairs to the next floor. Rollo was full of excitement and optimism. Perhaps his life was not over after all. Lenny tapped on a door and opened it onto a spacious, light room lined with books, and two men deep in conversation. Lenny addressed one of them, a thin-faced man a few years older than Rollo, untidily dressed in a way that reminded Rollo of his Oxford teachers. 'Forgive me for interrupting, sir, but I thought you might like to meet someone newly arrived from England.'

Allen turned to his guest and said in French: 'If you permit . . . ?'

The second man was younger, but more richly dressed, in a green tunic embroidered with yellow. He was strikingly good-looking, with light-brown eyes and thick blond hair. He shrugged and said: 'As you wish.'

Rollo stepped forward and offered his hand. 'My name is Rollo Fitzgerald, from Kingsbridge.'

'I'm William Allen.' He shook hands then indicated his

guest with a gesture. 'This is a great friend of the college's, Monsieur Pierre Aumande de Guise, from Paris.'

The Frenchman nodded coldly to Rollo and did not offer his hand.

Lenny said: 'Rollo lost his livelihood because he refused to sign the Thirty-Nine Articles.'

'Well done,' said Allen.

'And he wants to join us.'

'Sit down, both of you.'

Monsieur Aumande de Guise spoke in careful English. 'What education do you have, Rollo?'

'I was at Oxford, then I studied law at Gray's Inn, before entering my father's business. I did not take holy orders, but that is what I want to do now.'

'Good.' Aumande was thawing a little.

Allen said: 'The mission that awaits our students, at the end of their training, is to risk their lives. You do realize that? If caught you could be put to death. Please do not join us if you are not prepared for that fate.'

Rollo considered his answer. 'It would be foolish to treat such a prospect lightly.' He had the satisfaction of seeing Allen nod approvingly. He went on: 'But with God's help I believe I can face the risk.'

Aumande spoke again. 'How do you feel about Protestants? I mean personally.'

'Personally?' Rollo began to compose another judicious answer, but his emotions got the better of him. He clenched his fists. 'I hate them,' he said. He was so moved he found it hard to get the words out. 'I want to wipe them out, destroy them, kill every last one of them. That's how I feel.'

Aumande almost smiled. 'In that case, I think you may have a place with us.'

Rollo realized he had said the right thing.

'Well,' said Allen more cautiously, 'I hope you will stay with us for a few days, at least, so that we can get to know each other better; then we can talk some more about your future.'

Aumande said: 'He needs an alias.'

'Already?' said Allen.

'The fewer people who know his real name, the better.'

'I suppose you're right.'

'Call him Jean Langlais.'

'John the Englishman – in French. All right.' Allen looked at Rollo. 'From now on you are Jean Langlais.'

'But why?' said Rollo.

Aumande answered him. 'You'll see,' he said. 'All in good time.'

*

ENGLAND WAS IN the grip of invasion panic that summer. People saw the Papal Bull as an incitement to Catholic countries to attack, and any day they expected to see the galleons come over the horizon, teeming with soldiers armed to the teeth, eager to burn and loot and rape. All along the south coast, masons were repairing age-crumbled castle walls. Rusty harbour-mouth cannons were cleaned, oiled and test-fired. Sturdy farm lads joined the local militia and practised archery on sunny Sunday afternoons.

The countess of Shiring was in a different kind of fervour. On her way to meet Ned, Margery visualized the things they would do together, and she felt the anticipatory moisture inside her. She had once heard someone say that French courtesans washed their private parts every day and perfumed them, in case men wanted to kiss them there. She had not believed the story, and Bart had certainly never kissed her there; but Ned did it all the time, so now she washed like a courtesan. She knew, as she did so, that she was getting ready to commit mortal sin, again; and knew, too, that one day her punishment would come; but those thoughts gave her a pain in her head, and she thrust them away.

She went to Kingsbridge and stayed in the house Bart owned on Leper Island. Her pretext was seeing Guillaume Forneron. A Protestant refugee from France, Forneron made the finest cambric in the south of England, and Margery bought shirts for Bart and, for herself, chemises and nightdresses.

On the second morning, she left the house alone and went

to meet Ned at the home of her friend Susannah, now Lady Twyford. She still had the house in Kingsbridge that she had inherited from her father, and she usually stayed there when her husband was travelling. Ned had proposed this rendezvous, and both he and Margery felt sure they could trust Susannah to keep their secret.

Margery had got used to the knowledge that Susannah had once been Ned's lover. Susannah had been bashful when Margery revealed that she had guessed the truth. 'You had his heart,' Susannah had said. 'I just had his body, which, fortunately, was all I wanted.' Margery was living in such a daze of passion that she could hardly think straight about that or anything else.

Susannah received her in her parlour, then kissed her on the lips and said: 'Go on up, you lucky girl.'

An enclosed staircase led from the parlour up to Susannah's boudoir, and Ned was waiting there.

Margery threw her arms around him and they kissed urgently, as though starved of love. She broke the kiss to say: 'Bed.'

They went into Susannah's bedroom and pulled off their clothes. Ned's body was slender, his skin white, with thick dark hair on his chest. Margery loved just looking at him.

But something was wrong. Ned's penis was unresponsive, limp. This happened quite often with Bart, when he was drunk, but it was the first time with Ned. Margery knelt in front of him and sucked it, as Bart had taught her to do. It sometimes worked with him, but today with Ned it made no difference. She stood up, put her hands to his face, and looked into his golden-brown eyes. He was embarrassed, she saw. She said: 'What is it, my darling?'

'Something on my mind,' he said.

'What?'

'What are we going to do? What is our future?'

'Why think about it? Let's just love each other.'

He shook his head. 'I have to make a decision.' He put his hand into the coat he had thrown aside and took out a letter.

'From the queen?' Margery asked.

'From Sir William Cecil.'

Margery felt as if the summer day had been blasted by a sudden winter wind. 'Bad news?'

Ned threw the letter onto the bed. 'I don't know if it's bad or good.'

Margery stared at it. The letter lay on the counterpane like a dead bird, its folded corners sticking up like stiffening wings, the broken red wax seal like a spatter of blood. Intuition told her that it announced her doom. In a low voice she said: 'Tell me what it says.'

Ned sat up on the bed, crossing his legs. 'It's about France,' he said. 'The Protestants there – they're called Huguenots – seem to be winning the civil war, with the help of a huge loan from Queen Elizabeth.'

Margery knew this already. She was horrified by the relentless success of heresy, but Ned was pleased about it; Margery tried not to think about this or any of the things that divided them.

Ned went on: 'So, happily, the Catholic king is holding peace talks with the Protestant leader, a man called Gaspard de Coligny.'

At least Margery could share Ned's approval of that. They both wanted Christians to stop killing each other. But how could this blight their love?

'Queen Elizabeth is sending a colleague of ours called Sir Francis Walsingham to the conference as a mediator.'

Margery did not understand that. 'Do the French really need an Englishman at their peace talks?'

'No, that's a cover story.' He hesitated. 'Cecil doesn't say more in the letter, but I can guess the truth. I'll happily tell you what I think, but you can't tell anyone else.'

'All right.' Margery took part listlessly in this conversation, which had the effect of postponing the dreaded moment when she would know her fate.

'Walsingham is a spy. The queen wants to know what the king of France intends to do about Scottish Mary. If the Catholics and the Huguenots really do make peace, the king might turn his attention to Scotland, or even England.

Elizabeth always wants to know what people might be plotting.'

'So the queen is sending a spy to France.'

'When you put it like that, it's not much of a secret.'

'All the same I won't repeat it. But please, for pity's sake, what has this got to do with you and me?'

'Walsingham needs an assistant, the man must speak fluent French, and Cecil wants me to go. I think Cecil is displeased with me for staying away from London so long.'

'So you're leaving me,' Margery said miserably. That was the meaning of the dead bird.

'I don't have to. We could carry on as we are, loving one another and meeting secretly.'

Margery shook her head. Her mind was clear, now, for the first time in weeks, and she could think straight at last. 'We take terrible risks every time. We will be discovered one day. Then Bart will kill you and divorce me and take Bartlet away from me.'

'Then let's just run away. We'll tell people we're married: Mr and Mrs Weaver. We can take a ship to Antwerp: I have a distant cousin there, Jan Wolman, who will give me work.'

'And Bartlet?'

'We'll take him with us – he's not really Bart's son anyway.'

'We'd be guilty of kidnapping the heir to an earldom. It's probably a capital offence. We could both be executed.'

'If we rode to Combe Harbour we could be at sea before anyone realizes what we've done.'

Margery yearned to say yes. In the past three months she had been happy for the first time since she was fifteen. The longing to be with Ned possessed her body like a fever. But she knew, even if he did not, that he could never be happy working for his cousin in Antwerp. All his adult life Ned had been deeply engaged in the government of England, and he liked it more than anything. He adored Queen Elizabeth, he revered William Cecil, and he was fascinated by the challenges facing them. If she took him away from all that she would ruin him.

And she, too, had her work. In recent weeks she had, shamefully, used her sacred mission as a cover for adulterous meetings, but nonetheless she was dedicated to the task God had assigned her. To give that up would be a transgression as bad as adultery.

It was time to end it. She would confess her sin and ask God's mercy. She would rededicate herself to the holy duty of bringing the sacraments to deprived English Catholics. Perhaps in time she would come to feel forgiven.

As she reached her decision, she began to cry.

'Don't,' he said. 'We can work something out.'

She knew they could not. She embraced him and pulled him to her. They lay back on the bed. She whispered: 'Ned, my beloved Ned.' Her tears wetted his face as they kissed. His penis was suddenly erect. 'Once more,' she said.

'It's not the last time,' he said as he rolled on top of her.

Yes, it is, she thought; but she found she could not speak, and she gave herself up to sorrow and delight.

*

SIX WEEKS LATER, Margery knew she was pregnant.

17

SIR FRANCIS WALSINGHAM believed in lists the way he believed in the Gospels. He made lists of who he had met yesterday and who he was going to see tomorrow. And he and Sir Ned Willard had a list of every suspicious Englishman who came to Paris.

In 1572, Walsingham was Queen Elizabeth's ambassador to France, and Ned was his deputy. Ned respected Walsingham as he had Sir William Cecil, but did not feel the same breathless devotion. Towards Walsingham Ned was loyal rather than worshipful, admiring rather than awestruck. The two men were different, of course; but, also, the Ned who now served as Walsingham's deputy was not the eager youngster who had been Cecil's protégé. Ned had grown up.

Ned had undertaken clandestine missions for Elizabeth from the start, but now he and Walsingham were part of the rapidly growing secret intelligence service set up to protect Elizabeth and her government from violent overthrow.

The peace between Catholics and Protestants that had reigned in England for the first decade of Elizabeth's rule had been thrown into jeopardy by the Papal Bull. There had already been one serious conspiracy against her. The Pope's agent in England, Roberto Ridolfi, had plotted to murder Elizabeth and put Mary Stuart on the throne, and then marry Mary to the duke of Norfolk. The secret service had uncovered the plan and the duke's head had been chopped off a few days ago. But no one believed that was the end of the matter.

Ned, like all Elizabeth's advisors, feared more conspiracies. Everything he had worked for during the last fourteen years was now under threat. The dream of religious freedom could turn overnight into the nightmare of inquisition and torture, and England would again know the revolting smell of men and women being burned alive.

Dozens of wealthy Catholics had fled from England, and most of them came to France. Ned and Walsingham believed that the next plot against Elizabeth would be hatched here in Paris. It was their mission to identify the plotters, learn their intentions, and foil their plans.

The English embassy was a big house on the 'left bank', south of the river, in the University district. Walsingham was not a rich man, and England was not a rich country, so they could not afford the more expensive right bank where the French aristocracy had their palaces.

Today Ned and Walsingham were going to attend the royal court in the Louvre palace. Ned was looking forward to it. The gathering of the most powerful men and women in France was a rich opportunity to pick up information. Courtiers gossiped, and some of them let secrets slip. Ned would chat to everyone and chart the undercurrents.

He was just a little nervous, not on his own account, but on that of his master. Walsingham at forty was brilliant but lacked grace. His first appearance before King Charles IX had been embarrassing. A stiff-necked Puritan, Walsingham had dressed all in black: it was his normal style, but in the gaudy French court it was seen as a Protestant reproach.

On that first occasion, Ned had recognized Pierre Aumande de Guise, whom he had met at St Dizier with Mary Stuart. That had been eleven years ago, but Ned remembered Aumande vividly. Although the man had been good-looking and well-dressed, there was something creepy about him.

King Charles had pointedly asked Walsingham whether it was really necessary for Elizabeth to imprison Mary Stuart, the former queen of France, the deposed Queen of Scots, and Charles's sister-in-law. Walsingham should have known the book of Proverbs well enough to remember A *soft answer turneth away wrath*. However, he had responded with righteous indignation – always a weakness in Puritans – and the king had become frosty.

Since then Ned had made a special effort to be more easy-going and amiable than his unbending boss. He had adopted a style of dress appropriate to a minor diplomat without rigid religious convictions. Today he put on a pastel-blue doublet slashed to show a fawn lining, an unostentatious outfit by Paris standards but, he hoped, stylish enough to distract from the appearance of Walsingham, who clung stubbornly to his black.

From his attic window Ned could see across the Seine river to the towers of the cathedral of Notre Dame. Beside his smoky mirror stood a little portrait Margery had given him. It was somewhat idealized, with impossibly white skin and rosy cheeks; but the artist had captured her tumbling curls and the mischievous grin he had loved so much.

He still loved her. Two years ago he had been forced to accept that she would never leave her husband, and without hope his passion had burned low, but the fire had not gone out, and perhaps it never would.

He had no news from Kingsbridge. He had not heard from Barney, who was presumably still at sea. He and Margery had agreed not to torture themselves by writing to one another. The last thing Ned had done, before leaving England, was to quash the arrest warrant for Stephen Lincoln, which had been issued on the basis of evidence invented by Dan Cobley. If Margery felt it her sacred duty to bring consolation to bereft Catholics, Ned was not going to let Dan Cobley stop her.

Adjusting his lace collar in front of the mirror, he smiled as he remembered the play he had seen last night, called *The Rivals*. Highly original, it was a comedy about ordinary people who spoke naturally, rather than in verse, and featured two young men, both of whom wanted to abduct the same girl – who turned out, in a surprise ending, to be the sister of one of them. The whole thing took place in one location, a short stretch of street, in a period of less than twenty-four hours. Ned had not before seen anything so clever in London or Paris.

Ned was just about ready to leave when a servant came in. 'A woman has called, selling paper and ink cheaper than anywhere in Paris, she claims,' the man said in French. 'Do you care to see her?'

Ned used huge quantities of expensive paper and ink,

drafting and encoding Walsingham's confidential letters to the queen and Cecil. And the queen was as parsimonious with her spies as she was with everyone, so he was always looking for lower prices. 'What is Sir Francis doing right now?'

'Reading his Bible.'

'Then I have time. Send her up.'

A minute later a woman of about thirty appeared. Ned looked at her with interest. She was attractive rather than beautiful, modestly dressed, with a determined look softened by blue eyes. She introduced herself as Thérèse St Quentin. She took samples of paper and ink out of a leather satchel and invited Ned to try them.

He sat at his writing table. Both paper and ink seemed good. 'Where do you get your supplies?' he asked.

'The paper is made just outside Paris, in the suburb of Saint-Marcel,' she said. 'I also have beautiful Italian paper from Fabriano, in Italy, for your love letters.'

It was a flirty thing to say, but she was not very coquettish, and he guessed it was part of her sales pitch. 'And the ink?'

'I make it myself. That's why it's so cheap – though it's very good.'

He compared her prices with what he usually paid and found that she was, indeed, cheap, so he gave her an order.

'I'll bring everything today,' she said. Then she lowered her voice. 'Do you have the Bible in French?'

Ned was astonished. Could this respectable-looking young woman be involved in illicit literature? 'It's against the law!'

She responded calmly. 'But breaking the law no longer carries the death penalty, according to the Peace of St Germain.'

She was talking about the agreement that had resulted from the peace conference Ned and Walsingham had been sent to in St Germain, so Ned knew the details well. The treaty gave the Huguenots limited freedom of worship. For Ned, a Catholic country that tolerated Protestants was as good as a Protestant country that tolerated Catholics: it was the freedom that counted. However, freedom was fragile. France had had peace treaties before, all of them short-lived. The famously inflammatory Paris preachers ranted against every attempt at conciliation. This one was supposed to be sealed by a marriage – the king's rackety sister, Princess Margot, was engaged to the easy-going Henri of Bourbon, Protestant king of Navarre – but eighteen months later the wedding still had not taken place. Ned said: 'The peace treaty could be abandoned, and any day there could be a surprise crackdown on people like you.'

'It probably wouldn't be a surprise.' Ned was about to ask why not, but she did not give him the chance. She went on: 'And I think I can trust you. You're Elizabeth's envoy, so you must be Protestant.'

'Why do you ask?' Ned said cautiously.

'If you want a French Bible, I can get you one.'

Ned was amazed by her nerve. And as it happened, he did want a French Bible. He spoke the language well enough to pass as a native but sometimes, in conversation, he did not catch the biblical quotations and allusions that Protestants used all the time, and he had often thought he should read the better-known chapters to familiarize himself with the translation. As a foreign diplomat, he would not get into much trouble for owning the book, in the unlikely event that he was found out. 'How much?' he said.

'I have two editions, both printed in Geneva: a standard one that is a bargain at two livres, and a beautifully bound volume in two colours of ink with illustrations for seven livres. I can bring them both to show you.'

'All right.'

'I see you're going out – to the Louvre, I suppose, in that beautiful coat.'

'Yes.'

'Will you be back for your dinner?'

'Probably.' Ned felt bemused. She had taken control of the conversation. All he did was agree to what she proposed. She was forceful, but so frank and engaging that he could not be offended.

'I'll bring your stationery then, and two Bibles so that you can choose the one you prefer.'

Ned did not think he had actually committed himself to buying one, but he let that pass. 'I look forward to seeing them.'

'I'll be back this afternoon.'

Her coolness was impressive. 'You're very brave,' Ned commented.

'The Lord gives me strength.'

No doubt he did, Ned thought, but she must have had plenty to start with. 'Tell me something,' he said, taking the conversational initiative at last. 'How did you come to be a dealer in contraband books?'

'My father was a printer. He was burned as a heretic in 1559, and all his possessions were forfeit, so my mother and I were destitute. All we had was a few Bibles he had printed.'

'So you've been doing this for thirteen years?'

'Almost.'

Her courage took Ned's breath away. 'During most of that period, you could have been executed, like your father.'

'Yes.'

'But surely you could live innocently, selling just paper and ink.'

'We could, but we believe in people's right to read God's word for themselves and make up their own minds about what is the true gospel.'

Ned believed in that, too. 'And you're willing to risk your life for that principle.' He did not mention that if caught she would undoubtedly have been tortured before being executed.

'Yes,' she said.

Ned stared at her, fascinated. She looked back at him boldly for a few moments, then she said: 'Until this afternoon, then.'

'Goodbye.'

When she had gone, Ned went to the window and looked out across the busy fruit-and-vegetable market of the place Maubert. She was not as afraid as she might have been of a crackdown on Protestants. It *probably wouldn't be a surprise*, she had said. He wondered what means she had of finding out in advance about the intentions of the ultra-Catholics.

A few moments later she emerged from the door below and walked away, a small, erect figure with a brisk, unwavering step; willing to die for the ideal of tolerance that Ned shared. What a woman, he thought. What a hero.

He watched her out of sight.

*

PIERRE AUMANDE de Guise trimmed his fair beard in preparation for going to court at the Louvre Palace. He always shaped his beard into a sharp point, to look more like his young master and distant relative Henri, the twenty-one-year-old duke of Guise.

He studied his face. He had developed a dry skin condition that gave him red, flaking patches at the corners of his eyes and mouth and on his scalp. They had also appeared on the backs of his knees and the insides of his elbows, where they itched maddeningly. The Guise family doctor had diagnosed an excess of heat and prescribed an ointment that seemed to make the symptoms worse.

His twelve-year-old stepson, Alain, came into the room. He was a wretched child, undersized and timid, more like a girl. Pierre had sent him to the dairy on the corner to buy milk and cheese, and now he was carrying a jug and a goblet. Pierre said: 'Where's the cheese?'

The boy hesitated, then said: 'They haven't got any today.'

Pierre looked at his face. 'Liar,' he said. 'You forgot.'

Alain was terrified. 'No, I didn't, honestly!' He started to cry.

The scrawny maid, Nath, came in. 'What's the matter, Alain?' she said.

Pierre said: 'He lied to me, and now he's afraid of a thrashing. What do you want?'

'There's a priest to see you – Jean Langlais.'

That was the pseudonym Pierre had given Rollo Fitzgerald, the most promising of the exiles studying at the English College. 'Send him up here. Take this snivelling child away. And get some cheese for my breakfast.'

Pierre had met Rollo twice since that initial encounter, and had been impressed by him each time. The man was intelligent and dedicated, and in his eyes there was the burning light of a holy mission. He hated Protestants passionately, no doubt because his family had been ruined financially by the Puritans in Kingsbridge, the city from which he came. Pierre had high hopes for Rollo.

A moment later Rollo appeared, wearing a floor-length cassock and a wooden cross on a chain.

They shook hands, and Pierre closed the door. Rollo said: 'Is that young lady your wife?'

'Certainly not,' said Pierre. 'Madame Aumande de Guise was a lady-in-waiting to Véronique de Guise.' That was not true. Odette had been a servant, not a lady-in-waiting, but Pierre did not like people to know it. 'She's out.' Odette had gone to the fish market. 'The woman who admitted you is just a maid.'

Rollo was embarrassed. 'I do beg your pardon.'

'Not at all. Welcome to our humble dwelling. I spend most of my time at the Guise family palace in the rue Vieille du Temple, but if you and I had met there we would have been seen by twenty people. This place has one great advantage: it is so insignificant that no one would bother to spy on it.' In fact, Pierre was desperate to move out of this hovel, but had not yet managed to persuade the young duke to give him a room at the palace. He was now chief among the Guise family's counsellors but, as always, they were slow to grant Pierre the status his work merited. 'How are things in Douai?'

'Excellent. Since the Pope excommunicated Elizabeth, another fifteen good young Catholic Englishmen have joined us. In fact, William Allen sent me here to tell you that we're almost ready to send a group of them back to England.'

'And how will that be organized?'

'Father Allen has asked me to take charge of the operation.'

Pierre thought that was a good decision. Rollo clearly had the ability to be more than just a clandestine priest. 'What's your plan?'

'We will land them on a remote beach at dusk, then they'll travel through the night to my sister's castle – she is the countess of Shiring. She has been organizing secret Catholic services for years, and she already has a network of undercover priests. From there they will spread out all over England.'

'How reliable is your sister?'

'Totally, with anything that doesn't involve bloodshed. There she draws a line, I'm afraid. She has never understood that violence is sometimes necessary in the service of the Church.'

'She's a woman.' Pierre was pleased that Rollo evidently *did* understand the need for violence.

'And in Paris?' Rollo said. 'We in Douai have been worried by the news from here.'

'The Peace of St Germain was a major defeat for us, there's no denying that. The policy of Pope Pius V is quite clearly to exterminate all Protestants, but King Charles IX has rejected this in favour of peaceful coexistence.'

Rollo nodded. 'To some extent the king was forced into that by military defeat.'

'Yes. It's most unfortunate that Gaspard de Coligny has proved to be such a disciplined and talented general of the Huguenot armies. And the queen mother, Caterina, is another force for tolerance of vile heresy.' Sometimes Pierre felt as if every hand was against him. 'But we have seen edicts of tolerance before, and they have never lasted,' he added optimistically.

'Will Princess Margot marry Henri of Bourbon?'

Rollo asked all the right questions. Henri was the son of the late Antoine of Bourbon, and as king of Navarre he was the highest-ranking member of the pro-tolerance Bourbon–Montmorency alliance. If he married into the royal Valois family he might be able to preserve the Peace of St Germain. And the combined families of Bourbon, Montmorency and Valois would be enough to crush the Guises. 'We've done everything we can to delay the marriage,' Pierre said. 'But Coligny lurks in the background, a constant threat.'

'It's a pity someone doesn't stick a knife in his heart.'

'Many people would like to, believe me,' said Pierre. That included Pierre himself. 'But Coligny's not stupid, and doesn't give them much chance. He rarely comes to Paris.' He heard the bell of St Étienne's church strike ten. 'I have to attend court,' he said. 'Where are you staying?'

Rollo looked around. Clearly he had been expecting to

lodge at Pierre's house, but now realized the place was too small. 'I don't know.'

'The count of Beaulieu always welcomes English Catholics. You may meet people who could be useful to you at his house. But watch out for English Protestants, too.'

'Are there many in Paris?'

'Some, mainly at the embassy. Sir Francis Walsingham is the ambassador. He's a curmudgeon, but as sharp as a nail.'

'And a blaspheming Puritan.'

'I'm keeping an eye on him. But his deputy is more dangerous, because he has charm as well as brains. He's called Sir Ned Willard.'

Rollo reacted. 'Really? Ned Willard is deputy ambassador?'

'You obviously know the man.'

'He comes from Kingsbridge. I didn't realize he had become so important.'

'Oh, yes.' Pierre recalled the young man who had pretended to be a Scottish Protestant at St Dizier. Later Pierre had read, in a smuggled letter from Alison McKay, how Willard had gone to Carlisle Castle to tell Mary Stuart that she was a prisoner. And now the man had shown up in Paris. 'Ned Willard is not to be underestimated.'

'I used to flog him at school.'

'Did you?'

'I wish I'd beaten him to death.'

Pierre stood up. 'The count of Beaulieu lives in the rue St Denis. I'll point you in the right direction.' He led Rollo downstairs and out into the street. 'Come and see me again before you leave Paris. I may have letters for William Allen.' He gave Rollo directions to the Beaulieu palace, and the two men shook hands.

As Rollo walked away, Pierre noticed the back of a woman going in the same direction. She seemed familiar, but she turned the corner and was out of sight before he could place her.

However, she had not been richly dressed, so could not have been anyone important, and he went back inside and forgot about her.

He found Alain in the kitchen. Using a kinder tone of voice than usual, he said: 'Alain, I have something sad to tell you. There has been an accident. Your mother has been kicked by a horse. I'm afraid she is dead.'

Alain stared at him, wide-eyed, for a long moment, then his face crumpled in anguish and he began to wail. 'Mammy!' he cried. 'Mammy, Mammy!'

'There's no point in calling her,' Pierre said, reverting to the irritated tone he normally used with the boy. 'She can't hear you. She's dead. She's gone, and we'll never see her again.'

Alain screamed in grief. Pierre's deception was so effective that he almost regretted it.

A minute later Odette came rushing in with her fish basket. 'What is it, what is it, Alain?' she cried.

The boy opened his eyes, saw his mother and threw his arms around her. 'He said you were dead!' he wailed.

'You cruel swine,' Odette said to Pierre. 'Why did you do that?'

'To teach the boy a lesson,' Pierre said, pleased with himself. 'He lied to me, so I lied to him. He won't do it again in a hurry.'

*

THE LOUVRE WAS a square medieval fort with round cone-roofed corner towers. Walsingham and Ned crossed a drawbridge over a moat to enter the courtyard. Ned was alert, excited, eager. The power was here. In this building were the men who commanded armies and started wars, men who could raise their friends to high rank and destroy their enemies, men who decided who should live and who should die. And Ned was going to talk to them.

The late King Henri II had demolished the west wall of the square and replaced it with a modern palace in the Italian style, with fluted pilasters, immensely tall windows, and a riot of sculpture. There was nothing like it in London, Ned reflected. More recently Henri's son, Charles IX, had extended the new building, making an L-shape.

As always, the court gathered in a series of interconnecting spaces that delineated a hierarchy. Grooms, maids and bodyguards remained outside in the courtyard, whatever the weather. Ned and Walsingham entered the central door into the ballroom, which occupied the entire ground floor of the west wing. In this room were superior attendants such as ladies-in-waiting. Passing through, on his way to the next level, Ned was surprised to notice a stunning woman staring at him, her expression an odd mixture of shock, hope and puzzlement.

He looked hard at her. About his age, she was a classic Mediterranean beauty, with a mass of dark hair, heavily marked eyebrows, and sensual lips. Wearing bright red and black, she was easily the most flamboyantly dressed woman in the room, though her clothes were not the most expensive on display. There was something about her that made Ned think she was not merely a lady-in-waiting.

She spoke with an accent that was neither French nor English. 'No, you're definitely not Barney,' she said.

It was a confused statement, but Ned understood. 'My brother's name is Barney, but he's taller than I am, and handsomer.'

'You must be Ned!'

He placed her accent as Spanish. 'I am, Señorita,' he said, and bowed.

'Barney mentioned you often. He was very fond of his little brother.'

Walsingham interrupted impatiently to say: 'I'll go on. Don't be long.'

The woman said to Ned: 'I am Jerónima Ruiz.'

The name rang a bell. 'Did you know Barney in Seville?'

'Know him? I wanted to marry him. But it was not in the stars.'

'And now you're in Paris.'

'I am the niece of Cardinal Romero, who is here on a diplomatic mission for King Felipe of Spain.'

Ned would have heard about such a mission if it was official, so this must be something informal. Fishing for information, he said: 'I assume King Felipe doesn't want Princess Margot to marry a Huguenot.' In the chess game of international diplomacy, the king of Spain supported the Catholics in France just as the queen of England helped the Protestants.

'As a mere woman, I take no interest in such matters.'

Ned smiled. 'Answered like a skilled diplomat.'

She kept up the pretence. 'My role is to act as hostess at my uncle's table. The cardinal has no wife, obviously.' She gave him a provocative look. 'Unlike your English priests, who are allowed to do anything.'

She was alluring, Ned found. 'Why didn't you marry my brother?'

A hard look came over her face. 'My father died while being "interviewed" by the Inquisition. My family lost everything. Archdeacon Romero, as he then was, invited me to join his household. He saved me – but of course I could not think of marrying.'

Ned understood. She was not Romero's niece, she was his mistress. The priest had taken advantage of her at a moment when her world seemed to have collapsed. He looked into her eyes and saw pain there. 'You've been treated cruelly,' he said.

'I made my own decisions.'

Ned wondered whether her experiences had turned her against the Catholic Church – and, if that were the case, whether she might take her revenge by helping the Protestant cause. But he hesitated to ask her outright. 'I'd like to talk to you again,' he said.

She gave him an appraising look, and he had the unnerving feeling that she knew what was in his mind. 'All right,' she said.

Ned bowed and left her. He passed under the musicians' gallery, held up by four caryatids, and went up the stairs. What a beautiful woman, he thought, though she was more Barney's type than his. What is my type? he asked himself. Someone like Margery, of course.

He walked through the guardroom of the Swiss mercenaries who formed the king's personal protection squad, then entered a large, light room called the wardrobe. Here waited people who might or might not be admitted to the royal presence, minor nobility and petitioners.

Walsingham said grumpily: 'You took your time with that Spanish tart.'

'It was worth it, though,' Ned replied.

'Really?' Walsingham was sceptical.

'She's the mistress of Cardinal Romero. I think I may be able to recruit her as an informant.'

Walsingham changed his tone. 'Good! I'd like to know what that slimy Spanish priest is up to.' His eye lighted on the marquess of Lagny, an amiable fat man who covered his bald head with a jewelled cap. Lagny was a Protestant and close to Gaspard de Coligny. Aristocratic Huguenots had to be tolerated at court, at least until they did something overtly defiant of the king. 'Come with me,' Walsingham said to Ned, and they crossed the room.

Walsingham greeted the marquess in fluent, precise French: he had lived in exile for most of the reign of Elizabeth's Catholic elder sister, Queen Mary Tudor – 'Bloody' Mary – and he spoke several languages.

He asked Lagny about the topic on everyone's mind, the Spanish Netherlands. King Felipe's ruthlessly effective general, the duke of Alba, was mercilessly crushing the Dutch Protestant rebels. A French Protestant army led by Jean of Hangest, lord of Genlis, was on its way to help the rebels. Lagny said: 'Coligny has ordered Hangest to join forces with William of Orange.' The prince of Orange was the leader of the Dutch. 'Orange has asked Queen Elizabeth for a loan of thirty thousand pounds,' Lagny went on. 'Will she oblige him, Sir Francis?'

'Perhaps,' said Walsingham. Ned thought the likelihood was small. Elizabeth probably did not have thirty thousand pounds to spare and, if she did, she could think of better uses for it.

Ned was drawn away from the conversation by a richly dressed woman of middle age who spoke to him in English. 'Sir Ned!' she said. 'What a fine doublet.'

Ned bowed to Marianne, countess of Beaulieu, an English Catholic married to a French nobleman. She was with her daughter, a plump eighteen-year-old with a vivacious manner. Her name was Aphrodite: her father was a scholar of Greek.

The countess had a soft spot for Ned, and encouraged him to talk to Aphrodite. The countess would never let her daughter marry a Protestant, of course, but no doubt she thought Ned might convert. Ned liked Aphrodite well enough but had no romantic interest in her: she was a jolly, carefree girl with no serious interests, and she quickly bored him. Nevertheless, Ned flirted with both mother and daughter, because he longed to get inside the Beaulieu mansion in the rue St Denis, which was a refuge for exiled English Catholics, and might well be where the next plot against Queen Elizabeth was being hatched. But so far he had not been invited.

Now he talked to the Beaulieus about the worst-kept secret in Paris, the affair between Princess Margot and Duke Henri of Guise. The countess said darkly: 'Duke Henri is not the first man to have "paid court" to the princess.'

Young Aphrodite was shocked and excited by the suggestion that a princess might be promiscuous. 'Mother!' she said. 'You ought not to repeat such slanders. Margot is engaged to marry Henri of Bourbon!'

Ned murmured: 'Perhaps she just got the two Henris mixed up.'

The countess giggled. 'They have too many Henris in this country.'

Ned did not even mention the more shocking rumour that Margot was simultaneously having an incestuous relationship with her seventeen-year-old brother Hercule-Francis.

The two women were distracted by the approach of Bernard Housse, a bright young courtier who knew how to make himself useful to the king. Aphrodite greeted him with a pleased smile, and Ned thought he might suit her very well.

Ned turned away and caught the eye of the marchioness of Nîmes, a Protestant aristocrat. About Ned's age, and voluptuous, Louise de Nîmes was the second wife of the much older marquess. Her father, like Ned's, had been a wealthy merchant. She immediately gave Ned the latest gossip: 'The king found out about Margot and Henri de Guise!'

'Really? What did he do?'

'He dragged her out of her bed and had her flogged!'

'My goodness. She's eighteen, isn't she? It's a bit old for flogging.'

'A king can do what he likes.' Louise looked over Ned's shoulder and her face changed. Her smile vanished and she looked as if she had seen a dead rat.

The alteration was so striking that Ned turned to find out what had caused it, and saw Pierre Aumande. 'I guess you don't like Monsieur Aumande de Guise,' he said.

'He's a snake. And he's not a Guise. I'm from the same part of the world, and I know his background.'

'Oh? Do tell me.'

'His father is the illegitimate son of one of the Guise men. The family sent the bastard to school and made him the parish priest of Thonnance-lès-Joinville.'

'If he's a priest, how can he be Pierre's father?'

'Pierre's mother is the priest's "housekeeper".'

'So Pierre is the illegitimate son of an illegitimate son of a Guise.'

'And then, to cap it all, they made Pierre marry a servant who had been impregnated by another randy Guise.'

'Fascinating.' Ned turned again and studied Pierre for a moment. He was richly dressed in a lavender doublet pinked to show a purple lining. 'It doesn't seem to have held him back.'

'He's a horrible man. He was rude to me once, so I told him off, and he's hated me ever since.'

Pierre was talking to a tough-looking man who seemed not quite sufficiently well-dressed to be here, Ned saw. He said: 'I've always found Pierre a bit sinister.'

'A bit!'

Walsingham beckoned, and Ned left Louise and joined him as he moved to the doorway that led to the last and most important room, the king's private chamber.

*

PIERRE WATCHED Walsingham pass into the private chamber with his sidekick, Ned Willard. He felt a wave of revulsion almost like nausea: those two were the enemies of everything that kept the Guise family powerful and wealthy.

They were not noble; they came from a poor, backward country; and they were heretics – but, all the same, he feared and loathed them.

He was standing with his chief spy, Georges Biron, lord of Montagny, a little village in Poitiers. Biron was a minor peer with almost no income. His only asset was his ability to move easily in noble society. Under Pierre's tutelage he had become sly and ruthless.

Biron said: 'I've had Walsingham under surveillance for a month, but he isn't involved in anything we can use against him. He has no lovers, male or female; he doesn't gamble or drink; and he makes no attempts to bribe the king's servants, or indeed anyone else. He's either innocent or very discreet.'

'I'm guessing discreet.'

Biron shrugged.

Pierre's instinct told him the two English Protestants had to be up to something. He made a decision. 'Switch the surveillance to the deputy.'

'Willard.' The surname was difficult to pronounce in French.

'Same procedure. Twenty-four hours. Find out what his weaknesses are.'

'Very good, sir.'

Pierre left him and followed Walsingham into the audience chamber. He was proud to be one of the privileged. On the other hand, he remembered, with bitter nostalgia, the days when he and the Guise brothers had actually lived in the palace with the royal family.

We will return, he vowed.

He crossed the room and bowed to Henri, the young duke of Guise. Henri had been twelve when Pierre had brought him the news of the assassination of his father and assured him that the man responsible for the murder was Gaspard de Coligny. Now Henri was twenty-one, but he had not forgotten his oath of revenge – Pierre had made sure of that.

Duke Henri was very like his late father: tall, fair, handsome and aggressive. At the age of fifteen he had gone to Hungary to fight against the Turks. All he lacked was the disfigurement that had given Duke François the nickname Scarface. Duke Henri had been taught that his destiny was to uphold the Catholic Church and the Guise family, and he had never questioned that.

His affair with Princess Margot was a sure sign of courage, one court wit had said, for Margot was a handful. Pierre imagined they must make a tempestuous couple.

A door opened, a trumpet sounded, everyone fell silent, and King Charles came in.

He had been ten years old when he became king, and at that time all the decisions had been made by other people, mainly his mother, Queen Caterina. He was twenty-one now, and could give his own orders, but he was in poor health – they said he had a weak chest – and he continued to be easily led, sometimes by Caterina, sometimes by others; unfortunately, not by the Guise family at present.

He began by dealing with courtesies and routine business, occasionally giving a hoarse, unwholesome cough, sitting on a carved and painted chair while everyone else in the room remained standing. But Pierre sensed he had an announcement to make, and it was not long coming. 'The marriage between our sister, Margot, and Henri de Bourbon, the king of Navarre, was agreed in August the year before last,' he said.

Pierre felt Henri de Guise tense up beside him. This was not just because he was Margot's lover. The Bourbons were bitter enemies of the Guises. The two families had warred for supremacy under the French king since before either of these two Henris was born.

King Charles went on: 'The marriage will reinforce the religious reconciliation of our kingdom.'

That was what the Guises feared. Pierre sensed the peacemaking mind of Queen Caterina behind the formal words of the king.

'So I have decided that the wedding will take place on the eighteenth of August next.'

There was a buzz around the room: this was big news. Many had hoped or feared that the wedding would never happen.

Now a date had been set. This was a triumph for the Bourbons and a blow to the Guises.

Henri was furious. 'A blaspheming Bourbon, marrying into the royal family of France,' he said with disgust.

Pierre was downcast. A threat to the Guise family was a threat to him. He could lose everything he had won. 'When your Scottish cousin Mary Stuart married Francis it made us the top family,' he said gloomily to Duke Henri.

'Now the Bourbons will be top family.'

Henri's political calculation was correct, but his rage was undoubtedly fuelled by sexual jealousy. Margot was probably an exciting lover: she had that wild look. And now she had been taken from Henri – by a Bourbon.

Pierre was able to be calmer and think more clearly. And he saw something that had not occurred to young Henri. 'The marriage still may never happen,' he said.

Henri had his father's soldierly impatience with doubletalk. 'What the devil do you mean?'

'The wedding will be the biggest event in the story of French Protestantism. It will be the triumph of the Huguenots.'

'How can that be good news?'

'They will come to Paris from all over the country – those who are invited to the wedding, and thousands more who will want just to watch the procession and rejoice.'

'It will be a foul spectacle. I can just see them strutting through the streets, flaunting their black clothes.'

Pierre lowered his voice. 'And then we'll see trouble.'

Henri's face showed that he was beginning to understand. 'You think there may be violence between triumphant Protestant visitors and the resentful Catholic citizens of Paris.'

'Yes,' said Pierre. 'And that will be our chance.'

*

ON HER WAY to the warehouse Sylvie stopped at the tavern of St Étienne and ordered a plate of smoked eel for her midday meal. She also bought a tankard of weak beer and tipped the potboy to take it around the corner and deliver it to the back door of Pierre Aumande's house. This was the signal for Pierre's maid, Nath, to come to the tavern, if she could, and a few minutes later she appeared.

Now in her mid-twenties, Nath was as scrawny as ever, but she looked out at the world through eyes that were no longer frightened. She was a stalwart of the Protestant congregation in the room over the stables, and having a group of friends had given her a modest degree of confidence. Sylvie's friendship had helped, too.

Sylvie got straight down to business. 'This morning I saw Pierre with a priest I didn't recognize,' she said. 'I happened to be passing the door when they came out.' Something about the man had struck her vividly. His features were unremarkable – he had receding dark hair and a reddish-brown beard – but there was an intensity in his expression that made her think he was a dangerous zealot.

'Yes, I was going to tell you about him,' Nath said. 'He's English.'

'Oh! Interesting. Did you get his name?'

'Jean Langlais.'

'Sounds like a false name for an Englishman.'

'He's never been to the house before, but Pierre seemed to know him, so they must have met somewhere else.'

'Did you hear what they talked about?'

Nath shook her head. 'Pierre closed the door.'

'Pity.'

Nath looked anxious. 'Did Pierre see you, when you walked by?'

She was right to be concerned, Sylvie thought. They did not want Pierre to suspect how closely he was being watched by the Protestants. 'I don't think he did. I certainly didn't meet his eye. I'm not sure he'd recognize me from behind.'

'He can't have forgotten you.'

'Hardly. He did marry me.' Sylvie grimaced at the loathsome memory.

'On the other hand, he's never mentioned you.'

'He thinks I'm not important any more. Which suits me fine.'

Sylvie finished her meal and they left the tavern separately.

Sylvie walked north, heading for the rue du Mur. Ned Willard would be interested to hear about the visiting English priest, she guessed.

She had liked Ned. So many men regarded a woman selling something as a fair target for sexual banter, or worse, as if she would suck a man off just to get him to buy a jar of ink. But Ned had talked to her with interest and respect. He was a man of some power and importance, but he showed no arrogance; in fact, he had a rather modest charm. All the same she suspected he was no softie. Hanging alongside his coat she had seen a sword and a long Spanish dagger that looked as if they were not merely for decoration.

No one else was in sight in the rue du Mur when Sylvie took the key from behind the loose brick and let herself into the windowless old stable that had served her for so many years as a hiding place for illegal books.

Her stocks were running low again. She would have to order more from Guillaume in Geneva.

Her correspondence with Guillaume was handled by a Protestant banker in Rouen who had a cousin in Geneva. The banker was able to receive money from Sylvie and have his cousin pay Guillaume. Sylvie still had to sail down the Seine to Rouen to do business, but it was a lot easier than going to Geneva. She would collect her shipment personally and bring it upriver to Paris. With the help of the cargo broker Luc Mauriac she paid all the bribes necessary to make sure that her crates of 'stationery' were not inspected by customs. It was risky, like any criminal activity, but so far she had survived.

She found two Bibles and packed them into her satchel, then walked to the shop in the rue de la Serpente, a narrow street in the University district. She went in by the back door and called to her mother: 'It's only me.'

'I'm with a customer.'

Sylvie picked up the paper and ink ordered by Ned and stacked the parcels on a small handcart. She thought of telling her mother about the large order she had won from the charming Englishman, and found herself reluctant to do so. She felt a little foolish for being so taken with him after one short meeting. Isabelle was a strong character with decided opinions, and Sylvie always had to be ready either to agree or give good reasons for disagreeing. They had no secrets from one another: in the evening each would tell the other everything that had happened during the day. But by then Sylvie would have seen Ned again. She might not like him the second time.

'I have a delivery to make,' she called out, and she left the shop.

She pushed the handcart along the rue de la Serpente, past the grand church of St Severin, across the broad rue St Jacques, alongside the pale little church of St-Julien-le-Pauvre, through the crowded market of the place Maubert with its gallows, to the English embassy. It was hard work on the cobbled streets, but she was used to it.

It took only a few minutes, and when she arrived Ned had not yet returned from the Louvre. She unloaded his stationery from the cart and a servant helped her carry it upstairs.

Then she waited in the hall. She sat on a bench with her satchel at her feet. It had a strap that she sometimes fastened to her wrist, so that it could not be stolen: books were costly and Paris was full of thieves. But she reckoned she was safe here.

A few minutes later Walsingham came in. He had a hard, intelligent face, and Sylvie immediately put him down as a force to be reckoned with. He was dressed in black, and the white collar at his neck was plain linen, not lace. His hat was a simple cap without feathers or other decoration. Clearly he wanted everyone who looked at him to know immediately that he was a Puritan.

Ned came in behind him, in his blue doublet. He smiled when he saw her. 'This is the young lady I told you about,' he said to Walsingham, courteously speaking French so that Sylvie could understand. 'Mademoiselle Thérèse St Quentin.'

Walsingham shook her hand. 'You're a brave girl,' he said. 'Keep up the good work.'

Walsingham disappeared into an adjoining room and Ned led Sylvie upstairs to the room that seemed to serve him as both office and dressing room. His stationery was on his writing table. 'The king announced a date for the wedding,' he said.

Sylvie did not have to ask which wedding. 'Good news!' she said. 'Perhaps this peace treaty will be the one that lasts.'

Ned held up a cautionary hand. 'It hasn't happened yet. But it's scheduled for the eighteenth of August.'

'I can't wait to tell my mother.'

'Have a seat.'

Sylvie sat down. 'I have some news that may interest you,' she said. 'Do you know of a man called Pierre Aumande de Guise?'

'I certainly do,' Ned said. 'Why?'

'An English Catholic priest using the name Jean Langlais visited him this morning.'

'Thank you,' Ned said. 'You're quite right to think that interests me.'

'I happened to pass the house as the priest came out and I saw him.'

'What does he look like?'

'He wore a cassock and a wooden cross. He's a little taller than average, but otherwise I noticed nothing distinctive about him. I only glimpsed him.'

'Would you recognize him again?'

'I think so.'

'Thank you for telling me. You're very well informed. How do you know Pierre Aumande?'

The answer to the question was personal and painful. She did not know Ned well enough to go into that. 'It's a long story,' she said. To change the subject she asked: 'Is your wife with you here in Paris?'

'I'm not married.'

She made a surprised face.

He said: 'There was a girl I wanted to marry, in Kingsbridge, where I come from.'

'Is she the girl in the picture?'

Ned looked startled, as if it had not occurred to him that

Sylvie could see the little painting beside the mirror and draw the obvious conclusion. 'Yes, but she married someone else.'

'How sad.'

'It was a long time ago.'

'How long?'

'Fourteen years.'

Sylvie wanted to say *And you still have her picture?* But she bit back the comment and opened her satchel.

She took out the two books. 'The plain Bible is excellent,' she said. 'A good translation, printed clearly, perfect for a family without money to spare.' She opened the luxury edition, the one she really wanted to sell him. 'This edition is magnificent. It looks like what it is, a volume containing the word of God.' She liked Ned, but she still needed to make money, and in her experience the way to do that was to make a man feel that the expensive book would mark him, in the minds of others, as a man of distinction.

Modest though he was, he was not immune to her sales talk, and he bought the high-priced Bible.

She added up the total he owed and he paid her, then he walked her to the front door of the house. 'Where's your shop?' he asked. 'I might drop in one day.'

'Rue de la Serpente. We'd love to see you.' She meant it. 'Goodbye.'

She felt light of heart as she pushed the empty handcart home. A Catholic princess was going to marry a Protestant king right here in Paris! Perhaps the days of persecution really were over.

And she had found a new customer and made a good sale. Ned's gold livres chinked in her pocket.

He was so nice. She wondered if he really would come to the shop. How much did he still love the girl whose picture he had kept for so long?

She looked forward to telling her mother the news about the royal wedding. She was not sure what to say about Ned. She and her mother were very close, no doubt because they had been together through danger and destitution. Sylvie was rarely tempted to keep anything from Isabelle. But the problem was that she really did not know how she felt.

She got home and parked the handcart in the shed at the back of the house, then went in. 'I'm home,' she called. She went into the shop. A customer was just leaving.

Her mother turned and looked at her. 'My goodness, you look happy,' she said. 'Have you fallen in love?'

18

BARNEY WILLARD ANCHORED the A*lice* in the bay of the nameless town on the north coast of Hispaniola. He had come to see Bella.

He did not tie up at the jetty: that would make it too easy for a hostile force to board the ship from the land. He lined up with his starboard guns pointing directly at the little coral limestone palace that was still the main building. The guns on the port side usefully pointed out to sea at any vessel that might approach.

Barney was being cautious. He did not really expect trouble here.

A*lice* was a three-masted merchant ship, a hundred and sixty tons and ninety feet long. Barney had modernized the design, lowering the fore and aft castles. He had installed sixteen of the mid-weight cannons called culverins that fired eighteen-pound balls. He had specified long fifteen-foot barrels. Because the ship was only thirty feet across at its widest, the guns had to be staggered along the gun deck so that they did not crash into one another when they recoiled. But long barrels fired farther and more accurately, and Barney knew, from experience, that the only way to defeat a mighty Spanish galleon was to cripple it before it got close to you.

The A*lice* had only twenty crew. Most ships of the same size had forty or more. The vessel did not need so many, but captains usually made generous allowance for deaths on voyage, not just from battle but from the fevers that so often broke out. Barney took a different approach. He thought men were more likely to catch infections in crowded ships, and had proved to his own satisfaction that it was better to start with fewer men in cleaner conditions. He also carried live cattle and barrels of apples and pears, so that the men had fresh food, a policy he had copied from the pirate Sir John Hawkins. And when he did lose men, despite his precautions, he replaced them with new recruits, always available in port cities – which was how come the *Alice* now had three dark-skinned African sailors picked up at Agadir.

Towards the end of the afternoon he sent a boat party ashore. They bought chickens and pineapples, and scrubbed and filled the ship's water barrels at the bright stream that flowed through the town. They reported that the residents were excited to hear about the *Alice*'s cargo: scissors and knives made of Toledo steel; bolts of fine Netherlands cloth; hats, shoes, and gloves – luxuries and essentials that could not be manufactured on this Caribbean island.

Barney was sorely tempted to go ashore right away and look for Bella. On the long transatlantic journey, eager curiosity had grown into yearning. But he forced himself to wait. He did not know what to expect. It would be undignified for him to crash into what might be a cosy domestic scene. When he left Hispaniola she had been young and pretty; why would she not have married? On the other hand, she had a business of her own that made money, so she did not need a man to support her. Barney's hope was that she might have been reluctant to yield her independence to a husband. She was certainly feisty enough to take such an attitude.

If he approached her as an old friend, he would be able to deal with whatever he found. Should she have a husband, Barney would conceal his disappointment, shake hands, and congratulate the man on his good fortune. If she was single and alone – please, God! – he would take her in his arms.

In the morning he put on a green coat with gold buttons. It gave him a formal air and partly concealed the sword hanging from his belt, not hiding it but making it a little less ostentatious. Then he and Jonathan Greenland went to call on the mayor.

The town was bigger, but otherwise seemed unchanged. They were stared at crossing the central square, just as they had been nine years earlier, and probably by the same people. This time Barney stared back, looking for a beautiful African girl with blue eyes. He did not see her.

In the cool of the palace they were made to wait for a period long enough to impress them with the high status of the personage they wanted to see.

Then they were escorted upstairs by a man in a priest's cassock who was either Father Ignacio or a replacement – Barney did not remember the original well enough.

However, he vividly remembered the obese Alfonso, father of Bella. And the young man in the mayor's office was definitely not him.

'Don Alfonso is dead,' said the man in Alfonso's chair. 'Five years ago.' Barney was not surprised: immigrants to the Caribbean were highly vulnerable to strange tropical illnesses. 'I am the mayor now.' Alfonso's replacement was young but he, too, might be short-lived: he had the yellow-tinged skin that was a symptom of jaundice. 'My name is Don Jordi. Who are you?'

Barney made the introductions, then they went through the ritual dance in which Don Jordi pretended not to want a bribe and Barney pretended not to offer him one. When they had agreed a price for a 'temporary trading licence', the priest brought a bottle and glasses.

Barney sipped and said: 'Is this Bella's rum?'

'I have no idea,' said Don Jordi. 'Who's Bella?'

That was a bad sign. 'She used to make the best rum here.' Barney hid his disappointment. 'Perhaps she moved away?'

'Very likely. Is this not to your taste?'

'On the contrary. Here's to friendship.'

On leaving, Barney and Jonathan crossed the square to the house that had been Bella's home and distillery. They passed under the central arch into the rear yard. The business had expanded: there were now two stills dripping liquor into barrels.

A man with an air of authority came towards them. He was about thirty, and had dark African skin with straight hair, a combination that suggested he might be the son of a planter and a slave. He smiled in a friendly way. 'Good day,' he said. 'I

expect you've come to buy some of the best rum in the world.'
Barney thought apprehensively that this was exactly the kind
of man Bella might have married.

'We certainly have,' he said. 'And perhaps to sell you a pair
of Spanish pistols.'

'Come inside and taste the merchandise,' he said. 'I'm Pablo
Trujillo, proprietor.'

Barney could not control his impatience. 'What happened
to Bella?'

'I bought the business from her two years ago. I still use her
recipes, though.' He led them into the house and began to
squeeze limes just as Bella had.

'Where's Bella now?' Barney asked.

'She lives in a house on Don Alfonso's estate. He's dead, and
someone else owns the plantation, but Alfonso left her a
house.'

Barney had a feeling Pablo was holding something back. 'Is
she married?' he asked.

'I don't think so.' Pablo got out glasses and a bottle.

Barney was embarrassed to be asking so much about Bella.
He did not want people to think he was so soft-hearted as to
cross the Atlantic for the sake of a girl. He refrained from
further questions while they tasted the rum and agreed an
absurdly low price for two barrels.

When they were about to leave, he swallowed his pride and
said: 'I might call on Bella. Is there someone in town who
might lead me there?'

'Right next door. Mauricio Martinez takes a mule loaded
with supplies up to the plantation every few days.'

'Thank you.'

The neighbouring building was a fragrant general store
with barrels of rice and beans, herbs in bunches, cooking pots
and nails and coloured ribbons. Mauricio agreed to close the
shop right away and take Barney to the plantation. 'Must go
soon anyway,' he said. 'Flour and olive oil needed.' He spoke in
abbreviated sentences, as if to get the maximum said in the
time available.

Barney sent Jonathan back to take care of the *Alice*.

Mauricio saddled a horse for Barney, but he walked, leading the pack mule. They followed a dusty track out of town and up into the hills. Barney was not inclined for conversation, but Mauricio had plenty to say, in his condensed style. Fortunately, he did not seem to care whether Barney replied, or even understood. That left Barney's mind free to wander through his memories.

Soon they were alongside fields of sugar cane, the green stalks as high as Barney's head. Africans moved along the rows, tending the crop. The men wore ragged shorts, the women had simple shift dresses, and the children went naked. They all had home-made straw hats. In one field they were digging holes and embedding new plants, sweating under the sun. Barney saw another group operating a huge wooden press, crushing the cane stalks until the juice ran down into a tank below. Then he passed a wooden building in which fire flickered and steam billowed, and Mauricio explained: 'Boiling house.'

Barney said: 'In this weather, I wonder how people can survive, working in a place like that.'

'Many don't,' Mauricio said. 'Big problem, slaves dying in the boiling house. Costly.'

At last a plantation house came into view, a two-storey building made of the same yellow-white coral limestone as the palace in the town. As they approached it, Mauricio pointed to a small wooden house in the shade of a pleasant grove of palm trees. 'Bella,' he said. He rode on towards the big house.

Barney's throat felt constricted as he dismounted and tied his horse to a palm trunk. Nine years, he thought. Anything can happen in nine years.

He walked up to the house. The door was open. He stepped inside.

An old woman was lying on a narrow bed in the corner. There was no one else in the room. 'Where's Bella?' Barney said in Spanish.

The woman stared at him for a long moment then said: 'I knew you'd come back.'

The voice shocked him deeply. He stared at the old woman with incredulity and said: 'Bella?'

'I'm dying,' she said.

He crossed the little room in two strides and knelt beside the bed.

It was Bella. Her hair was thin almost to baldness, her golden skin had become the colour of old parchment, and her once-sturdy body was wasted away; but he recognized the blue eyes. He said: 'What happened to you?'

'Dandy fever.'

Barney had never heard of it, but it hardly mattered: anyone could see that she was close to death.

He leaned over to kiss her. She turned her head away, saying: 'I am hideous.'

He kissed her cheek. 'My beloved Bella,' he said. He felt so overwhelmed by grief that he could hardly speak. He fought back unmanly tears. Eventually he managed to say: 'Is there anything I can do for you?'

'Yes,' she said. 'I need a favour.'

'Anything.'

Before she could name it, Barney heard a child's voice behind him say: 'Who are you?'

He turned. A small boy stood in the doorway. He had golden skin, his curly African hair was reddish brown, and he had green eyes.

Barney looked at Bella. 'He's about eight years old . . .'

She nodded. 'His name is Barnardo Alfonso Willard. Look after him.'

Barney felt as if he had been knocked down by a charging horse. He could hardly catch his breath. Two shocks: Bella was dying, and he had a son. His life had been turned upside down in a minute.

Bella said: 'Alfo, this is your father. I've told you about him.'

Alfo stared at Barney, his face a mask of childish rage. 'Why did you come here?' he burst out. 'She's been waiting for you – now she'll die!'

Bella said: 'Alfo, be quiet.'

'Go away!' the boy yelled. 'Go back to England! We don't want you here!'

Bella said: 'Alfo!'

Barney said: 'It's all right, Bella. Let him yell.' He looked at the boy. 'My mother died, Alfo. I understand.'

The boy's rage turned to grief. He burst into tears and threw himself on the bed beside his mother.

Bella put a bony arm around his shoulders. He buried his face in her side and sobbed.

Barney stroked his hair. It was soft and springy. My son, he thought. My poor son.

Time went by without talk. Alfo eventually stopped crying. He sucked his thumb, staring at Barney.

Bella closed her eyes. That's good, Barney thought. She's resting.

Sleep well, my love.

19

Sylvie was busy – dangerously so.

Paris was full of Huguenots who had come for the royal wedding, and they bought a lot of paper and ink at the shop in the rue de la Serpente. They also wanted illegal books – not just the Bible in French, but the inflammatory works of John Calvin and Martin Luther attacking the Catholic Church. Sylvie was run off her feet going to the warehouse in the rue du Mur and delivering the contraband books to Protestant homes and lodging houses all over Paris.

And it all had to be done with total discretion. She was used to it, but not at this level of activity. She was risking arrest three times a day instead of three times a week. The increased strain was exhausting.

Spending time with Ned was like resting in an oasis of calm and security. He showed concern, not anxiety. He never panicked. He thought she was brave – in fact, he said she was a hero. She was pleased by his admiration, even though she knew she was just a scared girl.

On his third visit to the shop, her mother told him their real names and asked him to stay for midday dinner.

Isabelle had not consulted Sylvie about this. She just did it, taking Sylvie by surprise. Ned accepted readily. Sylvie was a bit taken aback, but pleased.

They closed and locked the street door and retired to the room behind the shop. Isabelle cooked fresh river trout, caught that morning, with marrow and aromatic fennel, and Ned ate heartily. Afterwards, she produced a bowl of greengages, yellow with red speckles, and a bottle of golden-brown brandy. They did not normally keep brandy in the house: the two women never drank anything stronger than wine, and they usually diluted that. Obviously Isabelle had quietly planned this meal.

Ned told them the news from the Netherlands, which was bad. 'Hangest disobeyed Coligny's orders, walked into an ambush, and was soundly defeated. He's a prisoner now.'

Isabelle was interested in Ned, not Hangest. 'How long do you think you'll stay in Paris?' she asked.

'As long as Queen Elizabeth wants me here.'

'And then I suppose you'll go home to England?'

'I'll probably go wherever the queen wants to send me.'

'You're devoted to her.'

'I feel fortunate to serve her.'

Isabelle switched to another line of enquiry. 'Are English houses different from French ones?' she said. 'Your home, for example?'

'I was born in a big house opposite Kingsbridge Cathedral. Now it belongs to my elder brother, Barney, but I live there when I'm in Kingsbridge.'

'Opposite the cathedral – that must be a pleasant location.'

'It's a wonderful spot. I love to sit in the front parlour and look out at the church.'

'What was your father?'

Sylvie protested: 'Mother, you sound like the Inquisition!'

'I don't mind,' Ned said. 'My father was a merchant with a warehouse in Calais, and after he died, my mother ran the business for ten years.' He smiled ruefully. 'But she lost everything after you French took back Calais from us English.'

'Are there any French people in Kingsbridge?'

'Persecuted Huguenots have sought asylum all over England. Guillaume Forneron has a factory making cambric in the suburb of Loversfield. Everyone wants a shirt from Forneron.'

'And your brother, what's his living?'

'He's a sea captain. He has a ship called *Alice*.'

'His own vessel?'

'Yes.'

'But Sylvie said something about a manor?'

'Queen Elizabeth made me lord of a village called Wigleigh,

not far from Kingsbridge. It's a small place, but it has a manor house, where I stay two or three times a year.'

'In France we would call you *Sieur de Wigleigh*.'

'Yes.' The name was difficult for French people to pronounce, like Willard.

'You and your brother have recovered well from your father's misfortune. You're an important diplomat, and Barney owns a ship.'

Ned must have realized that Isabelle was establishing his social and financial status, Sylvie thought, but he did not appear to mind; in fact, he seemed eager to prove his respectability. All the same, Sylvie was embarrassed. Ned might think he was expected to marry her. To bring the interrogation to an end she said: 'We have to open the shop.'

Isabelle stood up. 'I'll do that. You two sit and talk for a few more minutes. I'll call you if I need you, Sylvie.' She went out.

Sylvie said: 'I'm sorry about her prying like that.'

'Don't apologize.' Ned grinned. 'A mother is entitled to know all about a young man who becomes friendly with her daughter.'

'That's nice of you.'

'I can't possibly be the first man who has been questioned by her in that way.'

Sylvie knew that she had to tell him her story, sooner or later. 'There was someone, a long time ago. It was my father who questioned him.'

'May I ask what went wrong?'

'The man was Pierre Aumande.'

'Good God! Was he a Protestant then?'

'No, but he deceived us in order to spy on the congregation. An hour after the wedding we were all arrested.'

Ned reached across the table and took her hand. 'How cruel.'

'He broke my heart.'

'I found out about his background, you know. His father's a country priest, an illegitimate child of one of the Guise men. Pierre's mother is the priest's housekeeper.'

'How do you know?'

'The marchioness of Nîmes told me.'

'Louise? She's in our congregation – but she's never told me this.'

'Perhaps she's afraid to embarrass you by talking about him.'

'Pierre told me so many lies. That's probably why I haven't trusted anyone since then . . .'

Ned gave her an enquiring look. She knew it meant: *What about me?* But she was not yet ready to answer that question.

He waited a few moments, then realized she was not going to say any more. He said: 'Well, that was a lovely dinner – thank you.'

She got up to say goodbye. He looked crestfallen, and her heart leaped in sympathy. On impulse, she went around the table and kissed him.

She intended it to be a friendly peck, but it did not work out that way. Somehow she found herself kissing his lips. It was like sweet food: one taste made her desperate for more. She put her hand behind his head and pressed her mouth to his hungrily.

He needed no more encouragement. He put both arms around her and hugged her to him. She was swept by a sensation she had forgotten, the joy of loving someone else's body. She kept telling herself she would stop in another second.

He put both his hands on her breasts and squeezed gently, making a little sound in his throat as he did so. She thrilled to the feeling, but it brought her to her senses. She broke the kiss and pushed him away. She was panting. 'I didn't mean to do that,' she said.

He said nothing, just smiled happily.

She realized she had given him the message she had wanted to withhold. But now she did not care. All the same she said: 'You'd better go, before I do something I'll regret.'

That thought seemed to make him even happier. 'All right,' he said. 'When will I see you again?'

'Soon. Go and say goodbye to my mother.'

He tried to kiss her again, but she put a hand on his chest and said: 'No more.'

He accepted that. He went into the shop, saying: 'Thank you, Madame Palot, for your hospitality.'

Sylvie sat down heavily. A moment later she heard the shop door close.

Her mother came into the back room, looking pleased. 'He's gone, but he'll be back.'

Sylvie said: 'I kissed him.'

'I guessed that by the grin on his face.'

'I shouldn't have done it.'

'I can't think why not. I'd have kissed him myself if I were twenty years younger.'

'Don't be vulgar, Mother. Now he will expect me to marry him.'

'I'd do it quickly, if I were you, before some other girl grabs him.'

'Stop it. You know perfectly well that I can't marry him.'

'I know no such thing! What are you talking about?'

'We have a mission to bring the true gospel to the world.'

'Perhaps we've done enough.'

Sylvie was shocked. Her mother had never talked this way. Isabelle noticed her reaction and said defensively: 'Even God rested on the seventh day, after he made the world.'

'Our work isn't finished.'

'Perhaps it never will be, until the Last Trump.'

'All the more reason to carry on.'

'I want you to be happy. You're my little girl.'

'But what does God want? You taught me always to ask that question.'

Isabelle sighed. 'I did. I was harder when I was young.'

'You were wise. I can't marry. I have a mission.'

'All the same, regardless of Ned, one day we may have to find other ways of doing God's will.'

'I don't see how.'

'Perhaps it will be revealed to us.'

'It's in God's hands, then, isn't it, Mother?'

'Yes.'

'So we must be content.'

Isabelle sighed again. 'Amen,' she said, but Sylvie was not sure she meant it.

*

AS NED STEPPED out of the shop he noticed, across the street, a shabby young man lounging outside a tavern, on his own, doing nothing. Ned turned east, heading for the English embassy. Glancing back, he saw that the shabby man was going the same way.

Ned was in high spirits. Sylvie had kissed him as if she meant it. He adored her. For the first time, he had met a girl who matched up to Margery. Sylvie was smart and brave as well as warm and sexy. He could hardly wait to see her again.

He had not forgotten Margery. He never would. But she had refused to run away with him, and he had the rest of his life to live without her. He was entitled to love someone else.

He liked Sylvie's mother, too. Isabelle was still attractive in a middle-aged way: she had a full figure and a handsome face, and the wrinkles around her blue eyes gave character to her appearance. She had made it pretty clear that she approved of Ned.

He felt angered by the story Sylvie had told about Pierre Aumande. He had actually married her! No wonder she had gone so long without marrying again. The thought of Sylvie being betrayed like that on her wedding day made Ned want to strangle Pierre with his own hands.

But he did not let that bring him down. There was too much to be happy about. It was even possible that France might be the second major country in the world to adopt freedom of religion.

Crossing the rue St Jacques, he glanced behind and saw the shabby man from the rue de la Serpente.

He would have to do something about this.

He paused on the other side of the street to look back at the magnificent church of St Severin. The shabby man came scurrying across the road, avoiding Ned's eye, and slipped into an alley.

Ned turned into the grounds of the little church of

St-Julien-le-Pauvre. He walked across the deserted graveyard. As he turned around the east end of the church, he slipped into a recessed doorway that concealed him. Then he drew his dagger and reversed it so that the knob of the hilt stuck up between the thumb and forefinger of his right hand.

As the shabby man drew level with the doorway, Ned stepped out and smashed the knob of the dagger into the man's face. The man cried out and staggered back, bleeding profusely from his nose and mouth. But he recovered his balance quickly, and turned to run. Ned went after him and tripped him, and he fell flat. Ned knelt on his back and put the point of the dagger to his neck. 'Who sent you?' he said.

The man swallowed blood and said: 'I don't know what you mean – why have you attacked me?'

Ned pushed on the dagger until it broke the dirty skin of the man's throat and blood trickled out.

The man cried: 'No, please!'

'No one's looking. I'll kill you and walk away – unless you tell me who ordered you to follow me.'

'All right, all right! It was Georges Biron.'

'Who the devil is he?'

'Lord of Montagny.'

It rang a bell. 'Why does he want to know where I go?'

'I don't know, I swear to Christ! He never tells us why, just sends us.'

This man was part of a group, then. Biron must be their leader. He, or someone he worked for, had put Ned under surveillance. 'Who else do you follow?'

'It used to be Walsingham, then we had to switch to you.'

'Does Biron work for some great lord?'

'He might, but he doesn't tell us anything. Please, it's true.'

It made sense, Ned thought. There was no need to tell a wretch such as this the reasons for what he was doing.

He stood up, sheathed his weapon and walked away.

He crossed the place Maubert to the embassy and went in. Walsingham was in the hall. Ned said: 'Do you know anything about Georges Biron, lord of Montagny?'

'Yes,' said Walsingham. 'He's on a list of associates of Pierre Aumande de Guise.'

'Ah, that explains it.'

'Explains what?'

'Why he's having you and me followed.'

*

PIERRE LOOKED AT the little shop in the rue de la Serpente. He knew the street: this had been his neighbourhood when he was a student, all those years ago. He had frequented the tavern opposite, but the shop had not existed then.

Being here caused him to reflect on his life since then. That young student had yearned for many things that had since become his, he thought with satisfaction. He was the most trusted advisor to the Guise family. He had fine clothes and wore them to see the king. He had money, and something more valuable than money: power.

But he had worries. The Huguenots had not been stamped out – in fact, they seemed to grow stronger. The Scandinavian countries and some of the German provinces were firmly Protestant, as was the tiny kingdom of Navarre. The battle was still being fought in Scotland and the Netherlands.

There was good news from the Netherlands: the Huguenot leader Hangest had been defeated at Mons, and was now in a dungeon with some of his lieutenants, being tortured by the brutal duke of Alba. Triumphant Paris Catholics had devised a chant that could be heard every night in the taverns:

> Hang-est!
> Ha! Ha! Ha!
> Hang-est!
> Ha! Ha! Ha!

But Mons was not decisive, and the rebellion was not crushed.

Worst of all, France itself was lurching, like a drunk trying to go forwards but staggering back, towards the disgusting kind of compromise that Queen Elizabeth had pioneered in England, neither firmly Catholic nor Protestant but a permissive mixture. The royal wedding was just a few days away and had not yet provoked the kind of riot that might have caused it to be called off.

But it would. And when it did, Pierre would be ready. His black book of Paris Protestants had been augmented with visitors. And, in recent days, he and Duke Henri had made additional plans. They had worked out a matching list of ultra-Catholic noblemen who could be trusted to do murder. When the Huguenot uprising began, the bell of the church of Saint-Germain l'Auxerrois would ring continuously, and that would be the signal for each Catholic nobleman to kill his assigned Protestant.

All had agreed, in principle. Pierre knew that not every man would keep his promise, but there would be enough. As soon as the Huguenots revolted, the Catholics would strike. They would slay the beast by chopping its head off. Then the town militia could dispose of the rank and file. The Huguenot movement would be crippled, perhaps fatally. It would be the end of the wicked royal policy of tolerance towards Protestantism. And the Guises would once again be the most powerful family in France.

Here in front of Pierre was a new address for his black book.

'The Englishman has fallen in love,' Georges Biron had told him.

'With whom? Anyone we can blackmail?' Pierre had asked.

'With a woman stationer who has a shop on the left bank.'

'Name?'

'Thérèse St Quentin. She runs the shop with her mother, Jacqueline.'

'They must be Protestants. The Englishman would not dally with a Catholic girl.'

'Shall I investigate them?'

'I might take a look myself.'

The St Quentins had a modest house, he saw now, with just one upstairs storey. An alley the width of a handcart led, presumably, to a backyard. The façade was in good repair and all the woodwork was newly painted so presumably they were prospering. The door stood open in the August heat. In a window was an artistically arranged display: fanned sheets of paper, a bouquet of quill pens in a vase, and ink bottles of different sizes.

'Wait here,' he said to his bodyguards.

He stepped into the shop and was astonished to see Sylvie Palot.

It was definitely her. She was thirty-one, he calculated, but she looked a little older, no doubt because of all she had been through. She was thinner than before, having lost a certain adolescent bloom. She had the beginnings of wrinkles around her strong jaw, but her eyes were the same blue. She wore a plain blue linen dress, and beneath it her compact body was still sturdy and neat.

For a moment he was transported, as if by a magic spell, to that era, fourteen years ago: the fish market where he had first spoken to her; the bookshop in the shadow of the cathedral; the illegal church in the hunting lodge; and a younger, less knowing Pierre who had nothing but wanted it all.

Sylvie was alone in the shop. She was standing at a table, adding up a column of figures in a ledger, and at first she did not look up.

He studied her. Somehow she had survived the death of her father and the confiscation of his business. She had taken a false name and had begun a new enterprise of her own – which had prospered. It puzzled Pierre that God permitted so many blasphemous Protestants to do well in business and commerce. They used their profits to pay pastors and build meeting rooms and buy banned books. Sometimes it was hard to discern God's plan.

And now she had an admirer – who was a detested enemy of Pierre's.

After a while he said: 'Hello, Sylvie.'

Although his tone had been friendly, she gave a squeal of fright. She must have recognized his voice, even after all these years.

He enjoyed the fear on her face.

'Why are you here?' she said in a shaky voice.

'Pure chance. A delightful surprise for me.'

'I'm not afraid of you,' she said, and he knew, with pleasure, that she was lying. 'What can you do to me?' she went on. 'You've already ruined my life.'

'I could do it again.'

'No, you couldn't. We have the Peace of St Germain.'

'It's still against the law to sell banned books, though.'

'We don't sell books.'

Pierre looked around the room. There were no printed books for sale, it seemed; just blank ledgers like the one she was writing in and smaller notebooks called *livres de raison*. Perhaps her evangelical zeal had been stifled by the sight of her father burning to death: it was what the Church always hoped for. But sometimes such executions had the opposite effect, creating inspirational martyrs. She might have dedicated her life to continuing her father's mission. Perhaps she had a store of heretical literature somewhere else. He could have her followed, night and day, to find out; but, unfortunately, she was now forewarned, and would take extra precautions.

He changed his line of attack. 'You used to love me.'

She went pale. 'May God forgive me.'

'Come, come. You liked kissing me.'

'Hemlock in honey.'

He took a threatening step forward. He did not really want to kiss her – never had. It was more exciting to frighten her. 'You'd kiss me again, I know.'

'I'd bite your damned nose off.'

He had a feeling she meant that, but he kept up his banter. 'I taught you all you know about love.'

'You taught me that a man can be a Christian and a foul liar at the same time.'

'We're all sinners. That's why we need God's grace.'

'Some sinners are worse than others – and some go to hell.'

'Do you kiss your English admirer?'

That really did scare her, he saw to his gratification. Evidently it had not occurred to her that he might know about Sir Ned. 'I don't know who you're talking about,' she lied.

'Yes, you do.'

She recovered her composure with an effort. 'Are you

satisfied with your reward, Pierre?' She indicated his coat with a gesture. 'You have fine clothes, and I've seen you riding side by side with the duke of Guise. You've got what you wanted. Was it worth all the evil you had to do?'

He could not resist the temptation to boast. 'I have money, and more power than I ever dreamed of.'

'That wasn't really what you longed for. You forget how well I know you.'

Pierre suddenly felt anxious.

She went on remorselessly: 'All you wanted was to be one of them, a member of the Guise family that rejected you as a baby.'

'And I am,' he said.

'No, you're not. They all know your true origins, don't they?'

A feeling of panic began to creep over Pierre. 'I am the duke's most trusted advisor!'

'But not his cousin. They look at your fancy clothes, they remember that you're the illegitimate child of an illegitimate child, and they laugh at your pretensions, don't they?'

'Who told you these lies?'

'The marchioness of Nîmes knows all about you. She comes from the same region as you. You've married again, haven't you?'

He winced. Was she guessing, or did she know?

'Unhappily, perhaps?' she went on. He was unable to hide his feelings, and she read his face accurately. 'But not to a noblewoman. To someone low-born – which is why you hate her.'

She was right. In case he should ever forget how he won the right to use the Guise name, he had a loathsome wife and an irritating stepson to remind him of the price he had paid. He was unable to restrain the grimace of resentment that twisted his face.

Sylvie saw it and said: 'The poor woman.'

He should have stepped around the table and knocked her down, then called his bodyguards from outside to beat her up; but he could not summon the energy. Instead of being galvanized by rage he found himself helpless with self-doubt.

She was right, she knew him too well. She had hurt him, and he just wanted to crawl away and lick his wounds.

He was turning to leave when her mother came into the shop from the back. She recognized him instantly. She was so shocked that she took a step backwards, looking both fearful and disgusted, as if she had seen a rabid dog. Then her shock turned, with startling rapidity, to rage. 'You devil!' she shouted. 'You killed my Giles. You ruined my daughter's life.' Her voice rose to yelling pitch, almost as if she had been seized by a fit of insanity, and Pierre backed away from her towards the door. 'If I had a knife, I'd rip out your stinking guts!' she screamed. 'You filth! You discharge of an infected prostitute! You loathsome stinking corpse of a man, I'll strangle you!'

Pierre hurried out and slammed the door behind him.

*

RIGHT FROM the start, there was a bad atmosphere at the wedding.

The crowd gathered early on Monday morning, for Parisians would never actually stay away from such a spectacle. In the square in front of the cathedral of Notre Dame an amphitheatre had been constructed, made of timber and covered with cloth-of-gold, with raised walkways to the church and to the neighbouring bishop's palace. As a minor dignitary, Ned took his seat in the stand hours before the ceremony was due to begin. It was a cloudless day in August, and everyone was too hot in the sun. The square around the temporary construction was packed with sweating citizens. More spectators watched from windows and rooftops of neighbouring houses. All were ominously quiet. The ultra-Catholic Parisians did not want their naughty darling to marry a Protestant rotter. And their anger was stoked, every Sunday, by incendiary preachers who told them the marriage was an abomination.

Ned still could not quite believe it was going to happen. The crowd might riot and stop the ceremony. And there were rumours that Princess Margot was threatening a last-minute refusal.

The stand filled up during the day. At around three in the

afternoon he found himself next to Jerónima Ruiz. Ned had planned to talk to her again, after their intriguing conversation at the Louvre palace, but he had not had the opportunity in the few days since. He greeted her warmly, and she said nostalgically: 'You smile just like Barney.'

'Cardinal Romero must feel disappointed,' Ned said. 'The marriage appears to be going ahead.'

She lowered her voice. 'He told me something that will interest you.'

'Good!' Ned had been hoping that Jerónima might be persuaded to leak information. It seemed she did not need any persuading.

'The duke of Guise has a list of names and addresses of leading Protestants in Paris. One reliable Catholic nobleman has been assigned to each. If there are riots, the Huguenots will all be murdered.'

'My God! Are they that cold-blooded?'

'The Guise family are.'

'Thank you for telling me.'

'I'd like to kill Romero, but I can't, because I need him,' she said. 'But this is the next best thing.'

He stared at her, fascinated and a little horrified. The Guises were not the only cold-blooded ones.

The conversation was interrupted by a rumble from the crowd, and they turned to see the bridegroom's procession, coming from the Louvre palace, crossing the Notre Dame bridge from the right bank to the island. Henri de Bourbon, king of Navarre, wore a pale yellow satin outfit embroidered with silver, pearls and precious stones. He was escorted by Protestant noblemen including the marquess de Nîmes. The citizens of Paris watched in sullen silence.

Ned turned to speak to Jerónima, but she had moved away, and now Walsingham was next to him. 'I just learned something chilling,' he said, and repeated what Jerónima had told him.

'Perhaps we shouldn't be surprised,' Walsingham said. 'They have made plans – of course they have.'

'And now we know about their plans, thanks to that Spanish tart.'

Walsingham gave a rare smile. 'All right, Ned, you've made your point.'

King Charles came out of the bishop's palace with the bride, his sister, on his arm. He wore the same pale yellow satin as Henri de Bourbon, a sign of brotherhood. However, he had larger jewels, and more of them. As they approached, Walsingham leaned towards Ned and said disdainfully: 'I've been told that the king's outfit cost five hundred thousand ecus.'

Ned could hardly believe it. 'That's a hundred and fifty thousand pounds!'

'Which is half the annual budget of the English government.'

For once Ned shared Walsingham's disapproval of lavishness.

Princess Margot wore a velvet robe in a luminous shade of violet, and a blue cloak with a long train carried by three ladies. She was going to get hot, Ned thought. Every princess was said to be beautiful, but in her case it was true. She had a sensual face, with big eyes marked by dark eyebrows, and red lips that looked as if they wanted to be kissed. But today that lovely face was set in an expression of stubborn resentment. 'She's not happy,' Ned said to Walsingham.

Walsingham shrugged. 'She's known since childhood that she would not be allowed to choose her own husband. There is a price to pay for the obscenely extravagant life led by French royalty.'

Ned thought of Margery's arranged marriage. 'I sympathize with Margot,' he said.

'If the rumours about her are true, she won't let her marriage vows constrain her behaviour.'

Behind the king came his brothers, all wearing the same yellow satin. They were making sure the crowd got the point: from today on the Valois men and the Bourbons were going to be brothers. The bride was followed by at least a hundred noblewomen. Ned had never seen so many diamonds and rubies in one place. Every woman was wearing more jewels than Queen Elizabeth owned.

Still no one cheered.

The procession moved slowly along the raised walkway to the amphitheatre, and there the bride took her place beside the groom. This was the first time a Catholic had married a Protestant in a royal wedding, and a complex ceremony had been devised to avoid offending either side.

In accordance with custom, the wedding was performed outside the church. The cardinal of Bourbon administered the vows. As the seconds ticked by and the words were spoken, Ned felt the solemnity of the moment: a great country was moving, inch by painful inch, towards the ideal of religious freedom. Ned longed for that. It was what Queen Elizabeth wanted, and it was what Sylvie Palot needed.

At last the cardinal asked Margot if she would accept the king of Navarre as her husband.

She stared back at him, expressionless and tight-lipped.

Surely, Ned thought, she would not sabotage the whole wedding at this point? But people said she was wilful.

The groom shifted from one foot to the other impatiently.

The princess and the cardinal stared at one another for a long moment.

Then King Charles, standing behind his sister, reached forward, put his hand on the back of her head, and pushed.

Princess Margot appeared to nod.

This clearly was not consent, Ned thought. God knew that, and so did the watching crowd. But it was good enough for the cardinal, who hastily pronounced them man and wife.

They were married – but if something went wrong now, before the marriage was consummated, it could yet be annulled.

The bridal party went into the cathedral for the wedding Mass. The groom did not stay for the Catholic service, but emerged again almost immediately.

Outside the church he spoke to Gaspard de Coligny, the Huguenot general. They may have intended no offence, but their casual manner gave the impression that they were disdaining the service going on inside. That was certainly what the crowd felt, and they began to shout protests. Then they started their victory chant:

> Hang-est!
> Ha! Ha! Ha!
> Hang-est!
> Ha! Ha! Ha!

This was infuriating to the Huguenots whose leaders were being tortured in the dungeons of the duke of Alba.

The notables in the stand were milling around, chatting, but as the chanting grew, their conversations tailed off and they looked around anxiously.

A group of Huguenots on the roof of a nearby house retaliated by singing a psalm, and other voices joined in. In the crowd on the ground, a few young toughs began to move towards the house.

The scene had all the makings of a riot. If that happened, the pacific effect of the marriage could be reversed.

Ned spotted Walsingham's friend the marquess of Lagny, in his jewelled cap, and spoke to him urgently. 'Can't you stop those Huguenots singing?' he said. 'It enrages the crowd. We'll lose all we've gained if there's a riot.'

Lagny said: 'I could stop the singing, if the Catholics would stop chanting.'

Ned looked around for a friendly Catholic and saw Aphrodite Beaulieu. He buttonholed her and said: 'Can you get a priest or someone to stop the crowd doing the Hangest chant? We're heading for a nasty disturbance.'

She was a sensible girl and saw the danger. 'I'll go into the church and speak to my father,' she said.

Ned's eye lit on Henri of Bourbon and Gaspard de Coligny and he realized they were the root of the problem. He went back to Lagny. 'Could you tell those two to make themselves scarce?' he said. 'I'm sure they don't mean it, but they're provoking the crowd.'

Lagny nodded. 'I'll speak to them. Neither of them wants trouble.'

A couple of minutes later, Henri and Gaspard disappeared into the archbishop's palace. A priest came out of the cathedral and told the crowd that they were disturbing the Mass, and the chanting subsided. The Huguenots on the rooftops ceased their singing. The square became quiet.

The crisis was over, Ned thought – for now.

*

THE WEDDING WAS followed by three days of lavish celebrations, but no riots. Pierre was bitterly disappointed.

There were street fights and tavern brawls, as exultant Protestants clashed with furious Catholics, but none of the affrays turned into the city-wide battle he was hoping for.

Queen Caterina did not have the stomach for a violent confrontation. Coligny, like all the more cunning Huguenots, believed his best strategy was to avoid bloodshed. Together, milk-and-water moderates on both sides kept the peace.

The Guise family were desperate. They saw power and prestige slipping away from them permanently. Then Pierre came up with a plan.

They were going to assassinate Gaspard de Coligny.

On Thursday, as the nobility attended the tournament that was the climax of the festivities, Pierre stood with Georges Biron in one of the medieval rooms in the old part of the Louvre palace. The floors were dirt and the walls were rough stone.

Biron moved a table to a window for better light. He was carrying a canvas bag, and now he took from it a long-barrelled firearm.

'It's an arquebus,' said Pierre. 'But with two barrels, one below the other.'

'So if he misses Coligny with the first ball, he has a second chance.'

'Very good.'

Biron pointed to the trigger mechanism. 'It has a wheel-lock firing action.'

'Self-igniting, then. But will it kill him?'

'At anything up to a hundred yards, yes.'

'A Spanish musket would be better.' Muskets were bigger and heavier, and a shot from one of them was more likely to be fatal.

Biron shook his head. 'Too difficult to conceal. Everyone would know what the man was up to. And Louviers is not young. I'm not sure he can handle a musket.' It took strength to lift one: that was why musketeers were famously big.

Pierre had brought Charles Louviers to Paris. Louviers had kept a cool head in Orléans: the assassination of Antoine de Bourbon had failed through the dithering of King Francis II, not by any fault of Louviers's. Some years later, Louviers had assassinated a Huguenot leader called Captain Luzé and won a reward of two thousand ecus. And Louviers was a nobleman, which – Pierre thought – meant that he would keep his word, whereas a common street thug would change sides for the price of a bottle of wine. Pierre hoped he had made the right decisions.

'All right,' he said. 'Let's have a look at the route.'

Biron put the gun back in the bag and they stepped out into the courtyard. Two sides of the square were medieval castle walls, the other two modern Italian-style palaces. Biron said: 'When Gaspard de Coligny walks from his lodging to here, and from here back to his lodging, he is accompanied by a bodyguard of about twenty armed men.'

'That's going to be a problem.'

Pierre walked the way Coligny would have to go, out through the medieval gateway to the rue des Poulies. The Bourbon family had a palace immediately opposite the Louvre. Next to it was the mansion of the king's brother Hercule-Francis. Pierre looked along the street. 'Where does Coligny lodge?'

'Around the corner, in the rue de Béthisy. It's just a few steps.'

'Let's look.'

They walked north, away from the river.

The tension in the streets was still high. Even now Pierre could see Huguenots, in their sombre but costly outfits of black and grey, strolling along as if they owned the city. If they had any sense, they would not look so triumphant. But then, Pierre thought, if they had any sense, they would not be Protestants.

The ultra-Catholic people of Paris hated these visitors. Their tolerance was fragile, a bridge of straw holding up an iron-wheeled wagon.

Given a really good pretext, either side would run amok. Then, if enough people were killed, the civil war would start again, and the Peace of St Germain would be torn up, regardless of the marriage.

Pierre was going to provide that pretext.

He scanned the street for a vantage point from which a gunman might fire at someone walking along: a tower, a big tree, an attic window. The trouble was, the killer would need an escape route, for the bodyguards would surely go after him.

He stopped outside a house he recognized. It belonged to Henri de Guise's mother, Anna d'Este. She had remarried, and was now duchess of Nemours, but she still hated Coligny, believing him to have been responsible for the death of her first husband. Indeed, she had done as much as Pierre to keep alive young Duke Henri's yearning for revenge. She would undoubtedly cooperate.

He scrutinized the façade. The upstairs windows were overhung by wooden trellises bearing climbing plants, a pretty touch that surely came from the duchess. But today the trellises were draped with drying laundry, which suggested the duchess was not in residence. Even better, Pierre thought.

He banged on the door and a servant opened it. The man recognized Pierre and spoke in a tone of deference laced with fear. 'Good day to you, Monsieur de Guise, I hope I may be of assistance to you.' Pierre liked obsequiousness, but he always pretended not to notice it. Now he pushed past the man without replying.

He went up the stairs, and Biron followed, still carrying the long bag with the arquebus.

There was a large drawing room at the front on the upstairs floor. Pierre opened the window. Despite the laundry flapping in the breeze, he had a clear view of both sides of the street in the direction of the Louvre. 'Hand me that gun,' he said.

Biron took the weapon out of its bag. Pierre rested it on the windowsill and sighted along the barrel. He saw a well-dressed couple approaching arm-in-arm. He aimed the gun at the man. To his surprise he recognized the elderly marquess of Nîmes. Pierre moved the gunsight sideways and studied the woman, who was wearing a bright yellow dress. Yes, it was the Marchioness Louise, who had twice caused him to suffer humiliation: once long ago, when she had snubbed him at the Protestant service in the old hunting lodge; and again just a week ago, at the shop in the rue de la Serpente, when Sylvie had taunted him with secrets Louise had told her. He could get his revenge now, just by squeezing the trigger of the wheel-lock. He targeted her bust. She was in her middle thirties, but still voluptuous, and her breasts were, if anything, larger than before. Pierre yearned to stain that yellow dress with her bright blood. He could almost hear her screams.

One day, he thought; just not yet.

He shook his head and stood up. 'This is good,' he said to Biron, handing back the gun.

He stepped outside the room. The manservant was on the landing, waiting for orders. 'There must be a back door,' Pierre said to him.

'Yes, sir. May I show you?'

They went downstairs and through the kitchen and the wash-house to a yard with a gate. Pierre opened the gate and found himself in the grounds of the church of St-Germain l'Auxerrois. 'This is perfect,' he said to Biron in a low voice. 'You can have a horse waiting here, saddled ready, and Louviers can be gone a minute after firing the fatal shot.'

Biron nodded agreement. 'That'll work.'

They walked back through the house. Pierre gave the manservant a gold ecu. 'I wasn't here today,' he said. 'No one was. You saw nothing.'

'Thank you, sir,' said the man.

Pierre thought for another moment and realized that

money was not enough. He said: 'I don't need to tell you how the Guise family punish disloyalty.'

The servant looked terrified. 'I understand, sir, I really do.'

Pierre nodded and walked away. It was better to be feared than to be loved.

He went farther along the street until he came to a small graveyard behind a low wall fringed with trees. He crossed the street and looked back. He had a clear view of the Nemours house.

'Perfect,' he said again.

*

ON FRIDAY MORNING, Gaspard de Coligny had to go to a meeting of the royal council at the Louvre palace. Attendance was not optional, and absence was regarded as an act of disobedience offensive to the king. If a man were too sick to rise from his bed, and sent an abject apology, the king might sniff and say that if the illness was so bad, why had the man not died of it?

If Coligny followed his usual routine, he would walk past the Nemours house on his way back from the Louvre.

By mid-morning Charles de Louviers was installed at the upstairs window. Biron was at the back gate, holding a fast horse already saddled. Pierre was in the little graveyard, screened by trees, watching over the low wall.

All they had to do was wait.

Henri de Guise had given ready consent to Pierre's plan. Duke Henri's only regret was that he did not have the opportunity himself to fire the bullet that would kill the man responsible for his father's murder.

A group of fifteen or twenty men appeared at the far end of the street.

Pierre tensed.

Coligny was a handsome man in his fifties with a head of curly silver hair, neatly trimmed, and a beard to match. He walked with the upright bearing of a soldier, but right now he was reading as he went along, and in consequence moving slowly – which would be helpful to Louviers, Pierre thought with mounting excitement and apprehension. Coligny was surrounded by men-at-arms and other companions, but they did not seem notably vigilant. They were talking among themselves, glancing around only cursorily, appearing not to fear greatly for the safety of their leader. They had become slack.

The group walked along the middle of the street. Not yet, Pierre thought; don't fire yet. At a distance, Louviers would have difficulty hitting Coligny, for the others were in the way; but as the group approached the house, his vantage point on the upstairs floor gave him a better angle down.

Coligny came closer. In a few seconds the angle would be perfect, Pierre thought. Louviers would surely have Coligny in his sights by now.

About now, Pierre thought; don't leave it too late . . .

Coligny suddenly stopped in his tracks and turned to speak to a companion. At that moment a shot rang out. Pierre stopped breathing. Coligny's group froze in their positions. In the instant of shocked silence, Coligny roared a curse and grabbed his left arm with his right hand. He had been wounded.

Pierre's frustration was intense. That sudden unexpected stop had saved Coligny's life.

But Louviers's arquebus had two barrels, and a second shot came immediately afterwards. This time Coligny fell. Pierre could not see him. Was he dead?

The companions closed around him. All was confusion. Pierre was desperate to know what was happening but could not tell. The silver head of Coligny appeared in the middle of the throng. Had they lifted up his corpse? Then Pierre saw that Coligny's eyes were open and he was speaking. He was standing up. He was alive!

Reload, Louviers, and fire again, quickly, Pierre thought. But some of Coligny's bodyguard at last came to their senses and started to look about them. One pointed to the upstairs storey of the Nemours house, where a white curtain flapped at an open window; and four of them ran towards the house. Was Louviers even now cool-headedly loading his gun? The men ran into the house. Pierre stood looking over the graveyard wall, frozen to the spot, waiting for another bang; but none came. If Louviers was still there they must have overpowered him by now.

Pierre returned his attention to Coligny. He was upright, but perhaps his men were supporting him. Though only wounded he might yet die. However, after a minute he seemed to shake them off and demand some room, and they stopped crowding him. This enabled Pierre to get a better look, and he saw that Coligny was standing unaided. He had both arms clutched to his body, and blood on his sleeves and doublet, but to Pierre's dismay the wounds seemed superficial. Indeed, as soon as his men gave him space he began to walk, clearly intending to get home under his own power before submitting to the attentions of a doctor.

The men who had gone into the Nemours house now re-emerged, one of them carrying the double-barrelled arquebus. Pierre could not hear what they were saying, but he could read their gestures: head-shaking negation, shrugs of helplessness, arms waving in signs indicating rapid flight. Louviers had escaped.

The group came nearer to Pierre's hiding place. He turned around, hurried out of the graveyard by the far gate, and walked away, bitterly disappointed.

*

NED AND WALSINGHAM knew, as soon as they heard the news, that this could be the end of all they and Queen Elizabeth hoped for.

They immediately rushed to the rue de Béthisy. They found Coligny lying on a bed, surrounded by some of the leading Huguenots, including the marquess of Lagny. Several doctors were in attendance, notably Ambroise Paré, the royal surgeon, a man in his sixties with a receding hairline and a long dark beard that gave him a thoughtful look.

The usual technique for disinfecting wounds, Ned knew, was to cauterize them with either boiling oil or a red-hot iron. This was so painful that the patient sometimes died of shock.

Paré preferred to apply an ointment containing turpentine to prevent infection. He had written a book, *The Method of Curing Wounds Caused by Arquebus and Arrows*. Despite his success, his methods had not caught on: the medical profession was conservative.

Coligny was pale, and evidently in pain, but he seemed to have all his faculties. One bullet had taken off the top of his right index finger, Paré explained. The other had lodged in his left elbow. Paré had got it out – an agonizing procedure that probably accounted for how pale Coligny looked – and he showed it to them, a lead sphere half an inch across.

However, Paré said that Coligny was going to live, which was a huge relief. Nevertheless, the Huguenots would be outraged by the attempt on the life of their hero, and it would be a challenge to prevent them running riot.

There were several around the bed itching for a fight. Coligny's friends were thirsty for revenge. They were all sure that the duke of Guise was behind the assassination attempt. They wanted to go to the Louvre right away and confront the king. They were going to demand the immediate arrest of Henri de Guise, and threaten a national Huguenot uprising otherwise. There was even foolish talk of taking the king prisoner.

Coligny himself urged restraint, but it was the weak voice of a man wounded and supine.

Walsingham made an effort to hold them back. 'I have some information which may be important,' he said. He was the representative of the only major country in the world that was Protestant, and the Huguenot nobility listened to him attentively. 'The ultra-Catholics are prepared for your rebellion. The duke of Guise has a plan to put down any show of force by Protestants following the wedding. Each person in this room . . .' He looked around significantly. 'Each person in this room has been assigned his own personal assassin from among the more fanatical Catholic aristocracy.'

This was shocking news, and there was a buzz of horror and indignation.

The marquess of Lagny removed his jewelled cap and

scratched his bald head. 'Forgive me, ambassador Walsingham,' he said sceptically, 'but how could you know a thing like that?'

Ned tensed. He was almost completely sure that Walsingham would not reveal the name of Jerónima Ruiz. She might come up with further information.

Fortunately, Walsingham did not give away Ned's source. 'I have a spy in the Guise house, of course,' he lied.

Lagny was normally a peacemaker, but now he said defiantly: 'Then we must all be prepared to defend ourselves.'

Someone else said: 'The best defence is attack!'

They all agreed with that.

Ned was a junior here, but he had something worth saying, so he spoke up. 'The duke of Guise is *hoping* for a Protestant insurrection to force the king to breach the Peace of St Germain. You would be playing into his hands.'

Nothing worked. Their blood was up.

Then King Charles arrived.

It was a shock. No one was expecting him. He came without advance notice. His mother, Queen Caterina, was with him, and Ned guessed that this visit was her idea. They were followed in by a crowd of leading courtiers, including most of the Catholic noblemen who hated Coligny. But the duke of Guise was not with them, Ned noticed.

Charles had been king for eleven years, but he was still only twenty-one, and Ned thought he looked particularly young and vulnerable today. There was genuine distress and anxiety on his pale face with its wispy moustache and barely visible beard.

Ned's hopes rose a little. For the king to come like this was an extraordinary act of sympathy, and could hardly be ignored by the Huguenots.

Charles's words reinforced Ned's optimism. Addressing Coligny, the king said: 'The pain is yours, but the outrage is mine.'

It was obviously a rehearsed remark, intended to be repeated all over Paris; but it was none the worse for that.

A chair was hastily brought, and the king sat down facing

the bed. 'I swear to you that I will find out who was responsible—'

Someone muttered: 'Henri de Guise.'

'—whoever he may be,' the king went on. 'I have already appointed a commission of inquiry, and even now investigators are questioning the servants in the house where the assassin lay in wait.'

This was cosmetic, Ned judged. A formal inquiry was never a genuine attempt to learn the truth. No sensible king would allow independent men to control an investigation whose result could be so inflammatory. The commission was a delaying tactic, intended not to discover the facts but to lower the temperature – which was good.

'I beg you,' the king went on, 'to come to the Louvre palace, and be close to our royal presence, where you will be completely safe from any further harm.'

That was not such a good idea, Ned thought. Coligny was not safe anywhere, but he was better off here, among friends, than he would be under the dubious protection of King Charles.

Coligny's face betrayed similar misgivings, but he could not say so for fear of offending the king.

Ambroise Paré saved Coligny's face by saying: 'He must stay here, your majesty. Any movement could reopen the wounds, and he cannot afford to lose any more blood.'

The king accepted the doctor's ruling with a nod, then said: 'In that case, I will send you the lord of Cosseins with a company of fifty pikemen and arquebusiers to reinforce your own small bodyguard.'

Ned frowned. Cosseins was the king's man. Guards who owed loyalty to someone else were of highly doubtful value. Was Charles simply being naively generous, desperate to make a gesture of reconciliation? He was young and innocent enough not to realize that his offer was unwelcome.

However, one conciliatory gesture by the king had already been rejected, and etiquette forced Coligny to say: 'That is most kind of your majesty.'

Charles stood up to go. 'I shall revenge this affront,' he said forcefully.

Ned looked around the assembled Huguenot leaders and saw, by stance and by facial expressions, that many of them were inclined to believe in the king's sincerity, and at least give him a chance to prevent bloodshed.

The king swept out of the room. As Queen Caterina followed him, she caught Ned's eye. He gave the tiniest of nods, to thank her for keeping the peace by bringing the king here, and for an instant the corners of her mouth twitched in an almost imperceptible smile of acknowledgement.

*

NED SPENT MUCH of Saturday encoding a long letter from Walsingham to Queen Elizabeth, detailing the events of a worrying week and Queen Caterina's struggle to keep the peace. He finished late on Saturday afternoon, then left the embassy and headed for the rue de la Serpente.

It was a warm evening, and crowds of young men were drinking outside the taverns, jeering at passing beggars, whistling at girls, no different from boisterous lads in Kingsbridge with money in their pockets and energy to spare. There would be fights later: there always were on Saturday night. But Ned saw no conspicuous Huguenots. They were sensibly staying off the streets, it seemed, probably having supper at home behind locked doors. With luck, a riot would be avoided tonight. And tomorrow was Sunday.

Ned sat in the back of the shop with Sylvie and Isabelle. They told him that Pierre Aumande had visited them. 'We thought he had forgotten about us,' Isabelle said anxiously. 'We don't know how he found us.'

'I do,' Ned said, feeling guilty. 'One of his men has been following me. I must have led him here when I came for dinner last week. I'm so sorry. I didn't know I was being watched, but I found out after I left here.'

Sylvie said: 'How do you know the man following you worked for Pierre?'

'I knocked him down and put my knife to his neck and said I'd cut his throat unless he told me.'

'Oh.'

The two women were silent for a minute, and Ned realized that until now they had not pictured him involved in violent action. Eventually, he broke the silence by saying: 'What do you think Pierre will do?'

'I don't know,' Sylvie said. 'I'll have to be extra careful for a while.'

Ned described the scene when the king visited the wounded Coligny. Sylvie immediately focussed on the notion of a list of Protestants with their assigned killers. 'If the duke of Guise has such a list, it must have been made by Pierre,' she said.

'I don't know, but it seems likely,' said Ned. 'He's obviously the duke's chief spy.'

'In that case,' said Sylvie, 'I know where the list is.'

Ned sat up. 'Do you?' he said. 'Where?'

'He has a notebook he keeps at his house. He thinks it's safer there than at the Guise palace.'

'Have you seen it?'

Sylvie nodded. 'Many times. It's how I know which Protestants are in danger.'

Ned was intrigued. So that was where she got her information.

Sylvie added: 'But it has never included a list of murderers.'

'Could I see it?'

'Perhaps.'

'Now?'

'I can't be sure, but Saturday evening is usually a good time. Let's try.' Sylvie stood up.

Isabelle protested: 'It's not safe on the streets. The city is full of angry men, and they're all drinking. Stay home.'

'Mother, our friends may be murdered. We have to warn them.'

'Then, for God's sake, be careful.'

It was not yet dark when Ned and Sylvie left the shop and crossed the Île de la Cité. The dark mass of the cathedral brooded over the troubled city in the evening light. Reaching the right bank, Sylvie led Ned through the close-packed houses of Les Halles to a tavern next to the church of St Étienne.

She ordered a tankard of ale to be sent to the back door of a house in the next street – a signal, Ned gathered. The place was busy, and there was nowhere to sit, so they stood in a corner. Ned was full of nervous anticipation. Was he really about to get a look at Pierre Aumande's secret list?

A few minutes later they were joined by a plain, thin woman in her twenties. Sylvie introduced her as Nath, Pierre's housemaid. 'She belongs to our congregation,' she said.

Ned understood. Sylvie had subverted Pierre's servant and thereby gained access to his papers. Clever Sylvie.

'This is Ned,' Sylvie said to Nath. 'We can trust him.'

Nath grinned. 'Are you going to marry him?' she blurted.

Ned smothered a smile.

Sylvie looked mortified, but passed it off with a joke. 'Not tonight,' she said. She hastily changed the subject. 'What's happening at home?'

'Pierre's in a bad mood – something went wrong yesterday.'

Ned said: 'Coligny didn't die, that's what went wrong for Pierre.'

'Anyway, he's gone to the Guise palace this evening.'

Sylvie said: 'Is Odette at home?

'She's gone to see her mother and taken Alain with her.'

Sylvie explained to Ned: 'Odette is Pierre's wife, and Alain is his stepson.' Ned was intrigued by this glimpse into the private life of such a famous villain. 'I didn't know about the stepson.'

'It's a long story. I'll tell you another day.' Sylvie turned back to Nath. 'Ned needs to look at the notebook.'

Nath stood up. 'Come on, then. This is the perfect time.'

They walked around the block. It was a poor neighbourhood, and Pierre's home was a small house in a row. Ned was surprised by its modesty: Pierre was conspicuously affluent, with costly clothing and jewellery. But noblemen such as the duke of Guise sometimes liked to keep their advisors in humble quarters, to discourage them from getting above their station. And a place such as this might be useful for clandestine meetings.

Nath discreetly took them in through the back door. There were just two rooms on the ground floor, the living room and the kitchen. Ned could hardly believe that he was inside the private home of the dreaded Pierre Aumande. He felt like Jonah in the belly of the whale.

On the floor of the living room was a document chest. Nath picked up a sewing bag and took from it a pin that had been carefully bent into a hook shape. With the pin she unlocked the chest.

Amazing, Ned thought. Just like that. So easy.

Nath opened the lid of the chest.

It was empty.

'Oh!' she said. 'The book has gone!'

There was a moment of stunned silence.

Then Sylvie spoke. 'Pierre has taken it with him to the Guise palace,' she said thoughtfully. 'But why?'

Ned said: 'Because he's going to use it, presumably. Which means he's about to implement his plan of murdering every Protestant nobleman in Paris – probably tonight.'

Sylvie's face showed fear. 'God help us,' she said.

'You have to warn people.'

'They must get out of Paris – if they can.'

'If they can't, tell them to come to the English embassy.'

'There must be hundreds, including all the visitors who came for the wedding. You can't get them all into the embassy.'

'No. But in any event you can't warn hundreds of people; it would take you days.'

'What can we do?'

'We must do what's possible, and save as many as we can.'

20

By Saturday evening, Duke Henri was in a tantrum, possessed by the rage of a young man who finds that the world does not work in the way he confidently expected. 'Get out of my sight!' he yelled at Pierre. 'You're dismissed. I never want to see you again.'

For the first time ever, Pierre was as scared of Henri as he had been of Henri's father, Duke Scarface. He had a pain in his guts like a wound. 'I understand your anger,' he said desperately. He knew his career would be over unless he could somehow talk his way out of this.

'You predicted riots,' Henri roared. 'And they didn't happen.'

Pierre spread his arms in a helpless gesture. 'The queen mother kept the peace.'

They were at the Guise palace in the Vieille rue du Temple, in the luxurious room where Pierre had first met Duke Scarface and Cardinal Charles. Pierre felt as humiliated today as he had in this room fourteen years ago, when he was a mere student accused of dishonestly using the Guise name. He was on the brink of losing everything he had gained since then. He pictured the looks of pleasure and scorn on the faces of his enemies, and he fought back tears.

He wished Cardinal Charles were here now. The family needed his ruthless political cunning. But Charles was in Rome on Church business. Pierre was on his own.

'You tried to assassinate Coligny and failed!' Henri raved. 'You're incompetent.'

Pierre squirmed. 'I told Biron to give Louviers a musket, but he said it would be too big.'

'You said the Huguenots would rise up anyway, even though Coligny was only wounded.'

'The king's visit to Coligny's sickbed calmed them.'

'Nothing you do works! Soon all the visiting Huguenot noblemen will leave Paris and go home in triumph, and the opportunity will have been lost because I listened to you. Which I will never do again.'

Pierre scrambled to think clearly under the onslaught of Henri's fury. He knew what had to be done, but in this mood would Henri listen? 'I have been asking myself what your Uncle Charles would advise,' he said.

Henri was struck by that notion. His wrathful expression moderated a little, and he looked interested. 'Well, what would he say?'

'I think he might suggest that we simply act as if the Protestant rebellion has, in fact, started.'

Henri was not quick on the uptake. 'What do you mean?'

'Let's ring the bell of Saint-Germain l'Auxerrois.' Pierre held up the black leather-bound notebook in which he had written the names of the paired assassins and victims. 'The loyalist noblemen will believe that the Huguenots are in revolt, and they will slaughter the leaders to save the life of the king.'

Henri was taken aback by the audacity of this plan, but he did not immediately reject it, and Pierre's hopes rose. Henri said: 'The Huguenots will retaliate.'

'Arm the militia.'

'That can only be done by the Provost of Merchants.' The title meant the same as mayor. 'And he won't do it on my say-so.'

'Leave him to me.' Pierre had only a vague notion of how he would manage this, but he was on a roll now, carrying Henri with him, and he could not allow himself to stumble over details.

Henri said: 'Can we be sure the militia will defeat the Huguenots? There are thousands more staying in the suburbs. What if they all ride into town to defend their brethren? It could be a close-fought battle.'

'We'll close the city gates.' Paris was surrounded by a wall and, for most of its circumference, a canal. Each gate in the wall led to a bridge over the water. With the gates locked it was difficult to enter or leave the city.

'Again, only the Provost can do that.'

'Again, leave him to me.' At this point Pierre was ready to promise anything to win back Henri's favour. 'All you need to do is have your men ready to ride to Coligny's house and kill him as soon as I tell you that all is ready.'

'Coligny is guarded by the lord of Cosseins and fifty men of the king's guard, as well as his own people.'

'Cosseins is the king's man.'

'Will the king call him off?'

Pierre said the first thing that came into his head. 'Cosseins will *think* the king has called him off.'

Henri looked hard at Pierre for a long moment. 'You feel sure that you can achieve all this?'

'Yes,' Pierre lied. He just had to take the chance. 'But there is no risk to you,' he said earnestly. 'If I should fail, you will have mustered your men to no purpose, but nothing worse.'

That convinced the young duke. 'How long do you need?'

Pierre stood up. 'I'll be back before midnight,' he said.

That was one more promise he was not confident of keeping.

He left the room, taking his black notebook with him.

Georges Biron was waiting outside. 'Saddle two horses,' Pierre said. 'We've got a lot to do.'

They could not leave by the main gate, because there was a crowd of shouting Huguenots outside. The mob believed Henri was responsible for the assassination attempt, as did just about everyone, and they were baying for his blood – though not, as yet, doing anything bad enough to justify Henri's men opening fire. Fortunately, the house was huge, occupying an entire city block, and there were alternative ways in and out. Pierre and Biron left by a side gate.

They headed for the place de Grève, the central square where the provost lived. The narrow, winding streets of Paris were as convoluted as the design firming up in Pierre's mind. He had long plotted this moment, but it had come about in unexpected ways, and he had to improvise. He breathed deeply, calming himself. This was the riskiest gamble of his life. Too many things could go wrong. If just one part of his scheme miscarried, all was lost. He would not be able to talk himself out of another disaster. His life of wealth and power as advisor to the Guise family would come to a shameful end.

He tried not to think about it.

The provost was a wealthy printer-bookseller called Jean Le Charron. Pierre interrupted him at supper with his family and told him the king wanted to see him.

This was not true, of course. Would Le Charron believe it?

Le Charron had been provost for only a week, as it happened, and he was awestruck to be visited by the famous Pierre Aumande de Guise. He was thrilled to be summoned to the king, too much so to question the authenticity of the message, and he immediately agreed to go. The first hurdle had been surmounted.

Le Charron saddled his horse and the three of them rode through the twilight to the Louvre palace.

Biron remained in the square courtyard while Pierre took Le Charron inside. Pierre's status was high enough for him to get into the wardrobe, the waiting room next to the audience chamber, but no farther.

This was another dangerous moment. King Charles had not asked to see either Pierre or Le Charron. Pierre was not sufficiently high-born – by a long way – to have automatic access to the king.

Leaving Le Charron to one side of the room, he spoke to the doorkeeper in a confident, unhurried voice that suggested there was no question of disobedience. 'Be so good as to tell his majesty that I bring a message from Henri, duke of Guise.'

King Charles had not spoken to Henri, or indeed seen him, since the failed assassination. Pierre was betting that Charles would be curious to know what Henri might have to say for himself.

There was a long wait, then Pierre was called inside.

He told Le Charron to stay in the wardrobe until summoned, then he entered the audience chamber.

King Charles and Queen Caterina were at a table, finishing supper. Pierre was sorry Caterina was there. He could have fooled Charles easily, but the mother was smarter and more suspicious.

Pierre began: 'My noble master, the duke of Guise, humbly begs your majesty's pardon for not coming to court himself.'

Charles nodded acknowledgement of the apology but Caterina, sitting opposite him, was not so easily satisfied. 'What is his reason?' she asked sharply. 'Could it be a guilty conscience?'

Pierre was expecting this question and had his answer ready. 'The duke fears for his life, your majesty. There is a crowd of armed Huguenots outside his gates day and night. He cannot leave his house without risking death. The Huguenots are plotting their revenge. There are thousands of them in the city and suburbs, armed and bloodthirsty—'

'You're wrong,' the queen mother interrupted. 'His majesty the king has calmed their fears. He has ordered an inquiry into the shooting, and he has promised retribution. He has visited Coligny on his sickbed. There may be a few hotheads in the rue Vieille du Temple, but their leaders are satisfied.'

'That is exactly what I told Duke Henri,' Pierre said. 'But he believes the Huguenots are on the point of rising up, and fears that his only hope may be to mount a pre-emptive attack, and destroy their ability to threaten him.'

The king said: 'Tell him that I, King Charles IX, guarantee his safety.'

'Thank you, your majesty. I will certainly give him that powerful reassurance.' In fact, the assurance was more or less worthless. A strong king, feared by his barons, might have been able to protect Coligny, but Charles was physically and psychologically weak. Caterina would understand that, even if Charles did not, so Pierre directed his next sentence to her. 'But Duke Henri asks if he may suggest something further?' He held his breath. He was being bold: the king might hear advice from noblemen, but not normally in a message carried by an underling.

There was a silence. Pierre feared he was about to be thrown out for insolence.

Caterina looked at him through narrowed eyes. She knew

that this would be the real reason for Pierre's visit. But she did not reprimand him. In itself that was a measure of how tenuous was her grip on control and how close the city was to chaos.

At last the king said: 'What do you want?'

'Some simple security precautions that would guard against violence by either side.'

Caterina looked suspicious. 'Such as?'

'Lock the city gates, so that no one can come in from outside the walls – neither the Huguenots in the suburbs, nor Catholic reinforcements.' Pierre paused. The Catholic reinforcements were imaginary. It was the Huguenots he wanted to keep out. But would Caterina see that?

King Charles said: 'Actually, that's quite a good idea.'

Caterina said nothing.

Pierre went on as if he had received consent. 'Then shackle the boats on the waterfront, and pull the iron chains across the river that prevent hostile ships approaching the city. That way troublemakers can't get into Paris by water.' And Huguenots would not be able to get out.

'Also a sensible safeguard,' said the king.

Pierre felt he was winning, and ploughed on. 'Order the provost to arm the militia and place guards at every major crossroads in the city, with orders to turn back any large group of armed men, regardless of what religion they claim.'

Caterina saw immediately that this was not a neutral move. 'The militia are all Catholics, of course,' she said.

'Of course,' Pierre conceded. 'But they constitute our only means of keeping order.' He said no more. He preferred not to enter into a discussion about even-handedness, for in truth nothing about his plan was neutral. But keeping order was Caterina's main concern.

Charles said to his mother: 'I see no harm in such plainly defensive measures.'

'Perhaps not,' Caterina replied. She mistrusted the entire Guise family, but what Pierre suggested made sense.

'The duke has one more suggestion,' said Pierre. Duke Henri had not suggested any of this, but etiquette demanded that Pierre pretend the ideas came from his aristocratic master. 'Deploy the city artillery. If we line up the guns in the place de Grève, they will be ready to defend the city hall – or to be positioned elsewhere, if necessary.' Or to mow down a Protestant crowd, he thought.

The king nodded. 'We should do all these things. The duke of Guise is a sound military planner. Please give him my thanks.'

Pierre bowed.

Caterina said to Charles: 'You'll have to summon the provost.' No doubt she thought the delay would give her time to mull over Pierre's suggestions and look for snags.

But Pierre was not going to allow her that chance. He said: 'Your majesty, I took the liberty of bringing the provost with me, and, in fact, he is outside the door, waiting for your orders.'

'Well done,' said Charles. 'Have him come in.'

Le Charron came in bowing deeply, excited and intimidated to be in the royal presence.

Pierre took it upon himself to speak for the king, and instructed Le Charron to carry out all the measures he had proposed. During this recital Pierre feared that Charles or – more likely – Caterina might have second thoughts, but they only nodded assent. Caterina looked as if she could not quite believe that Duke Henri wanted only to protect himself and prevent rioting; but clearly she could not figure out what ulterior motive Pierre might have, and she did not dissent.

Le Charron thanked the king volubly for the honour of his instructions and vowed to carry them out meticulously, and then they were dismissed. Backing out, bowing, Pierre could hardly believe that he had got away with it, and every second he expected that Caterina would call him back. Then he was outside and the door was closed and he was another step closer to victory.

With Le Charron he walked through the wardrobe and the guardroom, then down the stairs.

Darkness had fallen by the time they stepped out into the square courtyard where Biron waited with their horses.

Before parting company with Le Charron, Pierre had one

more deception to perpetrate. 'Something the king forgot to mention,' he said.

That phrase on its own would have aroused instant suspicion in an experienced courtier, but Le Charron was overwhelmed by Pierre's apparent closeness to the monarch, and he was desperately eager to please. 'Anything, of course,' he said.

'If the king's life is in danger, the bell of Saint-Germain l'Auxerrois will ring continuously, and other churches with trustworthy Catholic priests will follow suit, all over Paris. That will be the alarm signal to you that the Huguenots have risen up against the king, and you must attack them.'

'Could that really happen?' Le Charron said, rapt.

'It could happen tonight, so be prepared.'

It did not occur to Le Charron to doubt Pierre. He accepted what he was told as fact. 'I will be ready,' he vowed.

Pierre took the book with the black cover from his saddlebag. He ripped out the leaves bearing the names of noble assassins and victims. The rest of the pages were devoted to ordinary Paris Huguenots. He handed the book to Le Charron. 'Here is a list of every known Protestant in Paris, with addresses,' he said.

Le Charron was amazed. 'I had no idea that such a document existed!'

'I have been preparing it for many years,' Pierre said, not without a touch of pride. 'Tonight it meets its destiny.'

Le Charron took the book reverently. 'Thank you.'

Pierre said solemnly: 'If you hear the bells, it is your duty to kill everyone named in that book.'

Le Charron swallowed. Until now he had not appreciated that he might be involved in a massacre. But Pierre had led him to this point so carefully, by such gradual and reasonable stages, that he nodded agreement. He even added a suggestion of his own. 'In case it comes to fighting, I will order the militia to identify themselves, perhaps with a white armband, so that they know each other.'

'Very good idea,' said Pierre. 'I'll tell his majesty that you came up with that.'

Le Charron was thrilled. 'That would be a great honour.'

'You'd better get going. You have a lot to do.'

'Yes.' Charron mounted his horse, still clutching the black book. Before leaving he suffered a troubled moment. 'Let us hope that none of these precautions proves necessary.'

'Amen,' said Pierre insincerely.

Le Charron trotted away.

Biron mounted his horse.

Pierre paused a minute, looking back at the Italian-style palace he had just left. He could hardly believe he had fooled its royal occupants. But when rulers were this close to panic, they were desperate for action, and eager to agree to any plan that was halfway promising.

Anyway, it was not over yet. All his efforts in the past few days had failed, and there was still time for tonight's even more complicated scheme to go awry.

He lifted himself into the saddle. 'Rue de Béthisy,' he said to Biron. 'Let's go.'

Coligny's lodging was close. The king's guards were outside the gate. Some were standing in line with arquebuses and lances; others, presumably resting, sat on the ground nearby, their weapons to hand. They made a formidable barrier.

Pierre reined in and said to a guard: 'A message from his majesty the king for the lord of Cosseins.'

'I will give him the message,' said the guard.

'No, you won't. Go and fetch him.'

'He's sleeping.'

'Do you want me to go back to the Louvre and say that your master would not get out of his bed to receive a message from the king?'

'No, sir, of course not, pardon me.' The man went off and returned a minute later with Cosseins, who had evidently been sleeping in his clothes.

'There has been a change of plan,' Pierre said to Cosseins. 'The Huguenots have conspired to seize the king's person and take control of the Government. The plot has been foiled by loyal men, but the king wants Coligny arrested.'

Cosseins was not as naive as Le Charron. He looked

sceptical, perhaps thinking that the duke of Guise's advisor was an unlikely choice as the king's messenger. 'Is there some confirmation of this?' he said worriedly.

'You don't have to arrest him yourself. The king will send someone.'

Cosseins shrugged. That did not require him to commit himself to anything. 'Very well,' he said.

'Just be ready,' said Pierre, and he rode off.

He had done everything he could. With a whole raft of plausible small deceptions, he had smoothed the way for Armageddon. Now all he could do was hope that the people he was trying to manipulate, from the king all the way down to the priest of Saint-Germain l'Auxerrois, would behave in accordance with his calculations.

The crowd in the Vieille rue du Temple had diminished with nightfall, but there were still enough angry Huguenots to cause Pierre and Biron to enter the palace by the side door.

The first question was whether Duke Henri would be prepared. The young duke was usually eager for action, but he had lost faith in Pierre, and it was possible that he had changed his mind and decided not to muster his men.

Pierre was relieved and thrilled to see fifty armed men assembled in the inner courtyard, grooms holding their saddled horses. He noticed Rasteau, the man with no nose, and his perennial companion Brocard. Blazing torches glinted off breastplates and helmets. This was a disciplined group of gentry and men-at-arms, and they remained quiet while they waited, in a scene of hushed menace.

Pierre pushed through the crowd to the centre, where Duke Henri stood. As soon as he saw Pierre he said: 'Well?'

'All is ready,' Pierre said. 'The king agreed to everything we wanted. The provost is arming the militia and deploying the city artillery as we speak.' I hope, he thought.

'And Cosseins?'

'I told him that the king is sending someone to arrest Coligny. If he doesn't believe me, you'll have to fight your way in.'

'So be it.' Henri turned to his men and raised his voice. 'We leave by the front gate,' he said. 'And death to anyone who gets in our way.'

They mounted up. A groom handed Pierre a sword belt with a sheathed weapon. He buckled on the belt and swung himself up into the saddle. He would try not to get personally involved in the fighting, if he could, but it was as well to be equipped.

He looked through the arch to the outer gateway and saw two servants swinging the great iron gates back. The mob outside was momentarily nonplussed. They had no plan for this situation: they were not expecting open doors. Then Duke Henri kicked his horse and the squadron pounded out with a sudden earthquake-rumble of hooves. The mob scattered in terror, but not all could get away. Amid screams, the big horses charged the crowd, the riders swinging their swords, and dozens fell wounded or dead.

The killing had begun.

They thundered through the streets at dangerous speed. Those few people out this late scurried out of the way for fear of their lives. Pierre was thrilled and apprehensive. This was the moment he had been working towards ever since King Charles had signed the disgraceful Peace of St Germain. Tonight's action would show everyone that France would never tolerate heresy – and that the Guise family could not be ignored. Pierre was scared, but full of desperate eagerness.

He worried about Cosseins. Pierre wished he had been able to win a pledge of cooperation from him, but the man was no fool. If he resisted now, there would be a fierce skirmish – which might give Coligny time to escape. The whole scheme could founder on that detail.

The Guise palace was on the east side of town, and Coligny's lodging was on the western edge, but the distance was small, and at that time of night there were few obstructions in the streets. In a few minutes the horsemen were in the rue de Béthisy.

Cosseins's men must have heard the hoofbeats at a distance, and now, as Pierre picked out Coligny's residence in the starlight, the guards presented a more orderly and formidable picture than they had half an hour ago, lining up in rows in front of the gate, lances and guns at the ready.

Duke Henri reined in and shouted: 'I am here to arrest Gaspard de Coligny. Open the gate in the name of the king!'

Cosseins stepped forward, his face lit fiendishly by the torches of the Guise men. 'I've had no such instructions,' he said.

Henri said: 'Cosseins, you are a good Catholic and a loyal servant of his majesty King Charles, but I will not take no for an answer. I have my orders from the king, and I shall carry them out, even if I have to kill you first.'

Cosseins hesitated. He was in a difficult position, as Pierre had calculated. Cosseins had been assigned to protect Coligny, yet it was perfectly plausible that the king had changed his mind and ordered the arrest. And if Cosseins now resisted Henri, and the two groups of armed men came to blows, much blood would be shed – probably including Cosseins's own.

As Pierre had hoped, Cosseins decided to save his own life now, and take any consequences later. 'Open up!' he shouted.

The gates came open, and the Guise men charged jubilantly into the courtyard.

The main entrance to the house had a large double door of heavy timber with iron reinforcements, and as Pierre rode into the courtyard he saw it slam shut. Coligny's personal bodyguards would be on the other side of it, he presumed. The Guise men began to attack the door with swords, and one shot out the lock. Pierre thought frustratedly how foolish they had been not to bring a couple of sledgehammers. Once again he fretted that the delay might allow Coligny to escape. No one had thought to check for a back entrance.

But the door yielded to force and burst open. There was fierce fighting up the stairs as half a dozen guards tried to keep the Guises back, but Coligny's men were outnumbered and in minutes they all lay dead or dying.

Pierre leaped off his horse and ran up the stairs. The men-at-arms were throwing doors open. 'In here!' one of them yelled, and Pierre followed the voice into a grand bedroom.

Coligny was kneeling at the foot of the bed, wearing a

nightgown, his silver hair covered with a cap, his wounded arm in a sling. He was praying aloud.

The men-at-arms hesitated to murder a man at prayer.

But they had all done worse things. Pierre yelled: 'What are you scared of? Kill him, damn you!'

A Guise man called Besme thrust his sword into Coligny's chest. When he pulled it out, bright blood pumped from the wound. Coligny fell forward.

Pierre rushed to the window and threw it open. He saw Henri down in the forecourt, still on horseback. 'Duke Henri!' he shouted. 'I am proud to tell you that Coligny is dead!'

Henri shouted back: 'Show me the body!'

Pierre turned into the room. 'Besme,' he said, 'bring the body here.'

The man put his hands under Coligny's arms and dragged the corpse across the floor.

Pierre said: 'Lift it up to the window.'

Besme complied.

Henri shouted: 'I can't see his face!'

Impatiently, Pierre grabbed the body around the hips and heaved. The corpse tumbled over the windowsill, fell through the air, and hit the cobblestones with a smack, face down.

Henri dismounted. In a gesture stinking with contempt, he turned the body over with his foot.

'This is he,' he said. 'The man who killed my father.'

The men around him cheered.

'It's done,' said Henri. 'Ring the bell of St-Germain l'Auxerrois.'

*

SYLVIE WISHED she had a horse.

Dashing from house to house, speaking to members of the congregation that met in the loft over the stable, she felt frustrated almost to the point of hysteria. Each time she had to find the right house, explain the situation to the family, persuade them that she was not imagining things, then hurry to the next nearest Protestant household. She had a logical plan: she was moving north along the rue St Martin, the main artery in the middle of the town, turning down side streets for short distances. Even so, she was managing only three or four calls per hour. If she had had a horse it would have been twice as quick.

She also would have been less vulnerable. It was hard for a drunk man to pull a strong young woman off a horse. But on foot and alone in the dark on the Paris streets she feared that anything could happen and no one would see.

As she approached the home of the marquess of Lagny, not far from her warehouse near the city wall, she heard distant bells. She frowned. What did that mean? Bells at an unexpected moment usually signified some crisis. The sound grew, and she realized that one church after another was joining the chorus. A city-wide emergency could mean only one thing: the apprehension that she and Ned had shared, when they found that Pierre's book was missing, was coming true.

A few minutes later she came to the marquess's house and banged on the door. He opened it himself: he must have been up, and his servants asleep. Sylvie realized this was the first time she had seen him without his jewelled cap. His head was bald with a monk's fringe.

He said: 'Why are they ringing the bells?'

'Because they're going to kill us all,' she said, and she stepped inside.

He led her into the parlour. He was a widower, and his children were grown and living elsewhere, so he was probably alone in the house apart from the servants. She saw that he had been sitting up reading by the light of a wrought-iron candle tree. She recognized the book as one she had sold him. There was a flask of wine beside his chair and he offered her some. She realized she was hungry and thirsty: she had been on the go for hours. She drank a glass quickly, but refused a second.

She explained that she had guessed that the ultra-Catholics were about to launch an attack, and she had been racing around the town warning Protestants, but now she feared it had begun, and it could be too late for warnings. 'I must go home,' she said.

'Are you sure? You might be safer to stay here.'

'I have to make sure my mother is all right.'

He walked her to the door. As he turned the handle, someone banged on it from the outside. 'Don't open it!' Sylvie said, but she was too late.

Looking over Lagny's shoulder she saw a nobleman standing on the doorstep with several others behind him. Lagny recognized the man. 'Viscount Villeneuve!' he said in surprise.

Villeneuve wore an expensive red coat, but Sylvie was scared to see that he held his sword in his hand.

Lagny remained calm. 'What brings you to my house at this time of night, Viscount?'

'The work of Christ,' said Villeneuve, and with a swift motion, he thrust his sword into Lagny's belly.

Sylvie screamed.

Lagny screamed too, in agony, and fell to his knees.

As Villeneuve struggled to pull his sword out of Lagny's guts, Sylvie ran along the hallway towards the back of the house. She threw open a door, dashed through, and found herself in a large kitchen.

In Paris, as everywhere, servants did not have the costly luxury of beds, but slept on the kitchen floor, and here a dozen staff were waking up and asking in scared voices what was going on.

Sylvie ran across the room, dodging the waking men and women, and reached the far door. It was locked, and there was no sign of a key.

She spotted an open window – letting air into a crowded room on an August night – and, without further thought, she scrambled through it.

She found herself in a yard with a henhouse and a pigeon loft. At the far side was a high stone wall with a gate. She tried to open the gate and found it locked. She could have wept with frustration and terror.

From the kitchen behind her she heard screams: Villeneuve and his men must have entered the kitchen. She guessed that they would assume all the servants were Protestants like their master – it was the usual way – and they would probably murder them all before coming after her.

She scrambled up onto the roof of the henhouse, causing a cacophony of squawking inside. Between the roof and the yard wall was a gap of only about a yard. Sylvie jumped it. Landing on the narrow top of the wall she lost her balance and fell to her knees painfully, but regained her balance. She dropped down the far side of the wall to a smelly lane.

She ran the length of the lane. It emerged into the rue du Mur. She headed for her warehouse, running as fast as she could. She reached it without seeing anyone. She unlocked the door, slipped inside, closed the door behind her, and locked it.

She was safe. She leaned on the door with her cheek against the wood. She had escaped, she thought with a strange sense of elation. A thought came into her mind that surprised her: I *don't want to die now that I've met Ned Willard.*

*

WALSINGHAM IMMEDIATELY saw the significance of the missing notebook, and assigned Ned and several others to call at the homes of prominent English Protestants in Paris, advising them to take refuge in the embassy. There were not enough horses for all and Ned went on foot. He wore high riding boots and a leather jerkin, despite the warmth of the night, and he was armed with a sword and a dagger with a two-foot-long sharpened blade.

He had completed his task, and was leaving the last of the houses assigned to him, when the bells began to ring.

He was worried about Sylvie. Pierre's plan required the murders only of aristocratic Protestants, but once men started to kill it was hard to stop them. Two weeks ago Sylvie might have been safe, for her life as a Protestant bookseller had been a well-kept secret, but last week Ned had led Pierre to her home, and now she was probably on Pierre's list. Ned wanted to bring her and her mother to the embassy for protection.

He made his way to the rue de la Serpente and banged on the door of the shop.

The upstairs window opened and a figure leaned out. 'Who is it?' The voice belonged to Isabelle.

'Ned Willard.'

'Wait, I'll come down.'

The window was shut and, a few moments later, the front door was opened. 'Come inside,' said Isabelle.

Ned stepped in and she closed the door. A single candle lit the shelves with their ledgers and ink bottles. Ned said: 'Where's Sylvie?'

'Still out warning people.'

'It's too late for warnings now.'

'She may have taken refuge.'

Ned was disappointed and worried. 'Where do you think she might be?'

'She was going to work her way north along the rue St Martin and end up at the home of the marquess of Lagny. She might be there. Or . . .' Isabelle hesitated.

Ned said impatiently: 'Where else? Her life is in danger!'

'There's a secret place. You must swear never to reveal it.'

'I swear.'

'In the rue du Mur, two hundred yards from the corner of the rue St Denis, there is an old brick stable with one door and no windows.'

'Good enough.' He hesitated. 'Will you be all right?'

She opened a drawer in the table and showed him two single-shot pocket pistols with wheel-lock firing mechanisms, plus half a dozen balls and a box of gunpowder. 'I keep these for when a drunk comes out of the tavern across the street and asks himself how hard it can be to rob a shop run by two women.'

'Have you ever shot anyone?'

'No. Waving the guns was always enough.'

He put his hand on the door handle. 'Bar the door behind me.'

'Of course.'

'Make sure all your window shutters are tightly closed and latched on the inside.'

'Yes.'

'Put out your candle. Don't open the door to anyone. If someone knocks, don't speak. Let them think the building is empty.'

'All right.'

'Sylvie and I will come back here for you then all three of us will go together to the English embassy.'

Ned opened the door.

Isabelle grabbed his arm. 'Take care of her,' she said, and there was a catch in her voice. 'Whatever happens, look after my little girl.'

'That's what I mean to do,' Ned said, and he hurried away.

The bells were still ringing. There were not many people on the streets of the left bank. However, as Ned crossed the Notre Dame bridge with its expensive shops, he was shocked to see two dead bodies in the street. A man and a woman in nightwear had been stabbed to death. Ned was sickened by the domesticity of the sight: husband and wife lying side by side, as if in bed, except that their nightgowns were soaked with blood.

The door of a nearby jewellery store stood open, and Ned saw two men emerging with sacks, presumably full of looted valuables. The men glared aggressively at him and he hurried past. He did not want to be delayed by an altercation with them, and they clearly felt the same, for they did not follow him.

On the right bank he saw a group of men hammering at a door. They had strips of white cloth tied to their arms in what Ned guessed was a form of identification. Most were armed with daggers and clubs, but one, better dressed than the others, had a sword. This one shouted in an educated voice: 'Open up, blaspheming Protestants!'

The men were Catholics, then, and they formed a squad led by an officer. Ned figured that they must be part of the town militia. Jerónima's information had suggested a mass slaughter of Protestant noblemen, but the house he was passing was an ordinary residence, that of a craftsman or small merchant. As he had feared, the killing was spreading beyond the original aristocratic targets. The result could be truly horrifying.

He felt cowardly sneaking past the scene, hoping the men with the white armbands would not see him. But no other action made sense. On his own he could not save the occupants of the house from six attackers. If he confronted them, they would kill him, then return their attention to the house. And he had to find Sylvie.

Ned followed the broad rue St Martin northwards, keeping his eyes peeled in the starlight, looking down the side streets, hoping to see a small woman with an upright stance and a brisk step coming towards him with a relieved smile. Glancing down an alley he saw another group of men with white armbands, three of them this time, rough-looking, none carrying swords. He was about to hurry past when something about the scene arrested him.

The men had their backs to him, looking at something on the ground, and Ned spotted what was horribly like the graceful shape of a young woman's leg.

He stopped and stared. It was dark, but one of the men held a lamp. As Ned peered more closely, he saw that a girl lay on the ground, and a fourth man was kneeling between her thighs. She was moaning, and after a moment Ned made out that she was saying: 'No, no, no . . .'

He felt a powerful impulse to run away, but he could not. It looked as if the rape had not actually begun. If he intervened in the next few seconds he could prevent it.

Or he could get killed.

The men were intent on the woman, and had not seen him, but at any moment one of them might glance backwards. There was no time to think.

Ned set down his lantern and drew his sword.

He crept up behind the group. Before fear could stop him, he stuck the point of his sword in the nearest man's thigh.

The man roared with agony.

Ned pulled his sword out. The next man was turning around to see what was happening, and Ned slashed at him. It was a lucky stroke, and the tip of the blade gashed the man's face from the chin up to the left eye. He yelled in pain and put both hands to his face. Blood spurted through his fingers.

The third spectator looked at his two wounded comrades, panicked, and ran away down the alley.

After a moment, the two men Ned had stabbed did the same.

The man on his knees jumped up and followed, holding up his breeches with both hands.

Ned sheathed his bloody sword, then knelt beside the girl and pulled her dress down over her legs, covering her nakedness.

Only then did he look at her face and realize she was Aphrodite Beaulieu.

She was not even a Protestant. Ned wondered what she had been doing on the street at night. Her parents would not have allowed her to wander around alone even in the daytime. Ned thought she might have had an assignation, and remembered how happily she had smiled at Bernard Housse in the Louvre. And she would probably have got away with it, had this not been the night that someone decided to let slip the dogs of war.

She looked at him and said: 'Ned Willard? Thank God! But how . . . ?'

He took her hand and pulled her to her feet. 'No time for explanations,' he said. The Beaulieu mansion was not far away in the rue St Denis. 'Let me take you home.' He picked up his lantern and took her arm.

She seemed too shocked to speak or even cry.

Ned looked about him warily as they walked. No one was safe.

They were almost at her house when four men with white armbands came out of a side street and accosted them. One said: 'Are you running away, Protestants?'

Ned's heart went cold. He thought of drawing his sword, but they had swords too, and there were four of them. He had taken the last lot by surprise, and scared them, but these four stood facing him with their hands on their hilts, ready for action. He did not stand a chance.

He would have to talk his way out of this. They would automatically suspect any foreigner, of course. His accent was good enough to fool people – Parisians thought he came from

Calais – but sometimes he made childish mistakes of grammar, and he prayed that he would not give himself away now by saying *le maison* instead of *la maison*.

He summoned up a sneer. 'This is Mademoiselle Beaulieu, you damn fool,' he said. 'She's a good Catholic, and the count of Beaulieu's mansion is right there. You lay a finger on her and I'll rouse the entire household.' It was not an empty threat: he was within shouting distance. But Aphrodite gripped his arm harder, and he guessed she did not want her parents to know that she had been out.

The leader of the group looked sly. 'If she's a Catholic noblewoman, what's she doing on the street at this time of night?'

'We'll get her father to answer that question, shall we?' Ned maintained his pose of confident arrogance, but it was a struggle. 'And then he can ask you what the devil you think you're doing pestering his daughter.' He took a deep breath and raised his head, as if about to shout for help.

'All right, all right,' said the leader. 'But the Huguenots have risen up against the king, and the militia has been ordered to seek them out and kill them all, so you'd both better get inside the house and stay there.'

Ned did not let his relief show. 'And you'd better be more careful how you address Catholic noblemen,' he said, and he escorted Aphrodite past the men. Their leader said no more.

As soon as they were out of earshot, Aphrodite said: 'I have to go in the back way.'

He nodded. It was as he had guessed. 'Is there a door unlocked?'

'My maid is waiting.'

It was the oldest of stories. Aphrodite's maid was helping her mistress have an unauthorized romance. Well, that was none of Ned's business. He walked her to the back of the house where she tapped on a high wooden gate. It was opened immediately by a young girl.

Aphrodite took Ned's hand in a fierce grip and kissed his fingers. 'I owe you my life,' she said. Then she slipped inside, and the gate closed behind her.

Ned headed for the Lagny home, even more wary than before. He was alone now, and therefore more suspect. He touched the hilt of his sword nervously.

Many houses were now showing lights. The inhabitants, alarmed by the bells, had presumably got up and lit candles. Pale faces appeared at windows, staring out anxiously.

Fortunately, the Lagny place was not far. As he walked up the steps to the front door the building was dark and silent. Perhaps Lagny and his servants were pretending the house was empty, as Ned had urged Isabelle to do.

When he knocked on the door it moved. Apparently it had not been fully closed and now it swung open, revealing a dark hall. Ned smelled a disgusting odour, like a butcher's shop. He held his lantern aloft and gasped.

There were bodies everywhere, and blood all over the tiled floor and the panelled wall. He recognized the marquess, lying on his back with stab wounds in his belly and chest. Ned's heart stopped. He held his lantern over the faces of the other corpses, dreading that one of them would be Sylvie. They were all strangers, and by their dress he guessed servants.

He went into the kitchen, where there were more. He saw an open window leading to a yard, and hoped that some of the household had escaped that way.

He searched the house, shining his light into every dead face. To his immense relief Sylvie was not there.

Now he had to find her secret place. If she was not there, he feared the worst.

Before leaving the building he ripped the lace collar off his shirt and tied it around his left arm, so that he would look like one of the militia. There was then a danger that he might be challenged and found out to be an impostor, but on balance he thought it was worth the risk.

He was beginning to feel desperate. In the few weeks he had known her she had come to mean everything to him. I lost Margery; I can't lose Sylvie, too, he thought. What would I do?

He made his way to the rue du Mur and located a plain brick building with no windows. He went to the door and tapped on the wood. 'It's me,' he said in a low, urgent voice. 'It's Ned. Are you there, Sylvie?'

There was silence. His heart seemed to slow down. Then he heard the scrape of a bar and the click of a lock. The door opened and he stepped inside. Sylvie locked it and replaced the bar, then turned to him. He held up the lantern to look at her face. She was distraught, scared and tearful, but she was alive and apparently unhurt.

'I love you,' Ned said.

She threw herself into his arms.

*

PIERRE WAS AWESTRUCK by the result of his machinations. The Paris militia was carrying out the slaughter of Protestants with even more force and spite than he had hoped.

His cleverness was not really the cause, he knew. Parisians were furious that the wedding had gone ahead, and popular preachers had told them they were right to feel as they did. The city had been ready to explode with hatred, waiting only for someone to ignite the gunpowder. Pierre had merely struck the match.

As dawn broke on Sunday, St Bartholomew's Day, there were hundreds of dead and dying Huguenots on the streets of the city. It really might be possible to kill all the Protestants in France. He realized, with a sense of triumph mingled with wonder, that this could be the final solution.

Pierre had gathered around him a small squadron of ruffians, promising them that they could steal anything they liked from those they killed. They included Brocard and Rasteau; Biron, his chief spy; and a handful of the street villains Biron used for such tasks as tailing suspects.

Pierre had given his black book to the provost, Le Charron, but he remembered many of the names and addresses. He had been spying on these people for fourteen years.

They went first to the premises of René Duboeuf, the tailor in the rue St Martin. 'Don't kill him or his wife until I say so,' Pierre ordered.

They broke down the door and entered the shop. Some of the men went upstairs.

Pierre pulled open a drawer and found the tailor's notebook containing the names and addresses of his customers. He had always wanted this. He would make use of it tonight.

The men dragged the Duboeufs downstairs in their nightwear.

René was a small man of about fifty. He had already been bald when Pierre first came across him thirteen years ago. The wife had been young and pretty then, and she was still attractive, even now, looking terrified. Pierre smiled at her. 'Françoise, if I remember rightly,' he said. He turned to Rasteau. 'Cut off her finger.'

Rasteau gave his high-pitched giggle.

While the woman sobbed and the tailor pleaded, a man-at-arms held her left hand flat on the table and Rasteau cut off her little finger and part of her ring finger. Blood spurted over the table, staining a bolt of pale grey wool. She screamed and fainted.

'Where is your money?' Pierre asked the tailor.

'In the commode, behind the chamber pot,' he said. 'Please don't hurt her any more.'

Pierre nodded to Biron, who went upstairs.

Pierre saw that Françoise now had her eyes open. 'Make her stand up,' he said.

Biron came back with a leather bag that he emptied onto the table in a puddle of Françoise's blood. There was a pile of assorted coins.

'He's got more money than that,' Pierre said. 'Rip off her nightdress.'

She was younger than her husband, and she had a good figure. The men went quiet.

Pierre said to the tailor: 'Where's the rest of the money?'

Duboeuf hesitated.

Rasteau said excitedly: 'Shall I cut her tits off?'

Duboeuf said: 'In the fireplace, up the chimney. Please leave her alone.'

Biron put his hand up the chimney – cold, in August – and

retrieved a locked wooden box. He broke the lock with the point of his sword and tipped the money on the table, a good heap of gold coins.

'Cut their throats and share out the money,' Pierre said, and he went back outside without waiting to watch.

The people he most wanted as victims were the marquess and marchioness of Nîmes. He would have loved to kill the man in front of his wife. What a revenge that would have been. But they lived outside the walls, in the suburb of St Jacques, and the city gates were locked, so they were safe from Pierre's wrath, for the moment.

Failing them, Pierre's mind went to the Palot family.

Isabelle Palot had done worse than insult him, when he had called at the shop a few days ago; she had scared him. And perceptive Sylvie had seen it. Now it was time for them to be punished.

The men were a long time dividing up the money. Pierre guessed they were raping the wife before killing her. He had observed, in the civil war, that when men started to kill they always raped as well. Lifting one prohibition seemed to lift them all.

At last they came out of the shop. Pierre led them south, along the rue St Martin and across the Île de la Cité. He recalled the words Isabelle had used to him: *filth, discharge of an infected prostitute, loathsome stinking corpse.* He would remind her of them as she lay dying.

*

SYLVIE'S STASH OF books was cleverly concealed, Ned saw. Anyone entering the warehouse would see only barrels stacked floor to ceiling. Most of the barrels were full of sand, but Sylvie had shown Ned that a few were empty and easily moved to reveal the space where the books were stored in boxes. No one had ever discovered her secret, she told him.

They snuffed out the light of Ned's lamp, for fear that a faint glow might leak through cracks and be seen outside, and sat in the dark, holding hands. The bells rang madly. Sounds of combat came to their ears: screams, the hoarse shouts of men fighting, and occasional gunfire. Sylvie was worried about her mother, but Ned persuaded her that Isabelle was in less danger at her house than Sylvie and he would be on the streets.

They sat for hours, listening and waiting. The street noises began to die away around the time that a faint light appeared around the edges of the door, like a picture frame, indicating dawn; and Sylvie said: 'We can't stay here for ever.'

Ned opened the door a few inches, put his head out cautiously, and looked up and down the rue du Mur in the morning light. 'All clear,' he said. He stepped out.

Sylvie followed him and locked the door behind her. 'Perhaps the killing has stopped,' she said.

'They might flinch from committing atrocities in broad daylight.'

Sylvie quoted a verse from John's Gospel: 'Men loved darkness rather than the light, because their deeds were evil.'

They set off along the street, side by side, walking quickly. Ned still had on his white armband, for what that might be worth. He placed more reliance on the sword at his side, and walked with a hand on the hilt for reassurance. They headed south, towards the river.

Around the first corner two men lay dead outside a shop selling saddles. Ned was puzzled to see that they were half-naked. The corpses were partly obscured by the figure of a grey-haired old woman in a dirty coat bending over them. After a moment Ned realized she was taking the clothes off the bodies.

Second-hand clothing was valuable: only the rich could buy new. Even worn and filthy underwear could be sold as rags to paper makers. This wretched old woman was stealing the garments of the dead to sell, he realized. She pulled the breeches off the legs of a body then ran away with a bundle under her arm. The nakedness of the stabbed bodies made the sight even more obscene. Ned noticed that Sylvie averted her eyes as they walked past.

They avoided the broad, straight main roads with their long sightlines, and zigzagged through the narrow, tortuous lanes of the neighbourhood called Les Halles. Even in these back streets there were bodies. Most of them had been stripped, and in some places they were piled one on top of another, as if to make room in the road for people to pass. Ned saw the tanned faces of outdoor workers, the soft white hands of rich women, and the slender arms and legs of children. He lost count of how many. It was like a painting of hell in a Catholic church, but this was real and in front of his eyes in one of the great cities of the world. The sense of horror grew like nausea in him, and he would have vomited if his stomach had not been empty. Glancing at Sylvie he saw that her face was pale and set in an expression of grim determination.

There was worse to come.

At the edge of the river, the militia were getting rid of bodies. The dead, and some of the helpless wounded, were being thrown into the Seine with no more ceremony than would have been used for poisoned rats. Some floated off, but others hardly moved, and the shallow edge of the water was already clogged with corpses. A man with a long pole was trying to push the bodies out into midstream to make room for more, but they seemed sluggish, as if reluctant to leave.

The men were too preoccupied to notice Ned and Sylvie, who hurried past and headed across the bridge.

*

PIERRE'S EXCITEMENT grew as he approached the little stationery shop in the rue de la Serpente.

He wondered whether to encourage the men to rape Isabelle. That would be a suitable punishment. Then he had a better idea: let them rape Sylvie in front of her mother. People felt more pain when their children suffered: he had learned that from his wife, Odette. It crossed his mind to rape Sylvie himself, but that might diminish his authority in the eyes of his men. Let them do the dirty work.

He did not knock at the door of the shop. No one in Paris was answering callers now. A knock only gave people time to arm themselves. Pierre's men smashed open the door with sledgehammers, taking only a few seconds, then rushed in.

As Pierre entered he heard a shot. That shocked him. His

men did not have guns: they were expensive, and normally only the aristocracy had personal firearms. A moment later he saw Isabelle standing at the back of the shop. One of Pierre's men lay at her feet, apparently dead. As Pierre watched, she raised a second pistol and carefully aimed it at Pierre. Before he had time to move, another of his men ran her through with his sword. She fell without firing the second gun.

Pierre cursed. He had planned a more elaborate revenge. But there was still Sylvie. 'There's another woman,' he shouted to the men. 'Search the house.'

It did not take long. Biron ran upstairs and came down a minute later. 'There's no one else here,' he said.

Pierre looked at Isabelle. In the gloom he could not see whether she was alive or dead. 'Drag her outside,' he ordered.

In the light of day he saw that Isabelle was pumping blood from a deep wound in her shoulder. He knelt over her and yelled angrily: 'Where is Sylvie? Tell me, bitch!'

She must have been in agony, but she gave him a twisted smile. 'You devil,' she whispered. 'Go to hell, where you belong.'

Pierre roared with anger. He stood up and kicked her wounded shoulder. But it was pointless: she had stopped breathing, and her eyes stared up at him sightlessly.

She had escaped.

He went back inside. His men were searching for the money. The shop was full of paper goods of all kinds. He went around pulling ledgers off shelves and emptying cupboards and drawers, piling paper up in the middle of the floor. Then he snatched a lantern from Brocard, opened it, and touched the flame to the paper. It caught immediately and flared up.

*

NED FELT THAT he and Sylvie had been lucky to reach the left bank without getting accosted. By and large the militia were not attacking people at random: they seemed to be using the names and addresses they had undoubtedly got from Pierre. All the same, Ned had been stopped and interrogated once, when he was with Aphrodite Beaulieu, and it could easily happen again, with unpredictable results. So it was with a sense of relief that he turned into the rue de la Serpente, with Sylvie at his side, and hurried towards the shop.

He saw the body on the street, and had a dreadful feeling he knew who it was. Sylvie did too, and she let out a sob and broke into a run. A moment later they both bent over the still form on the bloody cobblestones. Ned knew right away that Isabelle was dead. He touched her face: she was still warm. She had not been dead long, which explained why her clothes had not yet been stolen.

Sylvie, weeping, said: 'Can you carry her?'

'Yes,' Ned said, 'if you just help get her over my shoulder.' She would be heavy, but the embassy was not far away. And it occurred to him that he would look like a militiaman disposing of a corpse, and consequently would be less likely to be questioned.

He had his hands under Isabelle's lifeless arms when he smelled smoke and hesitated. He looked towards the shop and saw movement inside. Was there a fire in there? A flame flared up and lit the interior, and he saw men moving about with an air of purpose, as if looking for something; valuables, perhaps. 'They're still here!' he said to Sylvie.

At that moment, Ned saw two men step through the doorway. One had a mutilated face, his nose just two holes surrounded by puckered white scar tissue. The other man had thick blond hair and a pointed beard, and Ned recognized Pierre.

Ned said: 'We have to leave her – come on!'

Sylvie hesitated for one grief-stricken moment, then broke into a run. Ned ran after her, but they had been recognized. He heard Pierre shout: 'There she is! Go after her, Rasteau!'

Ned and Sylvie ran side by side to the end of the rue de la Serpente. As they passed the huge windows of the church of Saint-Severin, he glanced back over his shoulder and saw the man called Rasteau pounding after him, sword raised.

Ned and Sylvie raced across the wide rue St Jacques and into the graveyard of St-Julien-le-Pauvre. But Sylvie was tiring and Rasteau gained on them. Ned thought furiously. Rasteau was in his thirties, but big and strong, and his nose had obviously been chopped off in some fracas. He was probably a practised swordsman with long experience of combat. He would be a formidable opponent. In any fight lasting more than a few seconds, his greater size and skill would tell. Ned's only hope was to surprise him somehow and finish him quickly.

Ned knew his surroundings well. This was where he had trapped the man who had been tailing him. Turning around the east end of the church, he was out of Rasteau's sight for a moment. He stopped suddenly and pulled Sylvie into the deep shelter of a doorway.

They were both panting. Ned could hear the heavy running steps of their pursuer. In a moment he had his sword in his right hand and his dagger in the left. He had to judge this perfectly: he could not let the man go past. But there was no time to think. When it seemed that Rasteau must be almost upon them, Ned stepped out from the doorway.

His timing was not quite right. A moment earlier Rasteau had slowed his pace, perhaps suspecting a trap; and he was just out of Ned's reach. He could not stop, but he was able to swerve and avoid being impaled on Ned's blade.

Ned moved fast and lunged, and his point penetrated Rasteau's side. Momentum carried the man past Ned. The blade came out. Rasteau half turned, stumbled and fell heavily. Without conscious thought, Ned stabbed wildly. Rasteau swung his weapon in a wide sweep and knocked Ned's sword out of his hand. It flew through the air and fell on a grave.

Rasteau was up in a flash, moving fast for a big man. Ned glimpsed Sylvie coming out of the doorway and yelled: 'Run, Sylvie, run!' Then Rasteau came at him stabbing and slicing. Ned retreated, using his dagger to parry a thrust, then a swing, then another thrust; but he knew he could not keep it up. Rasteau feinted a downward cut then, with surprising agility, changed the stroke into a thrust that dipped under Ned's guard.

And then Rasteau stopped still, and the point of a sword came out through the front of his belly. Ned leaped backwards, avoiding Rasteau's sword, but it was not necessary, for the thrust lost all momentum as Rasteau screamed in agony and fell forward; and Ned saw, behind him, the small form of Sylvie, holding the sword Ned had dropped, pulling it out of Rasteau's back.

They did not wait to watch Rasteau die. Ned took Sylvie's hand and they ran across the place Maubert, past the gallows, to the embassy.

Two armed guards stood outside the house. They were not embassy employees: Ned had never seen them before. One of them stepped in front of Ned and said: 'You can't go in there.'

Ned said: 'I am the deputy ambassador and this is my wife. Now get out of my way.'

From an upstairs window came the authoritative voice of Walsingham. 'They are under the protection of the king – let them pass!'

The guard stood aside. Ned and Sylvie went up the steps. The door opened before they reached it.

They stepped inside to safety.

*

I married Sylvie twice: first in the little Catholic church of St-Julien-le-Pauvre, outside which she had killed the man with no nose; and then again in a Protestant service at the chapel in the English embassy.

Sylvie was a virgin at the age of thirty-one, and as if to recover lost time, we made love every night and every morning for months. When I lay on top of her she clung to me as if I were saving her from drowning, and afterwards she often cried herself to sleep in my arms.

We never found Isabelle's body, and that made it harder for Sylvie to mourn. In the end we treated the burned-out shop as a grave, and stood in front of it for a few minutes every Sunday, holding hands and remembering a strong, brave woman.

Amazingly, the Protestants recovered from St Bartholomew's Day. Three thousand people had been killed in Paris, and thousands more in copycat massacres elsewhere; but the Huguenots fought back. Towns with Protestant majorities took in crowds of refugees and closed their gates against the representatives of the king. The Guise family, as powerful Catholics on the side of the monarch, were welcomed back into the royal circle once more as civil war broke out again.

Services were resumed in the loft over the stable and in other clandestine locations all over the country.

Walsingham was recalled to London, and we went with him. Before we left Paris, Sylvie showed Nath the warehouse in the rue du Mur, and Nath took over the selling of illegal literature to Paris Protestants. However, my wife was not willing to abandon her mission. She announced that she would continue to order the books from Geneva. She would sail across the English Channel to Rouen, meet the shipments there, escort them to Paris, pay the necessary bribes, and deliver the cargo to the rue du Mur.

I worried about her, but I had learned from Queen Elizabeth that some women could not be ruled by men. Anyway, I'm not sure I would have stopped her if I could. She had a sacred mission, and I could not take that away from her. If she carried on long enough, one day, of course, she would be caught. And then she would die, I knew.

It was her destiny.

21

ROLLO STOOD ON THE deck of the *Petite Fleur* as the freighter approached the coast of England. This was the moment of greatest danger.

The ship, out of Cherbourg, was headed for Combe Harbour carrying barrels of apple brandy, huge rounds of cheese, and eight young priests from the English College at Douai.

Rollo wore a priest's robe and a pectoral cross. His hair was thinning on top, but to compensate he had grown a full beard. Over his shoulders was a white cloak, not very priestly: it was a prearranged signal.

He had made preparations with meticulous care, but too many things could go wrong in practice. He did not even know for sure whether the captain was trustworthy. The man was being paid handsomely for making this stop, but someone else – Ned Willard, or another of Queen Elizabeth's men – might have offered him a higher fee to betray Rollo.

He wished he was not relying so heavily on his sister. She was smart and well-organized and fearless, but in the end she was a woman. However, Rollo himself did not want to set foot on English soil, not yet, so he had to use her.

At dusk the captain dropped anchor in a bay with no name three miles along the coast from his destination. The sea was mercifully calm. In the bay close to the beach a small, round-ended fishing boat with a mast and oars was anchored. Rollo had known the vessel when his father had been Receiver of Customs at Combe Harbour: it had once been the *Saint Ava*, but was now simply called the *Ava*. Beyond the beach, in the cleft of a chine, stood a sturdy cottage of pale stone with smoke coming from its chimney.

Rollo waited anxiously, watching the cottage, looking for a

sign. His hope was so intense that it made his whole body taut and he almost felt he might throw up with fear of failure. This was the beginning of the end. The young men he was escorting were secret agents for God. They were a small advance party, but they would be followed by more. One day soon the dark years would come to an end, England would give up foolish notions of religious freedom, and once again the great mass of ignorant peasants and labourers would happily bow to the authority of the one true Church. The Fitzgerald family would be restored to its rightful position – if not better: Rollo might become a bishop, and his brother-in-law Bart a duke. In Kingsbridge there would be a purge of Puritans like the one in Paris on St Bartholomew's Day – though Rollo had to keep that part of his dream secret from Margery, who would have refused to take part if she had known what violence he had in mind.

At last he saw the agreed response to his white cloak: a white sheet was waved from an upstairs window.

It could have been a trick. Mal Roper, the staunch Catholic fisherman who lived in the cottage, might have been arrested by Ned Willard and tortured for information, and the white sheet could be the bait of a trap. But there was nothing Rollo could do about that. He and those with him were risking their lives, and they all knew it.

As the sky darkened, Rollo assembled the priests on deck, each with a bag containing his personal effects plus the items he would need to bring the sacraments to deprived English families: wafers, wine, oil for confirmation, and holy water. 'Complete silence until you reach the house,' he instructed them in a whisper. 'Even low voices carry across water. This bay is normally deserted except for the fisherman's family, but you never know, and your mission could end before you reach England.' One of the priests was the ebullient Lenny Price, the first man he had met at the college in Douai, and the oldest in this group. 'Lenny, you're in charge once you're on land.'

The captain lowered a boat and it splashed into the sea. The priests clambered down a rope ladder, Rollo last. Two sailors grasped the oars. The boat shushed through the waves. On the beach Rollo could faintly discern the figure of a small woman with a dog: Margery. He breathed more easily.

The boat bumped the slope of the beach. The priests jumped out into the shallows. Margery greeted them with a handshake, saying nothing. Her well-trained dog was equally silent.

Rollo remained in the boat. Margery looked at him, caught his eye, grinned, and touched her chin as if stroking a beard: she had not seen him like this before. Fool! he thought, and quickly turned away. The priests must not find out that Rollo was Margery's brother: they knew him only as Jean Langlais.

The sailors pushed off the beach and began to row back to the *Petite Fleur*. Rollo looked astern from the boat and watched Margery lead the priests stumbling across the pebbles, then into the cottage. They crowded through the front door and were lost from sight.

*

MAL ROPER, his wife Peg, and their three strapping sons knelt on the stone floor of the single downstairs room of the cottage while Lenny Price said Mass. Margery almost wept to see the joy of these simple believers as they received the sacraments. If she lost her life for the sake of this moment, she thought, it would be worth it.

She often thought of her great-aunt, Sister Joan, now dead. The troubled young Margery, sixteen-year-old bride, had climbed to the top floor of her father's house, where old Joan had turned two little rooms into a monastic cell and a chapel. There Joan had told her that God had a purpose for her, but she must just wait for him to reveal it. Well, Joan had been right. Margery had waited, and God had revealed his purpose, and this was it.

The demand for Catholic priests was huge. Margery talked to aristocratic and wealthy Catholics in London whenever Bart attended Parliament. Discreetly, she sounded them out, and soon found that many were desperate for the sacraments. In London Margery was careful to stay away from the French and Spanish embassies, to avoid the suspicion of conspiracy. She had persuaded Bart to be equally chary. He supported her mission. He hated Protestantism, but in middle age he had become lazy and passive, and he was happy to let her do all the work as long as she let him feel like a hero. Margery did not mind.

After the service, Peg Roper served them all a hearty fish stew in wooden bowls with coarse home-baked bread. Margery was glad to see the priests tucking in: they had a long way to go before daybreak.

The Ropers were not rich, but Mal refused money. 'I thank you, my lady, but we don't need payment to do God's will,' he said. Margery saw that he was proud to say this, and she accepted his refusal.

It was midnight when they left.

Margery had two lanterns. She led the way with one, and Lenny brought up the rear with the other. She headed due north along a familiar road. She urged silence on the men every time they approached a village or farmhouse, for she did not want them to be heard or seen. A group of nine people walking at night would arouse suspicion and hostility in the mind of anyone who saw them. Margery was particularly cautious near larger manor houses, where there might be men-at-arms who could be sent out with torches to question the travellers.

The night was mild and the road was dry. All the same, Margery found the walking hard. Ever since the birth of her second child, Roger, she had suffered occasional backache, especially when she had to walk a long distance. She just had to grit her teeth and bear it.

Every two or three hours she stopped at a preselected spot, far from human habitation, where they rested, drank water from a stream, ate some of the bread Peg Roper had given them for their journey, and relieved themselves before setting off again.

Margery listened hard as she walked along, alert for the sounds of other people on the road. In a city there would have been people skulking along the lanes, usually about some criminal business, but here in the countryside there was little to steal and therefore fewer criminals. All the same she remained cautious.

Margery had cried for a whole day when she heard about the St Bartholomew's Day Massacre. All those people murdered by Catholics! It was much worse than a battle, in which soldiers killed soldiers. In Paris the citizens had slaughtered defenceless women and children in their thousands. How could God permit it? And then, to make it worse, the Pope had sent a letter of congratulation to the king of France. That could not be God's will. Hard though it was to believe, the Pope had done wrong.

Margery had known that Ned was in Paris at the time, and she had feared for his life, but then it was announced that everyone in the English embassy had survived. Hard on the heels of that came the news that Ned had married a French girl. It made Margery sad – quite unreasonably, she felt. She had had the chance to run away with him and she had refused. He could not spend his life yearning for her. He wanted a wife and a family. She should be glad that he had found happiness without her. But she could not bring herself to rejoice.

She wondered what the new Mrs Willard was like. People said that French women were terribly sophisticated. Would she be beautifully dressed and dripping with jewellery? Margery found herself hoping that the girl was an empty-headed flibbertigibbet who would quickly bore Ned. What an unworthy hope, she thought. I should wish him happiness. I do.

A faint light was visible in the east as they approached New Castle, and she was able to make out the battlements against the sky. A feeling of weary relief came over her: it had been a long walk.

The road led directly to the entrance. As always, the rooks on the walls jeered at the visitors.

Margery hammered on the gate. A face appeared briefly at an arrow-slit window in the gatehouse, and a minute later a sleepy sentry hauled open the heavy wooden door. They went in, and the door was barred behind them. At last Margery felt safe.

She led her charges across the courtyard and ushered them into the chapel. 'In a few minutes the castle servants will bring you breakfast and bedding,' she told them. 'Then you can sleep – all day and all night, if you wish. But remember the need for secrecy. The people here are all Catholics, but even so, you should not ask their names, nor tell them yours. Don't ask questions about where you are or who owns the castle. What you don't know, you can't reveal – even under torture.' They had been told all this before by Rollo, but it could hardly be repeated too often.

Tomorrow she would take them out in pairs and set them on the roads for their different destinations. Two were going west to Exeter, two north to Wells, two north-east to Salisbury, and two east to Arundel. When she said goodbye they would be on their own.

She left the church and crossed the courtyard to the house. The arrival of the priests had already caused a flurry of activity, and the servants were up and busy. She went upstairs to the boys' room. They were asleep in side-by-side beds. She leaned over Bartlet, now seven, big for his age, and kissed his head. Then she moved to little Roger, not yet two, with fair hair. She kissed his soft cheek.

Roger opened his eyes. They were golden brown. The same as Ned's.

*

SYLVIE HAD BEEN looking forward to her first visit to Kingsbridge. This was the town that had made the man she loved. They had been married less than a year and she felt there was still much to be learned about Ned. She knew that he was brave and kind and clever. She knew every inch of his body, and cherished it all, and when they made love she felt as if she was in his head, and knew everything he was thinking. But there were gaps in her knowledge, topics he did not say much about, times in his life he rarely referred to. He talked a lot about Kingsbridge, and she was eager to see it. Most of all she wanted to meet the people who had been important to him, people he loved and hated; especially the woman in the little painting that had stood beside his shaving mirror in his room in Paris.

They were prompted to visit by a letter from Ned's brother, Barney. He had come home to Kingsbridge, he said, with his son.

'I didn't know he had a son,' Ned said, reading the letter in the parlour of the small house they had rented near St Paul's Cathedral.

Sylvie said: 'Does he have a wife?'

'I presume so. You can't have children otherwise. But it's odd that he doesn't mention her.'

'Can you get Walsingham's permission to leave London?' Sylvie knew that Ned and Walsingham were busy enlarging Queen Elizabeth's secret intelligence service, making lists of men who might conspire to overthrow the queen and replace her with Mary Stuart.

'Yes,' Ned said. 'He'll want me to make a few discreet inquiries about Catholics in the county of Shiring, especially Earl Bart, but I can manage that easily.'

They went from London to Kingsbridge on horseback, taking a relaxed five days for the journey. Sylvie was not yet pregnant, so there was no danger to her from horseback riding. She was disappointed that it was taking her so long to conceive, but happily Ned had not complained.

Sylvie was used to capital cities: she had always lived in Paris until she married Ned, and since coming to England they had lived in London. Provincial towns felt safer, more tranquil, less frenetic. She liked Kingsbridge immediately.

She was struck by the stone angel on top of the cathedral spire. Ned told her that, according to legend, the angel had the face of Caris, the nun who had founded the hospital. Sylvie wondered disapprovingly why the statue had not been beheaded like all the other idolatrous images of saints and angels. 'They can't reach it,' Ned explained. 'They'd need to build scaffolding.' He spoke lightly: he was somewhat lax about such matters. He added: 'But you should go up the tower one day. The view over the town is magnificent.'

Kingsbridge reminded her of Rouen, with its riverside

docks and the great cathedral at its heart. It had the same air of lively prosperity. Thinking of Rouen turned her mind to her plan to continue smuggling Protestant literature into Paris. She had received one letter from Nath, forwarded by the English embassy. It had been an enthusiastic missive: Nath was thriving as a clandestine bookseller, but for now she had plenty of stock, and she would write to Sylvie as soon as she began to run low.

Meanwhile, Sylvie had come up with another plan to run parallel with the first. There were thousands of Huguenot refugees in London, many of them struggling to learn English, and she thought she could sell them books in French. A foreigner would not be allowed to open a bookshop within the city of London, Ned told her, so she was looking for premises outside the walls, perhaps in the suburb of Southwark, where many of the refugees lived.

Sylvie liked Barney immediately: most women did, Ned told her with a smile. Barney wore a sailor's baggy breeches with tightly laced shoes and a fur hat. His red beard was luxuriant, covering most of his weather-beaten face. He had a rapscallion grin that Sylvie guessed would make many girls go weak at the knees. When they arrived at the house opposite the cathedral, he embraced Ned warmly and kissed Sylvie a little more enthusiastically than was quite appropriate.

Both Ned and Sylvie were expecting his son to be a baby, but Alfo was nine years old. He was dressed in a miniature version of Barney's seafaring outfit, including the fur hat. The child had light-brown skin, curly red hair like Barney's, and the same green eyes. He was obviously African, and even more obviously Barney's son.

Sylvie crouched down to talk to him. 'What's your name?' she said.

'I am Barnardo Alfonso Willard.'

Barney said: 'We call him Alfo.'

Sylvie said: 'Hello, Alfo, I am your Aunt Sylvie.'

'I am pleased to meet you,' the boy said formally. Someone had taught him good manners.

Ned said to Barney: 'And his mother?'

Tears came to Barney's eyes. 'The loveliest woman I ever knew.'

'Where is she?'

'In a graveyard in Hispaniola, New Spain.'

'I'm so sorry, brother.'

Alfo said: 'Eileen looks after me.'

The house was still cared for by the Fifes, now an elderly couple, and their daughter Eileen, who was in her twenties.

Ned smiled. 'And soon you'll go to Kingsbridge Grammar School, like your father and me, and you'll learn to write Latin and count money.'

'I don't want to go to school,' Alfo said. 'I want to be a sailor, like the Captain.'

'We'll see,' said Barney. To Ned he explained: 'He knows I'm his father, but on board ship he got into the habit of calling me Captain, as the men do.'

On the day after they arrived, Ned took Sylvie to meet the Fornerons, Kingsbridge's leading Huguenot family, and they all chattered in French. Sylvie's English was coming along fast, but it was a relief to be able to relax and talk without having to search for words. The Fornerons had a precocious ten-year-old daughter, Valerie, who took it upon herself to teach Sylvie some useful English phrases, which amused everyone.

The Fornerons wanted to know all about the St Bartholomew's Day Massacre, which was still being discussed with horror all over Europe. Everyone Sylvie met asked about it.

On the third day Sylvie received a costly gift, a bolt of fine Antwerp cloth, enough to make a dress, from Dan Cobley, the richest man in town. Sylvie had heard his name before: she and Ned had sailed from Paris to London on one of Dan's ships. 'He wants to ingratiate himself with me,' Ned said, 'just in case one day he needs a royal favour.'

Dan called the next day, and Sylvie took him into the front parlour, the room with the view of the cathedral, and gave him wine and cakes. He was a pompous fat man, and Ned spoke to him in uncharacteristically curt tones. When Dan had gone, Sylvie asked Ned why he disliked Dan so much. 'He's a hypocritical Puritan,' Ned said. 'He dresses in black and complains about kissing in plays, then he cheats people in business.'

A more important blank in the story of Ned's life was filled in when they were invited to dinner at the home of Lady Susannah Twyford, a voluptuous woman in her fifties. It took Sylvie about a minute to figure out that Susannah had been Ned's lover. She talked to him with an easy intimacy that could only come from a sexual relationship. Ned looked happy and relaxed with her. Sylvie felt bothered. She knew Ned had not been a virgin when they married, but actually seeing him smiling fondly at an old flame was a bit hard to take.

Susannah must have picked up Sylvie's anxiety, for she sat down next to her and held both her hands. 'Ned is so happy to be married to you, Sylvie, and I can see why,' she said. 'I always hoped he would meet someone courageous and bright as well as beautiful. He's a special man and he deserves a special woman.'

'He seems very fond of you.'

'Yes,' Susannah admitted. 'And I'm fond of him. But he's in love with you, and that's so different. I do hope you and I can be friends.'

'I hope so too,' said Sylvie. 'I met Ned when he was thirty-two, so I'd be foolish to imagine I was the first woman he fell for.'

'Funny, though, how we do sometimes imagine silly things when we're in love.'

Sylvie realized this woman was wise and kind, and she felt easier in her mind.

Sylvie entered the cathedral for the first time on Whit Sunday for the festival of Pentecost. 'This is wonderful,' Sylvie said as they walked along the nave.

'It's a magnificent church,' Ned agreed. 'I never tire of studying it.'

'It is, but that's not what I mean. There are no marble statues, no garish paintings, no jewelled boxes of ancient bones.'

'Your Huguenot churches and meeting halls are like that.'

Sylvie switched to French in order to express herself better. 'But this is a cathedral! It's huge and beautiful and hundreds of years old, the way churches are supposed to be, and it's Protestant too! In France a Huguenot service is a hole-in-corner affair in some kind of improvised space, never seeming to be quite the right thing. To have a Protestant service in a place where people have worshipped God for centuries makes me rejoice.'

'I'm so glad,' said Ned. 'You've been through more misery than any five other people. You're entitled to some happiness.'

They approached a tall man of about Sylvie's age, with a handsome face reddened by drink, his stout figure clad in a costly yellow coat. 'Sylvie, this is Bart, the earl of Shiring. An earl is the same as a count.'

Sylvie remembered that Ned had to check on the local Catholics, of whom Bart was the most prominent. She curtsied.

Bart smiled, inclined his head in a slight bow, and gave her a roguish look. 'You're a sly one, Ned, to come home with a pretty French wench,' he said.

Sylvie had an idea that the word *wench* was not quite polite, but she decided to ignore it. The earl had an expensively dressed little boy at his side, and she said: 'And who is this young man?'

'My son, Bartlet, the viscount,' Bart said. 'He's just had his ninth birthday. Shake hands, Bartlet, and say how do you do.'

The boy complied. He had the same vigorous physical presence as his father, despite being small. Sylvie smiled to see a wooden sword at his belt.

Ned said: 'And this is Countess Margery.'

Sylvie looked up and saw, with a shock, the woman in the little painting. It was a second jolt to realize that in real life she was much more striking. Although older than the painting – she had a few faint lines around her eyes and mouth, and Sylvie put her age at thirty – the living woman had an air of vivacity and charisma that was like the charged atmosphere of stormy weather. She had luxuriant curly hair, imperfectly tamed, and wore a little red hat at an angle. No wonder he loved you, Sylvie thought immediately.

Margery acknowledged Sylvie's curtsey, studying her with frank interest; then she looked at Ned, and Sylvie saw love in her eyes. Margery radiated happiness as she said hello to Ned. You haven't got over him, Sylvie thought. You'll never get over him. He's the love of your life.

Sylvie looked at Ned. He, too, looked happy. He had a big place in his heart for Margery, there was no doubt about that.

Sylvie felt dismayed. Susannah Twyford had been a bit startling, but had been no more than fond of Ned. Margery had far stronger feelings, and Sylvie was unnerved. She wants my husband, Sylvie thought.

Well, she can't have him.

Then Sylvie noticed a child of about two years, still unsteady on his legs, standing half-concealed by the full skirt of Margery's red dress. Margery followed Sylvie's look and said: 'And this is my second son, Roger.' She bent down and picked up the toddler with a swift motion. 'Roger, this is Sir Ned Willard,' she said. 'He's a very important person who works for the queen.'

Roger pointed at Sylvie. 'Is she the queen?' he said.

They all laughed.

Ned said: 'She's *my* queen.'

Thank you, Ned, Sylvie thought.

Ned said to Margery: 'Is your brother here?'

'We don't see much of Rollo nowadays,' Margery said.

'Where is he, then?'

'He has become a counsellor to the earl of Tyne.'

'I'm sure his legal training and business experience make him useful to the earl. Does he live at Tyne Castle?'

'He's based there, but the earl has properties all over the north of England, and I gather Rollo travels a lot on his behalf.'

Ned was still checking on the local Catholics, but Sylvie was looking at the little boy, Roger. There was something about him that bothered her, and after a minute she realized that the boy had a familiar look.

He resembled Ned.

Sylvie looked at Ned and saw him studying Roger with a faint frown. He, too, had noticed something. Sylvie could read his face effortlessly and she could tell, from his expression, that he had not yet figured out what was puzzling him. Men were not as quick as women to spot resemblances. Sylvie caught Margery's eye, and the two women understood one another instantly, but Ned was merely puzzled and Earl Bart was oblivious.

The service began with a hymn, and there was no further conversation until the ceremony came to an end. Then they had guests for dinner, and with one thing and another Sylvie did not get Ned on his own until bedtime.

It was spring, and they both got into bed naked. Sylvie touched the hair on Ned's chest. 'Margery loves you,' she said.

'She's married to the earl.'

'That won't stop her.'

'How can you say that?'

'Because she's lain with you already.'

Ned looked cross and said nothing.

'It must have been about three years ago, just before you came to Paris.'

'How do you know?'

'Because Roger is two.'

'Oh. You noticed.'

'He has your eyes.' She looked into Ned's eyes. 'That wonderful golden-brown.'

'You're not angry?'

'I knew, when I married you, that I was not the first woman you'd loved. But . . .'

'Go on.'

'But I didn't know you might still love her, or that she had had your child.'

Ned took both her hands in his. 'I can't tell you that I'm indifferent to her, or don't care about her,' he said. 'But please understand that you are all I want.'

It was the right thing to say, but Sylvie was not sure she believed him. All she knew was that she loved him and she was not going to let anyone take him away. 'Make love to me,' she said.

He kissed her. 'My goodness, you're a hard taskmaster,' he joked. Then he kissed her again.

But this was not enough. She wanted something with him that Susannah Twyford and Margery Shiring had never shared. 'Wait,' she said, thinking. 'Is there something you've always thought about doing with a woman?' She had never before talked like this to him – or to anyone. 'Something that excites you when you imagine it, but you've never done it?' She held her breath. What would he say?

He looked thoughtful and a little embarrassed.

'There is,' she said triumphantly. 'I can tell.' She was glad she could read his face so easily. 'What is it?'

'I'm embarrassed to say.'

Now he looked bashful. It was sweet. She wriggled closer to him, pressing her body against his. In a low voice she said: 'Then whisper.'

He whispered in her ear.

She looked at him, grinning, a little surprised but also aroused. 'Really?'

He shook his head. 'No, forget it. I shouldn't have said it.'

She felt excited, and she could tell he was, too. 'I don't know,' she said. 'But we could try it.'

So they did.

Part Four

1583 to 1589

22

NED STUDIED THE FACE of his son, Roger. His heart was so
full he could hardly speak. Roger was a child on the edge of
adolescence, starting to grow taller but still having smooth
cheeks and a treble voice. He had Margery's curly dark hair and
impish look, but Ned's golden-brown eyes.

They were in the parlour of the house opposite the
cathedral. Earl Bart had come to Kingsbridge for the spring
court of quarter sessions, and had brought with him the two
boys he thought were his sons: Bartlet, who was eighteen, and
Roger, twelve. Ned, too, had come for the court: he was the
Member of Parliament for Kingsbridge now.

Ned had no other children. He and Sylvie had been making
love for more than ten years, with a fervour that had hardly
diminished, but she had never become pregnant. It was a cause
of sadness to them both, and it made Roger painfully precious
to Ned.

Ned was also recalling his own adolescence. I know what
you have in front of you, he thought as he looked at Roger; and
I wish I could tell you all about it, and make it easier for you;
but when I was your age I never believed older people who
said they knew what the lives of younger ones were like, and I
don't suppose you will either.

Roger's attitude to Ned was, naturally, quite casual. Ned was
a friend of his mother's, and Roger regarded him as an
unofficial uncle. Ned could not display his affection except by
listening carefully to the boy, taking him seriously and
replying thoughtfully to what he said; and perhaps that was
why Roger occasionally confided in him – something that gave
Ned great joy.

Now Roger said: 'Sir Ned, you know the queen. Why does she hate Catholics?'

Ned had not expected that, though perhaps he should have. Roger knew that his parents were Catholics in a Protestant country, and he had just become old enough to wonder why.

Ned played for time by saying: 'The queen doesn't hate Catholics.'

'She makes my father pay a fine for not going to church.'

Roger was quick-thinking, Ned saw, and the little flush of pleasure he felt was accompanied by a painful stab of regret that he had to conceal his pride, most especially from the boy himself.

Ned said to Roger what he said to everyone: 'When she was young, Princess Elizabeth told me that if she became queen, no Englishman would die for his religion.'

'She hasn't kept that promise,' Roger said quickly.

'She has tried.' Ned searched for words that would explain the complexities of politics to a twelve-year-old. 'On the one hand, she has Puritans in Parliament telling her every day that she's too soft, and she should be burning Catholics to death, just as her predecessor Queen Mary Tudor burned Protestants. On the other hand, she has to deal with Catholic traitors such as the duke of Norfolk who want to kill her.'

Roger argued stubbornly: 'Priests are executed just for bringing people back to the Catholic faith, aren't they?'

Roger had been saving up these questions, Ned realized. He was probably afraid to challenge his parents about such matters. Ned was pleased the boy trusted him enough to share his worries. But why was Roger so concerned? Ned guessed that Stephen Lincoln was still living more or less clandestinely at New Castle. He would be tutor to Bartlet and Roger, and almost certainly said Mass regularly for the family. Roger was worried that his teacher might be found out and executed.

There were many more such priests than there had been. Stephen was one of the old diehards left over after Queen Elizabeth's religious revolution, but there were dozens of new priests, perhaps hundreds. Ned and Walsingham had caught seventeen of them. All had been executed for treason.

Ned had questioned most of the seventeen before they died. He had not learned as much as he wished, partly because they had been trained to resist interrogation, but mainly because they did not know much. Their organizer worked under the obvious pseudonym of Jean Langlais and gave them only the absolute minimum of information about the operation of which they were part. They did not know exactly where on the coast they had landed, nor the names of the shadowy people who welcomed them and set them on the road to their destinations.

Ned said: 'These priests are trained abroad and smuggled into England illegally. They owe allegiance to the Pope, not to our queen. Some of them belong to a hard-line ultra-Catholic group called the Jesuits. Elizabeth fears they may conspire to overthrow her.'

'And do they conspire?' Roger asked.

If Ned had been arguing with an adult, he would have responded disputatiously to these questions. He might have scorned the naivety of anyone who supposed that clandestine priests were innocent of treachery. But he had no wish to win an argument with his son. He just wanted the boy to know the truth.

The priests all believed that Elizabeth was illegitimate, and that the true queen of England was Mary Stuart, the queen of the Scots; but none of them had actually done anything about it – so far, at least. They had not tried to contact Mary Stuart in her prison, they had not called together groups of discontented Catholic noblemen, they had not plotted to murder Elizabeth.

'No,' he said to Roger. 'As far as I know, they don't conspire against Elizabeth.'

'So they are executed just for being Catholic priests.'

'You are right, morally speaking,' Ned said. 'And it is a great sadness to me that Elizabeth has not been able to keep her youthful vow. But politically it is quite impossible for her to tolerate, within her kingdom, a network of men who are loyal to a foreign potentate – the Pope – who has declared himself her enemy. No monarch on earth would put up with that.'

'And if you hide a priest in your house, the penalty is death.'

So that was the thought at the heart of Roger's worry. If Stephen Lincoln were caught saying Mass, or even proved to keep sacramental objects at New Castle, then both Bart and Margery could be executed.

Ned, too, was fearful for Margery. He might not be able to protect her from the wrath of the law.

He said: 'I believe we should all worship God in the way we think right, and not worry about what other people do. I don't hate Catholics. I've been friends with your mother – and father – all my life. I don't think Christians should kill each other over theology.'

'It's not just Catholics who burn people. The Protestants in Geneva burned Michel Servet.'

Ned thought of saying that the name of Servet was known all over Europe precisely because it was so unusual for Protestants to burn people to death; but he decided not to take that argumentative line with Roger. Instead he said: 'That's true, and it will be a stain on the name of John Calvin until the day of judgement. But there are a few people – on both sides – who struggle for tolerance. Queen Caterina, the mother of the king of France, is one, and she's Catholic. Queen Elizabeth is another.'

'But they both kill people!'

'Neither woman is a saint. There's something you must try to understand, Roger. There are no saints in politics. But imperfect people can still change the world for the better.'

Ned had done his best, but Roger looked dissatisfied. He did not want to be told that life was complicated. He was twelve years old, and he sought ringing certainties. He would have to learn slowly, like everyone else.

The conversation was interrupted when Alfo walked in. Roger immediately clammed up, and a few moments later politely took his leave.

Alfo said to Ned: 'What did he want?'

'He's having adolescent doubts. He treats me as a harmless friend of the family. How is school?'

Alfo sat down. He was nineteen now, and he had Barney's long limbs and easy-going ways. 'The truth is, a year ago the school had already taught me all it could. Now I spend half my time reading and the other half teaching the youngsters.'

'Oh?' It was clearly Ned's day for counselling young men. He was only forty-three, not old enough for such responsibility. 'Perhaps you should go to Oxford and study at the university. You could live at Kingsbridge College.' Ned was only mildly keen on this idea. He himself had never studied at a university, and he could not say that he had suffered much in consequence. He was as smart as most of the clergymen he met. On the other hand, he occasionally noticed that university-educated men were more agile than he in arguments, and he knew that they had learned that in student debates.

'I'm not cut out to be a clergyman.'

Ned smiled. Alfo was fond of girls – and they liked him, too. He had inherited Barney's effortless charm. Timid girls were put off by his African looks, but the more adventurous were intrigued.

English people were illogical about foreigners, Ned found: they hated Turks, and they believed Jews were evil, but they regarded Africans as harmlessly exotic. Men such as Alfo, who somehow ended up in England, usually married into the community, where their inherited appearance disappeared in the course of three or four generations.

'Going to university doesn't mean you're obliged to become a clergyman. But I sense that you have something else in mind.'

'My grandmother Alice had a dream of turning the old monastery into an indoor market.'

'That's true, she did.' It was a long time ago, but Ned had not forgotten looking around the ruins with his mother, imagining the stalls set up in the cloisters. 'It's still a good idea.'

'Could I use the Captain's money to buy the place?'

Ned considered. He had charge of Barney's wealth while Barney was at sea. He kept a lot of it in cash, but he had made some investments too – an orchard in Kingsbridge, a dairy in London – and had made money for his brother. 'I think we might, if the price is right,' he said cautiously.

'May I approach the chapter?'

'Do some research first. Ask about recent sales of building land in Kingsbridge – how much per acre.'

'I'll do that,' Alfo said eagerly.

'Be discreet. Don't tell people what you're planning – say I've asked you to look for a building plot for myself. Then we'll talk about how much to offer for the monastery.'

Eileen Fife came into the room with a packet in her hand. She smiled affectionately at Alfo and handed the packet to Ned. 'A messenger brought this from London for you, Sir Ned. He's in the kitchen, if you want him.'

'Give him something to eat,' Ned said.

'I've done so already,' Eileen said, indignant that Ned should think she might have omitted this courtesy.

'Of course you have, forgive me.' Ned opened the packet. There was a letter for Sylvie addressed in Nath's childlike handwriting, undoubtedly forwarded by the English embassy in Paris. It would probably be a request for more books, something that had happened three times in the last ten years.

Ned knew, from Nath's letters and from Sylvie's visits to Paris, that Nath had taken over Sylvie's role in more than bookselling. She still worked as maid to the family of Pierre Aumande de Guise, and she continued to watch Pierre and pass information to the Paris Protestants. Pierre had moved into the Guise palace, along with Odette, her son Alain, now twenty-two and a student, and Nath. This gave Nath extra opportunities for espionage, especially on English Catholics in Paris. Nath had also converted Alain to Protestantism, unknown to Odette or Pierre. All Nath's information came to Sylvie in letters such as this one.

Ned set it aside for Sylvie to open.

The other letter was for him. It was written in clear, forward-slanted script, the work of a methodical man in a hurry, and Ned recognized it as that of Sir Francis Walsingham, his master. However, he could not read it immediately because it was in code. He said to Eileen: 'I need time to compose a reply. Give the messenger a bed for the night.'

Alfo stood up. 'I'll make a start on our new project! Thank you, Uncle Ned.'

Ned began to decode his letter. There were only three sentences. It was tempting to write the decrypt above the coded message, but that practice was strictly forbidden. If a coded letter with its decrypt found its way into the wrong hands, the enemy would have a key to all other messages written in the same code. Ned's code-breakers, working on intercepted correspondence of foreign embassies in London, had benefited more than once from such carelessness on the part of the people on whom they spied. Ned wrote his decrypt with an iron pencil on a slate that could be wiped clean with a damp cloth.

He had the code in his head, and he was able to decipher the opening sentence rapidly: *News from Paris*.

His pulse quickened. He and Walsingham were eager to find out what the French would do next. All through the sixties and seventies, Queen Elizabeth had held her enemies at bay by pretending to consider marriage proposals from Catholic princes. Her latest victim had been Hercule-Francis, the brother of King Henri III of France. Elizabeth would be fifty this year, but she still had the power to fascinate men, and she had enraptured Hercule-Francis, even though he was still in his twenties, calling him 'my little frog'. She had toyed with him for three years, until he came to the conclusion reached eventually by all her suitors, that she had no intention of marrying anyone. But Ned felt she had played the marriage card for the last time, and he feared that her enemies might now do what they had been talking about for so long, and make a serious attempt to get rid of her.

Ned was beginning on the second sentence when the door was flung open and Margery burst in.

'How dare you?' she said. 'How dare you?'

Ned was thunderstruck. Margery's sudden rages were much feared by her servants, but he had never been subjected to one. His relationship with her was friendly to the point of affection. 'What on earth have I done?' he said.

'How dare you feed Protestant heresy to my son?'

Ned frowned. 'Roger asked me questions,' he said, reining in his indignation. 'I tried to answer him honestly.'

'I will bring up my sons in the faith of their forefathers and I won't have them corrupted by you.'

'Fine,' said Ned with some exasperation. 'But sooner or later someone's going to tell them that there's an alternative point of view. Be grateful it was me and not some bigoted Puritan such as Dan Cobley.' Even while he was annoyed with her he could not help noticing how attractive she was, tossing her abundant hair and flashing anger from her eyes. She was more beautiful at forty than she had been at fourteen, when he had kissed her behind the tomb of Prior Philip.

She said: 'They would recognize Cobley for the bull-headed blasphemer that he is. You pose as a reasonable man while you poison their minds.'

'Ah! I understand. It's not my Protestantism you object to, it's my reasonableness. You don't want your sons to know that men can discuss religion quietly, and disagree without trying to murder one another.' Even while he argued with her, he realized vaguely that she did not really think he was poisoning Roger's mind. In truth she was raging against the fate that had driven her and Ned apart so that they could not raise their child together.

But she was like a charging horse, and could not be stopped. 'Oh, you're so clever, aren't you?' she raved.

'No, but I don't pretend to be stupid, which is what you're doing now.'

'I didn't come here to argue. I'm telling you not to speak to my children.'

Ned lowered his voice. 'Roger is mine, too.'

'He must not be made to suffer for my sins.'

'Then don't force your religion down his throat. Tell him what you believe, and admit that good men disagree. He will respect you more.'

'Don't you dare tell me how to raise my children.'

'Then don't you tell me what I may and may not say to my son.'

She went to the door. 'I'd tell you to go to hell, but you're on your way there already.' She left the room, and a moment later the front door slammed.

Ned looked out of the window, but for once he did not enjoy the beauty of the cathedral. He was sorry to have quarrelled with Margery.

One thing they were agreed upon: they would never tell Roger the truth about his parenthood. They both felt it would be deeply disturbing to the boy – or even to the man, later on – to learn that he had been so deceived all his life. Ned would never have the joy of acknowledging his only son, but he had to make that sacrifice for the boy's own sake. Roger's welfare was more important than Ned's: that was what it meant to be a parent.

He looked down at his letter and transcribed the second sentence: *Cardinal Romero is back and his mistress with him*. That was significant. Romero was an informal envoy of the king of Spain. He must be plotting something with the French ultra-Catholics. And his mistress, Jerónima Ruiz, had spied for Ned at the time of the St Bartholomew's Day Massacre. Perhaps she would be willing to reveal what Romero was up to.

As he was working on the third sentence, Sylvie came into the parlour. Ned handed her the letter that had come with his own. She did not open it immediately. 'I heard some of your conversation with Margery,' she said. 'The louder parts. It sounded unpleasant.'

Ned took her hand, feeling awkward. 'I wasn't attempting to convert Roger. I just wanted to answer his questions honestly.'

'I know.'

'I'm sorry if you were embarrassed by my old flame.'

'I'm not embarrassed,' Sylvie said. 'I realized, a long time ago, that you love us both.'

That startled Ned. It was true, but he had never admitted it.

Reading his mind, Sylvie said: 'You can't hide that kind of thing from a wife.' She opened her letter.

Ned looked again at his own. With half his mind on Sylvie's words, he decoded the last sentence: *Jerónima will talk only to you*.

He looked up at Sylvie, and the right words came to him. 'As long as you know that I love you.'

'Yes, I do. This is from Nath. She needs more books. I have to go to Paris.'

'So do I,' said Ned.

*

SYLVIE STILL HAD NOT climbed the cathedral tower to look at the view. After the Sunday service, with a spring sun shining through the coloured windows, she looked for the staircase up. There was a small door in the wall of the south transept that opened on to a spiral staircase. She was wondering whether she should ask permission, or just slip through the door, when Margery approached her. 'I had no right to come storming into your house and make such a scene,' Margery said. 'I feel ashamed.'

Sylvie closed the little door. This was important and the view from the tower would always be there.

She felt that she was the lucky one, and therefore she should be magnanimous to Margery. 'I understand why you were so upset,' she said. 'At least, I think I do. And I really don't blame you.'

'What do you mean?'

'You and Ned should be raising Roger together. But you can't, and it breaks your heart.'

Margery looked shocked. 'Ned swore he would never tell anyone.'

'He didn't. I guessed, and he couldn't deny it. But the secret is safe with me.'

'Bart will kill me if he finds out.'

'He won't find out.'

'Thank you.' There were tears in Margery's eyes.

'If Ned had married you, he would have had a house full of children. But it seems I can't conceive. It's not as if we don't try.' Sylvie was not sure why she was having such a candid conversation with the woman who loved her husband. It just seemed pointless to pretend.

'I'm sorry to hear that . . . though I had guessed it.'

'If I die before Ned, and Bart dies before you, then you should marry Ned.'

'How can you say such a thing?'

'I'll look down from heaven and bless your marriage.'

'It's not going to happen – but thank you for saying it. You're a good woman.'

'You are too.' Sylvie smiled. 'Isn't he lucky?'

'Ned?'

'To have the love of both of us.'

'I don't know,' said Margery. 'Is he?'

*

ROLLO WAS AWESTRUCK by the Guise palace. It was bigger than the Louvre. With its courtyards and gardens it covered at least two acres. The place was thronged with servants and men-at-arms and distant relations and hangers-on, all of whom were fed daily and lodged every night. The stable block alone was bigger than the entire house Rollo's father had built in Kingsbridge at the height of his prosperity.

Rollo was invited there in June of 1583 for a meeting with the duke of Guise.

Duke 'Scarface' François was long dead, as was his brother Cardinal Charles. François's son Henri, aged thirty-two, was now the duke. Rollo studied him with fascination. By a coincidence that was regarded, by most Frenchmen, as divinely ordained, Henri had been wounded in the face, just like his father. François had been disfigured by a spear, whereas Henri had taken a bullet from an arquebus, but both had ended up with conspicuous marks, and now Henri, too, was nicknamed Scarface.

The famously cunning Cardinal Charles had been replaced, in the councils of the Guise family, by Pierre Aumande de Guise, the low-born distant relative who had been Charles's protégé. Pierre was patron of the English College, and had given Rollo his alias of Jean Langlais, the name by which he was always known when engaged in secret work.

Rollo met the duke in a small but opulent room that was hung with paintings of biblical scenes in which many of the women and men were naked. There was a distinct air of decadence that made Rollo uncomfortable.

Rollo was flattered, but somewhat intimidated, by the high status of the other attendees. Cardinal Romero was here to represent the king of Spain, and Giovanni Castelli the Pope. Claude Matthieu was the rector of the Professed Jesuits. These men were the heavy artillery of Christian orthodoxy, and he felt amazed to find himself in their company.

Pierre sat next to Duke Henri. Pierre's skin condition had worsened over the years, and now there were red flaking patches on his hands and neck as well as at the corners of his eyes and mouth, and he scratched himself continually.

Three Guise attendants served wine and sweetmeats as the notables took their seats, then stood by the door awaiting further orders. Rollo assumed they were thoroughly trustworthy, but all the same he would have made them wait outside. Secrecy had become an obsession with him. The only person in this room who knew his real name was Pierre. In England it was the opposite: no one knew that Rollo Fitzgerald was Jean Langlais, not even his sister, Margery. Rollo was theoretically employed by the earl of Tyne, who was a timid Catholic, devout but frightened of conspiracy; the earl paid him a salary, gave him indefinite leave of absence, and asked no questions.

Duke Henri opened the discussion with a statement that thrilled Rollo: 'We are here to talk about the invasion of England.'

This was Rollo's dream. The work he had been doing for the last ten years, smuggling priests into England, was important, but palliative: it kept the true faith alive, but did nothing to change the status quo. Its true value was as preparation for this. An invasion led by Duke Henri could return England to the Catholic Church and restore the Fitzgerald family to its rightful position in the ruling elite.

He saw it in his mind: the invasion fleet with banners flying; the armoured men pouring onto the beaches; the triumphal entry into London, cheered by the crowds; the coronation of Mary Stuart; and himself, in bishop's robes, celebrating Mass in Kingsbridge Cathedral.

Rollo understood, from his discussions with Pierre, that

Queen Elizabeth was a major nuisance to the Guises. Whenever the ultra-Catholics got the upper hand in France, swarms of Huguenots sought asylum in England, where they were welcomed for their craft skills and enterprise. Prospering there, they sent money home to their co-religionists. Elizabeth also interfered in the Spanish Netherlands, permitting English volunteers to go there and fight on the rebel side.

But Henri had another motive. 'It is insupportable,' he said, 'that Elizabeth, who has been declared illegitimate by the Pope, should rule England and keep the true queen, Mary Stuart, in prison.'

Mary Stuart, the queen of the Scots, was Duke Henri's cousin. If she became queen of England, the Guises would be the supremely powerful family of Europe. No doubt this was what was driving Henri and Pierre.

Rollo suffered a moment of doubt about the domination of his country by a foreign family. But that was a small price to pay for a return to the true faith.

'I see the invasion as a two-pronged fork,' Henri said. 'A force of twelve thousand men will land at an east coast port, rally the local Catholic noblemen, and take control of the north of the country. Another force, perhaps smaller, will land on the south coast and, again, muster the Catholics to take control. Both groups, supplied and reinforced by English supporters, will march on London.'

The Jesuit leader said: 'Very good, but who is going to pay for this?'

Cardinal Romero answered him. 'The king of Spain has promised half the cost. King Felipe is fed up with English pirates attacking his transatlantic galleons and stealing their cargoes of gold and silver from New Spain.'

'And the other half?'

Castelli said: 'I believe the Pope will contribute, especially if shown a credible war plan.'

Rollo knew that kings and popes gave promises more readily than they gave cash. However, right now money did not matter quite as much as usual. Duke Henri had just inherited half a million livres from his grandmother, so he was able to meet some of the expense himself, if necessary.

Henri now said: 'The invasion force will need plans of suitable harbours for the landing.'

Rollo realized that Pierre had choreographed this event. He already knew the answers to every question. The point of the meeting was to let each attendee know that all the others were willing to play their parts.

Now Rollo said: 'I will get the maps.'

Henri looked at Rollo. 'On your own?'

'No, duke, not alone. I have a large network of powerful and wealthy Catholics in England.' It was Margery's network, not Rollo's, but no one here realized that. And Rollo had always insisted on knowing where his priests were being sent, on the pretext of making sure they would be compatible with their protectors.

Henri said: 'Can you rely on these people?'

'Your grace, they are not just Catholics. They are men who are already risking the death penalty for harbouring the priests I have been smuggling into England for the last ten years. They are utterly trustworthy.'

The duke looked impressed. 'I see.'

'Not only will they supply maps: they will be the core of the uprising that will support the invasion.'

'Very good,' said Henri.

Pierre spoke for the first time. 'There remains one essential element: Mary Stuart, the queen of the Scots. We cannot embark on this enterprise unless we have a clear commitment from her that she will support the rebellion, authorize the execution of Elizabeth, and assume the crown herself.'

Rollo took a deep breath. 'I will undertake to make sure of her,' he said. He silently prayed that he would be able to keep this ambitious promise.

Henri said: 'But she is in prison, and her letters are monitored.'

'That's a problem, but not insuperable.'

The duke seemed satisfied with that. He looked around the room. With the brisk impatience common to powerful men, he said: 'I think that's all. Gentlemen, thank you for your attendance.'

Rollo glanced to the door and saw, to his surprise, that the three servants had been joined by a fourth person, a man in his early twenties whose hair was cut in the short style fashionable among students. He looked vaguely familiar. Whoever he was, he had presumably heard Rollo promise to betray his country. Unnerved, Rollo pointed and said loudly: 'Who is that man?'

Pierre answered: 'It's my stepson. What the devil are you doing here, Alain?'

Rollo recognized him now. He had seen the boy several times over the years. He had the blond hair and beard of the Guise family. 'My mother is ill,' Alain said.

Rollo watched with interest the procession of emotions over Pierre's face. At first, fleetingly, there was a look of hope, quickly repressed; then a mask of concern that did not quite convince Rollo; and finally an expression of brisk efficiency as he said: 'Summon a doctor immediately. Run to the Louvre and fetch Ambroise Paré – I don't care about the cost. My beloved Odette must have the best possible care. Go, boy, hurry!' Pierre turned back to the duke and said: 'If you have no further need of me, your grace . . .'

'Go, Pierre,' said Henri.

Pierre left the room, and Rollo thought: Now what was that pantomime about?

*

NED WILLARD HAD come to Paris to meet Jerónima Ruiz, but he had to be very careful. If she were suspected of passing secret information to Ned, she would be executed – and so might he.

He stood in a bookshop in the shadow of the Cathedral of Notre Dame. The shop had once been owned by Sylvie's father. Ned had not known Sylvie at the time, but she had pointed out the place to him in 1572, when they were courting. Now the shop was owned by someone else, and Ned was using it as a convenient place to loiter.

He studied the titles on the spines of the books and, at the same time, kept an anxious eye on the great west front of the church with its twin towers. As soon as the tall church doors opened he abandoned his pretence of shopping and hurried outside.

The first person to emerge from the cathedral was Henri III, who had become king of France when his brother, Charles IX, died nine years ago. Ned watched him smile and wave to the crowd of Parisians in the square. The king was thirty-one. He had dark eyes and dark hair already receding at the temples to give him a widow's peak. He was what the English called a 'politician' – in French *un politique* – meaning that he made decisions about religion according to what he thought would be good for his country, rather than the other way around.

He was closely followed by his mother, Queen Caterina, now a dumpy old lady of sixty-four wearing a widow's cap. The queen mother had borne five sons, but all had suffered poor health, and so far three had died young. Even worse, none of them had ever fathered a son, which was why the brothers had succeeded one another as kings of France. However, this bad luck had made Caterina the most powerful woman in Europe. Like Queen Elizabeth, she had used her power to arbitrate religious conflict by compromise rather than violence; like Elizabeth, she had had limited success.

As the royal party disappeared across the bridge to the right bank, there was a general exodus from the three arched doorways of the cathedral, and Ned joined the crowd, hoping he was inconspicuous among the many people who had come to look at the king.

He spotted Jerónima Ruiz in seconds. It was not hard to pick her out from the mob. She wore red, as usual. She was now in her early forties: the hour-glass figure of her youth had thickened, her hair was not so lush, and her lips were no longer full. However, she walked with a sway and looked out alluringly from under black eyelashes. She still radiated sex more powerfully than any other woman in sight – although Ned sensed that what had once been carelessly natural was now achieved with conscious effort.

Her eyes met his. There was a flash of recognition, then she looked away.

He could not approach her openly: their meeting had to look accidental. It also had to be brief.

He contrived to get close to her. She was with Cardinal Romero, though for the sake of appearances, she was not on his arm, but walking a little way behind him. When the cardinal stopped to speak to Viscount Villeneuve, Ned casually came alongside her.

Continuing to smile at no one in particular, Jerónima said: 'I'm risking my life. We can talk for only a few seconds.'

'All right.' Ned looked around as if in idle curiosity while keeping a sharp eye out for anyone who might notice the two of them.

Jerónima said: 'The duke of Guise is planning to invade England.'

'God's body!' said Ned. 'How—'

'Be quiet and listen,' she snapped. 'Otherwise I won't have time to tell you everything.'

'Sorry.'

'There will be two incursions, one on the east coast and one on the south.'

Ned had to ask: 'How many men?'

'I don't know.'

'Please go on.'

'There's not much more. Both armies will muster local support and march on London.'

'This information is priceless.' Ned thanked God that Jerónima hated the Catholic Church for torturing her father. It struck him that her motivation was similar to his own: he had hated authoritarian religion ever since his family had been ruined by Bishop Julius and his cronies. Any time his determination weakened, he thought of how they had stolen everything his mother had worked for all her life, and how a strong and clever woman had seemed to fade away until her merciful death. The pain of the memory flared like an old wound, and reinforced Ned's will.

He glanced sideways at Jerónima. Close up, he could see the

lines on her face, and he sensed a hard cynicism below her sensual surface. She had become Romero's mistress when she was eighteen. She had done well to maintain his affection into her forties, but it had to be a strain.

'Thank you for telling me,' he said. His gratitude was heartfelt. But there was something else he needed to know. 'The duke of Guise must have English collaborators.'

'I'm sure.'

'Do you know who they are?'

'No. Remember, my source of information is pillow talk. I don't get to ask probing questions. If I did, I would fall under suspicion.'

'I understand, of course.'

'What news of Barney?' she said, and Ned detected a wistful note.

'He spends his life at sea. He has never married. But he has a son, nineteen years old.'

'Nineteen,' she said wonderingly. 'Where do the years go?'

'His name is Alfo. He shows some signs of having his father's aptitude for making money.'

'A clever boy, then – like all the Willards.'

'He is clever, yes.'

'Give Barney my love, Ned.'

'One more thing.'

'Make it quick – Romero is coming.'

Ned needed a permanent channel through which to communicate with Jerónima. He improvised hastily. 'When you get back to Madrid, a man will come to your house to sell you a cream to keep your face young.' He was fairly sure he could arrange that through English merchants in Spain.

She smiled ruefully. 'I use plenty of that kind of thing.'

'Any information you give him will reach me in London.'

'I understand.' She turned away from Ned and beamed at the cardinal, sticking out her chest as she did so. They walked away together, Jerónima wiggling her ample behind. Ned thought they looked sad: a no-longer-young prostitute making the most of her tired charms to retain the affection of a corrupt, pot-bellied old priest.

Sometimes Ned felt he lived in a rotten world.

*

THE ILLNESS OF Odette excited Pierre even more than the invasion of England.

Odette was the only obstacle on his path to greatness. He was the duke's principal advisor, listened to more carefully and trusted farther than ever before. He lived in a suite of rooms in the palace in the Vieille rue du Temple with Odette, Alain, and their long-time maid Nath. He had been given the lordship of a small village in Champagne, which permitted him to call himself *sieur de Mesnil*, a member of the gentry though not of the nobility. Perhaps Duke Henri would never make him a count, but the French aristocracy had won the right to appoint men to high clerical office without approval from Rome, and he could have asked Duke Henri to make him abbot of a monastery, or even a bishop – if only he had not been married.

But perhaps now Odette would die. That thought filled him with a hope that was almost painful. He would be free, free to rise up in the councils of the mighty, with almost no limit to how high he might go.

Odette's symptoms were pain after eating, diarrhoea, bloody stools, and tiredness. She had always been heavy, but her fat had melted away, probably because the pain discouraged her from eating. Doctor Paré had diagnosed stomach fever complicated by dry heat, and said she should drink plenty of weak beer and watered wine.

Pierre's only dread was that she might recover.

Unfortunately, Alain took good care of her. He had abandoned his studies and rarely left her bedside. Pierre despised the boy, but he was surprisingly well liked by the staff of the palace, who felt sorry for him because his mother was ill. He had arranged to have meals sent to their suite, and he slept on the floor of her room.

When he could, Pierre fed Odette all the things Paré said she should avoid: brandy and strong wine, spices and salty food. This often gave her muscle cramps and headaches, and her breath became foul. If he could have had the exclusive care of Odette he might have killed her this way, but Alain was never absent long enough.

When she began to get better, Pierre saw the prospect of a bishopric receding from his destiny, and he felt desperate.

The next time Dr Paré called he said Odette was on the mend, and Pierre's heart sank farther. The sweet prospect of freedom from this vulgar woman began to fade, and he felt disappointment like a wound.

'She should drink a strengthening potion now,' the doctor said. He asked for pen, paper and ink, which Alain quickly supplied. 'The Italian apothecary across the street, Giglio, can make this up for you in a few minutes – it's just honey, liquorice, rosemary and pepper.' He wrote on the piece of paper and handed it to Alain.

A wild thought came into Pierre's head. Without working out the details he decided to get rid of Alain. He gave the boy a coin and said: 'Go and get it now.'

Alain was reluctant. He looked at Odette, who had fallen asleep on her feather pillow. 'I don't like to leave her.'

Could he possibly have divined the mad idea that had inspired Pierre? Surely not.

'Send Nath,' Alain said.

'Nath went to the fish market. You go to the apothecary. I'll keep an eye on Odette. I won't leave her alone, don't worry.'

Still Alain hesitated. He was scared of Pierre – most people were scared of Pierre – but he could be stubborn at times.

Paré said: 'Go along, lad. The sooner she drinks that potion, the sooner she will recover.'

Alain could hardly defy the doctor, and he left the room.

Pierre said dismissively: 'Thank you for your diligence, doctor. It's much appreciated.'

'I'm always glad to help a member of the Guise family, of course.'

'I'll be sure to tell Duke Henri.'

'How is the duke?'

Pierre was desperate to get Paré out of the room before

Alain returned. 'Very well,' he answered. Odette made a faint noise in her sleep, and Pierre said: 'I think she wants the piss pot.'

'I'll leave you, then,' said Paré, and he went out.

This was Pierre's chance. His heart was in his mouth. He could solve all his problems now, in a few minutes.

He could kill Odette.

Two things had kept him from doing it before she fell ill. One was her physical strength: he had not been sure he could overpower her. The other was the fear of Cardinal Charles's wrath. Charles had warned that if Odette died he would destroy Pierre, regardless of the circumstances.

But now Odette was weak and Charles was dead.

Would Pierre be suspected anyway? He took pains to play the role of devoted husband. Charles had not been fooled, nor had Alain, but others had, including Henri, who knew nothing of the history. Alain might accuse Pierre, but Pierre would be able to portray Alain as a bereaved son hysterically blaming his stepfather for a quite natural death. Henri would believe that story.

Pierre closed the door.

He looked at the sleeping Odette with loathing. Being bullied into marrying her had been his ultimate humiliation. He found himself shaking with a passionate desire. This would be his ultimate revenge.

He dragged a heavy chair across the room and pushed it up against the door so that no one could come in.

The noise woke Odette. She raised her head and said anxiously: 'What's happening?'

Pierre tried to make his voice soothing as he replied: 'Alain is getting you a strengthening potion from the apothecary.' He crossed the room to the bed.

Odette sensed danger. In a frightened voice she said: 'Why have you barred the door?'

'So that you're not disturbed,' Pierre said, and with that he snatched the feather pillow from under her head and put it over her face. He was just quick enough to stifle the scream that started from her throat.

She struggled with surprising energy. She managed to get her head out from under the pillow and draw a panicked breath before he was able to push it over her nose and mouth again. She wriggled so much that he had to get onto the bed and kneel on her chest. Even then she was able to use her arms, and she rained punches on his ribs and belly so that he had to grit his teeth to bear the pain and keep pressing the pillow.

He felt she might prevail, and he might fail to put an end to her; and that panicky thought gave him extra strength, and he pushed down with all his might.

At last she weakened. Her punches became feeble, then her arms dropped helplessly to her sides. Her legs kicked a few more times then went still. Pierre kept pressing on the pillow. He did not want to take the risk that she could revive. He hoped Alain would not return yet – surely it must take Giglio more time than this to make up the mixture?

Pierre had never killed anyone. He had been responsible for the deaths of hundreds of heretics and many innocent bystanders, and he still had bad dreams about the piles of naked bodies on the streets of Paris during the Massacre of St Bartholomew's Day. Even now he was planning a war with England that would kill thousands. But no one had died by his own hand until now. This was different. Odette's soul was leaving her body while he stopped her breathing. It was a terrible thing.

When she had been still for a couple of minutes he cautiously lifted the pillow and looked at her face, gaunt from her illness. She was not breathing. He put his hand on her chest and felt no heartbeat.

She was gone.

He was possessed by exultation. Gone!

He replaced the pillow under her head. She looked peaceful in death. There was no sign on her face of the violence of her end.

His thrill of triumph passed its peak and he began to think about the danger of discovery. He moved the chair from the door. He was not sure exactly where it had stood before. Surely no one would notice?

Looking around for anything that might cause suspicion, he saw that the bedclothes were unusually rumpled, so he straightened them over Odette's body.

Then he did not know what to do.

He wanted to leave the room, but he had promised Alain that he would stay, and he would look guilty if he fled. Better to feign innocence. But he could hardly bear to be in the room with the corpse. He had hated Odette, and he was glad she was dead, but he had committed a terrible sin.

He realized that God would know what he had done even if no one else did. He had murdered his wife. How would he obtain forgiveness for such a sin?

Her eyes were still open. He was afraid to look at them for fear they would look back. He would have liked to close them, but he dreaded to touch the corpse.

He tried to pull himself together. Father Moineau had always assured him of forgiveness, for he was doing God's work. Did not the same apply here? No, of course not. This had been an act of utter selfishness. He had no excuse.

He felt doomed. His hands were shaking, he saw – the hands that had held the pillow over Odette's face so firmly that she had suffocated. He sat on a bench by the window and stared out, so that he did not have to look at Odette; but then he had to turn around every few seconds to assure himself that she was lying still, for he could not help imagining her corpse sitting up in bed, turning its sightless face towards him, pointing an accusing finger, and silently mouthing the words *He murdered me.*

At last the door opened and Alain came in. Pierre suffered a moment of pure panic, and almost shouted It *was me,* I *killed her!* Then his usual calm returned. 'Hush,' he said, though Alain had made little noise. 'She's sleeping.'

'No, she's not,' said Alain. 'Her eyes are open.' He frowned. 'You straightened the bedclothes.'

'They were a bit rumpled.'

Alain's voice showed faint surprise. 'That was nice of you.' Then he frowned again. 'Why did you move the chair?'

Pierre was dismayed that Alain had noticed these trivial details. He could not think of an innocent reason for moving the chair, so he resorted to denial. 'It's where it always was.'

Alain looked puzzled but did not persist. He put a bottle on the little side table, and gave Pierre a handful of coins in change. He spoke to the dead body. 'I got your medicine, Mother,' he said. 'You can have some right away. It has to be mixed with water or wine.'

Pierre wanted to scream at him: *Look at her – she's dead!*

There was a jug of wine and a cup on the side table. Alain poured some of the potion into the cup, added wine from the jug, and stirred the mixture with a knife. Then – at last – he approached the bed. 'Let's get you sitting up,' he said. Then he looked hard at her and frowned. 'Mother?' His voice fell to a whisper. 'Blessed Mary, no!' He dropped the cup to the floor and the potion spilled oleaginously across the tiles.

Pierre watched him with horrid fascination. After a frozen moment of shock, Alain bounded forward and bent over the still form. 'Mother!' he shouted, as if a louder voice could bring her back.

Pierre said: 'Is something wrong?'

Alain grabbed Odette by the shoulders and lifted her. Her head flopped back lifelessly.

Pierre moved to the bed, judiciously standing on the side opposite Alain, out of striking range. He was not afraid of Alain physically – it was the other way around – but it would be better to avoid a brawl. 'What's the matter?' he said.

Alain stared at him in hatred. 'What have you done?'

'Nothing but watch over her,' Pierre said. 'But she seems to be unconscious.'

Alain laid her gently back on the bed, with her head on the pillow that had killed her. He touched her chest, feeling for a heartbeat; then her neck, for a pulse. Finally, he put his cheek next to her nose, to see if there was any breath. He stifled a sob. 'She's dead.'

'Are you sure?' Pierre touched her chest himself, then

nodded sadly. 'How terrible,' he said. 'And we thought she was recovering.'

'She was! You killed her, you devil.'

'You're very upset, Alain.'

'I don't know what you did, but you killed her.'

Pierre stepped to the door and shouted for a servant. 'In here! Anybody! Quickly!'

Alain said: 'I'm going to kill you.'

The threat was laughable. 'Don't say things you don't mean.'

'I will,' Alain repeated. 'You've gone too far this time. You've murdered my mother, and I'm going to get you back. If it takes me as long as I live, I will kill you with my own hands, and watch you die.'

For a brief moment, Pierre felt a chill of fear. Then he shook it off. Alain was not going to kill anyone.

He looked along the corridor and saw Nath approaching, carrying a basket, evidently back from the market. 'Come here, Nath,' he said. 'Quickly. A very sad thing has happened.'

*

SYLVIE PUT ON a black hat with a heavy veil and went to the funeral of Odette Aumande de Guise.

She wanted to stand beside Nath and Alain, both of whom were terribly upset; and she also felt an odd emotional link with Odette, because they had both married Pierre.

Ned did not come. He had gone to the cathedral of Notre Dame to see which prominent English Catholics were in Paris: perhaps the men who were collaborating with the duke of Guise might be foolish enough to reveal themselves.

It was a rainy day and the graveyard was muddy. Most of the mourners looked, to Sylvie, like minor Guise family members and maids. The only prominent ones who came were Véronique, who had known Odette since they were both adolescents, and Pierre himself, pretending to be stricken with grief.

Sylvie watched Pierre nervously, even though she felt sure he would not penetrate her disguise. She was right: he did not even look at her.

Only Nath and Alain wept.

When it was over, and Pierre and most of the mourners had departed, Sylvie, Nath and Alain stood under the canopy of an oak tree to talk.

'I think he killed her,' Alain said.

Alain had the Guise good looks, Sylvie noticed, even with his eyes red from crying. 'But she was ill,' Sylvie said.

'I know. But I left her alone with him for just a few minutes, to fetch a potion from the apothecary, and when I got back she was dead.'

'I'm so sorry,' said Sylvie. She had no idea whether what Alain said was true, but she felt sure Pierre was capable of murder.

'I'm going to leave the palace,' Alain said. 'I have no reason to stay now that she's not there.'

'Where will you go?'

'I can move into my college.'

Nath said: 'I have to leave, too. I've been dismissed. Pierre always hated me.'

'Oh, dear! What will you do?'

'I don't need employment. The book business keeps me run off my feet anyway.' Nath was indomitable. Since Sylvie had turned her into a spy, all those years ago, she had just become stronger and more resourceful.

But now Sylvie was perturbed. 'Do you have to leave? You're our most important source of information on Pierre and the Guises.'

'I've no choice. He's kicked me out.'

'Can't you plead with him?' Sylvie said desperately.

'You know better than that.'

Sylvie did. No amount of pleading would make Pierre reverse an act of meanness.

This was a serious problem – but, Sylvie saw immediately, there was an obvious solution. She turned to Alain. 'You could stay with Pierre, couldn't you?'

'No.'

'We need to know what he's doing!'

Alain looked tortured. 'I can't live with the man who murdered my mother!'

'But you believe in the true, Protestant religion.'

'Of course.'

'And it's our duty as believers to spread the word.'

'I know.'

'The best way for you to serve the cause might be to tell me what your stepfather is up to.'

He looked torn. 'Would it?'

'Become his secretary, make yourself indispensable to him.'

'Last week I swore to him that I would kill him in revenge.'

'He will soon forget that – too many people have sworn to kill Pierre. But surely the best way to avenge her death – and the way that would please the Lord – would be to cripple his efforts to crush the true religion.'

Alain said thoughtfully: 'It would honour my mother's memory.'

'Exactly.'

Then he wavered again. 'I'll have to think about it.'

Sylvie glanced at Nath, who discreetly pointed at herself in a gesture that meant *Leave this to me, I'll take care of it*. She probably could, Sylvie decided: she had been a second mother to Alain.

Sylvie said to Alain: 'I can't overstate how important it is for us to know about English Catholics who contact the Guise family.'

'There was a big meeting at the palace last week,' Alain said. 'They're talking about invading England.'

'That's terrifying.' Sylvie did not say that she already knew about the meeting. Ned had taught her never to let a spy know that there were other sources of information: that was a cardinal rule of the game. 'Were there any Englishmen at the meeting?'

'Yes, one, a priest from the English College. My stepfather has met with him several times. He's going to contact Mary Stuart and make sure she supports the invasion.'

Jerónima Ruiz had not known this crucial piece of information. Sylvie could hardly wait to tell Ned. But there was one more key fact she needed. 'Who is this priest?' she said, and she held her breath.

Alain said: 'He goes by the name of Jean Langlais.'

Sylvie breathed a sigh of satisfaction. 'Does he, now?' she said. 'Well, well.'

23

SHEFFIELD CASTLE WAS ONE of the more uncomfortable prisons in which Alison had spent the last fifteen years with Mary Stuart. It was three hundred years old, and felt it. The place was built at the confluence of two rivers and had a moat on the other two sides, and to say it was damp was a grim understatement. Its owner, the earl of Shrewsbury, had quarrelled with Queen Elizabeth about the meagre allowance she gave him for Mary's keep; and in consequence Shrewsbury provided the cheapest food and drink.

The only redeeming feature of the place was a deer park of four square miles just across the moat.

Mary was allowed to ride in the park, though she always had to be accompanied by an escort of armed guards. On days when she did not want to ride, for any reason, Alison was allowed to go into the park on her own: no one cared if she escaped. She had a black pony called Garçon who was well-behaved most of the time.

As soon as she had the avenue of walnut trees in front of her she galloped Garçon for a quarter of a mile, to burn off his excess energy. After that he was more obedient.

Riding fast gave her a feeling of freedom that was brief and illusory. When she slowed Garçon to a walk, she remembered that she lived in a prison. She asked herself why she stayed. No one would stop her if she went back to Scotland, or France. But she was a prisoner of hope.

She had lived her life in hope – and disappointment. She had waited for Mary to become queen of France, then that had lasted less than two years. Mary had come home to rule Scotland, but had never been truly accepted as queen, and in the end they had forced her to abdicate. Now she was the rightful queen of England, recognized as such by everyone – except the English. But there were thousands, perhaps millions, of loyal Catholics here who would fight for her and acclaim her as their queen, and now Alison was waiting and hoping for the moment when they would get the chance to do just that.

It was a long time coming.

As she was passing through a grove, a man she did not know stepped from behind a massive oak tree and stood in front of her.

He startled Garçon, who skittered sideways. Alison brought the pony under control swiftly, but not before the stranger had come close enough to grab the bridle.

'Let go of my horse, or I'll have you flogged,' she said firmly.

'I mean you no harm,' he said.

'Then let go.'

He released the bridle and stepped back a pace.

He was a little under fifty years old, she guessed; his hair thinning on top, his reddish beard bushy. He did not seem very threatening, and perhaps he had taken the bridle only to help her control the horse.

He said: 'Are you Alison McKay?'

She lifted her chin in the universal gesture of superiority. 'When I married my husband I became Lady Ross, and when I buried him a year later I became the dowager Lady Ross, but I was Alison McKay once, a long time ago. Who are you?'

'Jean Langlais.'

Alison reacted to the name, saying: 'I've heard of you. But you're not French.'

'I am a messenger from France. To be exact, from Pierre Aumande de Guise.'

'I know him.' She recalled a young man with waves of blond hair and an air of ruthless competence. She had wanted him on her side, and imagined them as a team, but that had not been their destiny. He was no longer young, of course. 'How is Pierre?'

'He is the right-hand man of the duke of Guise.'

'A bishop, perhaps, or even an archbishop? No, of course

not, he's married.' To a servant girl who had been impregnated by one of the rowdy Guise adolescents, she remembered. Much to Alison's regret.

'His wife died recently.'

'Ah. Now watch him rise. He may end up as Pope. What's his message?'

'Your imprisonment is almost over.'

Alison's heart leaped in optimism, but she suppressed her elation. It was easy to say: *Your imprisonment is almost over.* Making it happen was another thing. She kept her expression neutral as she said: 'How so?'

'The duke of Guise plans to invade England, with the backing of King Felipe of Spain and Pope Gregory XIII. Mary Stuart must be the symbolic leader of this army. They will free her and put her on the throne.'

Could this be true? Alison hardly dared to think so. She considered what she should say. To gain time she pretended to muse. 'Last time I saw Henri de Guise he was a little blond boy ten years old, and now he wants to conquer England.'

'The Guises are second only to the royal family in France. If he says he will conquer England, he will. But he needs to know that his cousin Mary will play to the full her role in this revolution.'

Alison studied him. His face was lean and handsome, but his looks gave an impression of flinty ruthlessness. He reminded her somewhat of Pierre. She made her decision. 'I can give you that guarantee here and now.'

Jean Langlais shook his head. 'Duke Henri will not take your word for it – nor mine, come to that. He wants it in writing, from Mary.'

Alison's hopes faded again. That would be difficult. 'You know that all her outgoing and incoming letters are read by a man called Sir Ned Willard.' Alison had met the young Ned Willard at St Dizier, with Mary's half-brother James Stuart, and then again at Carlisle Castle. Like Pierre, Ned had come a long way.

Recognition flickered in Langlais's eyes, and Alison guessed that he, too, knew Ned. He said: 'We need to set up a secret channel of communication.'

'You and I can meet here. I get to ride out alone about once a week.'

He shook his head. 'That might do for now. I've been observing the castle, and I see that security around Queen Mary is slack. But it may be tightened up. We need a means that is more difficult to detect.'

Alison nodded. He was right. 'What do you suggest?'

'I was going to ask you that. Is there a servant, someone who routinely goes in and out of Sheffield Castle, who might be persuaded to smuggle letters?'

Alison considered. She had done this before, at Loch Leven, and she could do it again. Many people called at the castle every day. They had to supply food and drink and everything else needed by Queen Mary and her entourage of thirty people – even an imprisoned monarch had a court. And that was on top of family and hangers-on of the earl of Shrewsbury. But which of the callers could be charmed, bullied or bribed into this dangerous business?

Alison's mind went to Peg Bradford, a plain, raw-boned girl of eighteen who came to collect the soiled linen and took it home to wash it. She had never before seen a queen, and made no secret of her worship of Mary Stuart. The queen of Scots was past forty now, and her beauty had gone; captivity had made her heavy, and her once-luxuriant hair had deteriorated so much that in company she wore an auburn wig. But she was still that fairy-tale figure, an ill-fated queen, nobly suffering cruelty and injustice, irresistibly seductive to some people. Mary played up to Peg almost automatically, hardly thinking about it: to such people she was always regal but friendly, so that they thought she was marvellously warm and human. If you were a queen, Alison knew, you did not have to do much to be loved.

'A laundress called Peg Bradford,' Alison said. 'She lives in Brick Street next to St John's church.'

'I'll make contact. But you need to prepare her.'

'Of course.' That would be easy. Alison could picture Mary

holding Peg's hand, talking to her in a low, confidential voice. She could imagine the joy and devotion on Peg's face when she was entrusted with a special task for the queen.

'Tell her that a stranger will come,' said Langlais. 'With a purse of gold.'

*

IN SHOREDITCH, JUST outside the east wall of the city of London, between a slaughterhouse and a horse pond, there stood a building called The Theatre.

When it was built no one in England had ever seen a structure like it. A cobbled courtyard in the middle was surrounded by an octagon of tiered wooden galleries under a tile roof. From one of the eight sides a platform, called a stage, jutted out into the yard. The Theatre had been purpose-built for the performance of plays, and was much more suitable than the inn yards and halls where such events were normally put on.

Rollo Fitzgerald went there on an autumn afternoon in 1583. He was tailing Francis Throckmorton. He needed to forge one more link in the chain of communication between the duke of Guise and the queen of Scots.

His sister Margery did not know that he was in England. He preferred it that way. She must never get even a suspicion of what he was doing. She continued to smuggle priests from the English College into the country, but she hated the idea of Christians fighting each other. If she knew he was fomenting an insurrection, she would make trouble. She might even betray the plot, so strongly did she believe in nonviolence.

However, all was going well. He could hardly believe that the plan was working with no snags. It had to be the will of God.

The laundress Peg Bradford had proved as easy to persuade as Alison had forecast. She would have smuggled letters in the laundry just to please Queen Mary, and the bribe Rollo gave her had been almost superfluous. She had no idea that what she was doing could lead her to the gallows. Rollo had felt a twinge of guilt about persuading such an unworldly and well-meaning girl to become a traitor.

At the other end of the chain, Pierre Aumande de Guise had arranged for his letters to Mary to be held at the French embassy in London.

All Rollo needed now was someone to pick up the letters in London and deliver them to Peg in Sheffield; and Throckmorton was his choice.

Admission to The Theatre was a penny. Throckmorton paid an additional penny to get into the covered gallery, and a third penny to rent a stool. Rollo followed him in and stood behind and above him, watching for an opportunity to speak to him quietly and inconspicuously.

Throckmorton came from a wealthy and distinguished family whose motto was *Virtue is the only nobility*. His father had flourished during the reign of the late Mary Tudor, but had fallen from favour under Elizabeth Tudor, just like Rollo's father. And Throckmorton's father had eagerly agreed to harbour one of Rollo's secret priests.

Throckmorton was expensively dressed, with an extravagant white ruff. He was not yet thirty, but his hair was receding into a widow's peak which, together with his sharp nose and pointed beard, gave him a bird-like look. After studying at Oxford, Throckmorton had travelled to France and contacted English Catholic exiles, which was how Rollo knew of his leanings. However, they had never actually met, and Rollo was far from certain that he could persuade Throckmorton to risk his life in the cause.

The play was called *Ralph Roister Doister*, which was also the name of the main character, a braggart whose actions never matched his words. His boasting was exploited, by the impish Matthew Merrygreek, to get him entangled in absurd situations which made the whole place rock with laughter. Rollo was reminded of the African playwright Terence, who had written in Latin in the second century BC. All students had to read the plays of Terence. Rollo enjoyed himself so much that for a few minutes he even forgot his deadly mission.

Then an interval was announced and he remembered.

He followed Throckmorton outside and stood behind him in a queue to buy a cup of wine. Moving closer, Rollo said quietly, 'Bless you, my son.'

Throckmorton looked startled.

Rollo was not wearing priestly robes, but he discreetly reached inside his shirt collar, grasped the gold cross that he wore under his clothes, showed it to Throckmorton for a second, then dropped it out of sight. The cross identified him as a Catholic: Protestants believed it was superstitious to wear one.

Throckmorton said: 'Who are you?'

'Jean Langlais.'

It had crossed Rollo's mind that he might use other false names, to confuse his trail even more. But the name of Jean Langlais had begun to acquire an aura. It represented a mysteriously powerful figure, a ghost-like being moving silently between England and France, working secretly for the Catholic cause. It had become an asset.

'What do you want?'

'God has work for you to do.'

Throckmorton's face showed excitement and fear as he thought what this might mean. 'What sort of work?'

'You must go to the French embassy – after dark, cloaked and hooded – and ask for the letters from Monsieur de Guise, then take those letters to Sheffield and give them to a laundress called Peg Bradford. After that you must wait until Peg gives you some letters in return, which you will bring back to the embassy. That's all.'

Throckmorton nodded slowly. 'Sheffield is where Mary Queen of Scots is imprisoned.'

'Yes.'

There was a long pause. 'I could be hanged for this.'

'Then you would enter heaven all the sooner.'

'Why don't you do it yourself?'

'Because you are not the only one who has been chosen by God to do his work. In England there are thousands of young men like yourself eager for change. My role is to tell them what they can do in the struggle to restore the true faith. I, too, am likely to go to heaven sooner rather than later.'

They reached the head of the line and bought their drinks. Rollo led Throckmorton away from the crowd. They stood on the edge of the pond, looking at the black water. Throckmorton said: 'I have to think about this.'

'No, you don't.' That was the last thing Rollo wanted. He needed Throckmorton to commit. 'The Pope has excommunicated the false queen, Elizabeth, and forbidden Englishmen to obey her. It's your holy duty to help the true queen of England regain her throne. You know that, don't you?'

Throckmorton took a gulp of wine. 'Yes, I know it,' he said.

'Then give me your hand and say you will play your part.'

Throckmorton hesitated for a long moment. Then he looked Rollo in the eye and said: 'I'll do it.'

They shook hands.

*

IT TOOK NED a week to get to Sheffield.

Such a distance, 170 miles, could be covered faster by someone who kept horses permanently stabled at intervals along the route, so that he could change mounts several times a day; but that was mainly done by merchants who needed a regular courier service between cities such as Paris and Antwerp, because news was money to them. There was no courier service between London and Sheffield.

The journey gave him plenty of time to worry.

His nightmare was coming true. The French ultra-Catholics, the king of Spain and the Pope had at last agreed on joint action. They made a deadly combination. Between them they had the power and the money to launch an invasion of England. Already spies were making plans of the harbours where the invaders would land. Ned had no doubt that discontented Catholic noblemen such as Earl Bart were sharpening their swords and burnishing their armour.

And now, worst of all, Mary Stuart was involved.

Ned had received a message from Alain de Guise in Paris, via the English embassy there. Alain continued to live with

Pierre and spy on him: this was his revenge. Pierre, for his part, treated his stepson as a harmless drudge, made him run errands, and seemed to like having him around as a dogsbody.

Alain's message said Pierre was rejoicing that he had succeeded in making contact with the queen of the Scots.

This was bad news. Mary's approval would give the whole treasonous enterprise a cloak of holy respectability. To many she was the rightful queen of England, and Elizabeth the usurper. Under Mary's auspices, a gang of foreign thugs became an army of righteousness in the eyes of the world.

It was maddening. After all that Elizabeth had achieved, bringing religious peace and commercial prosperity to England for twenty-five years, they still would not leave her be.

Ned's task of protecting Elizabeth was made more difficult by personal court rivalries – as happened so often in politics. His Puritan master, Walsingham, clashed with the fun-loving Robert Dudley, earl of Leicester. 'Secret codes, and invisible ink!' Leicester would jeer when he ran into Walsingham in the palace of White Hall or the garden of Hampton Court. 'Power is won with guns and bullets, not pens and ink!' He could not persuade the queen to get rid of Walsingham – she was too smart for that – but his scepticism reinforced her miserliness, and the work done by Walsingham and his men was never properly financed.

Ned could have reached Sheffield at the end of his sixth day of travel. However, he did not want to arrive muddy-stockinged and road-weary, in case he needed to impose his authority. So he stopped at an inn two miles outside the town. Next day he got up early, put on a clean shirt, and arrived at the gate of Sheffield Castle at eight in the morning.

It was a formidable fortress, but he was irritated to see that security was careless. He crossed the bridge over the moat along with three other people: a girl with two lidded buckets that undoubtedly contained milk; a brawny builder's lad carrying a long timber on his shoulder, presumably for some repair work; and a carter with a vertiginous load of hay. Three or four people were coming the other way. None of them was challenged by the two armed guards at the gate, who were eating mutton chops and throwing the bones into the moat.

Ned sat on his horse in the middle of the inner courtyard, looking around, getting his bearings. There was a turret house that he guessed would be Mary's prison. The hay cart rumbled over to a building that was clearly the stable block. A third building, the least uncomfortable-looking, would be where the earl lived.

He walked his horse to the stable. Summoning his most arrogant voice, he shouted at a young groom: 'Hey! You! Take my horse.' He dismounted.

The startled boy took the bridle.

Pointing, Ned said: 'I presume I'll find the earl in that building?'

'Yes, sir. May I ask the name?'

'Sir Ned Willard, and you'd better remember it.' With that Ned stalked off.

He pushed open the wooden door of the house and entered a small hall with a smoky fire. To one side an open door revealed a gloomy medieval great hall with no one in it.

The elderly porter was not as easy to bully as the groom. He stood barring the way and said: 'Good day to you, master.' He had good manners, but as a guard he was next to useless: Ned could have knocked him down with one hand.

'I am Sir Ned Willard, with a message from Queen Elizabeth. Where is the earl of Shrewsbury?'

The porter took a moment to size Ned up. Someone with nothing but 'sir' in front of his name was below an earl on the social scale. On the other hand, it was not wise to offend a messenger from the queen. 'It's an honour to welcome you to the house, Sir Ned,' said the porter tactfully. 'I'll go immediately to see whether the earl is ready to receive you.'

He opened a door off the hall, and Ned glimpsed a dining room.

The door closed, but Ned heard the porter say: 'My lord, are you able to see Sir Ned Willard with a message from her majesty Queen Elizabeth?'

Ned did not wait. He opened the door and barged in,

stepping past the startled porter. He found himself in a small room with a round table and a big fireplace – warmer and more comfortable than the great hall. Four people sat at breakfast, two of whom he knew. The extraordinarily tall fortyish woman with a double chin and a ginger wig was Mary Queen of Scots. He had last seen her fifteen years ago when he had gone to Carlisle Castle to tell her that Queen Elizabeth had made her a prisoner. The slightly older woman next to her was her companion Alison, Lady Ross, who had been with her at Carlisle and even earlier at St Dizier. Ned had not met the other two but he could guess who they were. The balding man in his fifties with a spade-shaped beard had to be the earl, and the formidable-looking woman of the same age was his wife, the countess, usually called Bess of Hardwick.

Ned's anger doubled. The earl and his wife were negligent fools who put at risk everything Elizabeth had achieved.

The earl said: 'What the devil . . . ?'

Ned said: 'I am a Jesuit spy sent by the king of France to kidnap Mary Stuart. Under my coat I have two pistols, one to murder the earl and one the countess. Outside are six of my men hiding in a cartload of hay, armed to the teeth.'

They did not know how seriously to take him. The earl said: 'Is this some kind of jest?'

'This is some kind of inspection,' Ned said. 'Her majesty Queen Elizabeth has asked me to find out how well you're guarding Mary. What shall I tell her, my lord? That I was able to enter the presence of Mary without once being challenged or searched and that I could have brought six men with me?'

The earl looked foolish. 'It would be better if you did not tell her that, I must admit.'

Mary spoke in a voice of queenly authority. 'How dare you act like this in my presence?'

Ned continued to speak to the earl. 'From now on she takes her meals in the turret house.'

Mary said: 'Your insolence is intolerable.'

Ned ignored her. He owed no courtesy to the woman who wanted to murder his queen.

Mary stood up and walked to the door, and Alison hurried after her.

Ned spoke to the countess. 'Go with them please, my lady. There are no Jesuit spies in the courtyard at the moment, but you won't know when there are, and it's as well to get into good habits.'

The countess was not used to being told what to do, but she knew she was in trouble, and she hesitated only a moment before obeying.

Ned pulled a chair up to the table. 'Now, my lord,' he said. 'Let us talk about what you need to do before I can give Queen Elizabeth a satisfactory account.'

*

BACK IN LONDON, at Walsingham's house in Seething Lane, Ned reported that Mary Stuart was now better guarded than she had been.

Walsingham went immediately to the heart of the matter. 'Can you guarantee that she is not communicating with the outside world?'

'No,' Ned said with frustration. 'Not unless we get rid of all her servants and keep her alone in a dungeon.'

'How I wish we could,' Walsingham said fervently. 'But Queen Elizabeth won't permit such harshness.'

'Our queen is soft-hearted.'

Walsingham's view of Elizabeth was more cynical. 'She knows how she could be undermined by stories about how cruel she is to her royal relative.'

Ned was not going to argue. 'Either way, we can do no more in Sheffield.'

Walsingham stroked his beard. 'Then we must focus on this end of the pipeline,' he said. 'The French embassy must be involved. See what English Catholics are among the callers there. We have a list.'

'I'll get on with it right away.'

Ned went upstairs, to the locked room where Walsingham kept the precious records, and sat down for a session of study.

The longest list was that of well-born English Catholics. It had not been difficult to make. All families who had prospered under Mary Tudor and fallen from favour under Elizabeth were automatically suspected. They confirmed their tendencies in several ways, often openly. Many paid the fine for not going to church. They dressed gaudily, scorning the sombre black and grey of devout Protestants. There was never an English-language Bible in a Catholic house. These things were reported to Walsingham by bishops and by lord lieutenants of counties.

Both Earl Bart and Margery were on this list.

But the list was too long. Most of these people were innocent of treason. Ned sometimes felt he had too much information. It could be difficult to separate the wheat from the chaff. He turned to the alphabetical register of Catholics in London. In addition to those who lived here, Walsingham received daily reports of Catholics entering and leaving the city. Visiting Catholics usually stayed at the homes of resident Catholics, or lodged at inns frequented by other Catholics. Doubtless the list was incomplete. London was a city of a hundred thousand people, and it was impossible to have spies in every street. But Walsingham and Ned did have informants in all the Catholics' regular haunts, and they were able to keep track of most comings and goings.

Ned leafed through the book. He knew hundreds of these names – lists were his life – but it was good to refresh his memory. Once again, Bart and Margery appeared, coming to stay at Shiring House in the Strand when Parliament sat.

Ned turned to the daily log of callers at the French embassy in Salisbury Square. The house was under surveillance day and night from the Salisbury Tavern across the road and had been ever since Walsingham had returned from Paris in 1573. Starting from yesterday and working backwards in time, Ned cross-checked every name with the alphabetical register.

Margery did not appear here. In fact, neither she nor Bart had ever been found to contact foreign ambassadors or other suspicious characters while in London. They socialized with other Catholics, of course, and their servants frequented a

Catholic tavern near their house called The Irish Boy. But there was nothing to link them with subversive activities.

However, many callers at the French embassy could not be identified by name. Frustratingly, the log had too many entries of the form *Unknown man delivering coal, Unidentified courier with letters, Woman not clearly seen in the dark*. Nevertheless, Ned persisted, hoping for some clue, anything.

Then he was struck by an entry two weeks ago: *Madame Aphrodite Housse, wife of the deputy ambassador*.

In Paris, Ned had known a Mademoiselle Aphrodite Beaulieu who appeared fond of a young courtier called Bernard Housse. This had to be the same person. And if it was, Ned had saved her from a gang of rapists during the St Bartholomew's Day Massacre.

He turned back to the alphabetical register and found that Monsieur Housse, the deputy French ambassador, had a house in the Strand.

He put on his coat and went out.

Two questions wracked him as he hurried west. Did Aphrodite know the name of the courier to Sheffield? And, if she did, would she feel sufficiently indebted to Ned to tell him the secret?

He was going to find out.

He left the walled city of London at Ludgate, crossed the stinking Fleet River, and found the Housse residence, a pleasant modest house on the less expensive north side of the Strand. He knocked at the door and gave his name to a maid. He waited a few minutes, considering the remote possibility that Bernard Housse had married a different Aphrodite. Then he was shown upstairs to a comfortable small parlour.

He remembered an eager, flirtatious girl of eighteen, but now he saw a gracious woman of twenty-nine, with a figure that suggested she had recently given birth and might still be breast-feeding. She greeted him warmly in French. 'It *is* you,' she said. 'After so long!'

'So you married Bernard,' Ned said.

'Yes,' she answered with a contented smile.

'Any children?'

'Three – so far!'

They sat down. Ned was pessimistic. People who betrayed their countries were normally troubled, angry individuals with massive grudges, such as Alain de Guise and Jerónima Ruiz. Aphrodite was a happily married woman with children and a husband she seemed to like. The chances were slim that she would give away secrets. But Ned had to try.

He told her that he had married a French girl and brought her home, and Aphrodite wanted to meet her. She told him the names of her three children, and he memorized them because he was in the habit of memorizing names. After a few minutes of catching up, he steered the conversation in the direction he wanted it to go. 'I saved your life, once, in Paris,' he said.

She became solemn. 'I will be grateful to you for ever,' she said. 'But please – Bernard knows nothing of it.'

'Now I'm trying to save the life of another woman.'

'Really? Who?'

'Queen Elizabeth.'

She looked embarrassed. 'You and I shouldn't discuss politics, Ned.'

He persisted. 'The duke of Guise is planning to kill Elizabeth so that he can put his cousin Mary Stuart on the throne. You can't possibly approve of murder.'

'Of course not, but—'

'There's an Englishman who comes to your embassy, collects letters sent by Henri de Guise and takes them to Mary in Sheffield.' Ned hated to reveal how much he knew, but this was his only chance of persuading her. 'He then brings back Mary's replies.' Ned looked hard at Aphrodite as he spoke, studying her reaction, and thought he saw a flicker of recognition in her eyes. 'You probably know the man,' he said insistently.

'Ned, this is not fair.'

'I have to know his name,' Ned said. He was dismayed to hear a note of desperation in his own voice.

'How can you do this to me?'

'I have to protect Queen Elizabeth from wicked men, as I once protected you.'

Aphrodite stood up. 'I'm sorry you came here, if your purpose was to get information out of me.'

'I'm asking you to save the life of a queen.'

'You're asking me to be a traitor to my husband and my country, and betray a man who has been a guest at my father's house!'

'You owe me!'

'I owe you my life, not my soul.'

Ned knew he was defeated. He felt ashamed for even trying. He had attempted to corrupt a perfectly decent woman who liked him. Sometimes he detested his work.

He stood up. 'I'll leave you,' he said.

'I'm afraid I think you should.'

Something was nagging at the back of his mind. He felt she had said something important that he had overlooked in the heat of the argument. He wanted to prolong his visit and ask more questions until she said it again, but she was looking angrily at him, visibly impatient to see the back of him, and he knew that if he did not go, she would just walk out of the room.

He took his leave and dejectedly returned to the city. He climbed Ludgate Hill and passed the Gothic bulk of St Paul's Cathedral, its grey stones turned black by the soot from thousands of London fireplaces. He came within sight of the Tower, where traitors were interrogated and tortured, then he turned down Seething Lane.

As he entered Walsingham's house, he remembered what Aphrodite had said: 'You're asking me to be a traitor to my husband and my country, and betray a man who has been a guest at my father's house!'

A man who has been a guest at my father's house.

The very first list Ned had made, when he arrived in Paris with Walsingham eleven years ago, had been a register of English Catholics who called at the home of the count of Beaulieu in the rue St Denis.

Walsingham never threw anything away.

Ned ran up the stairs to the locked room. The book containing the Paris list was at the bottom of a chest. He pulled it out and blew off the dust.

She must have been referring to her father's Paris house, must she not? The count had a country house in France but, as far as Ned knew, that had never been a rendezvous for English exiles. And Beaulieu had never appeared in the register of Catholics living in London.

Nothing was certain.

He opened the book eagerly and began to read carefully through the names, recorded in his own handwriting a decade ago. He forced himself to go slowly, recalling the faces of those angry young Englishmen who had gone to France because they felt out of place in their own country. As he did so he was assailed by memories of Paris: the glitter of the shops, the fabulous clothes, the stink of the streets, the extravagance of the royal entertainments, the savagery of the massacre.

One name struck him like a blow. Ned had never met the man, but he knew the name.

His heart seemed to stop. He went back to the alphabetical list of Catholics in London. Yes, one man who had visited Count Beaulieu's house in Paris was now in London.

His name was Sir Francis Throckmorton.

'Got you, you devil,' said Ned.

*

WALSINGHAM SAID: 'Whatever you do, don't arrest him.'

Ned was taken aback. 'I thought that was the point.'

'Think again. There will always be another Throckmorton. We will do all we can to protect Queen Elizabeth, of course, but some day one of these traitors will slip through our fingers.'

Ned admired Walsingham's ability to think one step ahead of the current situation, but he did not know where Walsingham was going with this. 'What can we do, other than be ever-vigilant?'

'Let's make it our mission to get proof that Mary Stuart is plotting to usurp Queen Elizabeth.'

'Elizabeth will probably authorize the torture of Throckmorton, given that he has threatened her throne; and Throckmorton will naturally confess; but everyone knows that confessions are unreliable.'

'Quite so. We must get incontrovertible evidence.'

'And put Mary Stuart on trial?'

'Exactly.'

Ned was intrigued, but he still did not know what Walsingham's devious mind was planning. 'What would that achieve?'

'At a minimum, it would make Mary unpopular with the English people. All but the most extreme ultra-Catholics would disapprove of someone who wanted to unseat such a well-loved queen.'

'That won't stop the assassins.'

'It will weaken their support. And it will strengthen our hand when we ask for the conditions of Mary's imprisonment to be made harsher.'

Ned nodded agreement. 'And Elizabeth will be less worried about being accused of unfeminine cruelty to her cousin. But still . . .'

'It would be even better if we could prove that Mary plotted not only to overthrow Queen Elizabeth but to murder her.'

At last Ned began to see the trend of Walsingham's thinking, and he was startled by its ruthlessness. 'Do you want Mary sentenced to death?'

'Yes.'

Ned found that chilling. To execute a queen was the next thing to sacrilege. 'But Queen Elizabeth would never execute Mary.'

'Even if we proved that Mary had conspired to assassinate Elizabeth?'

'I don't know,' said Ned.

'Nor do I,' said Walsingham.

*

NED PUT THROCKMORTON under twenty-four-hour surveillance.

Aphrodite had surely told her husband about Ned's call, and the French embassy must have warned Throckmorton. So, Ned figured, Throckmorton now knew that Ned suspected the existence of the correspondence with Mary. However, based on the same conversation, Throckmorton presumably believed that Ned did not know the identity of the courier.

The team tailing him was changed twice a day, but still there was a risk that he might notice them. However, he did not appear to. Ned guessed that Throckmorton was unaccustomed to clandestine work and simply did not think to check whether he was being followed.

Alain de Guise wrote from Paris to say that Pierre had sent an important letter to Mary Stuart by a courier. That letter would have to be smuggled to the imprisoned Mary by Throckmorton. If Throckmorton could be arrested with Pierre's letter in his hand, it might serve as objective proof of his treachery.

However, Walsingham wanted Mary, not Throckmorton. So Ned decided to wait and see whether Throckmorton got a reply from Mary. If she consented to a plot, and especially if she wrote words of encouragement, she would stand condemned.

One day in October, while Ned waited anxiously to see what Throckmorton would do, a gentleman of the court called Ralph Ventnor came to Seething Lane to say that Queen Elizabeth wanted to see Walsingham and Ned immediately. Ventnor did not know the reason.

They put on their coats and walked the short distance to the Tower, where Ventnor had a barge at the wharf waiting to take them to White Hall.

Ned fretted as they were rowed upstream. A peremptory summons was rarely good news. And Elizabeth had always been capricious. The blue sky of her approval could turn in an instant to lowering black clouds – and back again.

At White Hall, Ventnor led them through the guard room, full of soldiers, and the presence chamber, where courtiers waited, and along a passage to the privy chamber.

Queen Elizabeth sat on a carved and gilded wooden chair. She wore a red-and-white dress with a silver-gauze overdress, and sleeves slashed to show a lining of red taffeta. It was a youthfully bright outfit, but it could not hide the passage of time. Elizabeth had just passed her fiftieth birthday and her face showed her age, despite the heavy white make-up she used. When she spoke, she showed irregular brown teeth, several missing.

The earl of Leicester was also in the room. He was the same age as the queen but he, too, dressed like a wealthy youngster. Today he wore an outfit of pale-blue silk with gold embroidery, and his shirt had ruffs at the wrists as well as the neck. To Ned it looked absurdly costly.

Leicester seemed pleased with himself, Ned noticed with unease. He was probably about to score points off Walsingham.

Ned and Walsingham bowed side by side.

The queen spoke in a voice as cold as February. 'A man has been arrested in a tavern in Oxford for saying that he was on his way to London to shoot the queen.'

Oh, hell, thought Ned, we missed one. He recalled Walsingham's words: *Some day one of these traitors will slip through our fingers.*

Leicester spoke in a supercilious drawl that seemed to imply that everything was absurd. 'The man was armed with a heavy pistol, and he said that the queen was a serpent and a viper, and he would set her head on a pole.'

Trust Leicester to rub it in, Ned thought. But in truth the assassin did not sound seriously dangerous, if he was so indiscreet that he had been stopped when he was still sixty miles away from the queen.

Elizabeth said: 'Why do I pay you all this money, if not to protect me from such people?'

That was outrageous: she was paying only seven hundred and fifty pounds a year, nowhere near enough, and Walsingham financed much of the work himself. But queens did not have to be fair.

Walsingham said: 'Who is this man?'

Leicester said: 'John Somerfield.'

Ned recognized the name: it was on the list. 'We know of Somerfield, your majesty. He's one of the Warwickshire Catholics. He's mad.'

The earl of Leicester laughed sarcastically. 'So, that means he's no danger to her majesty, does it?'

Ned flushed. 'It means he's not likely to be part of a serious conspiracy, my lord.'

'Oh, good! In that case his bullets obviously can't kill anyone, can they?'

'I didn't mean—'

Leicester overrode Ned. 'Your majesty, I wish you would give someone else the task of protecting your precious person.' He added in an oily voice: 'It is the most important task in the kingdom.'

He was a skilled flatterer, and unfortunately Elizabeth was charmed.

Walsingham spoke for the first time. 'I have failed you, your majesty. I did not recognize the danger posed by Somerfield. No doubt there are many men in England who can do this job better. I beg you to give the responsibility to one of them. Speaking for myself, I would gladly put down the burden I have carried so long, and rest my weary bones.'

He did not mean this, of course, but it was probably the best way to handle the queen in her present mood. Ned realized he had been foolish to argue. If she was annoyed, then telling her she need not worry only irritated her further. Humble self-abnegation was more likely to please.

'You're the same age as me,' the queen shot back. However, she seemed mollified by Walsingham's apology; or perhaps she had been led to reflect that in fact there was no man in England who would work as hard and as conscientiously as Walsingham to protect her from the many people, mad and sane, who wanted to assassinate her. However, she was not yet ready to let Walsingham off the hook. 'What are you going to do to make me more secure?' she demanded.

'Your majesty, I am on the point of destroying a well-organized conspiracy against you by enemies of an order quite different from John Somerfield. These people will not wave their weapons in the air and boast about their intentions in taverns. They are in league with the Pope and the king of Spain, which I can assure you Somerfield is not. They are determined and well financed and obsessively secretive. Nevertheless, I expect to arrest their leader in the next few days.'

It was a spirited defence against the malice of Leicester, but all the same Ned was dismayed. This was premature. An arrest now would bring the conspiracy to an early halt, and in consequence they would not get evidence of Mary Stuart's complicity. Personal rivalry had interfered again.

The queen said: 'Who are these people?'

'For fear that they may be forewarned, your majesty, I hesitate to name names' – Walsingham looked pointedly at Leicester – 'in public.'

Leicester was about to protest indignantly, but the queen said: 'Quite right, I shouldn't have asked. Very well, Sir Francis, you'd better leave us and get back to your work.'

'Thank you, your majesty,' said Walsingham.

*

ROLLO FITZGERALD was anxious about Francis Throckmorton.

Throckmorton was not like the men who had been trained at the English College. They had made a life commitment to submit to the rule of the Church. They understood obedience and dedication. They had left England, spent years studying, taken vows, and returned home to do the job for which they had prepared. They knew their lives were at risk: every time one of them was caught by Walsingham and executed, the death was celebrated at the college as a martyrdom.

Throckmorton had made no vows. He was a wealthy young aristocrat with a romantic attachment to Catholicism. He had spent his life pleasing himself, not God. His courage and determination were untried. He might just back out.

Even if he stayed the course, there were other dangers. How discreet was he? He had no experience of clandestine work. Would he get drunk and drop boastful hints to his friends about his secret mission?

Rollo was also worried about Peg Bradford. Alison claimed Peg would do anything for Mary Queen of Scots; but Alison could be wrong, and Peg could prove unreliable.

His biggest worry was Mary herself. Would she cooperate? Without her the whole plot was nothing.

One thing at a time, he told himself. Throckmorton first.

He would have preferred to have no further contact with Throckmorton, for security, but that was not practicable. Rollo had to know whether everything was going according to plan. Reluctantly, therefore, he went to Throckmorton's house at St Paul's Wharf, downhill from the cathedral, one evening at twilight, when faces were hard to make out.

By bad luck Throckmorton was out, according to his manservant. Rollo considered going away and returning at another time, but he was impatient to know what was happening, and he told the man he would wait.

He was shown into a small parlour. A window looked onto the street. At the back of the room, a double door stood a little ajar, and Rollo looked through to a grander room behind, comfortable and richly furnished, but with a pungent smell of smoke: the manservant was burning rubbish in the backyard.

Rollo accepted a cup of wine and mused, while he waited, over his secret agents. As soon as he had established communication between Pierre in Paris and Mary in Sheffield, he would have to make a tour of England and visit his secret priests. He had to collect maps from them or from their protectors, and confirm guarantees of support for the invading army. He had time – the invasion would take place in the spring of next year – but there was much to be done.

Throckmorton came in at nightfall. Rollo heard the manservant open the door and say: 'There's a gentleman waiting in the parlour, sir – preferred not to give his name.'

Throckmorton was pleased to see Rollo. He took from his coat pocket a small package which he slapped on the table with a triumphant gesture. 'Letters for Queen Mary!' he said exultantly. 'I've just come from the French embassy.'

'Good man!' Rollo jumped up and began to examine the letters. He recognized the seal of the duke of Guise and that of Mary's man in Paris, John Leslie. He longed to read the contents, but could not break the seals without causing trouble. 'When can you take them to Sheffield?'

'Tomorrow,' said Throckmorton.

'Excellent.'

There was a banging at the front door. Both men froze, listening. It was not the courteous tap of a friendly caller but the arrogant hammering of someone hostile. Rollo went to the window and saw, in the light of the lamp over the door, two well-dressed men. One turned his head towards the light and Rollo instantly recognized Ned Willard.

'Hell,' he said. 'Walsingham's men.'

He realized in a flash that Ned must have had Throckmorton under surveillance. Throckmorton must have been followed to the French embassy, and Ned could undoubtedly figure out why he had gone there. But how had Ned got on to Throckmorton in the first place? Rollo realized that Walsingham's secret service was a good deal more effective than anyone imagined.

And in a minute Rollo would be in their hands.

Throckmorton said: 'I'll tell my man to say I'm out.' He opened the parlour door, but he was too late: Rollo heard the front door opening and the sound of demanding voices. Everything was moving too fast.

'Go and stall them,' said Rollo.

Throckmorton stepped into the entrance hall, saying: 'Now, now, what's all this racket?'

Rollo looked at the letters on the table. They were unmistakably incriminating. If they contained what he thought they did, they would condemn him and Throckmorton to death.

The entire scheme was in jeopardy, unless Rollo could get out of this in the next few seconds.

He picked up the letters and stepped through the half-open door into the back room. It had a window onto the yard. He opened it swiftly and clambered through. As he did so he heard the voice of Ned Willard, familiar to him since childhood, coming from the parlour.

In the middle of the yard was a fire of dead leaves, kitchen sweepings and soiled straw from the stable. Looking farther down the yard he saw, in the shifting red light of the bonfire, the outline of a man approaching through the trees. He must be a third member of Ned's team, Rollo reckoned: Ned was meticulous, and he would not have omitted to cover the back exit from the house.

The man shouted at Rollo: 'Hey, you!'

Rollo had to make a split-second decision.

Throckmorton was doomed. He would be arrested and tortured, and he would tell all he knew before he was executed. But he did not know the real identity of Jean Langlais. He could betray nobody except the laundress, Peg Bradford; and she was an ignorant labourer who would do nothing with her worthless life but give birth to more ignorant labourers. Crucially, Throckmorton could not incriminate Mary Stuart. The only proof against her was in the letters Rollo held in his hand.

He crumpled the letters and threw them into the bright yellow heart of the fire.

The third man ran towards him.

Rollo stayed precious seconds to see the paper flare up, blacken, and begin crumbling into ash.

When the evidence had been destroyed he surprised the third man by running straight at him. He gave the man a violent shove, causing him to fall to the ground, and ran on past.

Rollo ran down the length of the yard. It led to the muddy beach of the river Thames.

He turned along the waterfront and kept running.

*

IN THE SPRING of 1584, Pierre went to watch the marchioness of Nîmes being evicted from her house.

Her husband, the marquess, had got away with being a Protestant for decades, but Pierre had been patient. The country house in the suburb of St Jacques had continued to be a centre for heretical activities even after Pierre's great coup in 1559 when he had had the entire congregation arrested. But now, in 1584, Paris was in thrall to an unofficial group called the Catholic League, dedicated to wiping out Protestantism, and Pierre had been able to haul the marquess before the supreme court called the Parlement of Paris and have him sentenced to death.

Pierre had never really been interested in the old marquess. The person he really hated was Marchioness Louise, now a glamorous widow in her forties. The property of heretics such as the marquess was confiscated, so his execution had left her destitute.

Pierre had waited twenty-five years for this moment.

He arrived just as the marchioness was confronting the bailiff in the entrance hall. He stood with the bailiff's men, watching, and she did not notice him.

She was surrounded by the evidence of the wealth she had lost: oil paintings of country scenes on the panelled walls, carved hall chairs gleaming with polish, marble underfoot and chandeliers above. She wore a green silk gown that seemed to flow like water over her generous hips. When she was young every man had stared at her large bust, and she was still shapely.

'How dare you?' she was saying to the bailiff in a voice of authority. 'You cannot force a noblewoman to leave her home.'

The bailiff had undoubtedly done this before. He spoke politely, but he was unyielding. 'I advise you to go quietly, my lady,' he said. 'If you don't walk, you'll be carried, which is undignified.'

She moved closer to him and pulled back her shoulders, drawing attention to her breasts. 'You can use your discretion,' she said in a warmer voice. 'Come back in a week, when I will have had time to make arrangements.'

'The court gave you time, my lady, and that time is now up.'

Neither haughtiness nor charm had worked, and she allowed her despair to show. 'I can't leave my house, I have nowhere to go!' she wailed. 'I can't even rent a room because I have no money, not one sou. My parents are dead and all my friends are terrified to help me for fear that they, too, will be accused of heresy!'

Pierre studied her, enjoying the tears on her face and the note of panic in her voice. It was the marchioness who had snubbed young Pierre, a quarter of a century ago. Sylvie had proudly introduced him to the young Louise, he had uttered some pleasantry that had displeased her, and she had said: 'Even in Champagne, they should teach young men to be respectful to their superiors.' Then she had pointedly turned her back. The memory still made him wince.

He relished the reversal of position now. He had recently been made abbot of Holy Tree, a monastery that owned thousands of acres of land in Champagne. He took the income for himself and left the monks to live in poverty, in accordance with their vows. He was rich and powerful, whereas Louise was penniless and helpless.

The bailiff said: 'The weather is warm. You can sleep in the forest. Or, if it rains, the convent of St Marie-Madeleine in the rue de la Croix takes in homeless women.'

Louise seemed genuinely shocked. 'That place is for prostitutes!'

The bailiff shrugged.

Louise began to weep. Her shoulders slumped, she covered her face with her hands, and her chest heaved with sobs.

Pierre found her distress arousing.

At that point he came to her rescue.

He stepped out of the little group by the door and stood between the bailiff and the marchioness. 'Calm yourself, Madame,' he said. 'The Guise family will not allow a noblewoman to sleep in the forest.'

She took her hands from her face and looked at him through her tears. 'Pierre Aumande,' she said. 'Have you come to mock me?'

She would suffer even more for not calling him Pierre Aumande de Guise. 'I'm here to help you in your emergency,' he said. 'If you would care to come with me, I'll take you to a place of safety.'

She remained standing where she was. 'Where?'

'An apartment has been reserved, and paid for, in a quiet neighbourhood. There is a maid. It is not lavish, but you won't be uncomfortable. Come and look at it. I feel sure it will serve you temporarily, at least.'

Clearly she did not know whether to believe him. The

Guises hated Protestants: why would they be good to her? But after a long moment of hesitation she realized she had no other options, and she said: 'Let me put some things in a bag.'

The bailiff said: 'No jewellery. I will inspect the bag as you leave.'

She made no reply, but turned on her heel and left the room with her head held high.

Pierre could hardly contain his impatience. Soon he would have this woman under his control.

The marchioness was no relation to the Guises, and stood on the opposite side in the religious war, but somehow in Pierre's mind they were the same. The Guises used him as their advisor and hatchet man but, even now, they disdained him socially. He was their most influential and highly rewarded servant, but still a servant; always invited to a council of war and never to a family dinner. He could not be revenged for that rejection. But he could punish Louise.

She returned with a leather bag stuffed full. The bailiff, true to his threat, opened it and took everything out. She had packed dozens of pieces of beautiful silk and linen underwear, embroidered and beribboned. It made Pierre think about what she might be wearing beneath her green dress today.

With characteristic arrogance she handed the bag to Pierre, as if he were a footman.

He did not disillusion her. That would come, in good time.

He led her outside. Biron and Brocard were waiting with the horses. They had brought an extra mount for the marchioness. They rode out of the Nîmes estate, entered Paris through St Jacques Gate, and followed the rue St Jacques to the Petit Pont. They crossed the Île de la Cité and made their way to a modest house not far from the Guise palace. Pierre dismissed Biron and Brocard and told them to take the horses home, then he escorted Louise inside. 'You have the top floor,' he told her.

'Who else lives here?' she said anxiously.

He answered truthfully. 'A different tenant on each floor. Most of them have done work for the Guises in the past: a retired tutor, a seamstress whose eyesight has failed, a Spanish woman who does translations occasionally. All very respectable.' And none willing to risk losing their place by displeasing Pierre.

Louise looked somewhat reassured.

They went up the stairs. Louise was panting when they reached the top. 'This climb is going to tire me out,' she complained.

Pierre was pleased. That meant she was already accepting that she would live here.

The maid bowed them in. Pierre showed Louise the salon, the kitchen, the scullery, and finally the bedroom. She was pleasantly surprised. Pierre had said it was not lavish but, in fact, he had furnished the small apartment expensively: he planned to spend time here.

Louise was evidently confused. Someone she thought of as an enemy was being generous to her. Pierre could see from her face that nothing was making sense. Good.

He closed the bedroom door, and she began to understand.

'I remember staring at these,' he said, and put his hands on her breasts.

She stepped back. 'Did you expect me to become your mistress?' she said scornfully.

Pierre smiled. 'You are my mistress,' he said, and the words delighted him. 'Take off your dress.'

'No.'

'I'll rip it off you.'

'I'll scream.'

'Go ahead and scream. The maid is expecting it.' He gave her a powerful shove and she fell back on the bed.

She said: 'No, please.'

'You don't even remember,' he snarled. '*Even in Champagne, they should teach young men to be respectful to their superiors.* That's what you said to me, twenty-five years ago.'

She stared up at him in horrified incredulity. 'And for that, you punish me like this?'

'Open your legs,' he said. 'It's only just begun.'

*

AFTERWARDS, WALKING to the Guise palace, Pierre felt as he sometimes did after a feast: sated but slightly nauseated. He loved to see an aristocrat humiliated, but this had almost been too much. He would go back, of course; but perhaps not for a few days. She was rich food.

When he arrived home, he found, waiting for him in the parlour of his apartment, Rollo Fitzgerald, the Englishman he had codenamed Jean Langlais.

Pierre was irritated. He wanted an hour to himself, to get over what he had just done, and let his turbulent thoughts become calm again. Instead he had to go right to work.

Rollo was carrying a canvas case which he now opened to produce a sheaf of maps. 'Every major harbour on the south and east coasts of England,' he said proudly. He put the maps on Pierre's writing table.

Pierre examined them. They were drawn by different hands, some more artistic than others, but they all seemed admirably clear, with moorings, quays and dangerous shallows carefully marked. 'These are good,' he said, 'though they've been a long time coming.'

'I know, and I'm sorry,' Rollo said. 'But the arrest of Throckmorton set us back.'

'What's happening to him?'

'He's been convicted of treason and sentenced to death.'

'Another martyr.'

Rollo said pointedly: 'I hope his death will not be in vain.'

'What do you mean?'

'Is the duke of Guise still determined to invade England?'

'Absolutely. He wants to see Mary Stuart on the English throne, and so does almost every important European leader.'

'Good. Mary's jailers have raised the level of security around her, but I will find a way to re-establish communication.'

'So we could begin planning the invasion for next year, 1585?'

'Absolutely.'

Pierre's stepson came into the room. 'News from Picardy,' he said. 'Hercule-Francis is dead.'

'Dear God!' said Pierre. Hercule-Francis was the youngest

son of the late King Henri and Queen Caterina. 'This is a catastrophe,' Pierre said to Rollo. 'He was the heir to the throne.'

Rollo frowned. 'But there's nothing wrong with King Henri III,' he said. 'Why are you worried about his heir?'

'Henri is the third brother to be king. The previous two died young and without sons, so Henri may do the same.'

'So, now that Hercule-Francis is dead, who is the heir to the throne?'

'That's the disaster. It's the king of Navarre. And he's a Protestant.'

Rollo said indignantly: 'But France cannot have a Protestant king!'

'It certainly cannot.' And the king of Navarre was also a member of the Bourbon family, ancient enemies of the Guises, which was another compelling reason for keeping him far from the throne. 'We must get the Pope to disallow the claim of the king of Navarre.' Pierre was thinking aloud. Duke Henri would call a council of war before the end of the day, and Pierre needed to have a plan ready. 'There will be civil war again, and the duke of Guise will lead the Catholic forces. I must go to the duke.' He stood up.

Rollo pointed at his maps. 'But what about the invasion of England?'

'England will have to wait,' said Pierre.

24

ALISON WENT RIDING WITH Mary Stuart on Mary's forty-third birthday. Their breath turned to mist in the cold morning air, and Alison was grateful for the heat of her pony, Garçon, under her. They were accompanied by a squadron of men-at-arms. Mary and all her people were banned from speaking to anyone outside the group at any time. If a child offered the queen an apple, it would be snatched away by a soldier.

They had a new jailer, Sir Amias Paulet, a Puritan so rigid that he made Walsingham seem like a libertine. Paulet was the first man Alison had known to be immune to Mary's seductive charm. When Mary touched his arm, or smiled winningly at him, or talked lightly of such things as kisses or bosoms or beds, he stared at her as if she were mad, and gave no reply.

Paulet made no bones about reading all Mary's letters: he handed them to her opened, without apology. She was allowed to write to her relations and friends in France and Scotland, but under these conditions of course nothing could be said about invading England, rescuing her, executing Elizabeth and putting Mary on the throne.

Alison was invigorated by the ride but, as they turned for home, the familiar depression returned. This was the twentieth successive birthday Mary had passed in prison. Alison herself was forty-five, and had spent all those birthdays with Mary, each time hoping this would be the last for which they would be captives. Alison felt they had spent their lives waiting and hoping. It was a dismally long time since they had been the best-dressed girls in Paris.

Mary's son, James, was now twenty-one and king of Scotland. She had not seen him since he was one year old. He showed no interest in his mother and did nothing to help her, but then why would he? He did not know her. Mary was savagely angry with Queen Elizabeth for keeping her away from her only child for almost his entire life.

They approached their current penitentiary. Chartley Manor had a moat and battlements, but otherwise it was a house rather than a castle, a timber-framed mansion with many cheerful fireplaces and rows of windows to make it bright inside. It was not quite big enough for Mary's entourage plus the Paulet family household, so the men-at-arms were all lodged in houses in the neighbourhood. Mary and Alison did not feel perpetually surrounded by guards but, all the same, the place was still a prison.

The riders crossed the bridge over the moat, entered the broad courtyard, and reined in by the well in the centre. Alison dismounted and let Garçon drink from the horse trough. A brewer's dray stood to one side, and burly men were rolling barrels of beer into the queen's quarters through the kitchen entrance. Near the main door Alison noticed a little crowd of women. Lady Margaret Paulet was there with some of her maids, clustered around the figure of a man in a travel-stained coat. Lady Margaret was friendlier than her husband, and Alison strolled across the yard to see what was going on.

The man at the centre of the little crowd was holding open a travelling case full of ribbons, buttons and cheap jewellery. Mary came and stood behind Alison. The women were fingering the goods for sale, asking the price and chattering animatedly about which they liked. One of them said archly: 'Have you got any love potions?'

It was a flirtatious remark, and travelling vendors were usually adept at charming their female customers, but this one seemed embarrassed, and muttered something about ribbons being better than potions.

Sir Amias Paulet emerged from the front door and came to investigate. In his fifties, he was a bald man with a fringe of grey hair and a luxuriant ginger moustache. 'What is this?' he said.

Lady Margaret looked guilty. 'Oh, nothing,' she replied.

Paulet said to the salesman: 'Lady Margaret is not interested in fripperies.' Margaret and her maids moved away reluctantly, and Paulet added scornfully: 'Show them to the Scottish queen. Such vanities are more her type of thing.'

Mary and the women in her captive entourage ignored his rudeness, which was familiar. They were desperate for diversion, and they quickly crowded around the salesman, replacing the disappointed Paulet maids.

At that point Alison looked more closely at the man and repressed a gasp of shock as she recognized him. He had thinning hair and a bushy red-brown beard. It was the man who had spoken to her in the park at Sheffield Castle, and his name was Jean Langlais.

She looked at Mary and remembered that the queen had never seen him. Alison was the only one he had spoken to. She felt a thrill of excited hope. He had undoubtedly come here to talk to her again.

She also experienced a little spasm of desire. Since meeting him in the park she had entertained a little fantasy in which she married him and they became the leading couple at the court when Mary was queen of a Catholic England. It was silly, she knew, to have such thoughts about a man she had met for only a few minutes; but perhaps a prisoner was entitled to foolish dreams.

She needed to get Langlais away from the too-public courtyard and into a place where he could drop his pretence of being a travelling tinker and speak frankly.

'I'm cold,' she said. 'Let's go inside.'

Mary said: 'I'm still warm from the ride.'

Alison said: 'Please, madam, remember your weak chest, and step into the house.'

Mary looked offended that Alison should dare to insist; then perhaps she heard the hint of urgency in Alison's voice, for she raised a speculative eyebrow; and finally she looked directly at Alison, registered the message in Alison's widened eyes, and said: 'On second thoughts, yes, let's go in.'

They took Langlais directly to Mary's private chamber and Alison dismissed everyone else. Then she said in French: 'Your majesty, this is Jean Langlais, the messenger from the duke of Guise.'

Mary perked up. 'What does the duke have to say to me?' she asked him eagerly.

'The crisis is over,' Langlais said, speaking French with an English accent. 'The Treaty of Nemours has been signed, and Protestantism is once more illegal in France.'

Mary waved an impatient hand. 'This is old news.'

Langlais was impervious to the queen's dismissiveness. He carried on unruffled. 'The treaty is a triumph for the Church, and for the duke of Guise and the rest of your majesty's French family.'

'Yes, I know.'

'Which means that your cousin, Duke Henri, is free to revive the plan that has been his heart's desire for so long – to put your majesty on the English throne that is rightfully your own.'

Alison hesitated to rejoice. Too often she had celebrated prematurely. All the same, her heart leaped in hope. She saw Mary's face brighten.

Langlais went on: 'Once again our first task is to set up a channel of communication between the duke and your majesty. I have found a good English Catholic boy to be our courier. But we have to find a way to get messages into and out of this house without Paulet reading them.'

Alison said: 'We've done this before, but each time it gets more difficult. We can't use the laundry girls again. Walsingham found out about that ruse.'

Langlais nodded. 'Throckmorton probably betrayed that secret before he died.'

Alison was struck by how coldly he spoke of the martyrdom of Sir Francis Throckmorton. She wondered how many others of Langlais's fellow conspirators had suffered torture and execution.

She put that thought out of her mind and said: 'Anyway, Paulet won't let us send our washing out. The queen's servants have to scrub clothes in the moat.'

Langlais said, 'We'll have to think of something else.'

'No one in our entourage is allowed any unsupervised contact with the outside world,' Alison said gloomily. 'I was surprised that Paulet didn't throw you out.'

'I noticed barrels of beer being brought in here.'

'Ah,' said Alison. 'That's a thought. You're very quick.'

'Where do they come from?'

'The Lion's Head inn at Burton, the nearest town.'

'Does Paulet inspect them?'

'And look at the beer? No.'

'Good.'

'But how could we put letters in barrels of beer? The paper would get wet, and the ink would run . . .'

'Suppose we put the papers in sealed bottles?'

Alison nodded slowly. 'And we could do the same with the queen's replies.'

'You could put the replies back into the same bottles and re-seal them – you have sealing wax.'

'The bottles would rattle around in the empty barrels. Someone might investigate the noise.'

'You could find a way to prevent that. Fill the barrel with straw. Or wrap the bottles in rags and nail them to the wood to stop them moving.'

Alison was feeling more and more thrilled. 'We'll think of something. But we would have to persuade the brewer to cooperate.'

'Yes,' said Langlais. 'Leave that to me.'

*

GILBERT GIFFORD LOOKED innocent, but that was misleading, Ned Willard thought. The man seemed younger than twenty-four: his smooth face bore only the adolescent fluff of a beard and moustache, and he had probably never shaved. But Alain de Guise had told Sylvie, in a letter that came via the English embassy in Paris, that Gifford had recently met with Pierre Aumande in Paris. In Ned's opinion, Gifford was a highly dangerous agent of the enemies of Queen Elizabeth.

And yet he was behaving naively. In December of 1585, he crossed the Channel from France, landing in Rye. Of course he did not have the royal permission required by an Englishman to travel abroad, so he had offered the Rye harbourmaster a bribe. In the old days he would have got away with that, but things had changed. A port official who let in a suspicious character nowadays could suffer the death penalty, at least in theory. The harbourmaster had arrested Gifford, and Ned had ordered the man brought to London for interview.

Ned puzzled over the enigma while he and Walsingham faced Gifford across a writing table at the house in Seething Lane. 'What on earth made you imagine you would get away with it?' Walsingham asked. 'Your father is a notorious Catholic. Queen Elizabeth has treated him with great indulgence, even making him High Sheriff of Staffordshire – but, despite that, he refused to attend a service even when the queen herself was at his parish church!'

Gifford seemed only mildly anxious, for one facing an interrogator who had sent so many Catholics to their deaths. Ned guessed the boy had no idea of how much trouble he was in. 'Of course I know it was wrong of me to leave England without permission,' he said in the tone of one who confesses a peccadillo. 'I beg you to bear in mind that I was only nineteen at the time.' He tried a conspiratorial smile. 'Did you not do foolish things in your youth, Sir Francis?'

Walsingham did not return the smile. 'No, I did not,' he said flatly.

Ned almost laughed. It was probably true.

Ned asked the suspect: 'Why did you return to England? What is the purpose of your journey?'

'I haven't seen my father for almost five years.'

'Why now?' Ned persisted. 'Why not last year, or next year?'

Gifford shrugged. 'It seemed as good a time as any.'

Ned switched the line of questioning. 'Where in London do you plan to lodge, if we do not lock you up in the Tower?'

'At the sign of the Plough.'

The Plough was an inn just beyond Temple Bar, to the west of the city, frequented by Catholic visitors. The head ostler was in Walsingham's pay, and gave reliable reports on all comings and goings.

Ned said: 'Where else in England will you travel?'

'To Chillington, naturally.'

Chillington Hall was Gifford's father's residence in Staffordshire. It was half a day's ride from Chartley, where Mary Stuart was currently imprisoned. Was that a coincidence? Ned did not believe in coincidences.

'When did you last see the priest Jean Langlais?'

Gifford did not reply.

Ned gave him time. He was desperate to learn more about this shadowy figure. Sylvie had seen Langlais, briefly, in Paris in 1572 and had learned only that he was English. Nath and Alain had seen him a few times over the following years, and they described a man of slightly more than average height, with a red-brown beard and thinning hair, speaking French with the fluency of long practice but an unmistakable English accent. Two of the illicit priests Ned had interrogated had named him as the organizer of their clandestine entry into England. And that was all. No one knew his real name or where in England he came from.

Ned said: 'Well?'

'I'm trying to think, but I'm sure I don't know a man by that name.'

Walsingham said: 'I think I've heard enough.'

Ned went to the door and summoned a steward. 'Take Mr Gifford to the parlour and stay with him, please.'

Gifford left, and Walsingham said: 'What do you think?'

'He's lying,' said Ned.

'I agree. Alert all our people to be on the lookout for him.'

'Very good,' said Ned. 'And perhaps it's time for me to pay a visit to Chartley.'

*

ALISON FOUND Sir Ned Willard maddeningly nice during the week he spent at Chartley Manor. Now in his forties, he was courteous and charming even while he did the most obnoxious things. He went everywhere and saw everything. When she looked out of the window in the morning he was there in the courtyard, sitting by the well, eating bread and watching the comings and goings with eyes that missed nothing. He never knocked at a door. He walked into everyone's bedroom, male or female, saying politely: 'I do hope I'm not disturbing you.' If he was told that yes, he was disturbing someone, he would say apologetically: 'I'll be gone in a minute,' and then stay just as long as he pleased. If you were writing a letter he would read it over your shoulder. He walked in on Queen Mary and her companions at meals and listened to their conversations. It did not help to speak French as he was fluent. If anyone protested, he said: 'I'm so sorry – but, you know, prisoners aren't really entitled to privacy.' All the women said he was lovely, and one admitted to walking around her room naked in the hope that he would come in.

His meticulousness was particularly frustrating because, in recent weeks, Mary had started to receive letters in barrels from the Lion's Head in Burton, and it turned out that a huge backlog of secret correspondence had been piling up in the French embassy in London since the arrest of Throckmorton more than a year ago. Mary and her long-time secretary, Claude Nau, worked on the avalanche of mail day after day, updating Mary's confidential relations with powerful supporters in Scotland, France, Spain and Rome. This was important work: Alison and Mary knew that people could easily forget a hero who dropped out of sight. Now the courts of Europe were receiving lively reminders that Mary was alive and well and ready to take the throne that was rightfully hers.

When Sir Ned Willard arrived, all that had to stop. No letters could be written, let alone encoded, for fear that he might walk in and see a revealing half-written document. Numerous letters had already been sealed in bottles and placed in an empty barrel, ready to be picked up by the dray from the Lion's Head. Alison and Mary had a long discussion about what to do about them. They decided it might call attention to the barrel if they opened it to retrieve the bottles, so they left them as they were; but for the same reason they added no new ones.

Alison prayed that Ned would leave before the next delivery of beer. The man who called himself Jean Langlais had come up with the idea of hiding messages in barrels when he saw the beer being delivered; might not Ned think the same way, and just as quickly? Her prayer was not answered.

Alison and Mary were at a window, watching Ned in the courtyard, when the heavy cart arrived with three thirty-two-gallon barrels.

'Go and talk to him,' Mary said urgently. 'Distract his attention.'

Alison hurried outside and approached Ned. 'So, Sir Ned,' she said conversationally, 'are you satisfied with the security arrangements of Sir Amias Paulet?'

'He's a good deal more meticulous than the earl of Shrewsbury.'

Alison gave a tinkling laugh. 'I'll never forget you bursting in on us at breakfast at Sheffield Castle,' she said. 'You were like an avenging angel. Terrifying!'

Ned smiled, but Alison saw that it was a knowing smile. He knew she was flirting. He did not appear to mind, but she felt sure he did not believe her flattery.

She said: 'It was the third time I'd met you, but I'd never before seen you like that. Why were you so angry, anyway?'

He did not answer her for a moment. He looked past her at the brewer's men unloading the full barrels of beer from the dray and rolling them into Mary's quarters. Alison's heart was in her mouth: those barrels almost certainly contained incriminating secret messages from the enemies of Queen Elizabeth. All Ned had to do was stop the men, with his usual well-mannered determination, and demand that they open the barrels so that he could check the contents. Then the game would be up, and another conspirator would be tortured and executed.

But Ned did nothing. His attractive face showed no more emotion than it had when coal had been delivered. He returned his gaze to her and said: 'May I answer you with a question?'

'All right.'

'Why are you here?'

'What do you mean?'

'Mary Stuart is a prisoner, but you're not. You're no threat to the crown of England. You don't pretend to have a claim on the

English throne. You have no powerful relatives at the court of the king of France. You don't write letters to the Pope and the king of Spain. You could walk out of Chartley Manor and nobody would mind. Why do you stay?'

It was a question she sometimes asked herself. 'Queen Mary and I were girls together,' she said. 'I'm a little older, and I used to look after her. Then she grew into a beautiful, alluring young woman, and I fell in love with her, in a way. When we returned to Scotland, I got married, but my husband died soon after the wedding. It just seemed to be my destiny to serve Queen Mary.'

'I understand.'

'Do you?'

Out of the corner of her eye, Alison saw the men come back out with the empties – including one containing secret letters in bottles – and load the barrels onto the cart. Once again, all Ned had to do was give the order and the barrels would have been opened, revealing their secret. But Ned made no move to speak to the draymen. 'I understand,' he said to Alison, continuing their conversation, 'because I feel the same way about Queen Elizabeth. And that's why I was so angry when I found that the earl of Shrewsbury was letting her down.'

The brewer's men went into the kitchen for their dinner before setting off again. The crisis was over. Alison breathed easier.

Ned said: 'And now it's time for me to leave. I must get back to London. Goodbye, Lady Ross.'

Alison had not known he was about to leave. 'Goodbye, Sir Ned,' she said.

He went into the house.

Alison returned to Queen Mary. Together they watched through the window. Ned came out of the house with a pair of saddlebags presumably containing his few necessaries. He spoke to a groom, who brought out his horse.

He was gone before the deliverymen finished their dinner.

'What a relief,' said Queen Mary. 'Thank God.'

'Yes,' said Alison. 'We seem to have got away with it.'

*

NED DID NOT go to London. He rode to Burton and took a room at the Lion's Head.

When his horse was taken care of and his bags unpacked, he explored the inn. There was a bar opening on to the street. An arched vehicle entrance led to a courtyard with stables on one side and guest rooms on the other. At the back of the premises was a brewery, and a yeasty smell filled the air. It was a substantial business: the tavern was full of drinkers, travellers arrived and left, and drays were in and out of the yard constantly.

Ned noted that empty barrels from incoming drays were rolled to a corner where a boy removed the lids, cleaned the insides with water and a scrubbing brush, and stacked the barrels upside down to dry.

The owner was a big man whose belly suggested that he consumed plenty of what he brewed. Ned heard the men call him Hal. He was always on the move, going from the brewery to the stable, harrying his employees and shouting orders.

When Ned had the layout of the place in his head, he sat on a bench in the courtyard with a flagon of beer and waited. The yard was busy, and no one paid him any attention.

He was almost certain the messages were going in and out of Chartley Manor in beer barrels. He had been there for a week and had watched just about everything that went on, and this was the only possibility he could see. When the beer arrived he had been partly distracted by Alison. It could have been a coincidence that she chose to chat to him just at that moment. But Ned did not believe in coincidences.

He expected that the draymen would travel more slowly than he had coming from Chartley, for his horse was fresh and the carthorses tired. In the end it was early evening by the time the dray entered the courtyard of the Lion's Head. Ned stayed where he was, watching. One of the men went away and came back with Hal while the others were unhitching the horses. Then they rolled the empty barrels over to the boy with the scrubbing brush.

Hal watched the boy remove the lids with a crowbar. He

leaned against the wall and looked unconcerned. Perhaps he was. More likely, he had calculated that if he opened the barrels in secret his employees would know that he was up to something seriously criminal, whereas if he feigned nonchalance, they would assume it was nothing special.

When the lids came off, Hal looked into each barrel. Bending over one, he reached inside and brought out two bottle-shaped objects wrapped in rags and tied with string.

Ned allowed himself a satisfied sigh.

Hal nodded to the boy, then crossed the courtyard to a doorway he had not used before and went inside.

Ned followed rapidly.

The door led to a set of rooms that appeared to be the publican's home. Ned walked through a sitting room into a bedroom. Hal stood at an open cupboard, obviously stashing the two items he had taken from the barrel. Hearing Ned's step on the floorboards, he spun round and said angrily: 'Get out of here, these are private rooms!'

Ned said quietly: 'You are now as close as you have ever come to being hanged.'

Hal's expression changed instantly. He went pale and his mouth dropped open. He was shocked and terrified. It was a startling transformation in a big, blustering fellow, and Ned deduced that Hal – unlike poor Peg Bradford – knew exactly what kind of crime he was committing. After a long hesitation he said in a frightened voice: 'Who are you?'

'I am the only man in the world who can save you from the gallows.'

'Oh, God help me.'

'He may, if you help me.'

'What must I do?'

'Tell me who comes to collect the bottles from Chartley, and brings you new ones to send there.'

'I don't know his name – honestly! I swear it!'

'When will he next be here?'

'I don't know – he never gives warning, and his visits are irregular.'

They would be, Ned thought. The man is careful.

Hal moaned: 'Oh, God, I've been such a fool.'

'You certainly have. Why did you do it? Are you Catholic?'

'I'm whatever religion I'm told to be.'

'Greed for money, then.'

'God forgive me.'

'He has forgiven worse. Now listen to me. All you have to do is continue as you are. Give the courier the bottles, accept the new ones he brings, send them to Chartley, and bring back the replies, as you have been doing. Say nothing about me to anyone, anywhere.'

'I don't understand.'

'You don't need to understand. Just forget that you ever met me. Is that clear?'

'Yes, and thank you for being merciful.'

You don't deserve it, you money-grubbing traitor, Ned thought. He said: 'I'm going to stay here until the courier comes, whenever that may be.'

He arrived two days later. Ned recognized him instantly.

It was Gilbert Gifford.

*

IT WAS A dangerous business, recruiting men to join a conspiracy to kill the queen. Rollo had to be very careful. If he picked the wrong man he could be in the deepest kind of trouble.

He had learned to watch for a certain look in the eyes. The look combined noble purpose with a high-minded disregard for consequences. It was not madness, but it was a kind of irrationality. Rollo sometimes wondered whether he had that look himself. He thought not: he was cautious to the point of obsession. Perhaps he had had it when young, but he must surely have lost it, for otherwise he would by now have been hung, drawn and quartered like Francis Throckmorton and all the other idealistic young Catholics Ned Willard had caught. In which case, he would by now have gone to heaven, like them; but a man was not permitted to choose the moment he made that journey.

Rollo thought that Anthony Babington had the look.

Rollo had been observing Babington for three weeks, but from a distance. He had not yet spoken. He had not even gone into the houses and taverns that Babington frequented, for he knew they would be watched by Ned Willard's spies. He got close to Babington only in places that were not Catholic haunts, and among groups of people so large that one extra was not noticeable: in bowling alleys, at cockfights and bear-baiting, and in the audience at public executions. But he could not carry on taking precautions for ever. The time had come when he had to risk his neck.

Babington was a young man from a wealthy Derbyshire Catholic family that harboured one of Rollo's secret priests. He had met Mary Stuart: as a boy Babington had been a page in the household of the earl of Shrewsbury, at the time when the earl was her jailer; and the boy had been captivated by the charm of the imprisoned queen. Was all that enough? There was only one way to find out for sure.

Rollo finally spoke to him at a bullfight.

It took place at Paris Gardens in Southwark, on the south side of the river. Entrance was a penny, but Babington paid twopence for a place in the gallery, removed from the jostling and smell of ordinary folk in the stalls.

The bull was tethered in a ring but otherwise unconstrained. Six big hunting dogs were led in and immediately flew at the bull, trying to bite its legs. The big bull was remarkably agile, turning its head on the muscular neck, fighting back with its horns. The dogs dodged, not always successfully. The lucky ones were simply thrown through the air; the unlucky ones impaled on a horn until shaken off. The smell of blood filled the atmosphere.

The audience yelled and screamed encouragement, and placed bets on whether the bull would kill all the dogs before succumbing to its wounds.

No one was looking anywhere but the ring.

Rollo began, as always, by letting his target know that he was a Catholic priest. 'Bless you, my son,' he said quietly to Babington, and when Babington gave him a startled look he flashed the gold cross.

Babington was shocked and enthused. 'Who are you?'

'Jean Langlais.'

'What do you want with me?'

'It is time for Mary Stuart.'

Babington's eyes widened. 'What do you mean?'

He knew perfectly well what was meant, Rollo thought. He went on: 'The duke of Guise is ready with an army of sixty thousand men.' That was an exaggeration – the duke was not ready, and he might never have sixty thousand – but Rollo needed to inspire confidence. 'The duke has maps of all the major harbours on the south and east coasts where he may land his forces. He also has a list of loyal Catholic noblemen – including your stepfather – who can be counted upon to rally to the invaders and fight for the restoration of the true faith.' That was accurate.

'Can all this be true?' Babington said, eager to believe it.

'Only one thing is lacking, and we need a good man to supply the deficiency.'

'Go on.'

'A high-born Catholic whose faith is unquestionable must put together a group of similar friends and free Queen Mary from her prison at the moment of crisis. You, Anthony Babington, have been chosen to be that man.'

Rollo turned away from Babington, to give him a moment to digest all that. In the ring, the bull and the dead or dying dogs had been dragged away, and the climactic entertainment of the afternoon was beginning. Into the ring came an old horse with a monkey in the saddle. The crowd cheered: this was their favourite part. Six young dogs were released. They attacked and bit the horse, which tried desperately to escape their teeth; but they also leaped at the monkey, which seemed to tempt them more. The spectators roared with laughter as the monkey, maddened with fear, tried frantically to escape their bites, jumping from one end of the horse to the other, and even trying to stand on the horse's head.

Rollo looked at Babington's face. The entertainment was forgotten. Babington shone with pride, exhilaration and fear.

Rollo could read his mind. He was twenty-three, and this was his moment of glory.

Rollo said: 'Queen Mary is being held at Chartley Manor, in Staffordshire. You must go there and reconnoitre – but do not attract attention to yourself by attempting to speak to her. When your plans are made, you will write to her, giving the details, and entrust the letter to me. I have a way of getting papers to her secretly.'

The light of destiny shone in Babington's eyes. 'I'll do it,' he said. 'And gladly.'

In the ring the horse fell down, and the dogs seized the monkey and tore it apart.

Rollo shook Babington's hand.

Babington said: 'How do I get in touch with you?'

'You don't,' said Rollo. 'I'll contact you.'

*

NED TOOK GIFFORD to the Tower of London, his right arm roped to the left wrist of a guard. 'This is where traitors are tortured,' Ned said conversationally as they ascended the stone staircase. Gifford looked terrified. They went to a room with a writing table and a fireplace, cold in summer. They sat down on opposite sides of the table, Gifford still tied to the guard, who stood beside him.

In the next room, a man screamed.

Gifford paled. 'Who is that?' he said.

'A traitor called Launcelot,' said Ned. 'He dreamed up a scheme to shoot Queen Elizabeth while she rode in St James's Park. He proposed this murderous plan to another Catholic who happened to be a loyal subject of the queen.' The second man also happened to be an agent of Ned's. 'We think Launcelot is probably a lunatic working alone, but Sir Francis Walsingham needs to be sure.'

Gifford's smooth boyish face was deathly white, and his hands were shaking.

Ned said: 'If you don't want to suffer what Launcelot is going through, you just have to cooperate with me. Nothing difficult.'

'Never,' said Gifford, but his voice shook.

'After you collect the letters from the French embassy, you will bring them to me, so that I can make copies, before you take them to Chartley.'

'You can't read them,' Gifford said. 'Nor can I. They're written in code.'

'Let me worry about that.' Ned had a genius codebreaker called Phelippes.

'Queen Mary will see the broken seals on the letters and know what I've done.'

'The seals will be restored.' Phelippes was also a skilled forger. 'No one will be able to tell the difference.'

Gifford was taken aback by these revelations. He had not guessed how elaborate and professional Queen Elizabeth's secret service was. As Ned had suspected from the start, Gifford had no idea what he was up against.

Ned went on: 'You will do the same when you pick up the letters from Chartley. You will bring them to me, and I will have them copied before you deliver them to the French embassy.'

'I will never betray Queen Mary.'

Launcelot screamed again, and then the scream died away and the man began to sob and plead for mercy.

Ned said to Gifford: 'You are a lucky man.'

Gifford gave a snort of incredulity.

'Oh, yes,' said Ned. 'You see, you don't know much. You don't even know the name of the Englishman who recruited you in Paris.'

Gifford said nothing, but Ned guessed from his expression that he did have a name.

Ned said: 'He called himself Jean Langlais.'

Gifford was not good at hiding his feelings, and he let his surprise show.

'That is obviously a pseudonym, but it's the only one he gave you.'

Once again Gifford appeared disheartened by how much Ned knew.

'You're lucky, because I have a use for you, and if you do as you're told, you won't be racked.'

'I won't do it.'

Launcelot screamed like a man in hell.

Gifford turned away and threw up on the stone floor. The sour smell of vomit filled the little room.

Ned stood up. 'I've arranged for them to torture you this afternoon. I'll come and see you tomorrow. You'll have changed your mind by then.'

Launcelot sobbed: 'No, no, please, stop.'

Gifford wiped his mouth and whispered: 'I'll do it.'

'I need to hear you better,' Ned said.

Gifford spoke louder. 'I'll do it, God damn you!'

'Good,' said Ned. He spoke to the guard. 'Untie the rope,' he said. 'Let him go.'

Gifford could hardly believe it. 'I can go?'

'As long as you do what I've told you. You will be watched, so don't imagine you can cheat me.'

Launcelot began to cry for his mother.

Ned said: 'And the next time you come back here there will be no escape.'

'I understand.'

'Go.'

Gifford left the room, and Ned heard his hurried footsteps clatter down the stone stairs. Ned nodded to the guard, who also went out. Ned sat back in his chair, drained. He closed his eyes, but after a minute Launcelot screamed again, and Ned had to leave.

He went out of the Tower and walked along the bank of the river. A fresh breeze off the water blew away the smell of puke that had lingered in his nostrils. He looked around him, at boatmen, fishermen, street hawkers, busy people and idlers, hundreds of faces talking, shouting, laughing, yawning, singing – but not screaming in agony or sweating in terror. Normal life.

He crossed London Bridge to the south bank. This was where most of the Huguenots lived. They had brought sophisticated textile technology with them from the

Netherlands and France, and they had quickly prospered in London. They were good customers for Sylvie.

Her shop was the ground floor of a timber-framed building in a row, a typical London house, with each storey jutting out over the one below. The front door was open, and he stepped inside. He was soothed by the rows of books and the smell of paper and ink.

Sylvie was unpacking a box from Geneva. She straightened up when she heard his step. He looked into her blue eyes and kissed her soft mouth.

She held him at a distance and spoke English with a soft French accent. 'What on earth has happened?'

'I had to perform an unpleasant duty. I'll tell you, but I want to wash.' He went out to the backyard, and dipped a bowl in a rain barrel, and washed his face and hands in the cold water.

Back in the house, he went upstairs to the living quarters and threw himself into his favourite chair. He closed his eyes and heard Launcelot crying for his mother.

Sylvie came upstairs. She went to the pantry, got a bottle of wine, and poured two goblets. She handed him a glass, kissed his forehead and sat close to him, knee to knee. He sipped his wine and took her hand.

She said: 'Tell me.'

'A man was tortured in the Tower today. He had threatened the life of the queen. I didn't torture him – I can't do it, I don't have the stomach for that work. But I arranged to conduct an interrogation in the next room, so that my suspect could hear the screams.'

'How dreadful.'

'It worked. I turned an enemy agent into a double agent. He serves me now. But I can still hear those screams.' Sylvie squeezed his hand and said nothing. After a while he said: 'Sometimes I hate my work.'

'Because of you, men like the duke of Guise and Pierre Aumande can't do in England what they do in France – burn people to death for their beliefs.'

'But in order to defeat them I have become like them.'

'No, you haven't,' she said. 'You don't fight for compulsory

Protestantism the way they fight for compulsory Catholicism. You stand for tolerance.'

'We did, at the start. But now, when we catch secret priests, we execute them, regardless of whether they threaten the queen. Do you know what we did to Margaret Clitherow?'

'Is she the woman who was executed in York for harbouring a Catholic priest?'

'Yes. She was stripped naked, tied up, and laid on the ground; then her own front door was placed on top of her and loaded with rocks until she was crushed to death.'

'Oh, God, I didn't know that.'

'Sickening.'

'But you never wanted it to be this way! You wanted people with different beliefs to be good neighbours.'

'I did, but perhaps it's impossible.'

'Roger told me something you once said to him. I wonder if you remember the time he asked you why the queen hated Catholics.'

Ned smiled. 'I remember.'

'He hasn't forgotten what you told him.'

'Perhaps I did something right. What did I say to Roger?'

'You said that there are no saints in politics, but imperfect people can make the world a better place.'

'Did I say that?'

'That's what Roger told me.'

'Good,' said Ned. 'I hope it's true.'

*

SUMMER BROUGHT new hope to Alison, who brightened with the weather. Only the inner circle at Chartley Manor knew of the secret correspondence with Anthony Babington, but Mary's revived spirits heartened everyone.

Alison was optimistic, but not blindly so. She wished she knew more about Babington. He came from a good Catholic family, but that was about all that could be said for him. He was only twenty-four. Would he really be able to lead a rebellion against the queen who had held on firmly to power for twenty-seven years? Alison wanted to know the plan.

The details came in July of 1586.

After the initial exchange of letters that served to establish contact and assure both parties that the channel of communication was open, Babington sent a full outline of what he proposed. The letter came in a beer barrel, and was decoded by Mary's secretary, Claude Nau. Alison sat with Mary and Nau, in Mary's bedroom at Chartley Manor, and pored over the paper.

It was exhilarating.

'Babington writes of "this great and honourable action" and "the last hope ever to recover the faith of our forefathers", but he says more,' said Nau, looking at his decrypt. 'He outlines six separate actions necessary for a successful uprising. The first is the invasion of England by a foreign force. Second, that force to be large enough to guarantee military victory.'

Mary said: 'The duke of Guise has sixty thousand men, we're told.'

Alison hoped it was true.

'Third, ports must be chosen where the armies can land and be resupplied.'

'Settled long ago, I think, and maps sent to my cousin Duke Henri,' said Mary. 'Though Babington may not know about that.'

'Fourth, when they arrive they must be met by a substantial local force to protect their landing against immediate counterattack.'

'The people will rise up spontaneously,' Mary said.

Alison thought they might need prompting, but that could be arranged.

'Babington has given this some thought,' Nau said. 'He has selected men he describes as "your lieutenants" in the west, the north, South Wales, North Wales, and the counties of Lancaster, Derby and Stafford.'

Alison thought that sounded impressively well organized.

'"Fifth, Queen Mary must be freed",' Nau read aloud. '"Myself, with ten gentlemen and a hundred of our followers, will undertake the delivery of your royal person from the hands of your enemies."'

'Good,' said Mary. 'Sir Amias Paulet has nowhere near a hundred guards here, and anyway, most of them are lodged in the surrounding neighbourhood, not at the Manor. Before they can be mustered, we'll be long gone.'

Alison was feeling increasingly energized.

'And sixth, of course, Elizabeth must be killed. Babington writes: "For the dispatch of the usurper, from the obedience of whom we are by excommunication made free, there be six gentlemen, all my private friends, who for the zeal they bear to the Catholic cause and your majesty's service, will undertake that tragic execution." I think that's about as clear as it could be.'

It certainly was, thought Alison, and for a moment she was chilled to think of the murder of a queen.

'I must reply to this quickly,' said Mary.

Nau looked anxious. 'We should be careful what we say.'

'There is only one thing I can say, and that is yes.'

'If your letter should fall into the wrong hands . . .'

'It will be placed in safe hands, and written in code.'

'But if things should go wrong . . .'

Mary reddened, and Alison knew that the anger and frustration of the last twenty years were showing. 'I have to seize this opportunity. Otherwise there is no hope for me.'

'Your reply to Babington will be evidence of treason.'

'So be it,' said Mary.

*

THE BUSINESS OF espionage required a lot of patience, Ned reflected in July of 1586.

He had hoped, back in 1583, that Francis Throckmorton would lead him to hard evidence of the treachery of Mary Stuart. That hope had been disappointed when the malice of the earl of Leicester had forced Ned to arrest Throckmorton prematurely. Then, in 1585, he had found a new Throckmorton in Gilbert Gifford. This time the earl of Leicester was not in England to make trouble: Queen Elizabeth had sent him to the Spanish Netherlands at the head of an army to fight for the Dutch Protestant rebels against their Catholic Spanish overlords. Leicester was making a hash of the job – his talents were for flirting and charming, not fighting and killing – but it kept him from undermining Walsingham.

As a result, Ned was in a strong position. Mary thought she was sending and receiving secret letters, but Ned was reading everything.

However, it was now July and he had not yet found what he was looking for, despite six months of surveillance.

Treachery was *implied* in every letter Mary received or wrote, of course, whether she was corresponding with Pierre Aumande or the king of Spain; but Ned needed something no one could argue with. The letter Babington sent to Mary early in July was explicit, and he would undoubtedly hang for it. Ned waited in suspense to see how Mary would reply. Surely now she would have to make her intentions clear in writing? The exact wording of her response might finally condemn her.

Her reply came into Ned's hands on 19 July. It was seven pages long.

It was written by her secretary, Claude Nau, as always, and encoded. Ned gave it to Phelippes for deciphering and waited in a fever of impatience. He found he could not concentrate on anything else. He had a long letter from Jerónima Ruiz in Madrid about the internal politics of the Spanish court which he read three times without understanding a word. He gave up and left Walsingham's house in Seething Lane to walk across the bridge to his own home in Southwark for midday dinner. Being with Sylvie always soothed his soul.

She closed the shop and cooked some salmon in wine with rosemary. As they ate, in the dining room over the shop, he told her about Babington's letter and Mary's response. He had no secrets from Sylvie: they were spies together.

As they were finishing the fish, one of Ned's assistants arrived with the decrypt.

It was in French. Ned could not read French as effortlessly as he could speak it, but he went through it with Sylvie.

Mary began by praising Babington's intentions in general terms. 'That's already enough to convict her of treason,' Ned said with satisfaction.

Sylvie said: 'It's very sad.'

Ned looked at her with raised eyebrows. Sylvie was a crusading Protestant who had risked her life for her beliefs many times, yet she felt pity for Mary Stuart.

She caught his look. 'I remember her wedding. She was just a girl, but beautiful, with a wonderful future in prospect. She was going to be the queen of France. She seemed the luckiest young woman in the world. And look what has become of her.'

'She's brought all her troubles on herself.'

'Did you make good decisions when you were seventeen?'

'I suppose not.'

'When I was nineteen I married Pierre Aumande. How's that for bringing trouble on oneself?'

'I see your point.'

Ned read on. Mary went farther than general praise. She responded to each element of Babington's plan, urging him to make more detailed preparations to welcome the invaders, muster local rebels in support, and arm and supply everyone. She asked for a more precise outline of the scheme to free her from Chartley Manor.

'Better and better,' said Ned.

Most importantly, she urged Babington to give careful thought to exactly how the assassins of Queen Elizabeth would proceed with their murderous task.

When Ned read that sentence he felt as if a weight had been lifted from his aching back. It was incontrovertible proof. Mary was active in the planning of regicide. She was as guilty as if she wielded the knife herself.

One way or another, Mary Stuart was finished.

*

ROLLO FOUND Anthony Babington celebrating.

Babington was at the grand London home of Robert Pooley with several fellow conspirators, sitting around a table laden with roasted chickens, bowls of hot buttered onions, loaves of new bread and jugs of sherry wine.

Rollo was disturbed by their levity. Men who were plotting to overthrow the monarch should not get drunk in the middle of the day. However, unlike Rollo, they were not hardened conspirators but idealistic amateurs embarked on a grand adventure. The supreme confidence of youth and nobility made them careless of their lives.

Rollo was breaking his own rule in coming to Pooley's house. He normally stayed away from the Catholics' regular haunts. Such places were watched by Ned Willard. But Rollo had not seen Babington for a week and he needed to know what was happening.

He looked into the room, caught Babington's eye, and beckoned him. Uncomfortable in the home of a known Catholic, he led Babington out. Alongside the house was a spacious garden, shaded from the August sun by a small orchard of mulberry and fig trees. Even this was not secure enough for Rollo, for only a low wall separated it from the busy street, noisy with cartwheels and vendors and the banging and shouting of a building site on the other side of the road. He insisted they leave the garden and step into the shady porch of the church next door. Then at last he said: 'What's happening? Everything seems to have gone quiet.'

'Wipe that frown away, Monsieur Langlais,' said Babington gaily. 'Here's good news.' He took a sheaf of papers from his pocket and handed it over with a flourish.

It was a coded letter together with a decrypt written out by Babington. Rollo moved to the archway and read it in the sunlight. In French, it was from Mary Stuart to Babington. She approved all his plans and urged him to make more detailed arrangements.

Rollo's anxiety melted away. The letter was everything he had hoped for, the final and decisive element in the plan. Rollo would take it to the duke of Guise, who would immediately muster his army of invasion. The godless twenty-eight-year tyranny of Elizabeth was almost over.

'Well done,' Rollo said. He pocketed the letter. 'I leave for France tomorrow. When I return I will be with God's army of liberation.'

Babington clapped him on the back. 'Good man,' he said. 'Now come and dine with us.'

Rollo was about to refuse but, before he could speak, his instincts sounded an alarm. He frowned. Something was wrong. The street had gone quiet. The cartwheels had stopped, the vendors were no longer crying their wares, and the building site was silent. What had happened?

He grabbed Babington's elbow. 'We have to get away from here,' he said.

Babington laughed. 'What on earth for? In Pooley's dining room there's a keg of the best wine only half drunk!'

'Shut up, you fool, and follow me, if you value your life.' Rollo stepped into the church, hushed and dim, and quickly crossed the nave to a small entrance in the far wall. He cracked the door: it opened on to the street. He peeped out.

As he had feared, Pooley's house was being raided.

Men-at-arms were taking up positions along the street, watched in nervous silence by the builders and the vendors and the passers-by. A few yards from Rollo, two burly men with swords stood at the garden gate, clearly placed to catch anyone trying to flee. As Rollo looked, Ned Willard appeared and banged on Pooley's front door.

'Hell,' said Rollo. One of the men-at-arms began to turn towards him and he quickly closed the door. 'We're discovered.'

Babington looked scared. 'Who by?'

'Willard. He's Walsingham's right-hand man.'

'We can hide here.'

'Not for long. Willard is thorough. He'll find us if we stay here.'

'What are we going to do?'

'I don't know.' Rollo looked out again. Pooley's front door now stood open, and Willard had vanished, presumably inside. The men-at-arms were tense, waiting for action, looking around them warily. Rollo closed the door again. 'How fast can you run?'

Babington belched and looked green. 'I shall stand and fight,' he said unconvincingly. He felt for his sword, but he was not wearing one: Rollo guessed it was hanging on a hook in Pooley's entrance hall.

Then Rollo heard a sheep.

He frowned. As he listened, he realized it was not one but a flock of sheep. He remembered that there was a slaughterhouse along the street. A farmer was driving the flock to be butchered, a daily occurrence in every town in the world.

The sound came nearer.

Rollo looked out a third time. He could see the flock now, and smell them. There were about a hundred, and they filled the street from side to side. Pedestrians cursed them and stepped into doorways to get out of their way. The leaders drew level with Pooley's front door, and suddenly Rollo saw how the sheep might save him.

'Get ready,' he said to Babington.

The men-at-arms were angry about being shouldered aside by sheep, but they could do nothing. If humans had shoved them, they would have brandished their weapons, but already-terrified sheep could not be bullied into doing anything other than follow each other to their death. Rollo would have laughed if he had not been afraid for his own life.

When the leaders of the flock passed the two men standing by the garden gate, all the men-at-arms were trapped by sheep. At that point Rollo said: 'Now!' and flung open the door.

He stepped out, with Babington on his heels. Two seconds later their way would have been blocked by sheep. He ran along the street, hearing Babington's footsteps behind him.

A shout of 'Stop! Stop!' went up from the men-at-arms. Rollo glanced back to see some of them struggling to push through the sheep and give chase.

Rollo ran diagonally across the street and past the front of a tavern. An idler drinking a pot of ale stuck out a foot to trip him, but Rollo dodged it. Others just watched. Londoners were not generally well disposed towards men-at-arms, who were often bullies, especially when drunk; and some bystanders cheered the fugitives.

A moment later Rollo heard the bang of an arquebus, but he felt no impact, and Babington's pace did not falter, so the shot had missed. There was another shot, with the same lack of effect, except that all the bystanders scurried indoors to take cover, knowing well that bullets did not always go just where the gun was pointed.

Rollo turned into a side street. A man carrying a club held up a hand to stop him, shouting: 'City watch! Halt!' Members of the city watch had the right to stop and question anyone suspicious. Rollo tried to dodge past the man, but he swung his club. Rollo felt a blow on his shoulder, lost his balance, and fell. He rolled over and looked back in time to see Babington's arm swing through a half-circle that ended with a mighty punch to the side of the watchman's head, knocking him down.

He tried to rise but seemed too dazed, and he slumped on the ground.

Babington helped Rollo up and they ran on.

They turned another corner, ducked down an alley, emerged from it into a street market, and slowed to a walk. They pushed their way into the crowds shopping at the stalls. A vendor tried to sell Rollo a pamphlet about the sins of the Pope, and a prostitute offered to do them both together for the price of one. Rollo looked back and saw no one in pursuit. They had escaped. Perhaps some of the others had also managed to get away in the confusion.

'God sent his angels to help us,' Rollo said solemnly.

'In the shape of sheep,' said Babington, and he laughed heartily.

*

ALISON WAS ASTONISHED when grumpy Sir Amias Paulet suggested to Mary Stuart that she might like to join him and some of the local gentry in a deer hunt. Mary loved riding and socializing, and she jumped at the chance to do both.

Alison helped her dress. Mary wanted to look both pretty and regal for people who would soon be her subjects. She put on a wig over her greying hair and anchored it firmly with a hat.

Alison was allowed to go too, along with the secretary, Nau. They rode out of Chartley courtyard and across the moat, then headed over the moors towards the village where the hunt was to rendezvous.

Alison was exhilarated by the sun, the breeze, and her thoughts of the future. Previously, there had been several conspiracies aimed at freeing Mary, and Alison had suffered a series of bitter disappointments, but this one seemed different, for everything had been taken into account.

It was three weeks since Mary had replied to Anthony Babington giving her approval of his plan. How much longer did they have to wait? Alison tried to calculate how many days it would take the duke of Guise to assemble his army: two weeks? A month? Perhaps she and Mary would hear advance rumours of the invasion. Any day now, word might reach England of a fleet of ships assembling on the north coast of France, and thousands of soldiers going aboard with their horses and armour. Or perhaps the duke would be subtle, and conceal the fleet in rivers and hidden harbours until the last minute, so that the invasion would come as a shock.

As she was mulling this, she saw a group of horsemen at a distance, riding fast. Her heart leaped. Could this be the rescue party?

The party drew closer. There were six men. Alison's heart beat rapidly. Would Paulet put up a fight? He had brought with him two men-at-arms, but they would be outnumbered.

The leader of the group was someone Alison did not recognize. She noticed, despite her tumultuous excitement, that he was expensively dressed in a suit of green serge with extravagant embroidery. It must be Anthony Babington.

Then Alison looked at Paulet and wondered why he appeared unconcerned. The approach of a group of fast riders in open country was normally worrying, but he almost looked as if he had been expecting them.

She looked again at the riders and saw, with a horrible shock, that bringing up the rear was the slim figure of Ned Willard. That meant the riders were not a rescue party. Willard had been Mary's nemesis for a quarter of a century. Now approaching fifty, he had streaks of grey in his dark hair and lines on his face. Even though he was riding last, Alison felt he was the real leader of this group.

Paulet introduced the man in green serge as Sir Thomas

Gorges, an emissary from Queen Elizabeth, and Alison was seized by a fear as cold as the grave.

Gorges spoke what was obviously a rehearsed sentence. Addressing Mary, he said: 'Madam, the queen my mistress finds it very strange that you, contrary to the pact and engagement between you, should have conspired against her and her State, a thing which she could not have believed had she not seen proof of it with her own eyes and known it for certain.'

Alison realized that there was no deer hunt. Paulet had invented that as a way of separating Mary from the majority of her entourage.

Mary was horribly surprised. Her poise deserted her. Flustered, she spoke barely coherently. 'I have never . . . I have always been a good sister . . . I am Elizabeth's friend . . .'

Gorges took no notice. 'Your servants, known to be guilty too, will be taken away from you.'

Alison said: 'I must stay with her!'

Gorges looked at Willard, who gave a brief shake of his head.

Gorges said to Alison: 'You will remain with the other servants.'

Mary turned to Nau. 'Don't let them do this!'

Nau looked terrified, and Alison sympathized. What could one secretary do?

Mary got off her horse and sat on the ground. 'I will not go!' she said.

Willard spoke for the first time. Addressing one of his group, he said: 'Go to that house.' He pointed to a substantial farmhouse half-hidden by trees a mile away. 'They're sure to have a cart. Bring it here. If necessary, we'll tie up Mary Stuart and put her in the cart.'

Mary stood up again, giving in. 'I shall ride,' she said dispiritedly. She got back on her horse.

Gorges handed Paulet a piece of paper, presumably an arrest warrant. Paulet read it and nodded. He kept the paper, perhaps wanting proof – in case anything should go wrong – that he had been ordered to let Mary out of his care.

Mary was pale and shaking. 'Am I to be executed?' she said in a trembling voice.

Alison wanted to cry.

Paulet looked at Mary contemptuously. After a cruelly long pause he answered her question. 'Not today.'

The arresting party got ready to move off. One of them kicked Mary's horse from behind, causing the beast to start, jolting Mary; but she was a good rider, and stayed in the saddle as the horse moved off. The others went with her, keeping her surrounded.

Alison cried as she watched Mary ride away, presumably to yet another prison. How had this happened? It could only be that Babington's plot had been uncovered by Ned Willard.

Alison turned to Paulet. 'What is to be done with her?'

'She will be put on trial for treason.'

'And then?'

'And then she will be punished for her crimes,' said Paulet. 'God's will be done.'

*

BABINGTON PROVED elusive. Ned searched every London house where the conspirator had lodged without finding any clues. He set up a nationwide manhunt, sending a description of Babington and his associates to sheriffs, harbourmasters and lord lieutenants of counties. He dispatched two men to Babington's parents' home in Derbyshire. In every communication he threatened the death penalty for anyone helping any of the conspirators to escape.

In fact, Ned was not particularly concerned about Babington. The man was no longer much of a danger. His plot had been smashed. Mary had been moved, most of the conspirators were now being interrogated in the Tower of London, and Babington himself was a fugitive. All those Catholic noblemen who had been getting ready to support the invasion must now be putting their old armour back into storage.

However, Ned knew from long and dismal experience that another plot might readily grow in the ashes of the old. He had to find a way to make that impossible. The treason trial of Mary Stuart ought to discredit her in the eyes of all but her most fanatical supporters, he thought.

And there was one man he was desperate to capture. Every prisoner interrogated had mentioned Jean Langlais. All said he was not French but English, and some had met him at the English College. They described him as a tallish man of about fifty going bald on top: there seemed nothing very distinctive about his appearance. No one knew his real name or where he came from.

The very fact that so little was known about someone so important suggested, to Ned, that he was extraordinarily competent and therefore dangerous.

Ned now knew, from interrogating Robert Pooley, that both Langlais and Babington had been at Pooley's house minutes before the raid. They were probably the two seen, by the men-at-arms, running away from the neighbouring church, their escape aided by an obstructive flock of sheep. Ned had just missed them. But they were probably still together, along with the few conspirators remaining at large.

It took Ned ten days to track them down.

On 14 August a frightened rider on a sweating horse arrived at the house in Seething Lane. He was a young member of the Bellamy family, well-known Catholics but not suspected of treason. Babington and his fellow fugitives had turned up at the family's home, Uxendon Hall near the village of Harrow-on-the-Hill, a dozen miles west of London. Exhausted and starving, they had begged for shelter. The Bellamys had given them food and drink – compelled to do so under threat of their lives, they claimed – but had then insisted that the runaways leave the house and travel on. Now the family were terrified they would be hanged as collaborators, and eager to prove their loyalty by helping the authorities catch the conspirators.

Ned ordered horses immediately.

Riding hard, it took him and his men-at-arms less than two hours to reach Harrow-on-the-Hill. As the name suggested, the village was perched on top of a hill that stuck up out of the surrounding fields, and boasted a little school started recently by a local farmer. Ned stopped at the village inn and learned that a group of suspiciously bedraggled strangers had passed through earlier, on foot, heading north.

Guided by young Bellamy, the party followed the road to the boundary of the parish of Harrow, marked by an ancient sarsen stone, and through the next village, which Bellamy said was called Harrow Weald. Beyond the village, at an inn called The Hare, they caught up with their quarry.

Ned and his men walked into the building with swords drawn ready for a fight, but Babington's little group offered no resistance.

Ned looked hard at them. They were a sorry sight, having cut their hair inexpertly and stained their faces with some kind of juice in a poor attempt at disguise. They were young noblemen accustomed to soft beds, yet they had been sleeping rough for ten days. They seemed almost relieved to be caught.

Ned said: 'Which one of you is Jean Langlais?'

For a moment no one answered.

Then Babington said: 'He's not here.'

*

NED WAS FRUSTRATED to breaking point on the first day of February, 1587. He told Sylvie he was thinking of leaving the service of the queen. He would retire from court life, continue as member of Parliament for Kingsbridge, and help Sylvie run her bookshop. It would be a duller but happier life.

Elizabeth herself was the reason for his exasperation.

Ned had done everything possible to free Elizabeth from the menace of Mary Stuart. Mary was now imprisoned at Fotheringhay Castle in Northamptonshire and, although in the end she had been allowed to have her servants with her, Ned had made sure that the flinty Sir Amias Paulet also went with her to impose strict security. In October, the evidence he had assembled had been presented at Mary's trial, and she had been convicted of treason. In November, Parliament had sentenced her to death. At the beginning of December, news of the sentence had been broadcast all over the country to general rejoicing. Walsingham had immediately drafted the death warrant Elizabeth would need to sign to authorize the execution. Ned's old mentor William Cecil, now Lord Burghley, had approved the wording.

Almost two months later, Elizabeth still had not signed it.

To Ned's surprise, Sylvie sympathized with Elizabeth. 'She doesn't want to kill a queen,' she said. 'It sets a bad precedent. She's a queen herself. And she's not the only one who feels that way. Every monarch in Europe will be outraged if she executes Mary. Who knows what revenge they may take?'

Ned could not see it like that. He had devoted his life to protecting Elizabeth, and he felt she was rejecting his efforts.

As if to support Sylvie's point of view, ambassadors from both France and Scotland came to see Elizabeth at Greenwich Palace on 1 February to plead for Mary's life. Elizabeth did not want to quarrel with either country. She had recently signed a peace pact with King James VI of Scotland, who was Mary's son. On the other hand, Elizabeth's own life was still under threat. In January, one William Stafford confessed to plotting to poison her. Walsingham had publicized this, making it seem closer to success than it had ever really come, in order to bolster public support for Mary's execution. Exaggeration aside, it was still a chilling reminder that Elizabeth could never feel truly safe while Mary lived.

After the ambassadors had left, Ned decided to present Elizabeth with the death warrant again. Perhaps today she might be in the mood to sign it.

He was working with William Davison, who was standing in for Walsingham as secretary of state because Walsingham himself was ill. Davison agreed to Ned's plan – all Elizabeth's advisors were desperate for her to get it over with. Davison and Ned inserted the death warrant into the middle of a bundle of papers for her to sign.

Ned knew that Elizabeth would not be fooled by this little subterfuge. But she might pretend to be. He sensed that she was looking for a way to sign and then claim she had not intended to. If that was how she wanted it, he would make it easy for her.

She seemed in a good mood, he saw with relief when they

entered the presence chamber. 'Such mild weather for February,' she said. The queen was often too hot. Sylvie said it was her age: she was fifty-three. 'Are you well, Davison?' she said. 'Are you getting enough exercise? You work too hard.'

'I'm very well, and your majesty is most kind to ask,' said Davison.

She did not banter with Ned. She was aware that he was annoyed with her for prevarication. He could never hide his feelings from her. She knew him too well, perhaps as well as Sylvie did.

She had remarkable intuition, and now she gave a demonstration of it. Still addressing Davison, she said: 'That bundle of papers you're grasping to your bosom like a beloved child – does it include the death warrant?'

Ned felt foolish. He had no idea how she could have known.

'Yes,' Davison confessed.

'Give it to me.'

Davison extracted the paper from the bundle and handed it to the queen, bowing as he did so. Ned half expected her to berate them for trying to slip it past her, but she did not. She read the document, holding it at arm's length to compensate for her weakening eyesight. Then she said: 'Bring me pen and ink.'

Astonished, Ned went to a side table and picked up what she needed.

Would she really sign it? Or was she still toying with him, the way she had toyed with all those European princes who had wanted to marry her? She never had married: perhaps she never would sign the death warrant of Mary Stuart.

She dipped the quill he gave her in the inkwell he held out. She hesitated, looked at him with a smile he could not interpret, then signed the warrant with a flourish.

Hardly able to believe that she had at last done it, Ned took the document from her and handed it to Davison.

She looked sad, and said: 'Are you not sorry to see such a thing done?'

Davison said: 'I prefer to see your majesty alive, even at the cost of the life of another queen.'

Good answer, Ned thought; reminding Elizabeth that Mary would kill her if she could.

She said: 'Take that paper to the Lord Chancellor and have him affix the Great Seal.'

Even better, Ned thought; she was definitely in earnest.

'Yes, your majesty,' said Davison.

She added: 'But use it as secretly as may be.'

'Yes, your majesty.'

It was all very well for Davison to say yes, your majesty, Ned thought, but what on earth did she mean by telling him to use the document secretly? He decided not to ask the question.

She turned to him. 'Tell Walsingham what I've done.' Sarcastically she added: 'He will be so relieved it will probably kill him.'

Ned said: 'He's not that ill, thank God.'

'Tell him the execution must be done inside Fotheringhay, not on the castle green – not publicly.'

'Very well.'

A musing mood seemed to come over the queen. 'If only some loyal friend would deal the blow covertly,' she said quietly, not looking at either man. 'The ambassadors of France and Scotland would not blame me for that.'

Ned was shocked. She was proposing murder. He immediately resolved to have nothing to do with such a plan, not even by mentioning it to others. It would be too easy for a queen to deny she had made any such suggestion and prove the point by having the killer hanged.

She looked directly at Ned. Seeming to sense his resistance, she turned her gaze on Davison. He, too, said nothing. She sighed and said: 'Write to Sir Amias at Fotheringhay. Say that the queen is sorry he has not found some way to shorten the life of Mary Stuart, considering the great peril Elizabeth is subject to every hour of the day.'

This was ruthless even by Elizabeth's standards. 'Shorten the life' was hardly even a euphemism. But Ned knew Paulet better. He was a harsh jailer, but the rigid morality that led him to treat his prisoner severely would also hold him back from killing her. He would not be able to convince himself that murder was God's will. He would refuse Elizabeth's request – and she would probably punish him for that. She had little patience with men who did not obey her.

She dismissed Davison and Ned.

Outside in the waiting room, Ned spoke quietly to Davison. 'When the warrant has been sealed, I suggest you take it to Lord Burghley. He will probably call an emergency meeting of the Privy Council. I'm certain they'll vote to send the warrant to Fotheringhay without further consulting Queen Elizabeth. Everyone wants this done as soon as possible.'

'What will you do?' said Davison.

'Me?' said Ned. 'I'm going to hire an executioner.'

*

THE ONLY MEMBER of Mary Stuart's little court who was not crying was Mary herself.

The women sat around her bed all night. No one slept. From the great hall they could hear the banging of carpenters, who were undoubtedly building some kind of scaffold. Outside Mary's cramped suite of rooms, heavy boots marched up and down the passage all night: the nervous Paulet feared a rescue attempt and had posted a strong guard.

Mary got up at six o'clock. It was still dark. Alison dressed her by candlelight. Mary chose a dark red petticoat and a red satin bodice with a low neck. She added a black satin skirt and an overmantle of the same fabric with gold embroidery and sleeves slashed to show a purple lining. She had a fur collar to combat the chill of bleak Fotheringhay. Alison helped her don a white headdress with a long lace veil that fell down her back to the ground. It reminded Alison of the gorgeous train of blue-grey velvet she had carried at Mary's wedding in Paris, so many sad years ago.

Then Mary went alone into the little oratory to pray. Alison and the others stayed outside. Dawn broke as they waited. Alison looked out of a window and saw that it was going to be a fine, sunny day. Somehow that trivial detail made her angry.

The clock struck eight, and soon afterwards there was a loud and insistent knocking at the door of Mary's quarters. A man's voice called out: 'The lords are waiting for the queen!'

Until this moment Alison had not really believed that Mary would be killed. She had imagined it might all be a sham, a play put on by Paulet for some spiteful purpose; or by Elizabeth, who would issue a last-minute reprieve. She recalled that William Appletree, who had shot at Elizabeth while she was on a barge on the Thames river, had been dramatically reprieved as he stood on the scaffold. But if the lords were here to witness the execution, it must be real. Her heart seemed to turn into a lead weight in her chest, and her legs felt weak. She wanted to lie down and close her eyes and fall asleep for ever.

But she had to look after her queen.

She tapped on the door of the chapel and looked inside. Mary was on her knees in front of the altar, holding her Latin prayer book. 'Give me a moment longer, to finish my prayers,' she said.

Alison passed this message through the closed door, but the men outside were in no mood for concessions. The door was flung open, and the sheriff walked in. 'I hope she won't make us drag her there,' he said in a voice tinted with panic, and Alison sensed, in a moment of compassion that surprised her, that he, too, was distressed.

He opened the chapel door without knocking. Mary rose to her feet immediately. She was pale but calm, and Alison – who knew her well – felt reassured, at that moment, that the queen would maintain her regal bearing throughout the ordeal to come. Alison was relieved: she would have hated to see Mary lose her dignity as well as her life.

'Follow me,' said the sheriff.

Mary turned back momentarily and took an ivory crucifix from its hook on the wall over the altar. With the cross pressed to her heavy bosom and the prayer book in her other hand, she walked behind the sheriff, and Alison followed.

Mary was inches taller than the sheriff. Illness and confinement had made her portly and round-shouldered, but

Alison saw, with grieving pride, that she made a point of walking upright, her face proud, her steps unfaltering.

In the little antechamber outside the hall they were stopped. 'The queen goes alone from here,' said the sheriff.

Mary's servants protested, but the man was adamant. 'Orders from Queen Elizabeth,' he said.

Mary spoke in a high, firm voice. 'I do not believe you,' she said. 'As a maiden queen, Elizabeth would never condemn a fellow woman to die without any ladies to attend her.'

The sheriff ignored her. He opened the door to the hall.

Alison glimpsed a temporary stage about two feet high, draped with a black cloth, and a crowd of noblemen around it.

Mary passed through the doorway then stopped, so that the door could not be closed, and said in a carrying voice that rang in the hall: 'I beg your lordships, allow my servants to be with me, so that they may report the manner of my dying.'

Someone said: 'They might dip their handkerchiefs in her blood, to be used as blasphemous relics by superstitious fools.'

Someone was already worried about how to manage public reaction to this execution, Alison realized. No matter what they did, she thought savagely, those who took part in this vile performance would be regarded with hatred and loathing for all eternity.

'They will not do any such thing,' said Mary. 'I give you my word.'

The lords went into a huddle, and Alison heard murmured words, then the voice said: 'Very well, but only six.'

Mary gave in, pointed one by one at the people she wanted – starting with Alison – then walked forward.

Now Alison could see the entire hall. The stage was in the middle. Sitting on stage, on two stools, were men she recognized as the earls of Kent and Shrewsbury. A third stool, with a cushion, was clearly intended for Mary. In front of it, also draped in black, was the chopping block, and on the floor lay a huge woodcutter's axe, its blade freshly edged by the grindstone.

In front of the stage were two more seats, one occupied by Paulet and the other by a man Alison did not know. Standing to one side was a burly fellow in the clothes of a working man, the only person in the room dressed so; and after a moment's puzzlement Alison realized he must be the executioner. A heavy contingent of armed soldiers formed a circle around the stage. Outside the circle stood a large crowd of spectators: an execution had to be witnessed.

Among the crowd Alison spotted Sir Ned Willard. He had done more than anyone else to bring about today's horror. He had outwitted Elizabeth's enemies at every turn. He did not even appear triumphant. In fact, he looked aghast at the sight of the stage, the axe and the doomed queen. Alison would have preferred him to gloat: she could have hated him more.

Logs blazed in the massive fireplace, but failed to have much effect, and it seemed to Alison that the hall must be colder than the sunlit courtyard visible through the windows.

Mary approached the stage. As she did so, Paulet stood up and gave her his hand to help her up the steps. 'Thank you,' she said. But the cruel irony of his courtesy was not lost on her, for she then added bitterly: 'This is the last trouble I shall ever give you.'

She climbed the three steps with her head held high.

Then she calmly took her place on the execution stool.

While the commission for her execution was read out she sat motionless, her face without expression; but when a clergyman began to pray, loudly and pompously, asking God to convert her to the Protestant faith at the last minute, she protested. 'I am settled in the ancient Catholic Roman religion,' she said with queenly decisiveness, 'and I mean to spend my blood in defence of it.'

The man took no notice, but carried on.

Mary turned sideways on her stool, so that she had her back to him, and opened her Latin prayer book. She began to read aloud in a quiet voice while he ranted on, and Alison thought proudly that Mary was indisputably the more gracious of the two. After a minute, Mary slid off her stool to her knees, and continued to pray facing the execution block, as if it were an altar.

At last the prayers ended. Now Mary had to remove her

outer garments. Alison went onto the stage to help her. Mary seemed to want to undress quickly, as if impatient to get this over with, and Alison removed her overmantle and skirt as rapidly as possible, then her headdress with its veil.

Mary stood there in her blood-red underclothes, the very picture of a Catholic martyr, and Alison realized she had chosen the colour for exactly that effect.

Her servants were weeping and praying loudly, but Mary reproved them, saying in French: 'Don't cry for me.'

The executioner picked up the axe.

Another of the women brought a white blindfold and covered the queen's eyes.

Mary knelt down. Unable to see the block, she felt for it with her hands, then lowered her head into position, exposing her bare white neck. In seconds the axe would cut into that soft flesh. Alison was horrified to her soul.

In a loud voice Mary cried in Latin: 'Into thy hands, O Lord, I commend my spirit.'

The executioner lifted the axe high and brought it down hard.

He missed his mark. The blow did not sever Mary's neck, but bit into the bony back of her head. Alison could not contain herself and let out a loud sob. It was the most awful sight she had seen in a long life.

Mary did not move, and Alison could not tell whether she was still conscious. She made no sound.

The executioner lifted the axe and brought it down again, and this time his aim was better. The steel edge entered her neck at just the right place and went through almost all the way. But one sinew remained, and her head did not fall.

Horribly, the executioner took the head of his axe in both hands and sawed through the sinew.

At last Mary's head fell from the block onto the mat of straw that had been placed to receive it.

The man picked up the head by the hair, held it up for all to see, and said: 'God save the queen!'

But Mary had been wearing a wig, and now, to Alison's horror and revulsion, wig and head separated. Mary's head fell onto the stage, and the executioner was left holding her curly auburn wig. The head on the floor was revealed to be covered with short, grey hair.

It was the final, terrible indignity, and Alison could do nothing but close her eyes.

25

Sylvie felt sick when she thought about the Spanish invasion. She imagined another St Bartholomew's Day Massacre. In her mind she saw again the piles of naked corpses showing their hideous wounds on the streets of Paris. She had thought she had escaped from all that. Surely it could not happen again?

Queen Elizabeth's enemies had changed tactics. Instead of secret conspiracies they now favoured open action. King Felipe of Spain was assembling an armada. Felipe had long mooted this plan, but the beheading of Mary Stuart gave the invasion total legitimacy in the eyes of European leaders. The miserly Pope Sixtus had been so shocked by the execution that he had promised a million gold ducats towards the cost of the war.

Ned had known about the armada early, but by now it was the worst-kept secret in Europe. Sylvie had heard it discussed in the French Protestant church in London. King Felipe could not conceal the gathering of hundreds of ships and thousands of soldiers in and around the jump-off point of Lisbon. Felipe's navy was buying millions of tons of provisions – food, gunpowder, cannonballs, and the all-important barrels in which to store everything – and Felipe's purchasing agents were forced to scour Europe for supplies. They had even bought stores in England, Sylvie knew, because a Kingsbridge merchant called Elijah Cordwainer had been hanged for selling to them.

Ned was desperate to learn the Spanish king's battle plan. Sylvie had asked her contacts in Paris to be alert for any clues. Meanwhile, they heard from Barney. His ship, the *Alice*, had anchored briefly at Dover on its way to Combe Harbour, and

Barney had taken the opportunity to write to his brother to say that he would be in Kingsbridge within a few days, and he had a special reason to hope that he might see Ned there.

Sylvie had a competent assistant who was able to run the bookshop in her absence. Ned, too, was able to leave London for a few days. They reached Kingsbridge ahead of Barney. Not knowing exactly when he would arrive, they went to the waterfront every day to meet the morning barge from Combe Harbour. Barney's son, Alfo, now twenty-three, went with them. So did Valerie Forneron.

Alfo and Valerie were a couple. Valerie was the attractive daughter of the immigrant Huguenot cambric maker, Guillaume Forneron. She was one of numerous Kingsbridge girls who had been attracted to Alfo's Barney-like charm and exotic good looks. Sylvie wondered whether Guillaume had any misgivings about a suitor who looked so different from everyone else. However, it seemed that all Guillaume cared about was that Alfo was a Protestant. If Valerie had fallen for a Catholic boy, there would have been an explosion.

Alfo confided in Sylvie that he and Valerie were unofficially engaged to be married. 'Do you think the Captain will mind?' Alfo asked anxiously. 'I haven't been able to ask him.'

Sylvie thought for a minute. 'Tell him that you're sorry you haven't been able to ask for his approval, because you haven't seen him for three years, but you know he's going to like her. I don't think he'll mind.'

Barney arrived on the third morning, and he had a surprise for them. He got off the barge with a rosy-cheeked woman of about forty with a mass of curly fair hair and a big smile. 'This is Helga,' he said, looking pleased with himself. 'My wife.'

Helga immediately homed in on Alfo. She took his hand in both of hers and spoke in a German accent. 'Your father has told me all about your mother, and I know I will never replace her. But I hope you and I will learn to love each other. And I will try not to be like the wicked stepmother in the stories.'

It was just the right thing to say, Sylvie thought.

The story came out in fits and starts. Helga was a childless widow from Hamburg. She had been a prosperous dealer in the golden German wine the English called Rhenish. Barney had been first a customer, then a lover, then a fiancé. She had sold her business to marry him, but she planned to start a new enterprise here in Kingsbridge, importing the same wine.

Alfo introduced Valerie and, as he fumbled for the right words to say they were engaged, Barney forestalled him by saying: 'She's marvellous, Alfo – marry her, quick.'

Everyone laughed, and Alfo was able to say: 'That's what I'm planning, Captain.'

Sylvie enjoyed the occasion hugely: everyone hugging and shaking hands, news pouring out, several people talking at the same time, laughter and delight. As always on such occasions, she could not help contrasting Ned's family with her own. They had been just three, her parents and herself, and then two. At first she had been bewildered by Ned's crowd, but she loved it now, and it made her original family seem limited.

At last they all began the short walk uphill along the main street. When they reached the house, Barney looked across the market square and said: 'Hullo! What's happened to the monastery ruins?'

Alfo said: 'Come and see.'

He led the party through the new entrance in the west wall of the cloisters. He had paved the quadrangle, so that the crowds would not make it muddy. He had repaired the arcades and the vaulting, and now there was a market stall in each bay of the cloisters. The whole place was busy with shoppers.

Barney said: 'Why, this is my mother's dream! Who did it?'

'You did, Captain,' said Alfo.

Ned explained. 'I bought the place with your money, and Alfo turned it into the indoor market that Mother planned nearly thirty years ago.'

'It's wonderful,' Barney said.

Alfo said proudly: 'And it's making you a lot of money.'

Sylvie, who knew a great deal about the needs of shopkeepers, had given Alfo much advice on the indoor market. In the manner of young men, Alfo was not saying a lot about the help he had received; and, in the manner of kindly aunts, she did not remind him.

In fairness, Alfo had good commercial instincts. Sylvie assumed he had inherited them from his enterprising mother, who had apparently made the best rum in New Spain.

'The place is packed,' Barney said.

'I want to expand into the monks' old refectory,' Alfo said. Hastily he added: 'That is, if you approve, Captain.'

'It sounds like a good idea,' Barney said. 'We'll have a look at the numbers together later. There's plenty of time.'

They returned across the square and at last entered the house. The family gathered around the dining table for the midday meal, and inevitably the talk turned to the coming Spanish invasion.

'After all we've done,' Ned said with a gloom that tugged painfully at the strings of Sylvie's heart. 'We just wanted to have a country where a man could make his own peace with God, instead of mouthing prayers like a parrot. But they won't let us.'

Alfo said to Barney: 'Do they have slavery in Spain, Captain?'

Now where did that come from? Sylvie wondered. She recalled the moment when Alfo had become aware of slavery. He had been around thirteen or fourteen. His mother had told him that his grandmother had been a slave, and that many slaves were dark-skinned, as he was. He had been reassured to learn that slavery was not legally enforceable in England. He had not mentioned the subject since then, but Sylvie now realized that it had never left his mind. To him, England meant freedom; and the prospect of a Spanish invasion had renewed his fears.

'Yes,' Barney said. 'Spain has slavery. In Seville, where I used to live, every wealthy family had slaves.'

'And are the slaves dark-skinned?'

Barney sighed. 'Yes. A few are European prisoners-of-war, usually oarsmen in the galleys, but most are African or Turkish.'

'If the Spanish invade us, will they change our laws?'

'Most certainly. They will make us all Catholic. That's the point.'

'And will they permit slavery?'

'They might.'

Alfo nodded grimly, and Sylvie wondered if he would have

the possibility of slavery hanging over him all his life. She said: 'Can't we do something to prevent the invasion?'

'Yes,' said Barney. 'We shouldn't just wait for them to arrive – we should hit them first.'

Ned said: 'We've already put this proposal to the queen: a pre-emptive strike.'

'Stop them before they start.'

Ned was more moderate. 'Attack them before they set sail, aiming to do at least enough damage to make King Felipe think again.'

Barney said eagerly: 'Has Queen Elizabeth agreed to this?'

'She has decided to send six vessels: four warships and two pinnaces.' Pinnaces were smaller, faster craft, often used for reconnaissance and messages, not much use in a fight.

'Four warships – against the richest and most powerful country in the world?' Barney protested. 'It's not enough!'

'We can't risk our entire navy! That would leave England defenceless. But we're inviting armed merchant ships to join the fleet. There will be plunder, if the mission is successful.'

'I'll go,' Barney said immediately.

'Oh,' said Helga, who had hardly spoken until now. She looked dismayed. 'So soon?'

Sylvie felt sorry for her. But she had married a sailor. They led dangerous lives.

'I'll take both ships,' Barney went on. He now had two, the *Alice* and the *Bella*. 'Who's in charge?'

'Sir Francis Drake,' Ned told him.

Alfo said enthusiastically: 'He's the man for it!' Drake was a hero to young Englishmen: he had circumnavigated the Earth, only the second captain to do so in the history of the human race. It was just the daring kind of exploit to capture youthful imaginations, Sylvie thought. 'You'll be all right if Drake is with you,' Alfo said.

'Perhaps,' said Sylvie, 'but I'm going to pray that God goes with you too.'

'Amen,' said Helga.

*

No ONE SHOULD love the sea, but Barney did. He was exhilarated by the sensation of sailing, the wind snapping the canvas and the waves glittering in the sunshine.

There was something mad about this feeling. The sea was dangerous. Although the English fleet had not yet sighted the enemy, they had already lost one ship, the *Marengo*, during a violent storm in the Bay of Biscay. Even in good weather there was constant risk of attack by vessels of unfriendly countries – or even by pirates pretending, until the last minute, to be friendly. Few sailors lived to be old.

Barney's son had wanted to come on this voyage. Alfo wanted to be in the front line, defending his country. He loved England and especially Kingsbridge. But Barney had firmly refused. Alfo's real passion was commerce. In that he was different to his father, who had always hated ledgers. Besides, it was one thing for Barney to risk his own life; quite another to endanger his beloved child.

The treacherous Atlantic seas had become calmer as the fleet drew nearer to the warm Mediterranean. By Barney's reckoning the fleet was about ten miles from Cádiz, near Gibraltar on the south-western tip of Spain, when a signal gun was fired, and a conference pennant was raised on the flagship *Elizabeth Bonaventure*, summoning all captains to a council of war with vice-admiral Sir Francis Drake.

It was four o'clock on a fine afternoon, Wednesday 29 April 1587, and a good south-westerly breeze was blowing the twenty-six ships directly towards their destination at a brisk five knots. With reluctance Barney dropped the sails of the *Alice* and the ship slowed until it was becalmed, rising and falling on the swell in the way that made landlubbers feel so ill.

Only six in the convoy were fighting ships belonging to the queen. The other twenty, including Barney's two, were armed trading vessels. No doubt King Felipe would accuse them of being little better than pirates, and, Barney thought, he had a point. But Elizabeth, unlike Felipe, did not have the bottomless silver mines of New Spain to finance her navy, and this was the only way she could muster an attacking fleet.

Barney ordered his crew to lower a boat and row him across to the *Elizabeth Bonaventure*. He could see the other captains doing the same. A few minutes later, the boat bumped the side of the flagship and Barney climbed the rope ladder to the deck.

It was a big ship, a hundred feet long with massive armament – forty-seven guns, including two full-size cannons firing sixty-pound balls – but there was no stateroom anywhere near large enough to hold all the captains. They stood on deck, around a single carved chair that no one dared sit on.

Some of the fleet were straggling a mile or more behind, and not all the captains had arrived when the impatient Drake appeared.

He was a heavy-set man in his forties with curly red hair, green eyes and the pink-and-white complexion people sometimes called 'fresh'. His head seemed small for his body.

Barney took off his hat, and the other captains followed suit. Drake was famously proud, perhaps because he had risen to great heights from a humble farm in Devon. But the captains' respect for him was heartfelt. They all knew every detail of his three-year voyage around the world.

He sat on the carved chair, glanced up at the sky, and said: 'We could be in Cádiz before sunset.'

Cádiz was his target, rather than Lisbon where the Spanish fleet was gathering. Drake was like Barney's late mother in his obsession with news, and he had questioned the captains of two Dutch merchant ships encountered off Lisbon. From them he had learned that the supply vessels for the invasion were loading in Cádiz, and he had seized on this information. Supply ships would be easier to defeat, and – perhaps more important to the always greedy Drake – their cargoes would make more valuable plunder.

Drake's deputy was William Borough, a famous navigator who had written a book about the compass. He now said: 'But we don't even have our full numbers – several ships are miles behind us.'

Barney reflected that two men could hardly be more opposite than Drake and Borough. The deputy was learned, scholarly and cautious, a man for records and documents and charts. Drake was impulsive, scornful of timidity, a man of action. 'We have the wind and the weather on our side,' he said. 'We must seize the chance.'

'Cádiz is a large harbour, but the entrance to the bay is treacherous,' Borough argued. He flourished a chart which Drake did not condescend to look at. Borough pressed on. 'There is only one deep-water passage, and that goes close by the tip of the peninsula – where there is a fortress bristling with cannons.'

'We'll fly no flags as we enter,' Drake said. 'They won't know who we are until it's too late.'

'We have no idea what ships may be in the harbour,' Borough countered.

'Merchantmen, according to those Dutch captains.'

'There may be warships too.'

'They're all in Lisbon – which is why we're going to Cádiz.'

Borough found Drake's insouciance maddening. 'Then what is our battle plan?' he demanded angrily.

'Battle plan?' said Drake heedlessly. 'Follow me!'

He immediately began shouting orders to his crew. Barney and the rest of the captains hastily scrambled over the side to their boats, laughing with pleasure at Drake's boldness, eager for action themselves. An imp of anxiety in the back of Barney's mind whispered that Borough was right to be wary, but Drake's fighting spirit was infectious.

As soon as Barney was back aboard the *Alice*, he ordered the crew to set the sails. There were six, two on each mast, all of them square-shaped. The sailors climbed the masts like monkeys, and in less than a minute the breeze was filling canvas, the ship's prow was ploughing the waves, and Barney was happy.

He gazed forward. A smudge appeared on the horizon and gradually revealed itself to be a fortress.

Barney knew Cádiz. It was near the mouth of the Guadalquivir river eighty miles downstream from Seville, where he had lived with Carlos and Ebrima almost thirty years ago. A few miles inland was Jerez, source of the strong wine the English called sherry sack. The city of Cádiz, with its fort, stood at the end of a long peninsula that enclosed a large natural harbour. Two rivers emptied into a wide bay fringed with waterfront villages and settlements.

The ships of the fleet deftly eased into line behind Drake's flagship, warships first and merchantmen after. Without orders, they adopted the formation known as 'line ahead', or single file, so that an enemy directly in front – which was where the Spanish were for the moment – could fire at only one of them at a time. It also meant that if Drake found the correct passage through the shallows, they all would.

Barney was scared, but his fear had an odd effect: it excited him. It was better than sherry sack. In danger he felt more alive than at any other time. He was no fool: he knew the agony of wounds and he had seen the terrified panic of drowning men as a ship went down. But somehow none of that diminished the thrill he felt going into battle, getting ready to kill or be killed.

There was an hour left before sunset, he reckoned, when the *Elizabeth Bonaventure* entered the harbour of Cádiz.

Barney studied the fortress. He could see no movement around the guns, no hefting of cannonballs into muzzles, no scurrying to fetch gunpowder and swabbing buckets and the long screw-shaped cleaning tools called gun-worms. All he could make out was a handful of soldiers leaning on the battlements, gazing at the unidentified approaching fleet with mild curiosity. Clearly no alarm had sounded.

As the *Alice* entered the harbour behind the leading ships, Barney switched his gaze to the town. He could see what looked like a main square crowded with people. There were no guns there, for the obvious reason that they would have hit the close-packed ships moored side by side along the waterfront.

He was puzzled to notice that some of the ships had had their sails removed, leaving their masts naked. Why would that have been done? Sails needed repair now and again, but not all at the same time. He recalled Ned's saying that King Felipe had commandeered dozens of foreign ships for his armada, regardless of the wishes of their owners. Perhaps, Barney speculated, those vessels had to be prevented from sneaking away to freedom. But now they were immobilized, unable to flee from the English guns. They were doubly unlucky.

Peering in the evening light, Barney thought he could see that most of the people in the square had their backs to the water. They were in two groups and, as the fleet drew nearer, he saw that one crowd seemed to be watching a play being performed on a stage, and the other surrounded a troupe of acrobats. Cádiz had not seen battle in Barney's lifetime, nor for many years before, as far as he knew, and he guessed the people here felt safe. They were not going to turn around to look at the everyday event of ships arriving.

In the next few minutes they would suffer a horrible shock.

He looked around the bay. There were about sixty craft in harbour altogether, he reckoned. About half were large cargo ships; the rest were an assortment of smaller vessels, all moored at the quayside or at anchor offshore. Most of their crews would be ashore, eating fresh food and drinking in the taverns and enjoying female company. No doubt many of them were among the crowd in the main square. The English ships were foxes in a henhouse, about to pounce. Barney felt a leap of elation: what a devastating blow it would be to King Felipe's invasion plan if the English fleet could destroy them all!

He had turned almost a full circle, and was looking north, when he saw the galleys.

There were two of them, coming out of Port St Mary at the mouth of the Guadalete river. He knew what they were by their narrow profile and the lines of oars slanting from their sides, dipping into the water and out in perfect unison. Galleys would capsize in an Atlantic storm, but they were much used in the calmer Mediterranean. Manned by slaves, they were fast and manoeuvrable, and were independent of the wind, a big advantage over sailing ships.

Barney watched them speed across the bay. Their cannons were mounted at the front, so they could only fire ahead. They usually had a pointed iron or brass prow for ramming, after which their complement of pikemen and arquebusiers would board the crippled enemy ship to finish off the crew. But no one would send two galleys to attack twenty-six ships, so

Barney concluded that these had an investigative mission. They intended to question the leader of the incoming fleet.

They never got the chance.

Drake turned the Elizabeth Bonaventure towards the galleys in a perfectly executed manoeuvre. He might have been in trouble if there had been little or no wind in the bay, for sailing ships were helpless when becalmed, whereas galleys did not need wind. But Drake was lucky.

The other warships followed Drake with precision.

The merchantmen stayed on course, filing through the deep-water passage past the fort, then fanning out across the harbour.

Barney watched the galleys. Each had about twenty-four oars, he reckoned. One oar was manned by five slaves. Such men did not live long: chained to their benches, scorched by the sun, wallowing in their own filth, they were constantly afflicted by infectious diseases. The frail lasted a few weeks, the strong a year or two, and when they died, their bodies were unceremoniously thrown into the sea.

As the galleys approached the Elizabeth Bonaventure, Barney waited for Drake to act. Just as he began to fear that the vice-admiral might be holding his fire a little too long, a puff of smoke arose from the flagship, and a moment later the sound of a cannon boomed across the bay. The first ball splashed harmlessly into the water, as the gunner measured his range; artillery was an inexact art, as gunner Barney knew well. But the second and third missed, too, so perhaps Drake's man was incompetent.

The galleys did not return fire: their smaller guns were still out of range.

Drake's gunner was not incompetent. His fourth ball smashed into a galley amidships, and a fifth struck its prow.

They were deadly shots with heavy ammunition, and the galley began to founder right away. Barney could hear the screams of the wounded and the panicky shouts of those fortunate enough to remain unhurt. The soldiers threw their weapons away, jumped into the water, and made for the second galley, those who could not swim grasping pieces of floating timber. Within moments the crew were doing the same. A chorus of cries and pleas arose from the ranks of oarsmen as they begged to be unchained, but no one had time for them, and they were left, screaming piteously, to sink with the wreckage.

The second galley slowed and began to pick up survivors. Drake ceased firing, perhaps out of gentlemanly consideration for the helpless men in the water, but more likely to conserve ammunition.

Almost immediately more galleys appeared from Port St Mary, their oars dipping and rising with the repetitive grace of racehorses' legs. Barney counted six speeding across the calm harbour water. He gave credit to whoever was in command: it took a brave man to send six ships against twenty-six.

They came on line abreast – side by side – as was their normal tactic, for that way each protected the vulnerable sides of the two adjacent vessels.

The warships turned again, and all four began to fire as soon as the galleys were in range.

As battle was joined, Barney saw that a few of the ships in the bay were weighing anchor and setting their sails. Their crews had not yet gone ashore, Barney presumed, and their quick-thinking captains had realized Cádiz was under attack and decided to make a run for it. But most of the ships were stuck: they did not have time to round up their crews from the taverns and brothels, and a ship could not sail without a crew.

In the town square the people were panicking, some heading away from the waterfront to their homes, most running to the fortress for protection.

Barney was interested in the ships that did not move from their anchorages in the bay. They were probably guarded by only one or two nightwatchmen. He began to study them, and fixed his gaze on a smallish round-ended three-masted ship that looked built for freight rather than battle. He could see no activity on deck.

He directed his crew to reduce sail, slowing the *Alice*, and steer for the freighter. As they did so, Barney saw two men abandon the freighter: they scrambled down a rope to a boat, untied it, and rowed energetically for the shore. That confirmed his instinct. The ship would now be deserted.

He looked again across the bay to the warships, and saw that they had forced the galleys to retreat.

A few minutes later, the Alice was close enough to the freighter to drop its sails, becoming almost motionless. Barney's crew drew the two vessels together with boathooks and ropes. Finally, they were able to leap from one ship to the other.

There was no one aboard the freighter.

Barney's first mate, Jonathan Greenland, went down into the hold to investigate the cargo.

He came back looking woebegone, carrying strips of wood in one arm and metal hoops in the other. 'Barrel staves,' he explained disgustedly. 'And iron reinforcement rings.'

Barney was disappointed. As plunder this was not worth much. On the other hand, destroying this cargo would impair the invasion by creating a shortage of barrels for the armada's provisions. 'Fire the ship,' he said.

The crew brought turpentine from the Alice and splashed the inflammable liquid over the freighter's deck and below. Then they set fire to it in several places and hastily jumped back to their own vessel.

It was dark, but the blazing freighter lit up the ships nearby, and Barney chose a second target. Once again the Alice approached to find that the watchmen had fled. The crew of the Alice boarded, and this time Jonathan Greenland came up from the hold looking happy. 'Wine,' he said. 'From Jerez. Lakes and oceans of sack.'

English sailors were given beer to drink, but the lucky Spaniards got wine, and the invasion fleet would need thousands of gallons of it. But here was a cargo the armada would never receive. 'Take it all,' Barney said.

The crew lit torches and began the heavy work of bringing the barrels up from the hold and transferring them across to the Alice. They worked cheerfully, knowing that each of them would get a share from the sale of this costly cargo.

The enemy ship was fully stocked for a voyage, and Barney's

crew also took all its salted meat, cheese, and ship's biscuit for the stores of the *Alice*. It was armed, and Barney took its gunpowder. The shot was the wrong size for his guns, so he had the crew throw the cannonballs into the water, so that they would never be fired at English sailors.

When the hold was empty, he set fire to the ship.

Looking around the harbour, he could see another five or six vessels blazing. On shore, torches had been lit along the waterfront, and he saw guns from the fortress being towed, by teams of horses, to the dockside. The English raiders would still be out of range, but Barney figured the purpose was to discourage the attackers from coming ashore. He thought he could see troops being mustered in the square. He guessed that the townspeople presumed the attack on ships was only a prelude to an invasion, and had shrewdly decided to look to their landside defences. They could not know that Drake's orders were to destroy Spanish shipping, not to conquer Spanish cities.

But the upshot was that there was almost no resistance. Barney could see a massive ship firing back at several attacking English vessels, but it was exceptional: there was otherwise little gunfire, and mostly the raiders were able to loot and burn unhindered.

Barney looked around for another ship to destroy.

*

ENGLAND REJOICED at the news of Drake's sneak attack on Cádiz, but Margery's husband, Earl Bart, did not join in the celebrations.

Reports varied, but all said that around twenty-five major ships had been destroyed, and thousands of tons of supplies stolen or sent to the bottom. The Spanish armada had been crippled before it had even set out. No English sailors had been killed and only one wounded, by a lucky shot from a galley. Queen Elizabeth had even made a profit on the expedition.

'It was a day of infamy,' Bart raged at the dinner table in New Castle. 'No warning, no declaration of war, just outright murder and theft by a group of barefaced pirates.'

Bart at fifty reminded Margery painfully of the father-in-law who had raped her, except only that Bart was more red-faced and even fatter than his father had been. Now she said waspishly: 'Those ships were on their way here to kill us all – including both my sons. I'm glad they were sunk.'

Young Bartlet took his father's side, as usual. At twenty-three, Bartlet bore a resemblance to Margery's father, being tall and freckled, but he had all Bart's attitudes, unfortunately. She loved him, but he was hard to like, and that made her feel guilty. 'King Felipe only wants to return England to Catholicism,' Bartlet said. 'Most English people would welcome that.'

'Many would, but not at the price of being conquered by a foreign country,' Margery countered.

Stephen Lincoln was shocked. 'My lady, how can you say such a thing? The Pope approved the plan of the Spanish king.'

Stephen had proved a poor friend to Margery, but all the same she had some sympathy for him. He had spent thirty years as a secret priest, holding furtive services after dark and keeping the sacramentals in undignified hidey-holes as if they were shameful. He had dedicated his life to God but had spent it as a criminal, and that had left his face lined and gaunt and his soul bitter. But he was wrong about this, and so was the Pope. 'I think it's a mistake,' she said crisply. 'An invasion would actually turn people away from Catholicism, by linking it with foreign domination.'

'How can you know that?' Stephen meant *you, a mere woman*, but he did not dare to say it.

Margery replied: 'I know because it's what has happened in the Netherlands. Patriotic Dutch people fight for Protestantism, not because they care about doctrine, but because they want independence from Spain.'

Roger joined in. He had been such a pretty baby, Margery thought, but now he was seventeen, with a rapidly growing curly dark beard. Margery's impish look was reinterpreted, in her son, as a lively bantam confidence that made people smile. He had the golden-brown eyes of his biological father, Ned. It was fortunate that Bart, like most men of his type, never noticed the colour of people's eyes, and that anyone else who suspected Roger's parentage would never say it for fear of being run through by Bart's sword. Roger said: 'So, Mother, how do *you* think we could return our country to Catholicism?'

She was proud to have a son who could ask such a thoughtful and challenging question. He had a lively intellect, and was planning to go to Kingsbridge College, Oxford. Roger was a staunch Catholic and took an active part in the smuggling of the priests. All the same, Stephen, who was his tutor, had been unable to suppress the independence the boy had inherited from Ned.

She answered him: 'Left alone, English people will slowly and quietly make their way back to the old faith.'

However, the English were not destined to be left alone.

There was no Spanish armada in 1587 but, as summer turned to autumn, Margery and everyone else realized that they had celebrated too soon. They had imagined that Drake had prevented the invasion. But the raid on Cádiz had only postponed it. King Felipe was so rich that, to the consternation of the English, he simply started building new ships and buying replacement supplies.

Queen Elizabeth and her government began to prepare for a fight to the death.

All along the coast, defences were repaired that winter. Castles were reinforced, and new earth ramparts were thrown up around towns that had not seen battle for centuries. The walls of Kingsbridge were rebuilt, the old ones having long ago disappeared into a suburban sprawl. The rusting old cannons at Combe Harbour were cleaned and test-fired. Chains of hilltop beacons were built, from the coast to London, ready to transmit the dreadful news that the galleons had been sighted.

Margery was aghast. Catholics were going to slaughter Protestants, and vice versa. But being a follower of Jesus Christ was not supposed to be about cannons and swords, killing and maiming. In the gospel story only the enemies of Jesus shed blood.

Margery could not help brooding over the fact that Ned believed as she did, that Christians should not kill one another over doctrine. He claimed that Queen Elizabeth believed it too, even though he admitted that she had not always been true to her ideals.

Margery suffered agonies in the early months of 1588, as details trickled through of the size and strength of the new armada. It was rumoured to have more than one hundred ships, a figure that terrified the English, whose entire navy consisted of thirty-eight vessels.

The Government began interning notorious Catholics as a precaution. Margery hoped the men of her family would be put in prison where they would be safe. However, Bart was not considered dangerous. He had never been part of any conspiracy. It was Margery who had been the secret agent in New Castle, and she had been so careful that no one suspected her.

Then the weapons arrived.

Two carts loaded with hay trundled into the castle, but when the hay was forked off, it was found to conceal half a dozen battleaxes, forty or so swords, ten arquebuses, a sack of bullets and a small barrel of gunpowder. Margery watched the ordnance being carried into the house and stashed in the old bread oven, then said to Bart: 'What are these for?'

She genuinely did not know. Would her husband fight for his queen and country, or for the Catholic Church?

He quickly set her straight. 'I will muster an army of loyal Catholic gentry and peasants, and divide them in two. I will lead half of them to Combe Harbour to greet the Spanish liberators, and Bartlet will lead the other half to Kingsbridge where they will take over the town and celebrate Mass in the cathedral – in Latin.'

A horrified protest sprang to her lips, but she suppressed it. If she let Bart know how she felt, he would stop giving her information.

Bart believed she was merely squeamish about bloodshed. But she was more serious than that. She was not content merely to look away. She had to do something to prevent this.

Instead of protesting, she probed. 'You can't do all that on your own.'

'I won't be on my own. Catholic noblemen all over the country will be doing the same.'

'How can you know?'

'Your brother is in charge of it.'

'Rollo?' This was news to Margery. 'He's in France.'

'Not any more. He's organizing the Catholic nobility.'

'But how does he know whom to organize?' As she asked the question, Margery realized, with horror, what the answer would be.

Bart confirmed her fear. 'Every nobleman who has risked his life by harbouring a secret priest is willing to fight against Elizabeth Tudor.'

Margery found herself short of breath, as if she had been punched in the stomach. She struggled to hide her feelings from Bart – who, fortunately, was not observant. 'So . . .' She swallowed, took a deep breath, and started again. 'So Rollo has used my network of secret priests to organize an armed insurrection against Queen Elizabeth.'

'Yes,' said Bart. 'We thought it best not to tell you.'

Of course you did, Margery thought bitterly.

'Women dislike talk of bloodshed,' Bart went on, as if he were an expert on feminine feelings. 'But you were sure to find out eventually.'

Margery was angry and sick at heart, but she did not want Bart to know it. She asked a mundane question. 'Where will you keep the weapons?'

'In the old bread oven.'

'These aren't enough for an army.'

'There are more to come. And there's plenty of room behind the oven.' Bart turned to give instructions to the servants, and Margery took the opportunity to walk away.

Had she been stupid? She knew perfectly well that Rollo would not hesitate to lie to her, nor would Bart. But she had thought that Rollo, like her, wanted no more than to help loyal Catholics receive the sacraments. Should she have guessed at his real intentions?

Perhaps she would have seen through Rollo if she had been able to talk to him. But for years now she had only waved to him across the beach when he brought a new group of priests from the English College. The lack of contact had made it easier for him to fool her.

She felt certain of one thing: she would no longer smuggle priests from Rollo's college into England. She had done so in ignorance of their double role, but now that she knew the truth she would have nothing more to do with the business, nor with anything else her brother wanted. She would send him a coded message to that effect at the first opportunity. He would be furious, and that would give her some small satisfaction.

She lay awake that night and several succeeding nights, then she decided to stop reproaching herself and do something. She was under no obligation to keep Rollo's secrets, nor Bart's. Was there anything she could do to prevent bloodshed and keep her sons safe?

She resolved to speak to Ned Willard.

Easter was a few days away, and as usual she would go to Kingsbridge with Bart and the boys for the Easter Fair. They would all attend the special services in the cathedral. Bart could no longer avoid attending Protestant services: it was too dangerous and too expensive – the fine for not going to church was now £20.

She suffered a twinge of conscience as the family group approached Kingsbridge and the cathedral tower came into view over the treetops. Should she not be supporting this Spanish invasion and the associated Catholic rebellion? After all, the result might be that England would be Catholic again, and that had to be God's will.

Easter had become a dull affair under the Protestants. No longer were the bones of St Adolphus carried through the streets of Kingsbridge in a colourful procession. There was no mystery play in the cathedral. Instead, there was a troupe of actors in the courtyard of the Bell Inn every afternoon, performing a play called *Everyman*. The Protestants did not understand people's need for colour and drama in church.

But Margery at forty-five no longer believed that Protestantism was evil and Catholicism perfect. For her the important divide was between tyranny and tolerance; between people who tried to force their views on everyone else, and people who respected the faith of those who disagreed with them. Rollo and Bart belonged to the authoritarian group she despised. Ned was one of the rare people who believed in religious freedom. She would trust him.

She did not run into Ned on her first day in Kingsbridge, nor the second. Perhaps he would not come this Easter. She saw his nephew, Alfo, now proudly married to Valerie Forneron. She also saw Ned's German sister-in-law, Helga, but not Barney, who had returned from Cádiz with another small fortune in plunder and had gone back to sea after a short furlough. Margery was reluctant to question the family about Ned's plans. She did not want to give them the impression that she was desperate to talk to him. She was, though.

On Easter Saturday she was at the market in the old cloisters, now roofed over. She fingered a length of cloth in a dark wine-red colour that she thought might suit her now that she was, well, no longer a girl. Then she glanced across the quadrangle and saw the sturdy short figure of Ned's wife, Sylvie.

Sylvie was like Margery, and both women knew it. Margery did not have to be modest with herself, and she could see that both she and Sylvie were attractive women who were also intelligent and determined – in fact, rather similar to Ned's formidable mother. Sylvie was a Protestant, of course, and a crusading one; but even there Margery could see a similarity, for they both took terrible risks for the sake of their faith.

Margery wanted to speak to Ned, not Sylvie; but now Sylvie caught her eye, smiled, and came towards her.

It occurred to Margery that she could give Sylvie a message for Ned. In fact, that might even be better, for then no one could cast suspicion on Margery by reporting to Bart that she had been talking to Ned.

'What a pretty hat,' Sylvie said in her soft French accent.

'Thank you.' Margery was wearing a sky-blue velvet cap. She showed Sylvie the cloth she was contemplating. 'Do you like this colour?'

'You're too young to wear burgundy,' Sylvie said with a smile.

'That's kind.'

'I saw your two sons. Roger has a beard now!'

'They grow up too fast.'

'I envy you. I have never conceived. I know Ned is disappointed, though he doesn't complain.'

Sylvie's intimacy with Ned's unspoken feelings, so casually revealed, caused Margery to feel a hot wave of jealousy. You have no children, she thought, but you've got him.

She said: 'I'm worried about my boys. If the Spanish invade us, they will have to fight.'

'Ned says the queen's ships will try to prevent the Spanish soldiers landing.'

'I'm not sure we have enough ships.'

'Perhaps God will be on our side.'

'I'm not as sure as I used to be about whose side God is on.'

Sylvie smiled ruefully. 'Nor am I.'

Out of the corner of her eye Margery saw Bart enter the indoor market. She was forced to make a quick decision. 'Will you give Ned a message from me?'

'Of course. But he's here somewhere—'

'I'm sorry, there's no time. Ask him to raid New Castle and arrest Bart, Bartlet and Roger. He will find weapons stockpiled in the old oven – they're to support the invaders.' Her plan was risky, she knew, but she trusted Ned.

'I'll tell him,' Sylvie said, wide-eyed. 'But why do you want your sons arrested?'

'So that they won't have to fight. Better in prison than in the graveyard.'

Sylvie appeared startled by that thought. Perhaps she had not imagined that children might bring pain as well as joy.

Margery glanced at Bart. He had not yet noticed her. If she parted from Sylvie now he would not know that they had been talking. 'Thank you,' Margery said, and she walked away.

She did see Ned the following day, in the cathedral at the Easter service. His familiar slim figure was dear to her still, after all these years. Her heartbeat seemed to slow, and she was suffused by a mixture of love and regret that gave her joy and pain in equal measure. She was glad she had put on a new blue coat this morning. However, she did not speak to him. The temptation was strong: she longed to look into his eyes and see them crinkle at the corners when he said something wry. But she resisted.

She left Kingsbridge and returned to New Castle with her family on the Tuesday after Easter. On the Wednesday, Ned Willard came.

Margery was in the courtyard when a sentry on the battlements called out: 'Horsemen on the Kingsbridge road! Twelve ... fifteen ... maybe twenty!'

She hurried into the house. Bart, Bartlet and Roger were in the great hall, already buckling on their swords. 'It's probably the sheriff of Kingsbridge,' Bart said.

Stephen Lincoln appeared. 'The hiding place is full of weapons!' he said in a frightened voice. 'What am I to do?'

Margery had thought about this in advance. 'Take the box of sacramentals and leave by the back gate. Go to the tavern in the village and wait until you hear from us that the coast is clear.' The villagers were all Catholic, and would not betray him.

Stephen hurried away.

Addressing the boys, she said: 'You two are to say nothing and do nothing, do you hear? Leave it to your father to speak. Sit still.'

Bart said: 'Unless I tell them otherwise.'

'Unless your father tells you otherwise,' she repeated.

Bart was not the father of either boy, but she had kept that secret well.

She realized it was thirty years since she and Ned had met in this hall after he returned from Calais. What was the play they had seen? *Mary Magdalene*. She had been so excited after kissing him that she had watched the performance without taking any of it in. She had been full of hope for a happy life with Ned. If I had known then how my life was going to turn out, she thought, I might have thrown myself from the battlements.

She heard the horses enter the courtyard, and a minute later the sheriff walked into the great hall. It was Rob Matthewson, the son of old Sheriff Matthewson, who had died. Rob was as big as his father and equally determined not to be ordered around by anyone but the queen.

Matthewson was followed by a large group of men-at-arms, Ned Willard among them. Seeing Ned up close, Margery noticed that his face was beginning to show lines of strain around the nose and mouth, and there was a touch of grey in his dark hair.

He was letting the sheriff take the lead. 'I must search your house, Earl Bart,' Matthewson said.

Bart said: 'What the devil are you looking for, you insolent dog?'

'I have information that there is a Catholic priest called Stephen Lincoln here. You and your family must stay in this room while I look for him.'

'I'm not going anywhere,' Bart said. 'This is where I live.'

The sheriff went out again, and his entourage followed. Ned paused at the door. 'I'm very sorry this has happened, Countess Margery,' he said.

She went along with his act. 'No, you're not,' she said, as if angry with him.

He went on: 'But with the king of Spain getting ready to invade us, no one's loyalty can be taken for granted.'

Bart gave a disgusted grunt. Ned said no more and went out.

A few minutes later, they heard shouts of triumph, and Margery guessed that Ned had guided Matthewson to the hidey-hole.

She looked at her husband, who had obviously made the same guess. Consternation and anger appeared on Bart's face, and Margery knew there was going to be trouble.

The sheriff's men began to drag the weapons into the great hall. 'Swords,' the sheriff said. 'Dozens of them! Guns and ammunition. Battleaxes. Bows and arrows. All tucked away in a little secret room. Earl Bart, you are under arrest.'

Bart was apoplectic. He had been found out. He stood up and began to rage. 'How dare you?' he yelled. 'I am the earl of

Shiring. You cannot do this and expect to live.' Red in the face, he raised his voice even more. 'Guards!' he shouted. 'In here!' Then he drew his sword.

Bartlet and Roger followed suit.

Margery screamed: 'No!' She had done this to keep her sons safe but instead she had put their lives in danger. 'Stop!'

The sheriff and his men drew too.

Ned did not draw his sword, but held up his arms and shouted: 'Hold it, everyone! Nothing will be achieved by a fight, and anyone who attacks the sheriff's men will hang.'

The two groups faced each other across the hall. Bart's men-at-arms came in to stand behind their earl, and more of the sheriff's men appeared. Margery could hardly believe how quickly this had gone wrong. If they fought, there would be terrible slaughter.

Bart yelled: 'Kill them all!'

Then he fell over.

He went down like a tree, slowly at first then faster, hitting the stone floor with a sickening thud.

Margery had often seen him fall down drunk, but this was grimly different.

Everyone froze.

Margery knelt beside Bart and put her palm on his chest. Then she felt his wrist and his neck. There was no sign of life.

She stared at her husband. He was a self-indulgent man who had done nothing but please himself, heedless of others, during his fifty years on earth.

'He's dead,' she said.

And all she felt was relief.

*

PIERRE AUMANDE went to the apartment where he kept Louise de Nîmes, his mistress for the last four years. He found her richly robed, with her hair in an elaborate coiffure, as if she were going to court, which, of course, she was never permitted to do. He always made her dress formally, for that intensified the pleasure of degrading her. Anyone could humiliate a servant, but Louise was a marchioness.

He had not tired of the game, and he felt he never would. He did not often beat her, because it hurt his hands. He did not even fuck her much. There were more exquisite ways to give her pain. What he liked most was to destroy her dignity.

She had run away from him once. He had laughed: he knew what would happen. Her few friends and relations were terrified that if they took her in they, too, would come under suspicion of heresy, so she had nowhere to go. Born to privilege, she was utterly incapable of making a living on her own. Like so many destitute women, she had ended up prostituting herself to avert starvation. After one night in a brothel she had asked him to take her back.

Just for fun, he had pretended reluctance, forcing her to go down on her knees and beg. But of course she was too good to lose.

Today he was mildly surprised to see his stepson, Alain, at the apartment, sitting close to Louise on a sofa, talking intimately. 'Alain and Louise!' he said.

They both sprang up.

'What are you doing here?' he asked Alain.

Alain pointed to a gown draped over a chair. 'You told me to bring her that dress.'

That was true, Pierre recalled. He said: 'I didn't tell you to spend the afternoon gossiping here. Go back to the palace. Tell Duke Henri that I'm on my way to see him and I have learned the king of Spain's battle plan for the invasion of England.'

Alain raised his eyebrows. 'Who told you that?'

'Never mind. Wait for me outside the duke's apartment in the palace. You can take notes.'

He went up to Louise and casually fondled her breasts.

Alain left.

Both Alain and Louise were scared of Pierre. In moments of self-awareness he knew that was why he kept them around. It was not because of Alain's usefulness as a dogsbody, or Louise's sexual appeal. Those things were secondary. He liked their fear of him. It gave him a boost.

Did he care if they were friends? He saw no harm in it. He

could even understand why Alain might sympathize with Louise. She was an older woman, a mother substitute.

He squeezed her breasts harder. 'These were always your best feature,' he said.

She made a grimace of distaste. The expression was fleeting, and she suppressed it immediately, but he saw it, and he slapped her. 'Take that look off your face,' he said.

'I'm so sorry,' she said humbly. 'Would you like me to suck you off?'

'I don't have time. I came to tell you that I've invited someone to dine here tomorrow. I want to reward the man who told me the Spanish battle plan. You will serve us dinner.'

'Very well.'

'In the nude.'

She stared at him. 'Nude,' she said. 'In front of a stranger?'

'You will act perfectly normally, except that you will have no clothes on. I think it will amuse him.'

Tears came to her eyes. 'None at all?'

'You can wear shoes.'

She managed not to cry, but it was a struggle. 'Do you have any other requirements?'

'No. Just serve us.'

'Very well.'

Her distress made him horny, and he was tempted to stay longer, but he wanted to see Duke Henri as soon as possible. He turned away and left the room. As he closed the door he heard her sob, and smiled with pleasure as he went down the stairs.

*

NED WAS ELATED to receive a letter from Alain de Guise in Paris giving the battle plan of the king of Spain.

The Spanish armada would sail through the English Channel and anchor off Dunkirk. There they would rendezvous with the Spanish army in the Netherlands, led by Alessandro Farnese of Parma, the most successful general ever sent to the Netherlands by the king of Spain. Then the reinforced armada would turn around and sail due west, straight into the estuary of the river Thames.

Ned also got a letter from Jerónima Ruiz saying the Spanish armada had one hundred and twenty-nine ships.

Jerónima was in Lisbon, and she had seen the armada with her own eyes and counted the vessels in the harbour. She had gone there with the cardinal, who was one of a large contingent of priests needed to bless the ships and individually absolve each one of the twenty-six thousand sailors and soldiers for the sins they would commit in England.

Queen Elizabeth was devastated. Her entire navy consisted of thirty-eight ships. She did not see how she could defeat the invasion, and nor did Ned. Elizabeth would be destroyed, King Felipe would rule England, and the ultra-Catholics would dominate Europe.

Ned was mortified. He felt it was all his fault, for encouraging the execution of Mary Stuart.

Jerónima's information was corroborated by other spies. The numbers changed only a little from one message to the next.

Elizabeth wanted to know how many troops the duke of Parma had in the Netherlands, and how he planned to get them across the Channel. Ned had reports from several spies, but they disagreed, so he decided to go and see for himself.

He would be risking his life. If he were caught, and discovered to be an English spy, then hanging would be the best fate he could look forward to. But he had helped to create the catastrophe that loomed, and it was his duty to do what he could to avert it, including risking his life.

He took a ship to Antwerp. He found it a lively, cosmopolitan city: anyone was welcome, he guessed, as long as he paid his debts. 'And there's no nonsense about usury being a sin,' said Carlos Cruz.

Ned was intrigued to meet Carlos, the distant cousin about whom he had heard so much. He was fifty-one and heavy, with a bushy beard going grey. Ned thought he looked like a jolly peasant in one of those Dutch paintings of yokels merrymaking.

It was hard to imagine that Carlos and Barney had killed a sergeant in a fight over a card game.

Carlos lived in a large house near the waterfront with a huge ironworks in the backyard. He had a pretty wife, Imke, with a big welcoming smile. A daughter and son-in-law lived with him, plus two grandchildren. The men dressed sombrely but the women were draped in gorgeous colours, bright blue and scarlet, peach and lavender. The house was full of costly objects: framed oil paintings, musical instruments, mirrors, decorative jugs and bowls and glassware, leather-bound books, rugs and curtains. The Netherlands people seemed home-centred, and they showed off their wealth in a curiously domestic way that Ned had not seen elsewhere.

Ned needed Carlos's help for this mission, but he was not sure of getting it. Carlos was Spanish and Catholic. On the other hand, he had been forced by the Church to flee his homeland. Would he work against the armada? Ned would soon find out.

On the day Ned arrived, Carlos's long-time business associate, Ebrima Dabo, came to supper with his wife, Evi. Ebrima was seventy, and his curly hair was white. Evi wore a gold necklace with a diamond pendant. Ned remembered Barney saying that when Ebrima was a slave, he had been the lover of Aunt Betsy. What a life that man had led: first a farmer in West Africa, then a soldier, a prisoner of war, a slave in Seville, a soldier again in the Netherlands, and at last a rich Antwerp iron maker.

Carlos poured wine generously and drank a great deal of it himself. As they ate, it emerged that both Carlos and Ebrima were apprehensive about the Spanish armada. 'It's partly because of Queen Elizabeth that the Spanish have failed to pacify the Netherlands,' Carlos said, speaking French, which they all understood. 'Once the king of Spain has conquered England, he'll be free from her interference here.'

Ebrima said: 'When priests get to run the government, it's bad for business.'

Carlos said: 'And if our independence movement is defeated, there will be nothing to stop the Holy Inquisition.'

Ned was encouraged. It was good that they were worried. He judged this was the moment to make his proposition.

He had thought hard about it. He would be safer here if he travelled with Carlos, who spoke fluent Dutch, knew the country, and was himself known by hundreds of people in the region. But Carlos would be risking his life.

Ned took a deep breath. 'If you want to help England, there is something you could do,' he said.

'Go on,' said Carlos.

'I'm here to assess the strength of the Spanish forces getting ready to embark for England.'

'Ah,' said Ebrima in the tone of one who is suddenly enlightened. 'I wondered.'

Carlos said: 'The Spanish army is mostly around Dunkirk and Nieuwpoort.'

'I wonder if you would consider selling the Spanish a consignment of cannonballs. They must need thousands of them for the battle ahead. And if you and I arrived with several cartloads of ammunition, we'd be welcomed instead of suspected.'

Ebrima said: 'Count me out. I wish you well, but I'm too old for such adventures.'

That was a bad start, Ned thought grimly; it might encourage Carlos to decline.

But Carlos grinned and said: 'It will be like the old days.'

Ned relaxed and drank some more wine.

Next day Carlos loaded his entire stock of cannonballs onto carts, then scoured Antwerp for more. In the end, he had eight cartloads. He joined the carts in pairs in line, each pair pulled by two oxen. They set out on the third day.

The road to Nieuwpoort ran along the coast, and soon Ned began to see what he had come to look at: the preparations for the invasion. All along the shore were moored new flat-bottomed boats, and every boatyard was busy building more. They were crude, unwieldy craft, and they could have only one purpose: to move large numbers of men. There seemed to be hundreds of them, and Ned reckoned each would carry fifty to a hundred soldiers. How many thousands of troops did the duke of Parma have waiting? The fate of Ned's country depended on the answer to that question.

Soon Ned began to see the soldiers, camped inland, sitting around cooking fires, playing dice and cards, as bored as armies usually were. A group passed them on the road, saw the loaded carts, and cheered them. Ned was relieved by this confirmation that the cannonballs would be their passport.

He began to estimate numbers, but the camps seemed never to end. Mile after mile, as the plodding oxen pulled the heavy carts along the dirt road, there were more and more troops.

They bypassed Nieuwpoort and went on to Dunkirk, but the picture did not change.

They had no trouble gaining entry to the fortified town of Dunkirk. They made their way to the marketplace on the waterfront. While Carlos argued with an army captain over the price of the cannonballs, Ned went to the beach and looked across the water, thinking.

The number of troops here must more or less match the numbers embarking in Lisbon, he guessed. In total there must be more than fifty thousand men about to invade England. It was a vast army, bigger than anything Europe had seen for decades. The largest battle Ned could remember hearing about had been the siege of Malta, which had involved thirty or forty thousand Turkish attackers. He felt overwhelmed by the sense of an almighty power inexorably bent on the destruction of his home.

But they had to get to England first.

Could the flat-bottomed boats take the troops across the open sea to England? It would be hazardous – they would capsize in anything but calm water. More likely, their purpose must be to transport the soldiers to larger ships anchored near the shore – a process that would take weeks if all the galleons had to dock normally.

Ned stared at the harbour and imagined thousands of men being carried out to the galleons at anchor off the coast – and he realized that this was the weak point in the battle plan of the king of Spain. Once the army was embarked, the invaders would be an unstoppable force.

It was a gloomy prognosis. If the invasion succeeded, the burnings would resume. Ned would never forget the dreadful squealing sound Philbert Cobley had made as he burned alive in front of Kingsbridge Cathedral. Surely England would not go back to that?

The only hope was to stop the armada in the Channel before the troops could embark. Elizabeth's navy was outnumbered, so the chance was slim. But it was all they had.

26

ROLLO FITZGERALD SAW ENGLAND again at four o'clock in the afternoon of Friday 29 July 1588. His heart lifted in joy.

He stood on the deck of the Spanish flagship *San Martin*, his legs adjusting to the rise and fall of the waves without conscious effort. England was just a smudge on the horizon to the north, but sailors had ways of checking where they were. The leadsman dropped a weighted rope over the stern and measured its length as he paid it out. It was just two hundred feet when it hit the sea bottom, and its scoop brought up white sand – proof, to the knowledgeable navigator, that the ship was entering the western mouth of the English Channel.

Rollo had fled England after the collapse of his plot to free Mary Stuart. For several nail-biting days he had been only one step ahead of Ned Willard, but he had got out before Ned caught him.

He had gone immediately to Madrid, for it was there that the fate of England would be decided. Continuing to call himself Jean Langlais, he had worked tirelessly to help and encourage the Spanish invasion. He had a good deal of credibility. The reports of Don Bernardino de Mendoza, Spain's ambassador first to London, then to Paris, had made it clear to King Felipe that Langlais had done more than anyone to keep the Catholic faith alive in Protestant England. He was second in status only to William Allen, who would be archbishop of Canterbury after the invasion.

The launching of the armada had been postponed again and again, but it had at last sailed on 28 May 1588 – with Rollo aboard.

The king of Spain presented this as a defensive war: retaliation for the attacks of English pirates on transatlantic convoys, for Queen Elizabeth's help to the Dutch rebels, and for Drake's raid on Cádiz. But Rollo felt like a crusader. He was coming to free his country from the infidels who had seized it thirty years ago. He was one of many English Catholics returning with the armada. There were also 180 priests on the ships. The liberators would be welcomed, Rollo believed, by Englishmen who had stayed true, in their hearts, to the old faith. And Rollo had been promised the post of bishop of Kingsbridge, his reward for all those years of difficult and dangerous secret work under the nose of Ned Willard. Once again Kingsbridge Cathedral would see real Catholic services, with crucifixes and incense, and Rollo would preside over it all in the gorgeous priestly vestments appropriate to his status.

The admiral of the armada was the duke of Medina Sidonia, thirty-eight years old and prematurely bald. He was the richest landowner in Spain and had little experience of the sea. His watchword was caution.

When the position of the armada had been confirmed, Medina Sidonia hoisted a special flag on the mainmast, one that had been blessed by the Pope and carried in procession through Lisbon Cathedral. Then he flew the king's flag, a diagonal red cross, on the foremast. More flags blossomed on the other ships: castles from Castile, dragons of Portugal, the pennants of the noblemen aboard each vessel, and the emblems of the saints who protected them. They fluttered and snapped bravely in the wind, proclaiming the gallantry and strength of the fleet.

The *San Martin* fired three guns to signal a prayer of thanksgiving, then furled her sails and dropped anchor, and Medina Sidonia summoned a council of war.

Rollo sat in. He had learned enough Spanish in the past two years to follow a discussion and even to take part, if necessary.

Medina Sidonia's vice-admiral was the handsome Don Juan Martinez de Recalde, commanding the *San Juan de Portugal*. A lifelong naval officer, he was now sixty-two and the most experienced commander in the armada. Earlier today he had captured an English fishing vessel and interrogated the crew, and he now revealed that the English fleet was holed up in the mouth of the river Plym. This was the first large harbour on the south coast. 'If we dash to Plymouth now and surprise them, we could destroy half the English navy,' Recalde said. 'It will be revenge for Drake's raid on Cádiz.'

Rollo's heart leaped in hope. Could it really all be over that quickly?

Medina Sidonia was dubious. 'We have strict orders from his majesty King Felipe,' he said. 'We're to head straight for our rendezvous with the duke of Parma and the Spanish army of the Netherlands at Dunkirk, and not get diverted. The king wants an invasion, not a sea battle.'

'All the same, we know we're going to encounter English ships,' Recalde argued. 'They will surely try to prevent us making our rendezvous. Given a perfect opportunity to devastate them, it would be foolish to ignore it.'

Medina Sidonia turned to Rollo. 'Do you know this place?'

'Yes.'

Many Englishmen would now regard Rollo simply as a traitor. If they could have seen him, on the flagship of the invading force, helping and advising the enemy, they would have sentenced him to death. They would not understand. But he would be judged by God, not by men.

'The mouth of Plymouth harbour is narrow,' he said. 'Only two or three ships can pass through abreast, no more. And the entrance is covered by cannons. But, once inside, a few galleons could wreak havoc. The heretics would have nowhere to run.'

Spanish ships were armed with heavy, short-barrelled cannons, useless at any distance but destructive at close range. Furthermore, the decks of the armada were teeming with soldiers eager for action, whereas English warships were manned mainly by sailors. It would be a massacre, Rollo thought eagerly.

He finished: 'And the town of Plymouth has a population of about two thousand – less than a tenth of our manpower. They would be helpless.'

Medina Sidonia was thoughtful and silent for a long

moment, then he said: 'No. We'll wait here for the stragglers to catch up.'

Rollo was disappointed. But perhaps Medina Sidonia was right. The Spanish were overwhelmingly stronger than the English, so Medina Sidonia had no need to take risks. It hardly mattered when or where they engaged Elizabeth's navy: the armada was sure to win.

*

BARNEY WILLARD was at Plymouth Hoe, a park on top of low cliffs that overlooked the entrance to the harbour. He was one of a small crowd of men accompanying the admiral of the English fleet, Lord Howard. From the Hoe they could see their fleet, many of the vessels taking on supplies of fresh water and food. The few warships of the royal navy had been augmented by smaller armed merchant ships, including Barney's two vessels, the Alice and the Bella, and there were now about ninety craft in the harbour.

The breeze was from the south-west. It smelled of the sea, which always lifted Barney's spirits, but its direction was, unfortunately, perfect for the Spanish armada coming into the Channel from the Atlantic and heading east.

Queen Elizabeth had taken a huge gamble. In a meeting with her naval commanders – Lord Howard, Sir Francis Drake and Sir John Hawkins – she had decided to send most of her navy to meet the Spanish armada at the western end of the Channel. The eastern end – the 'Narrow Sea', where the duke of Parma planned to cross with his invading army – was left weakly defended by a few warships. They all knew how risky it was.

The atmosphere on Plymouth Hoe was tense. The fate of England was in their hands, and they faced an overwhelmingly stronger enemy. Barney knew that in a sea battle all expectations could be upset by the unpredictable weather; but the odds were against them, and they were worried – all but one: the vice-admiral, Drake, whose famous insouciance was on display now as he joined a group of local men in a game of bowls.

As Barney looked anxiously across the water, a pinnace appeared in the Sound. A small ship of about fifty tons, she had all sails raised, and flew across the water like a bird. Barney knew the ship. 'It's the *Golden Hind*,' he said.

There was a murmur of interest among the assembled company. The *Golden Hind* was one of several fast vessels assigned to patrol the westernmost approaches to England and watch for the invaders. There could be only one reason for her to dash back here, Barney thought, and apprehension prickled his skin.

He watched the ship enter the harbour, drop her sails, and moor at the beach. Before she was even tied up, two men disembarked and hurried into the town. A few minutes later, two horses moving at a brisk canter came up the slope to the park. Drake left his game and came across the grass, limping from an old bullet wound in his right calf, to hear what they had to say.

The senior man of the two introduced himself as Thomas Fleming, captain of the *Golden Hind*. 'We met the Spaniards at dawn,' he said breathlessly. 'We've been running before the wind ever since.'

The admiral, Charles Howard, was a vigorous fifty-two-year-old with a silver-grey beard. 'Good man,' he said to Fleming. 'Tell us what you saw.'

'Fifty Spanish ships, near the Scilly Isles.'

'What kind?'

'Mostly big galleons, with some supply ships and a few heavily armed galleasses with oars as well as sails.'

Suddenly Barney felt possessed by a bizarre sense of calm. The event that had been threatened so often and feared so long had at last happened. The most powerful country in the world was attacking England. The end of doubt came as a strange relief. Now there was nothing to do but fight to the death.

Howard said: 'In what direction were the Spaniards moving?'

'None, my lord. Their sails were struck, and they seemed to be waiting for others to catch them up.'

One of the attendant noblemen, Lord Parminter, said: 'Now, my man, are you sure of the numbers?'

'We did not get close, for fear we might get captured and be unable to bring you the news.'

Lord Howard said: 'Quite right, Fleming.'

Barney reckoned the Scilly Isles were a hundred miles from Plymouth. But Fleming had covered the distance in less than a day. The armada could not make the same speed, but they might get here before nightfall, he calculated anxiously, especially if they left behind their slower supply ships.

Parminter was thinking along the same lines. 'We must set sail at once!' he said. 'The armada must be confronted head-on before it can make landfall.'

Parminter was no sailor. Barney knew that a head-on battle was the last thing the English wanted.

Lord Howard explained with courteous patience. 'The tide is coming in, and the wind is in the south-west. It is very difficult for a ship to get out of the harbour against both wind and tide – impossible for an entire fleet. But the tide will turn at ten o'clock this evening. That will be the time to put out to sea.'

'The Spaniards could be here by then!'

'They could. What a good thing their commander seems to have decided to wait and regroup.'

Drake spoke for the first time. 'I wouldn't have waited,' he said. He was never slow to boast. 'He who hesitates is lost.'

Howard smiled. Drake was a braggart, but a good man to have alongside you in a fight. 'The Spanish have hesitated, but they are not yet lost, unfortunately,' he said.

Drake said: 'All the same, we're in a bad position. The armada is upwind of us. That gives them the advantage.'

Barney nodded grimly. In his experience, the wind was everything in a sea battle.

Howard said: 'Is it possible for *us* to get upwind of *them*?'

Barney knew how difficult it was to sail into the wind. When a ship was side-on to the wind with its sails at an angle, it could travel briskly in a direction ninety degrees to the direction of the wind. So, with a north wind, the ship could easily go east or west as well as south. A well-built ship with an experienced crew could do better than this, and travel north-east or north-west with sails trimmed in tightly, or 'close-hauled'. This was called sailing close to the wind – a challenge, because a slight error of judgement would take the ship into the no-go zone where it would slow down and stop. Now, if the English fleet wanted to head south-west into a south-westerly head wind, it would have to sail first south and then west in a zig-zag, a slow and tiresome process known as tacking.

Drake looked dubious. 'Not only would we have to tack into the wind, we'd also have to stay out of the enemy's sight, otherwise they'd change course to intercept us.'

'I didn't ask you if it would be difficult. I asked if it's possible.'

Drake grinned. He liked this kind of talk. 'It's possible,' he said.

Barney felt heartened by Drake's bravado. It was all they had.

Lord Howard said: 'Then let's do it.'

*

FOR MUCH OF Saturday, Rollo stood at the port rail of the *San Martin* as it sailed before a favourable wind along the English Channel towards Portsmouth. The armada formed a wide column, with the best fighting ships at the front and back, and the supply ships in the protected middle.

As he watched the rocky shores of Cornwall pass, Rollo was swamped by conflicting feelings of exultation and guilt. This was his country, and he was attacking it. He knew he was doing God's will, but a feeling at the back of his mind said that this might not bring honour to him and his family. He did not really care about the men who would die in the battle: he had never worried about that sort of thing – men died all the time, it was the way of the world. But he could not shake the fear that if the invasion failed he would go down in history as a traitor, and that troubled him profoundly.

This was the moment that English lookouts had been waiting for, and beacons burst into flame on the distant hilltops one after another, sending a fiery alarm along the coast faster than ships could travel. Rollo feared that the English navy, duly warned, might sail out of Plymouth harbour and head east to avoid getting trapped. Medina Sidonia's cautious delay had lost him an opportunity.

Whenever the armada sailed closer to the shore, Rollo saw crowds on the cliffs, staring, still and silent as if awestruck: in the history of the world no one had ever seen so many sailing ships together.

Towards evening, the Spanish sailors observed the shoal water and menacing black rocks of the dangerous reef called Eddystone, and veered away to avoid it. The famous hazard was due south of Plymouth. Soon afterwards, a few distant sails in the east, reflecting back the evening sun, gave Rollo his first heart-rending sight of the English fleet.

Medina Sidonia ordered the armada to anchor, to ensure that his ships remained to windward of the English. There would surely be battle tomorrow, and he did not want to give the enemy an advantage.

Few men slept aboard the *San Martin* that night. They sharpened their weapons, checked and re-checked their pistols and powder flasks, and polished their armour. The gunners stacked balls in lockers and tightened the ropes that lashed the cannons in place, then filled barrels with seawater for putting out fires. Obstacles were moved from the sides of the ships so that the carpenters could more quickly reach holes in the hull to repair them.

The moon rose at two a.m. Rollo was on deck, and he stared into the distance, looking for the English navy, but saw only vague shapes that might have been mist. He said prayers for the armada and for himself, so that he might survive tomorrow's battle and live long enough to become bishop of Kingsbridge.

The summer dawn came early, and confirmed that there were five English ships ahead. But as daylight brightened, Rollo looked back and suffered a frightening shock. The English navy was *behind* the armada. How the devil had that happened?

The five ships in front must have been decoys. The main body had somehow tacked around the armada, defying the wind, and now stood in the position of advantage, ready to do battle.

The Spanish sailors were astonished. No one had realized that the lower, narrower new design of English ships made such a difference to their manoeuvrability. Rollo was disheartened. What a setback – and so early in the battle!

To the north, he could see the last of the English fleet making its way along the coast to join the rest, with painfully short tacks to the south and north in the narrow passage available. To Rollo's astonishment, when the leading vessel reached the southernmost point of its zigzag, it opened fire on the northern flank of the armada. It emptied its cannons then quickly tacked north again. None of the Spanish ships was hit, so the English had wasted their ammunition; but the Spanish were doubly amazed, first by the seamanship then by the audacity of the English captain.

And the first shots of the battle had been fired.

Medina Sidonia commanded the gun-and-flag combination signal for the armada to come into battle order.

*

IT WAS THE TURN of the English to be astonished. The Spanish ships, heading east away from Howard's fleet, moved into defensive formation with a precision that no English navy had ever achieved. As if guided by a divine hand, they formed a perfect curve several miles across, like a crescent moon with its horns pointed menacingly back at the English.

Ned Willard watched from the deck of the Ark Royal. Ned was Walsingham's man on the flagship. The Ark was a four-masted galleon a little over a hundred feet long. The explorer Sir Walter Raleigh had built it, then sold it to Queen Elizabeth, though the parsimonious queen had not paid him but instead had deducted five thousand pounds from the money she said he owed her. The ship was heavily armed, with thirty-two cannons ranged on two gun decks and a forecastle. Ned did not have a cabin to himself, but he did have the luxury of a bunk in a room with four other men. The sailors slept on the decks, and the crew of three hundred plus more than a hundred soldiers struggled to find places on a ship only thirty-seven feet across at its widest point.

Watching the near-magical Spanish manoeuvre, Ned observed that the supply ships were in the middle and the fighting galleons either front-and-centre or at the tips. He saw at once that the English could only strike at the horns of the crescent, for any vessel entering within the curve would be vulnerable to attack from behind, with the wind taken from its sails. Every vessel but the last was guarded by the one behind. It was a carefully thought-out formation.

The Spanish armada unnerved Ned in other ways. The ships gleamed with paint in bright colours, and even from a distance he could see that the men on deck were all in their best finery, doublets and hose in crimson, royal blue, purple and gold. Even the slaves at the oars of the galleasses wore bright red jackets. What kind of people dressed for war as if they were going to a party? On the English ships, only the noblemen wore fancy clothes. Even commanders such as Drake and Hawkins had drab workaday woollen hose and leather jerkins.

Lord Howard stood on the poop deck of the *Ark*, an elevated position behind the mainmast from which he could see most of his ships and the enemy too. Ned stood close to him. Behind them the English fleet formed an unimpressively ragged line.

Ned noticed a sailor spreading sawdust on the main deck, and it took him a moment to figure out that this was to prevent the wood becoming slippery with blood.

Howard barked a command, and the *Ark* led the fleet into battle.

Howard headed for the northern horn of the crescent. Far to the south, Drake's ship *Revenge* chased the opposite tip.

The *Ark* came up behind the rearmost Spanish ship, a mighty galleon that Howard thought must be the *Rata Coronada*. As the *Ark* began to cross the stern of the *Rata*, the Spanish captain turned so that the two vessels passed broadside to broadside. They fired all their guns as they did so.

The boom of the cannons at close quarters was like a blow,

Ned found, and the smoke from all that gunpowder was worse than fog; but, when the wind cleared the view, he saw that neither ship had scored any hits. Howard knew that the Spanish wanted nothing more than to get close enough to board, and in taking care to avoid this disaster he had kept too great a distance to do any damage. The Spanish fire, from heavier, shorter-range guns, was equally harmless.

Ned had experienced his first skirmish at sea, and nothing had happened.

The ships following behind the *Ark* now attacked the *Rata* and three or four galleons close to it, but with little effect. Some of the English fire damaged the rigging of enemy ships, but no serious harm was done on either side.

Looking south, Ned could see that Drake's attack on the southern horn was having a similar result.

The battle moved eastward until the Spanish had lost all opportunity of attacking Plymouth, and with this objective achieved, the English withdrew.

However, it was a small gain, Ned thought gloomily. The armada was proceeding, more or less undamaged, towards its rendezvous with the Spanish army of the Netherlands at Dunkirk. The danger to England was undiminished.

*

ROLLO FELT MORE optimistic every day that week.

The armada sailed majestically eastwards, chased and harried by the English navy, but it was not stopped nor seriously delayed. A dog snapping at the feet of a carthorse can be a nuisance, but sooner or later it will get kicked in the head. The Spanish lost two ships in accidents and Drake, to no one's surprise, deserted his post long enough to capture one of them, a valuable galleon, the *Rosario*. But the armada was unstoppable.

On Saturday 6 August, Rollo looked ahead over the bowsprit of the *San Martin* and saw the familiar outline of the French port of Calais.

Medina Sidonia decided to stop here. The armada was still twenty-four miles from Dunkirk, where the duke of Parma was expected to be waiting with his army and flotilla of boats ready to join the invasion; but there was a problem. East of Calais, shoals and sandbars reached as far out as fifteen miles offshore, lethal for any navigator not intimately familiar with them, and there was a danger that the armada could be forced too far in that direction by westerly winds and spring tides. The cautious Medina Sidonia decided again that he did not need to take risks.

At a signal gun from the *San Martin* the ships of the great fleet all dropped their sails simultaneously and came to a choreographed halt, then dropped anchor.

The English came to a less impressive stop half a mile behind.

Sailing along the Channel, Rollo had watched enviously as small vessels appeared from the English coast bringing supplies to their fleet, barrels of gunpowder and sides of bacon being manhandled onto the ships. The Spanish had not been resupplied since Corunna: the French were under orders not to do business with the armada, because their king wanted to remain neutral in this war. However, Rollo had passed through Calais many times on his travels, and he knew that the people of Calais hated the English. The governor of the town had lost a leg thirty years ago in the battle to win Calais back from its English occupiers. Now Rollo advised Medina Sidonia to send a little delegation ashore, with greetings and gifts, and, sure enough, the armada was given permission to buy whatever it needed. Unfortunately, it was nowhere near sufficient: there was not enough gunpowder in all Calais to replace a tenth of what the armada had expended in the past week.

And then came a message that made Medina Sidonia mad with rage: the duke of Parma was not ready. None of his boats had any supplies, and boarding had not begun. It would take several days for them to prepare and sail to Calais.

Rollo was not sure that the commander's fury was justified. Parma could not have been expected to put his army on little boats and have them wait there for an indefinite period. It made much more sense to hold off until he knew that the Spanish had arrived.

Late that afternoon, Rollo was unpleasantly surprised to see a second English fleet sailing towards Calais from the north-east. This was the other part of Elizabeth's pathetic navy, he reasoned; those ships that had not been sent to Plymouth to meet the armada. Most of the vessels he could see were not warships but small merchant ships, armed but not heavily, no match for the mighty Spanish galleons.

The Spanish armada was still much stronger. And the delay was not a disaster. They had already held off the English navy for a week. They just had to wait for Parma. They could manage that. And then victory would be within their grasp.

*

THE ENGLISH NAVY had failed, Ned knew. The Spanish armada, almost intact and now resupplied, was on the point of meeting up with the duke of Parma and his Netherlands army. Once they had done that, they were less than a day from the English coast.

On Sunday morning, Lord Howard called a council of war on the deck of the *Ark Royal*. This was his last chance to stop the invasion.

A head-on attack now would be suicide. The armada had more ships and more guns, and the English would not even have their slight advantage of greater manoeuvrability. But at sea, on the move, the crescent shape of the Spanish force seemed invulnerable.

Was there anything they could do?

Several men spoke at once, suggesting fireships.

It was a course of desperation, Ned felt. Costly vessels had to be sacrificed, set on fire and driven towards the enemy. Capricious winds and random currents could easily send them off course, or the enemy ships might be nimble enough to get out of the way, so there was no certainty that fireships would reach their targets and achieve the objective of setting the enemy fleet alight.

But no one had a better idea.

Eight elderly vessels were selected to be forfeited, and they were moved to the middle of the English fleet in the hope of masking the preparations.

The holds of the ships were packed with pitch, rags and old timber, while the masts were painted with tar.

Ned recalled talking to Carlos about the siege of Antwerp, at which a similar tactic had been used by the Dutch rebels, and he suggested to Howard that the fireships' cannons should be loaded. The heat of the fire would ignite the gunpowder and fire the weapons, with luck at the moment when the fireships were in amongst the enemy fleet. Howard liked the idea and gave the order.

Ned supervised the loading of the guns in the way Carlos had explained, giving each a double charge, a cannonball plus smaller ammunition.

A small boat was tied to the stern of each fireship, so that the daring skeleton crews sailing towards the enemy could escape at the last minute.

The attempt to hide this activity failed, to Ned's dismay. The Spanish were not stupid, and they figured out what was going on. Ned saw several Spanish pinnaces and boats being steered to form a screen between the two navies, and guessed that Medina Sidonia had a plan for protecting his armada. However, Ned could not quite figure out how it was going to work.

Night fell, the wind freshened, and the tide turned. At midnight, wind and tide were perfect. The skeleton crews hoisted sails and steered the lightless fireships towards the glimmering lamps of the Spanish armada. Ned strained to see, but there was no moon yet, and the ships were dark blurs on a dark sea. The distance between the two fleets was only half a mile, but the wait seemed interminable. Ned's heart raced. Everything hung on this. He did not often pray, but now he sent a fervent request to heaven.

Suddenly light flared. One after another the eight ships burst into flame. Against the red conflagration Ned could see the sailors leaping to their escape boats. The eight separate blazes soon seemed to join together and become one inferno. And the wind blew the firebomb inexorably towards the enemy fleet.

*

ROLLO WATCHED WITH his heart thudding and his breath coming in gasps. The fireships approached the screen of small vessels that Medina Sidonia had deployed to hamper them. The smoke that filled Rollo's nostrils smelled of wood and tar. He could even feel the heat of the flames.

Two pinnaces now detached themselves from the screen and moved towards either end of the line of fireships. The crews, risking their lives, threw grappling irons onto the blazing vessels. As soon as they achieved a grip, each crew began to tow a fireship away. Even as he trembled for his own life, Rollo was awestruck by the courage and seamanship of those Spanish sailors. They headed for the open sea where the fireships could burn to ashes harmlessly.

Six fireships remained. Two more pinnaces, repeating the pattern, approached the outermost of the fireships. With luck, Rollo thought, all six might be detached in the same way, two by two, and rendered ineffectual. Medina Sidonia's tactic was working. Rollo's spirits rose.

Then he was shocked by a burst of cannon fire.

There was certainly no one alive on board the fireships, but their guns seemed to be going off by magic. Was Satan there, loading the cannons as the flames danced around him, helping the heretics? Then Rollo realized that the weapons had been pre-loaded, and had gone off when the heat ignited the gunpowder.

The result was carnage. Against the bright orange blaze of the fire he could see the black outlines of the men in the pinnaces jerk, like crazed devils cavorting in hell, as they were riddled with bullets. The cannons must have been loaded with shot or stones. The men appeared to be screaming, but nothing could be heard over the roar of the flames and the crash of the guns.

The attempt to capture and divert the fireships collapsed as the crews fell, dead or wounded, to their decks and into the sea. The fireships, carried by the tide, came on relentlessly.

At that point the Spanish had no choice but to flee.

Aboard the *San Martin*, Medina Sidonia fired a signal gun giving the order to weigh anchors and sail away; but it was superfluous. On every ship that Rollo could see in the orange light, the men were swarming up the masts and setting the sails. In their haste many did not raise their anchors but simply cut the arm-thick ropes with hatchets and left the anchors on the sea bed.

At first the *San Martin* moved with agonizing slowness. Like all the ships, it had been anchored head-on to the wind for stability; so first it had to be turned, a painstaking operation carried out with small sails. To Rollo it seemed inevitable that the galleon would catch fire before it could move away, and he got ready to jump into the water and try to swim to shore.

Medina Sidonia calmly sent a pinnace around the fleet with orders for all ships to sail north and regroup, but Rollo was not sure many would obey. The presence among them of blazing fireships was so terrifying that most sailors could think of nothing but getting away.

As they turned and the wind at last filled their sails, they had to concentrate on escaping without crashing into one another. As soon as they got clear, most ships fled as fast as wind and tide would carry them, regardless of direction.

Then a fireship sailed dangerously close to the *San Martin*, and flying sparks set the foresails alight.

Rollo looked down into the black water and hesitated to jump.

But the ship was prepared to fight fires. On deck were barrels of seawater and stacks of buckets. A sailor seized a bucket and threw water up at the burning canvas. Rollo grabbed another bucket and did the same. Others joined them, and they quickly extinguished the flames.

Then at last the galleon caught the wind and moved away from danger.

It stopped after a mile. Rollo looked back over the stern. The English were doing nothing. Safely to windward of the flames, they could afford to watch. The armada was still in the grip of confusion and panic. Even though none of the Spanish ships had caught fire, the danger was so immediate that it was impossible for anyone to think of anything but saving himself.

For the moment the *San Martin* was alone – and vulnerable.

It was dark now, and no more could be done. But the ships had been saved. In the morning Medina Sidonia would face the difficult task of re-forming the armada. But it could be done. And the invasion could still go ahead.

*

As DAWN BROKE over Calais, Barney Willard, on the deck of the *Alice*, saw that the fireships had failed. Their smouldering remains littered the Calais foreshore, but no other vessels had been burned. Only one wreck was visible, the *San Lorenzo*, drifting helplessly towards the cliffs.

A mile or so to the north he could make out the silhouette of the Spanish flagship, the *San Martin*, and four other galleons. The rest of the stupendous fleet was out of sight. They had been scattered, and their formation lost, but they were intact. As Barney looked, the five galleons he could see swung east and picked up speed. Medina Sidonia was off to round up his strays. Once he had done that, he could return to Calais in strength and still make his rendezvous with the duke of Parma.

And yet Barney felt the English now had a slim chance. The armada was vulnerable while its discipline was shattered and its ships were dispersed. They might be picked off in ones and twos.

If at the same time they could be driven towards the Netherlands sandbanks, so much the better. Barney had often negotiated those sandbanks as he sailed into Antwerp, and Drake was equally familiar with them, but to most Spanish navigators they were uncharted hazards. There was an opportunity here – though not for long.

To Barney's profound satisfaction, Lord Howard reached the same conclusion.

The *Ark Royal* fired a signal gun, and Drake's *Revenge* weighed anchor and raised sails. Barney shouted orders to his crew, who rubbed the sleep from their eyes and went into action all at once, like a well-trained choir commencing a madrigal.

The English navy set off in hot pursuit of the five galleons. Barney stood on deck, effortlessly keeping his balance in the heavy seas. The August weather was blustery, the wind constantly changing strength and direction, with intermittent driving rain and patchy visibility, as happened often in the Channel. Barney relished the feeling of racing across the water, the salty air in his lungs, cold rain cooling his face, and the prospect of plunder at the end of the day.

The fast English ships gained relentlessly on the galleons, but the Spanish flight was not fruitless, for as they passed through the straits into the North Sea they picked up more of their scattered armada. Nevertheless, they remained outnumbered by the English, who drew ever closer.

It was nine o'clock in the morning, and by Barney's calculation they were about seven miles off the Netherlands town of Gravelines, when Medina Sidonia decided that further flight was pointless, and turned to face his enemy.

Barney went down to the gun deck. His master gunner was a dark-skinned North African called Bill Coory. Barney had taught Bill everything he knew and now Bill was as good as Barney had ever been, perhaps better. Barney ordered Bill to prepare the gun crew of the *Alice* for a fight.

He watched Drake's *Revenge* bear down on the *San Martin*. The two ships were headed for a broadside pass like hundreds that had taken place in the last nine days with little effect. But this one was different. Barney became increasingly apprehensive as the *Revenge* took a course to bring it dangerously close to the Spanish ship. Drake had scented blood, or perhaps gold, and Barney feared for the life of England's hero as he came within a hundred yards of his target. If Drake were killed in the first clash of the battle, it could demoralize the English totally.

Both vessels fired their bow guns, small nuisance weapons that might disconcert and panic the enemy crew but could not cripple a ship. Then, as the two mighty vessels drew level, the advantage of the wind became apparent. The Spanish ship, downwind, heeled over so that its cannons, even at their lowest elevation, pointed up into the air. The English vessel, upwind, leaned towards its enemy, and at this close range its guns aimed at the deck and the exposed underbelly.

They began to fire. The guns of the two ships made different noises. The *Revenge* shot in a measured tattoo, like a drumbeat, each cannon on the deck firing as it reached the optimum position with a discipline that gladdened the artilleryman's heart in Barney. The *San Martin*'s sound was deeper but irregular, as if its gunners were saving ammunition.

Both ships rose and fell on the waves like corks, but they were so close now that even in heavy seas their guns could hardly miss.

The *Revenge* was struck by several huge balls. Because of the angle, the shots hit the rigging, but even that might cripple a ship if the masts were broken. The *San Martin* suffered a different kind of damage: some of Drake's guns were firing a variety of unconventional ammunition – packets of small iron cubes called dice shot that shredded the flesh; pairs of cannonballs chained together that whirled through the rigging and brought down the yard-arms; even lethal shards of scrap metal that could destroy sails.

Then the scene was obscured by the fog of gun smoke. Barney could hear the screams of maimed men between the bangs, and the taste of gunpowder was in his nose and mouth.

The ships drew apart, firing their stern guns as they did so. As they emerged from the smoke Barney saw that Drake was not going to slow his pace by turning around to attack the *San Martin* again, but was making a beeline for the next nearest Spanish ship. Barney deduced with relief that the *Revenge* was not badly damaged.

The second ship in the English line, the *Nonpareil*, pounced on the *San Martin*. Following Drake's example, its commander drew breathtakingly close to the enemy vessel, though not close enough to permit the Spanish to grapple and board; and the guns thundered again. This time Barney thought the Spanish fired fewer balls, and he suspected their artillerymen were slow to reload.

Barney had watched for long enough: it was time to join in. It was important for the *Alice* to be seen attacking Spanish ships, for that entitled Barney and his crew to a share of the spoils.

The *San Felipe* was the next galleon in the Spanish line, and it was already surrounded by English ships that were pounding it mercilessly. Barney was reminded of a pack of hounds attacking a bear in the English people's favourite entertainment. The ships were approaching so close that Barney saw one crazed Englishman jump across the gap to the deck of the *San Felipe* and immediately get cut to pieces by Spanish swords. He realized it was the only time in the past nine days that anyone had boarded an enemy ship – a measure of how the English had succeeded in preventing the Spanish from using their preferred tactics.

As the *Alice* swept into the attack, following in the wake of a warship called the *Antelope*, Barney glanced to the horizon and saw, to his consternation, a new group of Spanish vessels appearing over the horizon and racing to join the battle. To come to the rescue of an outnumbered fleet took courage, but it seemed the Spaniards had plenty of that.

Gritting his teeth, Barney yelled at his helmsman to approach within a hundred yards of the *San Felipe*.

The soldiers on the galleon fired their muskets and arquebuses, and were near enough to score several hits among the men crowded on the deck of the *Alice*. Barney dropped to his knees and escaped unscathed, but half a dozen of his crew fell, bleeding onto the deck. Then Bill Coory started firing, and the guns of the *Alice* thundered. Small shot raked the deck of the galleon, mowing down sailors and soldiers, while larger cannonballs smashed into the timbers of the hull.

The galleon replied with one large ball for the *Alice*'s eight smaller shots, and as it crashed into the stern, Barney felt the thud in the pit of his stomach. The ship's carpenter, waiting on deck for exactly this moment, rushed below to try to repair the damage.

Barney had been in battle before. He was not fearless – men without fear did not live long at sea – but he found that once the fighting started there was so much to do that he did not think about the danger until afterwards. He was possessed by high-energy excitement, yelling instructions at his crew, dashing from one side of the ship to the other for a better view, dropping down to the gun deck every few minutes to shout orders and encouragement to the sweating artillerymen. He coughed on gun smoke, slipped on spilled blood, and stumbled over the bodies of the dead and wounded.

He looped the *Alice* around behind the *Antelope* and followed the larger ship on its second pass, firing the port guns this time. He cursed as a shot from the galleon struck his rear mast. A fraction of a second later he felt a sharp stinging pain in his scalp. He reached up and pulled a splinter of wood from his hair. He felt the warm wetness of blood, but it was only a trickle, and he realized he had escaped with a scratch.

The mast did not fall and the carpenter hurried to brace it with reinforcing struts.

When the *Alice* was clear of the sulphurous smoke, Barney noticed that the armada was slowly moving into its crescent formation. He was amazed that the commanders and crews could summon up such discipline as they took a hellish pounding. The Spanish ships were proving worryingly hard to sink, and now reinforcements were about to arrive.

Barney looped the *Alice* around for another attacking run.

*

THE BATTLE RAGED all day, and by mid-afternoon Rollo was in despair.

The *San Martin* had been hit hundreds of times. Three of the ship's big guns had been dislodged from their mountings and rendered useless, but it had plenty more. The holed ship was being kept afloat by the divers, the bravest of the brave, who went into the sea with lead plates and hemp caulking to patch the hull while the gunfire raged. All around Rollo men lay dead or wounded, many calling on God or their favourite saint to release them from their agony. The air he breathed tasted of blood and gun smoke.

The *Maria Juan* had been so terribly damaged that it could not stay afloat, and Rollo had watched in despair as the magnificent ship sank, slowly but hopelessly, into the grey waves of the cold North Sea and disappeared from sight forever. The *San Mateo* was close to the end. In the effort to keep her afloat the crew were throwing everything movable overboard: guns, gratings, broken timbers, and even the bodies of their dead comrades. The *San Felipe* was so badly damaged that it could not be steered, and it was drifting helplessly away from the battle and towards the sandbanks.

It was not just that the Spanish were outnumbered. They were brave soldiers and skilled sailors, but they won their battles by ramming and boarding, and the English had figured out how to prevent them from doing that. Instead, they had been forced into a shooting battle, in which they were at a disadvantage. The English had developed a rapid-fire technique that the Spanish could not match. The larger Spanish guns were difficult to reload, sometimes requiring the gunners to hang from ropes outside the hull to insert the shot, and in the thick of a battle that was almost impossible.

The result was disaster.

As if to make defeat more certain, the wind had veered to the north, so there was no escape in that direction. To the east and south were only sandbanks, and the English were pressing them from the west. The Spanish were trapped. They were holding out bravely, but in time they would either sink under the English guns or run aground on the sandbanks.

There was no hope.

*

AT FOUR O'CLOCK in the afternoon the weather changed.

An unexpected squall blew up from the south-west. On the deck of Lord Howard's *Ark Royal*, Ned Willard was buffeted by strong winds and soaked by rain. He could have put up with that cheerfully, but what bothered him was that the Spanish armada was now hidden behind a curtain of rain. The English fleet moved tentatively to the place where the Spanish ought to be, but they had gone.

Surely they would not escape now?

After half an hour the storm moved on as quickly as it had arrived and, in the abrupt afternoon sunshine, Ned saw to his dismay that the Spanish ships were now two miles north and moving fast.

The *Ark* put on sail and gave chase, and the rest of the fleet followed, but it would take them time to catch up, and Ned realized there would be no more battle before night.

Both fleets stayed close to the east coast of England.

Night fell. Ned was exhausted and went to sleep, fully clothed, on his bunk. When dawn broke the next day he looked ahead to see that the Spanish were the same distance away, still racing north as fast as they could.

Lord Howard was in his usual place on the poop deck, drinking weak beer. 'What's happening, my lord?' Ned said politely. 'We don't seem to be catching up.'

'We don't need to,' Howard said. 'Look. They're running away.'

'Where will they go?'

'Good question. As far as I can see, they'll be forced around the northern tip of Scotland, then they'll turn south through the Irish Sea – for which there are no charts, as you know.'

Ned had not known that.

'I've been with you for every hour of the last eleven days, yet I don't understand how this has happened.'

'The truth, Sir Ned, is that it's very difficult to conquer an island. The invader is at a terrible disadvantage. He runs short of supplies, he is vulnerable as he tries to embark and disembark troops, and he loses his way on unfamiliar territory, or in unfamiliar seas. What we did, mainly, was to harry the enemy until the inherent difficulties overwhelmed him.'

Ned nodded. 'And Queen Elizabeth was right to spend money on her navy.'

'True.'

Ned looked across the water at the retreating Spanish armada. 'So we've won, then,' he said. He could hardly believe it. He knew he should jump up and down with joy, and he probably would when the news sank in, but for now he simply felt stunned.

Howard smiled. 'Yes,' he said. 'We've won.'

'Well,' said Ned, 'I'll be damned.'

27

PIERRE AUMANDE WAS AWAKENED by his stepson, Alain. 'There's an emergency meeting of the Privy Council,' Alain said. He seemed nervous, no doubt because he had to disturb the sleep of his snappish master.

Pierre sat up and frowned. This meeting was a surprise, and he did not like surprises. How come he had not known about it in advance? What was the emergency? He scratched his arms, thinking, and flakes of dry skin fell on the embroidered bedspread. 'What else do you know?'

'We got a message from d'O,' said Alain. The unusual name of François d'O belonged to King Henri III's financial superintendent. 'He wants you to make sure the duke of Guise attends.'

Pierre looked at the window. It was still dark and he could see nothing outside, but he could hear torrential rain drumming on the roof and spattering the windows. He was not going to learn more by lying in bed. He got up.

It was two days before Christmas 1588. They were in the royal château of Blois, more than a hundred miles south-west of Paris. It was a huge palace with at least a hundred rooms, and Pierre occupied a magnificent suite, the same size as that of his master, the duke of Guise, and almost as large as the king's.

Like the king and the duke, Pierre had brought with him some of his own luxurious furniture, including his voluptuously comfortable bed and his symbolically enormous writing table. He also had a treasured possession, a pair of wheel-lock pistols with silver fittings given to him by King Henri. It was the first and only time he had received a gift from a king. He kept them beside his bed, ready to fire.

He had an entourage of servants headed by Alain, now

twenty-eight, whom he had tamed completely and turned into a faithful aide. Also with him was his pleasantly cringing mistress, Louise de Nîmes.

Pierre had made Duke Henri of Guise one of the most important men in Europe, more powerful than the king of France. And Pierre's own status had risen along with that of his master.

King Henri was a peacemaker like his mother, Queen Caterina, and had tried to go easy on the heretical French Protestants called Huguenots. Pierre had seen the danger in this right from the start. He had encouraged the duke to establish the Catholic League, a union of ultra-Catholic confraternities, to combat the drift to heresy. The League had been successful beyond Pierre's dreams. It was now the dominant force in French politics, and controlled Paris and other major cities. So mighty was the League that it had been able to drive King Henri out of Paris, which was why he was now at Blois. And Pierre had managed to get the duke appointed lieutenant-general of the royal armies, effectively removing the king from control of his own military.

The Estates-General, the national parliament of France, had been in session here since October. Pierre advised the duke of Guise to pose as a representative of the people in negotiations with the king, though in fact he was the leader of the opposition to royal power, and Pierre's real aim was to make sure the king gave in to all demands made by the League.

Pierre was somewhat concerned that his master's arrogance was going too far. A week ago at a Guise family banquet Duke Henri's brother Louis, the cardinal of Lorraine, had proposed a toast to 'My brother, the new king of France!' The news of this insult had, of course, reached the king in no time. Pierre did not think King Henri had the nerve to do anything in retaliation but, on the other hand, such gloating tempted fate.

Pierre dressed in a costly white doublet slashed to show a gold silk lining. The colour did not show the white dandruff that fell constantly from his dry scalp.

Midwinter daylight came reluctantly and revealed black skies and relentless rain. Taking with him a footman to carry a candle, Pierre walked through the dim passages and hallways of the rambling château to Duke Henri's quarters.

The captain of the duke's night watch, a Swiss called Colli, whom Pierre was careful to bribe, greeted him pleasantly and said: 'He was with Madame de Sauves half the night. He got back here at three.'

The energetically promiscuous Charlotte of Sauves was the duke's current mistress. He probably wanted to sleep late this morning. 'I have to wake him,' Pierre said. 'Send in a cup of ale. He won't have time for anything else.'

Pierre entered the bedchamber. The duke was alone: his wife was in Paris, about to give birth to their fourteenth child. Pierre shook the sleeping duke by the shoulder. Not yet forty, Henri was still vigorous, and he came awake quickly.

'What is so urgent, I wonder, that the council can't wait until men have had breakfast,' the duke grumbled as he pulled on a grey satin doublet over his underclothes.

Pierre was unwilling to admit that he did not know. 'The king is fretting about the Estates-General.'

'I'd feign sickness, except that others might take advantage of my absence to plot against me.'

'Don't say *might*. They *would*.' That was the price of success. The weakness of the French monarchy, which had begun with the premature death of King Henri II thirty years ago, had given the Guise family tremendous opportunities – but whenever their power grew, others tried to take it away from them.

A servant came in with a tankard of ale. The duke drained it in one long swallow, belched loudly, and said: 'That's better.'

His satin doublet was not warm, and the corridors of the palace were chilly, so Pierre held out a cape for him to wear on the walk to the council chamber. The duke picked up a hat and gloves, and they left.

Colli led the way. The duke did not go without a bodyguard, even when moving from one apartment to another within the palace. However, men-at-arms were not allowed to enter the council chamber, so Colli remained at the top of the grand staircase while the duke and Pierre went in.

A big fire blazed in the hearth. Duke Henri took off his cape and sat at the long table with the other councillors. 'Bring me some Damascus raisins,' he said to a servant. 'I haven't had anything to eat.'

Pierre joined the advisors standing up against the walls, and the council began to discuss taxes.

The king had summoned the Estates-General because he needed money. The prosperous merchants who made up the Third Estate – after the aristocracy and the clergy – were obstinately reluctant to give him any more of their hard-earned cash. Insolently, they had sent accountants to examine the royal finances and had then declared that the king would not need higher taxes if only he would manage his money better.

The financial superintendent, François d'O, got straight to the point. 'The Third Estate must reach a compromise with the king,' he said, looking directly at Duke Henri.

'They will,' the duke replied. 'Give them time. Their pride won't allow them to give in immediately.'

This was all good, Pierre thought. When the compromise was eventually made, the duke would be the hero of the day for arranging it.

'But this is not *immediately*, is it?' said d'O stubbornly. 'They have been defying the king for two months.'

'They will come round.'

Pierre scratched his underarms. Why had the Privy Council been summoned so urgently? This was an ongoing discussion and it appeared that nothing new had happened.

A servant offered a plate to the duke. 'Your grace, there are no raisins,' he said. 'I've brought you some prunes from Provence.'

'Give them here,' said the duke. 'I'm hungry enough to eat sheep's eyes.'

D'O was not to be diverted. 'Whenever we tell the Third Estate that they must be reasonable, do you know what they reply?' he went on. 'They say they don't need to compromise, because they have the support of the duke of Guise.' He paused and looked around the table.

The duke took off his gloves and began to stuff prunes into his mouth.

D'O said to him: 'Your grace, you claim to be the peacemaker between king and people, but you have become the obstacle to settlement.'

Pierre did not like the sound of that. It was almost like a verdict.

Duke Henri swallowed a prune. For a moment he seemed lost for words.

As he hesitated, a door opened and Secretary of State Revol entered from the adjacent suite, which was the king's apartment. Revol approached Duke Henri and said in a low, clear voice: 'Your grace, the king would like to speak to you.'

Pierre was mystified. This was the second surprise of the morning. Something was going on that he did not know about, and he sensed danger.

The duke responded to the king's message with an audacious lack of urgency. He took from his pocket a silver-gilt confit box in the shape of a shell, and put some prunes into it to take with him, as if he might casually eat a snack while the king was talking to him. Then he stood and picked up his cape. With a jerk of his head he ordered Pierre to follow him.

A squad of the king's bodyguards stood in the next room, captained by a man called Montséry, who now gave the duke a hostile glare. These highly paid elite guards were called the Forty-Five, and Duke Henri, prompted by Pierre, had proposed they be disbanded to save money – and, of course, to further weaken the king. It was not one of Pierre's best ideas. The suggestion had been turned down, and the only consequence was that the Forty-Five hated the duke.

'Wait here in case I need you,' Duke Henri said to Pierre.

Montséry went to open the next door for the duke.

Duke Henri walked to the door, then stopped and turned again to Pierre. 'On second thoughts,' he said, 'go back to the Privy Council. You can let me know what they say in my absence.'

'Very good, your grace,' said Pierre.

Montséry opened the door to reveal King Henri standing

on the other side. Now thirty-seven, he had been king for fifteen years. His face was fleshy and sensual, but he exuded calm authority. He looked at Duke Henri and said: 'So here he is, the man they're calling the new king of France.' Then he turned to Montséry and gave a brief but unmistakable nod.

At that moment Pierre realized that catastrophe was about to strike.

With a swift, smooth motion, Montséry drew a long dagger and stabbed the duke.

The sharp blade passed easily through the duke's thin satin doublet and sank deep into his brawny chest.

Pierre was frozen with shock.

The duke's mouth opened as if to scream, but no sound came, and Pierre realized immediately that the wound must be fatal.

It was not enough for the guards, however, and they now surrounded the duke and stabbed him repeatedly with knives and swords. Blood came from his nose and mouth and everywhere else.

Pierre stared in horrified paralysis for another second. Duke Henri fell, bleeding from multiple wounds.

Pierre looked up at the king, who was watching calmly.

At last Pierre recovered his senses. His master had been murdered and he might well be next. Quietly but quickly he turned away and passed back through the door into the council chamber.

The Privy Councillors around the long table stared at him in silence, and he realized in a flash that they must have known what was going to happen. The 'urgent' meeting was a pretext for catching the duke of Guise unawares. It was a conspiracy, and they were all in on it.

They wanted him to say something, for they did not yet know whether the murder had been done. He took advantage of their momentary uncertainty to escape. He crossed the room swiftly, without speaking, and went out. He heard a hubbub break out behind him, cut off by the slamming of the door.

The duke's bodyguard, Colli, stared at Pierre in puzzlement, but Pierre ignored him and ran down the grand staircase. No one tried to stop him.

He was aghast. His breath came in short gasps and he found he was perspiring despite the cold. The duke was dead, murdered – and it had clearly been done on the orders of the king. Duke Henri had become overconfident. So had Pierre. He had been sure that the weak King Henri would never be so courageous or decisive – and he had been disastrously, fatally wrong.

He was lucky not to have been killed himself. He fought down panic as he hurried through the château. The king and his collaborators had probably planned no farther ahead than the assassination. But now that the duke was dead, they would think about how to consolidate their triumph. First they would want to eliminate the duke's brothers, Cardinal Louis and the archbishop of Lyon; and then their attention would turn to his principal advisor, Pierre.

But for the next few minutes all would be chaos and confusion, so Pierre had a brief chance to save himself.

Duke Henri's eldest son, Charles, was now duke of Guise, Pierre realized as he ran along a corridor. The boy was seventeen, old enough to step into his father's shoes – Henri himself had been only twelve when he became duke. If only Pierre could get out of here, he would do exactly as he had done with Henri: ingratiate himself with the mother, become the indispensable advisor to the youngster, nourish in both the seed of revenge, and one day make the new duke as powerful as the old.

He had suffered setbacks before, and had always returned stronger than ever.

He reached his quarters, breathing hard. His stepson Alain was in the sitting room. 'Saddle three horses,' Pierre barked. 'Pack only money and weapons. We must be gone from here in ten minutes.'

'Where are we going?' said Alain.

The stupid boy should have asked *why*, not *where*. 'I haven't decided yet, just *move*,' Pierre yelled.

He went into the bedroom. Louise, in her nightclothes, was

on her knees at the prie-dieu, saying her prayers with beads. 'Get dressed fast,' Pierre said. 'If you're not ready I'm going without you.'

She stood up and came to him, her hands still folded as if in prayer. 'You're in trouble,' she said.

'Of course I'm in trouble, that's why I'm running away,' he said impatiently. 'Put your clothes on.'

Louise opened her hands to reveal a short dagger and slashed Pierre's face.

'Christ!' He yelled in pain, but the shock was worse. He could not have been more surprised if the knife had moved of its own accord. This was *Louise*, the terrified mouse, the helpless woman he abused just for fun; and she had *cut* him – not just a scratch, but a deep gash in his cheek that was now bleeding copiously down his chin and neck. 'You whore, I'll slit your throat!' he screeched, and he lunged at her, reaching for the knife.

She stepped back nimbly. 'You fiend, it's all over, I'm free now!' she yelled; then she stabbed him in the neck.

With incredulity he felt the blade penetrate agonizingly into his flesh. What was happening? Why did she think she was free? A weak king had killed the duke and now a weak woman had knifed Pierre. He was bewildered.

But Louise was an incompetent assassin. She did not realize that the first thrust had to be fatal. She had bungled, and now she would die.

Rage directed Pierre's actions. His right hand went to his wounded throat while his left knocked aside her knife arm. He was hurt but alive, and he was going to kill Louise. He ran at her, crashing into her before she could stab again, and she lost her balance. She fell to the floor and the knife dropped from her hand.

Pierre picked it up. Trying to ignore the pain of his wounds, he knelt astride Louse and raised the dagger. He paused for a moment, hesitating over where to stab her: the face? Breasts? Throat? Belly?

He was struck by a powerful sideways blow to his right shoulder that threw him to the left. For a moment his right arm went limp, and it was his turn to drop the dagger. He fell heavily, rolling off Louise and over onto his back.

Looking up, he saw Alain.

The young man was holding in his hands the wheel-lock pistols given to Pierre by King Henri, and he was pointing both at Pierre.

Pierre stared at the guns for a helpless moment. He had fired them several times and knew that they worked reliably. He did not know how good a shot Alain was, but standing only two paces away he could hardly miss.

In an instant of quiet Pierre heard the drumming of the rain. He realized that Alain had known in advance about the assassination of the duke – that was how come he had asked *where* and not *why*. Louise had known, too. So they had conspired together to kill Pierre in his moment of weakness. They would get away with it, too: everyone would assume Pierre had been killed on the orders of the king, as the duke had been.

How could this be happening to him, Pierre Aumande de Guise, the master of manipulation for three decades?

He looked at Louise, then up again at Alain, and he saw the same expression in both faces. It was hatred mixed with something else: joy. This was their moment of triumph, and they were happy.

Alain said: 'I have no further use for you.' His fingers tightened on the long serpentine levers protruding below the guns.

What did that mean? Pierre had always used Alain, not vice versa, had he not? What had he failed to see? Yet again Pierre was bewildered.

He opened his mouth to shout for help, but no sound came from his wounded throat.

The wheel locks spun, both guns sparked, then they went off with a double bang.

Pierre felt as if he had been hit in the chest by a sledgehammer. The pain was overwhelming.

He heard Louise speak as if from a very great distance. 'Now go back to hell, where you came from.'

Then darkness descended.

*

EARL BARTLET NAMED his first son Swithin, after the child's great-grandfather, and his second Rollo, after the child's great-uncle. Both men had struggled bravely against Protestantism, and Bartlet was fiercely Catholic.

Margery was not pleased with either name. Swithin had been a loathsome man, and Rollo had deceived and betrayed her. However, as the boys' own personalities began to emerge, so their names morphed: Swithin became a very fast crawler and was nicknamed Swifty, and plump Rollo became Roley.

In the mornings, Margery liked to help Bartlet's wife, Cecilia. Today she fed Swifty a scrambled egg while Cecilia breastfed Roley. Cecilia tended to be anxious about the children, and Margery was a calming influence; probably all grandmothers were, Margery thought.

Her second son, Roger, came into the nursery to see his nephews. 'I'm going to miss these two when I go to Oxford,' he said.

Margery noticed how the young nurse, Dot, perked up in Roger's presence. He was quietly charming, with a wry smile that was very engaging, and no doubt Dot would have liked to ensnare him. Perhaps it was a good thing he was leaving for the university: Dot was a nice girl and good with the children, but her horizons were too narrow for Roger.

That thought made Margery wonder what Roger himself saw on his horizons, and she said: 'Have you considered what you might do after Oxford?'

'I want to study law,' Roger said.

That was interesting. 'Why?'

'Because it's so important. The laws make the country.'

'So what you're really interested in is government.'

'I suppose so. I was always fascinated by what father said when he came back from attending Parliament: how people manoeuvred and negotiated, why they took one side or the other.'

Earl Bart himself had never found Parliament very interesting, and had attended the House of Lords as an obligation. But Roger's real father, Ned Willard, was a political animal. Heredity was fascinating.

Margery said: 'Perhaps you might become the Member of Parliament for Kingsbridge, and sit in the House of Commons.'

'It's not unusual for the younger son of an earl. But Sir Ned is the MP.'

'He'll retire sooner or later.' He would be glad to do so, Margery guessed, if he could hand over to his son.

They all heard sudden loud voices downstairs. Roger stepped out and came back to say: 'Uncle Rollo just arrived.'

Margery was shocked. 'Rollo?' she said incredulously. 'He hasn't come to New Castle for years!'

'Well, he's here now.'

Margery heard glad cries down in the great hall as Bartlet greeted his hero.

Cecilia spoke brightly to her two children. 'Come and meet your great-uncle Rollo,' she said.

Margery was in no hurry to greet Rollo. She handed Swifty to Roger. 'I'll join you later,' she said.

She left the nursery and walked along the corridor to her own rooms. Her mastiff, Maximus, followed at her heels. Bartlet and Cecilia had naturally moved into the best rooms, but there was a pleasant suite of bedroom and boudoir for the dowager countess. Margery went into her boudoir and closed the door.

She felt a cold anger. After she had discovered that Rollo was using her network to foment a violent insurrection, she had sent him one short, coded message to say that she would no longer help smuggle priests into England. He had not replied, and they had had no further communication. She had spent many hours composing the outraged speech she would make if she ever saw him again. But now that he was here she suddenly did not know what to say to him.

Maximus lay down in front of the fire. Margery stood at the window looking out. It was December: servants crossed the courtyard muffled in heavy cloaks. Outside the castle walls, the fields were cold, hard mud, and the bare trees pointed forked limbs at the iron-grey sky. She had wanted this time to regain her composure, but she just continued to feel shocked. She picked up her prayer beads to calm herself.

She heard the sound of servants carrying heavy luggage along the corridor outside her door, and guessed that Rollo would be using his old bedroom, which was opposite her new one. Soon afterwards there was a tap at her door and Rollo came in. 'I'm back!' he announced cheerily.

He was bald now, she saw, and his beard was salt-and-pepper. She looked at him stone-faced. 'Why are you here?'

'And it's lovely to see you, too,' he said sarcastically.

Maximus growled quietly.

'What on earth do you expect?' said Margery. 'You lied to me for years. You know how I feel about Christians killing one another over doctrine – and yet you used me for that very purpose. You've turned my life into a tragedy.'

'I did God's will.'

'I doubt it. Think of all the deaths your conspiracy caused – including that of Mary Queen of Scots!'

'She's a saint in heaven now.'

'In any event, I will no longer help you, and you can't use New Castle.'

'I think the time for conspiracy is over. Mary Queen of Scots is dead, and the Spanish armada has been defeated. But, if another opportunity should arise, there are places other than New Castle.'

'I'm the only person in England who knows that you are Jean Langlais. I could betray you to Ned Willard.'

Rollo smiled. 'You won't, though,' he said confidently. 'You may betray me, but I can betray you. Even if I didn't want to give you away, I probably would under torture. You've been concealing priests for years, and it's a capital crime. You would be executed – perhaps in the same way as Margaret Clitheroe, who was slowly crushed to death.'

Margery stared at him in horror. She had not thought this far.

Rollo went on: 'And it's not just you. Both Bartlet and Roger helped smuggle the priests. So, you see, if you betray me, you would cause the execution of both your sons.'

He was right. Margery was trapped. Wicked though Rollo was, she had no choice but to protect him. She felt mad with frustration but there was nothing she could do. She glared at his smug expression for a long moment. 'Damn you,' she said. 'Damn you to hell.'

*

ON THE TWELFTH day of Christmas there was a big family dinner at the Willard house in Kingsbridge.

The tradition of an annual play at New Castle had fallen away. The earldom had become less and less rich through the years of anti-Catholic discrimination, and the earl of Shiring could no longer afford lavish banquets. So the Willard family had their own party.

They were six around the table. Barney was at home, flush with the triumph against the Spanish armada. He sat at the head of the table, with his wife Helga on his right. His son Alfo sat on his left, and Sylvie noticed that he was becoming plump with prosperity. Alfo's wife, Valerie, had a baby in her arms, a little girl. Ned sat at the end opposite Barney, and Sylvie sat beside him. Eileen Fife brought in a huge platter of pork roasted with apples, and they drank Helga's golden Rhenish wine.

Barney and Ned kept recalling episodes from the great sea battle. Sylvie and Valerie chatted in French. Valerie breastfed the baby while eating pork. Barney said the child was going to look like her grandmother Bella: that was unlikely, Sylvie thought, for only one of the child's eight great-grandparents was African, and at present she had unremarkable light pinky-tan skin. Alfo told Barney about further improvements he planned for the indoor market.

Sylvie felt safe, surrounded by her prattling family, with food on the table and a fire in the hearth. England's enemies were defeated, for now, though no doubt there would always be more. And Ned had heard from a spy that Pierre Aumande was dead, murdered on the same day as his master, the duke of Guise. There was justice in the world.

She looked around the table at the smiling faces and realized that the feeling that suffused her was happiness.

After dinner they put on heavy coats and went out. To

replace the play at New Castle, the Bell Inn had a company of actors to perform on a temporary stage in the large courtyard of the tavern. The Willards paid their pennies and joined the crowd.

The play, *Gammer Gurton's Needle*, was a broad comedy about an old woman who lost her only needle and could not sew. Other characters included a japester called Diccon who pretended to summon the devil and a servant called Hodge who was so frightened that he soiled his breeches. The audience laughed uproariously.

Ned was in a merry mood, and he and Barney left the courtyard to go into the tap-room and buy a jug of wine.

On stage, Gammer began a hilarious fist-fight with her neighbour Dame Chat. Sylvie's eye was caught by one man in the courtyard who was not laughing. She felt instantly that she had seen that face before. It had a gaunt look of fanatical resolve that she would not forget.

He met her eye and seemed not to recognize her.

Then she remembered a street in Paris and Pierre Aumande standing outside his little house, giving directions to a priest with receding hair and a reddish beard. 'Jean Langlais?' she muttered incredulously. Could it really be the man Ned had been hunting for so long?

He turned his back on the play and walked out of the courtyard.

Sylvie had to make sure it was him. She knew she must not lose sight of him. She could not allow him to disappear. Jean Langlais was the enemy of the Protestant religion and of her husband.

It occurred to her that the man might be dangerous. She looked for Ned, but he had not yet returned from the tap-room. By the time he came back, the man she thought might be Langlais could have vanished. She could not wait.

Sylvie had never hesitated to risk her life for what she believed in.

She followed.

*

ROLLO HAD DECIDED to return to Tyne Castle. He knew that he could no longer use New Castle for any secret purpose. Margery would not betray him intentionally – it would lead to the execution of her sons – but her vigilance might slip, and she would become a security risk. Better that she should know nothing.

He was still in the pay of the earl of Tyne, and in fact still carried out legal tasks for the earl from time to time to give credibility to his cover story. He was not sure what clandestine duties there might be for him to do now. The Catholic insurrection had failed. But he hoped fervently that sooner or later there would be a renewed effort to bring England back to the true faith, and that he would be part of it.

On his way to Tyne he had stopped over at Kingsbridge where he joined up with a group of travellers heading for London. It happened to be the twelfth day of Christmas, and there was a play in the courtyard of the Bell, so they were going to see the show then set off the following morning.

Rollo had watched for a minute, but he thought the play vulgar. At a particularly uproarious moment he caught the eye of a small middle-aged woman in the audience who stared at him as if trying to place him.

He had never seen her before and had no idea who she was, but he did not like the way she frowned as if trying to remember him. He pulled up the hood of his cloak, turned away, and walked out of the courtyard.

In the market square he looked up at the west front of the cathedral. I might have been bishop here, he thought bitterly.

He went mournfully inside. The church was a drab and colourless place under the Protestants. Sculptured saints and angels in their stone niches had had their heads chopped off to prevent idolatry. Wall paintings were dimly perceptible through a thin coat of whitewash. Amazingly, the Protestants had left the gorgeous windows intact, perhaps because it would have cost so much to replace the glass; but the colours were not at their best on this winter afternoon.

I would have changed all this, Rollo thought. I would have given people religion with colour and costume and precious jewels, not this cold cerebral Puritanism. His stomach churned with acid at the thought of what he had lost.

The church was empty, all the priests having gone to the play, he thought; but, turning around, he looked back the length of the nave and saw that the woman who had stared at him in the market square had followed him into the cathedral. When he met her eye again, she spoke to him in French, and her words echoed in the vaulting like the voice of doom. 'C'est bien toi – Jean Langlais? Is it really you – Jean Langlais?'

He turned away, mind racing. He was in terrible danger. He had been recognized as Langlais. It seemed she did not know Rollo Fitzgerald – but she soon would. At any moment she would identify him as Langlais to someone who knew him as Rollo – someone such as Ned Willard – and his life would be over.

He had to get away from her.

He hurried across the south aisle. A door in the wall there had always led to the cloisters – but now, as he jerked on the handle, it remained firmly shut, and he realized it must have been blocked off when the quadrangle had been turned into a market by Alfo Willard.

He heard the woman's light footsteps running up the nave. He guessed that she wanted to see him close up – to confirm her identification. He had to avoid that.

He dashed along the aisle to the crossing, looking for a way out, hoping to disappear into the town before she could get another look at him. In the south transept, at the base of the mighty tower, there was a small door in the wall. He thought it might lead out into the new market but, when he flung it open, he saw only a narrow spiral staircase leading up. Making a split-second decision, he went through the door, closing it behind him, and started up the steps.

He hoped the staircase would have a door leading to the gallery that ran the length of the south aisle, but as he went farther up he realized he was not going to be that lucky. He heard footsteps behind him, and had no option but to carry on up.

He began to breathe hard. He was fifty-three years old, and

climbing long staircases was more difficult than it had been. However, the woman chasing him was not much younger.

Who was she? And how did she know him?

She was French, evidently. She had addressed him by *toi* rather than *vous*, meaning either that she knew him intimately – which she did not – or that she did not think he was entitled to the respectful *vous*. She must have seen him, probably in Paris or Douai.

A Frenchwoman in Kingsbridge was almost certainly a Huguenot immigrant. There was a family called Forneron, but they were from Lille, and Rollo had never spent any time there.

However, Ned Willard had a French wife.

She must be the woman panting up the stairs behind Rollo. He recalled her name: Sylvie.

He kept hoping that, just around the curve, there would be an archway leading off the staircase to one of the many passages buried in the massive stonework, but the spiral seemed to go on forever, as if in a nightmare.

He was panting and exhausted when at last the steps ended at a low wooden door. He threw the door open, and a blast of cold air struck him. He ducked under the lintel and stepped out, and the door blew shut behind him. He was on a narrow stone-paved walkway at the top of the central tower that rose over the crossing. A wall no higher than his knees was all that stood between him and a drop of hundreds of feet. He looked down to the roof of the choir far below. To his left was the graveyard; to his right the quadrangle of the old cloisters, now roofed over to form the indoor market. Behind him, hidden from his view by the breadth of the spire, was the marketplace. The wind flapped his cloak violently.

The walkway ran around the base of the spire. Above, at the point of the spire, was the massive stone angel that looked human-sized from the ground. He went quickly around the walkway, hoping that there might be another staircase, a ladder, or a flight of steps leading away. On the far side he glanced down into the marketplace, almost deserted now that everyone was in the Bell watching the play.

There was no way down. As he arrived back where he started, the woman emerged from the doorway.

The wind blew her hair across her eyes. She pushed her locks off her face and stared at him. 'It *is* you,' she said. 'You're the priest I saw with Pierre Aumande. I had to be sure.'

'Are you Willard's wife?'

'He's been searching for Jean Langlais for years. What are you doing in Kingsbridge?'

His surmise had been right: she had no idea that he was Rollo Fitzgerald. Their paths had never crossed in England.

Until today. And now she knew his secret. He would be arrested, tortured, and hanged for treason.

And then he realized that there was a simple alternative.

He stepped towards her. 'You little fool,' he said. 'Don't you know what danger you're in?'

'I'm not afraid of you,' she said, and she flew at him.

He grabbed her by the arms. She screamed and struggled. He was bigger, but she was a spitfire, wriggling and kicking. She got one arm free and went for his face, but he dodged her hand.

He pushed her along the walkway to the corner, so that her back was to the low wall, and somehow she squirmed around him. Then his back was to the sheer drop, and she shoved him with all her might. He was too strong for her, and forced her back. She was screaming for help, but the wind took her cries, and he was sure no one could hear. He pulled her sideways, so that she was off balance, then got on the other side of her, and almost had her over the edge, but she foiled him by going limp, and slumping to the floor. Then she twisted out of his grasp, scurried away, got to her feet and ran.

He followed her, careering along the walkway, darting around the corners, with the fatal drop just one misstep away. He could not catch her. She reached the doorway, but the door had blown shut again and she had to stop to open it. In that split second he got hold of her. He grabbed her collar with one hand, and with the other grasped a fistful of the skirt of her coat, and jerked her out of the doorway back onto the walkway.

He dragged her backwards, her arms flailing, her heels

dragging along the stone floor. She repeated her trick of going limp. However, this time it did not work, only making it easier for him to pull her. He reached the corner.

He put one foot on the top of the wall and tried to drag her over. The wall was pierced at floor level by drain holes for rainwater, and she managed to get her hand into one and grab the edge. He kicked her arm and she lost her grip.

He managed to pull her until she was half over the edge. She was face down and staring at the drop, screaming in mortal terror. He released her collar and tried to grab her ankles so that he could tip her over. He got hold of one ankle but could not grasp the other. He lifted her foot as high as he could. She was almost over now, clinging to the top of the wall with both hands.

He grasped one arm and pulled her hand off the wall. She tipped over, but grabbed his wrist at the last minute. He almost went over the side with her, but her strength failed her and she released him.

For a moment he teetered, windmilling his arms; then he was able to step back to safety.

She overbalanced in the other direction and tilted, with nightmare slowness, off the parapet. He watched, with a mixture of triumph and horror, as she fell slowly through the air, turning over and over, her screams a faint cry in the wind.

He heard the thud as she hit the roof of the choir. She bounced, and came down again with her head at a queer angle, and he guessed her neck was broken. She rolled limply down the slope of the roof and off the edge, struck the top of a flying buttress, fell to the lean-to roof of the north aisle, tumbled off its edge, and at last came to rest, a lifeless bundle, in the graveyard.

There was no one in the graveyard. Rollo looked in the opposite direction; he saw nothing but rooftops. Nobody had seen the fight.

He stepped through the low doorway, closed the door behind him, and went down the steep spiral staircase as fast as he could. He stumbled twice and almost fell, but he had to hurry.

Reaching the bottom he stopped and listened at the door. He could hear nothing. He opened the door a crack. He heard no voices, no footsteps. He peeped out. The cathedral seemed empty.

He stepped into the transept and closed the door behind him.

He hurried along the south aisle, raising the hood of his cloak. He reached the west end of the church and cracked the door open. There were people in the market square but no one was looking his way. He stepped outside. Without pausing he walked south, past the entrance to the indoor market, deliberately not looking around him: he did not want to meet anyone's eye.

He turned around the back of the bishop's palace and made his way to the main street.

It crossed his mind to leave town instantly and never come back. But several people knew he was here, and that he was planning to leave in the morning with a group of travellers; so if he now left precipitately, it would be sure to throw suspicion on him. The town watch might even send horsemen to catch up with him and bring him back. He would do better to remain and act innocent.

He turned towards the market square.

The play had ended and the crowd was coming out of the Bell courtyard. He spotted Richard Grimes, a prosperous Kingsbridge builder who sat on the borough council. 'Good afternoon, alderman,' he said politely. Grimes would remember that he had seen Rollo coming up the main street from the direction of the riverside, apparently having been nowhere near the cathedral.

Grimes was surprised to see him after so many years, and was about to start a conversation, when they both heard cries of shock and dismay coming from the graveyard. Grimes went in the direction of the hubbub, and Rollo followed.

A crowd was gathering around the body. Sylvie lay with arms and legs visibly broken, and one side of her head a horrible mass of blood. Someone knelt beside her and felt for a heartbeat, but it was obvious that she was dead. Alderman

Grimes pushed through the press of people and said: 'That's Sylvie Willard. How did this happen?'

'She fell from the roof.' The speaker was Susan White, an old flame of Rollo's, once a pretty girl with a heart-shaped face, now a grey-haired matron in her fifties.

Grimes asked her: 'Did you see her fall?'

Rollo tensed. He had been sure no one was watching. But if Susan had glanced up she would probably have recognized him.

Susan said: 'No, I didn't see, but it's obvious, isn't it?'

The crowd parted, and Ned Willard appeared.

He stared at the body on the ground for an instant, then roared like a wounded bull: 'No!' He fell to his knees beside Sylvie. Gently, he lifted her head, and saw that part of her face was pulp. He began to weep then, still saying 'No, no,' but quietly, between sobs that came from deep inside.

Grimes looked around. 'Did anyone see her fall?'

Rollo got ready to make a run for it. But no one spoke. The murder had not been witnessed.

He had got away with it.

*

MARGERY STOOD at Sylvie's graveside as the coffin was lowered into the ground. The day was still and cold, with a feeble winter sun breaking through clouds intermittently, but Margery felt as if she were in a tornado.

Margery was heartbroken for Ned. He was weeping into a handkerchief, unable to speak. Barney stood on his right, Alfo on his left. Margery knew Ned, and she knew that he had loved Sylvie with all his being. He had lost his soulmate.

No one knew why Sylvie had chosen to climb the tower. Margery knew that her brother Rollo had been in town that day, and it crossed her mind that he might be able to answer the question, but he had left the day after Sylvie's death. Margery had casually asked several people whether they had seen Rollo before he left, and three of them had said something like: 'Yes, at the play, he was standing near me.' Ned said that Sylvie had always wanted to see the view from the tower, and perhaps she had disliked the play and had chosen that moment to fulfil her wish; and, on balance, Margery thought that was the likeliest explanation.

Margery's sorrow for Ned was made even more agonizing by this knowledge: that the tragedy might, in the end, bring her what she had craved for the last thirty years. She felt deeply ashamed of the thought, but she could not blind herself to the fact that Ned was now a single man, and free to marry her.

But even if that happened, would it end her torment? She would have a secret that she could not reveal to Ned. If she betrayed Rollo she would be condemning her sons. Would she keep the secret, and deceive the man she loved? Or would she see her children hanged?

As the prayers were said over the broken body of Sylvie, Margery asked God never to force her to choose.

*

It was an amputation. I would never get back the part of me that vanished when Sylvie died. I knew the feeling of a man who tries to walk having lost a leg. I would never shake off the sense that something should be there, where the missing limb had always been. There was a hole in my life, a great gaping cavity that could never be filled.

But the dead live on in our imaginations. I think that's the true meaning of ghosts. Sylvie was gone from this earth, but I saw her every day in my mind. I heard her, too. She would warn me against an untrustworthy colleague, mock me when I admired the shape of a young woman, laugh with me at a pompous alderman, and cry over the illness of a child.

In time the hurricane of grief and rage abated, and I was possessed by a calm, sad resignation. Margery came back into my life like an old friend returned from overseas. That summer she came to London and moved into Shiring House in the Strand, and soon I was seeing her every day. I learned the meaning of the word 'bittersweet', the acid taste of loss and the honey of hope in one bright fruit. We saw plays, we rode horses in the Westminster fields, we took river trips and picnicked in Richmond. And we made love – sometimes in the morning, sometimes in the afternoon, sometimes at night; occasionally all three.

Walsingham was suspicious of her at first, but she disarmed him with a combination of flirtatiousness and intellect that he found irresistible.

In the autumn, the ghost of Sylvie told me to marry Margery. 'Of course I don't mind,' she said. 'I had your love while I was alive. Margery can have it now. I just want to look down from heaven and see you happy.'

We were married in Kingsbridge Cathedral at Christmas, almost a year after Sylvie died. It was a subdued ceremony. Weddings are usually about young people starting out in life, but ours seemed more like an ending. Walsingham and I had saved Queen Elizabeth and fought for her ideal of religious freedom; Barney and I and the English sailors had defeated the Spanish armada; and Margery and I were together at last. It seemed to me that all the threads of our lives had drawn together.

But I was wrong. It was not over yet; not quite.

Part Five

1602 to 1606

28

Rollo Fitzgerald lived through the last decade of the sixteenth century in a fury of disappointment and frustration. Everything he had tried to do had come to nothing. England was more resolutely Protestant than ever. His life was a failure.

And then, with the turn of the century, he perceived that there was one last hope.

Queen Elizabeth was sixty-six when the new century began. It was a great age, and she was becoming haggard, pale and melancholy. She refused to look to the future, and made it an act of treason to even discuss the question of who would succeed to her throne. 'Men always worship the rising rather than the setting sun,' she said, and she was not wrong. Despite her prohibition, everyone was talking about what would happen when she died.

Late in the summer of 1602, a visitor from Rome came to see Rollo at Tyne Castle. It was Lenny Price, who had been a student with Rollo at the English College back in the seventies. The lively pink-faced youth of those days was now a grey-haired man of fifty-five. 'The church has a mission for you,' said Lenny. 'We want you to go to Edinburgh.'

They were standing on the roof of one of the castle towers, looking across farmland to the North Sea. Rollo's pulse quickened at Lenny's words. Scotland was ruled by King James VI, the son of Mary Stuart. 'Mission?' he said.

'Queen Elizabeth has no heir,' Lenny said. 'None of the three children of Henry VIII ever had a child. So King James is the likeliest candidate to succeed Elizabeth on the throne of England.'

Rollo nodded. 'He's had a book published explaining his

right to the throne.' James believed in the power of the written word, a useful philosophy for the king of a small, poor country such as Scotland.

'He's clearly manoeuvring for it. He's seeking support – so Rome thinks this is the moment to extract promises from him.'

Rollo felt a warm surge of hope, but forced himself to be realistic. 'Despite his mother, James is no Catholic. He was taken from Mary Stuart when he was a year old, and from then on, the poison of Protestantism was dripped daily into his childish ear.'

'But there's something you don't know,' said Lenny. 'Almost nobody knows, and you mustn't tell anyone.' He lowered his voice, even though they were alone. 'James's wife is a Catholic.'

Rollo was astounded. 'Anne of Denmark, the queen of Scotland, is a Catholic? But she was raised Protestant!'

'God sent a devout man to speak to her, and she saw the light.'

'You mean someone converted her?'

In a near-whisper, Lenny said: 'She has been received into the Church.'

'God be praised! But this changes everything.'

Lenny raised a cautionary hand. 'We don't think she'll be able to convert her husband.'

'Does he not love her?'

'Hard to say. Our informants in Scotland say they're fond of one another. And they have three children. But they also say that James is a pervert.'

Rollo raised an enquiring eyebrow.

'With young men,' Lenny explained.

Men who loved men committed a cardinal sin, but many of them were priests, and Rollo was not shocked.

Lenny went on: 'James knows his wife has become a Catholic, and he's accepted the fact. If we can't expect that he'll restore England to exclusive Catholicism, perhaps we can hope for tolerance.'

Rollo winced at the word *tolerance*. For him it was immorality, a mark of backsliding, error and decadence. How could the Catholic Church now be demanding *tolerance*?

Lenny did not notice. 'We must move to exploit this situation, and that's where you come in. You must take a message to Edinburgh from the Catholic Church in England. If James will promise us freedom of worship, we will not oppose his bid for the English throne.'

Rollo saw immediately that this was the right thing to do, and his heart lifted in optimism. But there was a snag. 'I'm not senior enough,' he said. 'The king of Scotland won't see me.'

'But the queen will,' said Lenny. 'She's one of us, now, so we can arrange it.'

'Is she so far committed?'

'Yes.'

'That's wonderful,' said Rollo. 'I'll go, of course.'

'Good man,' said Lenny.

Six weeks later Rollo was at the palace of Holyrood in Edinburgh. The house stood at the foot of a hill called Arthur's Seat. To the west, the road ran for a mile to another hill on which stood Edinburgh Castle, a much less comfortable home. King James and Queen Anne preferred to live at Holyrood.

Rollo dressed in priest's robes and hung a crucifix around his neck. He went to the west range of the palace and gave the name Jean Langlais to an assistant, together with an appropriate bribe. He was shown to a pleasant small room with tall windows and a big fire. Scotland was not so bad, he thought, if you were rich. It would have been quite another matter, in these cold winds, to be one of the barefoot children he had seen in the town.

An hour went by. Everyone knew that all royal servants pretended to be influential in order to solicit bribes, whether they had any real power or not. But Rollo was not relying only on his bribe. The priest who had converted Queen Anne to Catholicism was also supposed to tell her she should see Rollo. Nevertheless, she must first be told that Jean Langlais was here.

The woman who came in was not the twenty-seven-year-old queen but a gracious woman past sixty who looked familiar. 'Welcome to Scotland, Father Langlais,' she said. 'Do you remember me? It's been almost twenty years.'

When she spoke he recognized her as Mary Stuart's long-time

companion Alison. Her hair was grey now, but she had the same alert blue eyes. He stood up and shook her hand. 'Lady Ross!' he said.

'I'm Lady Thurston now.'

'I didn't expect to see you.'

'Queen Anne has been very good to me.'

Rollo got the picture. After the execution of Mary Stuart, Alison had returned to Scotland and married again. She had made herself useful to Queen Anne and become a lady-in-waiting. No doubt it was Alison who had introduced Anne to the Catholic priest who had converted her. 'I imagine it was you who suggested my mission today,' Rollo said.

'Perhaps it was,' Alison said.

This was good news. It improved Rollo's chance of success. 'Thank you for your help.'

'I owe you a great deal,' Alison said warmly, and the thought crossed Rollo's mind that she might have a soft spot for him. But he had never been very interested in romance. Love was a passion that seemed to have passed him by. He was wondering how to respond to Alison when Queen Anne came in.

She had a long oval face with a high forehead and curly light-brown hair. Her figure was good, and she wore a dress with a low neckline to show off her generous bust. 'I'm very glad to see you, Father Langlais,' she said pleasantly.

Rollo bowed low and said: 'Your majesty does me great honour.'

She corrected him. 'I do honour to the Church you represent.'

'Of course.' Royal etiquette was maddeningly difficult. 'Forgive me.'

'But let's sit down and talk.' She took a seat herself, and Rollo and Alison followed suit. The queen looked enquiringly at Rollo, waiting for him to open the conversation.

Rollo got straight to the point. 'His Holiness Pope Clement believes that your majesty may soon be queen of England.'

'Of course,' she said. 'My husband's title to the English throne is indisputable.'

It certainly was not indisputable. Mary Stuart had been

executed as a traitor, and it was generally accepted that the children of traitors could not inherit titles. Rollo said tactfully: 'And yet there may be men who oppose him.'

She nodded. She knew the facts.

Rollo went on: 'His Holiness has instructed English Catholics to support the claim of King James, provided only that he promises to allow us freedom of worship.'

'His majesty, my husband, is a man of tolerance,' she said.

A grunt of disgust escaped Rollo at the loathed word *tolerance*, and he had to smother the noise with a cough.

Queen Anne did not seem to notice. 'King James has accepted my conversion to the true faith,' she went on.

'Wonderful,' Rollo murmured.

'King James permits Catholic theologians at his court, and often engages them in debate.'

Rollo noticed Alison nodding discreetly to confirm this.

'I can assure you, without the least doubt,' Queen Anne said firmly, 'that when he becomes king of England, he will allow us Catholics freedom of worship.'

'That gives me great joy,' Rollo said with feeling. But in his mind he heard Lenny Price say: *But is it true?* Rollo really needed to hear it from King James himself.

Then the door opened and James walked in.

Rollo leaped to his feet and bowed low.

King James was thirty-six. He had the plump, fleshy face of a sybarite, and his heavy-lidded eyes had a sly look. He kissed his wife's cheek fondly.

Queen Anne said to him: 'Father Langlais, here, comes to tell us that his holiness the Pope supports your claim to the throne of England.'

James smiled at Rollo and spoke with a strong Scots accent. 'Thank you for bringing us this good news, Father.' He slobbered a little in his speech, as if his tongue might be too big for his mouth.

Anne said: 'I have been assuring him that you would grant freedom of worship to English Catholics.'

'Splendid,' said the king. 'My mother was a Catholic, you know, Father Langlais.'

'*Requiescat in pace*,' said Rollo, using the Latin formulation of 'Rest in peace' that was favoured by Catholics.

'Amen,' said King James.

*

NED WILLARD CRIED when Queen Elizabeth died.

She passed away at Richmond Palace on 24 March 1603, in the early hours of a rainy Thursday. Ned was in the room, which was crowded with courtiers, clergymen, and ladies-in-waiting: a queen was too important to die in peace.

Ned was sixty-three. His two patrons, William Cecil and Francis Walsingham, had died years ago, but the monarch still had need of secret intelligence, and Ned had continued to provide it. At the death bed he stood next to Elizabeth's diminutive, hunchbacked secretary of state Robert Cecil, aged forty, younger son of the great William. 'My pygmy,' Elizabeth had called Robert, with the casual cruelty of a monarch. But she had listened to him, for he was as brilliant as his father. Old William had said of his two sons: 'Thomas can hardly rule a tennis court, but Robert could rule England.'

We're all pygmies now, Ned thought sorrowfully; Elizabeth was the giant, and we just served her.

Elizabeth had been in bed for three days, and unable to speak for most of that time. She had fallen asleep at about ten o'clock the previous evening. Now it was three in the morning, and she had simply stopped breathing.

Ned could not control his sobs. The woman who had dominated his life was gone. For the first time in years he recalled the moment when he had glimpsed the young Princess Elizabeth getting out of her bath, and he was pierced by a pain that was almost physical to think that the lovely girl he had seen then was now the lifeless husk that lay in the bed in front of him.

Robert Cecil left the room the moment the doctors declared her dead, and Ned followed, wiping his wet face with the sleeve of his coat. They had no time to mourn. There was too much to do.

They took a painfully slow barge to London in the darkness.

Despite the royal ban on discussion of the succession, the council had agreed long ago that James of Scotland should be the next king of England. But it had to be done quickly. The ultra-Catholics knew the queen was dying and they, too, might have made elaborate plans.

There was no plausible rival to James as king, but there were other ways for the succession to be disrupted. The likeliest scenario was that the ultras would try to kidnap James and his eldest son, Prince Henry. Then they would either kill James or force him to abdicate, and declare his son king – which was how James himself had come to the throne of Scotland as a baby. Prince Henry was only nine years old, so, obviously, an adult would have to rule as his regent, and that would, of course, be one of the senior Catholic noblemen, perhaps even Ned's stepson, Earl Bartlet of Shiring.

Then the Protestants would form an army, civil war would break out, and England would see all the horror and bloodshed of the French wars of religion.

Ned and Cecil had spent the last three months taking precautions against this dreadful scenario. Ned had made a list of the most powerful Catholics and, with Cecil's approval, had put them all in jail. An armed guard had been set about the Exchequer. Cannons had been test-fired at the palace of White Hall.

Ned reflected that the three great women of the sixteenth century were now dead: Elizabeth, Queen Caterina of France, and Margherita of Parma, governor of the Netherlands. They had all tried to stop men killing one another over religion. Looking back, it seemed to him that their achievements had been pitifully limited. Evil men had always frustrated the efforts of the peacemakers. Bloody religious wars had raged for decades in France and the Netherlands. Only England had remained more or less at peace.

All Ned wanted to do, with what remained of his life, was to keep that peace.

Daylight dawned while they were still on the river. When they reached White Hall, Cecil summoned the Privy Council.

The council agreed a proclamation, and Robert Cecil wrote

it out in his own hand. Then the councillors went out to the green opposite the Tiltyard, where a crowd had gathered, no doubt having heard rumours. A herald read out the announcement that Elizabeth had died and James of Scotland was now king.

After that they rode to the city, where again crowds had gathered in places where proclamations were usually made. The herald read the statement outside St Paul's Cathedral then again at Cheapside Cross.

Finally, the council went to the Tower of London and formally took possession of the fortress in the name of King James I of England.

The reaction of Londoners was subdued, Ned observed with relief. Elizabeth had been popular, and they were sad. London merchants had prospered under Elizabeth, and their main wish was for no changes. James was an unknown quantity: a foreign king, though Scots was better than Spanish; a Protestant, but with a Catholic wife; a man, but rumoured to have womanly ways.

Queen Elizabeth's funeral was held while James was still on the long journey from Edinburgh.

A thousand official mourners escorted the hearse on its short journey to Westminster Abbey, and Ned estimated that at least a hundred thousand people watched the procession. The coffin was covered in purple velvet and surmounted by a coloured wax model of Elizabeth in formal robes.

Ned had a designated place in the cortege, but when they entered the cathedral he was able to slip away and find Margery. He held her hand during the service and drew strength from her like warmth from a fire. She was grieving too, for she had come to share Ned's conviction that peace between Christians was more important than doctrinal disputes, and Elizabeth had symbolized that life-saving creed.

When the coffin was lowered into its grave in the Lady Chapel, Ned wept all over again.

He considered what he was weeping for. It was partly for Elizabeth's idealism, which had also been his own. He grieved because those ideals had been so grubbily compromised, over the years, by the demands of everyday politics; for, in the end, Elizabeth had put to death almost as many Catholics as Queen Mary Tudor – 'Bloody Mary' – had killed Protestants. Mary had killed them for their beliefs, whereas Elizabeth had killed them for treason, but the line was too often blurred. Elizabeth was a flawed human being, and her reign had been a patchwork. All the same, Ned had admired her more than anyone else under heaven.

Margery passed him a handkerchief for his tears. It was embroidered with a design of acorns and he recognized it, with a little jolt of surprise, as one he had given her for the same purpose almost half a century ago. He wiped his face, but it was like trying to dry the beach at Combe Harbour: the tears kept flowing with the relentlessness of the incoming tide.

The chief officers of the royal household ritually snapped their white staves of office and threw the pieces into the grave after the coffin.

As the congregation began to leave, it struck Ned that his life had been worth living because of the people who had loved him, and of those the most important were four women: his mother, Alice; Queen Elizabeth; Sylvie; and Margery. Now he was stricken with grief because Elizabeth was the third of them to die; and he clung hard to Margery as they walked together away from the great cathedral, for he realized that she was all he had left.

*

A YEAR AFTER the death of Queen Elizabeth, Rollo Fitzgerald swore that he would kill King James.

James had broken his vows to Catholics. He had renewed Elizabeth's laws against Catholicism and had enforced them with extra savagery, as if he had never promised anyone tolerance or freedom of worship. Whether Queen Anne's undertakings had been sincere Rollo would never know, but he suspected not. Together James and Anne had duped Rollo, and the community of English Catholics, and the Pope himself. Rollo's rage came from the knowledge that he had been fooled, and had been used as the instrument of deceiving others.

But he was not going to give in. He would not concede victory to the lying James and the spiteful Puritans, the blasphemers and the rebels against the true Church. It was not over yet.

The idea of shooting or stabbing James was hazardous: in getting close to the king there was too much risk of being interfered with by guards or courtiers before the deed was done. On the roof of the tower at Tyne Castle, Rollo brooded over how the assassination could be managed, and as he did so his lust for revenge sharpened and his plan grew monstrously ambitious. How much better it would be to wipe out Queen Anne as well. And perhaps the royal children, too: Henry, Elizabeth and Charles. And the leading courtiers, especially Ned Willard. He wished he could shoot them all together with a double-shotted cannon as had been used against the armada. He thought of the fireships, and wondered if he could set light to a palace when they were all gathered together.

And, slowly, a plan began to form in his mind.

He travelled to New Castle and put the plan to Earl Bartlet and the earl's elder son Swifty, who was eighteen. As a boy, Bartlet had hero-worshipped Rollo, and Rollo still had strong influence over him. Swifty had been told since he was old enough to talk that the fortunes of the Shiring earldom had shrunk under Elizabeth. Father and son were grievously disappointed that James was continuing Elizabeth's persecution of Catholics.

Bartlet's younger brother, Roger, was not present. He worked in London for Robert Cecil and no longer lived at New Castle – which was a good thing. Much influenced by his mother Margery and his stepfather, Ned Willard, Roger might have disapproved of Rollo's plan.

'The opening of Parliament,' Rollo said, when the servants had gone and the three men were alone after dinner. 'We get them all together: King James, Queen Anne, Secretary of State Robert Cecil, Sir Ned Willard, and the members of that heretical blaspheming Parliament – all dead with one fatal blow.'

Bartlet looked puzzled. 'It's a tempting prospect, of course,' he said. 'But I can't imagine how it could possibly be achieved.'

'I can,' said Rollo.

29

NED WILLARD WAS ON the alert, looking anxiously around the chapel, studying the wedding guests, watchful for danger signs. King James was expected to attend, and Ned was as afraid for James's life as he had been for Elizabeth's. The secret service could never relax its vigilance.

It was three days after Christmas, 1604.

Ned did not much like King James. The new king had turned out to be less tolerant than Elizabeth, and not just of Catholics. He had a bee in his bonnet about witches – he had written a book on the subject – and he had brought in harsh legislation against them. Ned thought they were mostly harmless old women. All the same Ned was determined to protect James in order to prevent the civil war he dreaded.

The bridegroom was Philip Herbert, the twenty-year-old son of the earl of Pembroke. Philip had caught the eye of King James in the embarrassing way that charming young men often took the fancy of the thirty-eight-year-old king. A court wit had said: 'Elizabeth was king, now James is queen,' and this wisecrack had been repeated all over London. James had encouraged young Philip to get married, as if to prove that his interest in the boy was innocent – which no one believed.

The bride was Susan de Vere, granddaughter of the late William Cecil and niece of secretary of state Robert Cecil, Ned's friend and colleague. Knowing that James was coming, bride and groom waited at the altar, for the king had to be the last to arrive. They were at a chapel within White Hall Palace, where it would be all too easy for an assassin to strike.

Ned was hearing rumours from his spies in Paris, Rome, Brussels and Madrid: English Catholic exiles all over Europe were conspiring to get rid of King James who, they felt, had betrayed them. But Ned had not yet learned the details of specific plots so all he could do, for the time being, was keep his eyes open.

If he had thought, when young, of what life would be like when he was sixty-five, he would have assumed that his work would be done. Either he and Elizabeth would have succeeded, and England would be the first country in the world to have freedom of religion; or he would have failed, and Englishmen would again be burned at the stake for their beliefs. He had never anticipated that the struggle would still be as fierce as ever when he was old and Elizabeth was dead; that Parliament would still be persecuting Catholics and that Catholics would still be trying to kill the monarch. Would it never end?

He glanced at Margery beside him, a bright blue hat set at an angle on her silver curls. She met his eye and said: 'What?'

'I don't want the groom to see you,' Ned murmured teasingly. 'He may want to marry you instead of the bride.'

She giggled. 'I'm an old lady.'

'You're the prettiest old lady in London.' It was true.

Ned looked around the room restlessly. He recognized most of those present. He had been intimate with the Cecils for almost half a century, and he knew the groom's family almost as well. Some of the younger people at the back were only vaguely familiar, and he guessed they were friends of the happy couple. Ned found it increasingly difficult, as the years went by, to tell one youngster from another.

He and Margery were near the front, but Ned was not comfortable there, and he kept looking over his shoulder; so in the end he left Margery and went to the back of the room. From there he could watch everyone, like a mother pigeon studying the other birds, looking for the magpie that would eat her chicks.

All the men wore swords, as a matter of course, so any one of them could have been an assassin, in theory. This generalized suspicion was next to useless, and Ned racked his brains as to how he might learn more.

The king and queen came in at last, safe and sound, and Ned was relieved to see that they were escorted by a dozen men-at-arms. An assassin would have trouble getting past such a bodyguard. Ned sat down and relaxed a little.

The royal couple took their time walking up the aisle, greeting friends and favourites, and acknowledging the bows of others graciously. When they got to the front, James nodded to the clergyman to begin.

While the service was going on, a new arrival slipped into the chapel, and Ned's instincts sounded an alarm.

The newcomer stood at the back. Ned studied him, not caring whether the man knew he was being stared at. He was in his thirties, tall and broad, with something of the air of a soldier about him. However, he did not look stressed or even tense. He leaned against the wall, stroking his long moustache and watching the rite. He radiated arrogant confidence.

Ned decided to speak to him. He got up and walked to the back. As he approached, the newcomer nodded casually and said: 'Good day to you, Sir Ned.'

'You know me—'

'Everyone knows you, Sir Ned.' The remark was a compliment with an undertone of mockery.

'—I don't know you,' Ned finished.

'Fawkes,' said the man. 'Guy Fawkes, at your service.'

'And who invited you here?'

'I'm a friend of the groom, if it matters to you.'

A man who was about to kill a king would not be able to converse in this bantering manner. Nevertheless, Ned had a bad feeling about Fawkes. There was something about his coolness, his half-hidden disrespect, and his satirical tone that suggested subversive inclinations. Ned probed further. 'I haven't met you before.'

'I come from York. My father was a proctor in the consistory court there.'

'Ah.' A proctor was a lawyer, and a consistory court was a Church tribunal. To hold such a post, Fawkes's father would have to be an irreproachable Protestant, and must have taken the oath of allegiance that Catholics abhorred. Fawkes was almost certainly harmless.

All the same, as Ned returned to his seat he decided to keep an eye on Guy Fawkes.

*

ROLLO FITZGERALD reconnoitred Westminster, looking for a weak spot.

A collection of large and small buildings clustered around a court called Westminster Yard. Rollo was nervous about prowling around, but no one seemed to pay him much attention. The courtyard was a gloomy square where prostitutes loitered. No doubt other nefarious doings took place there after dark. The complex was walled and gated, but the gates were rarely closed, even at night. Within the precincts were all the Parliament buildings plus several taverns, a bakery, and a wine merchant's with extensive cellars.

The House of Lords, where the king would come to open Parliament, was a building on the plan of a squat letter H. The grand hall of the Lords, the biggest room, was the crossbar. One upright of the H was the Prince's Chamber, used as a robing room; the other was the Painted Chamber, for committee meetings. But those three rooms were on the upstairs floor. Rollo was more interested in the ground-floor rooms underneath.

Beneath the Prince's Chamber was a porter's lodge and an apartment for the Keeper of the King's Wardrobe. Alongside ran a narrow passage, Parliament Place, leading to a wharf called Parliament Stairs on the left bank of the Thames.

Rollo went to a nearby tavern called The Boatman and pretended to be a firewood dealer looking for storage space and willing to buy drinks for anyone who could give him information. There he gleaned two exciting nuggets: one, that the Wardrobe Keeper did not need his apartment and was willing to rent it out; and two, that it had a cellar. However, he was told, the place was reserved for courtiers, and was not available to common tradesmen. Rollo looked crestfallen and said he would have to search elsewhere. The regulars at the bar thanked him for the drinks and wished him luck.

Rollo had already recruited a co-conspirator, the courtier

Thomas Percy. As a Catholic, Percy would never be an advisor
to the king, but James had made him one of the Gentlemen
Pensioners, a group of ceremonial royal bodyguards. Percy's
support was a mixed blessing, for he was a mercurial character,
alternately full of manic energy or paralysed by gloom, not
unlike his ancestor Hotspur in a popular play about the youth
of Henry V; but now he proved useful. At Rollo's suggestion,
Percy claimed he needed the Wardrobe Keeper's rooms for his
wife to live in while he was at court and – after a prolonged
negotiation – he rented the apartment.

That was a big step forward.

Officially, Rollo was in London for a long-drawn-out
lawsuit between the earl of Tyne and a neighbour about the
ownership of a watermill. This was a cover story. His real
purpose was to kill the king. For that, he needed more men.

Guy Fawkes was just the type he was looking for. Fawkes's
staunchly Protestant father had died when little Guy was eight,
and he had been raised by a Catholic mother and stepfather. As
a wealthy young man Fawkes had rejected a life of idleness,
sold the estate he had inherited from his father, and set out to
look for adventure. He had left England and fought for Spain
against the Protestant rebels in the Netherlands, where he had
learned about engineering during sieges. Now he was back in
London, at a loose end, ready for excitement.

Unfortunately, Fawkes was under surveillance.

This afternoon he was at the Globe Theatre, on the south
side of the river Thames, watching a new play called *Measure
for Measure*. Two places along the bench from him was Nick
Bellows, an unobtrusive man in drab clothes, whom Rollo
knew to be one of Ned Willard's street stalkers.

Rollo was in the crowd of groundlings without seats. He
followed the play with disapproval. Its story of a strong ruler
who hypocritically breaks his own laws was blatantly designed
to encourage disrespect for authority. Rollo was looking for an
opportunity to speak to Fawkes without attracting the notice
of Bellows, but it was proving difficult. Bellows discreetly
followed when Fawkes left his seat, once to buy a cup of wine
and once to piss in the river.

Rollo still had not spoken to him when the play came to an end and the audience began to leave. The crowd choked the exit and the people shuffled along slowly. Rollo manoeuvred himself behind Fawkes and spoke in a low voice directly into his ear. 'Don't look around, whatever you do, just listen,' he said.

Perhaps Fawkes had been involved in clandestine activity before, for he did as Rollo said, only giving an almost imperceptible nod to show that he had understood.

'His Holiness the Pope has work for you to do,' Rollo said in the same low tone. 'But you're being followed by one of King James's spies, so first you have to shake him off. Go to a tavern and drink a cup of wine, to give me a chance to get ahead of you. Then walk west along the river, away from the bridge. Wait until there is only one boat at the beach, then hire it to take you across, leaving your tail behind. On the other side, walk quickly to Fleet Street and meet me at the York tavern.'

Fawkes nodded again once.

Rollo moved away. He went over London Bridge and walked briskly through the city and beyond its walls to Fleet Street. He stood across the street from the York, wondering whether Fawkes would come. He guessed that Fawkes would be unable to resist the call of adventure, and he was right. Fawkes appeared, walking with the characteristic swagger that made Rollo think of a prize fighter. Rollo watched for another minute or two, but neither Bellows nor anyone else was following.

He went inside.

Fawkes was in a corner with a jug of wine and two goblets. Rollo sat opposite him, with his back to the room; hiding his face was now an ingrained habit. Fawkes said: 'Who was following me?'

'Nick Bellows. Small man in a brown coat, sitting next but two to you.'

'I didn't notice him.'

'He goes to a certain amount of trouble not to be noticed.'

'Of course. What do you want with me?'

'I have a simple question for you,' Rollo said. 'Do you have the courage to kill the king?'

Fawkes looked at him hard, weighing him up. His stare would have intimidated many men, but Rollo was his equal in self-regard, and stared right back.

At last Fawkes said: 'Yes.'

Rollo nodded, satisfied. This was the kind of plain speaking he wanted. 'You've been a soldier, you understand discipline,' he said.

Again Fawkes just said: 'Yes.'

'Your new name is John Johnson.'

'Isn't that a bit obvious?'

'Don't argue. You're going to be the caretaker of a small apartment that we've rented. I'll take you there now. You can't go back to your lodging, it may be watched.'

'There's a pair of pistols in my room that I'd be sorry to leave behind.'

'I'll send someone to collect your belongings when I'm sure the coast is clear.'

'All right.'

'We should go now.'

'Where is this apartment?'

'At Westminster,' said Rollo. 'In the House of Lords.'

*

IT WAS ALREADY dark on a rainy evening, but the London taverns and shops were lit up with lanterns and blazing torches, and Margery knew she was not mistaken when she saw her brother across the street. He was standing outside a tavern called the White Swan, apparently saying goodbye to a tall man who Margery thought she recognized.

Margery had not seen her brother for years. That suited her: she did not like to be reminded of the fact that he was Jean Langlais. Because of this terrible secret she had almost turned down Ned's proposal of marriage fifteen years ago. But if she had done so, she would never have been able to tell him why. She loved him so much, but in the end what tipped the balance was not her love for him but his for her. He longed for her, she knew, and if she had turned him down, without plausible explanation, he would have spent the rest of his life being mystified and wounded. She had power over his life and she was unable to resist the temptation to make him happy.

She could not be comfortable with her secret, but it was like the backache that had afflicted her ever since the birth of Roger: it never ceased to hurt, but she learned to live with it.

She crossed the street. As she did so the second man left, and Rollo turned to go back into the tavern. 'Rollo!' she said.

He stopped suddenly at the door, startled, and for a moment he looked so fearful that she felt concerned; then he recognized her. 'It's you,' he said warily.

'I didn't know you were in London!' she said. 'Wasn't that Thomas Percy you were talking to?'

'Yes, it was.'

'I thought so. I recognized his prematurely grey hair.' Margery did not know what religion Percy adhered to, but some of his famous family were Catholic, and Margery was suspicious. 'You're not up to your old tricks, are you, Rollo?'

'Certainly not. All that is over.'

'I hope so.' Margery was not fully reassured. 'So what are you doing here?'

'I'm handling a protracted lawsuit for the earl of Tyne. He's in dispute with a neighbour over the ownership of a watermill.'

That was true, Margery knew. Her son Roger had mentioned it. 'Roger says the legal fees and bribes have already cost more than three watermills.'

'My clever nephew is right. But the earl is obstinate. Come inside.'

They went in and sat down. A man with a big red nose brought Rollo a cup of wine without asking. His proprietorial air suggested to Margery that he was the landlord. Rollo said: 'Thank you, Hodgkinson.'

'Something for the lady?' the man asked.

'A small glass of ale, please,' Margery said.

Hodgkinson went away, and Margery said to Rollo: 'Are you lodging here?'

'Yes.'

She was puzzled. 'Doesn't the earl of Tyne have a London house?'

'No, he just rents one when Parliament is sitting.'

'You should use Shiring House. Bartlet would be happy for you to stay there.'

'There are no servants there, just a janitor, except when Bartlet comes to London.'

'Bartlet would gladly send a couple of people up here from New Castle to look after you, if you asked him.'

Rollo looked peeved. 'Then they would spend his money on beef and wine for themselves and feed me bacon and beer, and if I complained, they'd tell Bartlet I was too high-handed and demanding. Frankly, I prefer a tavern.'

Margery was not sure whether he was irritated by her or by the thought of dishonest servants, but she decided to drop the question. If he wanted to stay in a tavern, he could. 'How are you, anyway?' she said.

'The same as ever. The earl of Tyne is a good master. How about you? Is Ned well?'

'He's in Paris right now.'

'Really?' said Rollo, interested. 'What's he doing there?'

'His work,' she said vaguely. 'I'm not really sure.'

Rollo knew she was lying. 'Spying on Catholics, I assume. That's his work, as everyone knows.'

'Come on, Rollo, it's your fault for trying to murder his queen. Don't pretend to be indignant.'

'Are you happy with Ned?'

'Yes. God in his wisdom has given me a strange life, but for the last fifteen years I have been truly happy.' She noticed that his shoes and stockings were covered with mud. 'How on earth did you get so dirty?'

'I had to walk along the foreshore.'

'Why?'

'Long story. And I have an appointment.' Rollo stood up.

Margery realized she was being dismissed. She kissed her brother's cheek and left. She had not asked him what his appointment was about, and as she walked away from the tavern she asked herself why. The answer came immediately: she did not think he would tell her the truth.

*

ROLLO IMPOSED STRICT security at the Wardrobe Keeper's apartment. Everyone arrived before dawn, so that they would not be seen entering. Each man brought his own food, and they did not go outside in daylight. They left again after dark.

Rollo was almost seventy, so he left the harder work to younger men such as Fawkes and Percy, but even they struggled. All were the sons of noble and wealthy families, and none of them had previously done much digging.

They had first to demolish the brick wall of the cellar, then scoop out the earth behind it. The tunnel needed to be large enough for a number of thirty-two-gallon barrels of gunpowder to be dragged inside. They saved time by making it no larger, but the disadvantage of that was that they had to work bent double, or lying down; and the confined space grew hot.

During the day they lived on salted fish, dried meat and raisins. Rollo would not let them send out for the kind of meal they were used to, fearing that they would draw attention to themselves.

It was muddy work, which was why Rollo had been embarrassingly dirty when he unexpectedly ran into Margery. The soil they removed from the tunnel had to be lugged up to ground level, then taken outside after dark and carried along Parliament Passage and down Parliament Stairs, from where it could be thrown into the river. Rollo had been unnerved when Margery asked about his filthy stockings, but she had seemed to accept his explanation.

The tunnellers were discreet, but not invisible. Even in the dark, they were sometimes seen coming and going by people carrying lanterns. To divert suspicion, Fawkes had let it be known that he had builders in, making some alterations that his master's wife had demanded. Rollo hoped no one would notice the improbably large quantity of earth being displaced by mere alterations.

Then they ran into a difficulty so serious that Rollo was afraid it might ruin the whole plan. When they had tunnelled into the earth for several feet, they came up against a solid stone wall. Naturally, Rollo realized, the two-storey building above had proper foundations: he should have anticipated this.

The work became harder and slower, but they had to go on, for they were not yet far enough under the debating chamber to be sure that the explosion would kill everyone there.

The stone foundations turned out to be several feet thick. Rollo feared they would not finish the job before the opening ceremony. Then Parliament was postponed, because of an outbreak of plague in London; and the tunnellers had a new deadline.

Even so, Rollo fretted. Progress was terribly slow. The longer they took, the more risk there was that they would be discovered. And there was another hazard. As they went farther, undermining the foundations, Rollo feared a collapse. Fawkes made stout timber props to support the roof – as he said he had done when digging under city walls in Netherlands sieges – but Rollo was not sure how much this fighting man really knew about mining. The tunnel might just fall in and kill them all. It could even bring down the entire building – which would achieve nothing if the king were not inside.

Taking a break one day, they talked about who would be in the chamber when the gunpowder went off. King James had three children. Prince Henry, who was eleven, and Prince Charles, four, would probably accompany their parents to the ceremony. 'Assuming they both die, Princess Elizabeth will be the heir,' said Percy. 'She will be nine.'

Rollo had already thought about the princess. 'We must be prepared to seize her,' he said. 'Whoever has her, has the throne.'

Percy said: 'She lives at Coombe Abbey, in Warwickshire.'

'She will need a Lord Protector, who will, of course, be the actual ruler of England.'

'I propose my kinsman the earl of Northumberland.'

Rollo nodded. It was a good suggestion. Northumberland was one of the great peers of the realm and a Catholic sympathizer. But Rollo had a better idea. 'I suggest the earl of Shiring.'

The others were not enthusiastic. Rollo knew what they were thinking: Bartlet Shiring was a good Catholic but did not have Northumberland's stature.

Too polite to denigrate Rollo's nephew, Percy said: 'We must plan uprisings in all parts of the country where Catholic peers are strong. There must be no opportunity for the Protestants to promote a rival for the throne.'

'I can guarantee that in the county of Shiring,' said Rollo.

Someone said: 'A lot of people will die.'

Rollo was impatient with men who worried about killing. A civil war would be a cleansing. 'The Protestants deserve death,' he said. 'And the Catholics will go straight to heaven.'

Just then there was a strange noise. At first it sounded like a rush of water overhead. Then it turned into a rumble as of shifting rocks. Rollo immediately feared a collapse. The other men clearly had the same instinctive reaction, for they all rushed, as if to save their lives, up the narrow stone staircase that led from the cellar to the apartment at ground level.

There they stopped and listened. The noise continued, intermittently, but the floor was not shaking, and Rollo realized they had overreacted. The building was not about to fall down. But what *was* happening?

Rollo pointed at Fawkes. 'Come with me,' he said. 'We'll investigate. The rest of you, stay quiet.'

He led Fawkes outside and around the building. The noise had stopped, but Rollo thought it must have come from roughly where their tunnel ran.

At the back of the building, a row of windows ran along the upper storey, lighting the debating chamber. In the middle of the row was a small door opening on to a wooden exterior staircase: it was not much used, for the grand entrance was on the other side. Under the staircase, at ground level, was a double wooden door that Rollo had hardly noticed before. If he had thought about it, he would have assumed that it gave access to the kind of storeroom where gardeners kept spades. Now for the first time he saw both doors wide open. A carthorse stood patiently outside.

Rollo and Fawkes stepped through the doorway.

It was a store, but it was huge. In fact, Rollo guessed, it was probably the same length and width as the debating chamber directly above. He was not quite sure because the windowless vault was dark, illuminated mainly by the light coming through the doorway. From what he could see, it looked like the crypt of a church, with massive pillars curving up to a low wooden ceiling that must form the floor of the room above. Rollo realized with dismay that the tunnellers had probably been hacking through the base of one of those pillars. They were in even more danger of collapse than he had feared.

The room was mostly empty, with odd pieces of timber and sacking lying around, and a square table with a hole broken through its top. Rollo immediately saw the explanation for the noise: a man whose face was black with dust was shovelling coal from a pile onto a cart. That was the cause of the noise.

Rollo glanced at Fawkes and knew they were both thinking the same thing. If they could get control of this room, they could place their gunpowder even nearer to the king – and they could stop tunnelling.

A woman of middle age was watching the carter work. When his vehicle was loaded, he counted coins with his sooty hands and gave them to her, evidently paying her for the coal. She took the coins to the doorway to examine them in the light before thanking the man. Then, as the carter backed his horse into the shafts of the cart, the woman turned to Rollo and Fawkes and said politely: 'Good day to you, gentlemen. Is there something I can do for you?'

'What is this room?' Rollo asked.

'I believe it used to be the kitchen, in the days when banquets were served in the grand chamber above. Now it's my coal store. Or it was: spring is coming and I'm getting rid of my stocks. You may like to buy some: it's the best hard coal from the banks of the river Tyne, burns really hot—'

Fawkes interrupted her. 'We don't want coal, but we're looking for somewhere to store a large quantity of wood. My name is John Johnson, I'm caretaker of the Wardrobe Keeper's apartment.'

'I'm Ellen Skinner, widow and coal merchant.'

'I'm pleased to make your acquaintance, Mrs Skinner. Is this place available to rent?'

'I've got it leased for the rest of the year.'

'But you're getting rid of your stock, you say, because spring is coming. Few people buy coal in warm weather.'

She looked crafty. 'I may have another use for the place.'

She was feigning reluctance, but Rollo could see the light of greed in her eyes. Her arguments were no more than negotiating tactics. He began to feel hopeful.

Fawkes said: 'My master would pay well.'

'I'd give up my lease for three pounds,' she said. 'And you'd have to pay the landlord on top of that – four pounds a year, he charges me.'

Rollo suppressed the impulse to say eagerly: *It's a bargain.* The price did not matter, but if they were seen to be throwing money around, they would attract attention and, perhaps, suspicion.

Fawkes haggled for the sake of appearance. 'Oh, madam, that seems too much,' he said. 'A pound for your lease at most, surely.'

'I might keep the place. I'll need a coal store come September.'

'Split the difference,' Fawkes said. 'One pound ten shillings.'

'If you could make it two pounds, I'd shake hands on it now.'

'Oh, very well,' Fawkes said, and held out his hand.

'A pleasure, Mr Johnson,' said the woman.

Fawkes said: 'I assure you, Mrs Skinner, the pleasure is all mine.'

*

NED WENT TO Paris in a desperate attempt to find out what was happening in London.

He continued to hear vague rumours of Catholic plots against King James. And his suspicion had been heightened when Guy Fawkes deftly shook off his surveillance and disappeared. But there was a frustrating lack of detail in the gossip.

Many royal assassination plots had been hatched in Paris, often with the help of the ultra-Catholic Guise family. The Protestants there had maintained the network of spies Sylvie had set up. Ned hoped that one of them, most likely Alain de Guise, might be able to fill the gaps.

After the simultaneous murders of Duke Henri and Pierre Aumande, Ned had feared that Alain would no longer be a source of information on exiled English Catholics; but Alain had picked up some of his stepfather's wiliness. He had made himself useful to the widow and befriended the new young duke, and so continued to live at the Guise palace in Paris and work for the family. And because the ultra-Catholic Guises were trusted by the English plotters, Alain learned a good deal about their plans, and passed the information to Ned by coded letters sent along well-established secret channels. Much of the exiles' talk came to nothing, but several times over the years Alain's tips had led to arrests.

Ned read all his letters, but now he was hoping to learn more by a personal visit. In face-to-face conversation random details could sometimes emerge and turn out to be important.

Worried though he was, the trip to France was nostalgic for him. It put him in mind of himself as a young man; of the great Walsingham, with whom he had worked for two decades; and, most of all, of Sylvie. On his way to meet Alain he went to the rue de la Serpente and stood for a while outside the bookshop that had been Sylvie's home, remembering the happy day he had been invited to dinner there and had kissed her in the back room, and the terrible day Isabelle had been killed there.

It was a butcher's shop now.

He crossed the bridge to the Île de la Cité, went into the cathedral, and said a prayer of thanks for Sylvie's life. The church was Catholic, and Ned was Protestant, but he had long believed that God cared little about such distinctions.

And nowadays the king of France felt the same. Henri IV had signed the Edict of Nantes, giving Protestants religious freedom. The new duke of Guise was still a child, and the Guise family had not been able to undermine the peace this time; and so forty years of civil war had come to an end. Ned thanked God for Henry IV, too. Perhaps France, like England, was slowly fumbling its way towards tolerance.

Protestant services were still discreet, and usually held

outside the walls of cities, to avoid inflaming ultra-Catholics. Ned walked south along the rue St Jacques, through the city gate, and out into the suburbs. A man sitting reading at the roadside was the signpost to a track that led through the woods to a hunting lodge. This was the informal church Sylvie had attended before Ned met her. It had been exposed by Pierre Aumande, and the congregation had broken up, but now it was again a place of worship.

Alain was already there, sitting with his wife and children. Also with him was his long-time friend Louise, the dowager marchioness of Nîmes. Both had been at the château of Blois when Duke Henri and Pierre had been murdered, and Ned suspected they had been in on the plot, though no one had dared to investigate either killing because of the presumed involvement of the king. Ned also saw Nath, who had taken over Sylvie's business in illegal books: she had become a prosperous old lady in a fur hat.

Ned sat next to Alain, but did not speak until the hymns, when everyone was singing too loudly to hear their talk. 'They all hate this James,' Alain murmured to Ned, speaking French. 'They say he broke his promises.'

'They're not wrong,' Ned admitted. 'All the same I have to stop them killing him. Otherwise the peace and prosperity that Elizabeth won with such a tremendous effort will be shattered by civil war. What else do you hear?'

'They want to kill the entire royal family, all but the little princess, whom they will declare queen.'

'The entire family,' Ned repeated, horrified. 'Bloodthirsty brutes.'

'At the same time they will kill all the leading ministers and lords.'

'They must be planning to burn down a palace, or something. They could do that while everyone was sitting at a banquet, or watching a play.' He was one of the leading ministers. Suddenly this had become about saving his own life as well as the king's. He felt a chill. 'Where will they do it?' he asked.

'I have not been able to elucidate that point.'

'Have you ever heard the name Guy Fawkes?'

Alain shook his head. 'No. A group came to see the duke, but I don't know who they were.'

'No names were mentioned?'

'No real names.'

'What do you mean?'

'The only name I heard was a false one.'

'And what was that?'

'Jean Langlais,' said Alain.

*

MARGERY WAS BOTHERED about Rollo. His answers to her questions had all been plausible, but just the same she did not trust him. However, she did not see what she could do about her unease. Of course, she could have told Ned that Rollo was Jean Langlais, but she could not bring herself to condemn her brother to the gallows just because he had muddy stockings.

While Ned was in Paris, Margery decided to take her grandson Jack, the son of Roger, on a visit to New Castle. She felt it was her duty. Whatever Jack ended up doing with his life, he could be helped by his aristocratic relations. He did not have to like them, but he had to know them. Having an earl for an uncle was sometimes better than money. And, when Bartlet died, the next earl would be his son Swifty, who was Jack's cousin.

Jack was an enquiring, argumentative twelve-year-old. He entered energetically into disputatious conversations with Roger and with Ned, always taking the view opposite to that of the adult he was talking to. Ned said that Jack was exactly like the young Margery, but she could hardly believe she had been so cocky. Jack was small, like Margery, with the same curly dark hair. He was pretty now, but in a year or two he would begin to turn into a man, and then his looks would coarsen. The pleasure and fascination of watching children and grandchildren grow and alter was the great joy of being elderly, for Margery.

Naturally, Jack disagreed with his grandmother about the need for this visit. 'I want to be an adventurer, like Uncle

Barney,' he said. 'Noblemen have nothing to do with trade – they just sit back and collect rents from people.'

'The nobility keep the peace and enforce the rules,' she argued. 'You can't do business without laws and standards. How much silver is there in a penny? How wide is a yard of cloth? What happens when men don't pay their debts?'

'They make the rules to suit themselves,' said Jack. 'Anyway, the Kingsbridge Guild enforces weights and measures, not the earl.'

She smiled. 'Perhaps you should be a statesman, like Sir Ned, rather than an adventurer.'

'Why?'

'You have such strong ideas about government. You could *be* the Government. Some of the most powerful men at court used to be clever schoolboys like you.'

He looked thoughtful. He was at the delightful age where anything seemed possible.

But she wanted him to behave himself at New Castle. 'Be polite,' she said as they approached. 'Don't argue with Uncle Bartlet. You're here to make friends, not enemies.'

'Very well, grandmother.'

She was not sure he had taken her warning to heart, but she had done her best. A child will always be what he is, she thought, and not what you want him to be.

Her son, Earl Bartlet, welcomed them. In his forties now, he was freckled like Margery's father, but he had modelled himself on Bart, who, he thought, was his father. The fact that Bartlet was in truth the result of rape by Earl Swithin had not completely poisoned the relationship between mother and son, miraculously. While Jack explored the castle, Margery sat in the hall with Bartlet and drank a glass of wine. She said: 'I hope Swifty and Jack get to know one another better.'

'I doubt they'll be close,' said Bartlet. 'There's a big age gap between twelve and twenty.'

'I bumped into your Uncle Rollo in London. He's staying in a tavern. I don't know why he doesn't use Shiring House.'

Bartlet shrugged. 'I'd be delighted if he would. Make my lazy caretaker do some work for a change.'

A steward poured Margery more wine. 'You'll be heading up to London yourself later this year, for the opening of Parliament.'

'Not necessarily.'

Margery was surprised. 'Why not?'

'I'll say I'm ill.' All earls were obliged to attend Parliament, and if they wanted to get out of it, they had to say they were too ill to travel.

'But what's the real reason?'

'I've got too much to do here.'

That did not make sense to Margery. 'You've never missed a Parliament, since you became earl. Nor did your father and grandfather. It's the reason you have a house in London.'

'The new king has no interest in the views of the earl of Shiring.'

This was uncharacteristic. Bartlet, like Bart and Swithin, would normally voice his opinion – loudly – without asking whether anyone cared to hear it. 'Don't you want to oppose any further anti-Catholic legislation?'

'I think we've lost that battle.'

'I've never known you to be so defeatist.'

'It's important to know when to fight on – and when to stop.' Bartlet stood up. 'You probably want to settle into your room before dinner. Have you got everything you need?'

'Yes, I think so.' She kissed him and went upstairs. She was intrigued. Maybe he was not like Bart and Swithin after all. Their pride would never have allowed them to say things like I *think we've lost that battle*. They would never admit that they might have been in the wrong.

Perhaps Bartlet was growing up.

*

THE MOST DIFFICULT and dangerous part of Rollo's plan came when he had to buy thirty-six barrels of gunpowder and bring them to Westminster.

With two of his younger conspirators he crossed the river

and walked to Rotherhithe, a neighbourhood of docks and shipyards. There they went to a stable and told an ostler that they wanted to rent a sturdy flatbed cart and two horses to pull it. 'We have to pick up a load of timbers from a demolished old ship,' Rollo said. 'I'm going to use them to build a barn.' Ships' timbers were often recycled this way.

The ostler was not interested in Rollo's story. He showed Rollo a cart and two sturdy horses, and Rollo said: 'Fine, that's just what I need.'

Then the ostler said: 'My man Weston will drive you.'

Rollo frowned. He could not accept this. A driver would witness everything. 'I'd rather drive myself,' he said, trying not to sound agitated. 'I have two helpers.'

The ostler shook his head. 'If Weston doesn't go with you, you'll have to pay a deposit, otherwise how do I know you'll bring the cart back?'

'How much?' Rollo asked for the sake of appearances – he was willing to pay more or less anything.

'Five pounds for each of the horses and a pound for the cart.'

'You'll have to give me a receipt.'

When the transaction was finalized, they drove out of the stable yard and went to a firewood supplier called Pearce. There Rollo bought faggots, irregular branches tied in bundles, and billets, which were more regular split logs, also roped together. They loaded all the wood onto the cart. Pearce was curious about Rollo's insistence on meticulously stacking the bundles on the cart in the shape of a hollow square, leaving an empty space in the middle. 'You must be picking up another load that you want to keep hidden,' he said.

'Nothing valuable,' said Rollo, as if he was afraid of thieves.

Pearce tapped the side of his nose knowingly. 'Enough said.'

They drove the cart to Greenwich, where Rollo had a rendezvous with Captain Radcliffe.

Guy Fawkes had calculated the amount of gunpowder required to be sure of completely destroying the House of Lords and killing everyone in it. A gentleman who owned a pistol or an arquebus might buy a box of gunpowder for his own use, and no one would ask any questions; but there was no legitimate way for Rollo to buy the quantity he needed without arousing suspicion.

His solution was to go to a criminal.

Radcliffe was a corrupt quartermaster who bought supplies for the royal navy. Half of what he purchased never went on board a ship, but was privately re-sold by him to line his own pockets. Radcliffe's biggest problem was hiding how rich he was.

The good thing about him, from Rollo's point of view, was that he could not babble about the sale of gunpowder, for if he did, he would be hanged for stealing from the king. He had to keep silent, for the sake of his own life.

Rollo met Radcliffe in the yard of a tavern. They loaded eight barrels onto the cart, stacking them two high in the middle of the square of firewood. A casual observer would assume the barrels contained ale.

'You must be expecting a war,' said Radcliffe.

Rollo had an answer ready. 'We're merchant sailors,' he said. 'We need to defend ourselves.'

'Indeed, you do,' said Radcliffe.

'We're not pirates.'

'No,' said Radcliffe. 'Of course not.'

Like Pearce, Radcliffe was inclined to believe whatever Rollo denied.

When they were done they completed the square and added wood on top, so that the secret load could not be seen even from a high window.

Then Rollo drove the cart back to Westminster. He went carefully. Crashes between wheeled vehicles were commonplace, usually leading to fistfights between the drivers which sometimes escalated into street riots. The London crowd, never slow to seize an opportunity, would often rob the carts of their loads while the drivers were distracted. If that happened to him, the game would be up. He drove so cautiously, always allowing another cart to go first, that other drivers began to look suspiciously at him.

He made it back to Westminster Yard without incident.

Fawkes was waiting and opened the double doors as they

approached, so that Rollo was able to drive the cart into the storeroom without stopping. Fawkes closed the doors behind the cart, and Rollo slumped with relief. He had got away with it.

He only had to do the same thing three more times.

Fawkes pointed to a new door in the wall, dimly visible by the light of a lamp. 'I made a passage from here to the Wardrobe Keeper's apartment,' he said. 'Now we can go from one to the other without stepping outside and risking being seen.'

'Very good,' said Rollo. 'What about the cellar?'

'I've bricked up the tunnel.'

'Show me.'

The two men went through the new doorway into the apartment, then down the stairs to the cellar. Fawkes had filled in the hole they had made in the wall, but the repair was visible even by candlelight. 'Get some mud or soot and dirty the new bricks,' Rollo said. 'And maybe hack at them a bit with a pickaxe, so that they look as if they've been damaged over the years.'

'Good idea.'

'I want that patch of wall to be indistinguishable from all the rest.'

'Of course. But no one is going to come down here anyway.'

'Just in case,' said Rollo. 'We can't be too careful.'

They returned to the storeroom.

The other two were unloading the gunpowder barrels and rolling them to the far end of the space. Rollo directed them to put the firewood in front of the barrels, stacking the bundles carefully so that the pile would remain stable. One of the young men stood on the broken table, careful not to put his foot through the hole, and the other passed bundles up to him to be placed at the top.

When it was done Rollo studied their work carefully. No one would suspect that this was anything other than a stack of firewood. He was satisfied. 'Even if someone were to search this place,' he said with satisfaction, 'they probably wouldn't find the gunpowder.'

*

NED AND MARGERY lived in St Paul's Churchyard, in a pleasant row house with a pear tree in the backyard. It was not grand, but Margery had made it cosy with rugs and pictures, and they had coal fires to keep the place warm in winter. Ned liked it because he could look out and see the cathedral, which reminded him of Kingsbridge.

Ned arrived back from Paris late one evening, tired and anxious. Margery made him a light supper and they went to bed and made love. In the morning he told her about his trip. She was shocked rigid by what he said, and struggled to hide her emotions. Fortunately, he was in a hurry to report to Robert Cecil, and he went out immediately after breakfast, leaving her free to think in peace.

There was a plan to kill the royal family, all except Princess Elizabeth, and at the same time all the leading ministers, which probably meant burning down a palace, Ned had said. But Margery knew more. Bartlet was going to miss the opening of Parliament, for the first time since he had become earl of Shiring. Margery had been puzzled by his decision, but now it made sense. The plotters would strike at Westminster.

The opening ceremony was ten days away.

How did Bartlet know about it? Ned had learned that Jean Langlais was involved, and Margery knew that Langlais was Rollo. Bartlet's uncle Rollo had warned him to stay away.

She knew it all, now, but what was she to do? She could denounce Rollo to Ned, and perhaps that was what she would have to do in the end, although she shuddered with horror at the thought of sending her brother to his death. However, there might be a better way. She could go and see Rollo. She knew where he was lodging. She could tell him she knew everything and threaten to reveal all to Ned. Once Ned knew, the entire plot was doomed. Rollo would have no choice but to give the whole thing up.

She put on a heavy cloak and stout boots and went out into the London autumn.

She walked to the White Swan and found the red-nosed landlord. 'Good day to you, Mr Hodgkinson,' she said. 'I was here a few weeks ago.'

The landlord was grumpy, perhaps because he had drunk too much of his own wine the night before. He gave her a look of indifference and said: 'I can't remember everyone who buys a cup of wine in here.'

'No matter. I want to see Rollo Fitzgerald.'

'There's no one of that name in the house,' he said tersely.

'But he was lodging here!'

He gave her a hostile look. 'May I ask who you are?'

Margery assumed an air of aristocratic hauteur. 'I am the dowager countess of Shiring, and you would do well to mind your manners.'

He changed his tune. No one wanted to quarrel with an aristocrat. 'I beg your pardon, my lady, but I can't recall ever having a guest of the name you mentioned.'

'I wonder if any of his friends stayed here. What about Jean Langlais?'

'Oh, yes!' said Hodgkinson. 'French name, though he spoke like an Englishman. But he left.'

'Do you know where he went?'

'No. Monsieur Langlais is not a man to give out unnecessary information, my lady. Close-mouthed, he is.'

Of course he was.

She left the inn. What was she going to do now? She had no idea where Rollo might be. There was now little point in denouncing him to Ned, for Ned would not be able to find him either. She racked her brains. People were going to commit an atrocity, and she had to stop them.

Could she give warning? Perhaps she could do that without condemning Rollo to death. She considered an anonymous letter. She could write to Ned, disguising her handwriting, and pretend to be one of the conspirators. She need not say anything about Rollo. The letter would simply warn Ned to stay away from the opening of Parliament if he wanted to live.

But that was implausible. Why would a Catholic conspirator want to save the life of a famous Protestant courtier?

On the other hand, if the letter went to a Catholic, he might approve of the plot and keep the news to himself.

What she needed was someone in between: a man who was

loyal to the king, but sufficiently friendly to Catholics that they would not want to kill him. There were several such people at court, and Margery thought of Lord Monteagle, a Catholic who wanted to be at peace with his Protestant countrymen. People such as Rollo and Bartlet spoke of him as a weak ditherer, but Margery thought he was sensible. If he were warned he would sound the alarm.

She decided to write him a letter.

She stepped out to one of the many stationery shops in St Paul's Churchyard and bought some paper of a type she did not normally use. Back in the house, she sharpened a quill with a pen knife. Using her left hand to disguise her writing, she began:

My Lord, out of the love I bear to some of your friends, I have a care of your preservation.

That was nicely vague, she thought.

Therefore, I would advise you as you tender your life to devise some excuse to shift off your attendance at this Parliament.

That was unmistakable: his life was in danger.

What would Rollo say in such a message? Something pious, perhaps.

For God and man have concurred to punish the wickedness of this time.

That seemed to have the right apocalyptic tone.

And think not slightly of this advertisement, but retire yourself into your country where you may expect the event in safety.

She needed to say something about the means by which the killing would be done. But all she knew was that Ned thought they planned to set the building on fire. She should hint at something like that.

For though there be no appearance of any stir, yet I say they shall receive a terrible blow this Parliament. And yet they shall not see who hurts them.

What else would a conspirator think about? Destroying the evidence?

This counsel is not to be condemned because it may do you good, and can do you no harm; for the danger is past as soon as you have burned the letter.

And how should she end? With something sincere, she decided.

And I hope God will give you the grace to make good use of it: to whose Holy protection I commend you.

She folded the letter and sealed it, pressing a coin into the soft wax and wiggling it a bit to make the impression unreadable, as if a seal ring had been carelessly applied.

Now she had to deliver it.

She would probably be seen by people at the house, and perhaps by Monteagle himself, who knew her, so she needed a disguise.

Margery and Ned employed a maid-of-all-work who was at present washing sheets in the backyard. Margery told her to take the rest of the day off and gave her sixpence to go to the bear-baiting.

She went to Ned's wardrobe. She put on a pair of his breeches, tucking her petticoats inside for bulk, and then a frayed old doublet. Ned was slim, but, nevertheless, his clothes were too big for her. However, a mere messenger would be expected to be badly dressed. She put on a worn-down pair of his shoes and stuffed them with rags to make them fit. Her ankles were too small for a man, she saw. She pinned up her hair and put on Ned's third-best hat.

It would be awkward if Ned were to come home now. But he would almost certainly be out all day: work would have piled up on his table while he was in Paris. And he was supposed to have dinner at Cecil's house. The likelihood of a surprise return was low – she hoped.

In the mirror she did not look much like a man. She was too pretty, and her hands were too small. She put a coal shovel up the chimney and brought down a quantity of soot, then used it to besmirch her hands and face. That was better, the mirror told her. Now she could pass for a grubby little old man of the kind who might well be used as a messenger.

She left the house by the back door and hurried away, hoping that any neighbours who glimpsed her would not recognize her. She went east to Ald Gate, and passed through it out of the city. She walked through fields to the village of

Hoxton, where Monteagle had a suburban house in a large garden. She went to the back door, as a scruffy messenger would.

A man with his mouth full of food came to the door. She handed the letter to him and said in her gruffest voice: 'For Lord Monteagle, personal and very important.'

The man chewed and swallowed. 'And who is it from?'

'A gentleman that gave me a penny.'

'All right, old boy, here's another.'

She held out her hand, small but dirty, and took the coin, then she turned away.

*

NED WILLARD AND most of the Privy Council were sitting around Robert Cecil's dining table when a servant came in to tell Cecil that Lord Monteagle needed to speak to him very urgently.

Cecil excused himself and asked Ned to go with him. Monteagle was waiting in a side room, looking anxious, holding a sheet of paper as if it might explode. He began with what was obviously a prepared sentence. 'The writer of this letter appears to think me a traitor,' he said, 'but I hope to prove I am not by bringing the letter to you, the secretary of state, within an hour of having received it.'

It struck Ned as ironic that the tall, strapping young Lord Monteagle was so visibly frightened of the dwarfish Cecil.

'Your loyalty isn't in doubt,' Cecil murmured pacifically.

That was not quite true, Ned thought; but Cecil was being polite.

Monteagle proffered the letter and Cecil took it. His high, white forehead creased in a frown as he began to read. 'By the Mass, this is untidy handwriting.' He read to the end, then passed it to Ned. Cecil's hands were long and fine-boned, like those of a tall woman.

Cecil asked Monteagle: 'How did this come to you?'

'My manservant brought it to me at supper. It was given him by a man who came to the kitchen door. My man gave the messenger a penny.'

'After you had read the letter, did you send someone to fetch the messenger back?'

'Of course, but he'd disappeared. Frankly, I suspect my servant may have finished his supper before bringing the letter to me, though he swore otherwise. At all events, we couldn't find the messenger when we looked for him. So I saddled my horse and came straight here.'

'You did the right thing, my lord.'

'Thank you.'

'What do you think of it, Ned?'

'The whole thing is plainly some kind of fake,' said Ned.

Monteagle was surprised. 'Really?'

'Look. The writer cares for your preservation, he says, out of the love he bears some of your friends. It seems a bit unlikely.'

'Why?'

'The letter is proof of treason. If a man knows of a plot to kill the king, his duty is to tell the Privy Council; and if he does not do so he may hang for it. Would a man endanger his own life for the sake of a friend of a friend?'

Monteagle was bewildered. 'I never thought of that,' he said. 'I took the letter at face value.'

Cecil smiled knowingly. 'Sir Ned never takes anything at face value,' he said.

'In fact,' Ned went on, 'I suspect the writer is very well known to you, or at least to someone to whom you might show the letter.'

Once again Monteagle looked out of his depth. 'Why do you say that?'

'No one writes like this except a schoolboy who has not yet gained full control of his pen. Yet the phrasing is that of an adult. Therefore the writing is deliberately disguised. That suggests that someone who is likely to read the letter knows the sender well enough to recognize his hand.'

'How dreadful,' said Monteagle. 'I wonder who it can be?'

'The sentence about the wickedness of the time is mere padding,' Ned went on, thinking aloud. 'The meat of the message is in the next sentence. If Monteagle attends

Parliament, he may be killed. That part, I suspect, is true. It fits with what I learned in Paris.'

Cecil said: 'But how is the killing to be done?'

'Key question. I believe the writer doesn't know. Look at the vagueness. "They shall receive a terrible blow . . . they shall not see who hurts them." It suggests danger from a distance, perhaps by cannon fire, but nothing more specific.'

Cecil nodded. 'Or, of course, the whole thing could be a figment of a madman's imagination.'

Ned said: 'I don't think so.'

Cecil shrugged. 'There's no concrete evidence, and nothing we can check. An anonymous letter is just a piece of paper.'

Cecil was right, the evidence was flimsy – but Ned's instinct told him the threat was real. Anxiously he said: 'Whatever we think, the letter must be shown to the king.'

'Of course,' said Cecil. 'He's hunting in Hertfordshire, but this will be the first thing he sees when he returns to London.'

*

MARGERY HAD ALWAYS known this terrible day would come. She had managed to forget the fact, even for years at a time, and she had been happy, but in her heart she had realized there would be a reckoning. She had deceived Ned for decades, but a lie always came back to you, sooner or later, and now that time had come.

'I know that Jean Langlais means to kill the king,' Ned said to her, worried and frustrated. 'But I can't do anything about it because I don't know who Langlais is or where to find him.'

Margery felt crucified by guilt. She had known that the elusive man Ned had been hunting most of his life was Rollo, and she had kept this knowledge to herself.

But now it seemed that Rollo was going to kill the king and queen and their two sons, plus all the leading ministers including Ned himself. She could not allow that to happen. Yet still she was not sure what to do, for even if she revealed the secret it might not save anyone. She knew who Langlais was but not where he was, and she had no idea how he planned to kill everyone.

She and Ned were at home in St Paul's Churchyard. They had eaten a breakfast of hen's eggs with weak beer, and Ned had his hat on, about to leave for Robert Cecil's house. At this moment in the day he often lingered, standing by the fire, to share his worries with her. Now he said: 'Langlais has been very, very careful – always.'

Margery knew that was true. The secret priests she had helped Rollo smuggle into England had known him as Langlais, and none of them had been told she was his sister. The same went for all the people he conspired with to free Mary Stuart and make her queen: they all knew him as Langlais, none as Rollo Fitzgerald. In being so cautious he was unlike most of his co-conspirators. They had approached their mission in a daredevil spirit, but Rollo had known the quality of the people he was up against, especially of Ned, and he had never taken unnecessary risks.

Margery said to Ned: 'Can't you cancel the opening of Parliament?'

'No. We might postpone it, or move it to a different location; though that would look bad enough: James's enemies would say the king is so hated by the people that he's afraid to open his own Parliament in case he might be assassinated. So James will make the decision himself. But the ceremony has to take place some time, somewhere. The country must be governed.'

Margery could bear it no longer. She said: 'Ned, I did a terrible thing.'

At first he was not sure how to take this. 'What?'

'I didn't lie to you, but I kept a secret from you. I thought I had to. I still think I had to. But you will be terribly angry.'

'What on earth are you talking about?'

'I know who Jean Langlais is.'

Ned was uncharacteristically bewildered. 'What? How could you – who is it?'

'It's Rollo.'

Ned looked as if he had been told someone had died. He

went pale and his mouth dropped open. He staggered and sat down heavily. At last he said: 'And you knew?'

Margery could not speak. She felt as if she were being strangled. She realized that tears were streaming down her cheeks. She nodded.

'How long?'

She gasped, sobbed, and managed to say: 'Always.'

'But how could you keep this from me?'

When at last she found words, they came fast. 'I thought he was just smuggling harmless priests into England to bring the sacraments to Catholics, then you found out he was conspiring to free Mary Stuart and Queen Elizabeth and he left the country, and he came back after the Spanish armada but he said it was all over and he wouldn't conspire any more, and if I betrayed him, he would reveal that Bartlet and Roger had helped smuggle priests.'

'You wrote the letter to Monteagle.'

She nodded. 'I wanted to warn you without condemning Rollo.'

'How did you find out?'

'Bartlet told me he's not coming to the opening of Parliament. He's never missed it before. Rollo must have warned him.'

'All this going on, and I didn't know. Me, the master spy, deceived by his own wife.'

'Oh, Ned.'

Ned looked at her as if she were the vilest criminal. 'And Rollo was in Kingsbridge the day Sylvie died.'

His words were like a bullet, and she found she could no longer stand. She sank to her knees on the rug. 'You want to kill me, I can tell,' she said. 'Go ahead, do it, I can't live now.'

'I was so angry when people said I could no longer be trusted to work for Queen Elizabeth because I had married a Catholic. What fools they were, I thought. Now it turns out that I was the fool.'

'No, you weren't.'

He gave her a look so full of rage that it broke her heart. 'Oh, yes, I was,' he said.

And then he went out.

*

NED AND CECIL saw King James on the first day of November. He received them at White Hall, in the Long Gallery that ran from the private rooms to the orchard. As well as paintings the gallery featured priceless draperies in gold and silver brocade, just the kind of thing James liked.

Ned knew that Cecil doubted the authenticity of the Monteagle letter, suspecting it might be no more than a piece of troublemaking. Cecil continued to believe this even when Ned told him that Earl Bartlet, a Catholic peer, was planning to miss the opening of Parliament for no plausible reason, and had probably been warned off.

Cecil's plan was to take all possible precautions, but not to reschedule the ceremony. Ned had a different agenda.

Ned wanted to do more than prevent the planned murders. Too often he had been on the trail of traitors only to see them scared off, after which they lived to plot another day. This time he wanted to arrest the conspirators. He wanted, finally, to get Rollo.

Cecil gave the Monteagle letter to James, saying: 'One would, of course, never keep something such as this from your majesty. On the other hand, it may not merit being taken seriously. It isn't backed by any facts.'

Ned added: 'No facts, your majesty, but there are supporting indications. I heard rumours in Paris.'

James shrugged. 'Rumours,' he said.

Ned said: 'You can't believe them, and you can't ignore them.'

'Exactly.' James read the letter, holding it up to the lamp, for the winter light coming through the windows was weak.

He took his time, and Ned's thoughts strayed to Margery. He had not seen her since her revelation. He was sleeping at a tavern. He could not bear the thought of seeing her or speaking to her: it was too painful. He could not even identify the emotion that swamped him, whether rage or hatred or grief. All he could do was look away and engage his mind with something else.

The king let the beringed hand holding the letter drop to his side, and he stood still for a minute or so, looking nowhere.

Ned saw intelligence in his eyes, and a determined line to his mouth, but a streak of self-indulgence was evidenced by his blemished skin and puffy eyes. It was hard, Ned guessed, to be disciplined and moderate when you possessed absolute power.

The king read the letter again, then said to Cecil: 'What do you think?'

'We could reinforce Westminster Yard with guards and cannons immediately. Then we could close the gates and search the precincts thoroughly. After that we could control and monitor everyone entering and leaving until the opening of Parliament is safely past.'

This was Cecil's preferred plan, but both he and Ned knew they had to give the king options, not instructions.

James was always conscious of his public image, for all his talk of the divine right of kings. 'We must take care not to alarm the public over what might be nothing at all,' he said. 'It makes the king look weak and frightened.'

'Your majesty's safety is paramount. But Sir Ned has an alternative suggestion.'

James looked enquiringly at Ned.

Ned was ready. 'Consider this, your majesty. If there is a plot, then perhaps the preparations are not yet complete. So if we act now we may fail to find what we're looking for. Worse, we may find incomplete preparations, which would give us only questionable evidence at a trial. Then the Catholic pamphleteers would say the charges were trumped up as a pretext for persecution.'

James did not yet get the point. 'We have to do something.'

'Indeed. In order to catch all the plotters and seize the maximum amount of incriminating evidence, we need to pounce at the last minute. That will protect your majesty both immediately and, importantly, in the future as well.' Ned held his breath: this was the crucial point.

James looked at Cecil. 'I think he may be right.'

'It's for your majesty to judge.'

The king turned back to Ned. 'Very well. Act on the fourth of November.'

'Thank you, your majesty,' Ned said with relief.

Ned and Cecil backed away, bowing, then the king was struck by an afterthought and said: 'Do we have any idea who is behind this wickedness?'

All Ned's frenzy at Margery came back to him in a tidal wave, and he struggled to suppress the shaking of his body. 'Yes, your majesty,' he said in a voice that was barely controlled. 'It's a man called Rollo Fitzgerald from Shiring. I'm ashamed to tell you that he's my brother-in-law.'

'In that case,' said James with more than a hint of menace, 'by God's blood, you'd better catch the swine.'

30

WHEN THE PLOTTERS heard about the Monteagle letter, on Sunday, 3 November, they started to accuse one another of treachery. The atmosphere became poisonous in the Wardrobe Keeper's apartment. 'One of us did this!' Guy Fawkes said belligerently.

Rollo feared that these aggressive young men would start fighting. 'Never mind who did it,' he said hastily. 'The man was certainly a fool rather than a traitor.'

'How can you be sure?'

'Because a traitor would have named us all. This idiot just wanted to warn Monteagle off.'

Fawkes calmed down. 'I suppose that makes sense.'

'The important question is how much damage has been done.'

'Exactly,' said Thomas Percy. 'Can we now go on with this plan, or should we abandon it?'

'After all we've done? No.'

'But if Cecil and Willard know . . .'

'I hear the letter was vague as to details, and Cecil isn't sure what to do about it,' Rollo said. 'There's still a strong chance for us. We can't give up so easily – success is within our grasp!'

'How can we check?'

'*You* could check,' Rollo said to Percy. 'Tomorrow morning, I want you to go on a scouting expedition. Visit your relative the earl of Northumberland. Think of some pretext – ask him for a loan, perhaps.'

'What's the point?'

'It's just a cover story, so that he won't guess that you're really trying to find out how much the Privy Council knows.'

'And how will I learn that?'

'By his attitude to you. If you're suspected of treachery, the earl will almost certainly have heard a rumour by now. He'll be nervous in your presence and eager to get you out of the house as fast as possible. He might even give you the loan just to be rid of you.'

Percy shrugged. 'All right.'

The group split up, leaving Fawkes in charge of the apartment. Next morning Percy went off to see Northumberland. On his return Rollo met him in a tavern near Bishop's Gate. Percy looked cheerful. 'I found him at Syon Place,' he said. Rollo knew that was the earl's country house not far west of London. 'He refused point-blank to give me a loan, told me I was a scapegrace, and invited me to dinner.'

'He has no suspicion, then.'

'Either that or he's a better actor than Richard Burbage.'

'Well done.'

'It's not really conclusive.'

'It's strongly suggestive, though. I'll go and give Fawkes the good news.'

Rollo headed across London. He did not feel safe – far from it: Ned Willard was coming too close for that. However, the stag was still ahead of the deerhounds, just. And he needed to stay ahead only a little longer – a few hours. By this time tomorrow it would be done.

But when he came within sight of the House of Lords he suffered a nasty shock.

At the rear of the building, where the storeroom entrance was, several well-dressed men were emerging from the upstairs debating chamber via the back door and coming down the wooden exterior staircase. Rollo could not recall ever having seen that door used.

He recognized the man leading the party. It was the earl of Suffolk, who, as Lord Chamberlain, had to make arrangements for the opening of Parliament.

With him was Lord Monteagle.

Rollo cursed. This was bad.

He stepped back around a corner out of sight. He fought down an urge to flee. He had to find out exactly what was going on. Whatever these men were doing was a terrible danger to his plan. He watched, half concealed, ready at any moment to run for his life.

They came down the steps and went to the double doors of the storeroom where the gunpowder was hidden. They were silent and alert, Rollo noted. Suffolk tried the door and found it locked. After some discussion, he ordered a servant to break it open.

So, Rollo thought with a sinking heart, this is a search party. It was maddening. Surely his plan would not be frustrated this easily?

Suffolk's servant deployed a crowbar. Rollo had not reinforced the door: the place was a storeroom, not a treasury, and the installation of iron bars or elaborate locks would have attracted attention. So the door came open with no great difficulty.

The group went inside.

Rollo hurried to the Wardrobe Keeper's apartment and ran through to the new passage Fawkes had created. He silently opened the door to the storeroom and looked in. The room was dim, as ever, and the lanterns of Suffolk's search party lit the large space only feebly.

However, they had seen Guy Fawkes.

God save us, Rollo prayed silently, or we're done for.

Fawkes was standing to one side, dressed in a cloak and a tall hat, carrying a lantern. It seemed Suffolk had only just spotted him, for Rollo heard the earl say in a startled voice: 'Who are you, man?'

Rollo held his breath.

'I am John Johnson, my lord,' said Fawkes. His voice was calm: he was a soldier, and had been in danger before.

Rollo wished he had not picked a name that sounded so obviously made up.

'And what the devil are you doing here, Johnson?'

'My master is tenant of this store, and of the apartment next door. I act as caretaker, you might say, when my master isn't here.'

It was a perfectly sensible story, Rollo thought hopefully. Was there any reason why Suffolk should not accept it?

'And for what purpose does your master use this vault?'

'To store firewood, as you can see.'

The members of the group looked at the firewood stack as if they had not previously noticed it – which was possible in the dim light.

Suffolk said: 'All this wood, just for an apartment?'

Fawkes did not respond to this rhetorical question. Rollo realized with dismay that he had overlooked this implausibility.

Suffolk said: 'Who is your master, anyway?'

'Thomas Percy.'

There was a little murmur of reaction from the search party. They would know Percy as a Gentleman Pensioner, and they would also know that he had Catholic relatives.

Rollo was so filled with dread that he felt nauseous. This was the moment of greatest danger. Would anyone think to look *inside* a pile of firewood? He remembered saying glibly: 'Even if someone were to search this place, they probably wouldn't find the gunpowder.' He was about to find out whether that was true. He felt tense enough to snap.

Suffolk took Monteagle aside, and the two men came closer to where Rollo stood behind the half-open door. He heard Monteagle say agitatedly: 'This involves the earl of Northumberland!'

'Keep your voice down,' Suffolk said more calmly. 'We can't accuse one of the greatest peers of the realm on the basis of an oversupply of firewood.'

'We must do something!'

'We must do nothing except inform the Privy Council of what we have seen.'

Rollo deduced that Suffolk had not thought of combing through the wood pile – yet.

Monteagle was calming down. 'Yes, of course, you're right, forgive me. I fear that all this is going to be blamed on me just because I was sent an anonymous letter.'

Rollo dared to hope that Monteagle's distress had distracted Suffolk from the search.

Suffolk patted Monteagle's shoulder. 'I understand.'

The two men rejoined the group.

There was some desultory conversation and then the search party left the building. Fawkes closed the broken door as best he could.

Rollo stepped into the storeroom. 'I heard everything,' he said to Fawkes. 'I was behind the door.'

Fawkes looked at him. 'Jesus save us,' he said. 'That was a close call.'

*

MARGERY WAS LIVING in a pit of misery. The bottom had dropped out of her world. After Ned left she drank little and ate nothing for a week. She saw no point in getting out of bed in the morning. If she forced herself up she just sat by the fireside, weeping, until it got dark outside and she could go back to bed again. Her life was over. She could have gone to her son Roger's house, but then she would have had to explain, and she could not face that.

But two days before the opening of Parliament she was seized by anxiety. Had Ned caught Rollo, or not? Would the ceremony go ahead? Would Ned be there? Would they all die?

She put on a coat and walked along the Strand to White Hall. She did not go into the palace, but stood outside, half-hidden by the gloom of a winter afternoon, watching for her husband. Courtiers came and went in their fur hats. Margery felt faint with hunger, and had to lean on a wall to stay upright. A cold mist came up from the river, but she was already so dejected that she hardly cared.

She wished with all her heart that she had not kept Rollo's secret so long. She should have told Ned the truth years ago. It would have been an earthquake, whenever she did it, but this was the worst time, after he had become so much a part of her that she could not manage life without him.

At last she saw him. He arrived with a small group of men in heavy coats – Privy Councillors, perhaps. His expression was grim. Perhaps it was an illusion, but he seemed to have aged in a week, his face creased with worry lines, grey stubble on pale cheeks.

She stepped in front of him and he stopped. She watched his face, reading his feelings. He was at first just startled. Then his expression changed and he looked angry. Instinct told her that he had been trying to forget about her and what she had done, and now he disliked being reminded. Was there any sign of softening, any hint of mercy? She was not sure.

She spoke the question she had come to ask. 'Have you found Rollo?'

'No,' said Ned, and he brushed past her and went inside.

Sadness engulfed her. She loved him so much.

She drifted away from the gates of the palace. In a daze of grief she wandered down to the muddy beach of the Thames. The river was tidal, and right now there was a fast downstream current, making the surface restless and troubled.

She thought about walking out into the water. It was almost dark now, and probably no one would see her. She had never learned to swim; her life would end in a few minutes. It would be cold, and there would be a long moment of gasping panic, but then her agony would be over.

It was a sin, a mortal sin, but hell could not be worse than this. She thought of a play she had seen in which a girl drowned herself after being rejected by the prince of Denmark, and a pair of comic gravediggers discussed whether she should have a Christian burial. There would be no burial for Margery if she went into the river now. Her body would be swept away by this strong current, perhaps all the way to the sea, where she would float gently down to the deep bottom, to lie with the sailors killed in the battle of the Spanish armada.

And who would say Mass for her soul? Protestants did not believe in prayers for the dead, and Catholics would not pray for a suicide. She would be damned as well as dead.

She stood there for a long moment, pulled painfully in opposite directions by her yearning for the peace of death and her horror of incurring God's eternal wrath. At last she seemed to see her great-aunt, Sister Joan, coming towards her across the mud, not as she had been in life but walking upright, without the aid of sticks. Although it was dark, Margery could see Joan's face, which was younger, and smiling. The vision did not speak, but silently took Margery's arm and led her gently away from the water. As they approached White Hall Margery saw two young men walking along together, laughing raucously at something; and she turned to ask Joan whether they, too, could see her; but Joan had gone, and Margery was alone again.

*

IN THE AFTERNOON of Monday, 4 November, Rollo sat with Guy Fawkes on the floor in the middle of the storeroom and gave Fawkes his final instructions.

Rollo produced a long match made of touchwood – dried rotted wood that was highly flammable – plus a tinder box. He took out his knife and notched the match in divisions each equal to the width of his thumb. Then he said: 'Fawkes, light the tinder, then say the Lord's Prayer, neither quickly nor slowly but just as you would in church.'

Fawkes lit the match. '*Pater noster*,' he began, and said the words of the prayer in Latin.

When he had finished the match had burned almost to the first mark. Rollo blew it out.

'Now,' said Rollo, 'how many paternosters will it take you to get clean away from here?'

Fawkes frowned. 'To leave here, close the doors, and walk to the river, two paternosters,' he said. 'To get into the boat, untie the rope, and deploy the oars, two more. Another six, maybe, to row far enough to be safe from the blast. Say ten altogether.'

'Then you must cut the match to a length of ten thumb widths.'

Fawkes nodded.

Rollo stood up. 'It's time to broach the gunpowder.'

Fawkes pulled the table over, stood on it, and started to remove bundles of firewood from the top. He passed them down to Rollo, rather than toss them on the floor, because they were needed intact to rebuild the barrier – just in case of a second search.

Rollo had a strange feeling in the pit of his belly. It was really happening, now, at last. They were going to kill the king.

After a few minutes they had made a passage through the stack to the barrels.

Rollo had with him a crowbar and a gardening tool like a small shovel. He levered off the top of a gunpowder barrel and tipped it over, spilling the dark grey powder on the ground. With the shovel he laid a trail of gunpowder from the barrel to the front of the stack. This would act as the fuse. He had been careful to pick a wooden shovel: an iron tool might have struck sparks from the slabs of the stone floor and blown them all up in a heartbeat.

It was now terrifyingly real, and Rollo felt his whole being thrill to the knowledge. Here was the gunpowder, and the match; above was the chamber; tomorrow was the day. The explosion would rock the kingdom and end English Protestantism. The triumph Rollo had sought for half a century was within his grasp. In just a few hours, his life's work would be done.

'We must put the firewood back carefully,' he said. 'The end of the gunpowder trail needs to be just under the front bundle.'

Together they rebuilt the stack and adjusted it until he was satisfied.

Rollo said to Fawkes: 'Tonight the rest of us leave for the shires, to be ready to start the uprising.'

Fawkes nodded.

'Tomorrow morning, as soon as you're sure the king is in the chamber above, you simply light the match, place it on the floor with the unlit end securely embedded in the powder trail, and leave.'

'Yes,' said Fawkes.

'You'll hear the explosion from the river.'

'Yes,' Fawkes said again. 'They'll hear it in Paris.'

*

IN THE LONG GALLERY at White Hall, just a few minutes' walk from Westminster Yard, there was calm, but Ned's instincts were sounding a raucous, insistent alarm.

Robert Cecil thought Thomas Percy was an untrustworthy character, but he saw no harm in a stack of firewood. The earl of Suffolk was worried about the political ructions that would result from a false accusation against the earl of Northumberland. But Ned was sure someone intended to kill the king, and he knew that person had not yet been found.

Fortunately, King James shared Ned's heightened sense of danger. He had an iron undershirt that he often wore in situations that made him feel vulnerable, and he decided he would wear it tomorrow to the opening ceremony. That was not enough for Ned, and late in the evening he got the king to agree to a second search of the House of Lords.

Those Privy Councillors still worried about causing unnecessary alarm insisted that the party be led by a Westminster Justice of the Peace, Thomas Knevett, and that he pretend to be looking for some missing ceremonial robes belonging to the king. Ned did not care what they pretended as long as he was part of the group.

The others carried lanterns, but Ned took a blazing torch, drawing frowns of disapproval from those worried about discretion. 'A search is a search,' he said stubbornly. 'If you can't see, you can't find anything.'

As they walked the short distance from the palace of White Hall to Westminster Yard, their lanterns casting restless shadows, Ned thought about Margery. She was always on his mind, even while he struggled to save the life of the king. He was terminally angry with her, but he missed her agonizingly. He hated going to a noisy tavern every evening and sleeping alone in a strange bed. He wanted to tell her things and ask her opinion. His heart ached for her. He was secretly glad to be living through a major emergency, for it occupied his mind and distracted him from his misery.

The party entered the House of Lords by the main door and searched the great hall and the two adjoining rooms, the Prince's Chamber and the Painted Chamber.

Unfortunately, Ned did not know what he was looking for. A concealed assassin? A hidden cannon? Nothing was found.

How will I feel, Ned wondered, if this really is a false alarm?

I will look foolish, but the king will live, and that's all that matters.

At ground level were various apartments. They searched the porter's lodge and the Wardrobe Keeper's apartment, rented by Thomas Percy; then they entered the storeroom, going in through the door Suffolk had broken down earlier. Ned was surprised at how large the place was, but otherwise it was as Suffolk had described it, even to the servant in cloak and hat guarding the place.

'You must be Johnson,' Ned said to the man.

'At your service, sir.'

Ned frowned. There was something familiar about Johnson. 'Have I met you before?'

'No, sir.'

Ned was not so sure, but it was hard to tell in the flickering torchlight.

He turned to the firewood stack.

There was a lot of it. Did Thomas Percy intend to start a conflagration? It would quickly blaze up to the wooden ceiling of the storeroom, which must be the floor of the chamber of the House of Lords. But this was an unreliable method of assassination. In all likelihood someone would smell smoke, and the royal family would be hustled out of the building in safety long before the place burned down. In order to be a serious danger, a fire would have to develop fast, with tar and turpentine, like a fireship, turning the building into an inferno before anyone could get out. Was there tar or turpentine here? Ned could not see any.

He moved closer to the stack. As he did so, he heard Johnson stifle a protest. He turned and looked at the man. 'Something wrong?'

'Pardon me, sir, but your torch is giving off sparks. Please take care not to set light to the wood.'

Johnson was unnecessarily jittery. 'If the wood catches fire you can stamp it out,' Ned said dismissively, and he went closer.

The wood was stacked with meticulous neatness. Something deep in Ned's memory was struggling to get out. This scene reminded him of another, long in his past, but he could not bring it to mind. He felt that he had stood like this, in a dark storeroom, looking at a pile of something, once before in his life, but he could not think when or where.

He turned away from the stack to see that everyone else was watching him in silence. They thought he was crazy. He did not care.

He looked again at Percy's caretaker and noticed that the man was wearing spurs. 'Going somewhere, Johnson?' he said.

'No, sir.'

'Then why are you wearing spurs?'

'I was on horseback earlier.'

'Hmm. Your boots seem remarkably clean, for a man who has been riding in November weather.' Without waiting for an answer, Ned turned back to the firewood.

An old table with a hole in its top stood near the stack, and Ned guessed that someone had stood on the table to place the topmost bundles carefully.

Suddenly he remembered.

It had been the terrible night of the St Bartholomew's Day Massacre in Paris. He and Sylvie had taken refuge in the warehouse in the rue du Mur where she kept her secret store of banned books. They had listened to the muffled sounds of riot in the city, the hoarse shouts of men fighting and the screams of those wounded, the pop of gunfire and the demented ringing of hundreds of church bells. In the warehouse, by the light of a lamp, Ned had looked at a stack of barrels that appeared to fill the space floor to ceiling and side to side.

But some of the barrels could be removed to reveal boxes of contraband literature.

'By the Mass,' Ned said softly.

He handed his torch to another of the search party and clambered onto the table, careful not to put his foot through the hole.

Once standing fairly securely on the table, he reached up and removed the top bundle of faggots. He threw it to the floor, then reached for another.

He heard a scuffle and turned.

John Johnson was making a run for it, dashing across the storeroom to the far end.

Ned shouted a warning, but one of his companions was already acting. It was Edmund Doubleday, he saw, and he was running after Johnson.

Johnson reached a door in the end wall, not previously visible in the dim light, and threw it open.

At that moment Doubleday launched himself through the air. He cannoned into Johnson with an audible thud. Both men fell to the floor.

Johnson tried to struggle up, and Doubleday grabbed his leg. Johnson kicked Doubleday in the face. Then the others surrounded them. As Johnson tried to get to his feet they shoved him down again. Someone sat on him. Another man grabbed his arms and a third sat on his legs.

Johnson stopped struggling.

Ned crossed the room and looked down at Johnson. His face was now clearly visible in the light of several lamps. 'I recognize you,' Ned said. 'You're Guy Fawkes.'

'Go to hell,' said Fawkes.

Ned said: 'Tie his hands behind his back and hobble his ankles so that he can walk but not run.'

Someone said: 'There's no rope.'

'Take off his breeches and tear them into strips.' A man with no breeches would not get far.

Something had triggered Johnson's sudden flight. 'What are you scared of?' Ned asked thoughtfully.

There was no reply.

It was when I threw down the second bundle of firewood, Ned thought. What was the significance of that?

'Go through his pockets,' he said.

Doubleday knelt beside Johnson and searched him. Doubleday had a large red mark on his face from the kick, and it was already beginning to swell, but he appeared not to have noticed it yet.

From inside Johnson's cloak Doubleday produced a tinder box and a touchwood match.

So, Ned thought, he was going to set fire to something. The

match was notched, as if for the purpose of timing its burning – perhaps so that the person who lit it would be able to get away before . . .

Before what?

Ned looked over at the firewood stack, then at the man who was holding his flaming torch, and a terrifying possibility occurred to him.

'Take my torch outside immediately, please, and put out the flames,' he said, just managing to keep his voice calm. 'Right now.'

The man to whom he had given the torch stepped smartly outside. Ned heard the hissing sound of flames being extinguished in water, probably a nearby horse trough, and he breathed a little easier.

The interior was still dimly lit by the lanterns held by the others in the search party. 'Now,' said Ned, 'let's see if this wall of firewood conceals what I think it does.'

The younger men started moving the bundles. Almost immediately Ned saw a dark-grey powder on the floor. It was almost the same colour as the stones of which the floor was made. It looked like gunpowder.

He shuddered to think how near to it he had stood with his flaming, sparking torch in his hand. No wonder Johnson had been nervous.

Behind the bundles was a space, just as in Sylvie's warehouse; but here it was not Bibles that were hidden, but barrels – dozens of them. One had been tilted off its base to spill a heap of powder on the floor. Ned held up a lamp to see more, and was awestruck. There were at least thirty barrels of various sizes – more than enough gunpowder to flatten the House of Lords and kill everyone inside.

Including Ned Willard.

He was surprised at how angry he felt at the thought that Rollo had planned to kill him, as well as the royal family and the rest of the Privy Council and most members of Parliament.

He was not the only one to feel that way. Doubleday said: 'They were going to murder us all!' Several others voiced their agreement.

One of the men standing over Fawkes kicked him in the balls, hard. Fawkes writhed in pain.

Ned understood the impetus but stopped the violence. 'We need him conscious and talking,' he said. 'He's going to give us the names of all his collaborators.'

'A pity,' one of the men said. 'I'd like to beat him to death.'

'Don't worry,' said Ned. 'In a few hours' time he'll be stretched on the rack. He'll suffer screaming agony before he betrays his friends. And when he's done that he'll be hung, drawn and quartered.' He stared at the man on the floor for a long moment. 'That's probably punishment enough,' he said.

*

ROLLO RODE THROUGH the night, changing horses when he could, and reached New Castle on the morning of Tuesday, 5 November. There he and Earl Bartlet waited anxiously for the messenger from London who would bring them the joyous news of the death of the king.

In the chapel that was part of the castle complex were dozens of swords, guns and armour. As soon as he heard that the king was dead, Bartlet would summon loyal Catholics and arm them, and they would march on Kingsbridge, where Rollo would hold a Latin Mass in the cathedral.

If something went wrong, and the news from London was not what Rollo expected, he had an alternative plan. A fast horse was standing by, and a pair of saddlebags packed with a few essentials. He would ride to Combe Harbour and take the first ship to France. With luck he would escape before Ned Willard closed England's ports in his hunt for the gunpowder plotters.

It was almost impossible that they would hear anything on the Tuesday, but all the same Rollo and Bartlet stayed up late just in case. Rollo spent a restless night and got up at first light on the Wednesday. Had the world changed? Was England in the midst of a revolution? They would surely know the answers before the sun went down today.

They found out earlier than that.

Rollo was at breakfast with Bartlet and the family when

they heard hoofbeats pounding into the compound. They all jumped up from the table, rushed through the house and ran out of the main door, desperately eager to know what had happened.

A dozen men and horses milled around the courtyard. For a moment it was not clear who was in charge. Rollo scanned the faces, looking for someone familiar. All the men were heavily armed, some with swords and daggers, others with guns.

Then Rollo saw Ned Willard.

Rollo froze. What did that mean? Had the plan gone wrong? Or had the revolution begun, and was Ned part of a desperate rearguard action by the tattered remains of the Protestant government?

Ned gave the answer immediately. 'I found your gunpowder,' he said.

The words hit Rollo like bullets. He felt shot in the heart. The plot had failed. Rage boiled up in him as he thought how Ned had frustrated him again and again through the years. He wanted more than anything else to get his hands around Ned's throat and squeeze the life out of him.

He tried to suppress his emotions and think straight. So Ned had found the gunpowder – but how had he known that Rollo had put it there? Rollo said: 'Did my sister betray me?'

'She kept your secret thirty years longer than she should have.'

Betrayed by a woman. He should never have trusted her.

He thought of the waiting horse. Did he have a slim chance of escaping from this crowd of strong young men, reaching the stable, and riding away?

Ned seemed to read his mind. He pointed at Rollo and said: 'Watch him carefully. He's been slipping through my hands for thirty years.'

One of the men lifted a long-barrelled arquebus and aimed it at Rollo's nose. It was an old gun with a matchlock mechanism, and he could see the glowing match ready to be touched to the firing pan.

At that point Rollo knew it was all over.

Earl Bartlet began a blustering protest, but Rollo felt impatient for the end. He was seventy years old and he had nothing more to live for. He had spent his life trying to destroy England's heretical monarchy, and he had failed. He would not get another chance.

Sheriff Matthewson, grandson of the sheriff Rollo remembered from his youth, spoke to Bartlet in a firm but calm voice. 'Let's have no trouble, please, my lord,' he said. 'It won't do anyone any good.'

The sheriff's reasonable tones and Bartlet's ranting both seemed to Rollo like background noise. Feeling as if he was in a dream, or perhaps a play, he reached inside his doublet and drew his dagger.

The deputy holding a gun on him said in a panicky voice: 'Drop that knife!' The arquebus shook in his hands, but he managed to keep it pointing at Rollo's face.

Silence fell and everyone looked at Rollo.

'I'm going to kill you,' Rollo said to the deputy.

He had no intention of doing anything of the kind, but he raised the knife high, careful not to move his head and spoil the deputy's aim.

'Prepare to die,' he said.

Behind the deputy, Ned moved.

The deputy pulled the trigger and the lighted cord touched the gunpowder in the firing tray. Rollo saw a flash and heard a bang, and knew instantly that he had been cheated of an easy death. At the last split-second the barrel had been knocked aside by Ned. Rollo felt a sharp pain at the side of his head and sensed blood on his ear, and understood that the ball had grazed him.

Ned grabbed his arm and took away the knife. 'I'm not finished with you,' he said.

*

MARGERY WAS summoned to see the king.

It would not be the first time she had met him. In the two years of his reign so far she had attended several royal festivities with Ned: banquets and pageants and plays. Ned regarded James as a voluptuary, interested mainly in sensual pleasure; but Margery thought he had a cruel streak.

Her brother, Rollo, must have confessed everything under torture, and therefore he would have implicated her in the smuggling of priests into England. She would be accused and arrested and executed alongside him, she supposed.

She thought of Mary Stuart, a brave Catholic martyr. Margery wanted to die with dignity as Queen Mary had. But Mary was a queen, and had been mercifully beheaded. Female traitors were burned at the stake. Would Margery be able to retain her dignity, and pray for her tormentors as she died? Or would she scream and cry, curse the Pope and beg for mercy? She did not know.

Worse, for her, was the prospect that Bartlet and Roger would suffer the same fate.

She put on her best clothes and went to White Hall.

To her surprise Ned was waiting for her in the anteroom. 'We're going in together,' he said.

'Why?'

'You'll see.'

He was tense, wound up tight, and she could not tell whether he was still angry with her. She said: 'Am I to be executed?'

'I don't know.'

Margery felt dizzy and feared she was going to fall. Ned saw her stagger and grabbed her. For a moment she slumped in his arms, too relieved to hold herself upright. Then she pushed herself away. She had no right to his embrace. 'I'll be all right,' she said.

He held her arm a little longer, then released her, and she was able to support herself. But he still looked at her with an angry frown. What did it mean?

She did not have long to puzzle over this before a royal servant nodded to Ned to indicate that they should go in.

They entered the Long Gallery side by side. Margery had heard that King James liked to have meetings in this room because he could look at the pictures when he got bored.

Ned bowed and Margery curtsied, and James said: 'The man

who saved my life!' When he spoke he drooled a little, a mild impediment that seemed to go with his sybaritic tastes.

'Your majesty is very kind,' Ned said. 'And of course you know Lady Margery, the dowager countess of Shiring and my wife of fifteen years.'

James nodded but did not say anything, and Margery deduced from his coolness that he knew of her religious affiliation.

Ned said: 'I want to ask your majesty a favour.'

James said: 'I'm tempted to say *Even unto the half of my kingdom*, except that the phrase has an unlucky history.' He was referring to the story of Salome, who had asked for the head of John the Baptist on a platter.

'I don't think I've ever asked your majesty for anything, although perhaps my service might have won me your good will.'

'You saved me from those evil gunpowder devils – me and my family and the entire Parliament,' said James. 'Come on, out with it – what do you want?'

'During the interrogation of Rollo Fitzgerald, he made certain accusations about crimes committed many years ago, during the 1570s and 1580s, in the reign of Queen Elizabeth.'

'What sort of crimes are we talking about?'

'He confessed to smuggling Catholic priests into England.'

'He's going to hang anyway.'

'He claims he had collaborators.'

'And who were they?'

'The late earl of Shiring, Bart; his then wife, Margery, who is now my wife; and their two sons, Bartlet, who is now the earl, and Lord Roger.'

The king's face darkened. 'A serious charge.'

'I ask your majesty to consider that a woman may be dominated by a strong-willed husband and an equally overpowering brother, and that she and her children are not entirely to blame for crimes committed under such strong masculine influence.'

Margery knew this was not true. She had been the leader,

not the follower. She might have said so, if her own life had been the only one at stake. But she bit her tongue.

Ned said: 'I ask your majesty to spare their lives. It is the only reward I ask for saving your own.'

'I can't say that this request pleases me,' the king said.

Ned said nothing.

'But the smuggling of priests took place a long time ago, you say.'

'It ended after the Spanish armada. From then on Rollo Fitzgerald did not involve his family in his crimes.'

'I would not even consider this were it not for the remarkable service you have rendered the crown of England over so many years.'

'My whole life, your majesty.'

The king looked grumpy, but at last he nodded. 'Very well. There will be no prosecutions of his collaborators.'

'Thank you.'

'You may go.'

Ned bowed, Margery curtsied, and they left.

They walked together, without speaking, through the series of anterooms and out of the palace into the street. There they both turned east. They went past the church of St Martin-in-the-Fields and along the Strand. Margery felt nothing but relief. All the lying and double-dealing was over.

They passed the palaces along the Thames shore and entered the less affluent Fleet Street. Margery did not know what was going on in Ned's mind, but he seemed to be coming home with her. Or was that too much to hope for?

They entered the city through Lud Gate and started up the rise. Ahead of them, on top of the hill, St Paul's Cathedral towered over rows of low, thatched houses like a lioness with cubs. Still Ned had not spoken, but Margery sensed that his mood had changed. His face slowly relaxed, the lines of tension and anger seemed to dissolve, and there was even a hint of his old wry smile. Emboldened, Margery reached out and took his hand in her own.

For a long moment he let her hold his hand without responding, and it lay limp in her grasp. Then, at last, she felt him squeeze her fingers, gently but firmly; and she knew it was going to be all right.

*

We hanged him in front of Kingsbridge Cathedral.

Margery and I did not want to join the crowd, but we could not be absent either, so we watched from the window of the old house. She burst into tears when they brought Rollo from the Guild Hall down the main street to the market square, and walked him up the scaffold.

When the support was jerked from beneath him, Margery began to pray for his soul. As a Protestant I never believed in prayers for dead souls, but I joined in for her sake. And I had done something more practical, also for her sake. Rollo should have been cut down and disembowelled while still alive, then hacked into pieces, but I had bribed the executioner, and so Rollo was allowed to choke to death before his body was ritually mutilated – to the disappointment of the crowd, who had wanted to see the traitor suffer.

After that I retired from court life. Margery and I came back to Kingsbridge permanently. Roger, who never found out that he was my son, took over from me as the Member of Parliament for Kingsbridge. My nephew Alfo became the richest man in Kingsbridge. I remained lord of Wigleigh – I had developed a strong affection for the people of my little village.

So Rollo was the last of the men I sent to the gallows. But there is one more part of the story to be told . . .

Epilogue

1620

AT THE AGE OF eighty, Ned spent a lot of time sleeping. He napped in the afternoon, he went to bed early, and he sometimes nodded off after breakfast in the front parlour of the Kingsbridge house.

The house was always full. Barney's son, Alfo, and Ned's son, Roger, both had children and grandchildren. Roger had bought the house next door and the youngsters treated the two houses as one home.

Someone had told them that Grandpa Ned knew everything, and his great-grandchildren often came running into the parlour with questions. He was endlessly intrigued by what they asked him: how long does it take to get to Egypt? Did Jesus have a sister? What's the biggest number?

He watched them with intense pleasure, fascinated by the random nature of family resemblances: one had Barney's roguish charm, another Alice's relentless determination, and one little girl brought tears to his eyes when she smiled just like Margery.

Inherited traits showed themselves in other ways, too. Alfo was mayor of Kingsbridge, as his grandfather Edmund had been. Roger was a member of King James's Privy Council. Over at New Castle, Earl Swifty was, sadly, as much of a swaggering bully as Swithin, Bart and Bartlet had been.

The family had grown like a spreading tree, and Ned and Margery had watched its progress together, until her life had come to a peaceful end three years ago. Ned still talked to her sometimes, when he was alone. 'Alfo has bought the Slaughterhouse Tavern,' he would say as he got into bed at the end of the day. Or again: 'Little Eddie is as tall as me, now.' It hardly mattered that she made no reply: he knew what she would have thought. 'Money sticks to Alfo like honey on his fingers,' she would have said, and: 'Eddie will be after girls any day now.'

Ned had not been to London for years, and would never go again. Strangely enough, he did not pine for the excitement of tracking down spies and traitors, nor for the challenges and intrigues of government. It was the theatre he missed. He had loved plays ever since he saw the story of Mary Magdalene performed at New Castle on that Twelfth Day of Christmas so long ago. But a play was a rare event in Kingsbridge: travelling companies came only once or twice a year, to perform in the yard of the Bell Inn. Ned's consolation was that he had some of his favourite plays in book form, so he could read them. There was one writer he particularly enjoyed, though he could never remember the fellow's name. He forgot a lot of things these days.

He had a book on his lap now, and he had fallen asleep over it. Wondering what had awakened him, he looked up to see a young man with Margery's curly dark hair: his grandson, Jack, the son of Roger. He smiled. Jack was like Margery in other ways: good-looking and charming and feisty – and far too earnest about religion. His extremism had gone in the direction opposite to Margery's and he was some kind of Puritan. This caused bad-tempered rows with his pragmatic father.

Jack was twenty-seven and single. To the surprise of his family he had chosen to be a builder, and had prospered. There were famous builders in the family's past: heritage again, perhaps.

Now he sat in front of Ned and said: 'I have some important news, Grandfather. I'm going away.'

'Why? You have a successful business here in Kingsbridge.'

'The king makes life uncomfortable for those of us who take the teachings of the Bible seriously.'

What he meant was that he and his Puritan friends stubbornly disagreed with the English Church on numerous points of doctrine, and King James was as intolerant of them as he was of Catholics.

'I'll be very sorry to see you go, Jack,' Ned said. 'You remind me of your grandmother.'

'I'll be sorry to say goodbye. But we want to live in a place where we can do God's will without interference.'

'I spent my life trying to make England that kind of country.'

'But it's not, is it?'

'It's more tolerant than any other place, as far as I know. Where would you go in search of greater freedom?'

'The New World.'

'God's body!' Ned was shocked. 'I didn't think you were going that far. Sorry about the bad language, you startled me.'

Jack nodded acknowledgement of the apology. He disapproved almost as much as the Catholics of the blasphemous exclamations Ned had learned from Queen Elizabeth; but he said no more about it. 'A group of us have decided to sail to the New World and start a colony there.'

'What an adventure! It's the kind of thing your grandmother Margery would have loved to do.' Ned felt envious of Jack's youth and boldness. Ned himself would never travel again. Luckily he had rich memories – of Calais, of Paris, of Amsterdam. He recalled every detail of those journeys even when he could not remember what day of the week it was.

Jack was saying: 'Although James will continue to be our king theoretically, we hope he will take less interest in how we choose to worship, since it will be impossible for him to enforce his rules at such a distance.'

'I dare say you're right. I wish you well.'

'Pray for us, please.'

'I will. Tell me the name of your ship, so that I can ask God to watch over it.'

'It's called the *Mayflower*.'

'The *Mayflower*. I must try to remember that.'

Jack went to the writing table. 'I'll note it down for you. I want us to be in your prayers.'

'Thank you.' It was oddly touching that Jack cared so much about Ned's prayers.

Jack wrote on a scrap of paper and put down the pen. 'I must leave you, now – I've got so much to do.'

'Of course. I'm feeling tired, anyway. I may take a little nap.'

'Sleep well, Grandfather.'

'God be with you, beloved boy.'

Jack left, and Ned looked out of the window at the glorious west front of the cathedral. From here he could just see the entrance to the graveyard where both Sylvie and Margery lay. He did not look down at his book. He was happy with his thoughts. They were often enough for him, nowadays.

His mind was like a house he had spent his life furnishing. Its tables and beds were the songs he could sing, the plays he had watched, the cathedrals he had seen, and the books he had read in English, French and Latin. He shared this notional house with his family, alive and dead: his parents, his brother, the women he had loved, the children. There were guest rooms for important visitors such as Francis Walsingham, William and Robert Cecil, Francis Drake, and of course Queen Elizabeth. His enemies were there, too – Rollo Fitzgerald, Pierre Aumande de Guise, Guy Fawkes – although they were locked in the cellar, for they could do him no more harm.

The pictures on the walls were of the times when he had been brave, or clever, or kind. They made the house a happy place. And the bad things he had done, the lies he had told and the people he had betrayed and the times he had been cowardly, were scrawled in ugly letters on the wall of the outhouse.

His memory formed the library of the house. He could pick out any volume and instantly be transported to another place and time: Kingsbridge Grammar School in his innocent childhood, Hatfield Palace in the thrilling year of 1558, the banks of the Seine river on the bloodstained night of St Bartholomew, the Channel during the battle with the Spanish armada. Strangely, the character of Ned that lived in those stories did not remain the same. It seemed to him sometimes that quite a different person had learned Latin, someone else had fallen under the spell of young Princess Elizabeth, another character had stabbed a man with no nose in the graveyard of the church of St-Julien-le-Pauvre, and yet another had watched the fireships scatter the galleons off Calais. But of course they were all just different versions of himself, the owner of the house.

And one day soon the place would fall down, as old buildings did, and then, quite quickly, it would all turn to dust.

With that thought he drifted off to sleep.

Acknowledgements

My historical advisors for A *Column of Fire* were: Mercedes García-Arenal on Spain; the late Roderick Graham on Scotland; Robert Hutchinson on England; Guy Le Thiec on France; and Geoffrey Parker on the Netherlands.

I was also helped by: Anne-Laure Béatrix and Béatrice Vingtrinier at the Louvre in Paris; Dermot Burke at Hatfield House; Richard Dabb and Timothy Long at the Museum of London; Simon Lennox, Trisha Muir and Richard Waters at Loch Leven Castle; Sarah Pattinson at Carlisle Castle; Les Read on English sixteenth-century theatre; and Elizabeth Taylor at the National Portrait Gallery in London.

My editors were: Cherise Fisher, Leslie Gelbman, Phyllis Grann, Neil Nyren, Brian Tart and Jeremy Trevathan.

Friends and family who gave advice included: John Clare, Barbara Follett, Emanuele Follett, Tony McWalter, Chris Manners, Charlotte Quelch, John Studzinski, Jann Turner and Kim Turner.

All of you helped me write a better book, and I give you my heartfelt thanks.

Who is Real?

Readers sometimes ask me which of the characters in a novel are real historical figures and which are fictional. For those who are curious about this, here's a list of the real people in *A Column of Fire*.

ENGLAND

Mary Tudor, queen of England
Elizabeth Tudor, her half-sister, later queen
Tom Parry, Elizabeth's treasurer
Sir William Cecil, advisor to Elizabeth
Robert Cecil, William's son
Sir Francis Walsingham, spymaster
Robert Dudley, earl of Leicester
Sir Nicholas Throckmorton
Nicholas Heath, Lord Chancellor
Sir Francis Drake, sea captain
Sir John Hawkins, naval commander, also said to be a
    pirate
Sir Francis Throckmorton
George Talbot, earl of Shrewsbury
Bess of Harwick
Sir Amias Paulet
Gilbert Gifford, spy
William Davison, temporary secretary of state to Queen
    Elizabeth
Anthony Babington, traitor
Margaret Clitheroe, Catholic martyr
Howard of Effingham, Lord High Admiral

Philip Herbert, earl of Pembroke, earl of Montgomery
Edmund Doubleday
Guy Fawkes
Thomas Percy

FRANCE

François, duke of Guise
Henri, son of François
Charles, cardinal Lorraine, brother of François
Marie de Guise, sister of François and mother of Mary Queen
    of Scots
Louis 'Bottles', Cardinal de Guise
Anna d'Este, duchess of Guise
Henri II, king of France
Caterina de' Medici, queen of France
Diane de Poitiers, mistress of King Henri II
Children of Henri and Caterina:
    Francis II, king of France
    Charles IX, king of France
    Henri III, king of France
    Margot, queen of Navarre
Mary Stuart, queen of Scots and queen of France
Antoine, king of Navarre
Henri, son of Antoine, later King Henri IV of France
Louis, prince of Condé
Gaspard de Coligny, admiral of France
Charles de Louviers, assassin
William Allen, leader of the exiled English Catholics
Ambroise Paré, royal surgeon
Jean de Poltrot, assassin
Jean de Hangest
Jean Le Charron, provost of Paris

SCOTLAND

James Stuart, illegitimate half-brother of Mary Queen of
   Scots
James Stuart, son of Mary Queen of Scots, later King James
   VI of Scotland and King James I of England
Anne of Denmark, queen of Scotland
John Leslie, bishop of Ross
Sir William Douglas
Lady Agnes, his wife
George 'pretty Geordie', their son
Willie Douglas, Sir William's illegitimate son

SPAIN

King Felipe II
Count of Feria, diplomat
Bishop Álvaro de la Quadra
Bernardino de Mendoza, ambassador to London
Alonso Pérez de Guzmán, 7th duke of Medina Sidonia,
   admiral of the Spanish armada

NETHERLANDS

Margherita of Parma, governor, illegitimate half-sister of King
   Felipe II
Pieter Titelmans, grand inquisitor

extracts reading groups
competitions books new
discounts extracts extracts
competitions reading groups
books new extracts discounts
reading groups events
events books
new extracts reading groups
books new titles reading groups
interviews events new
events extracts extracts books
discounts interviews new books
new books events events extracts
events new events

discounts extracts discounts

www.panmacmillan.com

extracts events reading groups
competitions books extracts new books